Catherine Clément

was born and educated in Paris. She has been a teacher, academic, journalist, TV producer and editor, and has published nine novels.

Praise for *Theo's Odyssey*:

'Clément provides a useful introduction to some aspects of religious history, and engages, through Theo, with fundamental spiritual concepts . . . *Theo's Odyssey* will perform a valuable service if it introduces its readers to the essential harmony and deep similarity of the world's faiths. At a time of heightened religious militancy, it is important that people learn to take others' faith seriously, and that secularists, like Theo, begin to realise that religion may be more congenial and less alien than they imagine.' KAREN ARMSTRONG, *Independent*

'Clément's rich storytelling guides Theo through an informative and deeply touching journey as he begins to understand others' relationships with God, as well as his own. Beneath the surface, this is a spiritual love story, one in which the love of family, a girlfriend, and God sustains and heals a dying boy.'
Amazon.com

'With its fluent and alert prose, this encyclopaedic novel will entrance any smart reader keen to extend their spiritual understanding.' *Madame Figaro*

'The questions posed in this book are those that concern us all, the explanations have a biblical simplicity to them, and, at a time when many men of God seem so fuelled by hate, Theo's journey of discovery makes for astonishing news.'
Elle

CATHERINE CLÉMENT

Theo's Odyssey

Translated from the French by
Steve Cox and Ros Schwartz

Flamingo
An Imprint of HarperCollinsPublishers

Flamingo
An Imprint of HarperCollins*Publishers*
77 - 85 Fulham Palace Road,
Hammersmith, London W6 8JB

Flamingo is a registered trade mark of
HarperCollins Publishers Limited

www.**fire**and**water**.com

Published by Flamingo 2000
9 8 7 6 5 4 3

First published in Great Britain by Flamingo 1999

First published in France as *Le Voyage de Théo* by Éditions du Seuil 1997

Copyright © Éditions du Seuil 1997
English translation copyright © Steve Cox and Ros Schwartz 1999

Catherine Clément asserts the moral right to be
identified as the author of this work

This novel is entirely a work of fiction. The names, characters
and incidents portrayed in it are the work of
the author's imagination. Any resemblance to actual persons,
living or dead, events or localities is entirely coincidental.

Photograph of Catherine Clément © John Foley/Seuil

The publication of this book is supported by the Cultural Service
of the French Embassy in London

institut français

ISBN 0 00 655135 1

Typeset in Garamond Book by Rowland Phototypesetting Ltd,
Bury St Edmunds, Suffolk

Printed and bound in Great Britain by Clays Ltd, St Ives plc

CONTENTS

Pour Titus la sardine

The Wrath
of the Gods

'Theo! Have you seen what time it is? THEO!'

'Theo wasn't really asleep. His head was under the covers and he was lost in the drowsy joys of waking up. At the moment when his mother entered his bedroom the skin of his feet was beginning to dematerialize, and he was going to be able to rise into the air without his body . . . What an incredible dream, and why should it stop, when he was hovering so comfortably between sleep and the daytime?

'All right, that's enough!' said Melina Fournay. 'This time you're getting up, or else . . .'

'No,' came a muffled voice. 'Don't shake the pillow!'

'It's always the same,' his mother protested. 'You go to bed too late, and then you can't wake up. It's your own fault.'

Theo struggled to get up. The hardest part was achieving the vertical position and facing the slight morning giddiness. One foot stuck out of the bed, then a leg, and then the whole of Theo, raking his fingers through his curly hair. He stood up . . . and staggered. His mother just caught him in time, and sat down with him on the edge of the bed. Sighing, she examined the books scattered over the blanket.

'*Dictionary of Ancient Egypt, Greek Mythology, Tibetan Book of the Dead.* . . These are horrific,' she grumbled. 'They're too old for you, Theo! How long did you stay up last night?'

'Ummm . . . Dunno,' grunted Theo sleepily.

'You read far too long and too late,' she murmured, knitting her thick black eyebrows. 'You'll end up making yourself ill, do you know that?'

'No, I won't,' said Theo with a yawn. 'It's just that I feel a bit hungry.'

'It's all on the table, and I've got your vitamins ready.' She hugged him and kissed him on the forehead. 'Fatou will be here soon, so get a move on. Wrap up well, it's awfully cold – oh, and don't forget to stop off at the chemist's and pick up your medicine. The prescription's on the table by the front door . . . Theo!'

But Theo was shambling to the bathroom, leaning on the walls along the way. Deep in thought, Melina walked back to the kitchen, where her husband Jerome was browsing through yesterday's paper.

'That child's not well,' she said, in a lowered voice. 'Not well at all.'

'Who, Theo?' said her husband, without looking up 'He's not a child any more, he's fourteen years old. What do you think is the matter?'

'Oh you, you never notice anything. He's looking terribly pale, he has trouble standing up . . .'

'Descartes couldn't bear getting up either. That didn't stop him becoming a philosopher.'

'But he seems to be having dizzy spells, and . . .'

'You know he stays up late reading,' Jerome broke in quietly.

'And have you seen what he's reading? A dictionary of mythology, the Tibetan Book of the Dead . . . the Book of the Dead!'

'Listen, darling, Theo hasn't had any religious education. You and I agreed on that principle . . . So it's quite natural that he should want to find out for himself. Let him get on with it! If he wants to choose a religion, that's for him to decide . . . And besides, he's shot up lately. Nothing came up in the annual medical check, as I recall . . . ?'

'You're joking, Jerome! The school medical check-up? Stethoscope, reflexes, one quick X-ray – though not always even that – and that's it. No, I'm definitely taking him to see Doctor Delattre.'

'Now wait a minute, Melina! You cram him full of tonics and coddle him like a baby. All right, so he stays up reading. Fine, I'm in favour of that. Sit down.'

'There's something wrong,' she muttered. 'I'm sure there's something wrong.'

'If you say so,' he sighed, folding his newspaper. 'Go to Delattre, fix up that blood test. And I'm going to the lab, if you don't mind. Do I get a kiss?'

Melina held out her cheek, without a word.

'And no more fussing about your favourite chick and his dizzy spells,' he ordered as he left.

Melina sat brooding over her coffee, waiting for Theo.

Theo's family

Until the previous winter, the Fournay family's outlook had been bright. Both parents working, no major disagreements. Theo's father was a director of research at the Pasteur Institute, a talented pianist, and the best of husbands. Melina was very lucky: she taught biology at the George Sand high school, the one that Theo attended, and where her colleagues were dedicated and her pupils well-behaved. Theo's sisters adored their brother. Irene, the eldest, had started a degree in economics. Athena, the youngest, was about to enter secondary school. Apart from a few tiffs about socks mixed up in the laundry basket, and pitched battles over clearing the table, Theo had no problems with his sisters. But he was delicate, that's all.

Before she married Jerome, Melina Chakros had come through some difficult times. She was only a child in 1967 when under threat from the Colonels' regime in Greece her parents – George Chakros, a journalist, and her mother Theano, a violinist – had been forced into exile in Paris, a town with neither olive trees nor sunshine. Then Melina had grown up, met Jerome, married Jerome, the children had been born, the Colonels' dictatorship replaced by democracy, and the Chakros parents had returned to Athens. In memory of the homeland regained, the Fournay children had Greek first names. That is why the eldest was called Irene, meaning peace, and the youngest Athena, or wisdom. Theo's full name was Theodore, which in Greek means 'gift of God'. Obviously that made things slightly awkward at school for Theodore and Athena, but their friends got used to calling them Theo and Attie.

If it hadn't been for Theo's health, it would all have been fine.

Theo's birth had been more stressful than he knew. Melina had been carrying twins, but they were born a good month premature, and only he had survived. The experience had left him a restless sleeper with really fragile health. Not wanting to upset him even more, Melina had decided not to tell him about his stillborn twin, and so he knew nothing of the baby's existence. Theo had been a beautiful baby, not sturdy, but with black curls and green eyes that were the envy of his sisters.

During her lifetime, Jerome's late mother Marie, Theo's French grandmother, had been fascinated by fairies and wood elves. She used to say that Theo had 'the devil's own beauty'. 'The beauty of the gods,' replied his Greek grandmother, Theano, who crammed her grandson's head full of classical mythology and Orthodox religion. Theo was so handsome and so vulnerable that when the two grandmothers cooed

3

in unison over their grandson's looks, Melina would surreptitiously cross herself, and touch wood in secret, to ward off bad luck, because although she did not believe in God, she was terribly superstitious.

Within the family, they all knew that there was something different about Theo. He always came top in his class, and he read all the time: even when he was very small, he always had his nose stuck inside some book or other. And when he could be prised away from his reading, it was only for him to settle in front of his Macintosh and explore his computer games with equal enthusiasm. Just lately, Theo had been glued to a mythological game called *Wrath of the Gods*, a present from his mother, in which a young hero confronts the whole Greek company of sirens, giants and monsters, while a red-haired Pythia, priestess of the Delphic oracle, offers misleading advice to keep the player guessing.

Despite her reservations about computer games, Melina had fallen for *Wrath of the Gods* because of the Greek theme. Theo spent hours roaming on screen through his mother's native land, in the shade of olive groves; he spent whole days questing for the identity of the Hero who resembled him like a brother, a handsome, very cunning, wiry young man forced to make forays into the underworld to find his true father, Zeus, the king of the Greek gods. When Jerome Fournay tried to compete with his son, he would find himself trapped for ever in the underworld, unable to get out. With the help of hidden gems, hammers of power, potions and magical rings, only Theo had the skills to track down the king of the gods on his Macintosh. Everyone knew that Theo was a brilliant boy.

That Theo was brilliant was nothing to be worried about, but he was also fragile, much too fragile. Melina ran through his illnesses. At the age of three, he had suffered a serious bout of illness. At seven, a severe attack of scarlet fever had undermined his strength for some time, but now he was fourteen years old, and that was ancient history. At ten, he had broken his shinbone playing football. Since then, he had shot up enormously, sports tired him out, his teachers talked about outgrowing his strength – in other words, Theo carried some hidden weakness. Was there some hereditary factor at work here? When she was fourteen, her mother had suffered from serious anaemia. Or was it simply hypoglycaemia? Or possibly mononucleosis . . . ?

Fatou

'Hello!' called a voice from the corridor. 'It's me, Fatou.'

Fatou was the Fournays' neighbour, a girl from Senegal, always chirpy in the morning. As usual, she was right on time, and as usual she came in panting for breath, and shaking her tiny plaits tipped by gold beads.

'Here already? I didn't hear you ring.'

'That's right,' said the girl, as she removed her school bag. 'I bumped into your husband and he let me in. Is Theo ready?'

'Of course not,' sighed Melina. 'You know Theo. Look, sit down and I'll pour you some coffee.'

'No time. We'll be late, and besides we have a history test this morning. I'll go and fetch him.'

'Knock first! He's in the bathroom,' Melina called out, but too late. As if the sight of Theo naked would come as a shock to Fatou. Ever since nursery school, they had grown up together. In the Rue de l'Abbé Grégoire, you never saw Fatou without Theo, or Theo without Fatou. Fatou was full of laughter all the time, except during demonstrations when some black or Arab kid had been killed on one of the housing estates. Then she would rush to see Theo and drag him off with her – 'Come on, Theo, we're going to the demo.' Theo could not do without Fatou, who took his mind off his books by telling him stories about Senegal.

The long prows of dugouts surfing the crest of the waves, the twisted arms of the baobabs, black straw-lofts perched on stilts, beaches where the fishermen unloaded their barracuda catches, the lumbering flight of the pelicans, the great red eyes of the hippos that emerged once every ten years onto the banks of the River Senegal ... Fatou talked and Theo dreamed. Mr Diop, Fatou's father, was a widower. A trained philosopher working for UNESCO, every now and then he would mention the African holidays they were sure to take together some day. But every year the two families found themselves back in La Baule, where Abdoulaye Diop would sit on the beach and gloomily compare the grey waves washing on the shores of France with the turquoise waves that jewelled the coasts of his homeland.

'MELINA!' Fatou yelled from the bathroom at the top of her voice. 'Come quick!'

Melina rushed in, and found Theo sprawled in a faint on the tiled floor. Fatou was patting at his cheeks, to no effect. Melina picked up a glass, filled it with a whoosh of the tap and dashed the water in Theo's face. He blinked and sneezed.

'Don't move, darling,' his mother whispered. 'Wait, and we'll help you get up.'

But as soon as he stood up, Theo's nose began to bleed.

'Tilt your head back, Theo,' Melina instructed curtly. 'Fatou, pick up that towel, please. Now wet it, really cold, and let me have it . . . There, on his forehead. It's nothing, darling. Don't worry.'

But her words belied her thoughts. No, this was not 'nothing': Theo was sick. And as the bleeding left off, she felt her son's neck. It felt thick with swollen glands. Melina's face tightened.

'Fatou, Theo won't be going to school this morning,' she decided. 'I'll give you a note to take to the Head.'

'Yes, of course,' said Fatou, petrified.

'Thank you, Fatou. Now, Theo, go and lie down again. I'll fetch you your breakfast in bed.'

'Great!' murmured Theo. 'Just what I like.'

'Lazybones,' said Fatou. 'I'll come back later. Don't worry, Theo.'

'But I'm not worried,' he replied. 'Should I be?'

A mystery illness

Doctor Delattre had checked Theo's blood pressure, tested his reflexes, felt the glands at the base of his neck, probed under his armpits and inside his groin, and paused for a moment when he came across a bruise on Theo's thigh.

'When did you hurt your leg?' he asked matter-of-factly.

But Theo, who knocked into things all the time, could not recall exactly where or when. After that, the doctor gave Theo's skin a thorough examination, and found another bruise on his stomach, which made him pause again. He listened to his chest, got him to flex his muscles and move his limbs, checked for stiffness in his neck, then stood up without a word and left without saying goodbye, which made Theo creep over to the door and eavesdrop on what the doctor was telling his mother.

As he left Theo's room, Doctor Delattre heaved a ponderous sigh.

'Until we run some tests, there's no knowing,' he said after a lengthy silence. 'I want you to call this number and ask them to come and do a blood test. Straight away.'

'Do you mean that I can't take him?' asked Melina in distress.

'I'd rather he stayed in bed. With nosebleeds, it's better to be careful.'

'Doctor, there's something the matter, isn't there?'

'Possibly,' the doctor evaded. 'As soon as I have the results I'll give you a call.'

'But what could it be?' sighed Melina.

'Stop tormenting yourself, Madame Fournay, and let's wait till tomorrow. And by the way, don't you have lessons today yourself?'

'Yes, in a couple of hours. But in the meantime . . .'

'In the meantime, keep him fed, give him what he wants, and let him be! It shouldn't be too serious.'

Theo went cheerfully back to bed. If it wasn't too serious, that meant he was due for a quiet week in bed with his books, his computer and the TV. Mum would bring him a tray of tea, toast and a boiled egg every morning, and he wouldn't have to tear himself away from his dreams. And that is exactly what happened this morning: Mum brought the tray, the egg, the toast soldiers and cup of tea, then she went off to school and Theo went back to sleep like a baby.

Naturally, before Mum left, the nurse had pricked his arm to take a blood sample, but that wasn't too high a price to pay for a whole day's enjoyment, and in any case Theo was used to injections.

The following day, Theo heard his mother call Doctor Delattre on the phone and then pull the door shut. What could the doctor be telling her?

Melina appeared, looking sad.

'Get dressed, Theo. We're going to the hospital for more tests. It's an urgent appointment.'

Hospital? Urgent? Theo felt daunted, but didn't want to let it show. The hospital spelled trouble. Still, at worst he was a year ahead in class.

'So what are they for, these tests?' he asked in a low voice.

'Nothing, darling. They want to take a bone marrow sample. It will hurt a little bit.'

'I think I can handle that. Can I have a sweetie if I promise not to cry?' Theo joked bravely.

Panic on board

When the test results came back from the hospital, everything changed.

The family went into a flap. Mum hid her tears, Dad came home very early in the afternoon, Attie kept popping in and out of her brother's room, and Irene cried. As for Fatou, she lost her laughter. Theo tried hard to tease her about her plaits coming half unravelled, but Fatou made do with a heartbreaking sad little smile. 'What's wrong with me?' he wondered.

Naturally, nobody told him anything. The funny thing was that he hadn't gone back to the hospital. A week went by. Theo didn't feel very much worse, or very much better. He drifted on a sea of weakness that didn't feel actively unpleasant. When Fatou asked him: 'So then, Theo, how are you feeling today?', he invariably answered: 'Just a bit tired, but I'll be OK.'

No question now of going back to school. Two days after the result of the bone marrow test, Dad had solved the problem in a trice. Fatou would bring the schoolwork, Theo would study at home and do his class work there: the teachers would mark it as usual, with the Head's approval. It wouldn't be hard to keep up.

Dad had it all worked out. He bought a desk designed for working in bed, a neat kind of drawing-board with feet that rested on the covers. He gave Theo a pen that slid across the paper extra smoothly . . . Yes, Dad took care of everything. But Theo favoured his own books over textbooks, and Fatou, who knew what he was doing, didn't seem to scold him at all.

One morning she brought him a necklace. 'A grigri from home,' she said as she hung it round Theo's neck. 'A kind of amulet. It's from my father. Wear it to please me. It will protect you, Theo.' It was a scorpion made of black pearls, dangling from a cord, an exotic-looking creature with studded white eyes. Theo liked to turn his protector this way and that between his fingers, thinking of the strange gods that watched over him from faraway Africa, the land of Fatou's birth.

Fatou had smiled on that day, but never once since then, and all this stress was taking its toll on Theo. The worst of it was Mum, summoning up her courage, eyes rimmed red with crying. Of course, Theo was taking medicine every day, but now that he no longer saw the boxes and instructions there was nothing he could learn. The doctor made regular calls, to inspect his skin, monitor the appearance of bruises, and feel his glands. Mum would bring the tablets, and the glass of water, sitting at his bedside without a word. One morning he asked whether he had Aids, and the question jolted Mum. No, he didn't have Aids, and then suddenly she fled, her eyes brimming with tears. No, all he knew was that he was ill, and that maybe, yes maybe he was going to die. But he wouldn't say that to anyone, and anyway it wasn't an absolute certainty.

CHAPTER 1

A Martha Kind
of Story

A crazy aunt

The second week, Theo went back to the hospital. Waiting room, blood test, waiting room, scanner, waiting room, X-ray, ultrasound, waiting room . . . there was no end to the routine. Theo was so frightened that he let it all wash over him. An object, that's what he'd become: they stretched him out, plugged him in, spread a clear cold jelly over his chest, stood him up again, whisked him off to another room, and so it went on. From time to time, Theo would ask whether it was a serious illness he had, but it only brought him noncommittal smiles. The nurses were kind, and Mum so gloomy that in order to stave off his own anxiety, Theo had brought his Egyptian mythology book with him.

'How can you read such dreary stuff?' his mother sighed. 'Why don't you try a good story? Something like *The Three Musketeers*.'

'Erm,' replied Theo. 'I've read it. It never even happened. All make-believe. Athos and Milady aren't real people.'

'Exactly! When it's not real it's more interesting! Anyway, what about your Egyptian gods? Do you think they really existed?'

'Well, yes,' Theo mumbled, and plunged back into a universe where ibises were scholarly, lionesses loving, and vultures were mothers. All the same, by the end of the day he was exhausted. Those big machines in the shadows, and those long, long silences.

One evening, when they came home, Dad waved a telegram to greet them.

9

'This time, at last, it's happening!' he cried. 'She'll be here tomorrow.'
'Who will?' asked Theo.
'Aunt Martha,' Mum replied. 'She's coming from Tokyo.'
'Tomorrow? What for?' he asked again.

No answer. They put him to bed, and shut themselves up in the study. There was something fishy going on, but then, when it involved Aunt Martha, that came as no surprise.

Aunt Martha was a rolling stone. When she was twenty, Martha Fournay had married a Japanese man whom she had met on the road in Thailand, while she was cycling round the world. Five years later, the Japanese husband had exited her life as unpredictably as he had entered it, and Aunt Martha had remarried, this time a rich Australian banker she had met in California somewhere between Los Angeles and San Diego. Aunt Martha had moved to Sydney with John Macquarie, and nothing more was heard from her, except at Christmas time. Then Uncle John had been killed in a car crash, and Aunt Martha had come into a huge fortune. Out of loyalty to John, whom she adored, she had sworn never to marry again, and because she had no children of her own she had transferred her affection on to her nieces and nephew, bombarding them with gifts from all over the world. Kimonos for the girls, American vitamins, special Japanese knives for slicing raw fish, matrioshkas, turquoise from China, spices from Indonesia . . . her inventiveness never ran dry.

But then she travelled all the time, she kept herself busy. After losing her husband, she had drawn on her knowledge of oriental languages to take up the study of traditional textiles. Aunt Martha had no need whatever to work, but she loved to roam the world, for her family's greater pleasure. Her personal life was a complicated fabric: she had friends all over the place, and talked about them with a wonderful directness that utterly exasperated her sister-in-law Melina, who felt she was pretentious. Aunt Martha was plump, and very lively, a sloppy dresser who adored jewellery, smoked cigarillos and practised yoga.

She was great company, but Dad thought she was slightly mad. 'Oh, it's another Martha kind of story,' he would say, when he thought something odd was going on. They seldom saw her, but she made a lot of phone calls, especially when a visit was due. 'I'll be with you in a month.' Then next day: 'No, in a couple of weeks, I've just got back from Kathmandu.' And the day after that: 'I'll be there on Friday night at eight, on the plane from Toronto.' And now Aunt Martha was flying in without any warning? The last time she'd done that had been when Grandad died.

For sure, she must have learned of Theo's illness.

Aunt Martha arrives

Draped in an Indian shawl that she unwrapped like a royal robe, Aunt Martha sank heavily into an armchair.

'Children, I'm frozen stiff,' she proclaimed. 'Melina, would you mind finding me some aspirin? Irene, what about making some tea, my dear? Look in the big bag and you'll find a packet from Japan, it's green tea. Attie, in my attaché case, the little red satin bag is for you, but you must look at it in your room. Now then, Theo, as for you . . .'

Lying on the living-room settee, Theo stared warily back at his aunt. They had all been dismissed without protesting, even Irene, who hated making tea. Aunt Martha heaved a mountainous sigh.

'Your present? We'll see about it later,' she said. 'So, you're not playing tricks on us, hmm? You're really sick? It's no joke?'

'How do I know?' answered Theo, twisting a lock of hair round his finger.

Squeezed into a tunic a size too small, and wearing an embroidered felt hat from Nepal, Aunt Martha was more ridiculous than ever. As if she were reading his thoughts, she met his eyes intently, and Theo felt guilty.

'But honest, Aunt Martha,' he stammered, 'nobody's told me a thing, nothing at all.'

'But you do have some idea, all the same.'

'Yes,' he admitted.

'And?'

Caught in the beam of Aunt Martha's stern gaze, suddenly Theo was sobbing.

'My poor child,' she sighed, and folded him in her arms. 'You don't suppose that I mean to stand by and do nothing?'

Theo couldn't stop the tears.

'My love,' Aunt Martha whispered, 'oh my little . . .' Then all at once she pushed him away from her. 'Stand up,' she commanded.

'I'm not allowed to,' he hiccuped.

'Rubbish!' she snapped. 'Now then, on your feet!'

Theo was goaded to his feet, and stood there like an idiot.

11

'There, you see,' she said with satisfaction. 'No, don't lie down again. Take a few steps . . . That's it. Very good. Now, jump.'

Aunt Martha really must be nuts. Jump, when he was ill, confined to his bed, doomed? . . . OK, why not? Theo performed a tiny little jump.

'Good. Not very high, but a jump all the same. Do you think you could manage that rucksack?' She pointed at a piece of overlooked luggage.

Without a murmur, Theo worked his arms through the straps of the black bag. It was quite heavy, and he tottered on his feet.

'It gives you some trouble,' she noticed. 'No wonder, you spend all your time in bed. It's just as I suspected.'

So what was Aunt Martha thinking? What did she have in mind? A thrill of sudden excitement ran through Theo.

'Do tell, Aunt Martha, have you brought me something?' he asked, running back to her welcoming arms.

'Yes, my boy,' she answered fondly. 'You'll know in a little while, at dinner time. In the meantime, go and get dressed. I prefer you in jeans.'

'You haven't brought me a tie, have you?' Theo asked. 'Because I can't stand wearing . . .'

'Don't be such an idiot. You can just put a scarf round your neck, that's fine with me.'

Surprises on the menu

Theo chose a red shirt, beige jeans and a black scarf. All right, they were warm weather clothes, but Aunt Martha was capable of switching on the summer in midwinter. In case it came in useful, while he was on his feet he turned on his computer, put *Wrath of the Gods* on the screen, and consulted the Pythia.

Smiling her catwalk smile, she charged him five points for the hint that might crack the riddle of the day. Theo paid up, and scanned the answer. 'Not your lucky day,' shrugged the Pythia, with a teasing grin. 'First you must journey through the Sacred Wood.' The Sacred Wood? Yet Theo thought he had explored the whole scenario. He exited the game and headed for the kitchen. Mum was tossing the salad.

'What are we having to eat tonight?' he asked her.

'Why, are you hungry, darling? There's minestrone, meze, and I've made a pie.'

'An apple pie?'

'No, pear, with meringue,' Melina answered anxiously. 'Will that do?'

As long as there was no red meat on the menu, it suited Theo. He prowled around the apartment, drifted into Irene's room, but as usual she had the cordless phone clamped to her shoulder, deep in conversation with her boyfriend. He backed out quietly and mooched off to tease Attie, as he had in the good old days, but Attie would only submit without a fight. That left Dad's study.

'What's this, you're out of bed?' he scolded. 'Listen, Theo, you can't be serious. Go and lie down, we'll call you when it's dinner time.'

Feeling discouraged, Theo skulked back to the living room and lay down on the big settee again. Dinner was dreary. Mum talked with phoney cheerfulness, Irene ate nothing, Attie just picked at her food, and Dad kept quiet. Aunt Martha, of course, was unstoppable, and over dessert she launched her attack.

'Well then, Theo,' she began, and ran her eye around the table. 'I've decided to take you round the world, just the two of us.'

Round the world! She really was a screwball, Aunt Martha!

'Do you know what you're saying?' Theo almost squeaked. 'What about school?'

'Pooh!' said Aunt Martha. 'School can wait. But I can't, I'm not immortal. Tell me if I'm wrong: you're a year ahead with your school work, aren't you?'

Theo was tongue-tied. He looked at his parents, but they were staring at their plates. As if in response to some invisible signal, Irene and Attie stood up and left the table.

'I'm ill, Aunt Martha,' Theo told her bravely. 'I don't believe that . . .'

'That's just it.' she insisted. 'These doctors are dummies. We're going to travel round the world and consult my kind of doctors – but not in hospitals, all right?'

This was another Martha kind of story! If not in hospitals, then where?

'Because this is no ordinary trip,' she pursued. 'Don't you go taking me for a tourist guide! You won't be seeing the Great Wall of China, or the Taj Mahal, or Niagara Falls . . .'

'Mum . . .' Theo appealed. 'Tell her!'

'I'm not a kidnapper either,' she broke in. 'You surely don't imagine that your parents aren't in favour? Isn't that right, Jerome?'

Theo's father gave a silent nod, but what would Mum say?

'Come on, Melina,' prompted Aunt Martha. 'Be brave.'

'Then I'm cured?' cried Theo, wild with delight.

'In any case, we'll call every day,' Aunt Martha ran on. 'I have a mobile

13

phone I bought in Tokyo, an amazing gadget, you'll see, there won't be a problem . . .'

'And you'll have blood tests done at every stop,' Mum continued. 'I have the names of all the hospitals, and . . .'

'Ah,' said Theo.

'There are excellent doctors all along the way, and you'll be taking the medicines with you, and . . .'

'Ah,' Theo sighed.

Aunt Martha shot a furious look at Melina.

'I don't want to hear another word about hospitals and drugs! Come on, let's clear the table. Girls! Come and lend us a hand.'

Aunt Martha could lay the law down when she wanted. As if by magic, Irene and Attie reappeared, and the table was empty in a flash.

'Jerome, please fetch that big folding map of the world that I've seen in your room, and I'll show you,' Aunt Martha ordered. '. . . Now, we start by . . .'

'Are we going to see the Pyramids?' Theo cut her short, suddenly very excited.

'Don't keep on interrupting! Attie, in my handbag there's a sheet of red stickers.'

'And the Kremlin?' Theo asked.

'You're interested in Lenin in his tomb?' replied Aunt Martha, busily sticking on the paper discs. 'I warn you, it's not on my itinerary.'

Fascinated, Theo watched the appearance of little red dots on the map of the world. Rome, Delphi, Luxor . . .

'I get it,' he said. 'It's a tour of the ancient world.'

'No it's not,' said Aunt Martha. 'Look here.'

'Am-rit-sar,' Theo deciphered. 'What's that?'

'The sacred city of the Sikhs,' Dad intervened. 'It's in Punjab.'

'Sikhs? What are they?'

'People who follow a religion you don't know about,' said Mum.

'Oh yes?' said Theo. 'I'd be surprised. With all the hassle it causes at school . . . Friday for the Muslims, Saturday for the Jews, Sunday for the rest – all that, and I don't know about religions!'

'We're listening,' smiled Aunt Martha. 'Go ahead.'

'The Jews are the oldest in the world,' Theo began. 'They pray on Saturday in a church they call a synagogue, and they were murdered by the Nazis in the war, it's called the Shoah. They lived in Jerusalem and they were forced to leave. Afterwards they were given back their country, Israel, but they fight all the time with the Muslims.'

14

'You might say that,' sniffed Aunt Martha. 'Who is their god?'

Theo fell silent.

Aunt Martha gave a silent ironic clap. 'Very good!' she said sarkily. 'The Jews have only one god, and they aren't allowed to make any sort of image of him, on any account, or even to name him. That's one point to remember. They are the chosen people of God, who made a covenant with them. That's two. And they're waiting for the Messiah who will come at the end of time, that's three. Keep going . . .'

'Wait,' said Theo. 'The Messiah, who's that?'

'The saviour of the world.'

'Then it's Jesus!' cried Theo.

'Not for the Jews, though, you see. Jesus is the Christians' Messiah. The Jews are still waiting.'

'But for the Muslims, no problem,' answered Theo, feeling put out. 'Their god is called Allah, he is great, and Muhammad is his prophet. They pray on Friday at the mosque, facing towards Mecca, their sacred city, where true Muslims go on pilgrimage once in a lifetime. Then they become hajis. They don't have priests, but marabouts.'

'That's better,' Aunt Martha conceded. 'But where did you get those marabouts from? They're only found in Africa.'

'My friend Fatou explained,' he answered proudly. 'She's a Muslim from Senegal.'

'And what about the Christians, Theo?'

'They believe in Jesus Christ, who was crucified by the Romans because he called himself "king of the Jews". Jesus was the Son of God the Father, who sent him to earth to redeem other people's sins. Christians go to mass on Sunday, they swallow the host, they kiss at the end, and the priests wear weird embroidered robes.'

'Let's say that's right,' sighed Aunt Martha. 'What difference do you see between the God of the Jews, the Christians and the Muslims?'

'Apart from the Jews and the Muslims seeming to believe in only one God, I've no idea,' he replied in a puzzled voice. 'Because for the Christians there are two, plus a dove called the Holy . . . I forget. Holy Father?'

'The Holy Ghost,' Melina corrected. 'You haven't been listening to Granny Theano.'

'What about other religions?' whispered Aunt Martha.

The Christians, Jews and Muslims, he had already mentioned. Aha, there were the Protestants, then the Orthodox Church, since the family was Greek, and then the Buddhists, the animists . . .

15

'Very good, Theo,' said his father.

'It's Fatou,' said Theo. 'She told me about the old gods of Africa. Well, when I say old, I don't mean . . .'

'And then?' Aunt Martha cut in.

'Then? Er . . . The Indians?'

'Which ones, in America or India?'

'America,' said Theo straight away. 'Because I've got the *Sacred Spirits* CD. And also, there's an episode of *Texas Ranger* when the ranger goes into a fire lodge and has the vision of an eagle, and he finds the boy who's been wounded by gangsters. But the Indian religion also exists on the other side, in India. What about that?'

'There are eight religions in India,' said Aunt Martha gently. 'You see, you don't know everything.'

'Zen!' announced Theo triumphantly. 'Irene's always saying that she's Zen!'

'All right,' Aunt Martha admitted. 'And in Brazil?'

Theo dried up. On China, he finally came up with Maoism.

'Not bad,' said Aunt Martha. 'A little bit out of date, perhaps, but that makes sense. You didn't mean "Taoism", by any chance?'

But Theo didn't know the word. The map caught his eye once again.

'Darjeeling?' he asked in surprise. 'I don't even know where it is! In Burma?'

'But Martha,' wailed Mum. 'What sort of hospital will Darjeeling . . .'

'Don't start that again, Melina. It's six hours by road from Calcutta and two hours from Delhi by plane. I've thought of everything.'

Silence fell around the table.

'Right,' said Theo. 'I've got it. We're making a tour of world religions. Is that it?'

That was it.

Mysterious preparations

But not all of it. The following day, as if the whole thing had been planned ages ago, the preparations started, and some really funny stuff began to happen. Aunt Martha made lists. Nothing odd about that. Lists of hotels, friends, trains, planes, boats, just what you'd expect.

But what about that list she only mentioned to her nieces, hmm?, and as soon as Theo appeared Irene hid these sheets of paper and Attie blushed, to the roots of her red hair. Why all these mysteries? Theo tried to grill Fatou.

16

'Theo, it's a secret. I've sworn not to tell.'

'Is it to do with my illness? Medicines or something?'

'Absolutely not!' Fatou insisted. 'It's a lot more fun than that.'

More fun than being ill? She came out with odd things did Fatou! As if Theo could have fun when he knew that he was very ill, and he might be going to – No, he didn't want to think about death. It must hurt a lot, death, otherwise no one would fear it. Loads of suffering, and then . . . Theo was sure that then came a windy voyage full of trials and complications. If you believed the ancient Egyptians and the Tibetans, life after death was no picnic . . . Grief choked his heart. The worst of it was that Mum would never bear it. And also that Theo might never see her again. No! The only solution was not to die.

One night when they thought he was in bed and he had come downstairs to fetch a yoghurt from the fridge, he overheard an odd conversation in the dining room.

'A scarab I said, not a tortoise!' Aunt Martha was insisting. 'I had it on the list. You'll have to go back to the shop.'

'All right, I'll find you your treasure. What stage is it for?'

'It's to hide under the . . .'

Intrigued, Theo stuck his head into the room and Aunt Martha stopped in midsentence.

'Back to bed, shrimp!'

Theo racked his brains for days, wondering why on earth Aunt Martha wanted to hide a scarab. He hunted for the list, to no effect, but he did notice that Aunt Martha had added a big padlocked bag to her luggage, and a locked casket. More secret cargo, twists in the plot. Were they presents? Surprises?

A month to go. Aunt Martha was spending her time in travel agencies. Some evenings she'd come home in a flap: 'Do you realize there's no air link between Bagdogra and Jakarta? You have to go via Calcutta. I don't believe it!' Or else she couldn't get a room in the hotel she'd chosen, which turned out to be either full, or closed down, or non-existent. At home, you'd find her using her mobile in impossible places, jabbering away at the top of her voice in English or German, with peculiar accents.

'Mahantji,' she bellowed into the phone, 'it's so good to hear you . . . Yes, I'm coming. No, in Paris for the time being. Oh, you have e-mail in Varanasi? OK, OK. But I won't be alone. My nephew will be travelling with me. Yes . . .' And here, all at once, she lowered her voice.

When she had finished her conversation with the invisible contact halfway round the world, she put down the handset with an air of satisfaction and proclaimed to all present: 'Mahantji is delighted.' Nobody knew who Mahantji might be, but Aunt Martha seemed so pleased that no one asked questions, especially because every day the phone was roping in another bunch of strangers delighted by the prospect of her visit – Miss Oppenheimer, Mrs Nasra, Rabbi Eliezer. 'OK,' she'd sigh, and riffle through her bulging address book. 'Brazil, let's try Brutus: Brutus Carneiro Da Silva . . .' and so it went on.

Theo's father, who had connections in the Foreign Ministry, organized a series of visas for his son, which took some fixing. Melina plucked up her courage and tackled the school principal. Mr Diop, Fatou's father, tackled the African section. Theo allayed his worries by consulting the Pythia on his computer.

The Pythia delivers a message

She wasn't giving too much away, the flame-haired oracle. Theo whizzed through the opening tests, which he knew by heart: giving a diamond to the beggar, putting an apple on the altar, and summoning up the serpent that taught him the language of the animals. Quickly the Hero ran northwards, carefully avoided the Kingdom of the Dead – Theo felt uneasy in the place – and plunged into a wood, a dark, uncanny place which had never come on screen before.

The Sacred Wood!

The Pythia winked, and put her finger to her lips. Then she gave her standard message: 'That will cost you five points . . .' OK, thought Theo. Come on, old girl, spit it out. Click on the Pythia. She continued: 'Take a ring with you and meet the king . . .'

The Pythia vanished and gave way to a heavenly country strewn with flowers and bathed in sunshine, a dream landscape that stretched beneath Greek olive groves. Near a ruined temple a shrouded figure awaited him. 'Have you brought the ring?' it asked in a cracked voice. 'If you have the ring and you meet the King, you will not die and you will meet up with your family again. If not . . .'

But Theo had no ring, and the scene faded into absolute darkness. Game over. For once, Theo had lost. He clicked and kept on clicking, but the Pythia did not wink again, and did not speak of a ring, and the shadow with the cracked voice did not reappear.

It gave him the shivers.

Christmas comes early

For over two days, Fatou never left the apartment. On the final evening there was a long commotion in the kitchen, where Theo was forbidden to set foot. Twenty minutes before dinner, Dad came in to warn him to 'look his best', and Dad was wearing a dinner suit, as if he was going to the opera. Theo complied: black jeans, T-shirt printed with a glorious tiger, white trainers, and Fatou's pearl scorpion.

When he opened the dining-room door, you'd think it was Christmas. Mum was wearing a long dress, the green one. Irene was a grown-up lady in a red bustier, Attie a ballerina in a blue tutu, Aunt Martha wore a black gandoura embroidered with white, and Fatou . . . Ah, Fatou. She had put on Theo's favourite robe – a boubou, she called it – the vermilion one with circles of gold. On the table, the couscous was ready, and in the corner a decorated Christmas tree twinkled above a nativity scene . . . Already?

'But it's too soon for Christmas!' he cried.

'We decided to bring the day forward,' Melina replied. 'Tonight is the tree and the presents.'

'Ah,' breathed Theo. 'Because by Christmas there's a chance I won't be . . . I mean . . .'

'Don't be such an idiot! Aunt Martha exploded. 'At Christmas we'll be off on our travels, that's all!'

'So where will Christmas be?' asked Theo suspiciously.

'You wait and see,' she hedged. 'And after that it'll be up to you to work out where we go next on our journey. All by yourself, like an adult.'

'But . . . But . . .'

'No buts. I've seen you playing that American game on your computer – what do you call the thing, with the red-haired Pythia?'

'*Wrath of the Gods*,' said Theo. 'What about it?'

'It's a real game you'll be playing,' his father told him. 'You'll have riddles of your own to be solved.'

'In each town we come to, you'll have to find something or meet someone,' Aunt Martha continued. 'It's you who'll work out our next destination.'

'No problem,' he answered. 'I already know about Rome, Luxor, Amritsar, Darjeeling and Delphi. You shouldn't have shown me!'

'I'm not as daft as you think.' she grinned. 'It's not going to be as easy as all that. For a start, I did show you various places on the map,

19

but that doesn't mean that we're going to visit them. And also, you'll have to solve riddles to find out where we're going next. For instance, supposing I tell you: "Go to the Sacred Heart of the city with the pyramid", what will you reply?'

'Cairo, of course!'

'Well, it's Paris,' she laughed. 'In Cairo there are several pyramids, but in Paris only one, the one in the Louvre courtyard . . . And didn't you think about the church of the Sacred Heart in Montmartre? You see it's not so simple . . .'

'But I don't know anything!' croaked Theo. 'I'm bound to make a hash of it.'

'Oh no you won't. We're taking a suitcase full of books to help you through. It will be hard work, I don't deny it, but your parents and I are agreed.'

'And if I can't work it out, then we go home?' asked Theo plaintively.

'Not on your life. If you're stumped, you can make a phone call to Fatou. She'll have some clues for you. Like the redhead on your screen.'

Fatou as the Pythia! That was the best news yet. Theo cheered up. But then she must already know everything . . . He jumped up to give her a hug, and Fatou backed away.

'Don't rely on me to tip you off,' she warned.

'No, but, just a cuddle, only five points,' he murmured, and led her away to his room.

'Sit down!' said Melina. 'You haven't finished your dessert.'

'Let them go,' said Jerome. 'They won't be seeing each other for a long time. If they ever see each other again . . .'

Melina's ring

After five minutes Jerome went to fetch Theo and Fatou.

'Now, Theo's presents,' he announced.

Crawling under the tall pine tree, Theo fumbled in the nativity scene. He jostled the donkey, overturned the ox, knocked down the Magi, gently shifted Mary and Joseph, and lifted the infant Jesus. The envelope was under the straw. A plane ticket from Paris to Tel Aviv, business class.

'Is that all?' he blurted in surprise.

'What more do you want?' Aunt Martha snapped.

'The rest is in your luggage, Theo,' said Dad. 'You'll find the presents in Jerusalem. It's the first test.'

'What for?' he cried. 'That's not fair.' And before he knew it, Theo was in tears.

'Mum,' he sobbed, 'I'm going away . . .'

Such ordinary words, 'I'm going away', but everyone in the room was close to tears: they all knew the other meaning, the meaning they must banish from their thoughts. As Melina walked him to his room, Theo whispered hoarsely:

'Mum, can I have one of your rings? Just any one, it doesn't matter which . . .'

Melina was puzzled.

'A ring?'

'One of yours, please, Mum . . .'

She looked down at her hand, which gleamed with a single gold band, her wedding ring. 'This one?' she murmured. 'Yes, of course,' and without hesitation she slipped it off her finger and slid it on to Theo's index finger.

'You know what it means, you won't lose it?'

'Promise,' breathed Theo. 'Now I'm certain to return.'

(Now I have the ring the Pythia wanted, he said to himself, closing his hand around his borrowed treasure. The ring that Dad had given to Mum was the most reliable of talismans.)

The why was still a mystery. The reason for the journey must have to do with those strange doctors who didn't work in hospitals. But surely Aunt Martha didn't mean to rely on miracles? It was another Martha kind of story, this whole trip.

All Theo knew was that he wasn't any better, that he was very ill, and that high hopes were pinned on the journey. He knew that, when it came to leaving, it was better to travel with Aunt Martha than to leave for the next world. And he also knew that here in Paris there would be lots more crying while he was solving the riddles.

He couldn't get to sleep. Now that he had the ring, what would the computer Pythia have to say? How could he escape the Kingdom of the Dead, how was he to avoid a meeting with the guardian of Hades, the ghastly skeleton called Charon?

He was still shuddering when Aunt Martha pushed the door open and poked her head through.

'Aunt Martha.' There was dread in Theo's voice. 'I want to ask you something. Am I going to die?'

'Now that is forbidden, my boy,' Aunt Martha replied, and ran her fingers through his curly hair.

CHAPTER 2

Next Year in Jerusalem

It was hard to say goodbye at the airport. Melina could barely quell her tears, while Jerome held her arm to support her. They mustn't make Theo break down. Mother and son were brave for one another, locked into the same silence, struggling to be cheerful . . . By chance, Fatou retrieved the situation.

'You're to bring me back those packs they give you on planes,' she ordered Theo, with a toss of her pigtails. 'You know, the ones with socks, and toothbrushes that come apart? I want them all!'

'Mm, yes,' said Theo, clearing his throat. 'What else should I look out for?'

'The miniature soaps and shampoos in the hotels, those little perfume samples, and . . . oh yes, the menus, please . . .'

'They're all yours. I'll phone you often . . .'

'That'll cost you five points! From now on, I'm your Pythia . . . Come and kiss me goodbye.'

On the plane, after the in-flight meal was served, Aunt Martha buried herself in her magazines. Theo tried all the buttons on the arm-rests, switched the overhead light on and off, summoned the hostess by mistake, adjusted the seat to recline, and dozed off. From time to time his head would loll on to Aunt Martha's shoulder, and he woke up with a jolt. 'Sleep, Theo,' she whispered.

But anxiety was practically choking him. Theo thought about Jerusalem, which appeared so often on TV with 'our special correspondent' posed in front of a golden dome, and away in the distance, pure white spires, and pink roofs so peaceful that it was hard to imagine the violence below, the gunfire and the bombs. Yet the special correspondent talked of nothing but killings and something called the Middle Eastern peace process.

'Aunt Martha,' he asked, 'what is that golden dome that overlooks Jerusalem?'

'The Dome of the Rock. It's one of the great holy places of Islam.'

'But the Jews also have their synagogue in Jerusalem. Is it smaller than the mosque, then?'

'First, the Dome of the Rock is not a mosque,' she corrected him. 'Second, the Jews did build their Temple in Jerusalem, but it was destroyed a very long time ago. Listen, don't start with your questions, you'll give me a headache!'

'Won't you at least tell me why we're starting with Jerusalem?'

'Of all the cities in the world, Jerusalem is the holiest,' she told him gravely. 'The most magnificent, the most moving, and the most badly torn apart. Just think: it is nearly three thousand years since King Solomon built the first Temple of the one god in Jerusalem on Mount Moriah. Solomon's Temple was plundered several times, then pulled down and rebuilt again, before it was razed by the Romans . . . It was to Jerusalem that Jesus came to carry the good word, and his followers spread palms in his honour, because he was the Son of God made man, which might sound confusing. There, in the holy city of the Jews, he was arrested, tried, and crucified on a hill, and it was in Jerusalem that he rose again . . . And then again, it was from a high rock in Jerusalem that the prophet Muhammad leaped into the sky on his winged donkey-mule. Will that do, shrimp?'

'I don't even know who King Solomon is,' Theo confessed. 'Or that Muhammad rode on a winged animal. It's amazing how little I know!'

'At least you know who Jesus is'

'Of course! He was born in a stable between the ass and the ox, his mother is the Virgin Mary and his father Joseph the carpenter, except that his real father was God. The rest is easy: he died, rose again, and then took off to heaven.'

'Took off!' Aunt Martha grumbled. 'Jesus rose to heaven, if you please. That day is called Ascension Day.'

'So if that's right, that makes two who flew away,' said Theo. 'Jesus and Muhammad. Who did the Jews have?'

'No one. The Jews have founding fathers, kings, prophets, heroes, martyrs and war chiefs, but none of them rose to heaven. To be with

God? Impossible, when you remember it's forbidden to look him in the face!'

'Really? But in that case, what do you do?'

'You listen to him. In Jerusalem, God speaks in several languages. In the Hebrew of the Jews, the Arabic of the Koran, the Latin, Armenian and Greek of the Christians . . . Sometimes it's difficult to hear him, because people are hard of hearing, and they chatter too much. Often, because of the difference in their languages, they don't understand each other and the result is killing. Do you know the story of the tower of Babel?'

'Vaguely,' he said. 'People decided to build a tower that reached all the way to heaven, so high that God was angry. Why he didn't like it, who knows? Anyway, he managed to stop the building.'

'He simply invented the languages of the world. Till then, all people had spoken the same language – it was easy, they all understood one another. But they tried to rival God, so God punished them. Bang! All at once there were languages. When they started their gigantic building again, they no longer understood each other and everything stopped.'

'So Jerusalem is the Tower of Babel?' Theo responded.

'But also the centre of the world, the place of the creation of Adam, the father of us all, the place where all the winds, before they go to blow across the earth, come and bow down in front of the Divine Presence. You've often heard me say that I don't believe in God, haven't you? Well, on the heights of Jerusalem it's different. These three religions that each express their love for God so powerfully, that breath of greatness that hovers over the ancient stones, those mouths that pray together and apart . . .'

'Those hands that plant bombs and fire machine guns,' Theo chimed in. 'If God does exist, then what is he up to? Couldn't he stop them?'

'It seems that the world is not ready. If we were ripe for peace, they tell us that God would grant it at once.'

'That doesn't make sense. If he can't even make peace, how do they prove that God exists?'

'This isn't the last time you'll want to ask that question. But I warn you, there's no answer . . .'

'The existence of God, a question without an answer?' laughed Theo. 'You must be kidding. What makes all those millions of people on earth believe in God? There must be a reason!'

Aunt Martha heaved a big sigh and said no more. The plane was over the Mediterranean. Through the window, Theo could see a scatter of islands whose names he did not know. The sky was a pale blue sea so close and so peaceful that Theo felt like diving into it.

'If God exists,' he whispered, 'I don't see why I'm going to die. Or maybe he's just not clever enough, Aunt Martha?'

Jews, Christians and Muslims

The plane landed at Lod airport, not far from Tel Aviv. Aunt Martha had warned Theo that the security precautions were exceptionally strict there, and every piece of baggage was searched.

After passport control, Aunt Martha spotted a young man dressed in a lightweight suit. She called and waved, and he came over.

'Martha, it's good to see you.'

'My dear friend,' gushed Aunt Martha. 'How kind of you to come and collect us. This is my nephew Theo. Theo, the French consul-general in Jerusalem.'

'Hello,' Theo mumbled, wondering how a consul could also be a general.

The official car and chauffeur were waiting outside. Aunt Martha subsided on to the seat, Theo sat in front, and they headed for Jerusalem.

'I suppose your car's still armoured?' Aunt Martha asked casually.

Bullet-proof, like a thriller! Theo couldn't believe his ears.

'Let's hope one day it will be unnecessary,' the Consul said. 'But you know, since the latest wave of attacks we've all been very careful. The Palestinians live in a state of permanent tension, and the religious community is not at all happy . . .'

'Religious community? What's that?' asked Theo as politely as he could.

'Theo! You don't interrupt grown-ups!' Aunt Martha scolded. 'But as I've told you about our journey, my friend, perhaps you could give him an answer . . .'

'What a question!' said the Consul. 'But I'll try. Here, young man, you are in the State of Israel. The great majority of its citizens are Jewish, and Judaism is the religion of the country.'

'Like the Roman Catholics at home,' Theo broke in.

'More than that,' said the Consul. 'In France, the Constitution of the Republic respects all religions equally, and the Catholic religion is simply the most widely practised. Here in Israel, there is no Constitution. Judaism is the official religion, but other religions are perfectly legal.'

'I don't understand,' said Theo. 'At home, religion and government are two different things. Isn't it the same in Israel?'

'Not exactly. The laws of Judaism are applied very strictly. I'll give you an example. In France, we don't work on Sunday because for Catholics it's the day of Christ's resurrection, but also so that everybody should have at least one day's rest.'

'The weekend,' Theo answered. 'It's sacred!'

'But in Israel, all activity ceases from sunset on Friday till the same time on Saturday. It's the day of Shabbat, the Sabbath, and it's taken very seriously . . . The Orthodox community want to apply the religious principles that require Jews to devote themselves to prayer throughout Shabbat, and not to light fires, use electricity, cook food or take the lift. It's very strictly enforced. But I should add that many Israelis are simply secular.'

'So they're atheists?' said Theo.

'Your nephew is clever, Martha,' the Consul remarked. 'But there's a big difference between an atheist and being secular, young man. To be an atheist means that you don't believe in God. To be secular means that you respect your country's civil laws and don't inject religion into everything you do. You can be Catholic and secular, Jewish and secular, Protestant and secular . . .'

'Muslim and secular too?' asked Theo.

'Theo knows a girl from Senegal,' Aunt Martha explained. 'But let's go back to the orthodox Jews.'

'Judaism is the religion of the State of Israel, but not all citizens practise it in the same way. Some are content to believe in the God of the Jews and to follow his commandments, others are atheists, and others are very devout. These are the ultra-orthodox. Their belief is very simple: as long as there is a single Jew on earth who does not observe the Sabbath rest, the Messiah will be unable to come and redeem the world. That is why they demand such total obedience to the laws. Most can be recognized by their full beard and by the skull cap they wear, a knitted *kippah*.'

'What's that?' asked Theo.

'Custom requires all Jewish men to cover their heads in the presence of God. Usually they wear the *kippah*, but some wear black hats, or hats edged with fur.'

'But what do the orthodox observe more than the rest do?'

'Their religion to the letter of the law, but on top of that, many dream of a Greater Israel,' the Consul sighed. 'They don't want Palestinians on their soil. It was an Orthodox Jew who murdered Itzhak Rabin, for example, because he was making peace with the Palestinians.'

'Who are all Muslim terrorists,' said Theo. 'I know that.'

'Then you know nothing,' flared Aunt Martha. 'Muslim terrorists don't represent all Palestinians. And besides, these Muslim extremists are just like the fundamentalists on the other side: they don't want peace. Also, Theo, there are Muslim Palestinians, but there are Christian Palestinians too.'

'Wait a minute,' said Theo. 'Christian Palestinians? OK, here, in the beginning, there were the Jews, right?'

'Depends on where you begin,' Aunt Martha answered. 'In the beginning there were the Canaanites who lived in the valley of Gehenna, worshipped gods and goddesses, and offered sacrifices to them to make the rain fall and water the earth, to bring good harvests. Some claim that they even sacrificed their own children . . .'

'What?' said Theo. 'Living children?'

'Mind what you say' said Aunt Martha. 'Not everybody thinks so. In any case, the idol-worshipping Canaanites made a covenant with the small Hebrew minority who worshipped a single god whose name it was forbidden to pronounce. You could only use his initials, "YHWH", otherwise he is sometimes called "Adonai" – "my Lord" – and sometimes "Hashem" – "the Name".'

'Yes!' cried Theo. ' "He who does not have a name." It's in the film. When a bush catches fire in front of Moses. I've seen that, with Charlton Heston and Yul Brynner. *The Ten Commandments*, Cecil B. De Mille, 1956.'

'What a mine of information!' said the Consul. 'But in that case, Theo, you know the whole . . .'

'No, because in the film, apart from God speaking through the fire with a voice like a man's, and being stronger than the gods of Egypt, you don't really know what he wants.'

'There's no easy answer,' the Consul confessed. 'Generally speaking, he wants his followers to worship him and him alone, to be worthy of him, and to obey his commandments.'

'So the Jews must have badly disobeyed him,' said Theo, 'if they ended up in slavery in Egypt.'

'They did disobey,' said the Consul, 'and God punished them harshly for it. You see, the relationship between the Jews and God hasn't always been free of violence. God often gets angry with his people . . .'

'But God gives them plenty of help, all the same,' Theo said. 'That time when Moses decided to lead them out of Egypt . . . The rod turned into a serpent, the foul stench rising from the rivers and seeping through the streets, and all the rest. Then they came back here. Is that it?'

'Came back, went away and came back again,' said the Consul. 'They were deported to Babylon by King Nebuchadnezzar, then driven out by the Romans after the fall of the Temple . . .'

'Will we see the Temple?' asked Theo excitedly.

'No, because it was destroyed on that occasion. It was then, when their Temple was pulled down, that the Jewish people, expelled from their homeland, dispersed for their long exile all over the world. First into Greece and Egypt, later to the Maghreb, Spain, Italy, Russia, Poland, India, China . . . Then to the USA, South America, Africa . . . century after century, truly everywhere. And all through the centuries they never ceased to be persecuted, especially between 1933 and . . .'

'I know,' Theo broke in. 'They told us at school. The Holocaust, in the last war. How the whole world let it happen, I will never understand.'

'No one ever has,' Aunt Martha said.

'Anyway,' the Consul continued, 'because this land had once been theirs, the international community decided to return to the Jews the country that became the State of Israel in 1948, because of the millions murdered by the Nazis.'

'They did quite right to return it,' cried Theo.

'Except that the land was peopled by Palestinians and many of them were forced into exile in their turn . . . There've been wars, truces, uprisings, suicide bombings, stones thrown by kids, bloody riots and negotiations . . . Today, Israelis and Palestinians are taking steps for peace, but on both sides it's hard to make progress. Among the Palestinians, the extremists don't want it, and among the Jews, the supporters of Greater Israel oppose it, whether they're secular or religious.'

'That doesn't tell me why,' said Theo. 'Don't they want to share?'

'No,' said the Consul. 'For the orthodox, this land belongs only to the Jews, as it is written in the Bible.'

'I still don't see where the Christian Palestinians come from,' said Theo.

'Well then, use your head,' Aunt Martha murmured.

Theo thought fast, and racked his memory. Christians believe in Christ, Christ was born . . .

'I've got it!' he cried. 'Christ was born in Palestine and died in Jerusalem. Palestine is also for the Christians.'

'Also,' said Aunt Martha. 'It's all in that little word "also".'

'Especially because it's also for the Muslims,' the pensive Consul remarked.

The route to Jerusalem ran along the edge of hillsides. Now and then a big Jeep would drive past, with people carrying guns.

'A thrice holy city,' said the Consul. 'Yerushalayim, "city of peace", holy for Jews, Jerusalem, holy for Christians, Al-Quds, "the shrine", holy for Muslims.'

'Holy for Jews, I understand,' said Theo. 'And for Christians too. But why for Muslims?'

'Patience,' said Aunt Martha.

A thought struck Theo. 'Didn't the Crusades happen around here?'

'Quite right,' the Consul agreed. 'In the days when the Muslims held Jerusalem, both sides fought over the tomb of Christ, you could say. When fifteen thousand crusaders under the orders of Godfrey of Bouillon stormed Jerusalem at the end of the First Crusade, to restore Christianity to the Holy Places, they sobbed with joy, but they also slaughtered the people inside. It happened on the fifteenth of July 1099, a dreadful night for Jerusalem. The Christian crusaders massacred tens of thousands of Muslims, burned the Jews shut up inside their synagogues, and piously washed their hands in the blood of their enemies.'

'That's awful,' said Theo. 'And they were Christians!'

'Oh yes, but afterwards they put on nice clean robes and walked barefoot where Jesus had trodden! The reign of the Christians lasted till the great Muslim leader Saladin recaptured Jerusalem in 1187, but – unlike the Crusaders – they spared the churches and allowed the Jews to return . . . So many battles over the tomb of Christ!'

'That's weird,' said Theo, 'when you think that, logically, either there's nothing inside it or else Christ didn't rise again.'

'That's just what the Jews and Muslims say,' the Consul nodded. 'That he was not a god but simply a prophet, as others had been before him. Of course, a prophet mattered to them. But there isn't only the tomb of Christ in Jerusalem, you know. There's also the Dome of the Rock, one of the most holy Muslim places . . . and also the Wailing Wall, where Jews come to weep before the remains of their lost Temple.'

'I've seen it on TV,' said Theo. 'They stuff bits of paper into cracks in the wall, with wishes written on them.'

'"Next year in Jerusalem",' Aunt Martha quoted solemnly. 'All Jews in exile have spoken those words on the day of Passover, the Jewish festival.'

'What's Passover?' asked Theo. 'I knew from school about their not working on Saturdays, but not about Passover.'

'Listen, and I'll tell you,' said Aunt Martha.

The angel of death and a few messiahs

Although it occurs around the same time as Easter, the two festivals are entirely unrelated. The Jews celebrate Passover in memory of the dreadful night during which they had fled from Egypt, where Pharaoh had held them in bondage for many years, whereas the Christians celebrate Easter in memory of the miraculous day when Jesus, having died on the cross three days before, rose again.

Passover consists of a special meal, eaten in a reclining position, in which a roast kid is served, together with bitter herbs and unleavened bread, which is bread made without a raising agent.

'Matzoh,' said Theo proudly. 'Dad brings some home now and then.'

The Christian Easter celebrates a day of rejoicing with a magnificent mass, held early in the morning of Easter Sunday. According to the story told to children in France, that is when the bells return from Rome, having been sent there for Lent, as a sign of mourning.

'Yes, well, that's only a custom, nothing more,' said Aunt Martha. 'Because there aren't any clocks in the New Testament.'

But it all required explaining, and when the Consul ran out of steam, Aunt Martha took over.

Passover night had been terrible in Egypt, not for the Jews but for the Egyptians, because in order to win the right to leave this country where the Jews had suffered dreadfully, Moses had cursed Pharaoh and brought down all sorts of plagues on Egypt, which Theo remembered clearly because of the film: swarms of locusts, rivers turned to blood, livestock dying, and finally the last and worst of all. At midnight on the fateful day, all of the firstborn in Egypt died, even Pharaoh's eldest son. That is why the Jews celebrated the feast of Passover in memory of the eve of their liberation, when they all stood ready to leave, wearing their sandals, with no time for the dough to rise. That is why the bread was baked without leaven, which produced a bread with no crust and no body, very flat and crumbly. As for the herbs, they had the bitterness of the slavery now at an end. Guided by Moses, the Jews set out at dawn, and it was not long before Pharaoh sent an army to recapture them.

'I remember,' said Theo. 'Moses divided the sea in two, the Jews passed through the waves, and when Pharaoh's soldiers followed, the sea closed in again. Served him right.'

And Christ died on the cross in Jerusalem because the Jews considered him an imposter, and a danger to Judaism. He claimed to be the son of God, and that was intolerable, so the Jews said. No one was the son of God. God had no face or body, and no family. Worse still, there were some who took Jesus for the Messiah, the saviour promised by God to his prophets, who would come to bring salvation to the world. Certainly some prophets had indeed foretold that one day the Messiah would come, but not this young man born in poverty, this nobody who dared to proclaim himself the Son of God. So the Jews asked the Romans to rid them of this troublesome Jesus, the son of Mary and of Joseph the carpenter.

Palestine was part of the Roman empire at that time. In theory the Romans did not interfere in religious affairs, except when the Jewish priesthood asked them to deal with threats to the established order. In this case the priesthood, under the high priest Caiaphas, accused Jesus of stirring up trouble in the country by allowing himself to be called 'king of the Jews', which was quite untrue. But Caiaphas had a powerful argument on his side, because in those days the only effective king of the Jews was the Roman emperor Tiberius. To all appearances, the Roman governor was not convinced of the guilt of the accused, a harmless dissident. All the same, it was the Roman who condemned Jesus to be crucified. But he solemnly washed his hands before pronouncing the sentence, as a sign that he did not endorse this injustice.

'This man was Pontius Pilate, wasn't he?' asked Theo. Dad often says: 'I wash my hands of this, like Pontius Pilate.'

So, for political reasons, Jesus was sentenced to be crucified, and he did not defend himself. They publicly scourged him, to make a fool of him they put a crown of sharp thorns on his head, and they made him carry the main beam of the cross all the way along the road that led to 'the place of a skull', Golgotha, where he was to die. Suspended by their hands, with their feet tied together, those sentenced to crucifixion were doomed to a slow and dreadful death: their shinbones were broken, the body was no longer supported, their lungs collapsed under the weight, they could not breathe and died of suffocation. The 'king of the Jews' came in for special treatment: though his legs were not broken, he was nailed to the wooden cross by his wrists and feet, which bled. His head also bled, because of the thorns in his crown. Flanked by two thieves condemned to the same punishment, Jesus died before they did, uttering a terrible cry. But he did not stay dead very long. Three days later, his tomb lay open, with his shroud discarded, and he appeared to a few wretched women who were weeping outside his tomb. Yet people might have understood that he was the Son of God, because at the exact hour of his death, after his cry of agony, there was a clap of thunder and the earth shook. So was Christ the Messiah, yes or no?

Yes, said the Christians, yes because he rose again from the dead. No, said the Jews, from that day onwards. No. The Jewish people saw Messiahs enough after Jesus. The Jewish communities in exile saw the rise of several charismatic figures who claimed to be the Messiah just as Jesus had done before them. Sometimes – in the sixteenth century, for example – their fate was to be burned at the stake as one of the many victims of the Inquisition, in the days when the Roman Catholic Church was conducting a frenzied persecution of the Jews. But there were some who rode a wave of success, as in the case of Sabbatai Zevi, who proclaimed himself the Messiah in 1648, and amassed a legion of followers among the exiled Jews of Europe. In the end he converted to Islam, when captured by the Turks and confronted with the choice of conversion or death.

'There, I'm confused,' said Theo. 'He, the Messiah, became a Muslim?'

Aunt Martha granted that Theo had reason for confusion. What he must realize was that the ages of waiting for the Messiah were bound to attract pretenders from among the Jewish people. To this day, some devotees were convinced that the Messiah, the real Messiah, was close at hand. In the 1990s he had nearly flown in from New York in the form of a very old and very holy American Rabbi called Menachem Schneerson. One morning in Jerusalem the news agencies had been notified that the Messiah was to arrive in Israel on the El Al flight from New York that same night. His house was ready; this would be a tremendous event. But he did not come, and then at the age of ninety-two he died in Brooklyn. You might think that faith in this Messiah of modern times would have died out – but not at all. Two years after his death, his followers were saying that Rabbi Schneerson had not died and that he would appear again. In Israel, others were saying that the Messiah – yet another Messiah – was about to appear in Judaea to redeem the whole world.

'In Judaea?' said Theo in amazement.

'That particular group wants to withdraw from Israel and found its own little State of Judaea,' the Consul intervened. 'But the strangest thing of all is the "Jerusalem syndrome". Do you realize, young man, that every year they record about three hundred barefoot cranks, Jews or Christians, dressed in tunics, who roam the streets of the holy city and proclaim the end of time, because they're all messiahs.'

'Madmen,' said Theo.

'That's what the children call after them in Arabic – *Majnun*. The demented one. They're usually harmless, but all the same one of them set fire to a famous mosque to hasten the end of time, so they have to keep an eye on them . . .'

'Yes,' resumed Aunt Martha, 'the Jewish people has got used to messiahs. But so have other peoples. Every now and then they have also appeared in the United States. For example, early in the nineteenth century, when he was fifteen years old, an American citizen who wasn't a Jew at all, Joseph Smith, claimed that he had received the first of what became a series of revelations. In one of these, God enabled him to discover in New York State a new gospel called the *Book of Mormon*, from the name of the previously unknown prophet who was said to have transcribed it. Ten years after his first vision, Smith founded his movement, which makes him either a new Moses or else a new Messiah, it's hard to say. In 1844 he was arrested for treason, then murdered by a lynch mob that broke into the jail where he was held. After his death, his successor organized and developed the new Mormon religion, the Church of Jesus Christ of Latter-Day Saints.'

'What is it?' asked Theo.

The Consul protested: Aunt Martha had no right to apply the word 'religion' to a sect that was certainly big but was not a true religion. Aunt Martha retorted that she saw no difference between a sect and a religion, except that an official religion was always a sect that had succeeded. Seeing that the Mormons numbered millions, that made them a religion in the USA.

Her words annoyed the Consul: was she by any chance suggesting that the Christian religion had been a sect at first, and then become very successful? That's right, Aunt Martha persisted. The Consul frowned.

'But sects are really dangerous,' Theo replied. 'On TV you see reports all the time . . . Their gurus are crooks! They rape women, and they have themselves treated like princes! Or else they kill each other, and kill other people with them . . . And whatever sort they are, they all steal their followers' money. How do these crackpots do it?'

'Generally, they have strange magnetic eyes,' Aunt Martha explained. 'They are good talkers, but they can also be silent when it will strengthen their hold on their disciples. They attract unhappy, unstable people the same way fly paper attracts flies . . . You can't unstick them from their guru!'

'So really they're hooked,' said Theo. 'Like a drug.'

'Something like that. It's as hard to remove a fool from his sect as it is to separate a fool from his drugs, because the followers need the guru just like a fix. Madness can be injected too.'

'And it kills,' Theo said. 'An awful lot of people.'

Neither of the adults could say that Theo was wrong, when they considered the deaths of David Koresh's Branch Davidians in Waco, Texas, and the collective suicides of the Solar Temple in Europe and Canada in the 1990s, not to mention – though it was before Theo's time – the deaths of more than nine hundred men, women and children in Jonestown, Guyana, in 1978, when the cult leader Jim Jones persuaded the followers of his 'People's Temple' to commit mass suicide. Most took cyanide, some were murdered.

'Yuck,' said Theo. 'That is disgusting. If that's what your Mormons are like, then sects are bad news.'

No, they assured him, the Mormons were different, and not the least bit dangerous. Aunt Martha and the Consul eventually agreed that time had a part to play, and that after two thousand years of existence the Christian Church no longer had much in common with the sect it once had been. As for the Mormons, let the best part of a millennium go by, then look again, but Aunt Martha pointed out that they had founded a town well known throughout the world, Salt Lake City.

The car had reached the outskirts of Jerusalem, under its layer of haze. The Consul glanced at his watch. A quarter of an hour to go: they would be just in time for lunch.

'By the way,' said Theo, 'the Roman Catholics also have a meal, like the Jews. Didn't they use to eat bread and drink wine at mass, in the beginning?'

That was quite true, the Consul agreed, but the Passover meal of the Jews could not be compared to the mass of the Christians, because the Christians celebrated mass every Sunday in memory of Christ's last supper. In fact, even though Jesus had celebrated the last supper in Jerusalem on the day of Passover, the two meals couldn't be more different: the Jews commemorated the end of a painful era, while the Roman Catholics commemorated the final events in the life of the Messiah, and therefore the beginning of a new age.

'Speaking of meals, what's for lunch?' asked Theo with a yawn.

In the beginning was confusion

The big gates swung slowly inwards under the gaze of the electronic cameras, and the car drove into the garden of the consulate. The steward came to collect their luggage and to inform the Consul that his meeting had already started, which sent their host hurrying away.

Theo's room was perched at the top of a spiral staircase, and Martha's further down. As they were climbing the stairs, suddenly Theo swayed and blacked out. The steward carried him up to his bed. Aunt Martha had turned pale.

'I'll fetch him a hot drink,' the steward whispered. 'Does the boy suffer from air sickness?'

Or perhaps, in their hurry, they had omitted one of Theo's drugs. Aunt Martha took out the list from her handbag and consulted it carefully.

'These damned medicines!' she said between her teeth. 'Oh, the day we get rid of them! There, we've forgotten one. Here's some water. Down with it!'

Down it went. Theo swallowed his capsule and closed his eyes. He didn't feel really tired, but his head was spinning hard. He felt like consulting his friend the Pythia, but he vaguely understood that in Jerusalem there were no monsters, giants, dragons or oracles, and that no ordeal out of Greek mythology would get the Jews and Christians to agree, not to mention the Palestinians, Christian or Muslim, who disagreed with both.

'He's asleep,' whispered Aunt Martha as she closed the door behind her. 'Don't bring anything for him, we won't disturb him.'

But Theo, who could not get to sleep, wondered what he was going to do in a country where people killed each other in a completely religious way, in the name of God, as if their god was not the same. Didn't Jews, Christians and Muslims all talk about a single god? Well then? Well, he'd probably understand tomorrow, or later, supposing he had time. Or never . . .

Oh no, it was much too soon to throw in the towel. Don't give in! Theo hadn't yet gone through his luggage, where the Christmas presents waited. He stood up carefully and opened the big bag that contained them all, each with its label attached. His father's present was a camera with built-in zoom, very light. Attie's was the latest kind of mobile phone, Irene's a radio-alarm showing the time all over the world. His mother had gone for the 'really useful' category, a parka and fur-lined boots. Fatou never went for the obvious: she had given Theo a tiny scroll of verses from the Koran, rolled up in a miniature leather case and threaded on a slim leather thong. Theo hung it round his neck straight away, on top of Fatou's first necklace, the grigri from Senegal.

At the bottom of the gift bag lay a notebook with a bright red cover and a pencil. The label had an unexpected inscription: 'From all your teachers'. It wasn't a bad idea he thought, as he picked up the pencil, turned to the first page and jotted: 'Jews and Muslims = one God. Christians believe the Messiah is Jesus, Jews are still waiting. Passover = memory of exodus from Egypt. Christian Easter = memory of resurrection of Jesus. Jerusalem holy city for Jews, Christians, Muslims.' But was the God of the Christians a single god or not? And did the Muslims also have a festival like Easter in memory of an important event? The journey was starting in a tangle.

'Next year in Jerusalem,' he mused as he fell asleep. 'Well, I don't know about New Year's Day, but I know for sure that for Christmas we'll still be in Jerusalem.'

There he was wrong, but he didn't know it yet.

Theo's first three guides

'Theo, do you know what time it is? THEO!'

Oh no, he'd overslept. Was he going to be late for school again? He sat up fast, swung one foot out of bed, and then the other, opened his eyes . . .

But it wasn't his mother who loomed at the foot of the bed, it was Aunt Martha, and Theo was not in the Rue de l'Abbé Grégoire in Paris, but in Jerusalem, where breakfast was waiting. Aunt Martha suggested a quick wash, a clean shirt, a scarf, a comb . . . and he'd better bring the parka, as it was cold outside.

'Careful on the stairs,' said Aunt Martha, taking his arm. 'Turn right . . . Keep going . . . There.'

The stairs led down to the terrace, from which they could see the shining white walls of the Old City, so beautiful that Theo was stopped in his tracks. It looked like a stronghold in a tale of knights and fairies. Beyond the ramparts rose onion domes, spires and towers, flanked by tall dark cypresses. The air was crystal-clear and on the parched grass the footpaths seemed to belong to a bygone age.

'Isn't it beautiful?' said a quiet voice behind him. 'From here you are looking at the Ottoman wall. Come with us, my son.'

Dazzled by the intensity of the light, Theo turned round and saw that three old gentlemen with beards and kindly smiles were standing on the terrace.

'This is Theo,' said Aunt Martha, shepherding him towards them. 'But first he has to eat. They've made us a buffet. Which would you prefer, tomato salad and cold chicken, or roast beef and mashed potatoes?'

'But aren't we expecting your friend the general consul?' asked Theo.

'Consul general!' his ruffled aunt replied. 'This isn't the Roman empire!'

'Never mind,' said Theo, 'with the Romans they were generals, then consuls, then they moved on to emperor, so . . .'

'Anyway, he sent to tell us that his meeting wasn't over,' said Aunt Martha. 'Go on, help yourself . . .'

Chicken salad.

Theo sat with his plate perched on his knees, wolfing down his food and inspecting the three men. Looking closer, he saw that they were not as old as he'd first thought. The impression had come from the three beards, one of them white over a long coat, one of them brown with a grey suit, the other fair, with a small round cap pinned to his hair, a *kippah*. What were they doing on the terrace?

'Let me introduce myself,' said the one with the fair beard. 'Rabbi Eliezer Zylberberg. Your aunt asked me to show you the Jerusalem of the Hebrews.'

'I am Father Antoine Dubourg,' said the man in the suit. 'We shall also visit the Jerusalem of the Christians.'

'And I am Sheikh Suleiman Al'Hajid,' said the third, whose voice was quite hoarse. 'I will show you the Jerusalem of the Muslims. But we'll all go together, shall we?'

'Then you're not angry with each other?' cried Theo in surprise. 'I thought . . . I've heard . . .'

'You heard that in Jerusalem we men of God are still fighting one another?' sighed the Sheikh. 'Some of us reject these stupidities. For many years, Jews and Muslims lived here on good terms. In the days of Turkish rule, the Jews lived in peace in this land . . . And at the end of the nineteenth century, when they started to return to settle in Palestine, the Arabs did not turn them away. Islam can be tolerant.'

'Do you think so?' Theo objected. 'That's not what we hear in Europe.'

'Of course not,' said Aunt Martha, 'with so many confrontations, and those terrorist attacks . . . Don't ask Theo to understand everything in advance! Don't forget that he's had no religious education, as I've told you before.'

'Then where do we start?' cried the Rabbi.

'We start with what unites us,' answered the Sheikh. 'You see, my boy, our three religions have in common a single God, the Creator. We don't call him by the same name, that is true. For the Jews, it is Elohim . . .'

'Adonai,' murmured the Rabbi. 'Adonai Elohim.'

'No complications,' growled the Sheikh. 'For Christians, it is God the Father, and for us Muslims, Allah. Our three sacred books all start with the same story, the one about Adam and Eve, the first two humans. The Creator explained that they could eat all the fruits in the garden of Paradise, except for one, the fruit of the tree of knowledge of Good and Evil.'

'That's the one about the serpent and the tree,' said Theo. 'They weren't supposed to eat the apple. God didn't want them to. Why not? Not much of a sin, to steal one fruit . . .'

'But Theo,' cried Aunt Martha. 'It's a sin to do something forbidden, that's very obvious.'

'There we agree,' Rabbi Eliezer intervened. 'When God gives an order, he has to be obeyed.'

'Really?' Theo was puzzled. 'Then why three separate religions?'

'Because,' said the Rabbi, 'we Jews do not believe that Jesus was the son of God.'

'Nor do we,' said the Sheikh. 'A prophet, yes. But the son of God, no!'

'I don't understand,' said Theo. 'What is it that keeps you apart?'

The three men glanced at each other, but did not speak.

'The simplest way,' Aunt Martha decided, 'is for each of you to explain the principles of his religion.'

'Then I'll begin,' said the Rabbi, 'because we Jews have the privilege of seniority. No one can take that away from us! Jesus and Muhammad came after us.'

'We count the Jewish prophets as our own!' the old Sheikh instantly protested.

'Hush, Suleiman,' murmured Aunt Martha. 'It isn't your turn.'

The Being who lays down the Law

'So, I was saying that we were the first to declare the existence of God,'
the Rabbi continued. 'What does that mean? Well, he is. He is being
itself.'

'Being,' said Theo with surprise. 'What an odd name for a god!'

'Because he is not *a* god, Theo, he is just God. Absolutely God. He
contains time. He is, do you see?'

'No,' said Theo.

'It's complicated, this concept of being. We humans, when we want
something done, it's not enough for us merely to speak – not at all! But
when God creates, he has only to say: "Let there be light", and there
is light.'

'Wait,' said Theo. 'If I say: "I'm Theo", don't I exist?'

'Which Theo are you talking about?' asked the Rabbi. 'Theo right
now, the child you were at birth, or the man you will become later on,
with the help of the Eternal? We *have* being, but we are not being
itself. You can tell that you yourself are not being. You develop, you
grow, time changes you, whereas God is all of time. The Eternal!'

'Provided you believe in him!' Theo objected.

'Even if you don't, that won't stop the Eternal from existing,' the
Rabbi replied. 'But it's you who will find it hard to live. What will you
turn to? Your parents? They will die one day. Your country? That may
disappear. To yourself? But you will change. Who will tell you the law?
Who will tell you what is forbidden? Will you give yourself permission
to kill somebody, Theo? You won't, will you? You probably imagine
that you won't kill simply because it is wrong and you are good-hearted
. . . Wrong! You will not kill because that is the sixth of the ten commandments of the Eternal. You will not kill because Judaism has given the
world its laws of morality towards other people. It is the same with the
nine other laws that make up the ten commandments, the Decalogue,
the heart of Judaism.'

'It seems to me that I would have put the ban on killing first,' murmured Theo. 'What commandments come before it?'

'The first is to love no god but the Eternal. The second is not to bow
down to any idol, any image, any false likeness. That is why we do
not picture the Eternal, because any image of the Being would be
false.'

'But people make portraits of Jesus!'

'Remember that in our view Jesus is not God,' said the Rabbi. 'The

40

fact that he is shown in pictures is proof enough, if proof were needed. Let's see, my boy . . . One may not even speak the name of the Eternal . . . That is the third commandment, not to take the name of the Eternal in vain. In fact, it is the same reason, because if you continually call on the name of the Being, eventually you will cheapen it into a shabby label, an imitation. So, no image or speaking of the name of the Eternal our God. The fourth . . . Ah! The fourth is very important, Theo: "Remember the Sabbath, to keep it holy; six days you will work, but the seventh day belongs to the Eternal." I am not one of those who want to stop cars being driven on Saturdays, but I know what the seventh day means.'

'Me too. People need rest, it's obvious!'

'No, my boy,' the Rabbi answered gently. 'The seventh day is the day of emptiness. You stop at last. You do nothing. Only then can you begin to do again. Because if you are *doing* all the time, tell me, is that a life? The seventh day is not for rest, it is the celebration of silence. The alternation between the world and yourself. A necessary blank.'

'A bit like sleep, then?'

'A very wakeful sleep! Because during Shabbat, Jews stay awake . . . Rather than sleep, I would talk about a vacation, because the word "vacation" also means emptiness. The seventh day is the day for vacations reserved for the Eternal. A blessed moment!'

'I like vacations. And the fifth commandment?'

'You'll like this one too,' said the Rabbi. ' "Honour your father and your mother, so as to prolong the life on earth that the Eternal gives you." Your future depends on it. To honour your parents means to respect their life, not to criticize it, to preserve its memory and open the future to your own children . . .'

'If all it takes is to honour your parents to prolong your own life, then I'm safe,' sighed Theo. 'But the doctors don't seem to agree, you see.'

'Doctors don't know the Eternal's plans.' The Rabbi's voice was urgent. 'Only he commands . . . And he commands well. He can decide to cure you.'

'You think so?' said Theo.

'I will implore him! After the honour due our parents comes the sixth commandment: "You shall not kill." Because if you don't accept the affirmation of the Eternal, if you don't respect the vacation of the Being, if you don't honour your parents, then you won't be in a position to understand why you must not kill. You are not the Eternal. No life belongs to you.'

'That's true,' murmured Theo. 'I hadn't thought of that.'

'The four other commandments forbid making love to another man's wife, stealing, giving false evidence, and coveting other people's goods. Do try to understand that, starting with respect for our parents, the Eternal also gives the law that governs our relations with others. You have no right to do them harm, no right to introduce falsehood into the truth of the Eternal, or to commit adultery, no right to steal, or lie, or envy: that is why we have laid the foundations of morality, we Jews. That is so true that our rabbis declare that, once they were spoken, the ten commandments were simultaneously translated into seventy languages so as to be understood throughout the world . . .'

'I didn't know that,' said Theo. 'Then the world has a lot to thank you for.'

'It hasn't exactly thanked us as yet,' said the Rabbi, with the trace of a smile. 'It has accused us of all sorts of crimes. The Bible says that we are the chosen people. Well, that gives rise to jealousy! Chosen people, that's dreadful, what about everybody else? Deprived of the Eternal, overlooked, unloved? They don't realize how dreadful it is for us too, for the Jews! We are always at fault with the Eternal . . . Do you know what Israel means?'

'The Jewish State?'

'Yes, but Israel is first of all the name given to his people by the Eternal. The word "Israel" comes from the contraction of two Hebrew roots, the words for "fight" and for "God". The first man to receive this name was called Jacob: one night he dreamed about a ladder that reached all the way to heaven, with angels climbing up and down it . . . The Eternal stood above it, and promised him possession of the land where he lay. Years afterwards, Jacob had to confront his own brother, Esau.'

'His brother?' said Theo. 'The chosen people have fighting between brothers?'

'Since the beginning of the world,' the Rabbi sighed. 'Cain, the son of Adam and Eve, killed his brother Abel. Esau and Jacob quarrelled with each other. And always the Eternal chooses his favourite: so it was with Abel, and with Jacob. During the night before the brothers were to confront one another again, an angel came down from heaven to wrestle with Jacob, and wounded him in the thigh . . . But Jacob fought bravely, and they were still wrestling at daybreak, when the angel asked

Jacob to let him go and Jacob demanded a blessing in return. It was after his fight with the angel that Jacob received the name given to him by the Eternal, which was Israel. "Because," said the angel, "you have fought with the Eternal, and you have conquered." Jacob was God's chosen one. Next day, Esau and Jacob were reconciled, but Israel's long battle began. Because the people of Israel are constantly at war with the Eternal their God.'

'I don't like this,' Theo protested. 'Why fight with God?'

'Because we're men,' the Rabbi replied. 'Because brothers fight over inheritances. Because no one obeys easily. Because, when all is said and done, it is hard to follow the commandments of the Eternal. All the commandments, ten of them together? Good luck! We have a long way to go. And the way is so long that it is simpler to believe in a messiah coming down to earth. See, the Messiah is coming, the Messiah is here: no more struggles, peace and quiet now. But that's not how it is. We are never finished with the Eternal. The fact is, the Eternal wanted his people to set an example and show the way to the rest of humanity. We are the chosen people – easy to say. We must take this impossible gamble . . . We are the standard for the world – well, do you see the hardship that involves? Ah, we have paid very dear for that responsibility! But we put up a solid resistance. It isn't for nothing that the Eternal calls us "a stiff-necked people" . . .'

'He's not very kind, the Eternal,' Theo decided.

'The Eternal has no virtues and no faults. The Eternal is Being itself!'

'It doesn't make sense, what you just said. God loses his temper, he patches it up again, he forgives, so he has virtues and faults. He's like a father, isn't he?'

'That is the image that we project on to him,' the Rabbi explained. 'Yes, the Bible asserts that God is great, wise, sad, disappointed, compassionate, all-powerful and jealous. Terrible in his anger and generous in his goodness. Sometimes he says a prayer to himself to calm his anger and become good again . . . No way to see him otherwise. The Bible inevitably has to speak the language of human beings in order to be understood at all. But people are free either to listen to the Eternal or to ignore him, Theo.'

'Free?' he asked doubtfully. 'When they have the commandments?'

'What does Jacob do? He wrestles with the angel . . . Yes, we are free in the face of the Eternal. That is what makes it interesting! The Eternal issues a call to us, he pursues us, summons us, and it is for us to reply – or else to be angry . . .'

'What? You mean there are Jews who are angry?'

'There was one,' said the Rabbi. 'His name was Job. He was so fervent a believer that the Eternal put him to the test, to see what would happen. He took away everything he had, covered his body with repulsive sores, reduced him to nothing, yet still, painful though it was, poor Job gritted his teeth and persisted in believing in the Eternal. But his friends thought that he must surely have sinned somehow, otherwise why all these dreadful punishments? Not at all, said Job. I have done nothing wrong. It is unjust. I believe in the Eternal, but I don't understand him.'

'Fantastically patient, this guy,' Theo said.

'Oh no! Job does complain and rebel! What does he want, the Eternal his God? What are Job's crimes? Why persecute him? On top of it all, the Eternal gives him a scolding. "Who are you to argue with my plans? Where were you when I created the earth?" And now, Job understands. "I will say no more," he replies. "I have talked too much. I am only a man." The crisis passes. Job regains his health and wealth, and he prospers again.'

'That's really disgusting,' said Theo, after a long pause. 'I hope the Eternal doesn't play the same trick on me.'

'I hope he does!' cried the Rabbi. 'That way, you'll be cured.'

The sacrificed God

'All right!' Aunt Martha broke in, with perfect timing. 'You've talked for a long time, Eliezer. Now, in the chronological order of appearance on earth, it's your turn, Father.'

'Our name, Christians, comes from the word "Christ",' Father Dubourg began. '*Chrestos* is in Greek the equivalent of *Mashiach* in Hebrew, and it means "the anointed one". In the Jewish religion it refers to the high priest consecrated by having his head bathed in holy oil, the only one who may present the offering to the Eternal in his Temple. But in the eyes of the Jews of his time, Jesus is not consecrated. He has not received the ritual unction . . . That is why Jesus is opposed by the high priest Caiaphas, the Lord's official anointed.'

'The baddy,' said Theo.

'No,' said the priest. 'The guardian of the Temple could not accept a man who called himself the Son of God and who was unanointed. Actually the fact is that Jesus did receive the unction, but in very unusual circumstances. It happened in Bethany. Mary Magdalene, a woman who

44

had sinned, knelt humbly at the feet of Jesus and bathed them in a very costly oil. The disciples complained. What a waste! All that money squandered on a gesture of love? But Jesus let her go on pouring the perfumed oil on his body, and finally over his head, and told them: "She is preparing my body to be buried."'

'They put oil on the body before they buried it?' asked Theo.

'Yes! Christ had not yet been condemned, and already he was thinking about his death, and about his glorious resurrection. Mary Magdalene knew nothing of all that, but she did not hesitate: by instinct, she anointed Jesus's head with the finest oil, as a serving maid would anoint a prince. Because the humble sinner had understood that Jesus was the Lord's Anointed.'

'Something like a king, you mean?'

'The high priests of Israel were indeed both kings and priests at once. The oil used for anointing had an olive-oil base: that is why Christians called Jesus "the holy olive", because he was pressed on the cross just like the fruit of the olive tree in the olive press, and the oil became his blood. For Jesus was more than a king, Theo, he was the Son of God! That is what matters. Instead of making an offering to the Temple, he offered himself as a sacrifice – himself, God ... And it is an ordinary sinner who marks him as "the Lord's Anointed" in a chance encounter! What divine madness! For the first time, God consented to be incarnated as a man. He became the father of a son who died and rose again. It's a radical change, but also a logical consequence of the Bible's message, as the Jewish people expected the Messiah.'

'And once he had landed on earth, the Messiah got rid of Judaism!' said Theo.

'Jesus did not break with Judaism, Theo, Jesus was born a Jew and did not deny the ten commandments ... On the contrary, he expanded them. Christ took a formulation of the last commandment from the Book of Leviticus – you remember, not to steal, not to covet another man's wife, not to do harm to another. "Love your neighbour as yourself." Very important! That means that you must first love yourself before you can love your neighbour. That people's natural selfishness, love of self, can and must apply to all people without exception. Perfect equality between oneself and others: what Jesus brings are God's commandments to the whole world.'

'The Jews already talked about the model for the world,' Theo reminded him.

'But Jesus is the Son of God! The Eternal is the Father who sends his son to earth in the shape of a man made of flesh, who drinks, eats, sleeps, suffers and dies. The Eternal is no longer only the invisible voice that commands: he brings himself close to his creation. It's a tremendous venture. God comes down among men. The Word is made flesh.'

'The word? As in grammar?'

'Yes, as in grammar: because in that saying, the word refers to an action. Now this is the point: both for Jews and for us Christians, the divine Word acts, because it creates. But before the birth of Christ, men communicated with God only by listening . . . In the Bible, God issues orders, gets angry, gives consolation, but he is not seen. That wasn't enough: people were still resisting. So the Word makes itself flesh: you can touch it, argue with it, follow it along the roads, share its meals, look it in the eye, see its blood flow . . . God is made man. What comfort! And the birth of God, what a story!'

'By the way,' said Theo, 'can you explain how you can be born to a virgin? A thing like that can't happen!'

'You're right,' said Father Dubourg. 'It shouldn't have happened. We know very little about Mary. She was a very young girl, dedicated to God according to a custom that Jews call Naziritism. You devote yourself to God for a given period of time, and don't touch a drop of wine, or eat grapes, or cut your hair. Mary lived in Nazareth, which possibly never existed, but anyway an obscure village, somewhere in the back of beyond. She was engaged to be married to Joseph the carpenter. God chose a completely obscure Jewish woman. Of course he did. Because the message of Jesus goes to the poor and the simple.'

'All right,' Theo objected, 'but all the same, how could she have a child without a man?'

'That is exactly what she asked the angel Gabriel when he told her that she was to bear the child conceived by God: "How shall this be, seeing I know not a man?"'

'She knew Joseph!' Theo replied.

'Well . . .' The cleric hesitated. 'In the gospel, "to know" means . . . it means to sleep with a man. Mary is simply saying that she is a virgin, do you see? The angel's answer arrives like a murmur: "That holy thing which shall be born of thee shall be called the Son of God." At that very moment, Mary realizes that the angel's breath has already passed into her belly. "This" has already happened! She believes him without hesitation. She sings her joy because she is God's chosen one. Do you know how old she is? Fourteen . . .'

'You are not telling me how God entered her,' Theo protested.

'I have just told you!' snapped Father Dubourg irritably. 'A breath, a murmur, a silence . . . The voice of God!'

'Right, then Mary is a female Moses, that's clear,' Theo concluded. 'She hears God. Incidentally, he doesn't often ask for people's opinion, God. He chooses, he decides . . .'

'He chose a virgin, Theo, to redeem the sin of another virgin, Eve. Irenaeus, one of the men we call "the Fathers of the Church" - great Christian scholars - wrote: "It was necessary that a virgin, by making herself a virgin's advocate, should destroy a virgin's disobedience by means of a virgin's obedience."'

'Woah there!' wailed Theo. 'Wait a bit . . . The virgin's disobedience, that's Eve. The obedience, Mary. But why the advocate?'

'Because Mary becomes the advocate of all those who have sinned. Always, she intervenes to plead the cause of humans with her son. She always has mercy. Because she never doubted for a single moment, God grants her rewards. Mary has the power to defend men, warn them and console them. Mary did not die as the rest of us do. She fell asleep and her body was taken up into heaven. We call her sleep the "Dormition", and her ascent into heaven the "Assumption", which means "Elevation".'

'So she did not really die,' said Theo.

'No,' Father Dubourg went on. 'Can you imagine the decay of the body of the mother of Jesus? Impossible! So impossible that, in the fourteenth century, the learned scholars of the Church declared that Mary herself had not been contaminated by the sin of our mother Eve. Her parents conceived her immaculate . . . God had prepared the birth of the chosen Virgin.'

'Tell me, if Jesus is also God, am I mistaken or is Mary her own son's daughter?'

'Why, certainly,' Father Dubourg replied. 'That's what Saint Augustine says.'

'And where does poor Joseph come in?' Theo was baffled.

'Ah, but Joseph came of a good family. He was descended from King David. He had to be, because the Bible stated that the Messiah would come from David's line . . . Furthermore, Joseph was a fine man, a very pious Jew. To him also, the angel spoke. When he told him: "Take with you Mary, take the infant and his mother", Joseph obeyed without question . . .'

'Except that he wasn't the true father of Jesus!'

'The father of Jesus is God. We believe in one God in three persons: the Father, the Son and the Holy Ghost.'

'I've been waiting for that!' cried Theo. 'What is the Holy Ghost exactly?'

'The breath of God,' said Father Dubourg. 'The voice of the angel who spoke to Mary. There is the Father who decides, the Son who saves, and the Holy Ghost who inspires: the Holy Trinity. God in three persons – one the God of the Jews, the other his only son, the Saviour of the World, and the third the inspiration that kindles inside us.'

'In the end, what did Jesus bring to men?' asked Theo. 'His being one of us? That's not enough!'

'No,' the priest answered. 'Jesus brings the hope of salvation, the sharing among ourselves that we call charity, and the vivid memory of his sacrifice, which we celebrate during mass. For during his last supper Jesus shared bread with his twelve apostles, and said: "Take, eat: this is my body." And he gave them all wine, and said: "This is my blood." The Word was made flesh, but it did much more than that, because the flesh of God is embodied in the bread and in the wine.'

'Eat my body, drink my blood, that sounds like what cannibals do,' said Theo.

'Not at all,' frowned the priest. 'Jesus sacrificed himself, but the substance of his body passes into the bread and the wine. The sacrifice of Jesus's body is the final, the ultimate gift. Because of that, we commemorate it with the bread and the wine of his life: "All of you, eat", he told us before he died. All, do you hear, Theo? To absorb the sacred body of Jesus is to take it into your mouth, touch it with your tongue, swallow it, it is an event that takes place in the body. The unleavened bread that we call the host is not human flesh, it is the transformed body of God . . . It is not a cannibal meal, it is a universal divine sharing, let us say!'

'Heck of a lot more complicated than the Jewish faith, your religion,' Theo concluded. 'Do you realize the number of miracles that have to be believed? A virgin conceived without sin, who conceives on her own with the Holy Ghost, a God made man, dying and rising again, whose flesh becomes bread and blood becomes wine . . . What is the purpose?'

'Closeness,' said Father Dubourg. 'To bring God closer to ourselves, and ourselves closer to each other. Because God came among us, we can imagine him – paint pictures of his birth, his life, his agony and his resurrection, sculpt his body, living or dead, pay actors to play his part in the cinema and restore him to our sight, both human and divine. The purpose of this repeated sacrifice is redemption from sin. Forgiveness. Erasing at a stroke the past sufferings of the people of Israel, and making a new pact of hope and brotherhood, a New Covenant. The point of God's sacrifice is to return to the Paradise he once expelled us from.'

The last revelation of God

'Over to you, my dear Suleiman,' said Aunt Martha, still controlling the debate. 'You're in luck, you will have the last word!'

'Inshallah,' the Sheikh replied, tweaking at his beard. 'If the Almighty wills it. And you're right, my dear friend, for we Muslims truly are the last. God's first revelation did not convert the Jewish people to obedience: as you made a point of saying, Eliezer, the Jews continued to fight with the Eternal. When the revelation of Jesus appeared, to sacrifice his life was not enough either, because there were still too many men and women in the world who did not believe in the one God. Isn't that true, my dear Antoine? That is why the Almighty chose Muhammad as his Prophet for his final revelation, after which no other is possible. Because to the Prophet the Almighty revealed the whole of his law.'

'What was there that hadn't been said?' Theo asked. 'I don't see . . .'

'To begin with, the Almighty does not forget anything, Theo. He recapitulates. When he dictates to Muhammad the text of the Koran, he recalls the line of the prophets – Adam, Abraham, Noah, Moses, Jesus – who all conveyed his Word. They are our prophets too. The ten commandments are ours. We too must never depict the face of God, or even of his prophets. In place of "You shall worship only the Lord your God", the divine Word: "There is no God but God and Muhammad is his Prophet." That means that the Revelation is completed. Muhammad was and will be the last of God's prophets.'

'What was special about your Muhammad?'

'Our prophet, peace be on him, did not call himself the son of God. How could God have a child? Like the Jews, we think that God is the Eternal Creator. But if he is the Creator, he is unbegotten, isn't that so?'

'Unbegotten . . .' Theo hesitated. 'No one begot him?'

'Exactly. No one begot the Creator, who begot no one, because he is subject neither to time nor life nor death. If he begot, if he was a father, the Eternal would enter into time, which is utterly inconsistent.

That is the reason why our Prophet does not call himself the son of God, but the chosen. Chosen by Allah, who sent the angel Gabriel to order him to establish a perfect and a just religion.'

'OK,' said Theo. 'But what else?'

'Who was he? A very poor man, born in Mecca in 570, and who to earn his living entered the service of a rich widow, Khadija. After he had married the woman he worked for, God spoke to him.'

'The way he spoke to Moses,' Theo commented.

'Yes. In the Arabia of his day, men fought each other savagely and mistreated women: they kidnapped and raped them. They worshipped more than three hundred idols made of stone or clay, gods and goddesses of harvests and the earth, as the Canaanites had done at the time of the birth of Judaism . . .'

'Then nothing had changed in all that time?' asked Theo.

'I'm afraid not,' sighed the Sheikh. 'They had to start again. The Almighty decided to have done with the worshippers of statues, once and for all. He inspired this man he had chosen as his messenger, tested his body and spirit to give him the strength to speak clearly. Actually it was a Christian monk who detected the first signs of his being divinely chosen. He was still in his youth when Bahira told him: "You are God's Envoy, the Prophet foretold by my Bible!" '

'Back to the messiah again!' murmured Theo.

'Prophet, Theo, not messiah,' the old man corrected him mildly. 'Muhammad was forty years old when he got into the habit of making solitary retreats to Mount Hira, near Mecca. At the beginning of the Revelation he endured some painful ordeals. The divine inspiration caused him dreadful suffering . . . The angel Gabriel, the very same angel who had brought the divine message to Mary, took possession of him. Muhammad believed that he was going mad, his head was on fire, and only his wife sustained him. Then the angel Gabriel dictated the Koran to him. But how was he to transmit the Revelation that passed through him, the simple man?'

'That's true,' said Theo. 'Moses had problems, Jesus died. What happened to Muhammad?'

'The Prophet was just and good. He had the gift of the Almighty in him, a compassionate heart, an invincible word that touched the poor. One of the first converts was a black slave, Bilal, who became the first caller to prayer, what we Muslims call a muezzin. The Bedouin started to follow Muhammad's teaching, then converted the unbelievers to a decent life, worthy of the Almighty. Guided by him, the Prophet triumphed over enemies numerically far stronger than his own followers, and founded the community of the faithful, the "Umma".'

'The Umma? Is that Arabic?'

'The Prophet lived in Arabia, so he received the Revelation in Arabic. The first Revelation had been expressed in Hebrew, the second in Greek, and the last is in Arabic. But mind, the Arabic of the Koran is not merely a language like all the rest. The inspiration of the Almighty that guided the Prophet expresses itself through beauty. The language of the Koran rings out like music, it envelops in its splendour, it protects! That is why the word Koran means "Reading aloud", or "Recitation": the text of the Revelation lives in the mouth of the believer. It is not enough to read it, it has to be spoken, breathed . . .'

'All right,' said Theo. 'Let's agree that, like Jesus, Muhammad is a prophet and he takes his teachings from the Bible and the Gospel, but what else does he do?'

'First you must understand that we do not accept the idea of the Son of God,' the old man insisted. 'It is with the Jews that we have been arguing for centuries. The covenant they have made with the Eternal is a war. A war of love, certainly, but a war all the same. In his final Revelation, the Almighty wanted to put an end to the war between himself and mankind. They have only to admit the truth - "There is no God but God and Muhammad is his Prophet" - and the war is over. The converted believer now returns to the Umma. And the Umma, Theo, is an extraordinary thing. Equality, justice, prayer, simplicity, sharing, total community . . . No clergy, no pope, no Church, no images, no statues . . . Every man lives in surrender to God, together with his brother, his equal. Yes, the fighting is ended between men and God. That is the Revelation of the Prophet.'

'No more fighting?' cried Theo. 'How much more do you need? Muslims spend their time fighting . . . What do they call it . . . The ji-something . . . jibad, is it?'

'Jihad,' sighed the Sheikh. 'Holy war. In the beginning the Prophet was compelled to defend the Revelation by force of arms, that's true. But "jihad" means making an effort, and first of all it means effort exerted on oneself. It is on himself alone that the believer must make war in order to respect the divine law. The message of Islam is ultimate peace. And what peace, Theo! Sweet, sustaining, deep as night, bright as the stars, perfect in fact . . . Yes, perfect, I see no other word.'

'But not the world: the world's not perfect,' Theo replied. 'You too have not succeeded.'

'Yet peace will come, Theo, peace for us all . . .'

'Then why so much fighting between Christians, Jews and Muslims?' Theo exclaimed. 'It's absolutely stupid.'

The three men of God exchanged smiles. There they did not disagree.

Wars and peace

'You haven't replied,' said Aunt Martha.

'Because,' said the Sheikh, 'the battles that have set us against one another for all these centuries are quarrels over territory and questions of power.'

'Because,' said the Rabbi, 'God is still testing us and makes us move slowly down the path to peace.'

'Because,' said the cleric, 'men don't know how to share what belongs to them.'

'Then why not tell them?' Theo protested.

'That's what we are doing,' he answered. 'But they don't always listen. What is to be done about Jerusalem? The Jews want it for themselves alone, the Muslims claim it for themselves, and the Christians strive to preserve the place where Jesus met his death. Share? Some day it will happen. When? We do not know, but we are working towards it.'

'That is why we have joined together to show you the three Jerusalems,' the Sheikh added.

'Now you must work out our timetable,' said Aunt Martha. 'What are you going to show Theo?'

They started to confer. In the Rabbi's view, the visit ought to be chronological. The Jews had more or less inaugurated Jerusalem three thousand years ago, so they would start with the Western Wall, all that remained of the Temple of Jerusalem, and a place of lamentation for all the Jews of the world. Father Dubourg felt that it would be more sensible, seeing that Theo was tired, to start with the Holy Sepulchre . . .

'The holy what?' said Theo.

'Sepulchre, it's another word for tomb,' said Aunt Martha.

'. . . the Holy Sepulchre, the tomb of Christ, where all the branches of Christendom join.'

'Not all,' Aunt Martha reminded him. 'Not the Protestants.'

The Sheikh took the opportunity to point out that Jerusalem was an Arab town occupied by the Israelis, and that in all fairness there should be recognition of the true protectors of the holy places, the Muslims.

'Careful now, everybody,' said Aunt Martha. 'I asked you not to tire my Theo. That leaves each of you with one or two visits. Sort it out between you!'

Father Dubourg suggested the Holy Sepulchre, the Mount of Olives where Jesus warned his disciples of his fate, and the Via Dolorosa, the road of the Stations of the Cross, the path he had followed to reach the place of his torment. Aunt Martha asked him to reduce the list.

The Rabbi raised his arms to the sky. How was he to choose between the Wailing Wall, the Israel Museum, the Yad Vashem memorial to the millions of Jews murdered by the Nazis, and the religious quarter of Me'a She'arim? It was asking the impossible! Aunt Martha told him briskly that the decision was up to him.

But the old Sheikh kept noticeably quiet, much to Aunt Martha's surprise.

'Nothing to say, Suleiman?'

'No,' he murmured. 'There's no point.'

'Either agree among yourselves,' she decided, 'or else let Theo choose.'

Three pairs of bright, sharp eyes focused on Theo, but his gaze had wandered towards the table where mouth-watering desserts soaked in honey were waiting to be eaten if only the bearded holy men could conclude their debate.

'Well?' said Aunt Martha.

'Well, we'll settle it the way we used to when I was small,' Theo replied, 'because I can't get my head round all these choices. Right, here we go.'

He pointed a finger as he counted: 'One, two, three, Bird's in the tree, Cat's in the branches but he can't catch me.' Oh 'me', his finger reached the Sheikh.

Aunt Martha laughed out loud. 'That's it,' she said. 'We'll start with you, Suleiman. I bet you've never made peace so easily before, you three!'

Abraham at the navel of the world

In the end, they had made up their minds. The Sheikh had opted for the Dome of the Rock, the Dominican for a visit to the Holy Sepulchre, and the Rabbi, after Aunt Martha assured him that Theo would be visiting synagogues on other stages of the journey, had reluctantly chosen the Wailing Wall and the Me'a She'arim quarter. So they made for the Dome of the Rock, as decided by Theo's counting rhyme. On the vast platform that overlooked the Wailing Wall, Theo saw the golden glow of one dome and the silver shimmer of another. Women walked there wearing long black robes with pink and red embroidery, and scarves that masked their faces; men in white headdresses bound by leather circlets took long majestic strides.

'Here we are,' said the Sheikh when the little band stopped in front of the sanctuary with the gilded roof. 'Over there, you can see the Al Aqsa mosque, built around the same time, in the seventh century. We are standing on the Dome of the Rock, at the very place where a fragment of Mount. Moriah still stands. This sacred place is called "the navel of the world", the rock that Allah chose in the garden of Paradise to make it the foundation of the universe. The souls of all our prophets are located in a well dug underneath the rock, and they pray there always. Those arches that you see between the dome and the mosque will support the scales to weigh our human souls at the moment of the final Event.'

'What event?' asked Theo in surprise. 'I thought that Islam had no expectations.'

'Yes, it does,' murmured the Sheikh. 'We expect the end of time itself. But for the moment, let us talk about the beginning, because it is here that the sacrifice of the prophet Ibrahim took place, whom the Jews and Christians call Abraham, peace be on him. I assume you know the story . . . ?'

'Er, not exactly,' Theo admitted.

'Abraham was a great prophet,' the Sheikh declared, 'the father of all the faithful. This is how we tell the story of Ibrahim. Because his wife Sarah was old and childless, she pressed her husband to conceive a child with her maid servant Hagar. Then Sarah herself gave birth to a son, so Abraham now had two sons: his son by his wife Sarah was named Isaac, and Hagar's son was Ishmael. But Sarah was jealous. She insisted that Hagar and her son must be driven out, and Abraham took them both out into the desert and left them in the care of the Almighty. Jews call themselves the children of Isaac, and Muslims the children of Ishmael, and that is why Abraham is the father of us all, the patriarch of patriarchs.'

'Do you remember, Theo,' murmured Aunt Martha. 'A few years ago, in Hebron, a Jewish fanatic with a submachine-gun murdered some of the congregation in a place called "the tomb of the Patriarchs", where Abraham is buried with his wife Sarah, and some say that Adam and Eve lie there too, in their eternal sleep . . . It was the only place in the world where Jews and Muslims could pray together.'

'They still can,' said the Rabbi, 'but with protection from our soldiers. I will not speak the name of the man who committed that atrocity. Abraham's tomb is the meeting-point of our religions. Because God wanted to put Abraham to the test: he ordered him to sacrifice his only son, Isaac . . .'

'But he had two sons!' Theo exclaimed.

'Hmm, well . . .' said the embarrassed Rabbi. 'The fact is that Isaac was the legitimate son, and according to our Bible the other was the son of a serving woman, in other words a bastard. But that distinction is not universally accepted, I agree. For us Jews, Isaac is the only son, otherwise the test that God imposes would not be meaningful. Isaac was born late, when his mother Sarah was nearly a hundred years old . . .'

'A hundred!' blurted Theo. 'You're kidding!'

'Sarah laughed too, when the angels told her that she was going to give birth to a child at that age. But it was true. So, Theo, imagine the suffering of that father, over a hundred years old, when God commanded him to take his son into the mountains, and there to cut his throat and sacrifice him as a burnt offering . . . And Abraham obeyed.'

'And that's your God?' said Theo. 'He's horrible.'

'He is hard to please,' the Rabbi replied. 'There's a difference. You know that he is good and proof of that is that when Abraham had tied up his son on the altar, and took out his knife, an angel stayed his arm . . . Then Abraham saw a ram with its horns caught in a bush, and instead of his son he sacrificed the animal. And God said to him: "I know now that you did not refuse me your son, your only son. And because of that, your descendants will be as numerous as the stars in the sky and the grains of sand on the sea shore." That happened beneath our feet.'

'You forgot to say that Isaac was suspicious about this strange kind of sacrifice,' said Father Dubourg. 'His father had saddled an ass, to carry the wood to burn the sacrifice, which would usually be a lamb. But there was no lamb! Isaac asked where the lamb was, not suspecting that the victim was himself. Later, when Christ came into the world, he accepted being the true lamb, sacrificed in truth on the cross. The Lamb of God.'

'I still don't like your God,' Theo complained. 'Why want the death of a child? Why want to sacrifice Jesus? Where's the sense in that?'

'Remember Job,' said the Rabbi. 'God puts us to the test. Demanding the death of a son may seem monstrous to us, but seeing that Isaac survived . . .'

'So he did,' said Father Dubourg. 'But Jesus did not. He knew he was going to die and he said yes.'

'Providing you accept that he was the son of God,' the Sheikh broke in. 'Providing you concede that Sarah was Abraham's favourite and Isaac his favourite son. That is not our belief. Because, according to the Koran, it was Ishmael who was spared by the Almighty so as to father countless future generations. We too, the children of Ishmael, descendants of Ibrahim and Hagar, are as numerous as the stars in the sky. And we do not believe that it is necessary to think in terms of the sacrifice of a son of God on the cross. Jesus is a prophet, and we recognize his greatness as the son of Mary, who received the Word of God, but the Creator cannot conceivably father a son incarnated in human form. That is impossible.'

'Then at the end of the stories, where is the truth in all this?' asked Theo. 'Abraham, Ibrahim, Jesus, Muhammad?'

In the long silence that followed Theo's question, a small flock of pigeons chose its moment to take to the air in a flutter of wings. And now Aunt Martha intervened, with a slight edge to her voice.

'Listen to me, Theo. It's my turn to speak up. And let me speak, the three of you! You won't agree, I know. For me, religion is not a matter of truth. You either believe, or you don't. For example, I do not believe in God. In any god. But I admit that religions have brought progress for humanity. Thanks to the Jewish people, that cruel God you so dislike has prevented some even more barbarous practices. Remember the Canaanites . . . The whole point about Isaac, the greatness of his sacrifice, is the very fact that he does not die. God makes a ram appear for the sacrifice. Man is no longer an animal that has its throat cut on an altar for the glory of a god. Isn't that better?'

'If you put it like that,' said Theo, 'I agree. But did it have to take so long for it to happen?'

'Oh yes, Theo!' cried the Rabbi. 'After thousands of years of barbarism, we were the first to believe that God had created man in his own image. His own image, which means that man contained a fragment of divinity . . . And it was Abraham who made the first pact between man and his God when he called him Adonai Elohim, the Lord our God. Before this Covenant, men and animals had equal value as sacrifices. After, it came to an end. The separation between men and animals is found first of all in our Bible.'

'Sin also comes from the Bible,' said Aunt Martha. 'God did not leave man in Paradise.'

'That is why God sacrificed his own son to mankind, to redeem that first sin,' added Father Dubourg. 'And no longer for a single chosen people, but for all people. That was a great step forward.'

'What need for such a bloody settlement?' sighed the Sheikh, with his hoarse voice. 'Why the crucifixion? Why did the covenant between the Jews and God fail to hold good from the start? What caused those rebellions and convulsions? Didn't the Prophet declare an end to the strife between God and men? Submission to the Almighty is enough . . .'

'So you say,' Theo grunted.

'So say Eliezer and Antoine too!' cried the Sheikh. 'All three of us recognize God's commandments. The only difference is what follows in the history of men . . . For Eliezer, it is waiting for the Messiah. For Antoine, it is the crucifixion of Jesus. For us, thanks to the Prophet – peace be on him – everything is said. Let me tell you about the Prophet's vision, then. He was walking on the terrace of his house in Mecca when his steed Buraq appeared, a creature like a horse, only with wings, and a woman's head . . .'

'I see,' said Theo. 'Winged like the horse Pegasus. I have that in my video game.'

'Will you let me finish, child?' said the Sheikh gently. 'So, the Prophet's steed appeared and brought him here. The Prophet hitched Buraq to the ramparts, and the animal struck the rock with its hoof and bounded into the air! The angel Gabriel – who in Islam is Jibril – brought the Prophet to the seventh heaven, where along the way he met Adam, Noah, Joseph and Moses before he found himself face to face with the patriarch Ibrahim. At last he heard Allah dictate the forms of Muslim prayers and worship to him, and returned to Mecca ecstatically transformed . . .'

'Are there any pictures of Muhammad in ecstasy?' asked Theo. 'I'd like to see one . . .'

'We never show the face of the Prophet,' the Sheikh explained. 'Sometimes you might come across popular illustrations of the sacred story, but his head is veiled in white. His ecstasy is too close to the Almighty to be portrayed. The Prophet's vision was divinely inspired. It is because of that exit from time, and the Prophet's leap beyond the bounds of human life, that Jerusalem is the third sacred city of Islam, after Mecca, where the Prophet was born, and Medina, where he died. And who built the dome above the Rock? Caliph Abd al-Malik in 685.'

'But King Solomon had built the first temple,' said the Rabbi. 'In the same place.'

'And the Crusaders built a gigantic cross here too,' said Father Dubourg. 'So, Theo, our three religions meet at the place of Abraham's sacrifice – the patriarch we have in common. We recognize the same sacred book, the Bible, whose name in Greek means Book. That is why we are called the three religions of the Book. And if you think about it, it is basically the same book.'

'Oh no! It is the Koran!'

'Where does that leave the Decalogue?'

They were arguing again. It tried Theo's patience, and he edged away to look over ramparts turned golden by the gently setting sun. The hazy air throbbed with the ringing of hundreds of bells that mingled with the call of the muezzins and the chanting of prayers. Jerusalem was a very complicated city, the scene of an ancient rivalry between believers in the one God, and in the Prophet, and in the Son of God.

'What are you thinking about?' said Aunt Martha, laying her hands on his shoulders.

'About this God who can't bring them all together,' said Theo.

CHAPTER 3

A Wall and a Tomb

Wailing for the lost Ark

The Rabbi had easily won priority over Father Dubourg, still citing history and chronology. To begin with, the three men of God would pay a visit to the place called the 'Wailing Wall', and the nearer they got to the wall, the more Theo felt a strange excitement take hold of him. For almost two thousand years Jews had been coming to weep before those great ancestral stones; for twenty centuries they had been wailing for their lost Temple. At a distance he heard the solemn murmur of an age-old prayer. As the Rabbi guided him towards the crowd of believers, all dressed in black, Theo shivered with anticipation.

'So that's the famous wall,' he breathed. 'It's a lot bigger than it looks on TV.'

'Yes,' murmured the Rabbi. 'The wall is immense – as great as the sorrow of the Jews. At dawn, the stones are covered with dew, which is the tears of the people of Israel driven from their holy land. Of the ten measures of suffering that the Eternal imparted to the universe, nine are for Jerusalem . . . Put this on your head, Theo, it's compulsory.'

'A *kippah*? It really looks great,' said Theo, placing the blue velvet cap on top of his curls.

'Let's join the queue on the left,' said Rabbi Eliezer. 'I'm afraid we'll have some time to wait.'

In front of them stretched a long line of men in black, some of them rocking backwards and forwards from the waist, others reading prayers in a low murmur, or chanting haunting dirges. On their heads they wore round hats made of black felt, or knitted skull-caps, or else odd little boxes made of leather and tied round their heads with leather straps. Some wore long curls that dangled in front of their ears. When they reached the high wall they laid their hands and leaned their foreheads on the stones and pushed messages written on little slips of paper into the cracks between the blocks of stone.

A little further to the right, women formed another, separate queue: many of them had their hair covered by a tightly knotted scarf. Sometimes they let out heart-rending cries. Aunt Martha stood to one side with Father Dubourg and Sheikh Al'Hajid, not far from the place where fax messages addressed to the Wall arrived from all over the world, on 02 62 12 22. The Wall was highly modernized.

The wall that Christians called the Wailing Wall and Jews the Western was all that remained of the third temple of Jerusalem. The first was the work of Solomon, king of Israel; the second was the one authorized by Cyrus, king of the Persians, after the destruction of the first; and the third was rebuilt by the king of Judaea who wanted it restored to its original splendour. That king, whose name was Herod, had been appointed by the Romans: he was only half Jewish by birth, and the Jews disliked him.

And then this last temple was not like the first. Certainly it was a splendid building, covered with plates of gold so brilliant that they dazzled the eye, but in the Holy of Holies, the Debir, the very heart of the Temple, only an empty space signalled the presence of God. The Ark of the Covenant, which contained the pact with God, was missing from the temple rebuilt by Herod.

'The same ark that Indiana Jones goes looking for in *Raiders of the Lost Ark*?' asked Theo. 'The one with radioactive powers locked inside it?'

'With what?' asked the Rabbi, who had not seen the film. 'Radioactive? Certainly not. The Ark of the Covenant between the Eternal and his people had been carried for many years in a cart drawn by white oxen, and King Solomon built the Temple to give it a permanent home not long after the Jews ended their journey in Jerusalem, in the time of King David. To honour the Ark, King David danced before it and played the harp. And yet, in spite of his famous victory when he used his shepherd's sling to kill the giant Goliath, the enemy champion, it was not little King David who built the Temple in Jerusalem, because he had committed a sin so serious that the Eternal refused him that pleasure.'

'And what was his sin?' asked Theo inquisitively.

'He had become infatuated with a beautiful woman, and caused her husband's death through concupiscence,' the Rabbi replied.

'Through what?'

'Concupiscence,' said the Rabbi testily. 'A desire forbidden by the commandments. Let's keep up with the queue!'

'He wanted to sleep with her, I suppose?' said Theo.

He supposed correctly, but the Rabbi chose not to pursue the subject. Rather than explain the word 'concupiscence' it was better to stick to the Ark of the Covenant, once kept so close to where they stood, whose contents had excited intense curiosity in the ancient world. Greek and Roman temples contained the statue of a god, one god to a temple. So this Ark that was not a statue was a mystery.

'But what was really in the Ark?' asked Theo, with his usual curiosity.

'The commandments that the Eternal gave to Moses on Mount Sinai after the flight from Egypt, that is all.'

'Nothing but words?'

'The word of the Eternal! After he had dictated it to Moses on Mount Sinai, the Jewish people knew what the Being wanted it to do.'

'But I thought that God had engraved them on tablets of stone,' said Theo, 'and then some time afterwards Moses broke them in a fit of temper, because while he was away the Hebrews had made a calf-god of gold, like an Egyptian divinity . . . Moses blew his top!'

But the tablets of the Law had been remade, then they had disappeared at the moment of the destruction of the Temple by Nebuchadnezzar. After that, the commandments had been transcribed on to long scrolls. Everything was included: what must be eaten, and what must not; what must be done and what must not be done. The voice of the Eternal had spoken to Moses with detailed precision, especially about the dietary laws, which according to the book of the Bible called Leviticus, the Manual of the Priesthood, forbade unclean animals, and especially the pig, the owl, the chameleon, the gecko, the centipede, the hawk, the stork and the hare . . .

'Jugged hare is unclean?' said Theo incredulously.

'All right,' said the Rabbi irritably, 'it isn't always easy nowadays to understand the exact meaning of a diet system three thousand years old, I admit – don't keep stopping, we'll lose our place . . . You see, when the Eternal speaks you don't talk back. He exchanges his protection for our respecting the rules that he lays down, and that's that. In the days when Moses received the commandments the Jewish people had shown enough signs of indiscipline to have made it necessary to force them to obey . . .'

For this was not the first time that the Eternal had made a covenant with his chosen people, the Rabbi went on. After their expulsion from Paradise, Adam and Eve had suffered all the hardships of living as a mortal man and woman. For generation after generation, humankind fell so low that the Eternal decided to punish his people by sending a Flood, so huge that it drowned the whole world. But in order to preserve his Creation the Eternal chose Noah, who was a just man. He ordered him to build a giant boat, and to take on board a pair of every kind of animal, as specimens of living species. This boat saved from the waters is called Noah's Ark, and it was the first Ark of the Covenant. Perched on the summit of Mount Ararat, it escaped the disaster. The Flood ceased, the sun returned, and an enormous rainbow appeared, an arch of light between the Eternal and humanity.

'I'm losing count,' said Theo. 'That makes how many covenants?'

'Three altogether,' said the Rabbi. 'The first was Noah's Ark, the second was concluded with Abraham, who agreed to be circumcised at the age of a hundred, and the third was the Ark of the Covenant containing the commandments dictated to Moses.'

'Circumcision, a covenant? Some condition!'

The first covenant did not last very long. There were other sins and other punishments. The Eternal decided to find a second just man, and that was Abraham, who had faith enough to be willing to sacrifice his only son. The second covenant, agreed with Abraham, required boys to be circumcised, so as to leave a permanent sign on the body of a Jewish man, the mark of God. One scrap of flesh removed, an emblem of the lack in man because he is not the Being.

The troubles of the last covenant

Now even this hallmark stamped on the flesh of the sons of Israel did not ensure obedience, so after the punishment of bondage in Egypt came the third covenant prescribed to Moses on Mount Sinai, down to the smallest detail.

That is why, after the flight from Egypt, during the long march back to the land promised by the Eternal to his people, wherever they went the Hebrews carried with them the Ark that contained God's commandments. By his order, it was built of acacia wood, plated inside and out with pure gold. Then it was installed in Jerusalem: kept separate from the rest of the Temple by a veil of blue and purple and scarlet hung on four pillars set on pedestals of silver, the Ark was forbidden to the eyes of the faithful. Hence the curiosity of non-Jews . . .

'I can understand that,' said Theo. 'It makes you long to see.'

'If only they'd done no more than feel curious!' the Rabbi sighed. 'But they didn't stop at that. After they conquered Palestine, the Greek rulers felt so much contempt for our religion that one of them put up a statue of Zeus in the second temple.'

'Yet in Greece, Zeus was the king of the gods,' Theo remarked. 'That's not so bad. What were the Hebrews complaining about?'

'You know very well that for Jews there is only one God,' the Rabbi answered patiently. 'Even the king of the gods is insignificant compared with the Eternal . . . The Hebrews would not bear that profanation, and they started a war to win back their Temple and their holy city. This they achieved, but alas, the Greeks were succeeded by the Romans, and it was they who gave Jerusalem to King Herod.'

'The half-Jew?'

'Yes, the bad man who wanted to kill all of the newborn Jews because the three Magi had told him that one of them would become the king of the Jews. As a puppet of the Romans, King Herod was the first persecutor of Jesus.'

'I see,' said Theo. 'A real collaborator, like the Vichy government in France in Hitler's time.'

'Certainly. But the Romans too were curious. The great Roman general Pompey was determined to enter the third Temple rebuilt by Herod, to see the famous Ark, which was no longer there. Pompey found nothing but an empty space.'

'Served him right,' said Theo. 'The Jews must have had a good laugh.'

'Oh no!' said the Rabbi. 'The Roman had passed through the veil, and that was sacrilege. The Jews did not forgive the Romans, or Herod either. They staged a rebellion. Then the day came when another Roman general decided to put an end to these fanatics. The Temple was destroyed, except for the wall. And Jerusalem became a Roman city under the name of Aelia Capitolina. The holy city was no more than a heap of ruins, but that was not enough. The emperor Hadrian ordered its total destruction. Six hundred thousand Jews were killed, and the survivors were forced into exile.'

'And they came back after the war,' said Theo.

'Which war?' the Rabbi answered. 'Jerusalem has seen so many . . . Some Jews never left Palestine. Most of them left, and then for many centuries they had to flee once more from the countries where they had found refuge, under the persecution of the Christian Church. So as to convert the heretics, in the Middle Ages a monk called Dominic founded the order of the Dominicans, who in their turn founded the Inquisition.'

'What is a heretic?'

'In the language of the Christians, a heretic was anybody who did not believe in the official creed of Christianity,' sighed the Rabbi. 'Heretics . . . well, they were us, the Jews, because of Jesus, of course – Careful, Theo, if you keep on hopping from one foot to the other you're going to bump into somebody! – Oh, I know that for the Inquisition we were not the only heretics, but we were its special targets. The Inquisition hounded us, controlled us, investigated our Jewish origins, tried us in its courts and burned us on its bonfires. At best, we were forcibly converted and had to observe the Sabbath in secret. The Church had decided to call us "New Christians", but the masses found us a better name: *marranos* – swine. To call a Jew a pig! What a disgrace!'

'What brutes! . . . No, more like swine themselves,' cried Theo.

'That was only the beginning . . . There has been worse since then. Yet exile didn't drive all the Jews away for ever. In 1492, when the king of Spain forced them to choose between conversion and expulsion, many Jews decided to return to Palestine, where the Ottoman empire allowed them freedom of worship. There was no more Temple and no more city, but it was still Jerusalem.'

'Are any of them left?' asked Theo.

'Descendants of the Jews who returned at that time? Yes, there are. The Eliachar family, for example. Four centuries later, after the long, long agony of Jerusalem, our city began its resurrection. It started around 1840, when the Ottoman empire granted the Jews equal rights with its other subjects, and allowed them to appoint a chief rabbi of Palestine: the first since the destruction of the Temple. – Don't keep jigging about, move on up! – I was saying that the Jews returned, and started to rebuild. They built hospitals, schools, neighbourhoods, they published newspapers, the whole world took notice.'

'But the State of Israel didn't exist,' said Theo.

'Not yet. The key event came in the late nineteenth century. A journalist called Theodor Herzl, an atheist Jew from Vienna, was sent to Paris – move up a bit, Theo, we're nearly there. Anyway, in Paris Herzl followed the court-martial of Captain Alfred Dreyfus, accused by the

French authorities of having betrayed military secrets because he was a Jew . . .'

'I know about the case,' said Theo. 'It was all a fabrication.'

'That's right. When Herzl returned to Vienna he wrote a book called *Der Judenstaat*, "The Jewish State". As he saw it, the only way to avoid persecution was for the Jews to have a State of their own. Zion is another name for Jerusalem, so Theodor Herzl founded the "Zionist" movement. At the time, the Jews of Vienna took him for a crank! But when he died, masses of poor Jews from Galicia and Poland came to attend his funeral. Herzl had not been mistaken: the Jewish State was a real possibility. More and more Jews returned to Jerusalem, until finally the Jewish State was born in 1948. And year after year the Wall where we mourn for our lost Temple has listened to the tears and sorrows of its visitors, and heard their wishes . . . Here it is now. Right in front of you.'

The message of the Wall

'It's your turn,' said the Rabbi. 'Have you brought a note to leave?'

The question took Theo by surprise. 'No, I haven't,' he stammered. 'But I'm not a Jew.'

'That doesn't matter,' said the Rabbi. 'I've brought my own petition: it's for you to be cured.'

He placed his hands on the stonework, leaned his forehead against the Wall, all the time murmuring a prayer, then slipped the note into a crack and made a deep pious bow. But when he stood and turned he was holding a little tube of paper in his hand.

'Something unusual has happened,' he whispered. 'When I left our little note, I found another lying on the ground. Here, take this message. It's for you.'

'For me?' said Theo, taken by surprise. 'From the Wall?'

He unrolled the piece of paper. *I am my own father, and I am an immortal bird. When you have found me you will know the country you are going to*. That was all it said.

A message in his own language? Absolute magic! Unless . . . What if it was the first clue in the treasure hunt?

'Aunt Marthal' he shouted. 'I've got the first message!'

'Marvellous,' she called. 'Now all you have to do is figure it out. In the meantime, we'd better get back.'

Father Dubourg came to meet them. 'Tell me, Eliezer, when you talked about Herod rebuilding the Temple, did you remember to mention that it coincided with the birth of the Infant Jesus?'

'I'm sorry,' said the Rabbi. 'I forgot.'

'On Christmas Eve! Aren't you ashamed of yourself, Rabbi?' Father Dubourg chided, not knowing whether to laugh or to frown.

Theo spoke up. 'Wait, Rabbi Eliezer, don't forget you told me about the wise men's prediction and the massacre of the newborn by that king!'

'So I did,' murmured the Rabbi. 'I'd forgotten.'

The priest was not placated. 'While I'm on the subject, Eliezer, did you talk about circumcision?'

'Of course, Antoine. I explained about the second covenant.'

'All the same,' said Theo, 'there's no need for a covenant with God to be circumcised – I had it done myself when I was little. Dad told me that a part of the skin there was too tight and had to be removed.'

'You know, Theo,' said Martha, 'there are quite a few religions that make marks or scars on their followers' bodies. Do you know that in many countries girls have some of their sexual parts cut away?'

'Fatou told me! It's horrible, excision . . . According to her, the Koran says nothing about it, and it's something that men have concocted to make life hard for women.'

'Sometimes they make it hard for themselves,' she said. 'In one Pacific tribe the men cut a slit in the skin of their penis every month, to make themselves bleed like women.'

'Those are appalling customs, and barbaric,' the Rabbi frowned. 'We merely take a useless scrap of flesh. And we aren't alone. Muslims also practise circumcision, don't they, Suleiman?'

'Yes,' he replied. 'Islam did not reject the rulings made by the first prophets, it added to them.'

'We Christians have refrained from levying a blood tax on the bodies of the faithful,' said Father Dubourg. 'For newborn children to enter the kingdom of God they only have to be immersed in water, after the example of John the Baptist, who practised conversion by dipping those who came to him into the River Jordan. Wearing animal skins and feeding on locusts and wild honey, he announced the coming of Jesus: "I am not the Messiah," he said, "because I baptize with water, and he will baptize you with the Holy Ghost." That is the New Covenant.'

'Baptism!' Theo cried. 'But why do you talk about immersion? They just sprinkle some water on the baby's forehead and a few grains of salt on the tongue!'

'In the early days of the Church they used to immerse the whole body, then later the ritual was simplified. Nowadays they no longer put salt on babies' tongues . . . That makes the baptism stronger: because it is the symbol of entering the Father's Kingdom.'

'Yes,' said the Rabbi. 'Symbolic, but not visible. The Eternal wants the body to keep an indelible sign of the Covenant – the true one.'

Theo looks back

Lying on his bed, Theo read and reread that puzzling note found in a crevice in the Wall. A bird that was its own father? Just as Mary was the daughter of her son? Honestly, Aunt Martha, this was going too far!

And Jerusalem, that went too far. To clarify his thoughts, Theo took out his notebook.

GOD OF THE JEWS = BEING WHO GIVES THE LAW TO THE MODEL PEOPLE. GOD OF THE CHRISTIANS = GOD THE FATHER GIVES HIS SON JESUS AS A SACRIFICE TO ALL PEOPLES THROUGH THE BREATH OF THE HOLY GHOST. GOD OF THE MUSLIMS = THE ALMIGHTY GIVES EQUALITY TO ALL MEN THROUGH HIS VERY LAST PROPHET, AS LONG AS THEY SUBMIT TO HIM. That was just about clear. Then it got more complicated. JEWS = FIRST REVELATION - WAITING FOR MESSIAH. CHRISTIANS = SECOND REVELATION - MESSIAH HAS ARRIVED. MUSLIMS = END OF REVELATION. what else? COVENANTS OF JEWS WITH GOD = 1 NOAH'S ARK. 2 CIRCUMCISION WITH ABRAHAM. 3 ARK OF MOSES. 4 CHRISTIANS: NEW COVENANT.

And where did the State of Israel come in? The fourth covenant, perhaps? There were still so many questions unexplained. Why was the Pope in the Vatican? Why did Muslims go to Mecca? And to think that they were all supposed to worship the same God!

Where could an immortal bird be found? What country did it come from? Was it India? Or possibly Greece?

The wrangles among the Christian Churches

Next morning, Aunt Martha woke Theo at dawn. If they wanted to avoid the tourists who came flocking to Jerusalem because of the Christmas season, they had to set off early. To go where?

'To the Holy Places,' said Aunt Martha. 'Well, that sounds odd, when you consider that the entire city of Jerusalem is holy. You'll see, the story of the Holy Places is a lot more convoluted than the history of the Jews.'

It was Father Dubourg's turn. The car stopped just around the corner from a little square where groups of visitors were already assembling, and Aunt Martha drew the Sheikh and the Rabbi aside.

'Our friend Antoine will have trouble enough explaining the whole situation,' she told them. 'Leave him alone with Theo, for once. If you get involved, it's out of my hands. You know what he's like, a heart of gold, but . . .'

'But touchy,' said the Rabbi. 'My dear Martha, you're quite right. Better to stay outside in the sun.'

'I will have something to say to Theo when they come out,' the Sheikh said quietly.

In front of Theo stood the church of the Holy Sepulchre, a massive building crowned by a large stone dome that was less massive than the Wall and less graceful than the shining golden Dome of the Rock. But it was here that Jesus had emerged alive from the kingdom of the dead.

'So we're going to see the tomb of Christ,' said Theo as they walked across the threshold.

'Not exactly,' answered Father Dubourg. 'For a start, one sees very little, because after the crucifixion of Jesus there was a Greco-Roman temple built on this site. Then a Roman emperor, Constantine, converted to Christianity in 312, and Jerusalem became the eastern capital of the new religion. The emperor's mother, St Helena, searched for the burial chamber there, and eventually found it, as well as the three crosses, where Christ was crucified, and the two thieves alongside him. The Greek temple was destroyed and a basilica built, which was itself destroyed by a caliph a few centuries later . . .'

'So this is the second,' said Theo, stopping in the entrance hall, which echoed with the prayers and footsteps of the faithful.

'No, it's the third, built by the Crusaders, and altered quite extensively since then. The basilica has had all kinds of problems, including a fire and an earthquake . . . On the original site, there have been chapels built in every nook and cranny of this huge building, because the Churches of Christendom have divided the place into so many separate territories that when you first come here it's difficult to find your way around. Look up above your head. Do you see that row of lamps hanging from ostrich eggs? There are four for the Greek Church, four for the Latin Church, which is what the Catholics are called here, and three for the Armenian Church.'

'All those churches for a single Christ?' said Theo out loud. 'Talk about a muddle . . .'

'Shhh,' said the priest. 'I'm here to explain things, but don't raise your voice, we are standing in a church . . .'

'So where is this tomb?' Theo whispered.

'Well, it's complicated,' Father Dubourg replied, 'but just in front of us, between the tall candle-holders, look at that red stone slab. Do you see that lady who appears to be wiping it clean? In fact she is using the cloth to soak up the holy water that people sprinkle on the slab, probably to heal a wound. That is the Stone of Unction. The whole of this space is called Golgotha, the place of the crucifixion. The red slab is where the body of Christ was anointed, but the Orthodox Christians think that it is the stone where his body was laid to remove the nails from his hands and feet. The Catholics don't agree.'

'Don't tell me that the Christians argue among themselves!' cried Theo.

'No more or less than the Jews of Israel do,' snapped Father Dubourg. 'We have an equal right to disagree!'

'OK, OK, no need to take offence . . . But don't they all believe in Jesus Christ?'

'As you will find out, Theo, there are several forms of Christianity. Not to mention the Protestants, who have nothing to do with this place.'

'Really,' said Theo in surprise. 'Why not?'

'Because for them, Theo . . . Oh, you'll go into that another time,' said Father Dubourg impatiently. 'No, I am telling you about the Christian Churches involved in the guardianship of the Holy Sepulchre, which you see spread around you with its chapels, convents, cloisters and rotundas. Those Churches are the Latin, the Orthodox, the Ethiopian, the Armenian, the . . .'

Hey,' said Theo. 'Slow down, I can't keep up.'

'All right, I'll explain as we go.'

The clamour of prayers and chanting rang beneath the domes. To the left of the entrance hall, already swarming with tourists, appeared a maze of pillars and partitions, walls cut into bare rock or faced with decorated marble. Theo walked faster.

'Slow down, Theo,' said Father Dubourg. 'The tomb is here.'

Theo stopped short.

'I can't see a thing,' he whispered, craning his neck. 'There are too many people.'

'But seeing's not the point, Theo. You pray there, that's all. Here, at least, all Christians can agree among themselves. Let's move forward. What is here called the Latin Church was historically the first, the one founded by St Peter, the first of the apostles. That is why it is called "apostolic", which comes from the word "apostle", meaning "envoy" – envoy of God. And as St Peter was crucified in Rome, our Church is therefore the Holy Latin Church, apostolic and Roman. It is the largest, and the most important.'

'Surely not!' Theo protested. 'That's not what my grandmother tells me. What about the Orthodox Church, where does that come in?'

'That's right, the boy's mother is Greek,' the priest muttered to himself. 'Your grandmother isn't mistaken, Theo, because the Orthodox Church was the first one to build a basilica – an early form of church building – in honour of the tomb of Christ, in the Byzantine era. That is why the general style here looks Byzantine. Theo, do you know about Byzantium?'

'Yes,' said Theo. 'In class we've learned about the fall of Byzantium. 1543 ... no, it was 1453, that's it. The Turks besieged the town the way the Serbs did with Sarajevo, except that they won in the end, not like the Serbs. A crisis in European history, though I'm not sure why.'

'Because the Christians had lost their most famous capital city, the centre of the Eastern Empire,' the Dominican explained. 'But long before the fall of Byzantium the Churches of Christ had been seriously divided. On one side, throughout Europe, the Catholic Church obeyed the pope, and on the other, in the Byzantine Empire, Christians obeyed the patriarch of Byzantium. Today, the city has kept its Turkish name, Istanbul, but I won't go into that, you'll see for yourself.'

'You mean I'll be going to Istanbul?' Theo's eyes shone with pleasure. 'I didn't see that in Dad's atlas!'

'Actually, Theo ... that's not what I meant,' said Father Dubourg awkwardly.

'Yes you did, I heard you correctly.'

'Shush, Theo. Yes, all right, you will see Istanbul. But don't go telling your aunt, or you'll get me into trouble.'

'I'll tell her you mentioned Byzantium, and she won't notice ...'

'A lie by omission, but still ... So, you realize that, before the fall of Byzantium, the Christian Churches had been divided over the role of the supreme leader: the pope for some, the patriarch for the rest. The outcome was what is called a schism, a word that means "split", or "separation". The first schism separated the Catholic from the Orthodox community in 1054, and the second, in 1439, separated the Catholic Churches of Europe from those of the Orient, even though the Churches of the Orient continue to obey the pope.'

'What a mess,' sighed Theo. 'And what did they fall out over this time?'

'About the marriage of priests, for example. The Eastern Churches allow it.'

'Like the Orthodox Church and the Protestants,' said Theo. 'It even causes trouble in France, priests being forbidden to marry. I wonder why they can't.'

'Because . . .' Father Dubourg ground to a halt. 'Your questions are starting to annoy me. So as not to get distracted by family concerns, that's why. The Latin and the Eastern Catholics disagree about baptism too. With them, as soon as an infant has been baptized it has the right to take communion, whereas we believe that boys and girls have to reach the age of reason before freely choosing to confirm their parents' choice. Isn't that sensible?'

'Yes, it is,' said Theo. 'My parents didn't even want us to be baptized, so that we could make our own decision. That is even more sensible.'

'All right,' said the tetchy priest. 'We are coming to a sector guarded by the Armenian Church. It is not the only Eastern Catholic Church, but Armenia was the first country to be converted to Catholicism, and that is why they have the honour of sharing in the upkeep of the Holy Sepulchre.'

'For once that's clear,' said Theo. 'And what about the Ethiopian Church?'

'It's a long story.'

The children of Balkis and King Solomon

They too represented a very ancient tradition, stemming from Africa, beyond the sources of the Nile, in Ethiopia.

It was in Ethiopia, the experts think, that Balkis lived – the Queen of Sheba, famous in the ancient world. An Ethiopian merchant gave her a description of the greatness of King Solomon so vivid that she decided to pay him a ceremonial visit. That was in the days of the building of the Temple; the king of the Hebrews was sending far and wide for the finest timber and the rarest metals. This wise man knew the most mysterious secrets of heaven and earth, the most sacred calculations and the most magical spells . . .

'King Solomon was a magician?' Theo was amazed.

A very wise and very powerful magus. Like all sovereigns, Solomon possessed a seal, an emblem of power and sacred authority. Solomon's seal comprised two triangles, one pointing upwards, representing fire, and the other pointing downwards, representing water.

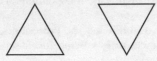

When the triangle of fire was truncated by the base of the other, that sign designated air; and when the triangle of water was similarly truncated, that gave the symbol for earth.

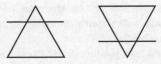

So fitting the two triangles together yielded a six-pointed star that symbolized all the elements in the universe.

'But I know that star!' cried Theo. 'It's on the blue and white flag of the State of Israel!'

Solomon's seal, known also as the star of David, did in fact appear on the Israeli flag. Such was the power and prestige of the great king that his image lingered on in the mind of the Jewish people. In fact he was so powerful that, according to the Koran, he used a lapwing as a spy: the bird brought him news from far away. So Solomon sent his lapwing Jaffur to spy on Balkis. After the bird had delivered an enthusiastic report on the grace and wisdom of the Queen of Sheba, the king made his mind up to accept Balkis's visit. But not before Balkis and Solomon tried to outwit one another, testing their powers. But it was an uneven match, because Balkis had no lapwing for a spy.

At last, dazzled by the unfathomable knowledge of the great king, Balkis set out on the long, exhausting journey to Israel, and was received with open arms by Solomon. Nevertheless, because he had heard it said that the women of the kingdom of Sheba had goat's hoofs for feet, he had her ushered on arrival into a room whose floor was covered with water: the Queen had to lift her robe so as not to get it wet. The still water acted as a mirror, and reflected the fact that Balkis had trim little feet with neither fur nor cloven hoofs. Solomon decided to house her in his palace, but the cautious Queen made him swear that he would not touch her, because she was a virgin.

'But not for long, I suppose,' commented Theo.

In return, Solomon made the Queen swear that she would take absolutely nothing while she was under his roof, other than what she was given. Then at the banquet in her honour he had Balkis served with foods so spicy that the following night she was on fire with thirst. She tiptoed over to a jar full of water that the cunning king had arranged to have placed in her bedchamber, and as soon as she drank a mouthful, Solomon appeared. By taking water from the jar, Balkis had broken her oath: now it was the turn of the great king to break his, and he entered her bed.

'Crafty so-and-so,' said Theo.

The enchanted lapwing Jaffur sang all night long. The encounter between the two sovereigns grew into a passionate romance, and out of that union came a son named Menelik, who became the first ruler of Ethiopia. When he returned to his own country, the young man took with him the Ark of the Covenant, removed by stealth from the temple erected by his father. The story goes that when Solomon saw what had happened he flew into a rage that subsided when he realized that his son was worthy of the Ark that he had stolen. That is why, according to the Ethiopians, the Ark of the Covenant vanished from the Holy of Holies: from that time onward it had lain hidden in Ethiopia, and it might very well still be there.

'That's why Indiana Jones went looking there!' cried Theo. 'I get it now!'

Ark or no Ark, Queen Balkis was converted to Judaism, which became established in her country. Many centuries later came Bishop Frumentius, who converted the Ethiopians to Christianity.

'Now,' Father Dubourg continued, 'as part of the legacy inherited from that long-ago encounter between Balkis and King Solomon, the Christians of Ethiopia describe themselves in the words of the Jews: they are the chosen people. In their country there is a huge basilica cut into the rock . . .'

'Inside a cave?'

'No, they dug it out of the living rock, into the base of a cliff. The processions are magnificent ... If only you could see them, Theo! Shaded by brocaded parasols, the priests wear crowns of gold and embroidered velvet copes, and they dance the dance of David, and accompany themselves on sistra and big drums . . .'

'I'd love to see that,' Theo murmured.

'When you're well again. The Christians of Ethiopia have called that place "Lalibela", in memory of a young martyred prince. But Lalibela is also, they say, the "new Jerusalem", because according to Ethiopian tradition the people of Africa are descended from King Solomon, and they managed to avoid the destruction of their own Jerusalem. Ethiopian priests look very impressive. You won't see them here in their full majesty, but come, I'll show you their monastery on the roof terrace.'

They climbed flights of stairs that grew more and more narrow until they emerged on to a terrace, and there at the end of it stood a number of little cells with green doors, in the shade of a pomegranate tree.

'Here we are,' said the Dominican. 'You know, the Ethiopians are among the oldest Christians in the world. This terrace is a very peaceful place, possibly the quietest in all the precincts of the Holy Sepulchre. Not so long ago there were also some very ancient communities in Ethiopia made up of African Jews descended from the legendary times of the Queen of Sheba – perhaps they came from Egypt in the days of bondage. These dark-skinned Jews are called "Falashas"; they carve statues of priests holding the Torah in their arms. Many have emigrated to Israel: some rabbis demanded that they should be re-educated, as if they had never been genuine Jews. We Christians have no reservations about our own Ethiopians. They have their rites, and we respect them.'

Apart from a few tall monks with ascetic faces, there was no one else on the terrace – not a single visitor. Theo took his first photograph with the automatic camera given to him by his father.

'It's fine up here,' said Theo. 'Did she have a black skin too?'

'Who do you mean?'

'The Queen of Sheba.'

'Most probably. She was very beautiful.'

'Yes,' mused Theo. 'Black and beautiful, like my friend Fatou. Shall we go down again? I suppose we've seen everything?'

'You didn't let me finish just now. There is still the Coptic Church, the Church of the Egyptian Christians. Most of the Egyptian Copts are Orthodox, except for a small Catholic minority. With the Christians of

Ethiopia, they form what is called the Alexandrian rite. Alexandria is in Egypt.'

'Egypt,' said Theo dreamily. 'It's funny, I have a feeling that I might find my bird there.'

'Your immortal bird?' answered Father Dubourg. 'Why not?'

Squabbles in the Holy Places

'Ah, there they are!' cried the Sheikh. 'At long last.'

'I need to sit down,' Theo sighed. 'The crowd, the incense, and then it was so dark and so confusing . . .'

'There's nothing I could do about that,' murmured the priest. 'There are so many different groups that look after the Holy Places, and we also visited the Ethiopians' roof terrace.'

'Talking of the Ethiopians,' said the Rabbi, 'I must tell you, Theo, that . . .'

'The Falashas?' said Theo.

'You've been talking about them?' The Rabbi was surprised.

'Of course,' smiled Father Dubourg. 'I never leave anything out.'

'Not even telling Theo who holds the key to the holy Places?' asked the Sheikh with the ghost of a smile.

'Good Lord, you're right, Suleiman,' said the Dominican. 'Listen, Theo, I forgot to tell you that the keys of the Holy Sepulchre are in Muslim keeping today.'

'The great family of the Nusseibahs,' said the Sheikh. 'To avoid strife among the Christian Churches, Caliph Omar, the caliph who built the Al Aqsa mosque, put them in charge of the keys in the seventh century of the common era, and for all this time it has been a Muslim who unlocks the doors at three in the morning and locks them at five in the evening.'

'That's really interesting,' said Theo. 'So religions can agree among themselves if they try.'

'Thank goodness!' Aunt Martha exclaimed. 'I suppose our friend Dubourg has told you about the quarrels inside Christendom? Your head must be stuffed with it all . . .'

'Yes!' cried Theo. 'Obey the pope or disobey the pope, marry or not marry priests, give babies communion or wait till they're older – honestly, it's hard to feel impressed. All that to keep control of a few old stones put together around a tomb that held Christ's body for a very short time!'

'If that's all you can remember of what I've taught you, Theo . . .'
Father Dubourg exploded. 'My dear Martha, I give up. The boy is too
recalcitrant to listen.'

'No, my friend,' said Aunt Martha, and took him by the arm. 'Why
not let bygones be bygones, admit that these battles are over and done
with . . . ? Don't be upset.'

'Over and done with, are they?' cried Father Dubourg. 'Then why all
that fighting in Yugoslavia – the Catholic Croats, the Orthodox Serbs,
the Bosnian Muslims?'

'I thought they each wanted a country of their own,' said Theo. 'Is
it true that they also fight because of their religion?'

'It's true in part,' Father Dubourg resumed. 'Don't think I enjoy having
to explain those long quarrels between us . . . And I'm not the only
one, you know! More than thirty years ago there was a pope who
decided to bring the Churches of Christ together.'

'John Paul II?' asked Theo.

'No,' said Aunt Martha. 'This one was called Pope John XXIII. He
died long before you were born.'

'Then why are you angry, Father Antoine?' said Theo. 'If you agree
with the pope . . .'

'All right, I lost my temper, I admit. But if you don't pick up a little
bit of history, then you stand no chance of understanding the world of
today. You'll see what I mean later on, Theo . . .'

'Do you really believe that I'll have time to see?' asked Theo quietly.

All at once he seemed so frail, and his assertiveness so sad, that Father
Dubourg was disarmed. The Sheikh had a lump in his throat, and the
Rabbi came over.

'Nice going,' murmured Aunt Martha. 'Antoine, you are incorrigible.
See what you've done!'

'Theo will have a lifetime to understand, I'm sure he will,' said the
priest, and put his arm round Theo's shoulder. 'God will not abandon
this child.'

'First of all,' said Aunt Martha, 'I don't know about God. Second: we
have an appointment at the hospital. And third: Theo is not a child, as
I've told you before.'

The hospital already? After only two days' travel? Theo's heart sank.
But Martha had promised Melina to have a blood test done and then
to tell her the results as soon as possible, and there was no getting
out of it.

Sarah the nurse

The hospital was just like in Paris, except that here they spoke Hebrew, the language of the country. In the process, talking to a nurse who had arrived in Israel from France when she was twelve years old, Theo learned the meaning of *aliyah*, going up, in other words returning to the Promised Land, because every Jew in the world had the right to go back home and become a citizen of Israel. You 'went down' when you left Jerusalem, and you 'went up' when you returned.

'On some conditions,' Aunt Martha explained. 'Since the murder of Prime Minister Rabin by a Jewish extremist, the law of return no longer applies without safeguards.'

After returning, the new citizen learned Hebrew, and at the age of eighteen had to do military service, men and women alike. Nurse Sarah Benhamin had worn the Israeli uniform. Theo strongly approved of this idea. While she was telling him what it had felt like to 'return', and about her military service, Sarah had unobtrusively slipped the needle into Theo's arm and gently filled the syringe with good red blood.

'You don't seem so sick,' she said as she stuck the label on the sample. 'I bet that you're going to recover.'

She was so bright and lively that Theo felt a lot more hopeful. He took her photo to remember her by.

'Do you believe in God?' he asked her.

'Do I what?' She laughed out loud. 'That's all I need! Lucky they don't ask that question the day we return. I'll tell you, Theo, right now I don't trust anyone who talks too much about respecting the Eternal's commandments. Sometimes our fundamentalists are too extreme. They won't have us dancing to rock music, or using electricity on the day of Shabbat . . . They want roadblocks put up to stop people driving their cars . . . You're not allowed to press the button to call the lift, just because on Shabbat it's forbidden to make sparks to light a fire. Can you believe it? In biblical times, electricity didn't exist!'

'That's true,' said Theo. 'They have no sense.'

'No, they have no tolerance. They make life hard in Jerusalem – well, take a look at Me'a She'arim, the Orthodox quarter, I guarantee you'll love it! What I say is that people have the right to believe in God without interfering with others.'

Which means that, thanks to Sarah, the blood test turned into a cheerful occasion. To keep the fresh air blowing, Aunt Martha decided that they would have lunch in the artists' quarter. 'Just the two of us?' asked Theo.

The two of them it was. Over the oriental bread and lamb kebabs, Theo tried hard to grill Aunt Martha about the mystery bird, but it got him nowhere. Aunt Martha joked and smiled, but refused to help. She would lend him a good dictionary, but that was all. Theo vented his frustration on the tender flesh of a baked fish by making a mess of the bones.

Nor did Aunt Martha give ground about the rest of Theo's day. An afternoon nap was compulsory, and she vetoed not only a walk on the Mount of Olives, but also a trip to Herod's Tomb. Maybe tomorrow. Meanwhile, to bed!

Mysteries of the dictionary

Theo slept for hours. When he woke up, night had fallen and Aunt Martha was there at his bedside, reading by the light of a lamp. She looked beautiful as she sat with her book, quite serious and still, wrapped in a big red cashmere shawl, with her face in shadow. Theo levered himself quietly up on one elbow, and watched as she turned the pages. Suddenly she snapped the book shut and looked up, to find Theo gazing back at her.

'Look at this nosy little shrimp,' she said. 'You're spying on me, Theo. How long have you been awake? Not too tired?'

'I'm OK,' said Theo. 'What are you reading?'

'A paperback dictionary, to see if it can help you,' she said. 'Here, you try.'

Theo looked up 'bird', and started to read out loud.

'"Aviary bird, rare bird, sea bird, bird of ill omen, bird of prey ... Bird of ill omen: bird seen in ancient times as a sign of some misfortune . . ." Bird of ill omen?'

'No,' said Aunt Martha. 'Absolutely not.'

'"Eagle, the king of the birds. Bird of Juno, the peacock. Bird of Minerva, the owl. Bird of Venus, the dove, the pigeon. Bell bird, butcher bird, hummingbird, bird of paradise . . ." Bird of paradise?'

'Not bad, but not right,' she said.

'"Bird in the hand, birds of a feather, strictly for the birds . . ." Now we're getting warm, right?'

'Very funny,' said Aunt Martha. 'Try something else.'

It was just like *Wrath of the Gods*: for every test the Hero had to sort through his bag on screen and pick the right object. But if you clicked on the lyre by mistake, instead of the sword, a chime sounded and a funny computer voice said: 'No, not that one. Choose something else.'

No. Not that one. Choose something else . . . 'Immortality: perpetual life; everlasting fame. In heraldry: immortality, phoenix on its pyre.'

'What does "in heraldry" mean?' asked Theo.

'Heraldry is about coats of arms, the ones that noble families have,' said Aunt Martha. 'And towns as well. Like the boat on a red and blue background for Paris.'

Feeling discouraged, Theo threw the dictionary on the floor.

'Why are you stopping?' she asked. 'That sounded interesting.'

But Theo had his face turned to the pillow. He'd had enough.

'Tell me, brave hero, in an emergency can't you consult the Pythia?' asked Aunt Martha. 'Besides, Fatou would love it.'

Fatou! He'd forgotten his friend! Theo took out his brand-new mobile and keyed the number.

The Pythia on the phone

'Is that you, Theo? Hi!' cried a familiar voice.

'Hi,' said Theo, with a rush of delight. 'Are you OK?'

'What about you, Theo? It isn't too tiring?'

'Not as much as school! Is it cold in Paris?'

'Icy, who am I, the weather forecaster? Talk about something else! You're not in need of a friend, by any chance?' said Fatou, with a laugh in her voice.

'I certainly am! Give me a clue, my lady, if you please.'

'You listen then. And pay attention, it's a long one. You'd better find something to write with. Here it is. To be born again, I light my own pyre by rubbing my wings together. I repeat . . .'

'No need to. Thank you, Fatou. Right . . . Well . . . Be seeing you.'

'You'd better,' said the voice. 'I'm counting on it.'

'Have you got it this time?' asked Aunt Martha, with a sparkle of mischief in her eye.

'No,' said Theo sheepishly. 'Not a thing. I don't know this bird.'

'Right!' she said, and rose to her feet. 'In the meantime it's Christmas Eve, and we're going to have a party on the terrace. Look your best, but put warm clothes on. I promise a surprise.'

A surprise?

Music in the night

On a terrace hung with fairylights in blue, white and red, the Consul was waiting, together with Aunt Martha. Eliezer, Antoine and Suleiman were there too, of course, but there were also some musicians, who smiled at Theo while they tuned their instruments.

'Good evening, young man,' said the Consul. 'We only have a small Christmas tree and not many presents to give you for Christmas. This one is from me' – he gestured towards the musicians. 'Let me introduce Elias, Ahmed, Amos and John.'

Elias sang and played guitar, Ahmed played the flute, John the tambourine, and Amos plucked the strings of an instrument with a big round belly. Elias had a voice as warm as a Greek summer night, and so sweet that it brought tears to Theo's eyes. Their music was strangely serene, as the muffled pulse of the tambourine beat time to the notes conjured out of the lute by Amos's fingers, and the melody that wafted from the flute. The Sheikh and the Rabbi nodded their heads in time, the lament wrung the hearts of the listeners on the terrace, and spun a web of happiness. Then the happiness stopped.

'That was just beautiful,' said Theo, after a long silence.

'Those were love songs,' murmured the Consul.

'Hey, that reminds me,' said Theo, turning to the trio of bearded holy men, 'you hardly mentioned love, the three of you!'

This drew a chorus of protest. Father Dubourg recalled the love of Christ for all his people, so great that he had accepted a cruel death for their redemption. The Sheikh spoke of the love of Allah the Compassionate, always ready to forgive his sinful believers if they truly repented. He added to this the love of Muhammad for his wives, which he had never sought to gloss over, never rejecting what Christians called the 'sins of the flesh'. The Rabbi said nothing.

'Why don't you speak, Rabbi Eliezer?' asked Theo in surprise.

'I was thinking that the most beautiful love song in the world appears in our own Bible,' he answered quietly. 'It is the Song of Songs, written by King Solomon, a hymn of betrothal, and the wonder of love between man and woman.'

'Say some of it for me,' Theo begged, and the Rabbi nodded, and began to speak in a low voice:

' "I am black, but comely, you daughters of Jerusalem. . . . ... As an apple tree among the trees of the wood, so is my beloved among young men . . . My beloved is like a gazelle, or a young hart . . ." That is what the girl says about the husband she is waiting for.'

'And he says?'

' "How beautiful you are, my love . . . How sweet are your caresses, my sister, my bride! How good they are, better than wine, and the smell of your perfumes, better than all spices! Your lips distil honey, my bride, honey and milk are under your tongue, and the smell of your robes is like the smell of Lebanon . . ." '

' "A garden closed is my sister, my bride," ' Aunt Martha continued, ' "a spring shut up, a fountain sealed. Your runnels are a paradise of pomegranates, with pleasant fruits, henna with nard, nard with saffron, calamus with cinnamon, with all the trees of frankincense . . ." '

'Aunty, you know it off by heart!' blurted Theo in amazement.

'Distant memories,' she sighed. 'One day you too will know the Song of Songs by heart.'

'I'm sure he wrote it for the Queen of Sheba,' said Theo conclusively.

'Who?' said the baffled Father Dubourg.

'King Solomon, of course! Because they loved each other.'

'The Bible doesn't say so!' the Rabbi protested.

'I don't care,' Theo insisted. 'Black and beautiful, like Fatou, his sister, his bride. Who else can she be except Balkis?'

'If you like,' the Rabbi conceded.

'Just one thing, though. What is nard?'

'A delicious aromatic oil,' the Rabbi answered.

'And cinnamon and calamus?'

'More kinds of perfume oils.'

'And the sealed fountain?'

'Hush . . .' murmured Aunt Martha. 'Don't disturb the night.'

Theo leaned on the wall of the terrace and looked out over Jerusalem, which glittered with lights. He could not see the Dome of the Rock, or the Holy Sepulchre, or the Wailing Wall, but the city wall built by the Ottoman Turks was bathed in golden light.

A pair of hands alighted on Theo's shoulders. 'Do you realize now why so many have fought over this city?' a hoarse voice rasped in his ear. 'Don't be so hard on us, Theo. The spirit of God blows in the air, no matter if we call him Allah, Adonai Elohim or Jesus.'

CHAPTER 4

The Night of the Just

'Aunt Martha!' yelled Theo at the foot of the bed.

'What's the matter?' groaned Aunt Martha, her head under the covers. 'What time is it?'

'Time to get up, old girl!' shouted Theo, hooting with laughter.

Aunt Martha sat up in a daze, forgetting to adjust the shoulder strap of her nightdress. Theo, up? Before her? And he'd called her 'old girl'? Never in the history of the Fournay family had Theo ever got up by himself. Aunt Martha deduced that Theo was feeling better.

'Don't be cheeky,' she grumbled. 'Did you fall out of bed?'

'Nearly. There's a fellow outside with the breakfast tray. Shall I let him in?

'Wait. Pass me my dressing gown, on the armchair.'

Breakfast turned into an endless argument. Theo wanted to go to Bethlehem, and Aunt Martha stubbornly refused.

'Out of the question,' she said. 'This morning we're going to Me'a She'arim, because the Rabbi said so.'

'You must be joking. You don't want to go to Bethlehem? Bethlehem, the town where Jesus was born? Isn't it the best place to go for Christmas?'

'No!' exclaimed Aunt Martha. 'I mean, yes . . . But we can't go there now.'

'Why not?'

'Listen Theo, our friends are waiting for us, we can't just ditch them,' replied Aunt Martha awkwardly. 'They're important people!'

'Yeah, yeah,' said Theo. 'Haven't your friends got a phone?'

'You're driving me mad!' burst out Aunt Martha. 'If you must know, we're going to Bethlehem this evening. I wanted it to be a surprise, but you're being such a pain that . . . now you know.'

Theo threw his arms around her neck and nearly knocked her over.

A special district

Theo had no idea what he was going to see that morning. Me'a She'arim, the name rang a bell. Who had told him something bad about it? Ah! It was Sarah, the nurse. It didn't sound exactly thrilling.

For the occasion, Aunt Martha had crammed her short hair under a headscarf tightly knotted under her chin and pulled down low over her forehead. With that getup, she looked like a Muslim woman, and a not very happy one either. When Theo asked her about this strange head-gear, she replied that no woman could enter this district of Jerusalem without completely covering her head.

'So it's a Muslim district,' concluded Theo.

'Quite the opposite,' replied Aunt Martha. 'You won't find any Jews more orthodox than those in Me'a She'arim.'

Here we go, thought Theo, what am I supposed to swallow now?

'Of course,' she murmured, 'it's not so easy to understand. The Rabbi will explain it to you, Theo.'

They met the Rabbi and his two colleagues under the sign that marked the entrance to the orthodox district. It was written plainly that women must cover their heads properly. The Rabbi inspected Aunt Martha's clothes and pushed a stray lock of hair inside her headscarf.

It looked like a village from long ago. Even though the white stone buildings were not very old, for some reason, it felt as though they were back in the eighteenth century. Wide-eyed, Theo stopped to gaze at this open-air theatre. Under their long, black caftans, the men wore knee-length breeches, with white hose and shoes. They wore wide-brimmed hats, and they all had beards. They seemed to be in a hurry, they walked quickly, and their eyes had a stern, intense expression. Sometimes, a boy wearing short trousers and quaint court shoes with a buckle, would dart across the road. Most of the women wore a sort of hairnet that came down low over their foreheads, held in place by a velvet hairband. Theo was very surprised to glimpse a little girl with a long plait down her back.

'Hey, Rabbi Eliezer, I thought that girls weren't allowed to show their hair?'

The Rabbi sighed. 'In this very special district,' he began, clearing his throat, 'live ultra-orthodox Jews who want to preserve the way of life of the ghetto intact.'

'The ghetto?' queried Theo.

'Of course,' replied the Rabbi, 'you don't know . . . I'd better begin at the beginning.'

Following the persecutions of the Spanish Inquisition, during the fifteenth century, nearly everywhere the Jews of Europe were herded into special districts called 'ghettos'. They were named after an area in Venice, where the first of these districts was established, towards the end of the Middle Ages.

'Mind you,' added the Rabbi, 'at first, the Jews preferred to keep to themselves, to preserve their customs and not mix with the other groups. Then, things turned sour.

'So sour that eventually, by order of the Pope, they no longer had the right to settle anywhere except in the Jewish quarters, the famous ghettos. Then, throughout Catholic Europe, they were made to wear a sign that would identify them. It was very useful when people wanted to throw them into prison or burn them at the stake. A yellow circle, for example, or a tall hat.'

'Or a star,' said Theo.

The star was the Nazis' idea. So, the ghettos were the Jewish quarters, and Me'a She'arim was certainly the last preserved ghetto, although, of course, nobody forced the inhabitants to follow the customs of a bygone era. There was only one place in the world where you could find the atmosphere of a European ghetto, and, strangely, this place was in Jerusalem, in the Me'a She'arim quarter, the quarter of the hundred gates, built at the time of the Reconstruction in 1874.

But fortunately, living conditions were much better than they used to be. For in the old days, the European Jews were often very poor and lived in overcrowded hovels. Then, in eighteenth-century Poland, the ghettos saw the growth of a powerful movement of inspired Jews who, to console themselves for the squalor of their living conditions, sought to know God directly.

'Know God directly?' exclaimed Theo.

'Yes, until then, the Jews had to read the holy books of Judaism. Books were the vehicle between the Jew and the Eternal. It wasn't just the Bible, but all sorts of books written during the exile. The Talmud, a collection of learned commentaries. Or, at the other end of the spectrum, the Kabbala, based on mystical tradition . . .'

'Don't burden him with the Kabbala so soon,' protested Father Dubourg. 'You'd have to explain so many other influences, we'd never hear the end of it!'

'To cut a long story short, it was Jewish tradition to read books. People wrote commentaries on them and discussed them endlessly, and that was the way it had been since they wept in exile for Jerusalem, after the destruction of the Temple. But the Jews of Poland, Lithuania and Russia were not so fond of books. They were happy just to sing and dance. Accompanied by followers who sang and clapped, the rabbis would whirl majestically until their heads spun, and that was when they entered into direct communion with God. They were called the Hasidim. It was a powerful, mystical movement.'

'Mystical?' asked Theo. 'You mean like the New Age, with crystals and incense?'

Aunt Martha told Theo that he'd do well to remember the word 'mystical' because he'd be coming across it every few seconds. A mystic is someone who can communicate directly with God.

'Amazing,' retorted Theo. 'You mean without the rabbis?'

'No . . . not at all. The Polish rabbis taught these communication techniques to others. They were all great teachers and their portraits are actually here.' And the Rabbi stopped outside a gloomy shop, with posters on the wooden shutters. And on the posters were the faces of teachers of Hasidism, with turbans, fur hats, and often long white beards.

'OK,' said Theo, 'but, Rabbi Eliezer, you haven't answered my question. I asked you about the women's hair, and you took me through the ghettos of Europe.'

The Rabbi heaved another great sigh. 'Well, in the Jewish tradition of the ghettos of Central Europe, there were very strict rules for women. When married, a woman must keep herself for her husband, and for him alone. To keep them from temptation, a strange custom was gradually introduced which consisted of shaving a wife's head the day after her wedding. After that, she wore a wig to go out.'

'It's not true,' said Theo. 'He's making it up, isn't he, Aunt Martha?'

But the Rabbi had not made up anything at all. To this day, women had their heads shaved in certain parts of Jerusalem, and even in Europe, in Strasbourg, Paris, London. They were not allowed to show their own hair. Besides, he added, Islam did exactly the same.

'It's true,' confirmed the Sheikh. 'Except that we don't shave women's heads. We just cover them, and then only in public, not at home.'

'But sometimes,' cried the Rabbi, 'in some countries, you put a leather mask over their faces! That's no better!'

The conversation grew heated. Aunt Martha became extremely annoyed, decreed that these outdated ideas on women's hair were neither in the holy books nor in the Bible nor in the Koran, and that they had not come to Me'a She'arim to collect religious idiocies. Whatever would Theo think?

'That if that's what religion's about, you can all go and take a jump!' cried Theo. 'Shaving women's heads? Making them wear leather masks? Are you crazy? What about the Song of Songs, was that a joke then?'

'There,' remarked Aunt Martha calmly, 'well done all of you! How are you going to explain the rest to him after that?'

The blue flames

The Sheikh and the Rabbi exchanged anxious glances. Indeed, how were they going to make up for their behaviour?

'My dear Eliezer,' began the Sheikh, 'I think you should talk about the Baal Shem.'

'Oh yes! The Baal Shem! Excellent idea,' agreed Father Dubourg.

'The Baal Shem,' concluded Aunt Martha. 'There's no other option. Let's go on a little. It's easier to understand when you're walking.'

Weird name, thought Theo. Perhaps they were talking about the immortal bird in the riddle, after all. The Bayulshem?

'The Baal Shem,' began the Rabbi, carefully picking his way among the pot-holes, 'was the nickname given in Poland . . .'

Suddenly he tripped over a stone and nearly lost his balance. The Sheikh caught him just in time.

'Before going any further, we must reassure our young friend,' he whispered in the Rabbi's ear as he helped him steady himself.

'You're right!' exclaimed the Rabbi, planted firmly on his feet. 'Theo, let me tell you this. There are two ways to find out about religions. The first consists of sticking to what you see with your eyes. You see the worst, and you're put off. The other consists of trying to find out more, to understand the grain of truth that is hidden beneath the excesses, like a jewel under a pile of straw. Me'a She'arim is not only the district of intolerance, it is here that we discover how the Jews kept their faith in exile, how the unhappy Jews preserved the *Shekhinah*, the presence of God. Without the inspired discipline of the Hasidim, our faith would not have survived with all its vitality. Yes, they danced and sang to reach the Eternal. And thus they preserved the essence of our religion, faith in exile, the *Shekhinah*. For in our language, the *Shekhinah* is a very beautiful woman, wearing a black veil and weeping. She represents the feminine side of the Eternal. You see, you shouldn't just judge by appearances.'

'Very good,' approved the Sheikh. 'Go on, Eliezer.'

'The Baal Shem,' continued the Rabbi, 'is none other than the founder of Hasidism. His full name, the Baal Shem Tov, means "Master of the Good Name". He communicated by singing, or by using the supernatural powers he'd been endowed with. On one feast day, the Baal Shem Tov's disciples danced and drank so much that they kept on asking for more wine to be brought up from the cellar. The Rabbi's wife had had enough, and said to her husband that soon there would be no more wine left for Shabbat. "That's true," laughed the Master. "Well, tell them to stop!" The Rabbi's wife went into the room where the disciples were jigging around and what did she see? A ring of tall, blue flames dancing above their heads. So she rushed down to the cellar herself to bring up more wine. The Master had caused this miracle to show her that communion with God must not be interrupted.'

'So they were allowed to drink wine?' said Theo. 'In other words, they were tight as newts.'

'Ecstasy is a form of intoxication, and we do not forbid wine. On another occasion, the Baal Shem Tov went into an ecstatic trance that made him tremble from head to foot. A disciple touched the fringe of his shawl: it was trembling. The disciple looked at the water in the bowl on the table: it was trembling. Ecstasy is a divine trembling and the Master was drunk on God without having touched a drop of wine.'

'Drunk on God,' murmured Theo. 'Sometimes music makes me tremble too.'

'And on another occasion, the Baal Shem was taking his ritual bath in the bath house, by the light of a single candle. It was so cold that icicles had formed on the inside walls. The Baal Shem splashed around in the water for a long time, and the candle was burning lower and lower. "Master, the candle's about to go out!" cried an anxious disciple. "Fool!" replied the Baal Shem, "Just take an ice candle from the eaves! Talk to the ice and it will be kindled!" The disciple obeyed, for you must always obey the master. And the ice candle burned with a beautiful clear flame.'

'It's not a true story, is it?' asked Theo.

'Who knows?' said the Rabbi, stopping in front of a large building with open windows. 'It all depends on whether or not you believe. But you probably noticed the Baal Shem called his disciple a fool, for masters are duty-bound to be strict with their pupils. Now, come over here. Look through the window.'

Theo raised himself up on tiptoe. Seated in an orderly fashion around a wooden table, little schoolboys swayed as they stumbled through the text they were reading aloud, and their curly locks danced on either side of their heads in a regular motion.

'A school,' remarked Theo. 'But it's funny, they're swaying.'

'That way the body learns at the same time,' said the Rabbi. 'Compulsory discipline. Watch them carefully. Here you can understand the spirit of the Jewish exile, preserved over the centuries. The body played an important part In Hasidism. The masters turned slowly, one arm raised and the other over one ear: it was their way of praying. They were all called "Zaddik", which means "Just" in Hebrew.'

'Like Oskar Schindler, the good Nazi?' inquired Theo.

'Yes, Schindler was a Just man, it's the same word. They say it would only take ten Just men to save the whole world. But at the time of Hasidism, the Just men were the Jewish masters at divine encounters. When people are in exile, they have to find a way of preserving the faith of their ancestors, and that's what they were doing with their miracles, their stories, their dancing and their drunkenness. The Jerusalem we are walking in today was no more than a faraway neglected little town, but they still had the celestial Jerusalem, the inner Jerusalem that every Jew carries in their body. So, when they celebrated, the Just were commemorating their inner Jerusalem.'

'But what about now they've got it back?' asked Theo.

'They haven't got their Jerusalem back, Theo. They have a divided city in a modern state called Israel. They still dream of a Jerusalem of light and faith where the rebuilt Temple shines in a city ready to welcome the Messiah. Often, some will not even recognize the existence of the State of Israel.'

'They're crazy!'

'No!' cried the Rabbi. 'What they can't accept is that a government, laws, an army and courts have been established by the people, instead of God. These people refuse to do military service and won't even speak the official language, which is Hebrew.' .

'So what do they speak, then?' asked Theo in astonishment.

'Yiddish, the language of the European Jews, the only language able to express their ideal. That is why they have recreated the world of the Polish Hasidim, to preserve the inner Jerusalem, which they prefer to the real one. For this Hasidic world died in Auschwitz, Theo. There are almost no Jews left in Poland, they were all slaughtered.'

'Are the only ones left all here?' asked Theo.

'Oh no!' interrupted Aunt Martha. 'You can also find them in America and Europe. The celestial Jerusalem is not about to die out, nor are the rapturous dances of the Hasidim.'

'There are other Jews who have chosen to live in the past,' added the Rabbi. 'The Samaritans, for example. We may meet some in the streets, you'll recognize them by their turbans and heavy coats. They are very unusual. When most of the Jews went into exile after the destruction of the first Temple, they chose to mingle with the occupying forces at the time of the Assyrians. But when the Jews returned, they rejected those they considered as traitors.'

'I remember something about a good Samaritan,' said Theo. 'He was very wicked, but Jesus stood up for him . . . is that right?'

'The Samaritans weren't wicked, but people disapproved of them during Christ's time, because they had collaborated with the occupying forces. So they decided to break their ties with the Jews and build their own temple on Mount Gerizim where, according to them, Abraham had agreed to sacrifice Isaac, and only to marry among themselves. But this type of marriage always leads to the same thing: fewer and fewer children. Nowadays there are less than a thousand of them. They speak a very ancient form of Hebrew and they only recognize part of the Bible.'

'So what are they, then?' queried Theo.

'They have recently become reintegrated into the institutions of Israel. What do you expect, Theo? Every religion has its dissidents. Is it really bad? It can also be enriching, you know.'

'We have that too,' chimed in the Sheikh. 'We also have our miracles, our inspired beings and our legends. We have masters who dance and whirl until they reach ecstasy – the dervishes. You see a lot of them in Istanbul.'

'Istanbul!' exclaimed Theo. 'Are they sometimes called "immortal birds" by any chance?'

'No, Theo,' replied the Sheikh with a little laugh. 'Istanbul isn't where you'll find your bird.'

'Drat,' said Theo. 'Yet I'd have thought . . .'

'But the dervishes aren't birds. Actually, the master of the dervishes is very similar to the Polish Baal Shem. He was Turkish, he lived in the twelfth century and was called the Maulana, which means "our master". He too told all sorts of stories and he too was harsh with his disciples. The main thing is for the master to set an example. He embodies the image of the Almighty.'

'Besides,' added the Rabbi, 'while we're on the subject of the Baal Shem Tov, there's a wonderful story about him. In Paradise, the souls of all men to come were contained in Adam's body. When the serpent appeared by the tree of knowledge, the Baal Shem's soul escaped from Adam's body and did not eat the cursed fruit.'

'And nor did Jesus?' asked Theo.

'Ah! That I don't know,' replied the Rabbi.

'What about Father Dubourg? Have you got any stories like that?' queried Theo.

'Of course,' the priest replied. 'All the saints are heroes, and each one has a story. Saint Martin was a Roman soldier who cut his coat in two to give half to a poor man who was naked. Saint Agatha, the martyr, had both her breasts cut off. Saint Anthony was a monk who was exposed to every kind of temptation and resisted them all, Saint Blandine of Lyon was devoured by lions in a Roman arena, Saint Genevieve saved Paris from the invasion of the Barbarians, Saint Cecilia was a musician. No religion can do without its saints. That is why, in Christianity, they are officially recognized. It's easier.'

'Let me tell you something, Theo,' interrupted Aunt Martha. 'There's God, who is not always easy. He can be kind and fatherly, but he can also be angry and harsh. And to get closer to God, it's better to follow the example of men who are simply generous, inspired and good.'

'Like Sister Emmanuelle in Cairo. Except that she's a woman.'

'Men or women, they are cantankerous,' went on Aunt Martha. 'They don't get on with politicians, they tell their President, Sultan, or High Priest a few home truths, but come what may, they comfort the poor.'

'I like that,' said Theo. 'Is there a portrait of the Baal Shem in the shop over there?'

There was. Theo grabbed the roll of paper from which the Master gazed at him with his mischievous expression. They had walked for well over an hour, and Aunt Martha was worried about her Theo and decided it was time to go back. The journey to Bethlehem was not far, but on Christmas Eve, it was wise to leave in good time and have an early lunch.

The solution to the first riddle

On returning to his little room perched at the top of the French Consulate, Theo dreamed of the Master jumping up and down surrounded by a circle of disciples and imagined himself among them, drinking and dancing, his feet encased in heavy, snow-laden boots. How good it must be to let oneself go . . .

He picked up his notebook and added a few jottings: MYSTIC = SOMEONE WHO COMMUNICATES DIRECTLY WITH GOD. GHETTO: QUARTER WHERE EUROPEAN JEWS WERE FORCED TO LIVE. HASIDIM: POLISH, RUSSIAN AND UKRAINIAN MASTERS WHO PREFERRED DANCING AND DRUNKENNESS TO STUDY. BAAL SHEM: AN AMAZING GUY! MUSLIM SAINTS = WHIRLING DERVISHES. CHRISTIAN SAINTS: CHARITABLE, BRAVE, MARTYRS. WOMEN'S HAIR = PROBLEMS. HOLY SEPULCHRE = BAZAAR! CHURCHES: CATHOLIC, ARMENIAN, GREEK ORTHODOX, ETHIOPIAN AND . . .

There was one missing. And Theo still had not found the bird that rubbed its wings together to kindle its pyre. Just as he was about to pick up the dictionary again, the telephone rang. It was Mum.

'How are you, darling? Not too tired? How did it go at the hospital? They didn't hurt you, I hope. Are you taking your medicine? And . . .'

'Stop, Mum,' sighed Theo. 'That's enough! Will you get off my back?'

'Oh!' said Melina, shocked. 'I'll put your father on.'

After Dad, Irene, then Attie who passed him on to Fatou.

'Well, have you found it, Theo?'

'I haven't had time,' he replied defensively. 'Am I allowed two clues?'

'That'll cost you five poi-ints,' replied Fatou, imitating the voice of the Pythia in the video game. 'Five points off your total sco-ore.'

'Don't care!' retorted Theo, 'Out with it!'

'*Don't confuse me with the scribe bird,*' declared Fatou in an inspired tone. 'There. Big kisses.'

'And to you,' muttered Theo, putting down the receiver. Hard.

A scribe bird . . . that vaguely rang a bell. Where had Theo met a god of writing in the form of a bird? In Egypt, of course! The scribe bird was the god Thoth with the head of an ibis. If the two birds were likely to be confused, then the immortal one was in Egypt!

'Aunt Martha!' yelled Theo, rushing into the other room.

'What's the matter, darling?'

'The bird, it's in Egypt, isn't it?'

'Well done! And about time too . . . We're leaving soon for Cairo. How did you guess?'

'It was Fatou, the second clue, the scribe bird.'

'Of course. You know the gods of Egypt well. And what's the name of the immortal bird that rubs its wings?'

'That I don't know,' murmured Theo.

'You read it in the dictionary . . . a bird, a pyre . . .'

'The phoenix!' cried Theo.

'Yes, Theo, the phoenix, which is its own father and which never dies. The phoenix is born at the source of the Nile, lights its own funeral pyre in the delta and rises again from the ashes.'

'And rises again from the ashes,' echoed Theo sadly. 'I wish I could be that bird.'

Christmas in Bethlehem

On the road from Jerusalem to Bethlehem, the traffic was already reduced to a crawl. The Consul had decided to drive Theo and Aunt Martha in his bullet-proof car, while the three friends would follow in the Dominican's car. Soon, the first checkpoints appeared, manned by soldiers carrying submachine guns.

'The frontier,' said the Consul. 'We're leaving Israel and entering the territories that are under Palestinian jurisdiction. This is likely to take some time.'

A diplomatic vehicle with a special number plate, no search. Slowly, the car overtook the waiting vehicles and drove between the two chicanes spanning the road. Ten kilometres of tailbacks before they reached Bethlehem, where Father Dubourg had arranged accommodation at the Saint Joseph Inn – very simple rooms, narrow beds, a table, a pitcher of water, a bowl and a chair. They would spend the rest of the night there after Midnight Mass.

In Manger Square, surrounded by sheer walls, rose the huge basilica with its dark ochre pediment, decked with countless Palestinian flags and garlands of fairy lights strung between the houses. There was already a large crowd. Television crews wandered around with their heavy gear bumping into passers-by, bearded young men, tourists in lightweight clothing and women dressed in black. The Consul elbowed his way through to ensure they had seats, because of Theo. In the meantime, the rest of the troop would go and visit the Grotto of the Milk, where the Holy Family had apparently taken refuge before fleeing to Egypt. In fact, it was no longer a grotto, but a simple chapel.

'Wait,' called Theo, 'Let me think. The Holy Family, you mean Joseph the carpenter, Mary and the Baby Jesus. They were on their way to Egypt because a bad guy wanted to kill all the babies.'

'King Herod,' said the Sheikh.

'The same one who rebuilt the Temple?' asked Theo in amazement.

'The very same,' replied Father Dubourg. 'The same one who gave the order to kill all Jewish babies under the age of two.'

'So they set off, and on the way, Jesus was born here.'

'Not at all, Theo!' exclaimed Aunt Martha. 'Jesus was born in the Grotto of the Nativity, inside the basilica. Where we're going to hear Midnight Mass – if our friend the Consul has managed to get us seats!'

The Consul had done wonders. Despite the crowds milling through all the streets of Bethlehem, he managed to shepherd his little group into the basilica itself, where the civil and military authorities sat alongside government representatives and religious dignitaries, not forgetting the President of the Palestinian Authority and his wife, a Christian woman with a lovely, luminous face under a black lace mantilla. Because he represented France, the Protector of Holy Places, the Consul always had the place of honour in the front row. Compared with the ornate choir and the officiants in their gold chasubles, the altar, covered in white, was very simple. Wearing a mauve skullcap, the Latin patriarch praised the virtues of peace, reconciliation between Christians and Muslims, the hope of Light and the symbol of the nativity at the back of the nave, where, at the end of the Mass, he would take the statue of the Infant Jesus whose arms were outstretched towards an invisible heaven. It was dreadfully hot, and the hubbub of the crowds outside disturbed the majestic ceremony of the Nativity.

All the world's television stations had sent their crews to film the event: Midnight Mass in Bethlehem, the holy city of Christianity and a Muslim town. The joyful clamour of the crowd, the fireworks in the night, the stars in the reddish sky, the firecrackers let off by the children and the intensity of the celebrations, it was all deafening. And even if this riotous crowd was far removed from the simplicity of the first Nativity, even if there was no comparison between the straw-filled manager, the donkey and the ox and the sumptuous churches of Bethlehem, there was a mysterious connection between the dawn of time and today, the appearance of a holy infant and the memory of his birth. Despite her disbelief, Aunt Martha went so far as to brush away a tear, and Theo, thrilled, wanted to linger in the streets a little longer.

At last they had to go back to the Saint Joseph Inn. Aunt Martha observed her nephew out of the corner of her eye, noticing the dark circles under his eyes. But Theo had barely lain down, his head still full of stars of Bethlehem, when the door opened and the Sheikh entered.

No more 'whys'

'Sssh!' he said mysteriously, his finger to his lips. 'I know it's very late, Theo, but you always find it hard to get to sleep at night, don't you?'

'How do you know?' asked Theo, sitting up in amazement.

'I've been keeping a close eye on you, my child,' answered the Sheikh. 'When you stop tormenting yourself at night, you will be halfway there. May I sit down for a moment?'

And without waiting for an answer, he sat down on the wooden chair.

'You've heard so many things over the last two days, Theo,' he began, 'but there's been so little mention of God!'

'What do you expect?' sighed Theo.

'So little, and so inadequate,' said the Sheikh gravely, smoothing out his jellaba. 'Forget the fury, forget the wars and massacres, and see what we have in common. We have only one God, and he has spoken to us. For he spoke to Abraham, Moses, Jesus and Muhammad. God has spoken to man through his messengers. Of course, each one is different. Moses had his wrath, Jesus his goodness, and Muhammad his sense of justice.'

'Muhammad, justice?' cut in Theo.

'I feared so,' sighed the Sheikh. 'In your country, Islam is not understood, and besides, my two friends had so much to tell you. I preferred to listen to you. And I heard your resistance, which won't help you to get to sleep. Let me tell you about Muhammad again.'

'But you've already told me!'

'Muhammad was like his predecessors: he was seeking to unite God and man with simple rules. Moses heard God dictate to him the tablets of the law, Jesus preached the good news in the Gospels and the Angel Gabriel dictated the Koran to Muhammad. Moses introduced the idea of law, Jesus that of charity, and Muhammad the notion of justice. For all, God is love.'

'Why talk to me about that now?' murmured Theo.

'To reconcile you with all of us, my child,' replied the Sheikh. 'To soothe that little mind that is forever contradicting. Oh! Don't think I want to stop you thinking. But the disease gnawing at you can go away, Theo. I'm not asking you to believe in God. That won't cure you. But just be aware that you too are a little bit of God. Breath is in you as it is in each of us, Theo. Seek the way. Find the breath.'

'I'd love to,' said Theo, 'but why?'

'Sometimes you have to know when to stop asking why,' replied the Sheikh. 'You're too old to be forever asking questions, you're not five any more! Calm down. To find the breath, you have to let yourself go. Let yourself go, Theo, otherwise you'll never get better.'

'Do you think so?' murmured Theo, panic-stricken.

'Somewhere in the world, one of us will cure you, I know it,' said the Sheikh, raising his voice. 'Your illness will go back where it came from, brought by an evil spirit. But if you resist with your 'why's, then none of us will be able to save you. I'm asking you to believe in the breath, that is all.'

'In the breath?' asked Theo, perplexed. 'What does that mean?'

'Another question!' exclaimed the Sheikh with authority. 'Will you agree for once to obey me without asking any questions?'

'Yes,' replied Theo without hesitation.

Then, closing his eyes, the Sheikh placed his hands on Theo's chest. After a moment, Theo felt an unfamiliar heat on his back, like a warm towel after bathing in the sea, the sun on the Greek beaches, the softness of Fatou's cheek. He fell asleep.

'Praised be the Almighty,' murmured the Sheikh, as he stood up. 'We'll save you, Theo. Don't ever forget that.'

And he tiptoed out of the room with a light heart.

CHAPTER 5

A Solar Boat and Ten Seeds

Goodbye Jerusalem

The three of them stood there, the Rabbi, the Dominican and the Sheikh, in front of the passport control desks, in the place where their ways and Theo's were to part. He took out his camera and hit the flash button, and all three blinked in unison.

'Right, well, so long, Suleiman,' said Theo, shaking the old man's hand. 'I meant to say . . . About the breath . . . I'll never forget Christmas night.'

'So long to you too,' murmured the Sheikh, and bowed his head. 'May the blessing of the Almighty protect you.'

'You've been really kind,' said Theo to the Rabbi. 'But there's still some stuff I haven't really grasped.'

'Oh, I know! You haven't even been inside a synagogue! You haven't taken part in Shabbat! I haven't talked to you about the seven-branch candlestick, or the Torah, or the letters with the crowns, and what they mean, or the mezuzah, or . . .'

'Rabbi, that's enough!' Aunt Martha protested. 'Don't confuse him . . . Others will complete what you've begun.'

'But where?' asked the Rabbi suspiciously. 'Will they be good Jews?'

'They will be in the diaspora, no worse and no better than you are,' Aunt Martha told him firmly.

'Diaspora? What's that?' Theo cut in.

'It's the name we use to refer to all those Jews, wherever they are, who have not yet returned to Israel,' said the Rabbi.

'They're the ones who have chosen to practise their Judaism in their own country,' Aunt Martha continued. 'Diaspora means "dispersion" in Greek. Those Jews have been dispersed, but they want to stay in the place where they live, the country they were born in, you see. That is their right.'

'They will return,' assured the Rabbi.

'In any case, I promise you that we will be meeting some of them in Europe,' Aunt Martha assured him. 'And Theo will take part in Shabbat.'

'Let us hope so,' said the Rabbi. 'You too will return, Theo, but so will your health! Do you remember the nine-tenths of the burden of suffering doled out to Jerusalem? I didn't tell you the whole story. Jerusalem also received nine-tenths of human happiness. When I was little and we were living in exile, my father would raise the seder plate above my head and say: "This year, here, son of slavery. Next year in Jerusalem, son of freedom." When you return to Jerusalem, next year, you will be freed from the slavery of your illness, my son.'

'All right,' Aunt Martha murmured, in a voice that failed to hide her distress. 'Next year in Jerusalem, if all goes well.'

'You too, Father Antoine, you've been kind, and patient too,' said Theo. 'I hope you're not feeling offended.'

'Offended, me?' cried Father Dubourg. 'What an idea! Come here and give me hug. I will pray for you, my son.'

It was time to go. Aunt Martha shepherded her nephew to the passport desk, with the Consul at their heels. When they were through, Theo turned round.

'The main thing is, you all remain good friends!' he called.

He waved his arms above his head in a last salute, and then he was gone.

'What a little firecracker,' sighed the Rabbi. 'Rebellious, but so intelligent. If only our friend can find a cure.'

'Only God knows,' said Father Dubourg.

'Inshallah,' the Sheikh declared. 'He will survive, I tell you.'

Amal the Egyptian

A pair of sharp eyes swept to and fro across the dense throng of porters and veiled women. Aunt Martha was looking for someone. On the plane from Tel Aviv to Cairo, she had laughed out loud when Theo asked who was to be their guide in Egypt. All he could get out of her was: 'A marvellous character, and that's all I'm saying.'

Theo's head throbbed with the clamour of voices and the background airport smell of dirty grease, and his eyes were distracted by imitation bas-reliefs plonked on top of yellow imitation marble, as he too kept a lookout for Mr X. Another bearded sage? Another consul? A professor of Egyptian history? All at once Aunt Martha shouted: 'Amal! Amal! Over here!'

But Amal's face was beardless. Amal was a big woman with beautiful white hair and bright dark eyes. She wore a bright green suit and stylish golden earrings, and she was not the French consul, but a professor of Greek civilization at al-Azhar university. She had the kind of understated energy that takes control yet has no need to shout. A rusting old trolley to stow the luggage, an Egyptian pound to pay for it, customs check, the yells of porters, 50 piastres, taxi.

'We'll go straight home,' she said, 'and Theo can rest, inshallah! Do you like Karkade?'

She was talking to Theo with all the warmth and affection of someone who had known him since his childhood. By now she had her arm around his shoulder and he found himself nestling companionably against his new friend's broad hips.

'I don't think Theo's come across Karkade,' said Aunt Martha.

Karkade was a soft drink of a beautiful raspberry colour, made from plants grown in Nubia. It was an Egyptian speciality, like the *moulukhiya* that Theo would discover at supper time. *Moulukhiya*? Ah, it couldn't be described, you had to taste it. It was one of those pleasures unlike anything else.

Amal's talk was as buoyant as her humour: she paid no attention to the giant traffic jams that took them at a crawl past lorries, cars, young buffaloes with curved horns, and little trotting donkeys, towards Brazil Street, in the district of Zamalek, on Gezira Island. The taxi drew up in front of Amal's house, and the city noises faded, the blare of car horns replaced by the song of unseen birds hidden in clouds of jasmine. The house was not new. The paintwork on the wooden door was fading, and the blue and white floor tiles showed signs of wear, but as soon as he crossed the threshold Theo's head almost swam with a tantalizing scent. Amal's house had the heady charm and individual smell of old houses long occupied and lived in, but this was something different, and he ran to trace its source.

In the drawing room, the leather settees were well worn and the carpets fraying. On the table stood a vase full of long stiff stems bristling with spikelets of white stars. The scent was here. Theo plunged his face into the sprays of stars and breathed in so hard that the old settee had to catch him on the rebound.

'So, what do you say?' breathed Aunt Martha as she flopped down beside him.

'Obviously it's not so fine a house as the French consulate in Jerusalem,' said Amal.

'Nah,' said Theo, with vast indifference. 'What are those flowers?'

'They're tuberoses,' Amal replied. 'They smell like a million jasmines.'

She took them to their rooms, and Theo was instructed to lie down and rest. In his room a huge bed stood against a wall papered with golden branches and flowers. When he threw himself down on the sheets, his teeth almost rattled, the mattress felt so hard. A proper bed of nails.

'All right, sleep well,' said Aunt Martha.

The two old friends went back down to the drawing room and sank onto the comfy settees. Amal lit a red candle and Aunt Martha a cigarillo. It was late afternoon, an ideal time for scheming.

'How I've missed you,' Amal began. 'When did you leave?'

'Not so long ago,' Aunt Martha replied. 'I wouldn't have come back so soon if it hadn't been for Theo.'

'How is he getting on?' asked Amal, lowering her voice.

'The tests in Jerusalem weren't brilliant. All the same, I think he's looking more lively. He's so inquisitive, and what with our visits, the crowds, and all these new experiences, he's very excited.'

'We mustn't overdo it. What do you want to show him here?'

'The Tutankhamun treasure. He's longing to see it. Otherwise, not a whole lot. The Coptic quarter?'

'And a mosque, too. If not he'll forget that Egypt is a Muslim country. And what about the City of the Dead?'

'No,' said Aunt Martha, very firmly. 'No City of the Dead, no mummies, no underground exploring in the Valley of Kings, no expeditions to visit the dead.'

'*Yaani*. Poor child, I wasn't thinking,' said Amal in confusion. 'Tell me, what are you really hoping to do?'

'To make him well. In the old days, when a growing boy fell ill, they would send him away on his travels. Sometimes he would die, but sometimes he would be healed by the mysterious power of the journey. And that's what I intend.'

'But you talked to me about a tour of the world of religions.'

'It's the same thing,' said Aunt Martha decisively, stubbing out her cigarillo.

The pillar sitters

At dinner, Theo felt at home. When the *moulukhiya* was served, he liked it so much that he ate three helpings and asked all sorts of questions. What was the recipe? Fry onions and cloves of garlic in a pan, add sweet pepper, rice, and plenty of the green herb *moulukhiya*, well chopped, and when it is cooked to a soup, serve with roast chicken. What exactly was *moulukhiya*? A herb, an Egyptian herb. You know what a herb is!

'He's always like this,' Aunt Martha told her friend. 'When my friend Dubourg emerged after the visit to the Holy Sepulchre he was practically seething with exasperation. What was the difference between the Armenian Church and the Coptic and Ethiopian Churches, and did the queen of Sheba . . . ?'

Theo defended himself. 'I'm travelling to learn, so I'm bound to ask questions.'

'But I hear you already know everything about ancient Egypt,' said Amal.

'I wish! I just know two or three gods. Hathor the cow, Sebek the crocodile, Sekhmet the lioness, Anubis the jackal, Thoth the ibis, Ra the sun, Apis the bull, Bastet the cat, Khnum the ram . . .'

'Two or three gods?' said Amal. 'That's nine already!'

'So many animal gods,' said Theo proudly. 'And there are others. Tauert the hippopotamus, Apopis the serpent . . .'

'Even Apopis?' said Amal. 'Now there, you really surprise me. But you haven't mentioned Isis or Osiris, and they are the greatest of the gods.'

'Yes, but they haven't got animal heads,' Theo replied. 'With them, it's a different story. Osiris had an evil brother who cut him up in pieces, and his wife Isis searched for them far and wide. She found everything except his willie.'

'Theo!' said Aunt Martha, scandalized.

'OK, then,' said Theo, 'what should I say? The phallus?'

'Right,' said Amal. 'And what happened after that, Theo?'

'After that she conceived a son – his name was Horus – all by herself. Sometimes he has a funny-looking lock of hair that sticks out from his shaven head, but he usually has the head of a falcon. But Osiris never comes back to life. He's a kind of unfinished Jesus.'

'Not bad,' said Aunt Martha. 'And what about the pharaohs?'

'Rameses, Amenophis, Tutankhamun, Pepsi . . .'

'Pepi!' his Egyptian hostess laughed as she corrected him. 'But you haven't come here to learn the names of all the pharaohs. In Cairo you will see some Coptic churches.'

'Again?' cried Theo. 'But I've seen them already in Jerusalem.'

'Coptic means literally "Egyptian",' Amal told him. 'And what you saw in Jerusalem was just a little chapel in that beehive of the Holy Sepulchre. Without the Copts, you'll never understand the first thing about the birth of Christianity. It was here, in the desert, that the anchorites came to live, only a few at first, and then whole armies, recruited by the first bishops.'

'That word anchorite,' said Theo. 'Doesn't it sound Greek?'

'Yes, it comes from a Greek word meaning "withdraw". An anchorite is a solitary monk – though sometimes a nun – in a hermitage. Sometimes, when he lives on top of a pillar up to eight metres high, out in the desert, he is called a "stylite".'

'A guy who lives on a pillar?' said Theo. 'What about food?'

'They go without. They fast, they pray, and they meditate. Others draw a circle ten metres across, and vow never to leave it. Others settle in the hollow of a tree, and only put their head out to eat.'

'Then they're crazy,' Theo decided.

'Yes, but they're crazy for God,' Amal replied. 'They were the first Christians in this land. There were great saints among them. Later they turned more violent. To erase the very memory of the ancient Egyptians, they smashed up the bas-reliefs in temples. They made war on what they called "paganism". All the most sacred creations of ancient Egypt, and everything that Greece had given to the world, they were determined to destroy.'

'So tell him the story of Hypatia,' Aunt Martha suggested.

'Poor Hypatia. She was beautiful and clever, and an outstanding philosopher, but she was also a pagan. The Christian bishop disliked her, because she argued so brilliantly. It did no harm to anybody, except that because of her, Greek philosophy was making great strides and getting in the way of Christianity.'

'Why?' asked Theo.

'Because Greek philosophy did not believe in this tale of a god-made man, then dying on the cross and rising again on the third day. In order to get rid of her, the bishop set a pack of monks on Hypatia, and they sliced her to pieces using oyster shells as knives.'

'Fascists,' said Theo.

'Or something like it. The Christians won out in the end. A Roman emperor called Theodosius published an edict banning paganism, and the Coptic Christian Church reigned in Egypt for a long time. But later there were divisions in the Churches, and . . .'

'I've seen that myself,' said Theo.

'. . . and when Islam conquered Egypt, it was the Copts' turn to lose.'

'And a good thing too. They shouldn't have attacked other people.'

'But the Copts are important, Theo!' said Aunt Martha. 'They are the only ones to preserve a little of the writing of the ancient Egyptians, they created a beautiful kind of decorative art that led to the Byzantine style that you've seen in Greek churches, and even the Romanesque churches in your own country owe something to the Copts. Their numbers are fewer today, but they play a great part. And besides, the caliphs were also destructive. Isn't that right, Amal?'

'Yes,' she conceded ruefully. 'Like all the rest.'

'What about you, Amal?' asked Theo. 'What are you?'

'Egyptian and Muslim, but Egyptian first.'

'Look at her, Theo,' Aunt Martha prompted. 'Doesn't she resemble the female figures on the frescoes you've seen pictures of in books?'

'Yes,' said Theo. 'Without the earrings, but with big breasts and no blouse.'

'He *is* observant,' said Amal, and so he was, but the hour was growing late. They made plans for the following day, and decided that they would travel backwards in time, starting with the Copts, then making a detour through the Bible, before they reached the ancient Egyptians.

Two halves and three elements

'This is the main entrance,' said Amal. 'Past the nailed gate, we're in the Babylon Fortress fort, inside the wall of the old Coptic quarter.'

'Very very ancient,' was Theo's expert verdict. 'You can see that straight away.'

'But much less ancient than the Pyramids,' Amal informed him. 'Don't forget that ancient Egypt is the oldest civilization on earth - five thousand years old - and this place is less than two thousand years old, because it was Christians who built it. Let's go and look at the churches, the synagogue and the mosque.'

'Wait!' said Theo. 'Do I get an explanation?'

'Of what? The synagogue and the mosque? Well, if you've seen Jerusalem you'll have noticed that every religious building has been destroyed, and then rebuilt, and then destroyed again, and so on. That's what happened with the Ben Ezra synagogue, which was built under the Romans, then converted into a church, then reconverted into a synagogue in the twelfth century. As for the mosque, it was the oldest in the whole of Egypt when it was first built, out of brick, and before it was rebuilt in the fifteenth century.'

'Like Jerusalem,' said Theo. 'So how much is actually left?'

'A few dilapidated stones, memories, those two towers that date from Roman times, and some history books,' said Amal with a sigh in her voice. 'But that's what happens with all religious monuments. The temples crumble, the names of the gods fade away. Only the people remain.'

'But the Pyramids are still there,' said Theo. 'And anyway, I've had it up to here with all that fighting between Christians!'

Amal did not answer as she guided Theo and Aunt Martha down narrow streets lined with bougainvillaea. They entered the first church, where Theo was reluctant to hang about because in Greece he had seen any number of very similar churches. When they emerged, he sat down on the steps with a sulky expression.

'I'm not interested in this,' he said rebelliously. 'I want to see the Pyramids.'

'But during their flight to Egypt, Joseph and Mary stopped here, in the crypt,' said Amal. 'Isn't that something worth seeing?'

'No!' cried Theo. 'I want to see the Pyramids.'

'But the history of the Copts is so important, and so fiery,' urged his guide. 'You just don't realize. Think, Theo. Egypt had been one of the first great civilizations, not just for hundreds but thousands of years, then it absorbed the Greeks, and then the Romans, and still it lived on, and developed into one of the jewels of the later ancient world. And now came the Christian Church of Egypt, and it might have become the most powerful in the world, and maintained a great empire in the Orient, when . . . but it's all too complicated.'

'Oh?' said Theo curiously. 'What happened?'

'It's going to seem completely idiotic,' said Aunt Martha.

'Maybe I'm not that slow.'

'No one said you were,' said Amal. 'Right. Are you ready? Then I'll begin. You know that for Christians, Jesus is God made man. In today's world, everyone is accustomed to this old idea, familiar with it. But imagine how it was in the beginning, the mental confusion. God made man? Then how much is God's share, and how much is man's, in Jesus, hmm?'

'Half and half?' guessed Theo.

'The question obsessed the theologians. If human nature is full of faults, what comes uppermost in Jesus – the divine or the human? Did Jesus have faults or did he not? They came up with all sorts of theories. According to some, man is the bad, and God the good. That's pretty much your theory, half and half. Except that after a few centuries, little by little, as a result of separating Jesus into these two halves – the bad side human, the good divine – some Christians decided they had to make the bad side wither away in order to liberate the good. So they committed suicide by starving their bodies, the incarnation of evil. They called themselves Cathars, which means "pure ones".'

'Purity again!' said Theo. 'And this was in Egypt?'

'No, but the theory was born not so very far from here, in the third century, in the mind of a man called Mani. This way of thinking is called Manichaeism, and the Catholic Church classes it as a heresy. Do you know what a heresy is?'

'Something to do with sects?'

'Yes, but officially condemned by an assembly of the Church. Here, the disagreement was between the school of thought that rejected the divine nature of Christ without going so far as to destroy the evil bodily side, and those who claimed that his divine nature absorbed his human nature and made it divine.'

'Wait a minute,' said Theo. 'There's one version that sees Christ as just a man, and therefore not altogether good, and another that sees him as God, and therefore totally good: is that right?'

'Exactly right. The first were the Arians, named after their chief thinker, Arius, a priest in the city of Alexandria, less than two hundred kilometres northwest of where we stand. The second were the monophysites, which means "one nature". Not to mention the Nestorians, who flatly denied the unity of Christ and reverted to Mani's theory. For centuries, religious battles raged in Egypt over the nature of Christ.'

'You see how idiotic it sounds,' Aunt Martha said.

'Not really, though,' said Theo. 'I'd never seen the problem before. What about the Catholics, what do they claim?'

'That it is a divine mystery,' Amal replied. 'The heart of the mystery is based in the Holy Trinity – God in three persons.'

'That reminds me,' said Aunt Martha. 'Once, in a play, I heard an irresistible definition of the Trinity. It was spoken by a man who was playing the part of Jesus. Whenever he mentioned the Trinity, it was always "the Old One, the dove, and me".'

'Come to think of it,' said Theo, 'this bringing in the dove is not a bad idea. With two equal halves it's sure to be complicated, but add a third element and you can sort it out, it seems to me. It's like a family with the parents and the child.'

The women exchanged glances of surprise.

Theo gave a yawn and a stretch. 'All right,' he said, 'so tell me whose side the Copts are on, and then we'll go on to the Pyramids.'

The Copts had kept their monophysite view, and as a result they had been condemned by the Church, which later reinstated them. But this long struggle had exhausted Egypt, and so it was easily conquered by the Muslims. The Copts led a precarious existence: sometimes persecuted, sometimes abandoned, they did not regain their place until the birth of modern Egypt, which granted equal rights to all its citizens, no matter what their religion.

Their final visit was to Amr's Mosque, and it delighted Theo, because anybody who could pass through the narrow space between two sacred pillars there was considered to be virtuous, and Theo was so thin that he slipped through, and then slipped back again to say: 'As I'm the virtuous one, I get to make the decision. WE'RE GOING TO THE PYRAMIDS!'

Resistance was useless now. Tutankhamun was postponed till tomorrow, and they decided to have lunch in the Mena House Oberoi, the famous hotel where Winston Churchill once stayed. The subject of the British wartime leader monopolized the conversation, but Theo hardly noticed. He was too busy peering this way and that past office and apartment blocks along the road, occasionally glimpsing the three silhouettes that played hide and seek behind the buildings.

The solar boat of Cheops

Suddenly there they were, white under the midday sun. Theo was very surprised that they did not look larger, but Amal assured him that they would not seem small when their shadows reached out across the sand of the desert and he was circling around them on camelback. It was nearly one o'clock in the afternoon when they came to the foot of the

Great Pyramid. In order to see it, you had to tilt your head back and use your hand to shade your eyes against the sun. Even then, the vast tomb seethed with light. And in spite of the chorus of tourist voices, speaking more languages than he could ever identify, as well as the postcard vendors, the donkey drivers tugging at his elbow, and the hawkers of amulets, Theo was lost in wonder at the mass of stone that loomed out of the sky.

'He hasn't brought a hat,' said Aunt Martha. 'This is crazy. I'm going to buy him one right now.'

'Don't stay too long in the sun,' warned Amal. 'You'll feel faint.'

Theo made no reply. Aunt Martha haggled with one of the vendors, and bustled back in triumph holding out her trophy.

'Quick, put it on,' she commanded, but Theo made no move, and just as she was about to cram it on to his head, he crumpled, then fell into her arms. Aunt Martha was starting to panic when Amal dealt Theo a sharp smack that brought a flush of colour to his cheeks.

'We're going straight back,' decreed Aunt Martha. 'It's all my fault, I should have remembered a hat.'

Amal disagreed. She took Theo's pulse, peered into his eyes, and then heaved a sigh of relief. Such incidents were not unusual in the presence of the Great Pyramid, and there hadn't been time for Theo to suffer from sunstroke.

'But no camel ride, Theo, you'd get seasick. And you'd better forget about visiting the interior of the Pyramid. It's stifling in there, and you have to stoop all the time.'

'I don't care about that,' croaked Theo. 'All I want to see is the boat. The one the pharaoh sails by night with his friend the sun, and after, when he rises.'

There was no arguing with that, and the three of them walked slowly towards the side of the pyramid where the Cheops boat was kept. Theo peered intently at the huge wooden craft.

'It was found in 1954, completely dismantled, in one of two pits that were sealed by big blocks of limestone,' said Amal. 'It took years to reassemble it, and they haven't yet opened the second pit, where its twin must still be waiting in the dark. No one really knows what its purpose may have been.'

'But they must do,' said Theo. 'It's not so very complicated. Either it was used for Cheops's funeral, to carry him to the eternal shore, or it is there to ferry him through the night, or else it really did transport the pharaoh's body from Memphis to Giza, and then was used for pilgrimages, but to find that out would mean setting it afloat again on the Nile, and who is going to take a risk like that?'

'Where did you get all that from?' asked Aunt Martha.

'From the encyclopedia of Egyptian civilization in the library in Paris. One thing I'd like to know is how the Egyptian dead managed to travel all night long, as well as cultivating the sacred fields, and eating all the food left ready in their tombs.'

'Well?' said Amal.

'Well, I couldn't handle all that,' he whispered sadly. 'Out of all those, when I die I will choose to sail the night, that's what I'd like.'

'That's enough, Theo,' said Aunt Martha. 'Come on, we're leaving.'

'What a fine voyage it must be,' Theo mused. 'The sun has left the earth, the serpent Apopis creeps through the dark to try to sting him, the living pray for his return, and meanwhile the dead escort him, all in their boats. Millions and millions of friends to watch over the sleeping sun.'

'I said that's enough,' Aunt Martha exploded.

Amal took Theo by the hand. 'Come on,' she said, 'there will be other boats to see. You're going to see the Nile, and feluccas. Let's go.'

Theo left the place with regret. Amal suggested that they make a donkey ride to see the Sphinx of Giza, the guardian of the pyramid. Theo wanted to go for a ride around it, but this time by himself, and the two women sat and waited nearby.

'He knows everything about Egypt,' sighed Aunt Martha.

'*Malaish*! I'd be surprised,' Amal told her. 'Does he know what's the matter with him?'

'No,' said Aunt Martha. 'He just knows he's very ill.'

'Then he must have suspected it,' said Amal. 'That's why he was interested in Egypt, the land of the dead.'

'What shall I do, Amal?'

'Show him that there was also *life* in ancient Egypt,' said Amal forcefully, 'and that there is today. Sail on the Nile, and trust the river. When he sees the women on the banks and the peasants working in the fields, he will realize that this Egypt, our Egypt, is not dead.'

Clinging on tight, perched on the back of his donkey, which moved at a cheerful trot, Theo came back a bit shaken, but smiling. It wasn't so much the great Sphinx that had entertained him, but the donkey and its driver. The donkey had a whitish hide, an artful expression, liquid eyes: it was the shrewd one in the partnership, while its driver played the fool.

'And the Sphinx?' asked Aunt Martha.

'It's only a stupid lion with a broken nose,' flared Theo. 'This big chief who brings a hundred thousand slaves to build his pyramid. If the Egyptians didn't like him, it serves him right.'

'Who are you talking about?' asked Aunt Martha.

'Chephren of course,' said Theo. 'The pharaoh who ordered the Sphinx's face to be carved as a portrait of himself.'

Theo discovers the Underworld

Back at the house in Brazil Street, Theo went upstairs to rest, under protest. As soon as he went to his room, Aunt Martha picked up the telephone to change their reservations on the Cairo–Luxor train, but it was too late to bring them forward, so at dinner they made plans for the following day. The train was due to leave at 19.40. That left the morning free.

'We're going to see Tutankhamun,' said Theo, in the same decisive mood that had brought them to the Pyramids.

'Well now,' said his aunt hesitantly. 'You see, the Egyptian Museum is a very tiring place to visit.'

'It's not the whole museum I want to see, Aunt Martha, only the Tutankhamun galleries.'

'Can you tell us what draws you to those?' Amal joined in.

'Those objects found in his tomb, the beds, the tables, the stools,' said Theo. 'And the golden shrine with the four goddesses. Oh, and the wreath of dried flowers that his wife left on his chest. You see, I know what to look for!'

'We realized that already,' said Aunt Martha. 'How long have you been so interested in Egypt?'

'Ever since Zappa. It was last June, just when grandad died. Our history teacher left to have a baby, and her replacement had a moustache and bushy black eyebrows, so we called him Zappa. He was mad about Egypt.'

'And it was Zappa who told you about the solar boat and its journey?'

'Him and the encyclopedia.'

'*Yaani*,' said Amal. 'Listening to you, anyone would think that the afterlife in ancient Egypt is a thousand times better than life. You go boating, you eat, you till the fields . . . that's true, but only if you are a good soul. Because if you aren't . . . Did this Zappa of yours tell you about the Underworld of ancient Egypt? Obviously not. Well, if you'd committed an injustice in your lifetime, you were boiled alive, quartered, impaled, and eventually annihilated.'

'I didn't know that,' said Theo. 'All the same, since I passed between the pillars I'm virtuous, so I run no risk.'

'One injustice, Theo, one is all it takes.'

'Only one? Help!'

'Naturally, as the pharaoh was deified, no one would think of condemning him to the Underworld.'

'Then we're going to see Tutankhamun! Hurray!' Theo cheered.

'And I suppose you know his story?' asked Amal.

'No, I don't. All I know is that he died very young. Can I telephone Fatou?'

'On your mobile!' Aunt Martha called. Already he was halfway up the stairs.

Since arriving in Egypt, he had not said a word about his family. He had not made a single phone call, or even spoken Fatou's name. Aunt Martha breathed a sigh of relief.

'Well done, Amal. With your description of the Underworld, you've made him stop and think. At least he won't be dreaming any more about the joys of death in Egypt.'

'It isn't enough, though,' said Amal. 'It's going to take more than that . . . When are we supposed to send the next message?'

'In Luxor,' answered Aunt Martha. 'But I don't quite know where yet, or how.'

'Perfect!' her friend exclaimed. 'Then leave it to me. I have an idea.'

The seeds of resurrection

As soon as they entered the first room in the Egyptian Museum, Theo set off at such a trot that the two women could hardly keep up.

'Wait, Theo!' cried Aunt Martha, already out of breath.

'It's so I won't keep stopping all the time,' Theo explained. 'I've found an antidote.'

The antidote worked so well that Theo did not spare a glance for the statues whose dark bulk loomed above his head. He stopped only once, at the door to the room where the mummies of pharaohs were displayed, but Amal moved to block him.

'Not the mummies, Theo,' she commanded, with unusual authority, placing her hands on his shoulders and steering him away.

'But I want to see them!'

'They are a hideous sight,' she told him. 'It's nothing to enjoy. And think of those poor dead people dragged from their graves to lie in a museum.'

'That's true,' said Theo.

'The worst part is the tourists, peering down into their faces, examining them like specimens in a dissecting room. You'd feel very uncomfortable.'

Theo nodded. 'Yes,' he said, 'I think I would,' and trotted off again. On the first floor of the Tutankhamun treasure, he finally slowed down. He lingered, in a state of trance, in front of each display case.

'Just like the books,' he kept repeating. 'It's tremendous. Zappa was right.'

A grave expression came over his face when he entered the rooms where the three sarcophagi were kept. He leaned over to stare silently down at the famous mask of gold with the boyish smile, and had to be removed by force from the young pharaoh.

'I would like to have seen his true face,' he sighed as they left. 'Where is his mummy? Down below?'

'No,' answered Amal. 'It was sent back in state to his tomb in the Valley of the Kings, across the Nile from Luxor and Karnak. Come and look at the Osiris garden. I expect you know what it means.'

But for once, Theo dried up about the Egypt of his dreams. In front of a chest moulded in the form of a human body sprouting ancient grasses, Amal explained the nature of the strange human garden he was seeing.

'The mummified body of Osiris stands for the land of Egypt. Every year, it is fertilized by the flooding of the Nile, and the fields grow green again. Every year, in these chests in the image of the god the Ancient Egyptians planted seeds that grew in the season of the floods. And in every tomb they would plant an Osiris garden, so as never to forget that even though death may follow life, so too does life always follow death. To this day, during the winter Egyptians push lentils into wads of cotton wool so as to watch them grow in springtime. It brings good luck.'

'Let's do the same before we leave, shall we? I can take the seeds with me, and then . . .' The rest of the sentence stuck in his throat.

'Yes,' said the Egyptian woman, 'you'll see the lentils grow, inshallah! We'll buy some straight away.'

Theo planted them before lunch, ten pink seeds in a transparent plastic jar with a snap-on lid. He had to water them every day, and only put the lid on during journeys.

CHAPTER 6

The Archaeologist and the Sheikha

Aunt Martha loathed last-minute departures. It was not yet 4 p.m. when she went on the warpath, hounding Amal to get ready. Her friend had to dig her heels in to persuade her not to start out till five o'clock, to catch an express train that left at seven forty. According to Aunt Martha, anything might happen, including an Egyptian train leaving ahead of time. Even if no such event had been recorded in all the annals of Egypt, nothing could stop Aunt Martha from leaving good and early.

With its soft music piped to each compartment, its disco bar and snug couchettes, train no. 86 deserved its reputation. Aunt Martha, who loved her creature comforts, heaved a contented sigh. Amal had brought along some lessons to prepare for the following week, while Theo was already immersed in his little notebook, which he had not touched since arriving in Egypt.

'By the way, what did Fatou have to say?' said Aunt Martha out of the blue.

'Mmm,' grunted Theo, without looking up. 'Apparently it's snowing in Paris.'

'Is that all? What about the family?'

'Nothing worth mentioning,' he uttered. 'Oh yes, Irene has the flu.'

'And your mother?'

'Will you give me a break?' he suddenly flared. 'You can see I'm writing.'

'Oh well, if his lordship is busy,' said Aunt Martha sarcastically.

113

Moses and Joseph, two Egyptian Jews

Theo was updating his notes. JESUS = DIVINE NATURE AND HUMAN NATURE. ARIANISTS = HALF & HALF. MONOPHYSITES = ONE NATURE. NESTORIANS . . .

They'd slipped his memory. Ah! . . . CATHARS = CRAZY KIND OF SECT WHO LET EVIL BODY DIE TO LIBERATE GOOD SPIRIT. COPTS = CHRISTIANS OF EGYPT. MONKS IN DESERT = ASCETICS. MONKS ON PERCHES = STYLITES. MONKS MURDER BEAUTIFUL PHILOSOPHER, SMASH STATUES. MONKS GOOD DECORATORS. EARLY COPTIC MONKS = HALF GOOD, HALF BAD. BEN EZRA SYNAGOGUE: SITE WHERE PHARAOH'S DAUGHTER RESCUED MOSES. MOSQUE WITH PILLARS OF VIRTUE . . .

'How are you getting on, Theo?' asked Aunt Martha.

Just great, if she'd leave me to it!

In the restaurant car he kept quiet. Amal and Aunt Martha chattered about making arrangements for Luxor, but Theo took no notice.

Aunt Martha would say: 'You do want to see the Son-et-Lumière at Karnak, don't you, Theo?' Or: 'We'll hire a felucca on the Nile, shall we, Theo?'

Each time his train of thought was interrupted, his response was an impatient 'Huh?', or a gruff 'What's that?'

In the end, Amal couldn't resist remarking:

'Honestly, Theo, anyone would think that you'd lost interest in Egypt.'

'It's not that,' he replied, 'it's just that I'm looking for the link between ancient Egypt and Judaism. I need to find people who combine both Jewish and Egyptian, and there aren't any.'

'What do you mean?' Aunt Martha disagreed. 'I can think of at least two, and one of them you know a lot about.'

'An Egyptian Jew?'

'Go back to the beginning,' said Amal. 'A Jewish Egyptian.'

'Somebody born in Egypt, and Jewish too . . . It's Moses!' exclaimed Theo. 'And the other?'

'The other's name is Joseph,' Aunt Martha began. 'He was the youngest of Jacob's children, and he was a dreamer, a bit like you. One day he told one of his dreams to his brothers, and they hated him for it, because in the dream Joseph saw himself standing in front of his brothers while they all bowed down to him.'

'You mean that Joseph dreamed about binding sheaves of corn, and only his own stood upright,' her Egyptian friend corrected.

'OK, I'm simplifying,' Aunt Martha admitted. 'Now, Joseph's brothers were so furious that they decided to sell him as a slave to a passing merchant caravan, out in the desert.'

'But first they tried to murder him,' Amal continued. 'They threw him down into a pit – you can see it inside the Citadel, in Cairo.'

'Yes, but I'm trying to keep it short,' said Aunt Martha huffily. 'Anyway, Joseph's elderly father fell for the brothers' story about his youngest son being eaten by a wild animal, but Joseph was not dead. The merchants sold him as a slave, and he had all sorts of adventures, and went to prison, but came through it all so well that he became a kind of court astrologer to Pharaoh.'

'Which means that he had a marvellous gift for interpreting other people's dreams,' said Amal. 'It made him enormously powerful.'

'Who's telling this story?' Aunt Martha burst out. 'You or me? As you know so much, go ahead!'

Amal jumped at the chance:

'It's very simple. Because of his genius for dreams, and his intelligence, Joseph was promoted to the rank of governor under Pharaoh. He married an Egyptian woman and they had two children. Then, far away in Palestine, which in those days was called the land of Canaan, a famine hit the Hebrews, and the brothers came to sell some of their livestock in Egypt, to buy corn.'

'And I bet it was Joseph they tried to sell to!' cried Theo.

'Yes, but they didn't recognize him, and there they were, in front of him, bowing down to the ground, begging to be allowed to buy food. Joseph's dream had come true.'

'Then he got his revenge,' Theo guessed.

'No, he didn't take revenge. First of all he fed them, then he told them who he was, and ordered them to break the news to old Jacob, his father, that his son Joseph was not dead. Jacob was reunited with his son in Egypt, and ended his days there. Some years later, when the persecuted Jews left Egypt, they carried Joseph's bones when they fled.'

'You've missed out a chapter,' said Theo. 'You tell me about Jacob, then suddenly it's the exodus, and look, Joseph's bones are leaving Egypt. Your story's weird! Why does it all go so well for the Jews with Joseph, and then go so wrong later on?'

'The Jews had prospered and multiplied,' Amal explained. 'In fact, Joseph governed Egypt so ably that he extended his master's territory. No one in Egypt was more powerful. Imagine it, Theo: when Jacob died, and Joseph went to Palestine to bury him, Pharaoh's whole court came with him. Then Joseph died in his turn, at the age of a hundred and ten. At last Pharaoh died, and others succeeded him, and the Jewish people experienced a population explosion . . .'

'A baby boom, you mean?'

'That's right, as is happening today in India, and also here in Egypt. But one day a pharaoh appeared who wasn't like Joseph's kind master. He'd stop at nothing to lessen the influence of these cuckoos in the nest. First he ordered the midwives to kill the sons of Jewish mothers at birth, and when the midwives refused to cooperate he gave orders for all first-born sons to be killed. Moses survived, hidden by his mother in a basket made of bulrushes, and was taken in by the evil pharaoh's daughter. Later he learned that he was Jewish, and freed his people by returning them to . . .'

'Don't waste your breath,' Theo broke in. 'Moses is Joseph in reverse. Act One, go down from Palestine to Egypt; Act Two, go up from Egypt back to Palestine. And that makes two Egyptian Jews. Thanks a lot.'

'Tell me, Amal,' cooed Aunt Martha, 'haven't you left out Potiphar's wife?'

'*Malaish!* She's not essential,' Amal replied.

'You think not?' said Aunt Martha. 'You listen, Theo. When he was first sold into slavery, Joseph was employed by a worthy Egyptian called Potiphar, who trusted him and put him in charge of his household. Potiphar's wife wanted to go to bed with Joseph, but he refused, so fearing he would go to her husband and denounce her, Potiphar's wife got in first. She accused Joseph of trying to seduce her, and that's how Joseph came to be in prison. Isn't that a key point, Theo?'

'Not really,' he told her. 'It's like in the sitcoms on TV. A girlfriend of mine played just the same trick to come between Fatou and me, but it didn't work.'

'Children aren't children any more,' Aunt Martha sighed. 'Potiphar's wife in the classroom!'

'Poor Martha,' said Amal. 'You'll have to do some catching up!'

'Be quiet, girls!' Theo cut in. 'Leave the squabbling to the churches. They've had a lot more practice!'

The two friends fell silent. Theo did not like quarrels.

'Just you eat your orange,' mumbled Aunt Martha.

The absent archaeologist

On the railway platform at Luxor, the porters had grabbed all of Aunt Martha's luggage, Theo's big bags, and Amal's small suitcase, but Amal was refusing to move. The archaeologist friend whom she was determined to wait for was often late, but he was coming, she felt sure . . . Half an hour later, she gave him up for lost. Her friend wasn't young anymore: maybe he'd sprained his ankle working on his dig in Karnak.

'What about telling us his name?' Aunt Martha suggested.

'He's French, very competent, a bit cranky but a nice man, you'll see. And a great scholar.'

It seemed that they could learn a whole lot about the archaeologist, except for his name, which Amal forgot to mention. In the meantime the taxi had dropped them at the Winter Palace hotel, where Aunt Martha was a familiar face, and which had style, so she said. In the lobby, in front of the sweeping staircase, the mysterious archaeologist was waiting. You couldn't mistake him: a silver-haired old man dressed up in a dusty fedora, short waistcoat, lightweight boots, and a pair of black spectacles – a comic-strip figure, especially when visibly fuming with exasperation.

'Well, here you are!' he erupted when he caught sight of Amal. 'So you finally deigned to turn up.' But as soon as he heard how long they had hung about in the station, the old boy apologized profusely, and laid the blame on his legendary absentmindedness. Yes, come to think of it, it wasn't here that he'd been supposed to meet them.

'And this charming young man – Theo, I believe? He's not too tired? Can he come and pay a visit to the dig? And Madame Macquarie – his aunt, I think? – she will come too?' he said gauchely, shifting from one foot to the other.

'First one thing, then another, and now what?' muttered Aunt Martha, pushing Theo up the stairs. 'He didn't even introduce himself! Well, I'm not budging an inch without a shower. Amal, we're going to our rooms.'

An hour later, the old archaeologist was doing his level best to cram all four of them into his little car, which was so full of papers, files and assorted bits and pieces that it hardly had room for its driver. Amal's suggestion of a horse-drawn carriage was gladly accepted, and they both set off, the car in fits and starts, the horses almost ambling. Out on the river, felucca sails spread their elegant wings to the breeze. Beyond the opposite bank, hidden at the foot of barren mountains, lay the tombs of the necropolises of Thebes, the ancient capital of the Egyptian empire. You couldn't see them, but you knew that they were out there, light-years away from the romantic barouche that idled along the tree-lined avenues, with their hotels and groups of elderly tourists. Car and carriage passed by the temple of Luxor without stopping and turned sharp right. Soon they were drawing up in front of the entrance to the temples. They had arrived at Karnak.

The veteran archaeologist was in a talkative mood. He lectured for some minutes on the building they had driven past – the Franco-Egyptian Centre – before turning into the town. Aunt Martha tried in vain to learn the identity of their absent-minded host, who wanted to give them a thorough tour of this site, despite the two women's objections. No, they did not want to make a close inspection of the bases of the ram-headed sphinxes with the recycled blocks that might date from Roman times, nor did they want to know about the history of the porches, or about excavation policy since the opening of the site.

'But I thought . . .' their new companion swallowed his disappoint-ment. 'Then we're to go straight to the great hypostyle hall, and no stopping along the way?'

'And the sooner the better!' thought Aunt Martha, cursing her friend Amal. This rambling old pedant was going to ruin everything, Theo would lose interest . . . But Theo was very much at ease as he strolled from gate to pylon gate, now and then running a fingertip over the leg of a god whose carved relief had walked these walls for thousands of years. Theo was standing on the floor of his own Egypt, strolling through its heart. In front of one strange figure of a god, he paused for so long that Aunt Martha turned back to find him.

'Who's that?' he asked, pointing at the erect phallus of one carved figure.

'His name is Min, the god of Fertility,' Aunt Martha told him. 'The old religions always insist on the sacred aspect of the penis.'

'I can see that he has one hand raised, but it's funny, with the other hand it looks as if he's touching himself . . .'

'Come on, don't keep us waiting,' she chided, tugging at his elbow. 'Look over there instead, isn't that a marvellous sight?'

Past the ruins ahead they could see through to the world-famous forest of giant columns in the great hypostyle hall of the temple of Karnak. Theo stopped still on the threshold, taking time to absorb the impact of the vast structure. The columns of sand and gold were crushingly heavy, yet they rose lightly into the sky, and formed a design so harmonious that the palm trees in the background seemed to have been somehow shrunk to a dwarfish scale to accentuate their vastness.

'What do you think?' Aunt Martha prompted.

There was a silence before Theo spoke.

'You feel a bit like an ant. It's mostly all that sky that feels so sweird. They wouldn't have seen it, the worshippers who came here because in those days the temple had a roof. Was it here that the sacred boats were brought?'

The archaeologist pricked up his ears: the boy really knew something. Soon they were chatting like a pair of old friends, leaving the women to trail in their wake.

'He'll tire the boy out,' Aunt Martha fretted.

'They seem so delighted,' said Amal. 'My friend doesn't often come across teenagers.'

'By the way,' said Aunt Martha, 'either you tell me the name of your batty friend, or I don't take another step from here.'

'Didn't I tell you?' said the startled Egyptian. 'His name is Jean-Baptiste Laplace. He's a widower.'

'Fine,' said Aunt Martha thoughtlessly, as she moved on. 'But where have they vanished to?'

'We mustn't be too late at the sacred lake,' said Amal. 'Someone is waiting for us there.'

The Sheikha's message

When the two women reached the sacred lake, they found Theo and Professor Laplace already conversing with a strange old lady dressed in a green robe and seated in front of the huge granite scarab. Amal hurried to meet her.

'*Salaam aleikhum*, Sheikha,' she said, raising her hand to her forehead in greeting.

'*Aleikhum salaam*,' the woman replied, with a faint smile. 'I see the child we spoke of. Is this the moment?'

And without waiting for an answer she pointed at a small scarab hidden beneath the big one. Theo bent down and discovered a piece of paper under the fetish animal. It was a message wrapped around a blue earthenware figurine and written in hieroglyphics.

'Here's my next riddle!' he announced, and sat down on the ground.

'Now I have to work it out. Do you think you could help me, Monsieur Jean-Baptiste?'

The intrigued archaeologist needed no persuading, and sat down next to Theo. While scholar and student conferred, the lady in green took Amal to one side.

'Come herc, daughter,' she said gravely. 'That child is very ill. You haven't summoned me here just to deliver a coded message, have you? You've brought me here to make him well!'

'Yes, Sheikha,' Amal answered humbly. 'I know that you can.'

'If Allah wills!' sighed the old woman. 'I will try. But the musicians will have to be paid, and that comes expensive, you know. Also, he knows nothing of our ways . . . With one of our own people I would feel sure of the outcome. But with this young foreigner . . .'

'Nothing ventured, nothing gained,' said Amal, spreading her hands. 'And in any case, they've told the family that he's terminally ill.'

'Then the doctors at home can do nothing? In that case . . . Meet me outside my house, at seven o'clock.'

She turned away, and was soon out of sight behind a pillar. Aunt Martha had observed the conversation at a distance, and was curious, but Amal would say nothing, and asked her friend to trust her. They were going to attempt a treatment specific to Egypt, and which worked wonders in the slum districts of the country. Of course it was strange, and it might be tiring, but if there was no other prospect of a cure for Theo . . .

'I see,' sighed Aunt Martha. 'To tell you the truth, I've got nothing against these ways of healing. I imagine they involve ointments, and massage?'

Amal refused to answer.

'All right,' Aunt Martha conceded, 'but I hope you're not going to get me in a tizz, because if there's magic involved . . .'

'Hush,' Amal cut in. 'Here he comes.'

Isis, Amun, Aten

'Finished!' cried Theo. 'Here's what the message says: *I flew all the way to the seven hills*. But I don't get it.'

'Seven hills, young man,' said the archaeologist. 'Well now, that's not too hard. The most likely seven hills are . . .'

'Not another word!' ordered Aunt Martha. 'Theo must find the answer for himself. He just has to focus on the way he found the message.'

'Under the scarab,' Theo mused, 'and . . . the figurine! I left it behind.'

After racing back to the lakeside, he called from the distance: 'It's Isis!' Clad in a tall headdress with three feathers, and holding the infant Horus in her arms, the tiny blue earthenware Isis wore an enigmatic smile. Theo was no wiser than before. What foreign city with seven hills would an Egyptian goddess fly to? He felt stumped.

'Help me, please,' he pleaded, turning to the scholar again.

'You know I'm not allowed to,' Professor Laplace protested. 'All I can say is that there was a cult of Isis in the city you're seeking. Her worship spread all over Europe in those days.'

'She wouldn't by any chance have come across the sea with Cleopatra?' Theo suggested.

Laplace had to stall. 'Well,' he began, 'I don't say you're wrong, but . . .'

'Then the city is Rome,' Theo decided. 'Cleopatra went there to join Julius Caesar. She had their son Caesarion on her knee, and I know that for a fact!'

He'd found it – on his own. After congratulating such an intelligent pupil, Professor Laplace drew him into a long discussion about the comparative merits of the gods of Egypt, because it must not be forgotten that the family of Osiris with his wife Isis and Horus their son had been recognized fairly late in the day, whereas the great god Amun, lord of the Karnak temples, was very much older and greater than Osiris. Not only that, but when Amenhotep, the fourth pharaoh of that name, decided to worship a single god, the Sun, instead of the old god Amun and his family of gods, Egypt had witnessed a true revolution.

'Leave him in peace,' said Amal. 'You'll tire him out.'

'Me?' Theo protested. 'Not likely! I want to learn all there is to know about Amenhotep IV!'

In fact, this exceptional personage was better known by the name of Akhenaten. Theo remembered some details: Akhenaten, the husband of Nefertiti, was a pharaoh with a long face, drooping belly and elongated hands. On the bas-reliefs there were some very cute girls, with long chins, just like Fatou.

'Mm-yes,' the old gentleman allowed, 'that is what's known as the Amarnian style, because the pharaoh decided to build a new capital city far away from here, on a site now called Tell el Amarna. It's often been claimed that that was the birth of realist art, and that Akhenaten refused to let any of his defects be glossed over, but that is a gross overstatement.'

And the Sun god's name was Aten. Aunt Martha, never reluctant to

121

speak, chipped in to stress that Akhenaten's chief claim to fame was that he had invented monotheism long before the Hebrews, the Christians and the Muslims. Overnight he had expelled the countless gods of Egypt in favour of the Sun god, the source of all existence.

'Yes,' Laplace corrected, 'but the Sun already occupied an essential place in the original myth system. The creation of the world depends on it, because the Sun – hatched from an egg by breaking through its shell – rides the sky by day in its chariot, and disappears at night before it is recalled by human prayer. Amun, the god of the great temple at Karnak, is also a Sun figure.'

'In that case,' Theo pounced, 'where does the revolution come in?'

'Good question,' the scholar approved. 'It comes in because the name Aten does not refer to a figure with a humanoid body: Aten is portrayed in the form of a symbol, the sun disc. And as a result, for Akhenaten to inflict on his people the worship of an image so stripped of humanity became an act of tyranny . . . So I repeat, for the pharaoh's subjects, it was a real revolution.'

'Then, if it was a revolution, it was because there were injustices in Egypt? If not, why do you suppose the idea would have occurred to Akhenaten?'

'That is a possibility,' the cautious archaeologist conceded. 'It's true that the priests of the god Amun were immensely wealthy, and we can't rule out the notion that they exploited the people of Egypt, even though that word and the concepts it implies are quite anachronistic under the Eighteenth Dynasty, over three thousand years ago . . . Still, let's say you're right. On the other hand, young fellow, it is not true that Akhenaten invented monotheism, because monotheism is never far removed from Egyptian thinking. No, the novelty in his case is the worship of an abstract entity. Much of the rest is speculation.'

'All the same,' Aunt Martha protested, 'Akhenaten was an instinctive revolutionary. We have him to thank for his radical departure from the older ways of worship, and for a new kind of art. Otherwise why try to obliterate him from the record after his death? After his fall, Akhenaten was cursed by the priests, his cult forbidden, his capital destroyed and his mummy scattered and lost!'

'That is a fact,' Professor Laplace agreed. 'He is certainly the only pharaoh whose soul is suffering in the Underworld. Between ourselves, he asked for it.'

'You've really got it in for Akhenaten!' cried Aunt Martha. 'What do you hold against him?'

'He was a rotten pharaoh,' the archaeologist growled. 'Under his reign the empire went to pieces. He undermined the whole administration, demoralized his people – it was sheer anarchy! And he's far too much in fashion nowadays. They make him out to be a martyr, praise him to the skies, and in the process they ignore the humble virtues of the ordinary workaday religion. A revolutionary, in ancient Egypt? I ask you . . .'

A fuming Aunt Martha pointed out that the founder of psychoanalysis, Sigmund Freud himself, had put forward an interesting hypothesis in the twentieth century, linked to the pharaoh Akhenaten and to his chief disciple, Moses. Freud had suggested that the great Moses, the saviour of the Hebrews, was not Jewish by birth, but Egyptian.

'Obviously,' said Theo. 'Because he was adopted by Pharaoh's daughter.'

But instead of a Moses born into a family of slaves, Freud had theorized that the great hero of the Jewish people was actually Egyptian by birth, and of noble family. Having risen to high office under Akhenaten, he made up his mind to preserve the spiritual heritage left endangered after the death of the outcast pharaoh.

'In secret, you mean?' said Theo. 'Now that is interesting. So he made the Jews the solution to his problem?'

Exactly. And since the Egyptians wanted nothing more to do with the Sun god, this Moses who was Akhenaten's disciple had gone over to the Jewish people, who refused to worship the many Egyptian deities with their animal heads, just as the outcast pharaoh had done. Freud's theory was that Moses had made himself the guide of that persecuted people, and having betrayed his native land in the name of the one god, he decided to go with them when they fled.

'Rubbish,' her opponent retorted. 'Not a scrap of serious evidence has ever been found to support it.'

'Let me remind you that, after Freud, an Israeli scholar proved it not ten years ago!' Aunt Martha insisted.

'Then that makes one more idiot!' barked Laplace. 'These people aren't Egyptologists! It only goes to show what kind of drivel the Akhenaten legend has spawned.'

'Even so, he did write some superb hymns to his god,' murmured their Egyptian companion, who had kept quiet till now.

This time the old partisan said nothing. No one could dispute the lyrical power of Akhenaten's hymns.

'One thing I do see,' said Theo, taking a snapshot of his disgruntled expression, 'is that you don't like revolutionaries. Perhaps you're too old . . .'

The furious archaeologist announced that he would leave them to find their own way back to the hotel.

'When shall we meet again?' called Aunt Martha as he stalked away.

'We'll see,' his answer floated over his shoulder.

She cupped her hands to hail him. 'Our cruise on the Nile leaves the landing stage at ten tomorrow morning. Do come and wish us goodbye . . .'

'He really looks hurt,' said Theo. 'I may have gone too far.'

Theo's dance

They spent the afternoon on their first boat trip on the Nile. Theo lounged on the deck of the felucca and watched the boatman's busy hands as they worked the vast white sails. Around five o'clock, as the Sun god embarked into the night, they returned to the hotel. At six, they left for an unknown destination. On the outskirts of Luxor they stopped in front of a large tent embroidered with white circles and crimson triangles. Outside, wrapped in a long veil, the mysterious woman in green stood waiting for her visitors.

'*Salaam*,' she said, touching her hand to her forehead. 'Welcome, my child. This ceremony is for you.'

'Great,' said Theo. 'Will there be any music?'

'Count on it,' she answered. 'And dancing too. But you too will dance, little bride.'

'Hey, watch it,' he jibbed, 'I'm not a girl.'

'Girl or boy, it makes no difference here,' replied the Sheikha, propelling him forward. 'You are sick, so you are the bride. That is required in our dances.'

'I'll have to learn fast then,' murmured Theo. 'I can't dance.'

Inside the tent, ten or twelve men lay on cushions, puffing at their nargilehs, while a little knot of women sat round a brazier and warmed the taut skins of tambourines in front of the flames. The old woman whom Amal called Sheikha had her three guests remove their shoes. After that, they could sit on the ground. Then she started to beat on a heavy drum, chanting as she did so, and the musicians followed. When the cymbals and the tambourines struck up, the Sheikha drew Theo to his feet and led him to stand in the middle of the tent.

124

'Just let it happen,' she whispered in his ear. 'Remember, there's nothing to fear.'

Intrigued, Theo saw her pick up an earthenware bowl full of live embers and sprinkle some pellets of incense into it, while she recited a prayer. She passed the bowl under Theo's legs, then ran it beneath his armpits and his hands. A fragrant warmth swept over him. A sickly-looking woman levered herself to her feet and began to dance beside him in a slow whirl. It was an effort for Theo to keep his eyes open. All at once the woman's neck swivelled violently to and fro, and the Sheikha threw a long, spotless shawl over her head. To Theo's alarm, the dancer now collapsed, showing the whites of her eyes.

'What's the matter with her?' he cried.

'Hush,' murmured the Sheikha. 'Her sickness has gone away. Look at her. See how she smiles. Her cousin from the underworld came to pay her a visit to heal her. It's your turn now, my son. Send for your cousin. Dance!'

Caught in a panic, Theo broke into a clumsy dance, guided by the expert hands of the Sheikha, who flexed his shoulders to make them sway. Then he slowed to a halt, exhausted.

'His cousin won't come out. The bride's legs need fresh blood,' cried the Sheikha. 'Lift up the cockerel!'

Held out at arm's length, the terrified creature frantically flapped its wings. Theo flinched, but the Sheikha clung to him. When the oldest of the men in the tent cut the animal's throat, Theo screwed his eyes shut, and then rough fingers daubed a warm, sticky liquid on to his forehead, hands, and the upper surface of his feet. 'The cockerel's blood!' he gasped in terror. A void seemed to open, and he fell into it.

'He's fainted!' screamed Aunt Martha. 'Stop!'

'No,' said Amal, and would not let her stir. 'It has to happen. His invisible cousin has come, and you can't interfere.'

Acting with infinite care, the Sheikha picked Theo up and laid him gently on the cushions. He looked as pale as a ghost, except for the deep purple rings under his eyes, and splashes of blood on his forehead. Aunt Martha was petrified.

'Madness,' she moaned. 'This is madness. You'll kill the boy.'

'No, no,' breathed her friend.

With practised ease, the Sheikha was massaging Theo, who had not yet come out of his faint. Then she sprinkled him with rose water and wafted incense under his nose. Around them, the musicians pounded on the hollow skins of their drums, whose heavy beat throbbed louder and louder in the close air. Aunt Martha sat with her heart in her mouth, waiting for her nephew to revive.

When he finally opened his eyes again, a boy of about his own age was twirling with easy grace in the middle of the tent, his heavy skirt flaring and shimmering like a great solar disc trembling behind a veil of cloud. Theo sat up and smiled.

'Would you like to go and dance with him?' asked the Sheikha softly, as she helped him to his feet.

This time, Theo found the rhythm at once. With outspread arms, a flush on his cheeks and a wide smile, he spun effortlessly, airily, round and round, his eyes half shut, a look of joy on his face. And it was unbelievable to see him dance so lightly, as if illness had never brushed him with its wing . . . With every twirl, Aunt Martha shuddered with dread. Where was Theo dredging up this new supply of energy?

The music stopped. Theo found himself standing and tipsily swaying.

'What came over me?' he asked, and rubbed his eyes. 'Have I been dancing, then? Really dancing?'

'It's all right, young man,' said the Sheikha. 'Now, go and say thank you to the musicians. Off you go!'

Trays laden with glasses of tea were passed around. Squatting beside the musicians, Theo examined their discarded instruments. He seemed fully recovered from his blackout.

'The colour's come back to his cheeks,' Aunt Martha remarked in relief.

'His cousin from the Underworld came to pay a visit,' murmured the Sheikha. 'The rest is in Allah's hands.'

'Can he be cured already?'

'*Malaish*!' said the Sheikha. 'You foreigners do not believe in invisible powers. But perhaps the child has found his way. We have done all we could.'

'This is for the musicians and the dancers,' said Amal at once, reaching for her purse. 'Thank you for your kindness, Sheikha. We will never forget it.'

Theo was reluctant to leave, and had to be dragged from the tent. When the three of them were back in the car, he asked a spate of questions. What was the point of the whirling? Why had he fainted so suddenly? Why had the Sheikha called him 'the bride', when he was a boy?

'Slow down, Theo,' said Amal. 'One thing at a time. You were the focus of the Zar ceremony. It's a very ancient ritual, invented to heal the sick by ridding them of evil genies – djinns.'

'Ah,' said Theo. 'I have an evil genie inside me.'

'Yes,' said Amal cautiously, 'because if we recognize the existence of these djinns that cause illnesses, then it isn't only medicines that can cure the body.'

'I agree,' said Theo. 'The lady was my doctor, but a different kind.'

The Zar was an age-old ceremony, originating possibly in ancient Egypt, possibly in Ethiopia or Black Africa – no one could say for sure. At some point the ritual had become incorporated into the Muslim religion, which didn't exactly acknowledge it, but tended to turn a blind eye, because it often produced a cure. It was practised in the shanty towns of Egypt where unemployed young people had all kinds of diseases, and not enough money to consult a doctor.

'That's terrible,' said Theo. 'Now tell me about the dance.'

The effect of the whirling was to numb the dancer's spirit, so that the body would let go of its sickness without noticing. The fainting was essential, or else the body would not obey the dance. The dance was completely in charge.

'In a way, that's better than Ecstasy,' said Theo. 'But could the cockerel's blood be a drug?'

No, because the blood was not drunk. Sacrificing a cockerel was one of those distant legacies of ancient and possibly prehistoric rituals that were common to this day throughout the world. And, male or female, the sick took the name of 'bride' because the ceremony in question derived from the craft and lore of women.

'Says you!' said Theo. 'The musicians are all men.'

The musicians, no doubt, but the Sheikha was a woman, and it was she who took charge. As for the word 'Zar', it stood for a combination of 'visit', 'spirit' and 'ritual'.

The odd thing was that Theo did not ask a single question about his cousin from the Underworld.

'Tell us the truth,' said Aunt Martha. 'What did you feel?'

'Scared stiff!' was Theo's answer. 'When I saw the cockerel's wings, and its feathers all bristling . . . there I was really afraid. But after that, it was like a cradle, very soft . . . it felt really great.'

'What about the cousin?' said Amal softly.

'There was somebody there,' Theo murmured. 'But it was as if the someone was myself. A heart beating right next to mine – a weird sensation. It felt just like a twin.'

127

Aunt Martha gave a start. Theo knew nothing about the circumstances of his birth, and had no idea about his stillborn twin. Let's hope that Amal doesn't get too inquisitive . . .

Which is exactly what happened. 'Have you got a twin, Theo?' she now enquired.

'Oh really, Amal, don't talk such nonsense,' snapped Aunt Martha nervously. 'Theo, we'll have to get that dried blood cleaned off. You've got it all over you.'

Back at the hotel, they found a message waiting. Professor Laplace had called, intending to invite them to the Son-et-Lumière, but seeing no sign of them he had gone away again. Theo decided that when it came to Son-et-Lumière he'd rather have seen the Zar ceremony from the inside than the temple of Karnak in lights.

Flowers for Amal

Next morning Aunt Martha and Theo boarded the *Tutankhamun* on a five-day cruise from Luxor to Aswan, where they had a flight booked to the capital. Theo had slept like a prince. Amal was returning to Cairo, where her students were waiting.

A week from now, Aunt Martha and Theo would be back in Brazil Street. Naturally, old Laplace had forgotten the time again. Theo kept an eye open for him.

'It's a shame,' he said at last. 'Wish him goodbye for me, Amal, and tell him I was only teasing about his age. He's not so very old!'

Amal watched them climb on board, Martha in that silly hat of hers, all the way from Tibet, Theo wearing the straw hat bought at the foot of the Pyramids. There was no way of knowing whether any good would come of the strange ceremony performed at Amal's request, but it had certainly done no harm.

The steamer had cast off and was on its way upriver when Laplace turned up at last, with an armful of flowers from the souk.

'Don't tell me they've left!' the old archaeologist exclaimed. 'Am I late?'

'A good hour late,' Amal told him. 'My friend Martha sends her regards.'

'And the boy?' he asked sharply.

'Theo? He sends his best wishes, and wants you to know that, come to think of it, you're not so very old after all.'

'An unusual young man,' he murmured with feeling. 'And remarkably sharp. He'll make a first-class Egyptologist, I am sure . . .'

'*Inshallah,*' she sighed.

'What am I to do with all these useless flowers?' the old man bumbled. 'They were meant to be a gift for the New Year . . . Oh, take them, my dear friend, they're yours.'

And with a clumsy gesture he thrust the flowers into the Egyptian woman's hands.

CHAPTER 7

Seven Hills, One Rock

The crocodiles and the birds

When they returned from their cruise on the Nile, Amal came to meet them, looking very elegant in a black and green silk dress. Theo gave her a hug.

'Don't you look well!' said Amal. 'You've caught some sun!'

'That's more than Auntie has,' Theo replied. 'She and the sunshine don't get along!'

'That's enough from you,' said Aunt Martha. 'It's fine for you, but for a woman's skin, sun-bathing is very harmful. Anyway, I think Theo's been enjoying himself. Am I right?'

'Oh yes!' he cried. 'Especially the New Year's Eve party on the boat, it was great!'

In the car going back to Brazil Street, Theo was more forthcoming about the trip. The finest temple was Kom Ombo, because of a sanctuary full of the mummies of sacred crocodiles. Had he set eyes on one of his beloved goddesses? Yes, a beautiful Sekhmet with a lioness's head and her hands placed sedately on her knees. And what about the Abu Simbel pharaohs? 'Well they're certainly big,' said Theo with no great conviction.

What did he like best?

'The banks of the Nile,' he answered at once. 'The women in the fields looked like the princess who rescued the baby Moses. And those white birds nesting in the papyrus reeds. I'm told they're not true ibises, but never mind, they're the same shape, so . . .'

Amal was delighted with Theo's responses, partly because, with the exception of the crocodiles, there was no more mention of mummies, or the solar boat. Back at the house, he shut himself up in his room to phone Fatou.

'I think he's making progress,' said Amal. 'I can't wait to hear the results of the next set of tests.'

'Oh dear,' sighed Aunt Martha. 'I know he's looking well, but he fainted again on the boat.'

'In the sun? On deck?'

'Yes . . . And he had a nosebleed too.'

'This time it really must have been sunstroke. The sun is scorching hot on the Nile. That kind of incident is quite common.'

'Please God,' said Aunt Martha.

The Egypt game

Fatou was fine, so was Mum, so was Dad, the whole family was zooming along as if there was nothing the matter, and Theo felt neglected. Were they putting up a front so as not to upset him, or had they got used to his fate? After all, he was ill, wasn't he? And if he ever did recover, would they still treat him with the same attention?

And what if he didn't get better? What if his visitor from the Underworld, the cousin whose unseen presence he had glimpsed, were to let go of his hand? Supposing he relapsed as soon as they left Egypt? Rome was all very well, but it would be cold there in mid-winter. Obviously Aunt Martha had plans of her own, but Theo would rather stay in Egypt.

Egypt was certainly an ideal place for his little notebook. He could even make sketches. Theo had drawn six statues with animal heads. Horus-vulture, Sekhmet-lioness, Bastet-cat, Anubis-jackal, Sebek-crocodile, Thoth-ibis. Up above these gods he placed Isis and Osiris with their human faces, the parents. At the top he drew a disc with rays: Akhenaten's single god. He only had to draw a star of David round the sun, and the plan was complete. It made a fine drawing. EGYPT = ANIMALS – HUMAN. AKHENATEN = SUN GOD, THEN MOSES.

That left death. Theo sketched the solar boat, but when he went to add the mummy that it carried, his fingers let go of the pencil. 'No!' breathed a voice in his ear. 'Don't do that, little brother! Don't draw the figure of death!'

Theo spun round in surprise. No one was there.

132

An eye-shaped pendant

Next morning it was time to say goodbye. Tears brimmed in Amal's eyes, and she hugged him hard and long. He'd better not forget to keep in touch, he must phone her whenever he could, and make sure . . .

'*Malaish*!' said Theo, planting a kiss on her face. 'Don't worry, Amal, we'll meet again.'

'Wait!' she exclaimed, and fumbled in her handbag. 'Theo, this is for you.'

It was a pendant, an eye with a black pupil on a fragment of deep blue pottery. Amal insisted as she tied it round his neck that Theo must never, ever, part with it. This made three emblems around his neck: the black pearl scorpion, Fatou's little Koran, and now Amal's eye.

'It's an amulet, you see. Well . . . *Yaani*! I don't know how to tell you . . .'

'*Malaish*!' Theo repeated. 'I know what you're trying to say.'

Once past the airport formalities, all that was left of Amal was a waving hand. Theo realized that on every stage of the journey he would be leaving behind new friends that he might never see again.

'Tell me about your man in Rome, Aunt Martha. What will I make of him?'

'Dom Ottavio Levi? You'll take to him, you'll see. He's a cardinal in the Curia.'

'A cardinal? Another priest? You've got your own supply!'

'Be quiet, cheeky! Dom Ottavio is a really nice man, very open-minded, very progressive.'

'Priests aren't too popular in our house,' Theo muttered. 'Dad says . . .'

'Your father can't talk!' snapped Aunt Martha. 'Because he wouldn't teach you about religions, see what a dunce you can be!'

What with the Cardinal and the winter weather, Theo had no great expectations of Rome. He sulked on board the plane, but Aunt Martha was engrossed in the city pages and took no notice. Only the view from the window consoled him. Through gaps in the cloud, occasional mountains looked like outsize rats, and tiny ships rode the crests of the waves, painting their streaks of white over a grey-green sea.

When the plane landed at Fiumicino airport, a storm of applause broke out in the cabin, as the Egyptians celebrated their safe deliverance from the sky boat.

The Cardinal and the pagans

Dom Ottavio Levi was a stout, energetic little man who collected his two visitors with garrulous efficiency. He hugged Martha, kissed Theo on both cheeks, shot off a volley of questions without waiting for the answers, and informed them that their schedule was booked solid. In two shakes the high-powered Cardinal had everything under control: their luggage located and stowed, the car already waiting to take them to the Hassner-Villa Medici hotel near Piazza di Spagna. And while the ecclesiastical limousine drove on towards the capital, Dom Ottavio presented the programme he had devised.

'To keep to the chronological order, *bambino*, we shall begin with the catacombs, which are the tombs of the earliest Christians, underground basilicas – two hours, *basta così*. Then the heart of the Christian world: Saint Peter's church, Bernini's bronze canopy – it's very fine, you'll see. Then the Vatican museum, another two hours. That leaves San Giovanni in Laterano, plus a few other churches, the ab-so-lute-ly unmissable ones – got it, *bambino*?'

'Don't call me *bambino*,' said Theo. 'I'm not a five-year-old.'

The prelate roared with laughter. 'What an amusing boy. Do you approve of the programme?'

'Dunno,' said Theo warily. 'I'd certainly like to see the Forum and the Capitol.'

'Hmm,' said the Cardinal. 'That's got nothing to do with Christendom, *bambino*.'

'But before Saint Peter there were gods in Rome, and anyway I'm not a *bambino*,' Theo grumbled.

'All right. And do you know about the Roman gods?'

'Not all of them,' said Theo. 'I know about Jupiter because in Greece he is Zeus, Juno who is Hera, his wife, Diana who is Artemis, the virgin, Venus who is Aphrodite, the goddess of Love, Mercury who is Hermes, the messenger, and that's all. In my book on mythology they also mention the Lares, but I can't make out who they are.'

'I see,' said the Cardinal thoughtfully. 'You're very well-informed for your age. The Lares are the gods who protect the household. But you know, the Roman religion went through several phases. At first there were ordinary little gods, then the high gods of Greece invaded the city, and later, under the Empire, there are the Asiatic cults and the mysteries, a whole pandemonium . . .'

'Pandemonium? What's that?'

'A riot of demons, *bambino*!' laughed Dom Ottavio. 'I'm sorry, I can show you some books, but otherwise, all we have left are some ruins. There's almost nothing left of the cult of Isis, or of Astarte the Syrian, or the goddess Cybele with her turreted crown, and still less of the god of the Thracians, Mithra. For him, they sacrificed live bulls. Their blood came spurting out across the worshippers, as they crouched beneath a hurdle.'

'Disgusting!'

'Do you know that Christendom owes a great deal to Mithra? Mithra worship was a real cult of purification. The sacrifice of the bull was considered to bring salvation to the world, like the death of Jesus Christ on the cross. In early Christendom, the great goddesses also lent us a helping hand: Isis because she raises Osiris from the dead, Astarte who weeps for her lover Adonis, and brings him back to life . . . They promoted the idea of resurrection that culminated in Jesus.'

'But you're keeping unusually quiet about the goddess Astarte and the details of her rituals,' Aunt Martha intervened.

'Oh come!' the flustered Cardinal protested. 'Is that really necessary?'

'No censorship,' she reproved, with a wink in Theo's direction. 'Why keep my nephew in the dark about such a fine story? The handsome Adonis had been killed and mutilated by a wild boar. So in memory of that dreadful death, the priests felled a pine tree and carried it in procession through the streets, wailing as they went. Then, to pay homage to Astarte's lover, drugged by the music and lost in a trance, the priests voluntarily castrated themselves, Theo.'

'Castrated?' Theo was appalled. 'The way they do with cats and dogs? Does that mean that they cut their balls off?'

'Exactly,' said Dom Ottavio. 'At least Christendom avoided these pagan barbarities. With their gaudy robes, and their drums and metal sistra, the processions of the great goddesses must have made a deep impression on the community, but the rites were too bloody and the mutilations too frequent. The ancient Romans detested this behaviour: to them it was just vulgar. Christianity is simpler and more humane. We are content to sacrifice bread, which is the body of Christ, and wine, which is his blood. And we share him in a single meal.'

'Only the bread,' said Theo. 'It's the priest who drinks the wine on the quiet, I saw it once at Mass!'

Dom Ottavio was running out of patience. This nephew of Martha's was a tough nut to crack. Luckily they had reached the hotel, and Theo was quickly deposited in a room with red curtains. Aunt Martha closed

135

the shutters so that he could rest, but the communicating door to her room was a bad fit, and the sound of arguing filtered through.

'But this child knows far too much about it for his age!' Dom Ottavio whispered. 'What with the tests, the clinic and the X-rays, I don't see how we can visit the Forum. And the meeting' – his voice grew louder – 'have you thought about who's coming? It's the day after tomorrow. We'll never have the time! And when they're here, he'll be far too excited!'

'Shhh,' said Aunt Martha. 'He'll hear us.'

They? Somebody coming? Theo's heart began to pound. Who could it be? His friends? A surprise? If only the weather would improve! A sunbeam for a *bambino* in distress, if you please, Lady Isis, give me back some life!

'I warn you, Martha,' the Cardinal resumed, 'don't overload him. In any case, I've already made the appointment at the clinic, because the scanner needs to be booked well in advance.'

'All right,' agreed Aunt Martha, and heaved a big sigh. 'Then we'll expect the car in two hours.'

Theo curled up beneath the blankets. 'They' were doctors, 'they' were going to do another blood test and sacrifice him to the gods of medicine. All he would see on his first day in Rome was a nurse and yet more doctors.

The Vestals and the cult of fire

As Theo was being very cooperative, the tests went fairly quickly. When they left the clinic Aunt Martha made a detour to the elegant circular Temple of Vesta.

'It's one of the few still standing,' she explained. 'Vesta was the goddess of the hearth, and her priestesses, the Vestals, had to stay virgins to guard the sacred flame. Because fire is basic. Anywhere in the world, its extinction is a threat to life. The Indians of South America tell how the jaguar gave the first humans its eyes of fire in exchange for a human wife. In ancient Persia, which we now call Iran, religion was totally devoted to the god of Fire. And in India there are communities of the last followers of that religion, so persecuted by Islam that they emigrated there: they are called Parsis – Persians – because they came from Iran, or Zoroastrians, in memory of their prophet Zoroaster, who is also called Zarathustra.'

'Weird name,' said Theo. 'Sounds like a comic strip hero.'

136

'Zarathustra was a very great prophet! Back in the sixth century before Christ he withdrew into the desert, saw visions there, and soon put forward the idea of a single good god, Ahura Mazda – "the Wise Lord". That's why the religion of the Zoroastrians is also called Mazdaism. The principle is simple: two armies are at war – in white, the armies of Good, in black, the armies of Evil. Dressed in white linen, the fighters for Good must refrain from sacrificing animals, and especially the ox, protected by Zoroaster.'

'The ox? Why?'

'Because people should let it graze in peace, and then use what it gives them,' Aunt Martha replied. 'You'll see just the same thing in India with cows. No doubt the Zoroastrians' respect for the soul of the ox is the reason why they fled to India. The Indian Parsis who worship fire are very good and very moral people. They're also very reserved. For instance, so as not to pollute the earth, they don't bury their dead, and so as not to pollute fire, they don't burn them either. Corpses are simply exposed on top of towers, the Towers of Silence, and there . . .'

'There what?'

'There vultures come and eat them very quickly,' murmured Aunt Martha. 'But apart from the Parsis themselves, no one is allowed to attend this ceremony.'

'I don't see why,' said Theo. 'Burial isn't much better. Rotting away in the ground, no thanks! The Parsi way, at least the birds fly up into the sky.'

'Anyway,' Aunt Martha hurried on, 'fire worship is one of the oldest religions in the world. Do you know the story of Prometheus?'

'The one whose liver was pecked by Zeus's eagle?'

'It was his punishment for stealing fire from the gods. The theft of fire from the gods is a legend found in many cultures. That's why the Vestals guarded the flame so jealously, and why they stayed pure. If one of them ever took a lover, the penalty was to be buried alive. There was once a Vestal who was loved by the emperor himself, but when the truth came out she was buried all the same. You didn't fool around with Vesta's servants!'

'Does that happen to nuns as well?' asked Theo. 'They have to be celibate too!'

'Not these days, Theo. It's a thing of the past. But you're right to compare the Vestal virgins to nuns. The Vestals were dedicated to the goddess of the Hearth just as nuns are to their husband Jesus.'

'But why were the Vestals forbidden to have children?'

'They say that a baby takes all its mother's love,' said Martha. 'Vestals or nuns, as sacred priestesses the idea is that keeping them childless makes better use of the love they might have given them. But I'm not in the best position to speak about maternal love.'

'That's true, you've got no children,' Theo sympathized. Then something caught his eye. 'What's that over there?'

Set in the portico of a church a sinister bearded face, carved in marble, glowered menacingly back at Theo. Aunt Martha explained that in olden times its gaping mouth, known as the Bocca della Verità, the Mouth of Truth, was used as an ordeal for suspected criminals. Their hand was forced inside it, and if they lied the mouth was supposed to clamp shut. The old superstition had survived, and brave people still dared to reach inside, and take their chances. Theo extended a finger, then realized that the sight had made him ravenously hungry.

'A useful affliction,' said Aunt Martha, and they went to find a cure in the nearest trattoria, over red and white checked paper tablecloths. Theo downed his platcful of spaghetti with relish, and started to grill his aunt. Who were the mysterious 'they' that she had discussed with the Cardinal?

'You can be such a pest,' she grumbled, 'always insisting on knowing all there is to know! There's plenty of time.'

'No,' he retorted. 'That's not true. I haven't got very much time. Go and stick your hand in the Mouth of Truth, fibber!'

Aunt Martha looked away to hide the tears that brimmed in her eyes.

In the streets, Romans strolled beneath a dark sky streaked with red. He didn't want to go to bed, and felt like prolonging the night, buying a strawberry ice cream and roaming aimlessly around, viewing the floodlit monuments, but that was not allowed. He dreamed of priests in white tunics spattered with blood, baying around a felled pine tree whose needles swayed to the rhythm of the drums. All veiled in black, the goddess Astarte wore no face except the face of death, and that is what jolted Theo out of a restless sleep to hear the throb of an African tom-tom lost somewhere outside in the Roman darkness.

The first Christians

Next morning Dom Ottavio reappeared, his cassock fluttering in the wind.

'So, are you ready for the catacombs, *bambino*? I suppose you know what they are?'

'They're tunnels dug beneath the city,' Theo told him. 'We have them in Paris too.'

'But in Rome they are the burial places of the first Christians. We have to leave the city, because in ancient times it was forbidden to bury the dead inside the sacred boundary.'

'Listen, when it comes to graveyards we had our share in Egypt,' Aunt Martha protested. 'Let's look at the underground basilicas instead.'

They drove until they saw the cypresses and stone pines of the Appian Way, where the grass was sparse and yellow. Pale sunlight filtered through a break in the grey sky on to the Roman mausoleums. The neon sign over a nearby trattoria read 'Quo Vadis'.

'What an odd name,' said Theo. 'Quo Vadis?'

'Ah!' said the Cardinal. 'Those are the words spoken by Saint Peter on this very spot, when Jesus appeared to him on the road.'

'Right here?'

'So the story goes. He bowed down in front of his Lord and asked him: "*Quo vadis, domine*?" – Where are you going, Lord? And Jesus answered: "I go to Rome to be crucified in your place." After that, the apostle turned back again and went to his death.'

'What does that mean, apostle?'

'That is the name for the first twelve disciples of Christ, all excepting Judas, who betrayed him to the Romans, and who was replaced by Saint Matthias.'

'What? There was one who betrayed Christ?'

'Yes indeed, *bambino*. By kissing him. That was the signal to the Roman soldiers. "Whoever I kiss, that will be Jesus," he told them. Betrayed by a kiss, for money . . . Later on, Judas was racked by remorse, and hanged himself. As for Peter, he did not turn traitor, but three times running he lied. He claimed that he'd never heard of Jesus, on the very night his master was arrested.'

'And he was an apostle all the same?'

'The greatest of all! Jesus knew about the weakness in the human heart. That is why he chose a weak man to set it an example. When he sees that his life is in danger, the apostle Peter starts by running away, but he pulls himself together and decides to die like Christ.'

'That was brave,' Theo admired. 'And where do the catacombs come in?'

'The Romans used to cremate their dead on bonfires, but Christians believe in the resurrection of the dead in the form of their glorified bodies. So they have to remain intact, and that's why they are buried, so that they can rise from the dead the way they were, only better.'

'How better?' asked Aunt Martha.

'Radiant, luminous, transparent . . .'

'With wings?' said Theo.

'Who knows?' said the Cardinal. 'In any case, before the Christians, the Jews had their own catacombs in Rome.'

This took Theo by surprise. 'Then there were also Jews in Rome?' he asked.

'Quite a lot of them, *bambino*. They were persecuted under several emperors – Tiberius, Nero . . . People from many foreign lands had come to Rome, all with their own religion. Because they came from the Middle East, the Jews were lumped together with the vast category of the Asiatic sects that were eating away at the Roman religion, gradually eroding it.'

'Asia is China and Japan,' Theo declared. 'They got it wrong.'

'No, *bambino*, because the Romans didn't know that those countries existed. From their point of view, modern Turkey, Syria, Egypt, Iraq and Palestine were located in Asia, and they saw the Asiatic religions as ugly superstitions. But these foreign cults were thriving. The emperors spent quite some time trying to defend the religion of ancient Rome, then when they saw themselves being submerged under the spread of those oriental sects, they did what they could to assimilate the new religions either by accepting being deified themselves or else by endorsing the great goddesses who came from other places.'

'That worked fairly well,' said Aunt Martha. 'And it was useful too.'

'Except for Christianity, which did not accept the deification of a man, because the only god-man was Jesus. So the emperors started to persecute the Christians, and that continued right up to the point when Christianity became so widespread that in the fourth century the emperor Constantine decreed it the official religion. But here we are.'

To enter the catacombs of San Callisto they went down narrow steps, and found a maze of tunnels quarried out of soft volcanic rock. Burial niches were hewn out of the walls, one above the other, with Latin inscriptions that Dom Ottavio obligingly translated – '*Vivas in Deo:* May you live in God' – or symbols he was able to explain – 'Here, an anchor, symbol of a good landfall in the port of heaven; over there, a jar of water, to ease the ordeal'.

Theo shuddered. The ordeal of death – would he be facing it soon? Water to stave off pain, not much help there . . . DON'T THINK ABOUT IT.

140

Down a huge staircase, you came to a crypt supported by two white pillars. Dom Ottavio walked over to a large marble slab engraved with names.

'The Crypt of the Popes,' he whispered. 'Nine pontiffs are buried here, and nearly all are martyrs. Look at the graffiti, carved by a pilgrim. It says in Latin: "Jerusalem, city and ornament of martyrs."'

'Yet another Jerusalem!' cried Theo. 'One in Jerusalem, another in Ethiopia, in Lalibela, and this one makes three. Does that mean that the catacombs are the Christians' Jerusalem?'

'Jerusalem is more than just a city, *bambino*, it's also an idea. Jerusalem is the gathering of the faithful, Christians and Jews alike. It took a long time to separate Judaism from Christianity: same provenance, same population, same origin. Jews and Christians have the Bible and Jerusalem in common.'

'Now you're going too far!' Aunt Martha rebelled. 'All through the centuries, who else if not the Christians persecuted the Jews? What about the Inquisition?'

'And the Pope in the days of the Nazis, what about him?' Theo persisted caustically. 'Dad told me that in the war he didn't lift a finger to save the Jews.'

'That verdict is too harsh,' the churchman protested awkwardly. 'The German priests were admirable.'

'But the popes,' Aunt Martha challenged. 'Just look at the popes! The ones who lie under this slab, fair enough, but you can't excuse some of the later ones. When I think of the dogma of papal infallibility! Because – Theo, are you ready for this? – the Pope is infallible. He never makes mistakes about religious matters!'

'My dear friend, you are twisting this young man's arm,' Dom Ottavio erupted. 'And besides, you told me that he had no religious education, but that was a lie, Martha. He plainly has one, and it is totally anticlerical!'

'You know me well enough to know that I share those views,' Aunt Martha challenged. 'Religions are fine to begin with, but once they organize themselves into hierarchies, then priesthoods appear, and they're always intolerant.'

'I agree with that,' said Theo. 'Can I help it if I don't like priests?'

'Theo!' cried Aunt Martha. 'Please don't be so rude!'

'Make up your mind,' he grumbled. 'All right, I apologize, Father.'

'You're supposed to say "Cardinal".'

'Oh, leave him in peace!' barked Dom Ottavio. 'What do you expect?

You're the first to complain about the Church, then you insist on his using my title! It doesn't make sense!'

'Quite right!' Theo seconded. 'Now, what's this story about popes not making mistakes?'

'I'll try to explain. The Pope is the guide for all Catholics, and he is infallible, but only when he is speaking formally, in the name of God on earth, about topics related to the Church and its doctrines. After all, there are questions that must be settled: there has to be some source of truth! For us it is the Holy Father. In other cases he is only a man, just like anybody else. Now over this matter of anti-semitism and the Inquisition, it so happens that John Paul II, a Pope of the twentieth century, has put an end to the ancient quarrel with the Jewish people.'

'Then the other popes before him were wrong,' said Theo.

'You can see it that way if you want to,' the prelate reluctantly conceded. 'The Church consists of people, and the divine message is the captive of human history, I won't deny it. But that episode is finally over: Jews are no longer called "deicides", "killers of God", and our views have reverted closer to where we began. The Jews set out on the right path before the Christians did, that's all. The day when Pope John Paul II made a solemn visit to the synagogue in Rome was a great event for the whole world.'

'Very well,' Aunt Martha intervened. 'But you must admit that for centuries the Church was anti-semitic.'

'Let us say that with its mind set on obeying its universal vocation and converting what it used to call the heathen, the Church has sometimes resorted to dubious methods.'

'Yes, for instance when it burned the Indians in Brazil to verify whether they had a soul . . .'

'And during that same period, the Indians were drowning their invaders for the same reason,' the Cardinal retorted. 'This is stale news, and you know it.'

'STOP!' cried Theo. 'I can't breathe. It's stifling in here!'

Aunt Martha and her cardinal hurried back up to the surface, where Theo sat on the ground and inspected the movements of a goat as it rooted for tufts of grass. A stray, like himself.

Tongues of fire and all the tongues of earth

'Does it feel cooler out here?' asked Aunt Martha, trying to sound casual. 'You know, Ottavio and I are always bickering.'

'*E vero*,' the prelate nodded. 'Friendships are strengthened by quarrels. Don't take it to heart.'

'You get on my nerves, the pair of you!' Theo scolded. 'It's confusing enough already, the stuff you're talking about, so if you lose your tempers too . . .'

Aunt Martha sat down next to Theo, with a sheepish expression, while the Cardinal, armed with a handkerchief, busied himself by dusting off a rock so as not to dirty his purple habit. Silence fell.

'The Jews and the Indians,' Theo resumed. 'All right, you didn't persecute them on purpose. But there's something I don't understand. Why you were so dead set on converting them.'

'I told you, *bambino*: because the Church is universal, which means that it is valid all over the world. You know the word "Catholic", but do you know what it stands for in Greek? That's right – universal. Obviously you've heard of Pentecost.'

'Pentecost?' said Theo. 'A long weekend in May.'

'Good gracious,' murmured Dom Ottavio. 'The child knows hardly anything. But it's such a beautiful story . . . After his resurrection, Jesus had been taken up to heaven. Fifty days later the disciples were gathered in a room, behind closed doors, when a clap of thunder sounded in the sky. A wind of incredible power rushed through the house, and tongues of fire sprang up on the heads of all twelve of the apostles.'

'Now I remember,' said Theo. 'It's the pigeon at work.'

'The Holy Ghost, a pigeon!' the Cardinal chided. 'A dove, I'll grant you, but a pigeon . . .'

'It isn't my word, it's Aunt Martha's.'

'Oh?' grunted the baffled Cardinal. 'Very well then. Now it was a feast day in Jerusalem, and believers had arrived from every nation – Egyptians, Cretans, Arabians, Romans, Assyrians . . . This mystifying noise brought them flocking to the spot in curiosity. Then the apostles emerged from the house and spoke, and all their listeners heard themselves addressed in their own tongue. It was a complete miracle to hear them speak languages unknown to them only a few minutes earlier.'

'No kidding,' said Theo. 'They'd learned them just like that?'

'The tongues of fire had brought the gift of tongues, *bambino*. Some said they must have had too much to drink, but Peter pointed out that it was only the third hour of the day – far too early for drunkenness. No, they weren't drunk: they had received the revelation of the universal scope of the New Covenant. From that moment on, they were able to preach in every language on earth. And that is why Pentecost is the feast of the universal.'

'The phenomenon isn't unique,' Aunt Martha pointed out. 'It even has a scholarly name – glossolalia. Sick people who present the same symptom appear from time to time in psychiatric hospitals, and when you priests were torturing so-called witches in seventeenth-century Europe, they too would start to speak in unknown tongues.'

'Perhaps, but in terms of the brain the thing is unaccountable, and as long as there's no scientific explanation you won't prevent me thinking that divine inspiration is involved. Lately there's been a return to those beginnings. The Christian movement known as charismatic renewal has been reviving the tradition of the early days: during their meetings it's not unusual for someone or other in the congregation to start speaking in tongues. Doesn't that demonstrate the universality of the Christian Church?'

'I'm interested in this learning thing you mentioned, this colossalalia,' said Theo. 'I have trouble enough just with German!'

'Glossolalia, Theo,' Aunt Martha corrected. 'And it isn't available on prescription! You can't expect to pick it up so easily.'

'Why not?' Dom Ottavio broke in. 'Didn't Christ say: "Let the children come to me"?'

'Tough luck!' said Theo. 'Never mind, I won't speak Hebrew, but I can speak pig Latin, do you know it, Ardinalcay?'

'Sorry,' said the Cardinal, and smiled. 'I'm only a poor priest of the Roman Curia, a Catholic bureaucrat, only just competent enough to explain about the universal meaning of Pentecost. Oh, and by the way, you know how when Pope John Paul II travels abroad he has a habit of kissing the ground as soon as he steps off the plane? That's his way of showing that the earth is blessed no matter where it is.'

'I've seen him on TV,' said Theo. 'The last few times, he couldn't kneel down any more, poor guy.'

'But he has continued to travel, even though he was badly wounded in an attempt on his life, and you must have seen his pope-mobile with its bullet-proof windows. John Paul II has visited every corner of the globe, because Christendom contains no no-go areas: anybody can become a Christian. There are some closed religions: if you're not born into them it will be hard to join. And there are religions open to all, and that is the case with Christianity. Anyone can become a convert, and that is why we are universal.'

The prelate sat back and rearranged his cassock. A perfect demonstration, and finally the boy seemed impressed.

Martyrs and conquerors

A sudden frown crossed Theo's face. 'Anyone can if they want to, but why force them?'

'That's something else again,' the Cardinal exclaimed. 'You never run short of questions, do you, *bambino*? It's a long story. Am I to tell it, my dear Martha?'

'Go ahead, Ottavio,' said Aunt Martha. 'I can't wait to hear your reply.'

'Very well,' Dom Ottavio conceded. 'In the beginning, Christians converted by example. When other religions had mystery cults that only the rich could take part in, Christendom was open to the destitute, the dispossessed, the slaves. People were people: that was all, and that was convincing enough. Later the Christians showed such courage under the persecutions they suffered that they became martyrs, and each martyr brought further conversions. The word "martyr" in Greek simply means "witness": the martyr bears true witness to his faith. So this new God must be powerful indeed, to give so much strength to his believers. The first Christians went looking for martyrdom – they sometimes felt ashamed to die in their beds!'

'Personally, I would prefer my bed to hungry lions,' Theo murmured.

'Me too,' the Cardinal admitted. 'We're only human. But the Church is built on its early martyrs, the sowers of the seed. They became the saints in the calendar.'

'And people used to squabble over their relics,' Aunt Martha added. 'Scraps of cloth, bits of bone, yellow teeth, all for conspicuous devotion. Don't tell me that wasn't paganism in disguise, Ottavio!'

'To some extent,' the Cardinal admitted. 'But that has no bearing on the true meaning of martyrdom. Look at the greatest of our martyrs, Saint Peter. He decided to let himself be crucified head-downwards, so as not to copy his master's sacrifice.'

'And that's why he's the greatest of the saints?'

'Not only for that. When they met for the first time, Christ changed his name from Simon, and told him: "You are Peter, and on this rock I will build my Church." That is what happened. The greatest Christian basilica is built over Peter's tomb, in the Vatican. And yet, Simon Peter was a coward: when Christ was arrested on the Mount of Olives, he ran away . . .'

'A liar, a coward . . . Some saint!' said Theo.

'Wait, *bambino*. The true meaning of martyrdom is that a poor human being can suffer and die in the name of the living God. It took a plain man like Peter to build the universal Church: someone who could stand for all the rest, with all their faults. That's why, when he revealed himself to him by the Sea of Tiberias, after his resurrection, Jesus said to Peter: "Feed my lambs." '

'Who weren't capable of feeding themselves?' asked Theo.

'Who might not find the pasture. He was making Peter the shepherd-in-chief of the Christian flock.'

'Who are all sheep,' said Theo.

'Defenceless creatures!' snapped Dom Ottavio. 'Keep up this sniping, Theo, and you'll start to annoy me.'

'Hey,' said Theo, 'you called me by my name. We're making progress.'

'Listen to me, *bambino*. I haven't got Peter's forbearance, I warn you. He is the Prince of the apostles – "Princeps", the first among them. Thanks to him, the meaning of Rome was transformed. The Rome of the Romans had been "the city of the seven hills". Now it was the city of the one rock, the first rock of the Church.'

'Why Rome, why not Venice or Timbuktu?' said Theo. 'It's a sheer accident!'

'The popes have not always lived in Rome, *bambino*. They too have been persecuted. They have been forced to flee, and leave the Holy City. In the fourteenth century, they took refuge in Avignon for seventy years. In the nineteenth century, one pope was even taken hostage by Napoleon and forcibly shipped off to France. Don't think it's been nothing but success!'

'Then your tale of the rock doesn't stand up,' Theo pounced.

'But the Church according to Jesus is not a building: it's the gathering of all the Christians in the world. The very first among them died in Rome, so it fell to Rome to found the Church of Christ. Later, after the phase of persecutions, Christianity became the religion of the Roman state. From that time on, it was a powerful force.'

He paused for a moment. Here came the tricky bit.

'After that, the conversions often had military causes, and warfare became holy. Islam behaved no differently, and the Koran refers to "Jihad", holy war, aimed at converting the Infidels. You conquer some region of the globe, and if too few conversions occur, well then, you force them to occur.'

'But why?' Theo insisted.

'Because you're sure you have right on your side, obviously.' The Cardinal's voice was subdued. 'The history of religions is also the history of intolerance, and our own has not escaped, any more than Judaism in its time, or expansionist Islam. We too have passed through this cycle. The worst is summed up in a comment made by a Catholic war leader appointed to crush the Cathar rebellion. The Cathars were a visionary sect whose hatred of the material world was so extreme that they advocated suicide as deliverance from Evil.'

'I remember,' said Theo. 'Father Dubourg told me about them in Jerusalem.'

'My word! And I thought I was teaching you something new! Well, one of those sects, with a doctrinaire contempt for human life, was still flourishing up until a little while ago. That's how it happened.'

'Exactly what happened?' asked Theo.

'This war leader, whose name was Armaud-Amaury, slaughtered communities wholesale in southwestern France – communities that also contained Catholics. To justify his actions, he made a terrible remark: "Kill them all, God will recognize his own!"'

'That's why I'm on the side of religious minorities,' said Aunt Martha. 'When a religion is on top, it's bound to be unjust. When it's a minority – that's when it protects the weak.'

'Martha,' said the Cardinal. 'You are in Rome, in the heart of the Catholic and universal Church. Cheer up. Christendom no longer means conquest. These are the days of dialogue between religions.'

'I do hope you're right,' prayed Aunt Martha. 'You don't fight the battle for tolerance with a weapon in your hand.'

Theo was fetching fresh grass for the goat, staring the devil's creature deep in its wide brown eyes.

'Some feed lambs,' he announced, 'and I feed goats.'

CHAPTER 8

Glory and the Poor

Tomorrow had come, 'they' were expected next day, and Theo was chafing with impatience. Who would emerge from nowhere to deliver the next message? What new wizards would pop out from behind a Roman pillar? Yesterday evening, at dinner, Dom Ottavio and Aunt Martha had argued on and on about politics, the Mafia, and of course priests, whom Aunt Martha had demolished – for the sake of annoying Ottavio – with the same relish as her ravioli and truffles. Theo had dozed off at table, and been whisked off to bed.

As soon as Aunt Martha had eased his bedroom door shut behind her, Theo felt beneath the pillow for his telephone, but in vain. His parents were out – maybe they'd gone to the cinema – and it was too late to call Fatou, who always went early to bed. So no luck there, and then to cap it all it was the patter of rain that woke him up next morning. Theo put his lentils out on the balcony, just in case. He thought nostalgically about the cloudless skies of Egypt, then started to daydream about his missing twin. Who knew when he'd return, but without the sun, surely he would not want to surface.

A special kind of State

Breakfast went badly. Theo would rather have slept late, but no chance of that. Aunt Martha put her foot down, and he dressed in slow motion. The Cardinal was ready and waiting in the lobby downstairs – on your marks, get set, go!

'Did you sleep well, *bambino*?'

'Yes thanks, old man,' Theo retaliated. 'How about you?'

'Not bad,' said the Cardinal. 'You're not too tired?'

'I'm all right. What's happening today?'

'We're leaving Italy,' the prelate answered grandly.

'Then we're catching a plane?'

'Not at all. We're going to the Vatican. Because that is a State, *bambino*. Forty-four hectares, but with its own government, its currency, its flag, its stamps, its radio station, its newspaper . . .'

'*L'Osservatore Romano*,' Aunt Martha cut in. 'The official organ of the Papacy. But as States go, you could wrap it all up in a handkerchief!'

'Ah! Obviously there isn't a customs post, but to enter the Vatican is to enter another world.'

'A world where you are a minister, Dom Ottavio?' asked Theo inquisitively.

'Assistant under-secretary – small fry, really.'

'And how many inhabitants there?'

'Seven or eight hundred,' the Cardinal replied.

'Not a super-power, then,' said Theo.

'But we have our own laws, and our customs. And we also have our own elections, when the Pope dies.'

'Then if you have elections, you're a democracy!' Theo decided.

'Not quite,' Aunt Martha intervened. 'Tell him how a Papal election works.'

'All the cardinals in the world gather in strict isolation, and stay there till the new Pope has been elected. It's known as a conclave, and it can last for a very long time. There have even been times in the course of history when the cardinals were walled in to hurry them up! Because this election is a very great event. To choose the representative of Christ is a decision with no small implications for the world. After each vote, a little fire is lit. If the vote is inconclusive the smoke that comes out of the building is black; if positive, the smoke is white. That means that a new Pope has been elected.'

'Though there's just one more detail to be checked,' said Aunt Martha. 'They check in the proper place to make sure that he really is a man.'

'What an odd idea!' said Theo. 'Isn't it obvious?'

'Well,' growled the Cardinal, 'the legend goes that once, by mistake, they elected a woman, Pope Joan. But your aunt will be furious, I'll be bound: after all, why not a female Pope?'

'Yes, after all, why not?' Theo agreed. 'And why are priests always men? Why aren't they married?'

'Here we go!' the Cardinal sighed. 'In the early days of the Church, priests often lived with women, and it didn't work out very well – they neglected their duty, they had their minds on other things, and that was forbidden. What am I to say? The priest must be available to all, and if he chooses a wife he inevitably has a preference. That is why priests are forbidden to marry.'

'Then what is left for women in Catholicism, my poor friend?' Aunt Martha cut in.

'What, Martha? You're not serious. Take a good look at the role of women in the Bible! Without Sarah, old as she was, Abraham would not have been the first patriarch; without Rachel, that fine woman, Jacob would not have been the second. Jesus would have had no body without Mary! And let's not forget the great heroines – Judith, who saved her people by seducing and then beheading the enemy chief, Esther who married a pagan king and won him over to toleration towards Jews, and the lesser women, the obscure ones . . . Here, take Ruth the Moabite, and her mother-in-law Naomi. Here's a poor girl who isn't a Jew, a pagan woman asked by her late husband's ageing mother to perpetuate the family name because her sons are dead. The two women are in exile, destitute, starving. Ruth doesn't know what to do. Then it comes to her that Boaz, who is a kinsman of her late father-in-law, and a wealthy man, would make an honourable father, and Naomi approves.'

'Ah, here it comes!' said Theo. 'There's got to be a husband!'

'It's one of the most touching stories in the Bible. Ruth goes to glean barley in Boaz's field, after the harvest, and he notices this beautiful woman hard at work. At mealtime, he gives her bread and wine. She's almost there, but there's one thing that stands in her way: under Jewish law, it's forbidden to marry a pagan.'

'Ouch,' said Theo. 'So now she's had it.'

'But Naomi sees what to do. Ruth must lie at Boaz's feet while he is sleeping on the threshing floor, after the harvest feast, and give herself to him. Ruth obeys. She waits till after nightfall and comes to Boaz. At midnight he wakes up with a start and asks her: "Who are you?" . . . because he can't see her in the darkness. "I am Ruth, your maidservant," she tells him. "Spread your wing over your servant." And the Jew Boaz will take Ruth for his wife, in defiance of the religious laws, because he hears the prayer of humility.'

'That means he sleeps with her in the dark,' Theo interpreted.

'Isn't it wonderful? In the morning he tells her: "Now, my daughter, do not fear. I will do for you all that you ask, because you are virtuous" – virtuous, this pagan woman who seduces a rich man in his sleep! And the Bible celebrates the virtue of the woman whose great grandson will be King David! I find that . . . I can't express it, Theo. Magnificent! Thrilling!'

'Such fulsome enthusiasm!' said Aunt Martha coldly. 'When it boils down to saying that a woman is only good for making babies.'

'But men don't bear them, don't give birth to them!' the Cardinal flared. 'How can you care so little about motherhood? It gives life! Motherhood is divine!'

'OK,' said Theo. 'In that case there's no reason to ban a woman from being a priest, is there, Dom Ottavio?'

The Cardinal offered no reply. No doubt Aunt Martha would think of one. She would rant about the misogyny of the Church, and bring up the movement for the ordination of women, and the injustice done to the first woman, Eve the apple lover, blamed for the sins of the world . . .

Aunt Martha played her part to perfection. She raged for a quarter of an hour, the Cardinal sat out the storm, and Theo enjoyed every moment.

The largest church in the world

The car drew up in front of Bernini's colonnade. Gleaming in the rain, the square was almost deserted, except where some bobbing umbrellas sheltered a cluster of devoutly scurrying nuns.

'I love this place when it's empty,' Aunt Martha remarked, as they walked across the square. 'You see the scale of the columns, and the harmony is overwhelming. Theo, you're looking at the heart of the Catholic Church: the largest church in the world, built on top of Saint Peter's tomb.'

'And will we see the Pope on the balcony?'

'No,' said the Cardinal. 'He doesn't appear every day. But I imagine that you must have seen him on television at Easter, for the *Urbi et Orbi* blessing?'

'Urbiwhat?' asked Theo.

'It's from the Latin: *urbs*, the city, *orbis*, the world. The Pope's blessing reaches out *urbi et orbi* – to the city and to the world, to our universe, which gives us the word "universal". On that day the Pope, the visible head of the entire Church, pronounces his blessing in all the languages spoken by Christians, like the apostles long ago, on the day of Pentecost.'

'So there were Christians in ancient Egypt,' Theo now said.

Dom Ottavio frowned. 'Of course not! Christianity was born three thousand years later.'

'Then why the obelisk in the middle of the square?'

'You don't miss a thing, *bambino*. The obelisk does come from Egypt. It was one of the ornaments of Nero's Circus, where Saint Peter was crucified. It was moved to this site, and a piece of the cross of Christ was added to the top.'

'Recycled,' said Theo. 'It looks good, anyway. Shall we go in?'

He couldn't suppress a gasp of wonder when they entered the vast basilica. Buzzing with cheerful tourists and costumed prelates, the nave seemed designed to make room for a thousand worlds. The ceilings, with their indecipherable scenes, were so high, and so animated, that it made your head spin to look up at them. When Theo's gaze had taken in this space, it came to rest on the great black canopy, standing on gilded spiral columns.

'This is not a church,' he murmured, obviously impressed.

'So what do you think it is?' Aunt Martha asked.

'I don't know,' he said. 'A church is simple and white, with an altar, a crucifix, and bouquets of flowers placed in front of it. And also it's peaceful, a church. But this . . . !'

'There's truth in what you say, *bambino*,' the Cardinal admitted. 'Everything in this place is intended to express the power and glory of God. If you were to see the ceremonies in all their splendour! The Pope sits on his throne, surrounded by the cardinals in full dress, the choirs sing wonderful melodies, and we celebrate God the Supreme at the height of his glory. You're right, this basilica is not a church, it is a masterpiece of Christendom. Michelangelo, the most powerful of all Italian artists of the Renaissance, drew up the plans, but it took so long to build that he never saw it completed. The world's finest statues are here, the greatest painters and the greatest sculptors are represented here, and what you see there, the *baldacchino*, the pontifical canopy, is one of the wonders of the Vatican.'

'I don't like it,' said Theo. 'It's too big.'

'Right! Then I'll show you something else,' said the Cardinal, and tugged Theo over to his right, into a chapel at the side of the nave. Here, behind a thick glass screen, with tourists clustered round it, Theo found himself looking at a statuary group carved in pure white marble.

'The Pietà,' the Cardinal whispered. 'Michelangelo carved those figures. They represent Mary, the mother of Christ, and her son, who has just died. Look at that woman's face, so beautiful, and so sad in her suffering. Isn't that a touching sight?'

'You'd think they were the same age,' murmured Theo.

'Mary was actually very young when she was visited by the Angel who told her the good news, so when Jesus died she was not old.'

'He looks very peaceful in death. Why are they shut in a cage?'

'Because not so long ago, someone tried to destroy them. Michelangelo's sculpture had to be protected. In olden days the barbarians who invaded Rome would smash up Christian statues. So nothing much has changed. As for the medieval statue of Saint Peter . . . well, you'll see for yourself.'

The saint's eyes gazed out at the horizon, but one of his dark bronze feet seemed to have been polished smooth by some crude hand. The faithful's lips had brushed it so very many times, for so many centuries, that they had kissed away the metal. To Theo, that was a definite miracle.

The Cardinal pressed on. Here a statue, there a monument, now a tomb, and now another, then another.

'Not too much longer,' fussed Aunt Martha. 'He'll get tired.'

'Not at all! He's doing fine,' said the Cardinal, as he towed his *bambino* in his wake, and now Aunt Martha realized that her nephew was fighting for breath.

'Ottavio, stop!' she commanded. 'The boy's worn out. Can't you see how shaky he is? Look, he can hardly stand.'

Suddenly repentant, the prelate decided to carry Theo out to the gardens, where he could sit down. Ignoring his protests, he bent over, pulled Theo's arm over his shoulder, and picked him up in a fireman's lift. Theo struggled, but he was helpless.

'Stop fighting me, *bambino*!' cried Dom Ottavio. 'You're weak, and I'm strong enough to carry you. Let this be a lesson in humility . . .'

But as soon as Dom Ottavio tried to stand him on his feet again, Theo collapsed in a faint. With a pounding heart, his aunt went rushing over, and while the Cardinal ran for help she rubbed her nephew's temple with a Chinese balsam that she was never without – a yellow ointment with a reek of camphor.

'Don't go, Theo,' she pleaded, 'it isn't time . . . Come back!'

Seconds crawled by. Then Theo half-opened his eyes, blinked in a ray of winter sunlight, and horrified his aunt by announcing:

'Hey, this time I didn't die.'

'But Theo,' she gasped, 'does this happen to you often?'

'Quite often,' he murmured. 'I'm used to it. It's my illness, you see. One day I won't wake up.'

'I forbid you . . .'

'You're not God,' he replied. 'There's nothing you can do.'

'I promise you there is,' she retorted. 'But we must leave this place. Where has Ottavio got to?'

The Cardinal was returning, flanked by three nuns, one carrying an oxygen bottle, the others with a stretcher. At the first aid post a doctor examined him, noticed the patches of blue all over his body, frowned as he checked his blood pressure, and stood up with an anxious shake of his head.

'All right, that's it,' said Theo, with tears in his eyes. 'I'd like some tea and bread and butter, please. And no more glum faces!'

'Good boy,' said the Cardinal, very moved. 'Quick, tea, bread and butter, *presto!*'

A touch of colour crept into Theo's cheeks as he munched his bread and butter methodically and drank his tea in sips like medicine. The Cardinal hovered in the background, and Aunt Martha was still furious.

'I warned you, Ottavio,' she scolded. 'You can be so pig-headed!'

'But, my dear . . .'

'Be quiet and pray!' she boomed.

The Cardinal complied, and lapsed into a painful meditation.

Messages for Theo

Martha wanted to return to the hotel, but Theo wouldn't hear of it. Yes, he was back on his feet and could walk; no, he didn't feel sleepy and wasn't going to faint again. But he was absolutely determined to find out who 'they' were.

'Listen, Theo, they're not here yet,' said Aunt Martha awkwardly. 'They won't be long, so try to be patient. What if we go and look for the next message instead?'

To please his aunt, Theo agreed. The Cardinal took him very carefully by the arm and walked him slowly along. They would go to the Fountain of the Popes, and after that they would take the car, and no arguing, even if it was only for two hundred metres.

The new riddle nestled between two big tiaras of grey stone, just above the twin mouths gushing their jets of clear water. The paper was slightly damp, and in fact some words had been blotted out, so that the message now read: *Sitting on my sacred ... I am the eternal dancer. Come to the banks of my river, come to the oldest city in the world. I am worshipped there, and I ... Come!*

'Sitting on his bottom?' asked Theo.

'A sacred bottom? Surely not, Theo,' said Aunt Martha.

'What about a throne? A tree? A drum?'

None of those. Aunt Martha admitted that the plot had thickened more than it was meant to, and suggested that Theo should appeal to his Pythia when they got back to the hotel. Attentive now, the Cardinal took Theo to his car.

'Tell me, sir, what is this whole shebang good for?' asked Theo after a long silence.

'So I'm no longer Dom Ottavio, *bambino*?' the prelate responded sadly.

'If you like,' said Theo magnanimously. 'But answer my question first.'

The Cardinal peered scrupulously down at his own hands. When he replied, it was in an altered voice.

'By "shebang" you mean the Vatican City, I imagine. To be honest, there are times when I wonder myself. I know that we celebrate the glory of God in all its splendour here, but I wonder what a younger mind may make of it.'

'That it's fantastically rich, for a start,' said Theo.

'That's it!' sighed Dom Ottavio. 'Do you know what Jesus Christ's message is? I bet you don't.'

'Yes I do!' said Theo. 'He was the son of God, he died to save the world, redeem our sins and all that. His mother was a virgin and his father Joseph adopted him. Mostly, it's quite a good story.'

'If you're not too tired, we could go for a spin in town. It's quite a good place.'

They drove along the Tiber to Castel Sant'Angelo, where high on the roof the Archangel Michael looks down and sheaths his sword for all eternity. The Cardinal spoke no word of explanation. Then the chauffeur took a road out of town, and still Dom Ottavio said nothing. From time to time Aunt Martha drew Theo's attention to some famous monument or church. Suddenly they were gliding past pine trees and cypresses, in the area where the catacombs began. The chauffeur pulled up.

'You surely don't intend to make us get out and walk again!' cried Aunt Martha.

The Cardinal sat back on the grey cushions and finally broke his silence.

'Forgive me for bringing you here,' he apologized, 'but I don't know of a better place to talk to Theo about the message of Our Lord. Along this ancient road it's possible to imagine the shepherds watching their flocks – we could almost be in the country. Jesus was a man of fields and valleys, a man who knew the sands of the desert and saw the flowers return in springtime. If you're trying to pick up his trail, you won't find it in present-day Jerusalem.'

'Not any more,' said Theo.

'You'll find it wherever you feel a sense of peace.'

'Peace wasn't all he brought,' Aunt Martha answered. 'He demanded a lot. He drove out the traders who turned the floor of the Temple into a market for sacred knick-knacks.'

'And made a scourge to whip them,' Dom Ottavio confirmed. 'But that's because he rejected pomp and glory. He wanted equality among his people: in an age ruled by slavery, injustice and inequality, that was a revolution! And to stress this fundamental equality, to highlight it, he, the Son of God, invented baptism. Have you been baptized, Theo?'

'No,' replied Theo. 'My parents told me that I can choose when I grow up – well, if I grow up.'

'Ah,' murmured the Cardinal. 'Of course. But you see, it wasn't through baptizing others that Jesus invented baptism: it was through consenting to *be* baptized, by John the Baptist. First, water washes away sin, but what the water of baptism does most of all is to welcome each candidate into the community. That is why Jesus, who was God made human, chose to be baptized himself.'

'To show that he was equal?' asked Theo.

'More or less. And later, to reinforce the message, Jesus saved the outcasts, the rejected. He turned none of them away – not the repentant prostitute, the shunned Samaritan or the adulterous woman, not the poor or the sick. He simply healed or consoled them, with a word and a look.'

'And he brought a dead man back to life,' Theo added. 'I've forgotten his name.'

'Lazarus. When Jesus called the dead man's name, he came out of his tomb, even though he had been buried for four days. Jesus wanted to conquer death, and he succeeded, to prove that he was truly the Son of God. Equality, the resurrection and the life: that is his message. Do you know the Beatitudes, Theo?'

'Er . . .' Theo faltered. 'Is it when you're happy?'

'Exactly. Jesus had just chosen his first twelve disciples, and he came down from the mountain where he had been praying to his Father. We always pray better on the heights, Theo, you'll find that all over the world. The true visionaries are often on the mountain tops.'

'Oh yes! Moses on Mount Sinai!' cried Theo.

'Moses, or the god Shiva in India, and many others . . . And down at the foot of the mountain, a crowd was waiting. So then he told them about happiness. Blessed are the poor, and the hungry, and those who mourn, and those who are hated and cursed and excluded for the sake of the Son of man. Because the kingdom of God belongs to you, he told them.'

'Wait,' said Theo. 'The Son of man? I thought he was the son of God.'

'Yes, but not exclusively that. Because he was born of a woman, he was also a man. As the Son of man, he also knew about the griefs of human life. So happiness would belong to the most wretched of the earth, and that was the core of the message.'

'I'm all for that,' Theo admitted. 'But there are wars.'

'I'm coming to that. Jesus went on to talk about intelligence, or at any rate the way people think about it. Blessed are the simple in mind. Blessed are the little children. Those who make themselves as small as children will be the greatest in the kingdom of heaven.'

'Here,' said Theo, 'are you suggesting that children are idiots?'

'I've never said any such thing!' the Cardinal protested. 'Ah! It's because of the simple in mind. But Theo, Jesus was referring to simplicity in itself. Children come straight to the point. They ask straightforward questions, they're not wily.'

'You think not?' said Theo.

'You, for example, Theo. You're gifted for your age, but your mind is direct. You don't hesitate, you come right out and ask your questions . . .'

'Then I haven't been getting on your nerves?' asked Theo, sounding rather disappointed.

'No,' declared the prelate. 'In spite of all your efforts, you haven't. You have a pure heart, as children do. Like the lilies of the field and the birds of the air. In medieval Italy, in his convent in Assisi, little Saint Francis extended the love of Jesus to the animals. He spoke to titmice, blackbirds and warblers, and preached the Gospel to them as well as to the poor, and to children . . . You're an odd bird, Theo, but a simple soul.'

'OK,' said Theo uncomfortably. 'And what else did Jesus say?'

'He talked about sorrow too. Woe to the rich, he said, woe to the full bellies, and to those too accustomed to praise.'

'That was the world upside-down!' said Theo.

'Revolutionary! And the people in power were quite aware of it: because it was the establishment of the day that condemned Jesus. He was getting in their way: he criticized priests, merchants, the clergy and the institutions.'

'Jesus is like Che Guevara,' said Theo.

The Cardinal was dumbstruck. Aunt Martha sat back in her corner and managed not to smile.

Love your enemies

'Have I put my foot in it?' Theo inquired.

'What do you think, Ottavio?' asked Aunt Martha wryly.

'No, *bambino*, you haven't,' the Cardinal resumed. 'Some rebels who defend the poor by force of arms are in fact looking to the revolutionary side of Jesus. And some priests have supported them out of sympathy for the have-nots. In Latin America they developed a version of Catholicism called liberation theology.'

'Theology, what does that mean?'

'Discourse about God. Ever since the birth of Judaism, there's been one long argument among God's people! The pope is there to introduce some element of order into those debates. Over the issue of priests taking up arms, he has come down hard: peace is paramount. Let's talk about wars, then. Jesus also said that we are to love our enemies, and that if anyone strikes us on one cheek, we should offer them the other. And in those days, my son, that was the very opposite of the Jewish religion, you see. The Jews practised what's known as the law of talion – an eye for an eye, a tooth for a tooth. You give as good as you get.'

'That's not correct,' Aunt Martha intervened. 'The true interpretation of the law of talion is basically: "Do as you would be done by. Don't strike if you'd rather not be struck." You're offering a very simplistic view of that law!'

'All right, but if war comes in answer to war, then how will war end? Jesus does not ignore the existence of wars. He calls them "birth-pangs". Nation against nation, kingdom against kingdom, betrayals, false prophets, earthquakes, famines . . . Jesus predicts all those. But when the kingdom of heaven prevails throughout the world, then wars will cease, he says. The message of Jesus is universal peace. Anyway, we in the Vatican have our own diplomats: we often negotiate peace deals, and it isn't easy. Apart from the Swiss Guard, a relic of the papal army of old, we have no soldiers among us. Do you remember what Stalin said after winning the Second World War? "How many divisions has the pope?" The answer is simple. None. But we have the strength of the spirit.'

Theo looked sceptical. 'Through loving enemies? And it works?'

'Jesus says: Love your enemies, do good to those who hate you.'

'That reminds me of a remark I once read about, made by Roberto Rossellini, the filmmaker,' said Aunt Martha. ' "If you have enemies, plague them with love." It's a pretty good solution.'

'If you like,' the prudent Cardinal conceded. 'It's true that there's no great virtue, as Jesus says, in loving those who love you. Whereas loving your enemies . . . !'

'I couldn't do it,' said Theo. 'And anyway, what's the point?'

'The point is to imitate God the Father, who forgives. To bring back peace. That's better, don't you think?'

'No, I don't,' Theo retorted. 'If someone does you harm, they shouldn't get away with it.'

'If someone does you harm, let them be. That was the martyrs' big idea, and it's with us to this day. There are cases of nuns being tortured in Argentina or Algeria, or monks who are murdered, when all they've done is help. Maybe you remember the seven candles that were kept burning in Notre Dame? Seven flames for the lives of seven monks kidnapped in Algeria. Eventually we learned that all seven had had their throats cut. Then Cardinal Lustiger blew out the candles one by one, and solemnly recalled that we must love our enemies.'

'That's not fair,' said Theo.

'Fairness is something that only God really knows about. Jesus talks about charity. Sharing, giving to others, not keeping what we have to ourselves. That's why his message spread so fast: it spoke to the poor.'

'Come on, you're kidding me,' cried Theo. 'After all the treasures you were showing me before? And your car, and your beautiful robes, eh?'

'OK,' said the Cardinal. 'But the faithful have to be taught, and that's for the Church to take care of. Giving to the poor needs organization, giving orders needs order, and order requires a hierarchy.'

'That's feeble, Ottavio, very feeble,' Aunt Martha remarked.

'But we've got rid of all sorts of useless vestments, we've removed the ostrich feathers from the papal throne, and we've simplified the ceremonial. We humbly wash the feet of the poor . . . Even the Pope!'

'Once a year!' Aunt Martha objected.

'But we give a vast amount! We run a tremendous number of charities.'

'Don't start again, you two,' Theo broke in. 'Anyway it's true, I know some Catholics who take care of homeless people.'

'Aha!' said the Cardinal triumphantly.

Aunt Martha now raised the subject of the continual rebellions faced by the Catholic Church over repeated accusations that it had forgotten the message of the Gospels. The Church was too rich, it exploited the poor instead of helping them, it flaunted its gold, and its affluent monasteries: it made itself hated, and was sometimes overthrown.

The Cardinal retorted that there were popes who had set out to reclaim the truth of the message, and that Pope John XXIII, for example, had profoundly transformed and rejuvenated the Catholic Church in the middle of the twentieth century, so it wasn't too old. In any case, the faithful had good reason to shake the old tree and to lop the dead branches, because pruning a tree makes it bear fruit. And that was also the meaning of the death and resurrection of Christ, who, like the lamb of the sacrifice, had allowed himself to be killed.

'Lamb or shepherd?' asked Theo. 'It's not the same thing!'

'Yes, it is,' the Cardinal replied. 'He is shepherd and lamb at the same time. Shepherd of God, because he rescues the lost sheep, the poor and forsaken, and lamb of God, sacrificed in place of all the rest.'

'So if Jesus is the shepherd, then you are one of the sheepdogs?' said Theo.

'Some sort of dog, OK,' said the prelate. 'A plump, well-fed one, as you see. I can bark, but I don't bite.'

Nightfall was coming. The chauffeur started the car, and they headed for the city. When they drove past a patch of waste ground where children were playing by the light of street lamps, Dom Ottavio pointed out that here were the new disinherited of the earth – not in the country, or in the city, but in the space between.

Theo had fallen asleep in the car. As he carried him up to his room, the Cardinal commented on his pink cheeks and fresh complexion. He stayed asleep till dinner time. Aunt Martha and Dom Ottavio sat facing each other at his bedside, watching him sleep.

'You really think he's looking better?' she asked. 'I'm so afraid.'

'If only you could pray!' the Cardinal whispered.

'But I do pray, Ottavio, in my own way,' she murmured.

161

'They' arrive

The sound of the doorbell roused Theo from his sleep, and he blinked his eyes. Sunshine was slanting through a chink in the curtain: it was daytime. A chair scraped. There was someone in his room. Breakfast time already? How he'd slept!

Someone? A silhouette like Mum's. No, couldn't be, she was in Paris. He was dreaming . . .

'So, how's our travelling reporter?' said his father's voice.

Theo woke up and shot upright. It wasn't a dream, they were here!

'Wow!' he said, reaching up to hug them. 'So "They" were you! I never guessed.'

CHAPTER 9

Images of God

Reunion

Melina sank on to the bed and smothered her son with kisses. Jerome blinked back a tear, groped for words, failed to find any, and patted Theo's hand. Yes, here they were; no, they wouldn't stay long, just for the weekend. Their visit had been planned all along: Paris to Rome was such a short hop, a two-hour flight, easy enough. Whereas after . . .

'After Rome?' said Theo. 'Then if you can't fly out to see me from here on, it's because we'll be too far away.'

Melina sighed. What about food, at least? How was his appetite? Was he sleeping well? And wasn't he getting tired of blood tests at every stopover?

'Just you ask Aunt Martha,' he grunted.

Putting on a brave face, Melina suggested that after breakfast they might try a quiet stroll round the block, then come back to the hotel for a rest.

'No fear!' said Theo. 'I'm sick of resting.'

'OK,' said Jerome, 'we'll do some sightseeing. Get dressed.'

Theo made a dive for the shower.

'Jerome, this isn't sensible,' said Melina.

'The platelet count has risen,' said Jerome. 'We may not be able to explain it, but we have the results.'

'But they may have made a mistake. Italian hospitals . . .'

'Stop it! All over the world, we've selected the best. Would you rather watch him waste away in some hospital bed in Paris? No? Then calm down.'

'Where are we going?' came Theo's voice, muted by the towel he was using to dry his tousled hair after the shower. 'I'm starving!'

Theo's first assessment

Croissants, bread and butter, two sorts of jam, Theo wolfed it all down under his mother's delighted eye. There was an unmistakable improvement. The least they could say was that Aunt Martha's unorthodox therapy was starting to have an effect.

'So tell us about it,' said his father. 'What's the most interesting thing you've seen?'

'Where do I start?' Theo enthused. 'I've seen mosques and churches, I've seen the banks of the Nile, sailed past ibises standing on their black legs, peasant women balancing jugs on their heads, papyrus reeds growing . . . oh, and I've seen the Pyramids!'

'Nothing too religious there,' Jerome remarked. 'Sounds more like a tourist trip to me.'

'Well you're wrong there, Dad,' said Theo. 'Because the most interesting part is the people, Aunt Martha's friends. She knows loads of people, Aunt Martha. Rabbi Eliezer, Father Antoine, Sheikh Suleiman, Amal, she's terrific, this batty old guy who does archaeology in Luxor, and even this funny Cardinal she calls by his first name . . .'

'Who do you like best?' asked Melina. 'Amal?'

'Oh, they're all really nice,' Theo replied. 'Amal told me lots of stuff about Egyptian mythology. I do like her. But the others aren't bad either, you know . . .'

'You're bound to have your favourite though,' said Dad. 'I know you.'

'Hmm,' said Theo. 'Not really. They're all very religious, except for Amal. Even the archaeologist is religious in his way.'

'What do you mean?'

'He believes in the Egyptian gods, of course!' Theo declared. 'And so do I!'

'OK, fine,' said Dad. 'What about the other religions?'

'They're all the same,' said Theo. 'They believe in God, they want what's best for the human race, and they spend their time quarrelling. They talk about peace, and they're always picking on each other. Take the Christians. Did you know there were so many different kinds?

Armenians, Copts, Ethiopians, Greek Orthodox, Russian Orthodox, it just goes on and on . . .'

'That's right,' Dad laughed. 'What a mix-up, eh?'

'Not when you think about it,' said Theo. 'At first, Christianity was only a small bunch of people, but when they got settled all over the place, that's when they each started fighting for their own way of life. They had different traditions, you can see how it happened. So with a mess like that, it naturally took a while to sort it out.'

'Naturally,' his father echoed thoughtfully. 'And what did you make of Judaism?'

'Oh,' said Theo, 'I do enjoy Joseph, who is kind, and Moses, because he's always right. I'm going to read their Bible – it's full of stories. The one about Ruth I like a lot, because God really gets in a twist there. He tells Jews not to marry pagan women, then fixes it to happen all the same. God is very strange. Sometimes he's an ogre – a bit like you when you're feeling bad-tempered about something – and sometimes a friend, like you when you give me a hug. The Jews don't speak his name, not ever, they love him so much. They're meant to obey him, but it's easier said than done . . . They take their punishment as if they've got it coming, but they don't half make life complicated for themselves.'

'I don't suppose you took too kindly to Islam,' said Melina.

'Why not?' asked Theo. 'One night, my friend the Sheikh came to visit me, and there was something so reassuring about his being there, that I slept like a baby.'

'Ah,' said Melina with a frown. 'So you haven't come across any Muslim fundamentalists yet. Well, you'll see . . .'

'Melina!' Jerome warned. 'Let Theo judge for himself.'

'Ah, but this is Mum's Greek blood talking,' said Theo with a big smile.

'What gives you that idea?' asked Dad in surprise.

'It's because after the fall of Constantinople the Ottoman Turks occupied Greece, and they were Muslims,' Theo explained. 'The Greeks resisted, and they were Orthodox. Isn't that it?'

Jerome and Melina exchanged glances. Theo was as precocious as ever.

'Why stuff your head so full of notions?' said Melina, under her breath. 'Couldn't you just enjoy the travelling?'

Theo had not heard her appeal. 'Anyway,' he continued, 'religions must always resist. That's how they get strong, I've noticed that. Without persecution, there's no religion. They need mart — '

'Can't you give your brain a rest?' his father broke in.

'I'd like to,' said Theo, 'but I can't stop . . . Oh but I can though. Once, in Luxor . . . hey, I'd forgotten this . . .'

He stopped. All of a sudden his fuzzy memories of the Sheikha's dance came rushing into focus once again, and his mind spun off at a delicious tangent.

'Theo!' said Mum. 'Stop your daydreaming!'

He made no answer. The cockerel's blood, its throat slit open, the acrid smoke, the giddy feeling . . . The drumbeat, the smell of roses and incense, his cousin from the Underworld, the bride . . .

'Theo!' His mother sounded anxious.

'Yes,' he replied distractedly. 'You know, Mum, I didn't tell you, but now I have a twin.'

'God help us,' she gasped.

'I felt him there,' Theo continued. 'I was the bride, and I danced with him . . . My twin from the Underworld. In Luxor.'

Melina spilled her coffee on the tablecloth. Jerome took her hand and held it tight.

'Lucky for you, then,' he tried to smile. 'Still, I wouldn't let it get to you, son.'

'I don't,' said Theo. 'It's just that he makes me feel better.'

Martha's got some explaining to do, thought Jerome. What's she been up to now?

A god with a cobra round his neck

Aunt Martha had gone out on business for the day, after suggesting that they should take Theo sightseeing. Jerome decided to visit Hadrian's Villa, some way east of the city, but its legion of statues left Theo cold.

'Superb, aren't they, Theo?' his father enthused when they stopped in front of the Etruscan reclining figures.

'I suppose so,' Theo replied.

'Are you feeling bored?'

'A bit,' said Theo. 'When do we see Aunt Martha again?'

Then it was the Forum. Theo still felt bored. On the Capitol he listened dutifully to Jerome when he talked about the geese that warned the Romans of danger, about the Tarpeian Rock, which symbolized the fall from glory, and about the primitive huts of Romulus and Remus, the twin founders of Rome.

'Where's Aunt Martha?' he repeated as they walked back down the hill.

This was too much for Melina. 'Shut up about Martha!' she barked.

'That's right, Theo,' said his father awkwardly. 'We've come all the way from Paris to see you. Pay us some attention!'

'All right. But I've got to phone Fatou. Unless you help me to decipher the latest message . . .'

'There's lots of time,' said Dad. 'Look where you are! This is the Eternal City.'

'I don't care,' said Theo mulishly. 'I want to understand my message.'

They had to stop in a café, sit down at a table, unfold the piece of paper and read the spattered message. Sitting on my sacred . . . I am the eternal dancer.

For the first smudged word, Dad suggested that it must refer to some animal.

'A horse?' asked Theo.

'No,' said Dad. 'Think!'

'A donkey? A cow?'

'You're burning!'

'A bull,' said Theo. 'Zeus transformed into a bull? But Zeus doesn't dance.'

It wasn't Zeus, and the rest was no clearer.

Come to the banks of my river, come to the oldest city in the world.

'There are rivers all over,' said Theo. 'I've seen the Nile, and ditto the Tiber in Rome. The world's oldest city is Thebes, in Egypt. Are we going back to Egypt?'

But it wasn't Egypt. Theo dialled Fatou's number.

Clue three: snake, trident

'Is that you, Theo?' purred the distant voice. 'How are you?'

'I'm fine,' said Theo. 'Except I'm having trouble with the third message. Also, there are three words smudged by drops of water.'

'That's a shame. Do you want your clue?'

'I'll say I do,' said Theo. 'No choice.'

'Wait . . . Message number three . . . Here it is. I wear a snake round my neck, and I carry a trident in my hand.'

'Oh hell. Who's that? Nothing else?'

'Yes,' said the voice. Look at the pictures in the dictionary of mythology. Will that help?'

167

'It'll have to,' sighed Theo. 'What about you? How are you?'

'I miss you,' said the voice. 'I'd really love to see you.'

'Me too. But you know, I'm feeling OK.'

'I'm glad. Are you going to get well?'

'I wish I knew. We'll have to wait and see.'

'Lots of love,' the voice whispered. 'As ever.'

A click, and Fatou was gone. Theo brushed at a tear and asked to return to the hotel to consult his books. In the dictionary there were gods sitting on rocks, birds and thrones, perching on branches, lying in boats, impaled on spears and bristling with arrows. Round their necks they wore nothing but necklaces. Though Theo pored over the pages he could not find the dancer with a snake coiled round his neck – not only that, but riding on a bull!

Feeling frustrated, he snapped the book shut just as Aunt Martha came sailing in. She leaned over to give him a kiss.

'So, Sherlock Holmes, are you stumped?'

Theo reached up to her. 'Darling Aunt Martha,' he entreated, 'I really need your help.'

'Why this rush of affection, Theo?' she whispered, stroking his hair.

'I see you two are getting along,' said Melina, with a trace of jealousy.

'Come on, Theo.' Aunt Martha looked embarrassed. 'Make an effort!'

'I can't find it,' he said pathetically. 'Help me.'

Aunt Martha opened the book again and turned to a particular page.

'There,' she said. 'See what a small picture it is. That's why you missed it.'

It was a completely naked god, with blue skin and two pairs of arms. One held a trident, another a small drum, a third a flame, a fourth a sort of rattle. He was laughing, and he had a snake coiled round his neck – a smiling cobra, with its hood spread.

'He's fantastic,' said Theo. 'Who is he? Shiva. But he isn't dancing.'

'Yes he is,' said Aunt Martha. 'He doesn't seem to be, but his two legs are dancing.'

'But why has he got four arms and only two legs?'

'We're off again,' she said. 'Questions, always questions! By the way, there's one you haven't asked me, Theo. You haven't asked where we're going next.'

'To India,' Theo instantly replied. 'The article says so. So the river is the Ganges, and the town is Benares, because I knew that from the start. It's obvious. Hey, but there are still words missing in the message. "I am worshipped there, and I . . ." I what?'

'"Set free",' said Dad. 'The smudged words say "set free". It'll come to you later. Meanwhile, you can go and lie down, and no nonsense!'

Melina's fury

As soon as the door swung closed behind her son, Melina exploded. Her sister-in-law had broken her word. Hadn't she sworn never to tell Theo about his twin who'd died at birth? How could she . . .

'But Melina, I swear . . .' Martha's voice shook with anxiety. 'I didn't tell him anything!'

Melina refused to believe her. Theo had talked about his twin. Not only that, he thought he had met him. Well . . . ?

'Well, you remember me telling you that Theo took part in a Zar ceremony in Luxor . . .'

'That's right,' said her brother. 'You also said that Theo felt better when he came out of it. I don't see the connection.'

'Well . . .'

At first Aunt Martha faltered. The connection wasn't easy to explain, and the whole story would probably sound unbelievable to them. Martha had seen Theo pass out without warning, then come alive again by dancing . . .

'Alive again?' Melina was shocked by the words. 'But he wasn't dead!'

Finally, when he came out of his trance, Martha had distinctly heard Theo refer to his twin. Facts were facts.

'Theo in a trance,' said Jerome. 'Basically it isn't surprising. He's such a dreamer.'

'Yes, isn't he?' said Martha with relief. 'Anyway, according to the Sheikha he really did meet his twin. I wonder if you shouldn't tell him the truth.'

'No!' cried Melina. 'He's too highly strung.'

'But what if this hidden twin was drawing him into the underworld kingdom without your knowing?' Aunt Martha murmured. 'Family secrets sometimes do so much harm . . .'

'And what if the truth did even more?' Jerome replied. 'Theo is seriously ill, you know.'

'Of course I do,' she told him. 'Only too well. And I'd be the last to upset him. Let's leave things as they are.'

'That's more like it,' said Melina at once. 'The main thing is that the results are improving, and I don't see what my dead baby has to do with blood tests.'

Aunt Martha was on the point of saying that the stillborn twin wasn't exactly irrelevant either, but she restrained herself. Martha had her own ideas about the way to cure her nephew, and the first stage had fulfilled all her hopes.

The god whose wife caught fire

Dom Ottavio reappeared next day, and as the news of the medical tests was good he suggested a short visit to the Vatican Museums.

'Not every one of them,' he added. 'I've learned my lesson! Just the ethnological part. I think you'll be interested, *bambino*.'

'Provided you don't hold my hand. And that we stop when I want to. Promise?'

The Cardinal promised.

'The buildings of the Ethnological Missionary Museum are completely new,' Dom Ottavio explained as they entered the foyer of a modern building. 'They contain gifts presented to many popes, as well as some quite rare collections. All the world's religions are represented here, *bambino* – it's an illustrated guide to your journey.'

'But there are Christians in every country,' Aunt Martha added. 'That's why this museum is called "missionary" too: you'll see all the ancient gods that the Roman Catholic priesthood wanted to replace with their own God.'

'All gods lead to a single God,' the Cardinal murmured. 'The key thing is belief in divinity. We've had this whole debate a hundred times, Martha. Let Theo find things out for himself.'

Theo stroked a pair of Chinese lions, strolled past the model of the Temple of Heaven in Beijing, paused for a moment in front of the altar to the ancestors, glanced at the Buddhist statues, and swept straight through the Japanese section as if it wasn't there . . .

'You're going too fast!' called Martha.

'I'm looking for somebody,' said Theo, hurrying on. 'Tibet . . . No. Mongolia, certainly not. Indochina . . . Ah, found it. India.'

And he came to a stop in front of the statue of a god with a snake coiled round his neck, a big cobra with its head reared up. And he really was riding on a bull.

'That's him,' he said. 'My Indian god. Hey look, the name's not spelled the same.'

'There are several ways of writing Indian names,' said the Cardinal. 'Siva with an S or Shiva, it's the same name. But he isn't just Indian: he belongs to the Hindu religion. His bull is called Nandi.'

'The bull has a name as well?'

'Nandi is divine, *bambino*. He has shrines of his own.'

'And the lady next to Shiva?'

'She is his wife, Parvati,' Aunt Martha replied. 'Hindu gods are hardly ever single. Shiva's first wife was a goddess named Sati, but her father wanted nothing at all to do with his divine son-in-law, because Shiva is a savage, brutal god, with no manners at all. Sati's pride as a wife was so injured that she decided to burn herself alive, to take revenge on her tyrannical father.'

'And did she do it?' asked Melina in horror. 'These myths are so cruel!'

'She burst into flames and was swallowed by the earth.'

'Poor Shiva!' said Theo. 'He was all alone.'

'No, because later on Sati was reincarnated under the name of Parvati. Now, ever since losing his wife, Shiva had been plunged into an endless meditation that nothing could rouse him from. To win back her husband, Sati – who had now become Parvati – endured some incredible ordeals. She stood on one leg for so many millions of years that plants started growing over her body and she became like a tree. In the end, touched by the wife he had failed to acknowledge, Shiva emerged from his trance and married her.'

'Wait,' said Theo. 'You're saying she was the same woman?'

'Yes and no. Hindus believe that once it leaves the body the soul is instantly reincarnated in another. The soul doesn't change, but the body is different.'

'That's a marvellous idea,' said Theo. 'How many times can you be reincarnated?'

'Millions of times,' said Aunt Martha. 'Until the soul has come far enough along the road to reach perfection and finally dissolve into thin air. Because, don't get this wrong, Theo, the ideal of the Hindus is to put an end to reincarnation. And Shiva happens to be the one god with the power to stop the cycle.'

'He sets free,' Theo continued. 'I get it. "I am worshipped there, and I set free." But I don't want to be set free. I'd rather be reincarnated.'

Melina shuddered. Jerome put an arm around her shoulders. The Cardinal cleared his throat before cutting in to say:

'There's no hurry, *bambino*. Besides, the Hindus have a tremendous sense of life – don't you agree, Martha?'

'Oh yes,' she sighed. 'Shiva is the god of Life and Death, and Dance and Music, all at the same time. That tells you a lot!'

'I've seen films shot in Benares, with people swarming all along the Ganges to bathe – it looks tremendous,' said Theo, suddenly excited. 'Could I bathe too?'

'We'll see,' said Aunt Martha. 'I'll take you to see my friend the high priest. He'll explain the rites much better than I can.'

'My word!' the Cardinal whistled. 'A high priest? You certainly do have contacts everywhere!'

'High priest of the temple of the monkey god, if you please . . .'

'A monkey god!' said Theo thoughtfully. 'Then in India there are gods who are men?'

'Any number!' Aunt Martha replied. 'They can be monkeys, cows, bulls, eagles, horses . . . stones, even.'

'Isn't that precisely what you call idolatry, Cardinal?' asked Jerome, with a grin.

The Cardinal shrugged his shoulders. Christendom was more tolerant of animal gods than Islam and Judaism: it accepted images of God.

'Idols just anticipate the human form, that's all,' he answered after a brief silence. 'In time, people discovered the Son of man, created in God's image. The divine is everywhere present . . . It's nothing to kick up a fuss about.'

'Actually, in Egypt they have a cat goddess,' said Theo. 'So it's just the same in India and Egypt? Great!'

Theo absolves the Cardinal

It was the last day in Rome. Theo used his camera and snapped his parents – then he could take them with him, he said. In fact he ambushed them in bed in the early morning, and woke them with his flash. At table the Cardinal – determined, come what may, to complete his pupil's apprenticeship – tried in vain to fit the Gospel parables in.

'But they're so beautiful,' Dom Ottavio pleaded, brandishing his fork. 'Let me tell you the parable of the fig tree . . .'

'Figs are out of season,' said Theo with his mouth full of spaghetti.

'Then what about the wise virgins? No? The three servants . . . ?'

'Another time,' said Theo gently. 'Otherwise I'll get in a muddle, you see?'

'He's right, Ottavio. And we'll be seeing other Christians in other places,' Aunt Martha reminded him.

'A pity,' said the Cardinal. 'It's still better in Rome.'

'Sin of pride!' said Jerome, raising his glass ironically. 'Isn't that wrong, Cardinal?'

'Look here!' the Cardinal protested. 'I'm the confessor here. Don't get our roles confused, Mister Director of Research!'

'I've never understood what confessing meant,' said Theo.

'Christians can have all their sins forgiven,' Dom Ottavio answered earnestly. 'They have only to go to a priest and tell him their sins, and he gives absolution in the name of God. "Absolution" means "total solution", and therefore dissolution, erasure.'

'That's convenient,' said Theo. 'That way, you can do anything you please. And what about you, don't you ever sin?'

'Of course,' said the Cardinal. 'Except I have the power to take confession, and your father hasn't. There you are – I have no wife or children, but I can give absolution. One can't have everything.'

'It's sad, all the same,' said Theo.

'Do I seem sad, Theo?' the Cardinal asked. 'Seriously, tell me . . .'

'No,' said Theo. 'Deep down, you have a great sense of humour.'

'Splendid!' the Cardinal exclaimed. 'A great sense of humour, for the greater glory of God!'

'Cardinals like you make one feel more sympathetic to the Church,' Jerome admitted. 'And I'm not fond of priests . . .'

'So I've noticed,' the prelate cut in. 'Your son has mentioned it often enough. Well, you'll find that he ends up as a believer in spite of you.'

'It's a bet,' said Theo. 'Believer in what, do you think?'

'That, I don't know,' Dom Ottavio replied. 'But what I'm convinced of is that if you look hard into all the faces of God, you'll find one you can't look away from.'

'If that happens, I'll write and let you know,' Theo promised.

The Cardinal takes over

Theo's parents flew back to Paris on the same day that he and Aunt Martha were due to fly to Delhi. At the airport, Melina wept so hard that her son burst into tears. Jerome and Aunt Martha did not dare to part them. Time was running short.

Then the Cardinal produced his handkerchief – a big white cotton one.

'Blow your nose,' he ordered Theo, in a tone so authoritative that the tears dried up and Theo took the handkerchief.

173

'You too, Madame,' the Cardinal instructed, as he handed the object to Melina. 'You do yourself no good with all these tears. Crying is all very well, but not in excess.'

Melina blew her nose and dried her tears.

'Excellent,' said the Cardinal, methodically folding his handkerchief again. 'Now, go ahead and kiss each other nicely. There. *Bambino*, kiss your father . . . Madame, go that way with your husband, if you will. And you, Theo, come this way, with your aunt.'

Everything was sorted out, and Martha was impressed.

'My friend,' she murmured, 'what a wonderful master of ceremonies you make. You settled all that in a trice.'

'When it comes to managing events, the Vatican is a first-class training ground,' the Cardinal whispered. 'We've had quite a bit of practice, you know.'

'Mum!' called Theo, running over to Melina. 'Take my seeds of lentils. They'll sprout for you!'

'Thank you, darling,' said Melina softly. 'I'll take good care of them. Off you go, my precious . . .'

CHAPTER 10

India's Seven Faces

Aunt Martha's anxieties

As soon as they were settled in the plane, Theo fell fast asleep. As a seasoned long-distance flyer, Aunt Martha took off her shoes at once, stretched her legs, and opened the *Herald Tribune*, but her heart wasn't in it. What if the only outcome of their expedition turned out to be the shortening of Theo's life? What if she was totally mistaken, and the doctors . . .

'Get a grip, girl,' she told herself. 'The specialists have admitted defeat. They've given him up for lost, but they can't say why. Unknown virus . . . Tropical-type poisoning, possible airline vector . . . Come on! I know I'm right.'

But the Indian stage of the trip would not be easy. The shock of sheer vastness, the density and pressure of the crowds, the strange-looking gods, the fervent devotion to so many divinities . . . Martha ticked off her plan of action point by point. First, talk Theo into agreeing to wait before they faced the dangers of Benares, for the banks of the Ganges were lined with funeral pyres. She stared hard into the blue of the sky, and thought about the tongues of flame in the night, and the ashes scattered in the water.

'He won't see the pyres,' she muttered. 'I know that there are much better things in Benares for my Theo.'

But however much she knew, she could not help trembling in advance. It was not for nothing that the city of Benares worshipped the god of Destruction! In what form might he reveal himself? Death or life?

'Stick to the omens on the Stock Exchange, my girl,' Martha told herself, and skimmed abstractedly through the prices of her shares in Frankfurt and Tokyo.

The eight religions of india

Six hours of flying, six hours of airline meals, a film, and a howling chorus of babies. Theo woke up and eyed the Indian mothers who paraded their kids up and down with a glorious lack of concern, and the tall girls with their raven braids plaited with silver threads. Strange old men clad in three-piece suits, and with turbans pointed at the front, bought tax-free beauty products.

'Aunt Martha,' he whispered, 'why do they keep their beard in a net?'

'Because they're Sikhs,' she murmured. 'Their religion forbids them to cut any of their hair. Under the turban they wear a topknot, and when the beard is long they fold it up to keep it tidy. That's what the net is for – and they also use one for their hair . . .'

'More rules about hair!' Theo exclaimed. 'Why do they have to keep controlling it?'

'But this time it isn't the women who have to obey, it's the men. They swear an oath in memory of the persecution their ancestors suffered in the past, and because their master ordered them to be constantly ready to defend themselves. Their hair identifies them as warriors, and they are not the only example: the same myth appears in the Bible. Do you know the story of Samson?'

'The guy whose girlfriend cuts his hair off to take away his strength?'

'This chap was a Nazirite of God. You remember they had to let their hair grow, because hair gave a man the strength of his God. Well, Samson fell in love with an enemy of the Jews, a woman of the Philistine tribe. Worse luck for him. Delilah cut his hair while he was asleep, so no more link with God. He was captured, and they gouged out his eyes, and chained him, and put him in prison. Some time later the Philistines held a festival in the temple of their god, Dagon, and to make a mockery of Samson they brought him there, and made him stand between two pillars. But he'd been in prison for a long time, and his hair had started to grow again. Then . . .'

'I know!' cried Theo. 'His strength came back, and he pulled the pillars down, and the temple collapsed and crushed them all.'

'You see, hair often ties believers to their god. In India, it's a tuft in the crown of a Brahman's shaven head.'

Theo acknowledged that this was an interesting question, and turned his attention to a Buddhist monk in a crimson robe. Then his eyes strayed, first to a fair-skinned American woman wearing a turban as immaculate as her long trousers and tunic, and then to the rings that glittered on every finger of a well-fed Indian sprawled fast asleep in his seat. This flight to India was no ordinary journey.

'What an odd religion,' he remarked, for want of anything better to say.

'Whose do you mean?'

'The Indian religion.'

Aunt Martha rolled her eyes. 'Come on now, *Theo mio*, haven't I told you that there's not just one religion in India?'

'Oh yes.' He tried to sound contrite. 'How many did you say?'

'At least eight,' said Aunt Martha. 'Hinduism, Buddhism, Jainism, Islam, Zoroastrianism, Sikhism, Christianity, and even Judaism.'

'I can't keep up,' wailed Theo. 'Can we go over it again?'

With unfeigned patience, Aunt Martha explained that the oldest roots were in Brahmanism.

'But you didn't say that name just now!' Theo protested.

'I know, and that's because it no longer exists in its archaic form. Brahmanism had grown so old, and so outdated, that it reformed itself in the third century under the name of Hinduism. Right now, more than seven hundred million of the Indian people are Hindus.'

'Wow!' said Theo. 'That's a lot of people.'

One of the most extraordinary things about India was the sheer number of people everywhere. The city of Calcutta alone had more inhabitants than the whole of Austria, and before too long the whole population would have crossed the billion mark. There were single states in India with more people than the whole of France, and . . .

'Stop!' said Theo, 'you're making my head spin.'

And no wonder. Especially when his aunt told Theo that in Hinduism there were more than a million gods – some would put the figure as high as three hundred and thirty million. In other words, no one could really say. But he needn't panic, there were some he'd get to know.

'I only know two,' said Theo. 'Shiva and Parvati.'

That wasn't so bad. The main thing was to understand the core of Hinduism, which Aunt Martha summed up as three concepts: respect for the cosmic order, obedience to one's fate, and – dominating every

177

action in life – the duty of purity, laid down at birth by the gods for all Hindus, according to their caste of origin. Because purity was not the same for everyone. The pyramid of social categories, or '*varna*', specific to India divided Hindus into three high orders – priests and scholars, warriors and rulers, farmers and traders – and a lower order containing the menial castes that served them. Only the purest, the Brahmans, were allowed to read the sacred texts and supervise their strict application. The warriors exercised political power and defended the national territory, and the traders took care of business. All male members of the three high *varna* were 'twice-born', which meant that at the age of eight, eleven and fourteen respectively they passed through an initiation ceremony seen as a second birth, which transformed them, and them alone, into pious Hindus.

Beneath the three *varna* of the twice-born were the thousands of menial castes, classified by their levels of increasing impurity, down to the lowest tolerable degree of humanity. But below the human level came the others – all the others. Lowest on the list of the excluded were the most impure, those who attended to the dead: because when the soul had departed the body remained – the ultimate impurity. In the traditional conception, these people were so dirty, so 'defiled', that the system shut them out altogether: they had no caste, and therefore no place. During the colonial period the British referred to them as 'untouchables', so wide was the gulf between them and other Hindus. Fate had imposed on them the most slavish of possible existences, never to be evaded. For the lives of all Hindus were a function of their status at birth, totally dictated by the nature of the cosmic order and by the caste system that guaranteed the general social purity – a fabric strenuously preserved by the twice-born, and especially by their topmost grade, the Brahmans, to whom the knowledge of the sacred texts belonged.

Admittedly, in order to uphold the careful balance between the privileged pure and the unranked impure, the Hindu deities had multiplied. Yet as Professor Laplace, the archaeologist, had explained about the Egyptian religion, they related to a unique idea of divinity, the Absolute – known to all Hindus, whatever their caste of origin, as 'Brahman'. Brahman was pure being, the boundless, the infinite, the All, which has no form. And all individuals contained within themselves their own reflection of the Absolute, the *atman*, or true Self, the individual soul fated to rejoin the All through the release of death before the next reincarnation, before the ultimate freedom, and at last perhaps to take leave of life altogether. The plural Brahmans – members of the priestly caste – took their name from the singular Brahman, the Absolute, whose guardians they were. And so, by performing the sacred rites they guaranteed to all Hindus communion with the unique Absolute.

But there was more. Before Brahmanism there was only a single goddess in India, and she was Aditi, the Mother, the source of life, whose name in Sanskrit, the classical language of ancient India, means boundlessness. Then, it was said, the Brahmans took charge of India and the great goddess vanished under the influx of masculine gods. Of course, the Hindus respected the order of nature; to every god, his goddess. They invented divine couples: to each god his wife, and to each wife her function. But if you spoke to a pious urban Hindu you found that the image of the single divinity had not disappeared: because if the good Hindu decided to dedicate his life to the gods of his choice, his individual soul sought the Absolute, as it does throughout the world. Assisting the various tasks within society, the Hindu deities each symbolized an element of life: for every activity there was a god, or a goddess. For wealth, the goddess Lakshmi; for the arts, the goddess Sarasvati; for the home and business, the god Ganesa, and so on . . .

'Handy,' said Theo. 'I'll have to find one for myself.'

But now that they had surveyed the Hindu deities, others remained. 'Buddha?' said Theo.

'The Buddha was not a god!' Aunt Martha exclaimed. 'The Buddha was a prince, born of a queen, before he renounced the world. When he ventured outside the royal household he discovered human suffering in the form . . . Well, Theo, the form of two dreadful forces, disease and old age. Then, along the way, he met a monk with a peaceful face, and the experience caused him to withdraw from the world, to meditate until he reached enlightenment. Later in his life, many disciples came to him and began to worship him.'

'Right,' said Theo. 'So the Buddha became a god.'

But Aunt Martha felt guilty, because she had deliberately omitted the third form of suffering, the one which had led the young Prince Gautama to renounce his former life: the sight of a corpse. Dismissing her remorse, she proceeded to tell Theo how in the same era and not far from the Buddha's birthplace lived another young prince who also renounced the world and, under the name of Mahavira, established Jainism, a religion related to Buddhism. But the most striking feature of both men was that they did not belong to the Brahman order, the guarantors of purity, but to the order of princes and warriors, just a notch below. This went some way to explaining why it was that, in their concern for equality, Mahavira and the Buddha invented two religions that were open to all, without distinction of caste. These were important steps forward.

Mahavira, the great teacher of Jainism, preached absolute respect for living creatures, which it was forbidden to harm. Therefore the Jains were strict vegetarians, eating neither eggs nor roots, and their greatest fear was of killing any animal, no matter how small. They would sweep the road in front of them so as not to kill an insect, and they wore a white muslin mask over their mouths for fear of inadvertently swallowing some invisible microscopic life form.

'That's nice, you must admit,' said Theo.

'It's nice,' Aunt Martha agreed, 'but it's awkward too. Also, they're divided into two branches: the white-clothed and the space-clothed – in other words, those who go totally naked.'

'Nudists?' said Theo. 'Why not?'

'Of course . . . Except that nudists don't go naked all their life, but the space-clothed never wear clothes.'

Theo started counting on his fingers. 'Hinduism, Buddhism, Jainism, plus the three I've met, Jews, Christians and Muslims, that makes six religions. And Zoroaster's people you've talked about already – that's seven.'

That left only Sikhism, whose god was worshipped in the form of a living Book.

'Living?' said Theo. 'You're joking!'

In Sikh temples, called gurdwaras – meaning 'doorway to the guru' – Theo would see the sacred book with his own eyes. There were no fewer than seventeen million Sikhs in India, almost as many as there were Christian – twenty million. There were one hundred and twenty million Muslims, four million Jains, five million Buddhists, and fewer than a hundred thousand Zoroastrians, better known as Parsis. As for the Jews, there were only a few thousand left – a handful. The rest had emigrated to Israel.

'Because of persecutions,' said Theo.

'Actually no. If there's one country where Jews have never, ever, been persecuted, that country is India, Theo. The Jews of India have emigrated on their own initiative, simply because they too wanted to return to Jerusalem.'

'After hearing "next year in Jerusalem" so often, they were bound to want to go. But I'm glad if people are allowed to do what they want in India.'

Aunt Martha winced. 'Er, yes and no. Between Hindus and Muslims it isn't that simple. Trivial causes lead to terrible events. Pigs and cows can trigger massacres . . . Don't give me that look, Theo, I did say pigs and cows. Every now and then, to stir up trouble, Hindus throw a pig's tail over the wall of a mosque, because in Islam the pig is strictly forbidden, as it is in the Bible. That leads to the Muslims throwing a piece of beef over the Hindu temple walls, because in Hinduism the cow is sacred.'

'That's true,' said Theo. 'Will we see any cows?'

They certainly would. Two hundred million sacred cows were pretty hard to ignore. But they weren't much like their European cousins: quite skinny, and they didn't give much milk.

'So what are they used for?' Theo asked.

Milking was allowed, but in general cows did whatever they felt like. They could browse, wander, dawdle, lie down in the middle of the railway tracks – in other words, they were free.

'It's great, a country like that,' said Theo admiringly. 'What about other animals?'

Nearly all of them were depicted as gods, except for dogs, which got nothing but sticks and stones, because these poor animals were seen as reincarnations of the souls of thieves. In India you could find a sacred monkey, a sacred bull, an eagle god, a horse god, an elephant god, and even gods in the form of hordes of rats. In Bikaner these charming animals were worshipped in a temple consecrated to the souls of a low caste which had somehow been promoted to the level of rodents. The story didn't indicate the caste they had started from.

'Fleas?' Theo suggested. 'Worshipping rats is weird, you must admit!'

'It's not the last weird thing you'll find in India,' Aunt Martha replied.

'And the lady in white over there, with her funny turban, what's she?'

'Oh, she'll be British or American,' said Aunt Martha dismissively. 'She must belong to the "Daughters of Brahma" sect. They're quite harmless. When they feel really cut off, some Westerners love to buy their soul a new disguise, so they fly away to India, to designer retreats made specially for them, with group trances and orgies of worship, and the Indians make a whole lot of money out of them. They're very good at business. They've even come up with a very funny name for what the customers are buying: "Karma-Cola".'

'Karma-Cola? Like Coca-Cola?'

181

'Yes, except that in Hinduism the word "karma" means something like the fate of the individual. I'm sure you must have heard the word before.'

'Yes,' said Theo. 'Mum has a screwy kind of friend who talks about her karma all the time – as if everything revolved around her, Dad says. She makes him laugh.'

'He's quite right,' said Aunt Martha. 'But it makes Indians laugh even harder. Because you can't become a Hindu. You're either born a Hindu, or you're not, and that's all there is to it. So naturally, when they see these Westerners in fancy dress . . .'

'What harm does it do them?' asked Theo.

'None, but in India everybody knows what it's about. It's just possible that a Westerner might be reborn as a Hindu in a later incarnation, but this time around there's nothing to be done!'

'Reincarnation,' said Theo dreamily. 'Think what it could mean. So you have several lives – maybe thousands of lives.'

'Better ones if you're good, and worse if you misbehave,' Aunt Martha grumbled. 'Don't start, please!'

'But I haven't done anything!' Theo defended himself. 'I'm trying to understand, that's all. It's a hassle to keep up with all this stuff!'

Certainly, all this stuff made a complicated picture, but as each religion had its own rites and its own dress codes there were pointers to stop you getting lost. Though they should also add to the list of eight religions the huge population of animists dispersed throughout most of the country and peacefully worshipping their many fetish deities, just as they do in Africa.

'And what am I going to do with my notebook?' asked Theo, scratching his head. 'How do I make room for millions and millions of gods?'

Aunt Martha smiled. Theo would soon understand that in the case of India it was simply impossible to put it all in order in his notebook, or anywhere else.

Ila, and some animals

At four in the morning, as they walked down the gangway and into the airport, a gust of warm air with a smell of tar and honey wafted into Theo's face. A crush of people pressed against the barriers, many holding up notices with names printed in capital letters. Aunt Martha pushed her trolley through the jostling crowd, and cursed under her breath: arriving in Delhi was always a hassle.

'Martha!' a woman's voice shouted.

'Ah, there she is,' sighed Aunt Martha with relief.

A young woman wearing the traditional baggy trousers and tunic in bright pink came rushing up to Martha and gave her a huge hug before turning to Theo with a look of cheerful welcome.

'Meet my friend Ila,' said Aunt Martha.

Ila pressed her palms together and bowed. How beautiful she was – like the goddess Hera in *Wrath of the Gods*. In the corner of her right nostril shone a tiny diamond stud in the form of a daisy. Her whole face smiled – her dark eyes, raven hair, dazzling white teeth, even the beauty spot by the corner of her mouth. Theo's delighted response was to press his hands together in return.

'You say "*Namaskar*",' Aunt Martha taught him. 'That means Hello.'

'*Namaskar*,' Theo repeated gravely. 'How do you do?'

'I'm fine,' she said politely. 'The *sardar* is waiting with his taxi.'

The *sardar* was a bearded young man with long curly hair. In the car, Ila explained to Theo that all Sikhs had the title of *sardar*, that they often drove taxis, and that she liked them a lot, because they were reliable.

'Look, Aunt Martha, he isn't wearing a turban,' Theo whispered. 'He's not a real Sikh.'

'Who said the turban was compulsory?' Aunt Martha answered tartly. 'The beard and hair, yes. The turban, no.'

Muffled shadows trudged along the side of the road, hard to make out in the dawn mist. Suddenly the pale hind quarters of a cow appeared in the headlights, and the car slowed down.

'A sacred cow!' cried Theo.

'Yes, and a nuisance it is too,' Aunt Martha grumbled. 'Really, can't it just move along a bit?'

The *sardar* edged carefully past the animal, which started to nibble a sheet of tattered newspaper. When a giant shape loomed up out of the mist, at first Theo mistook it for a truck – a terribly slow, rhythmically swaying truck. But as the car overtook it, Theo saw a flapping ear and a trunk, and realized that this was an elephant carrying a load of foliage.

'Well done, Theo!' said Ila. 'Seeing an elephant is a very good omen. They bring good luck.'

'What other animals might we see?' asked Theo, all excited.

An army of monkeys, two or three flop-eared goats, a flock of sheep driven by a shepherd, queues of cars, and a chorus of honking. And a whole lot of people. Wherever he looked Theo saw little bonfires with

183

people gathered round them. Long threads of smoke twined upwards through the treetops; the air seemed infinitely blue before the light took on tinges of pink above the city. Before they reached the Taj Palace hotel. Theo glimpsed a flight of apple-green parrots, three or four black kites soaring in search of prey, and higher still a flock of white-backed vultures, wheeling on wide dark wings.

The car pulled up at the foot of a marble staircase, and a bearded warrior wearing a plumed turban leaned majestically down to open the door of the car. Theo couldn't help gaping, and he was no less amazed by the scale of their suite, with its vast drawing room where a bowl of fruit lay on the table beside a vase of flowers that Theo knew by their smell before he even saw them.

'Tuberoses!' he shouted in delight. 'I'm hungry!'

Ila unzipped a banana, sliced open a green and yellow pawpaw to reveal its pinkish flesh, and warned Theo that you should never eat fruit in India without peeling it first. As for water, he must be careful never to drink anything but bottled mineral water, and to use it even for brushing his teeth.

'Is your water so dangerous?' Theo inquired.

In India, water was a serious problem. Ila's house had its own supply of drinking water, but it cost so much that only the well-to-do could afford it.

'And what do you do for a living?' asked Theo, logically.

Ila looked after her family and wrote novels, which didn't make much money, but her husband Sudhir was an airline pilot, and that was a well-paid profession. Ila was telling Theo about her two children when Aunt Martha decided that it was time to rest. It took some time before he fell asleep. So many animals. So many different kinds of people.

Theo picks the elephant god

Just after midday Aunt Martha woke Theo out of a deep sleep. Through the window he discovered a majestic copper dome, flanked by colonnades. A Hindu temple!

'Not exactly,' Aunt Martha told him. 'That's the dome of the presidential palace, where the viceroys lived in the days of the British Empire. If it's a temple, then it's the temple of Indian democracy!'

So where were the temples? Martha stretched out an arm to point to various small pear-shaped buildings dotted about the garden-city's greenery. India's largest temples were not in the capital, nor in Benares. They were all much further south: huge complexes of courtyards and pools, majestically surrounded by colossal carved elevations. You had to remove your shoes when you entered these shrines, and in summer time the sun-scorched ground would burn your feet.

'Take off your shoes?' said Theo.

In India you entered all places of worship barefoot, as a sign of respect. No doubt the custom derived from Hinduism, because once inside the temple grounds the wearing of leather, made from cowhide, was forbidden. Later, when the Mughal emperors – Muslim conquerors – occupied much of India, the faithful took their shoes off to enter mosques, as Islam required. Even in churches and synagogues you went barefoot. Perhaps it was just so as not to foul these sacred places with dirt from the street.

'That's why I made you bring so many pairs of socks,' Aunt Martha concluded. 'For when it's too hot or too damp. When the floor of a temple has only just been sluiced down, you'll be grateful! Now it's time for your pills. After that, we're going to eat Chinese.'

The Chinese restaurant was full of women dressed in saris of all colours and covered with jewels, worn even in their nostrils.

'Aunt Martha, why do they wear diamonds in their noses?' asked Theo suddenly.

'It's like an earring, only they pierce the nostril. Ila says it doesn't hurt. Don't you think it looks pretty?'

'Yes, I do,' said Theo. 'I'd like to bring one back for Mum.'

They spent the afternoon in an unusual crafts museum. Part of it was a large village where craftsmen worked in the open air, some casting metal for figurines, others carving statues or painting fine miniatures, using a brush with three hairs.

'You must buy a god,' Aunt Martha decided. 'Take your pick.'

Theo hesitated. The little statues didn't really appeal to him.

'Why do the gods have so many arms?' he inquired.

'Simply to represent movement,' Aunt Martha replied. 'And also to perform contradictory actions – like creating with one arm and destroying with the other, for example. It also enables each hand to carry a weapon or a symbol. Take your Shiva, the god of Asceticism and Dance: one hand for the trident, the symbol of meditation, another for the little twin-sided drum, symbol of the creative impulse, and the other two for balance. Look at this one that comes from Bengal.'

Mounted on a lion, the ten-armed goddess brandished a different weapon in each hand – an axe, a sword, a spear, a harpoon, and so on – as she struck down a demon with an animal body.

Theo was startled and impressed. 'Doesn't she look frightening?' he murmured.

'So she is, in that shape,' said Aunt Martha. 'Her name is Durga, she who is hard to approach. The gods created her to destroy a buffalo-demon that was wreaking havoc on the world. That is why Indians also call her "the Mother", because she protects. Look at the other goddess next to her. Do you see the one I mean?'

This was a goddess with dishevelled hair and bulging eyes, whose enormous tongue protruded through a hideous smile. In her eight arms she held weapons that dripped with blood, and she was trampling on a pale bloodless body. Her tongue lolled out so far that it reached her neck.

'She's ghastly,' said Theo, pulling a horrified face.

'Kali always has that effect,' Aunt Martha smiled. 'She was created by the greatest of the gods, who combined their efforts to rid the earth of its demons. Kali is the most venerated of the mother goddesses of India. After all, every mother has two faces, hasn't she – one smiling and one angry?'

'No,' said Theo. 'I've never seen Mum stick her tongue out.'

'Ah! Kali's tongue is a strange story. When she walked on to the stage of the world to destroy the illusory demons there, Kali was so fighting mad that by mistake she trod on the body of Shiva, her husband and one of her creators. So she gaped with surprise, and stuck out her tongue . . .'

'Sort of, "My God, what the hell have I done"?'

'Really, Theo, do watch your language. But it's true that Kali felt stunned by what she'd done. Then afterwards, when she realized that a Shiva in bodily form was not truly the god himself, her fighting spirit soared and she wiped out whatever came against her . . . If you look closely, you'll see Shiva under her feet. And Kali's tongue has stuck out ever since.'

'When I stick *my* tongue out, it doesn't reach the end of my chin,' said Theo, and extended it, not very far.

'To manage that, you've got to be a yogi,' said Aunt Martha. 'Come and sit down, it takes some explaining.'

Yogis were holy men who withdrew from the world and practised a special physical exercise that required control of the body and breathing to achieve a state of trance. Their technique was spectacular, but its purpose was always meditation. In their three thousand years of practice, they had perfected all sorts of techniques to cleanse the body, prevent it from ageing, and completely purify it, for instance by absorbing salt water through the nostrils, or swallowing a strip of cloth about six metres long, which they would then remove . . .

'Wait a minute,' said Theo. 'That's downright impossible!'

'Well, if you like you can have some lessons. They'd be really good for you.'

'And where does this sticking your tongue out come in?'

'It's quite complicated. To reach the state of trance, you have to be able to hold your breath for a very long time. Well, the yogis actually block up the opening to their throat by folding back their tongue, and in order to do that they cut the little muscles that attach it to the lower jaw.'

'That's crazy!' said Theo. 'You mean they cut open their tongue?'

'Just the opposite. They release it. Very gradually, day after day, with the edge of a dry leaf. It takes years to achieve, but it works. Kali sticks her tongue out because she is a *yogini*, a goddess inspired by yoga. Is that clear?'

'It is and it isn't,' said Theo, rising to his feet. 'But I've never seen a figure more contorted than these are. I don't want Durga or Kali. Find me something else!'

No sooner said than done. Aunt Martha reached out to an odd-looking statue with a human body, an elephant's head, and a trunk curled down to tickle its pot belly.

'He's a hoot!' Theo cried.

'More like a trumpet,' said Aunt Martha. 'I thought you'd like him.'

The elephant-god was called Ganesa. According to one story he was created by Shiva's wife, Parvati, after a domestic quarrel. To get even with her husband she modelled a son out of clay and stood him in the doorway of her bedroom to keep her husband out. The furious Shiva decapitated the child of clay at a stroke, but to soothe Parvati's tears he promised to give Ganesa the head of the first living creature that happened along.

'It was an elephant!' cried Theo.

Naturally Ganesa started to grow, and he grew so big that he had to sit down. He became the god of children, the home and success. Also, Ganesa was a glutton for sugar and milk. One year – it wasn't long ago – all the statues of Ganesa started to drink the milk that their worshippers

187

offered. For two days, crowds queued outside the temples to witness this miracle: the child-god drinking milk.

'Dad says we shouldn't believe in miracles,' said Theo. 'All the statues? Even the wooden ones?'

'No,' smiled Aunt Martha. 'The wooden Ganesas went thirsty.'

'With marble and metal, that figures,' said Theo. 'We've done that in physics. You bring them close, and the liquid gets absorbed on contact. Kids' stuff.'

Kids' stuff. On the second day of the miracle a famous journalist had caused a ruckus on morning TV by inviting his shoemaker neighbour on to the programme to show how his cobbler's last, made of brass, could drink milk quite easily. It was a clear demonstration, but the religious parties brought an action against him for sacrilege. Because in India the miraculous was a part of everyday life, and Ganesa was the most popular of all the gods in the Hindu pantheon.

'It's true he looks friendly,' said Theo. 'I'll take him.'

The little god was made of polished brass, with a tall diadem and earrings. He had only one tusk, and Theo wanted to return it to the stall-holder, but Aunt Martha stopped him: it wasn't faulty workmanship. Long ago, Ganesa had given the other tusk to a poet, for use as a pen to write the first of his country's great epics.

Religious panorama

On the second day, Aunt Martha and Ila took Theo round the city on a whistle-stop visit to the religions of India.

'I've worked out a schedule for a tour,' she said. 'But mind, we've got to be back before sunset, six o'clock at the latest. Otherwise it's too tiring.'

First stop, the Hindu temple, where Ila made an easygoing guide. Theo must first take his shoes off, then ring the bell, then bow low in front of each altar. Worshippers in a hurry shed their shoes in a trice, touched the bell perfunctorily, but joined their hands when they came to the altars, to pray in silence and with passionate intensity. What devotion, Theo thought. Yet there was nothing very impressive about these particular gods. Draped in red satin and garlanded with fresh flowers, each had a doll-like face, with black enamel eyes and a smile of joy. Ila named them one by one: this god was Rama, with his wife Sita; that one was Krishna, with his mistress Radha . . .

'She isn't his wife?' asked Theo.

No. Each of them was married to someone else. But as Krishna was a god, he was entitled to be, and the mortal Radha had been quickly deified.

'It's great to be a god, all the same,' Theo remarked.

Second stop, the Sikh gurdwara. You didn't just walk straight in off the street, you had to remove your shoes and wash your feet. Theo was nettled at first, but when he came to the steps that led to the sacred pool, he changed his mind. Shining in the sun, the white gurdwara was alive with Sikhs dressed in blue, with swords or daggers at their sides, and wearing huge turbans jewelled with crescents of gold. Worshippers prayed and sang hymns to the Book. Long queues of cheerful pilgrims gossiped while they waited their turn.

'Look at that!' Theo cried. 'It's lively in here!'

Ila smiled. Although she was a Hindu, the Sikhs were her favourite Indian people. And yet they were warriors . . . She felt that this paradox needed accounting for.

'The Sikhs took their inspiration from Islam and Hinduism,' she began.

'Hold on,' said Theo. 'Explain.'

So Ila told the wonderful story of Guru Nanak, so noble and holy a man that when he died in 1539 both the Hindu and the Muslim communities claimed him for their own. By drawing on both Hinduism and Islam together, Guru Nanak conceived a new religion in which he combined the ideal of purity, aid to the poor, and equality for all, which played no part in Hinduism, because of the caste system. But, claiming that Islam did not allow religious intrusions from elsewhere, a Muslim emperor slaughtered many Sikhs.

'More killing!' said Theo.

The tenth guru gathered the last of the faithful to test their courage. He mustered them in front of a big tent and asked who was willing to die: those who came forward were to have their throats cut on the spot. There were only six volunteers – former untouchables. The guru ushered them into the tent, and the rest stood there petrified, listening to the dull thud of falling bodies and seeing streams of blood flow from inside. But when the guru opened the flaps of the tent the six brave men stood there alive and well: in their place lay six decapitated sheep.

'Hey, it's Isaac times six,' Theo remarked.

But the story ended differently, because the guru gave orders that from then on Sikhs must display the same courage as the six volunteers, and must hold themselves ready for battle. So they always wore a dagger, and often a sword, to defend themselves in case they were attacked.

After that, the tenth guru commanded Sikhs to venerate as his successor the last living guru, who would not be himself, but a Book. This was the Guru Granth Sahib, the sacred Book of the Sikhs, which was attended and prayed to each day, and ceremonially closed and put to rest at nightfall. So the Sikhs belonged to the monotheist religions, from which they had inherited the transition from human sacrifice to the Book and a single God.

'That makes four monotheist religions, and not three,' Theo concluded.

'Not to mention some others,' Aunt Martha teased. 'Including two you know – the religion founded by Akhenaten and the one preached by Zarathustra. And that's not all . . .'

Third stop, the Muslim city of Nizamuddin. The car drove down a narrow street in a squalid shanty town. This time, when she got out, Ila took shelter behind Aunt Martha's broad back.

'My word, you're frightened,' Aunt Martha reproved her.

Ila looked embarrassed. 'N . . . no,' she said. 'But I'm a Hindu, and they know it.'

Aunt Martha shrugged her shoulders and strode forward, shielding her eyes with one hand. Clusters of children hung around street stalls selling hot pancakes, garlands of red roses, and fine silk almond-green scarves. Aunt Martha was looking for someone.

'But I told him we were coming,' she murmured. 'Where is he hiding? Ah, here he comes.'

The man who approached them and took hold of Aunt Martha's hand in a fervent clasp was as thin as a rake, and dressed in a black tunic and a fake fur hat. Once again they had to take their shoes off.

'I warn you, Theo,' Aunt Martha whispered as they unlaced their shoes, 'it's a depressing sort of passageway we have to go through. Remember that in this village it's forbidden to give alms to beggars. Be guided by our friend Nizami.'

Mr Nizami waved an arm to open a path. In the narrow alley entire families of wretched people stretched out their hands. Sleeping beggars swarmed with flies, and the undersized, emaciated women seemed to be starving. Mr Nizami walked past without stopping. Theo's heart was in his mouth, and he trembled with distress. Whichever way he looked . . . And then the long corridor ended in brightness, and Theo was so dazzled by the glare that he had to stop.

The Sufi village

In the middle stood the shrine of the saint called Nizamuddin. The women pressed up against its marble outer walls, and murmured prayers. The men were entitled to enter the building and meditate in front of the long tomb covered in green veils fringed with gold. Over to one side sat a curious group of men wearing hats embroidered with an assortment of copper coins; they gaped and rolled their eyes in all directions. At the far end, leaning against walls so intricately carved that they might have been made of lace, some stately elders were telling their beads in silence. The whole place seethed with life, yet at the same time it was utterly serene.

'We're visiting the Sufis,' Aunt Martha explained. 'These are Muslims who have made the love of God their ideal, and tolerance their law. Their Islam is not exclusive: its acceptance of those who love God is unconditional, as long as they seek to encounter him directly. Here all religions are admitted. Hindus come to worship the Muslim saint, and over there, at the top of the steps, they care for the mentally ill from all over India, no matter what their religion.'

'Mad people?' Theo was perplexed. 'In a church?'

'A church?' his aunt corrected him. 'Don't you see the little mosque, there to our right? But let me tell you something. In medieval Europe, our churches gave shelter to lunatics, because in the shadow of God the mentally ill live at peace.'

'Those over there?' asked Theo, nodding towards the group with the rolling eyes.

'That's right. They're called fakirs, which means poor men, dependent on God. They're mad, but they aren't dangerous. They're left alone, and when they do get upset they can be soothed by singing.' Their guide gave a nod to Aunt Martha, and she turned to Theo. 'Our friend Nizam says it's time.'

She sank down on to the little wall surrounding the shrine, and Theo sat down on a mat, feeling a little apprehensive. Time for what?

A sudden commotion brought the answer. It was the arrival of the *qawwali*, the Sufi singers. To the sound of drums and a portable harmonium they chanted the songs composed by the saint, making broad ritual gestures as they sang. The madmen broke into smiles: the marvellous singing eased their suffering and pacified their minds. Those who were not mad listened with equal delight, and some shed uninhibited tears of happiness. One old man began to turn his head from side to

191

side faster and faster with an ecstatic smile. The joy that rang in the singers' voices shone in the faces of their listeners.

'Take a good look, Theo,' Aunt Martha whispered. 'All these people practise a kind of singing called *dhikr*, which means "remembrance" in Arabic. For Sufis it has come to mean the breath of divine love. All the way from Black Africa to Indonesia, Morocco to the Middle East, all the Sufis in the world know this form of prayer. It's a kind of rhythmic recitation backed by music and continually repeating the same saying, which is part of the *shahada*, the Muslim statement of faith: "*la ilaha illa Allah*" – there is no god but God. Do you see that old man, the one who keeps turning his head? That's his way of praying. Some people can run out of breath and get winded through repeating the chant over and over, and it's quite common for them to fall into trances.'

'With music, it's easy,' Theo told her. 'Do you think techno musicians know about stuff like that? I think there's some resemblance.'

'I doubt if in techno they chant the name of God,' she answered cautiously. 'But there's something in it, because there is no religion without music.'

'Aha! I just knew it,' said Theo triumphantly.

'The chant of the *qawwali* is simple and powerful. Their voice comes from the heart, and you see how they smile as they sing . . . I don't know any more beautiful way to express the love of God.'

'So you do believe in him, then?'

'Here, Theo,' said Aunt Martha, slipping a 100-rupee note into his hand. 'Go and give this to the musicians.'

'I daren't,' he whispered, but he set out anyway, tiptoed across the marble floor, and put the note on top of the harmonium's cardboard folds. The singers' smiles of thanks were so dazzling that Theo's shyness melted into pleasure.

'There, you see, it wasn't so hard . . .'

'It's so nice in here,' said Theo.

The *qawwali* stopped chanting and the muezzin gave the call to prayer. The sun was sinking fast, and the men stood together to pray in chorus in front of the shrine. If they wanted to be back before dark it was high time to leave. Mr Nizami claimed Aunt Martha's hand for the second time, then put his hand on his heart and bowed to Ila, who returned the bow.

'I have one question,' said Theo in the car. 'Why is it forbidden to give to beggars?'

192

'Because the Nizami family collects all donations from the faithful,' Aunt Martha replied. 'The office has been hereditary ever since the thirteenth century, and the men of the family have administered the shrine for centuries. The money goes to the school, the medical service, maintaining the graveyard, and running the soup kitchen. They're very efficient.'

'The cemetery? The school? Where are they?' Theo asked. 'And what about the soup kitchen? I didn't see that.'

The soup kitchen opened at sunset outside the shrine. The school was in the alleyway; they had walked right past the doorway in the gloom. And the graveyard was just behind the musicians: the marble latticework screened a number of tombs several centuries old. The medical centre was at the back of the shrine, nestling between two trees and five graves. In Nizamuddin, life, death, love and music harmonized wonderfully well.

Theo sighed. A young Westerner could not set up house in a Sufi village of the thirteenth century. Too bad.

Dinner with the family

Caught up in the excitement of coming to India, Theo had not said a word about Benares. On the third day, visits to the synagogue, a church and the Baha'i temple left Theo uninspired. The synagogue was tiny, and located in a concrete building, a far cry from the glories of Jerusalem. The church was built on classical European lines, but not much to write home about. As for the immense Baha'i temple, it was almost new, shaped like a white lotus, very clean, and attended by paramilitary guards who kept a close eye on the visiting pilgrims. In the middle of the great shrine there was nothing but a carpet and a microphone.

'What kind of worship is this?' Theo asked. 'I don't see any god!'

The founder of the Baha'is, who called himself the Bab - the Gate - was born in Iran in the early nineteenth century. As a young man, he attracted crowds by proclaiming that he was a new prophet of Islam. The Bab was gentle; he was executed in Tabriz in 1850. After his death, his disciple Baha'ullah developed his faith into a new religion. Two years later, the Bab's followers suffered cruel persecution in an attempt by the Shah to suppress them. They were tortured by having their flesh ripped open and lighted fuses inserted, and when the torturer threatened one father that he would cut the throats of his two sons before his eyes if he would not renounce his faith, the elder son bared his neck and demanded to be executed first.

Theo was horrified. 'What had they done to deserve that?' he asked.

They preached a universal religion that gave precedence to none of the existing religions. Their vision was of a world government able to arbitrate between all nations, and a new language that would bring all people together. But above all they demanded equality of the sexes, and orthodox Islam does not accept this. That was the reason for their early martyrdom. They managed to gain acceptance in Iran until the hostility of the new Islamic Republic after 1979 forced them to emigrate to countries such as India and Israel. Their meeting places were starkly austere.

'Not bad,' said Theo. 'Those poor people . . .'

But as they were leaving the place a uniformed figure gave him a violent shove.

'There's no need to have cops throwing their weight about!' Theo exploded. 'I'm sick of this. When do we leave for Bena . . . ?'

'By the way, Ila,' Aunt Martha cut in hastily, 'are we still dining at your house tonight?'

While Ila dashed off to attend to her kitchen they had time to return to the hotel for a shower and change of clothes before the taxi picked them up. Since the 1950s the city had been divided into geometrical districts, the 'colonies', and Ila lived in one of these. When she opened the door, Theo hardly knew her. She was wearing a fabulous pink silk sari, with a single row of miniature black pearls round her neck, and a pair of immense golden earrings, set with rubies. Her eyes and smiling mouth were vividly made up.

'The goddess is you,' said Theo, open-mouthed in amazement at the transformation.

'Pink is my colour,' Ila answered modestly.

She took him to her children's rooms and introduced him first to her daughter Pallavi and then to her son Shiv, who was just Theo's age. Soon Shiv and Theo had their eyes riveted on the screen as they played a Japanese computer game. Ila's husband always came home very late, and they would not be waiting for him for dinner. Ila had affectionately remembered and cooked Aunt Martha's favourite dishes: chicken with almond sauce, lamb curry, nan, and tomatoes with yoghurt. They helped themselves, and balanced their plates on their knees. For dessert, Ila had bought barfi. Theo had started carefully peeling off the silver on one side when Ila stopped him – in India, you also ate the silver leaf.

'You eat metal?'

'Only gold and silver,' she explained. 'It's a very old Indian medical tradition: gold and silver are used as medicines.'

'At home we use an academic word for them,' said Aunt Martha. 'We call them oligo-elements. In the West they're given as pills, but here they're eaten raw. Give it a try!'

Theo tried, and so successfully that he polished off half the sweets all by himself. When he had finished he looked up and saw that Ila and Aunt Martha were watching him fondly, as if, when he swallowed the silver leaf, he had also absorbed a dose of life. Silence descended. A lump rose in Theo's throat when he thought about Paris, and dinner time in the family apartment, and realized that he had not phoned home for two days.

CHAPTER 11

Mahantji

'Mum?'

'Darling, it's you . . . We've been wondering. Are you all right?'

'Mm . . . yes,' Theo stalled.

'You're taking your medicine, anyway? You don't feel tired? You're sleeping well?'

And so on. Then Mum went quiet, and her silence was worse than her questions. Theo heard her faltering breathing, and guessed at the handkerchief screwed up in her hand, and the grief she could no longer hide.

'Mum,' he told her in a piercing whisper, 'I love you, you know . . .'

'Yes,' she sniffled. 'Don't worry, I'm brave and I won't let you down. Let me speak to your aunt.'

As usual, they wrangled. Aunt Martha slammed the phone down with a huff of exasperation, and it rang again almost at once. This time it was her nieces, straining to be casual, before Dad came on. He was always more relaxed. Aunt Martha described their first two days in Delhi, promised to phone more often, promised something else in a tetchy kind of voice, and hung up again.

When the storm was over, Theo called his favourite Pythia. As he had no question to ask, he simply declared that he missed her, and that one day when they were both grown up he would love to return to India with her. Fatou just said yes. Aunt Martha had slipped tactfully out of the room. When Theo put the phone down his eyes were bright with tears. This was no time to tell him about tomorrow's medical tests.

'The tests can wait,' Aunt Martha decided. 'Too bad, we'll postpone them till we get back – it won't be long.' Better to allow Theo to go to sleep with Fatou's voice in his ear. Next day, instead of taking him to the hospital she let him have a long lie-in. The plane for Benares left in the late afternoon, and Aunt Martha did the packing.

Captain Lumba's cockpit

A big surprise awaited Theo. Right after take-off, as soon as he, Aunt Martha and Ila had unfastened their seat belts, the captain made an unusual announcement.

'Good afternoon, ladies and gentlemen, and welcome aboard your Indian Airlines flight. I am Captain Lumba, and I wish you a very good trip to Varanasi. We are on schedule to touch down there in an hour. Let me bid a special welcome to our guest of honour, young Theo . . .'

Theo, who had been paying no attention till now, almost sprang out of his seat. The captain had spoken his name. And if Theo was a guest of honour, didn't that mean . . . ?

'Go ahead,' said Ila, waving him forward, and Theo obeyed in a daze.

When he reached the front the door to the cockpit opened, and the captain turned round with a broad smile. 'Hi, Theo. Sit down.' He pointed at the narrow seat behind him, and Theo didn't need asking twice. Soon he was listening while the captain explained that the green crosses on the control screen showed the flight path, that visibility was clear for the moment, but by the time they reached Benares they would be landing through cloud. All through the flight he kept up the same running commentary, as if it was the most natural thing in the world to have this unknown French boy visiting his cockpit.

At last, as the plane was starting to descend, the captain called for silence in the cockpit, and in the evening mist Theo saw the most spectacular panorama of earth and sky: beneath the dark blue dome of night a cathedral of light outlined in deeper darkness, thousands of red and white fireflies – the landing strip. The captain gave a few quiet orders and the plane touched down with a butterfly's lightness.

Ila's head appeared in the cockpit, and then the rest of her, as she leaned down to kiss the captain, who was her husband Sudhir. He put on his cap with military briskness and took Aunt Martha's flight bag in a vigorous grip.

'So that's your husband?' Theo whispered, almost in awe. 'I think he's great!'

'Me too!' said Ila, with only a trace of a blush.

Captain Lumba made short work of the landing formalities, crammed baggage, wife and guests into two taxis, and in double quick time they were on their way to the city of Benares, whose Indian name is Varanasi. Night had fallen, and there was nothing much to see: a murky landscape, unlit villages, cows by the wayside, and the muffled shadows that trudge along the roads and paths of India. There was no sign of the river. The Taj hotel stood in a landscaped garden, and though it smelled musty inside, the rooms were pleasant and the staff very friendly. But they hadn't passed the river on the way, nor could it be seen from the windows. The captain led his little band to the restaurant, and soon he was deep in conversation with Martha, so Theo had a chance to talk to Ila.

The four heads of the god Brahma

'Can I ask you a question?' he said to Ila quietly. 'What caste do you belong to?'

'Oh . . .' The question took her by surprise. 'I'm a Brahman. But you know, we don't talk about castes any more.'

'Are you sure? On TV they talk about the caste war in India.'

She paused before replying. 'Yes. You're right to ask. It is a bad system, abolished by the constitution of 1950, but so ancient that it left a deep mark. As a legacy of their original function the Brahmans have held on to education, and also learning. They are often teachers and professors, and in fact it is Brahmans who have governed the country since independence despite the abolition of the caste system, out of sheer habit. You don't change three thousand years of tradition in half a century! Except that now the lower castes want their own turn to govern, which is only natural.'

'But where do they stand, in your system?' asked Theo.

'Ah, that is the question! To understand the answer, you need to know the myth of foundation. The god of Creation, whose name was Brahma, divided people according to the structure of his own body: for his mouth, the Brahmans; for his arms, the leaders and warriors; for his thighs, the traders and farmers. And for the rest – his belly, legs and feet – the god made the lower castes.'

'Well, that doesn't strike me as a very good start,' said Theo.

'No good at all. And there was worse to come, because down below the caste system was the enormous mass of the untouchables. As their name indicates, and as if to be impure was contagious, they were for-bidden to touch a man or woman of the higher castes, forbidden to share their food, or cook for them, or even look them in the eye. It was even forbidden for their shadow to fall across the shadow of a Brahman. They had no rights at all.'

'My aunt told me that,' said Theo, after a silence. 'And does that still exist?'

'No, because India became a democracy based on the principle of equality. But in some remote villages, sometimes the higher castes . . . Well, it's as you'd expect with privileged people; they're conservatives. Getting rid of the old habits is a long battle. It started in Mahatma Gandhi's time . . .'

'I saw the film!' Theo interrupted. 'He was outstanding!'

The Mahatma had tried hard to improve the condition of the untouch-ables, and gave them the name of 'Harijans' – 'children of God'. In late twentieth-century India the untouchables and the lower castes were joining forces in the bid for power, and that wasn't easy. Except that the vice-president of the republic actually was a man from the lowest caste, who had become a scholar and a diplomat.

'That's good,' said Theo. 'The Mahatma would have been glad.'

Ila did not fail to add that the strangest feature of the creator of the castes, the god Brahma, was his four heads. The legend said that the god's four heads represented his efforts to follow the darting movements of his own daughter, when he fell in love with her.

Theo was stunned by this story. 'Shame on him! And he was the great creator of the whole system?'

'That's right. But unlike all the other gods, Brahma has hardly any temples in India, even though the other two supreme gods are wor-shipped everywhere.'

'Who are they?' asked Theo, yawning at the end of a long day.

Ila opened her mouth to tell him about Vishnu, preserver of the universe, and Shiva, the destroyer, god of Death, but before she could speak Theo's head had flopped onto the table and he was fast asleep. Captain Lumba took him in his arms and carried him to bed.

The high priest of the monkey god

Aunt Martha snapped awake with the thought that this day was going to be the hardest, and longed for it all to go smoothly. When she looked into Theo's room a plea came from under the sheets:

'When are we going to see the Ganges?'

'First, eat your toast and scrambled eggs,' she retorted, with a tremor in her voice.

The taxi that took them to the river crawled through a sea of bicycles, most of them pulling tiny carriages in which plump women wearing saris reclined. Ila explained that these vehicles were rickshaws, and that in the old days, instead of cycling, their drivers, the 'rickshaw wallahs', took hold of the shafts and ran to carry their passengers. Right now the bicycles were being replaced by auto-rickshaws, small three-wheeled vehicles whose engines belched foul black fumes. Engrossed in the bicycle tide, Theo listened to the tinkling din of their thousands of bells. Slowed to a snail's pace by the press of people and traffic, the journey to the river was interminable. Then all at once, just as they had begun to see the sparkle of sunshine on water, the car turned into a narrow side street and dropped them there. They had to continue on foot.

'Put your hat on, Theo,' said Aunt Martha. 'We're going to pay a visit to my friend the high priest. But when we find him, you'll do exactly as I do. Promise?'

'Do what, exactly?'

'Touch his feet with your right hand.'

'But I thought you only had to press your palms together . . .'

'With a man of God you have to touch his feet,' she insisted. 'You also use his title when you speak to him: you'll call him Mahantji.'

A *mahant* was a high priest, and *-ji* was a suffix expressing respect and affection, which could be applied to anybody.

'So I could call you Martha-ji?'

'It doesn't sound right,' said Aunt Martha. 'Anyway, seeing how you treat me it would be much too respectful!'

Then the maze of city streets was behind them and they were standing on a terrace – a *ghat*, Aunt Martha called it later – where under a giant banyan tree stood four immaculate temples no taller than Theo, housing statues of the gods, and a small bull that he recognized straight away.

'Nandi! It's Nandi!' he cried, dancing from one foot to the other. 'Doesn't he look sweet!'

'Look over there,' said Aunt Martha. Theo looked eastwards, and there flowed the slow broad River Ganges, shimmering under a cloudless sky.

Dazzled by sparkling reflections, he shaded his eyes with one hand and watched scores of black boats, full of chanting pilgrims, drift past. Further on, a bigger boat with patched sails glided smoothly down-river. The opposite shore was deserted, a landscape of pale yellow banks,

201

and beyond them green fields. Untroubled by the temple bells that rang across the city behind them, the air was absolutely calm. Aunt Martha gave Theo a sudden nudge with her elbow, and he turned round to encounter the bright dark gaze of an old man dressed in a white tunic. It was Mahantji.

The breathing lesson

When Martha bent down to touch his feet, Mahantji raised her at once, with a shake of his head. Ila did the same, and this time Mahantji laid his hand on her head in blessing. But when Theo went to follow his aunt's instructions and kneel, Mahantji caught him by the shoulders. The high priest's face was pitted, his moustache bleached yellow with age, and his eyes shone with a goodness that Theo could feel. When he spoke, it was with a silky voice, and in English:

'So, my boy, you are the Theo I have heard so much about.'

Mahantji gave audiences in a spacious room in the middle of his house. He sat cross-legged on a wide platform draped with white cotton cloth; Martha, Ila and Theo sat on seats. A servant brought tea and biscuits. No one spoke. Mahantji's eyes were still fixed on Theo, but it was to Martha that he addressed a stream of questions. This time the conversation was too difficult for Theo's schoolboy English to follow, but he picked up enough words to know that they were talking about 'health', and 'doctors', and 'illness' as Mahantji listened gravely to Aunt Martha's long account.

'But at this moment, Mahantji,' Aunt Martha concluded, 'it would help if you could explain your vision of Hinduism to my nephew.'

Ila whispered a translation to Theo.

The high priest's piercing eyes bored into Theo's, and caused him to wriggle where he sat. Then he unfolded his long legs, and signalled Theo to follow. He walked towards a doorway at the back, which opened on to a narrow corridor. Before they left the room, Theo saw that the rear wall was decorated with a painting of Shiva, dressed in a leopard skin, dancing with his legs in the air and a cheerful smile on his face. Mahantji passed by without stopping, and guided Theo through a maze of dark corridors and out on to a miniature terrace where a shapeless idol stood in a small alcove at ground level, with a pair of sandals placed in front of it. Mahantji sat down on the low outer wall of the terrace, and it was then that Theo noticed that he had a club foot.

'Sit here, my boy,' said the high priest, beckoning Theo to join him.

Theo perched next to Mahantji. Just above his head a bell hung suspended between two uprights of rough stone. Below them flowed the Ganges, its breezes thousands of whispered prayers. Now and then men walked stealthily past them, touched Mahantji's feet, bowed to the shapeless deity, and struck the bell, so softly that it hardly broke the tranquil silence. Mahantji put an arm round Theo's shoulder, pulled him close, and wrapped him in his big white shawl. A long silence followed before he whispered in Theo's ear:

'You will not understand what I am going to say, will you, young man?'

'Yes,' said Theo boldly. 'I am sure that I can understand.'

'*Shanti-i*,' said Mahantji solemnly, holding him tighter. 'The meaning of *shanti* is peace.'

All right, thought Theo, but what is this word *shanti*?

'May your spirit be in peace for ever,' said Mahantji. 'Do you understand?'

'You make a wish for me.'

'Now, take a breath,' said Mahantji, and took a deep breath himself. Theo breathed in and out, but not very hard.

'From here,' Mahantji ordered, placing his hand on his stomach.

So Theo inflated his stomach, and suddenly his lungs pushed outwards, so hard that it hurt his shoulders.

'Good,' smiled Mahantji. 'Do it again.'

The second time started a feeling inside him as of petals ready to unfold. The third time brought a surge of wellbeing. And the fourth time caused a fit of frantic coughing.

'Very good,' said Mahantji, with a beaming smile, then reached up his hand and rang the bell.

'Let's go,' he said, and stood up with authority.

In the room by the edge of the river, Aunt Martha and Ila were waiting anxiously.

'Well?' said Aunt Martha. 'What did he say?'

'Nothing much,' said Theo. 'He only gave me a breathing lesson. Oh yes, and he also talked about peace. It could be connected to castes and the gods.'

Ramayana

The next meeting with Mahantji was timed for sunset, in his temple. Meanwhile they returned to the hotel for lunch and an afternoon nap. At table Theo fizzed with questions. Who was the unknown god in the little alcove? Why did Mahantji limp? What was this funny kind of breathing through your stomach all about? What god did Mahantji have charge of? What was the name of the huge tree with those three white temples underneath . . . ?

'Steady, my lad,' said Aunt Martha. 'You're making us dizzy. One thing at a time if you please.'

The god in the alcove was not a god at all, but a man, one of India's greatest poets, Tulsidas, who in the sixteenth century translated texts from Sanskrit, the language of learning, into Hindi, a popular language. And as he had lived in Benares they had built him an altar there, where they worshipped his sandals.

Mahantji had been born lame, but it didn't prevent him from walking each morning at daybreak down the hundred steps that led to the river, and then climbing back up again. Besides, Aunt Martha added, ever since the ancient Greeks, and all over the world, great visionaries had often had disabilities: lame and one-eyed people were blessed by the gods, and Mahantji was no exception to the rule. Armed with a will of iron, he had tamed his club foot just as he had tamed his hoarse voice, which he had retrained by means of musical exercises.

And this gave a clue to the purpose of the breathing lesson the high priest had given Theo, because in the West most people breathed with the upper body, while in India they practised breathing from the stomach, the only way to fill the lungs with oxygen completely. For three thousand years, Indians had learned the basic skill of breathing: with the help of breath, everything could be cured. Theo thought back to the Sheikh in Jerusalem.

As for the tree, it was a sacred pipal, one of the fig-tree family.

'What about Mahantji's god?'

The god that Mahantji worshipped was not quite a god, but a divine monkey called Hanuman, and thereby hung a tale that Ila was longing to tell. There once was a king who had three sons and two wives. As usual, the second wife grew so jealous of the first one's children that she insisted that the eldest, Prince Rama, should be sent into exile. Young and handsome, and married to the beautiful Princess Sita, Prince

Rama dutifully obeyed his father and left for the forest, accompanied by his brother Lakshmana. The stepmother had won.

'Things will work out, though,' said Theo knowingly.

They did work out, but not in a hurry. Because Sita was rash enough to be lured away from the safety of their forest retreat in pursuit of a golden gazelle. That was a fatal mistake, because in reality this beautiful creature was Ravana, the hideous demon king of Lanka (now Sri Lanka), a very clever, very evil Brahman who had become infatuated with Rama's wife. He carried her off to his island kingdom, Prince Rama set off in search of his vanished wife, and now began an endless war, with the demons – called *rakshasas* – on one side, and on the other the three brothers, helped by an army of monkeys.

'Aha!' cried Theo. 'This is where Mahantji's monkey comes in!'

The mighty monkey Hanuman was commander-in-chief of the monkey forces. He turned his body into a giant bridge to carry his troops across the water to the island of Lanka; he acted as a messenger by leaping from tree to tree, and then across the ocean and high over the wall of Lanka to find the captive princess; he was so wholehearted, so dedicated, that for ever after he became the symbol of ideal loyalty. When a temple to the monkey god Hanuman was built in Benares in the sixteenth century, its guardianship went to Mahantji's great-great-great-great-grandfather. So Mahantji worshipped the god of Devotion.

'All the same, though, a monkey . . .' Theo was puzzled. 'How does he get by with a face like that?'

Easily enough, because it was thanks to Hanuman that Prince Rama finally slew the demon Ravana and rescued his wife. Therefore the monkey god had moved out of the animal state and advanced into the human world. Often he was portrayed pulling open his chest to reveal his faithful heart, shining a brilliant red. Hanuman was worshipped as a good servant of Rama. After his victory, Prince Rama re-entered his kingdom in triumph. This epic story was called the *Ramayana*. The great Tulsidas translated it into Hindi, and every year, starting in October, it was performed all over India for forty nights, acted by youths in costume – but not by girls. The story played to enthusiastic audiences, loudly absorbed in the action, and ended with the burning of the demon Ravana in the form of a giant cardboard effigy stuffed with fireworks.

'It's a marvellous sight!' Ila assured him.

'But ever so smoky,' Aunt Martha added. 'It makes you cough.'

Later on, the story took a darker turn, when Rama accused his wife of having given in to her demon seducer and poor Sita had to endure an ordeal by fire to prove her innocence. Ila claimed that she emerged unscathed from the fire and it all ended happily, but Aunt Martha swore that she had read the authentic version in which Sita, outraged by this monstrous accusation, appealed to her mother the earth, who gaped open and swallowed her up. But Rama had eventually revealed himself as a god, and not just a prince, and there was no argument about that.

For Rama was one of the many expressions of the god Vishnu, guardian of the order of the universe, who was often portrayed lying fast asleep on the ocean, guarded by the seven-headed serpent king Sesha. Every billionth year or so, Vishnu came down to earth and incarnated himself in an earthly form: these manifestations were called 'avatars'. In this way he had taken the shape of a turtle, a lion, a wild boar, as well as human forms such as Rama, Buddha, Krishna, and some even added Jesus Christ.

'Krishna?' said Theo. 'Like those cranks who shuffle down the Boulevard Saint-Michel banging cymbals and chanting "Hare Krishna"?'

Exactly. Except that the cranks in question were only Westerners dressed up, but the true god Krishna was central to the life and mind of a nation. Ila could hardly wait to tell Theo just a few of the many stories about Krishna's boyhood, his pranks and mischief, what a lovable young scamp he'd been, and then about the eleven thousand *gopis* – shepherdesses – who had all become his mistresses in the sacred groves of Vrndavana.

'Eleven thousand?' Theo was flabbergasted. 'That's quite a man you're talking about!'

Not a man, but a god. Krishna had the power to multiply himself myriad times: none of the shepherdesses was disappointed, because the god embraced them all in his thousands of guises. Later on, after his wild adolescence, Krishna had become the most cunning of all the gods, and the best adviser to men. To them he taught courage, and the sense of sacrifice and duty. And when men resisted him, if they refused to do battle, then he revealed himself in his true identity: like Prince Rama, Krishna was Vishnu – sea and stars, beginning and end, high and low; birds, octopuses, the river and its banks, the world in its diversity . . . Dazzled by the god's revelation, men would then fulfil their duties, to the point of killing each other willingly, setting aside their personal qualms to respect the god-given order of the world. Lord Krishna's sermon to a hesitant warrior was called the *Bhagavad Gita*, and this was the text that all Hindus had recited at sunrise for over two thousand years.

'I wouldn't jump to it so fast,' said Theo. 'I'd want to know how and why. I'd want to see!'

Talking about divine visions, Aunt Martha interrupted to suggest that it was time to find out what his afternoon rest had to tell him, and this time Theo didn't need prompting. It was a far cry from his friend Mahantji to all these stories of warring gods who forced men to obey. He dreamed about a monkey with a human face and an affectionate smile, who leaned over him to straighten his pillow.

The monkey god's blessing

At five in the afternoon, Ila shook him gently awake. It was time to meet Mahantji again in his temple.

They went through the stately entrance and into a series of courtyards that teemed with worshippers. In the middle of each courtyard stood clusters of little temples where priests with yellow scarves round their necks took the offerings, blessed them and presented them to the gods. To all the gods, and among them the monkey god with the smiling face, weeping with compassion. The crowd thronged quietly up against the walls, touching or stroking the statues, and the sound of bells kept splashing through the background murmur like raindrops on the river.

Suddenly Theo spied Mahantji, tallest of all the priests, his head high above the crowd, except when he stooped to raise up visitors bowing at his feet. He came limping up to Theo and greeted him with hands joined in front of his forehead. Then he picked up the boy like a feather and handed him over to a priest who had been trailing him around. The little band climbed a long staircase that emerged on to the temple roof, and there Theo was deposited on a white mattress, with cushions supporting his back. Aunt Martha sat down gingerly, while Ila folded her legs in a trice. At a signal from Mahantji, attendants brought some tiny tables, set with doll's-house meals – a little yoghurt, a meatball, a banana, and a sweet.

'*Prasad*,' Ila explained in a low voice. 'The priests eat nothing but the food the faithful bring, once the gods have consumed its essence. It is blessed, Theo. Eat!'

'Aunt Martha, is it like the host at Mass?' Theo whispered as he nibbled his meatball.

'No,' she replied. 'These aren't the flesh or blood of a god, just consecrated offerings.'

'Anyway, it all tastes delicious,' he told her, and didn't leave a crumb.

Then, when the meal was finished, Mahantji started to speak. The god he worshipped looked like a monkey, but what look did people give to the gods? For Mahantji, any representation of god was god, and every human being contained a scrap of godhood. Mahantji loved Hanuman because the monkey god stood for compassion: that was why he had offered a sacrifice to heal Theo, and the food that Theo had just wolfed down was his offering, blessed by Hanuman. But Mahantji also venerated the three great gods of India: Vishnu, from whom derived Krishna, the symbol of courage and youthful passion; Brahma, the symbol of creation; and Shiva, lord of life and death, symbol of the cosmic dance and meditation. Mahantji loved all the gods because between them all they formed a single god. And he broke into English to say that was why Hinduism was essentially 'catholic'. This gave Theo a jolt. Catholic? He didn't get it.

But the high priest explained with a smile that in English 'Catholic' meant universal: that was the meaning of the original Greek word. Theo wanted to say that Cardinal Ottavio had also mentioned the word 'universal' in the Vatican, but he didn't have time. While Mahantji spoke, musicians had appeared surreptitiously, and now they began to play. Light hands beat rhythmic patterns on the skins of two small drums, and plucked strings shivered in the fallen darkness. With one hand resting on his knees, Mahantji raised the other like an outspread wing, and his husky voice reached to the stars. One by one, the temple lights blinked out, leaving only the gleam of the thousands of oil lamps burning in the courtyards below. Moonlight shone across the dense foliage of the mango trees, Mahantji sang, and feeling flowed through Theo.

As it had done in Jerusalem, when he saw the city ramparts in the night, and in Luxor, after the bridal dance. And once again Theo heard the voice of his Underworld twin, a vibrant young voice that talked about life and resurrection. He had returned! He was cradling him so peacefully . . .

'He's fallen asleep,' Aunt Martha whispered.

'It's Hanuman's blessing,' said Ila softly. 'Let's be sure not to wake him.'

CHAPTER 12

Lessons of the River

The Ganges at dawn

When they carried him to the car, Theo grunted, but stayed asleep. Aunt Martha glanced at her watch. Next morning, breakfast at four, and sunrise over the Ganges.

Dawn had not yet broken when the taxi set out through empty streets. As they approached the river, Benares was starting to stir: women swept the ground outside their doorways, vendors set out their vegetable stalls, beggars claimed their places, and Hindus made their way towards the Ganges to perform their first devotions of the day. The taxi pulled up in front of an enormous terrace sloping down to the water where numerous boats lay waiting. Ila chose one that she seemed to know, though she still gave boat and crew a quick inspection. Across the river rose a screen of milky white mist.

The bank consisted of a gigantic flight of tall steps, bustling with people. Men and women stood in the water with hands joined in prayer, waiting for the return of the sun whose crimson dome peeped over the horizon. They completely immersed themselves in the sacred river, ducking out of sight once, twice, three times . . . Theo began to count: twelve times. The twelfth time they raised their cupped hands high and let water spill out. Then they emerged and dried themselves. The sun became a ball of red.

Young people soaped themselves vigorously; women washed their

209

saris and spread them all along the bank; soap stung some children's eyes, and they bawled. The climbing sun turned orange.

Hawkers and pedlars appeared, selling tea, pancakes, figurines, candy floss and quack medicines. Under broad parasols of patchwork palm leaves, curious figures stood still and read the sacred texts aloud in return for money. It was an open-air temple, a sacred swimming pool, a public bath, a giant marketplace, a monumental crush as more and more pilgrims kept flocking down the steps to bathe in the river and pray. The sun blazed down on the water out of a blue sky. Further downriver, plumes of white smoke climbed high into the sky – the funeral pyres. Theo asked no questions. He was too fascinated with the bathers at prayer – hundreds in front of him, thousands along the river.

'And do Hindus do this every day?' he asked.

All the days that God sends, to summon the sun back to earth, as they did in ancient Egypt, and keep the world in order. In India, there was nothing more important than the prayer at daybreak, the first act of life. After that, you went to work. Even the yogis, who had their own ways of being busy. Aunt Martha suggested paying them a visit. Naturally the boatman haggled over the price, but while Aunt Martha bargained with him, the youngest oarsman, with a cheeky grin, slipped a little scroll of paper into Theo's hand. A message!

Theo sat down on a step, unrolled the paper, read and reread what it said, and was totally baffled. *Up there, neither coming nor going, nor time, nor death, nor rebirth. Follow the middle way.*

Quite automatically, he looked upwards. High up above, on temple roofs, stray pipal seedlings grew out of crevices in statues. Pigeons' wings scythed and whirred through the warm air, and vultures wheeled. Insects and birds, coming and going, the sky above Benares was full of life: the answer wasn't there. Theo stowed the message deep in his pocket – no getting it wet in the Ganges! – and followed Aunt Martha in search of her yogi.

'Come on,' she muttered to herself as they climbed the steps, 'I'm sure it was here we said we'd meet . . .'

But on the first flat terrace to their left along the river, the only meditating figure belonged to a woman, a Muslim in a mauve chador, facing the sun. Pursued by hawkers offering badges, incense, statuettes, Aunt Martha made her way to the second level, and there she found her yogi, wearing a loincloth, with his legs folded in the lotus position. Without a word, he joined his hands in greeting. Then, silent as ever, he rose to his feet, donned a shabby woollen cap, wrapped himself in a threadbare blanket, and trotted along in Aunt Martha's footsteps. He would give his lesson back at the hotel, in their room.

Professor Wacko's demonstration

'But I haven't asked for anything,' said Theo in the corridor. 'What is this wacko going to do to me?'

'You can call me "wacko" if you like, it doesn't upset me at all,' said the yogi in fluent French. 'Your aunt has made up her mind that our knowledge might help you, but it all depends on you, young man. Do you agree?'

'Show me first,' Theo answered. 'Then we'll see.'

'Show you?' said the yogi. 'All right.'

He sat down in the lotus position, with his left foot resting on his right thigh and his right foot resting on his left thigh, palms turned upwards and eyes closed. Theo waited. Nothing happened. The yogi's face remained inscrutable. An endless time passed by, and then he opened his eyes and smiled.

'Is that all?' Theo exclaimed.

'Our practice concerns knowledge,' the yogi said. 'The word "yoga" signifies union – yoking together. The yoke is the solid frame that holds the two horses together to pull a cart. The cart is your body, the horses your feelings. The driver is thought, and the reins your intelligence. Yoga tries to hold the team of horses firmly under the yoke by guiding them through thought. Now, you who wanted to see yoga, tell me, what did you see?'

'A man who kept still,' said Theo timidly.

'Good answer,' said the yogi. 'The ability to keep still takes practice, careful exercises, all designed to achieve absolute peace of thought. You can't see that, but I can show you the positions you can use to achieve stillness. Take care! Don't be deceived by the resemblance to gymnastics: what you will take for acrobatics is simply a means of achieving stability. Are you ready?'

'Yes,' said Theo, impressed by the yogi's assurance.

The lesson began. Standing on one leg, the yogi raised the other leg effortlessly behind his head, and stood perched like a heron. Then he unfolded again, placed his hands on his knees and rotated his stomach very fast, so quickly and deeply that Theo was startled to see the ridge of his backbone outlined against the skin of his stomach. The yogi worked his way methodically through a series of positions. Standing on

211

his head, he did the splits horizontally, then touched the ground behind his head with his knees. Lastly, with his arms and legs so closely intertwined that Theo couldn't make out the pattern, he stuck out an enormous tongue and rolled protruding eyes. Theo burst out laughing and got a dig in the ribs and an irate 'Hush!' from Aunt Martha.

Unfazed, the yogi stretched out on the ground and closed his eyes.

'That's the relaxation position, the last one,' Ila whispered in Theo's ear.

'And you want me to learn all this stuff?' asked Theo. 'What for?'

Back in the lotus position, the yogi explained. The principle was simple: the posture was intended to equip the body with the relaxation necessary to meditate, but without effort. Now this ephemeral machine that people called their body was not prepared for stillness – on the contrary. It took some effort just to relax it, let alone forget it. Each of the yoga positions worked on the spinal column, but yoga also acted on the muscles, and even on the internal organs. For instance, in an upside-down position the blood flowed down to irrigate the brain, and the nape of the neck, by resting on the ground, massaged the thyroid gland on which the regulation of humour depended.

'Good humour?' asked Theo.

Both good and bad: the idea was to regulate the passions. Rotating your stomach massaged the intestines, the liver and the spleen, and produced perfect digestion. Yoga did not ignore a single muscle, bone or organ. For the heart, you learned to suspend your breathing, which rested the cardiac muscle. By exercising the throat and vocal chords, you could even make sounds vibrate in your head, and so hear an inner music whose effect was to bring you peace of mind.

'And sticking your tongue out, and making your eyes bulge, what does that do?' Theo asked.

Ah, said the yogi, that was simply a means of stretching and controlling the muscles of the tongue and eye-sockets. This exercise was called 'the lion': quite a lot of yoga positions were inspired by animals. To show what he meant, he squatted down with his hands on his knees, and walked without raising his heels: the crow. He lay on his stomach and leaned on his hands to lift his upper body off the ground: the cobra. Then he knelt down with his torso folded forwards, his hands flat on the ground, and his head retracted into his shoulders: the tortoise. For over two thousand years, yogis had imitated the long series of animal species that, following the metamorphoses of the god Vishnu, had led up to the human race.

'It's funny,' said Theo, 'but I still don't see what use it is.'

The body is sacred, the yogi told him. 'Enter the temple of your body' was the starting-point of his discipline. Yoga was a prayer of mind and body whose ultimate aim was to achieve fusion with the universe. Then the mind dissolved completely, the self disappeared, and the individual, that ephemeral blend of soul and matter, no longer existed.

'Which means that if I go that far I won't be myself any more?' Theo protested. 'Thanks, but no thanks!'

It came as no surprise to the yogi to find Westerners unable to accept an ideal whose aim was the total eradication of their precious individuality. But he explained to Theo that for Hindus, the body was only a temporary lodging, which the soul would leave so as to enter another body, another lodging, until its final release from its burden of matter enabled it to rejoin the universal soul from which it had been parted.

'I get it,' said Theo. 'One day you're going to be reincarnated. But here and now, what do I have to gain?'

The answer was peace of mind: the health of the body depended on it. By practising the art of breathing every day, yogis achieved such close control of their cardiac rhythm that they were able to suspend their heartbeat, make a long transition into the pattern of a deep sleep, and stay buried underground for several days as if they were dead, except that they eventually returned to life.

'Do you do that?' Theo marvelled.

No, Aunt Martha's yogi was not one of those human guinea pigs who fascinated American scientists. He would not have consented to be shut up in a tank and watched by an army of observers with eyes glued to their monitor screens. He was content to seek knowledge, to control his pair of harnessed horses, and to practise non-violence, love of others, avoidance of anger, and indifference to material goods – which was plenty to get on with, after all. And he proposed to teach Theo the art of spiritual repose.

'Sounds like sleeping,' Theo muttered. 'That I can do.'

It wasn't sleep that the yogi meant, even though most people did not know the art of sleeping. True repose was something quite different: a sense of calm after struggle, a mind adrift on the tide. It also involved kindling the energies, hidden inside oneself, that strengthened mind and body both at once. For yogis had a special concept of the human body that viewed the whole length of the spinal column as containing energy centres, the *chakras*, each of which ruled a level of the organism. These circles could be wakened one by one, and if you reached the

213

last of them, just above the crown of the head – the position of the fontanelle in babies – then you opened up the last of the *chakras*, the dazzling white, thousand-petalled lotus. The exercise was extremely difficult, because it called for waking an inner serpent coiled in the 'sacred' region known in the Western system of anatomy as the 'sacrum', at the base of the spine.

The yogi explained that it was close to the sacrum that the testicles were located in the human foetus. The aim in yoga was to force the serpent, the *kundalini*, to climb upwards to the brain. The inner serpent was female – a particular form of all-powerful female energy. No intervention on earth by the god Shiva could do without the manifestation of that female power, or *shakti*, which was present in all bodies, men's as well as women's. It was this power, in serpent form, that had to be channelled to the crown of the head.

'A serpent at the base of the spine,' Theo mused. 'Could that have something to do with sperm, by any chance?'

The yogi smiled: Theo had guessed correctly. But in the yoga view, sperm was also present in women, because female energy was shared equally between the two sexes. Sometimes, in certain Hindu sects, in order to increase it, intercourse was deliberately prolonged in order to make sperm rise into the head.

'Unbelievable,' Theo gasped. 'Wait till I tell Fatou!'

But the yogi quickly pointed out to him that this practice was reserved for a few advanced initiates, and needed years of training. On the other hand, the simple awakening of inner energy was available to ordinary people.

'Including you?' asked Theo.

The yogi humbly confessed that he counted these precious moments on the fingers of his two hands, but the rest of the time he was content to worship the deity as best he could, by way of his own body.

'It boils down to saying that yoga is a religion for the individual alone,' Theo decided. 'God is ourselves. People should even be able to do without God altogether. Is that it?'

No, said the yogi, in India it was impossible to do without the idea of divinity. But a young Westerner could try yoga without believing, most certainly.

'OK,' said Theo. 'For health and peace of mind, it's worth trying. Teach me.'

Theo and his guru

The yogi told Theo to sit down cross-legged and asked him to place his left foot on his right thigh, then his right foot on his left thigh, and then to lower his head, keeping his neck straight, and repeat after him a series of vowels, starting with 'a' and ending with 'om'. A-om. On 'om' he must close his mouth and smile: then, said the yogi, Theo should feel his lips vibrate.

'A-om,' Theo repeated. 'I can't feel anything. A-om . . .'

'The smile,' the yogi reminded him.

'A-o-om.' Theo smiled when he chanted. 'It vibrates! Aunt Martha, tell me what all this monkeying around is for . . . I'm not a Hindu!'

Monkeying around: the phrase was well chosen, said the yogi. Because the human race had no special priority in the order of the universe, and the yoga tradition was glad to make room for all living species: monkey, lion, bird, insect, and even the deadly cobra.

'If it's eco-friendly that's good,' Theo admitted.

Breathing exercises. Breathe very hard through the nostrils to clear them properly, hold your breath, breathe out. Stop up one nostril and breathe in through the other, hold your breath, stop up the other nostril and breathe out. Hold your breath with your stomach expanded . . . But at this point Theo winced.

The yogi frowned and felt his stomach.

'I feel something wrong in the blood,' he said with concern. 'The winds are not blowing through the proper channels. Let me see what I can do.'

True yogis had access to supernatural powers, called *siddhi*, which some of them could use to heal the sick. The yogi told Theo to lie on the ground, and laid both hands on his left side.

'Can you feel anything, young man?'

'Warmth,' Theo answered.

'All right,' said the yogi. 'Now, you're going to do just as I say. Feet apart, hands by the side of your body, palms upward. Close your eyes. Let your tongue lie loose in your mouth. Relax your toes, ankles and calves . . .'

Soon Theo was feeling as heavy as lead. The yogi spoke in a murmur about a gardener who cleared out the irrigation channels in a garden, and about a water lily that opened gladly, floating on the water. Now Theo was light as a feather, and he felt himself float in his turn. When his breathing evened out, he fell asleep.

215

'The boy is tired,' said the yogi. 'Very tired. But death has called a halt.'

'It's strange,' said Aunt Martha. 'In order to heal him, you made him assume the posture you call "the corpse". Can you tell me why?'

The yogi smiled. Only the corpse posture enabled the dread of death to be mastered, he told her. Then Theo woke up of his own accord, and the yogi made sure to ask him to flex his toes before asking him to stand up slowly, in case he might feel dizzy.

'So how do you feel?' asked Aunt Martha.

'I'm all right,' said Theo. 'I feel a bit funny though – the way I did when I was little, and Mum used to bathe me. It's cool.'

The yogi recited the final prayer then joined his hands and bowed: the lesson was over. He put on his cap, picked up his blanket and draped it neatly round himself, then walked away.

'Now you have a guru,' said Ila, who had not said a single word till now.

'Me?' said Theo, taken by surprise.

'Guru means teacher,' she said. 'You have a teacher.'

'But I don't even know his name!'

'His name is Mr Kulkarni,' said Aunt Martha. 'He came all the way from Bombay. But you must be respectful, and call him Guru-ji.'

'Mr Kulkarni,' said Theo. 'So I've got a guru of my own. That's too much! Wait till I ring Fatou – she'll crack up when I tell her!'

Right in the middle, a tea

Theo had already picked up his mobile when Aunt Martha's gesture halted him.

'Before you call Fatou, what about seeing to your message?'

'My message . . . I'd forgotten. Can you give me any help?'

'No I can't. No cheating!'

Theo scrabbled in his pocket and found the slip of paper. *Neither coming nor going, nor death, nor rebirth . . .*

'*Neither coming nor going* – sounds like yoga,' he said. '*Nor death, nor rebirth.* So does that, if I heard him right. But that doesn't tell me where the next town is.'

'You're forgetting the middle,' said Aunt Martha.

'The middle of the bed?'

'The middle way,' she stressed. 'The way, Theo.'

'A road? A path? A footpath, a motorway . . .'

'Not bad,' said Aunt Martha. 'Keep going.'

'You're nagging!' said Theo. 'I'd rather call Fatou, and I'm going to!'

Aunt Martha sheepishly admitted that she ought to have waited before expecting Theo to rack his brains for answers, but Fatou was already on the line.

'Yes, it's me, it's Theo.' He raised his voice. 'Can't hear me? I'm a long way away – too far, Fatou . . . In Benares. You're getting an echo? Not me, you sound fine.'

He cupped his hands around the phone.

'I've learned some incredible stuff,' he whispered. 'If you knew how . . . I said some incredible stuff. I've found myself a guru . . . Still can't hear? OK, I'm going to shout. I SAID I'VE FOUND A GURU. Really? It doesn't surprise you? He taught me how . . . I said HE TAUGHT ME HOW TO WAKE UP A SNAKE DEEP DOWN INSIDE YOU. Yes, you keep a snake inside your hips. I said YOU HAVE A SNAKE TOO. Listen, I'll show you. Am I OK? I think so. I said I THINK SO. Oh, and if you could give me my clue, now's the time . . . What? Say again. The way of what? Of tea? The way of tea? Are you sure? All right, kisses all over. I said A BIG FLOCK OF KISSES, FLYING YOUR WAY! Yes. Me too.'

Theo was panting for breath, and scowling at his cell-phone.

'It's always like that when you call from Benares,' Aunt Martha informed him. 'Did you get your clue?'

'Yes,' said Theo, his annoyance already dissolved. 'The way is the way of tea. I don't get it. The middle, and tea?'

'Look at the map,' Aunt Martha suggested. 'You never know.'

He opened his atlas, scanned the map of China, and pointed to a spot.

'Here,' he decided. 'They drink tea there, and it's the capital of the Middle Kingdom. It's got to be Beijing.'

'Not a bad guess,' she said, shaking her head. 'But it's not the Middle *Kingdom*, Theo, it's the Middle *Way*.'

'Then I don't know.' Theo looked baffled and discouraged.

'Drop it for now,' she advised, ruffling his hair. 'You've got till tonight. Time for lunch, and your afternoon rest.'

Weddings and freedom

At five o'clock Aunt Martha woke Theo and announced that she had arranged a twilight boat ride. The boat would deliver them to the river-side stairway that led up to Mahantji's house, so that they could wish him goodbye.

'Already?' said Theo. 'But I haven't decoded my message yet.'

'Maybe the Ganges will whisper in your ear,' was all Aunt Martha said in reply.

Taxis and people, bicycles and people, rickshaws threading their way through even more people. Women snatched their children from under the wobbling wheels of cycles looking for a way through, and the tea vendors manoeuvred their portable urns with practised skill. The tangled lines of vehicles slowed to a stop.

'Traffic jam,' said Ila. 'Bound to be a wedding . . . There, what did I tell you? It's a wedding.'

A band of uniformed musicians ambled towards them, playing ophi-cleides. They were followed by a white horse, decked in red velvet and ridden by a turbaned young man with his face veiled in glittering tinsel garlands, a huge paper garland round his neck, and a child sitting in front of him. Liveried attendants carried lighted neon torches. Then came some women dressed in festive saris and dancing in time to the music. At the tail of the procession came an open-topped van with a poor fellow pedalling furiously on a bicycle mounted at the back.

'That's a wedding?' said Theo. 'Where are the bride and groom?'

In India, they weren't on view at this stage of the wedding. You could just about detect the husband's features concealed behind the various garlands. Because he was the star of the occasion, leaving the paternal home astride a white stallion. The child was the youngest in his family . . .

'And the paper garland?'

The garland consisted of banknotes, good omens for wealth. As for the poor wretch toiling on the bicycle, as he pedalled he was turning a tiny generator to keep the neon torches lit. And all this was only day two of a wedding – Indian-style – just like thousands of others being celebrated all over the subcontinent at the height of the season.

'But where's the bride?'

She was waiting in her father's house, with her head bowed in a posture of traditional modesty.

'In a white dress?'

'No,' said Ila. 'In India, white is the colour of mourning. Red, the colour of life, is reserved for the bride's sari. When I was married I wore a bright pink sari, with lots of jewels in my ears, my nose, my hair, on my fingers – all over! Sudhir wore a turban, and he looked so embarrassed it was funny. But when the priest tied us together with a piece of thread, and when we walked seven times round the altar to seal our marriage in front of the gods, we both felt very moved, you know . . .'

'Like all new couples everywhere,' Aunt Martha said. 'Except that you and Sudhir were in love already.'

'Yes,' she agreed with a blush. 'We were lucky.'

'Lucky?' said Theo, taken by surprise. 'To be in love when you were married? That's the usual thing, isn't it?'

Ila sighed. No, in India it was not usual to marry for love. By long tradition, it was the parents who chose a bride for their son, judging by standards that had to include religion, caste, wealth and education . . . Often the bride and groom had never set eyes on each other before, and marriage for love was exceptional.

'So in India you can't choose your own wife!' Theo was scandalized.

Ila did her best to explain. In India, the Hindu religion left no choice – you might say that it didn't know the meaning of the word. Before they were born, all human beings were predestined to carry out their *dharma*, the rightful duty that custom and the universal order required. To depart from that, and follow one's personal choice, was an insult to the gods. And if you wanted, for example, to escape from your original caste, then you could convert to one of the other religions of India, all of them based on individual equality. That was why so many Muslims came from the lower castes, who for centuries had been converting to Islam so as to regain their dignity. That was how, more than ten years after Independence, the leader of the untouchables, a true Buddhist, launched a movement of conversion to Buddhism so as to achieve equality. As for marriage, it was still so thoroughly controlled by the traditional criteria that the government sometimes awarded prizes for mixed marriages, whether between castes or between religions. The battle for equality was still being fought in India, and it was far from being won . . .

Theo thought for a while, then turned and said to Ila: 'Don't think it's over in France, though, because it isn't.'

The jam disentangled and the taxi moved off again. The procession had gone by.

219

Funeral pyres

By the time they reached the river the sun had set. Hawkers cleared their trays and stalls and packed up their wares by the dim lights shining on the steps. Bells rang and gongs sounded for the evening prayer, while pilgrims hurried up the ghats, wrapped in their long brown shawls. The boatman waited on the river bank, where little girls swarmed around other barges, offering for sale little boats made of leaves sewn together, then filled with rose petals and fitted with tiny candles for masts. Aunt Martha bought three of them – one each for Theo and Ila.

'Here, little shrimp,' she said, lighting the candles one by one. 'Launch your boat and make a wish. If it floats downriver without sinking, your wish will come true.'

Theo complied, Ila too, and the Ganges caught and spun their two small craft, which stood still for a moment, then skimmed downstream till they flickered out of sight in the darkness.

'Cast your bread upon the waters,' Aunt Martha murmured, and placed her own boat gently on the stream.

All three had travelled safely.

'There she goes!' cried Theo. 'Then some day I'll marry Fatou.'

The splashing of oars was lost in the silence that lay across the water, darker than the sky overhead. The town appeared to be sleeping, except for the distant flames that danced in the night.

'Look,' said Theo. 'There's something on fire. It's strange, on the bank of the river.'

Neither woman spoke.

'Unless it's for cremation,' he suggested. 'Yes, I'm sure they're funeral pyres.'

Aunt Martha caught her breath, but Theo just turned casually away, leaned over the side of the boat, and trailed his fingers in the water.

'Don't worry so much, old thing,' he continued. 'I knew the other day you were wondering if I'd noticed the smoke. You didn't want me seeing the bonfires, did you? Well, you blew it, and so what? It's just like it is in the films!'

Ila took his hand, and Theo leaned to whisper in her ear: 'She thinks I'm a sissy, you know. But given that after you die you live another life, then . . .'

'Then you're terrific in this one,' said Ila.

'I know,' he grinned. 'Better a bit less terrific, but cured.'

WATERSTONE'S BOOKSELLERS
174 - 176 Argyle Street
GLASGOW
G2 8BT
Tel.No: 0141 248 4314
Fax No: 0141 248 4622
VAT No: 710 6311 84

108 CASH-1   8376 0099 001

THEO'S ODYSSEY   QTY 1   6.99
              TOTAL   6.99

Cash   10.00
              CHANGE   3.01
www.waterstones.co.uk

27.03.01 13:16

Searching for
a book?

www.waterstones.co.uk

Visit us 24 hours
a day at

www.waterstones.co.uk

Any book at the
touch of a button

www.waterstones.co.uk

Visit us 24 hours
a day at

www.waterstones.co.uk

Free delivery to
any branch

www.waterstones.co.uk

The boat drew up to the river bank in near pitch darkness. They had arrived.

Mahantji delivers the message

At this point the steps were really steep. Theo skipped up them like a goat, and the two women followed more slowly.

'Don't go so fast!' Aunt Martha panted.

'Hey, it's me who's supposed to be ill,' Theo called out from the top. 'Get a move on, slowcoach!'

The slowcoach toiled upwards, pausing on every step.

'When I think of the yoga I've done,' she puffed. 'I'm much too fat!'

'A proper whale,' said Theo, poker-faced, and came to take her arm.

Wrapped in his white shawl, Mahantji waited under the pipal tree. The white of the miniature temples had turned to pale blue, and a dancing thread of moonlight had begun to trickle across the water. Mahantji sat down by the edge of the terrace and invited his guests to join him. Then he asked Ila a whole string of questions that meant nothing to Theo because it was Hindi they were speaking. Every now and then, Mahantji would shake his head and open his eyes in surprise; sometimes he burst out laughing. When his face clouded over, Theo realized that he was the cause. Eventually he shot a glance at Theo and asked a final question.

'Mahantji would like to know how you are feeling today,' Ila said. 'He has been praying for you.'

'Tell him it's been a good day,' said Theo, 'and I feel fine. Except that I still haven't worked out my message, but apart from that . . .'

Ila translated. Mahantji smiled, and offered his assistance.

'He knows the answer?'

'Of course,' said Ila. 'He set the question.'

'Wow!' said Theo.

Mahantji explained through Ila that the first time he had been to Paris it was only to change planes at Roissy airport, and all he recalled was the sight of some men with dark skins and blue overalls, sweeping the ground. Years later, a French friend of his had decided to give him a different view, and invited him to Normandy. Mahantji had discovered winding roads, green meadows, apple trees, and plump cows grazing in the fields. He had enjoyed the visit so much that he told his friend: 'For this life, it's getting late, but next time I'd love to be reincarnated in France.'

'What was the best part?' asked Theo.

Mahantji pointed to the shimmering river. The finest sight, he said, was the moonlight reflected in the sea below Mont Saint-Michel. The Middle Way.

It was time to solve the message. For thousands of years, Hindu philosophy had been searching for the meeting point between the soul and its absolute. In order to arrive there, certain philosophers had developed a logic in the form of a dual negation that they expressed as 'Neti. . . Neti' – neither . . . nor, not this, not that. Neither coming nor going, nor death, nor rebirth. This asceticism of renunciation they combined with an asceticism of the body, designed to give rigorous control. One day a prince forsook his palace and became a perfect ascetic. Then, realizing that this was not enough to achieve the absolute, he saw that extreme solutions were worthless, and that the Middle Way must be practised in everything.

'Got it,' said Theo. 'It's Buddha.'

Buddha it was. Now all he had to do was reach the place. Where were Buddhist temples found? In the mountains, 'up there'.

'Brilliant!' cried Theo. 'We're going to Tibet.'

Unfortunately, Lhasa was out of the question. The altitude was too dangerous for his health, and the doctors had objected. But in India there was a Buddhist town in the Himalayas, more than two thousand metres above sea level, in a region where a world-famous variety of tea was grown. All Theo had to do was to identify this special kind of tea.

'A tea known all over the world?' said Theo. 'I'm an expert, you'll see. Earl Grey. No, it's an English name. Orange Pekoe? Doesn't sound like a place.'

Assam was a good guess, but wrong. Lapsang Souchong was Chinese. When Theo dried up, Mahantji spoke the name of the town, which lay at the heart of vast tea plantations: Darjeeling.

'What a thicko!' said Theo, clapping his hand to his forehead. 'And Aunt Martha even mentioned the place. When do we leave?'

Oh, not directly, because the weather was cold up there. The plan was to stay a bit longer in Benares, then return to Delhi for Theo's medical check-up, and then fly to Silguri, and drive up into the mountains by car. The reason for having to say goodbye to Mahantji was that he would be leaving next day to attend a world conference on river conservation, because in civilian life the high priest was also a water pollution control engineer, and the Ganges was one of the worst polluted rivers in the world. For many years, Mahantji had been fighting like Hanuman himself on behalf of his sacred river, the mother, inundated every day with waste water from the city of Benares.

According to legend, the Ganges was a goddess who came down from the Himalayas to water the parched earth, but the young Ganga was a wilful girl, and she decided to give a mighty leap and flood the earth, just for fun. The gods got worried – she would ruin all their work – so Shiva planted himself on the spot where the obnoxious brat was going to land, and caught her in his tangled hair. Once she was tamed, Ganga grew docile, and became the most generous of mothers. The water of the divine river was pure by definition. For pilgrims, it was an article of faith that the Ganges was the soul of purity, so Mahantji had to keep repeating that religious and physical cleansing did not necessarily coincide – there was purity and purity, the first a spiritual, the second a scientific fact. As a high priest, Mahantji protected the purity of Ganga; as a scientist he fought hard for the purity of the river. All it required was to divert the waste water . . .

Theo gazed down in disappointment at the wake of the moon in the river. Was it conceivable that those shining waters were a home for millions of bactcria? Was the Ganges nothing but a dangerous illusion?

'*Maya*,' sighed Mahantji, as if reading Theo's thoughts. 'Illusion.'

Then, after explaining that the whole world was nothing but illusion, a veil of appearances, he took Theo to stand in front of the tiny altar where the sandals of the poet Tulsidas were worshipped. It was time for the final evening sacrifice. A priest used an iron hoop set with burning torches to draw a circle of fire in the air. Reflections danced redly over the stone, the priest kept a crowd of little bells ringing softly, Mahantji put an arm round his shoulder, and Theo felt his tension dissolve. The river might be polluted, but the sky above Benares remained as pure as Mahantji's heart.

CHAPTER 13

Demons and Wonders

Bells and bazaars

Mahantji had gone away, but even without him the rest of their stay in
Benares went like a dream. Aunt Martha's regime was inflexible. Wake
up at 7, with tea in bed, an English custom still preserved in India –
strong tea to dissolve the haze of sleep. At 7.30, yoga lesson with
Professor Wacko; 8.30, shower and breakfast; 9, outing till midday.
Compulsory siesta. Late afternoon, visit the city bazaars.

After three days, Theo could stand on his head, and the relaxation
was starting to take effect. With breathing, the boy had trouble, but Mr
Kulkarni was so persuasive that he managed to teach him the vital
method of breathing through the stomach that opened his lungs and
straightened his shoulders. In less than a week, Theo was hooked on
his guru. Mr Kulkarni joined in all their expeditions, and because he
knew so many things he had a fund of stories to tell.

They set out into the green surrounding countryside to explore the
vast sacred zone called Kashi, the original name of Benares. Kashi the
radiant, Kashi the glorious, Kashi the City of Light, was the geographical
heart of Hinduism: the true Hindu must set out on foot along a series
of stages, each of them marked by a temple, and sleep in very ancient
dormitories built specially for pilgrims. The winding pilgrimage passed
through little villages where intrigued peasants stared at this odd party
made up of an elderly memsahib, a beautiful Indian woman very much
at ease with foreigners, a yogi wrapped in his threadbare blanket and

armed with a staff of peace, and a young man with curly black hair who but for the green of his eyes would have resembled Lord Krishna. But when it came to Westerners, the peasants of Benares had seen it all before.

All along their route, the four companions entered the little temples and rang on their waiting bells, and Mr Kulkarni prayed with equal fervour, whether to Durga, to Shiva, or to Ganesa. If he could not identify the god of the place, he worshipped the unknown. Sometimes the temples stood by lakesides where steps led down to the water; the women bathed, or did their washing, while the men splashed around; all of them prayed there, with their hands together, as pilgrims did in the Ganges. Because there was not a river in India, nor any lake or stream, that was not a distant descendant of our mother Ganga. As a necessity of life, and so of prayer, all water was sacred.

But what Theo liked best was their twilight strolls through the bazaars. The lanes were so narrow that when a cow ran down them, tossing its horns, pedestrians had to flatten themselves against the wall. They were too bold for Theo's liking, and like the children of Benares he got into the habit of giving them a smack on the rear – not that it ever seemed to worry them. Theo bought a diamond nose stud for his mother. Aunt Martha spent a fortune in the emporium owned by her favourite silk merchant. Theo admired the careless, practised gestures that set bolts of silk unrolling in a salon whose walls were covered in white cotton. The owner served his customers with a drink called *lassi*, yoghurt mixed with water, in an earthenware bowl.

All this was delightful, but best of all were the posters of gods, the smiling, dark-eyed Hindu gods, plump and bursting with health. Theo set out to collect them, starting with his very own elephant-god. Then he tackled Shiva when, caught in the flowing locks of the blue-skinned god, he found the beautiful face of Ganga, with river water gushing from her helpless mouth. There were angry Shivas, furiously brandishing their tridents, Shivas with their eyes closed, meditating, with the snowy Himalayas in the background. He even found a very strange one, divided down the middle, one half a woman, the other a man. Mr Kulkarni explained that the great god was both female and male, and that the image expressed how much of the other sex was present in every human being.

'So I'm supposed to have some female in me?' said Theo in surprise. 'I don't see where . . .'

'But in Luxor, just before the dance, didn't the Sheikha call you "the bride"?' Aunt Martha reminded him.

226

Theo remembered and looked flustered, for his underworld twin chose that moment to surface once again. It was the time of day when the bells began to ring. The red-streaked sky over Benares was darkening fast, and birdsong answered the call of the night. 'I'm here, little brother,' whispered the quiet voice from nowhere. 'I won't leave you . . .'

'Theo, what's the matter? Are you dreaming?' said Aunt Martha.

Yes, he was dreaming. For the first time, it occurred to Theo that the twin brother who had risen from the depths of the dance in Egypt might have been a twin sister. Then his eye alighted on another poster, where Shiva stood flanked by Ganesa on one side, and on the other by a shining young man, armed with a spear.

'Hey look, a new one,' he said. 'Who's he?'

Two guardians at the door

Then Mr Kulkarni sat down: it was going to be a long explanation.

The young man's name was Skanda, and he was Shiva's unwanted son. One day, the gods needed a warrior to fight demons, and they requested Shiva to sire a son. Shiva agreed, and he married Parvati, but because he was an ascetic he spent a thousand years in congress with her, but did not conceive a son.

'I don't understand,' said Theo. 'Congress for a thousand years. What's that about?'

While Mr Kulkarni suffered a sudden fit of coughing, Aunt Martha came to the rescue. As ascetics alone had the power to retain their semen and channel it up to the brain, they could lie with a woman for a long time, and yet do nothing. Theo was none the wiser.

'Without going all the way,' said Ila, blushing.

'Oh,' said Theo, 'you mean without ejaculating? Why didn't you say so?'

Now it was clear, and Mr Kulkarni could relate how the impatient gods interrupted the holy exercise, distracting Shiva, whose seed fell into the fire, which consigned it to the water, which passed it to the reeds, until at last it gave birth to Skanda, whose name meant 'gush of semen'. Actually, as a devotee of the goddess Ganga the good yogi preferred a shorter version: seeing Ganga leap down from heaven, the god found her so beautiful that he ejaculated into the river, from which Skanda was born . . . Anyway, this meant that Shiva had two children: Ganesa the fat and Skanda the handsome.

'How many stories are there about Ganesa?' Theo asked.

All sorts, especially because the elephant-god had travelled a lot, and turned up in China and Tibet in the shape of a pot-bellied child dressed in red and armed with Shiva's trident, but as a god of the Kitchen. In Japan, as in India, he was the god of Good Luck, but also of Wealth, a jolly little man standing on two sacks of rice. But he always had a door to guard: his mother Parvati's, or the door of a temple or kitchen. On the other side of the door, Skanda also kept watch. For any door there were two guardians: Skanda the handsome, born of his father's seed, and Ganesa the greedy, offspring of his mother's intimacy. One sprang from the paternal fire, the other from the maternal waters.

'Now we're nearly in China,' Aunt Martha interrupted. 'There, two principles rule the order of the universe: the Yin shadow and female, the Yang sun and male, as you'll see.'

'Another Ganesa story,' Theo begged.

The tale of the god's missing tusk came in all sorts of variations. According to the best-known account, Ganesa pulled it out to give it to the very first writer, so becoming the god of literature. In a different version, one day Ganesa was out riding on his rat, when a big snake crossed his path. The rat took fright and threw his rider, whose swollen belly, stuffed with sweetmeats, burst, and scattered some of its contents over the ground. To save the rest, and hold himself together, the elephant-god took hold of the snake and used it for a belt. He looked so silly that the whole sky rang with the Moon god's glee, till Ganesa lost his temper, broke off a tusk and hurled it at the jeering yellow face, which went dark and disappeared. Ever since that day, the Moon has periodically gone missing.

A whole new treasury of stories. Theo was fascinated.

On another evening, when Theo stopped in front of a poster of Vishnu, Mr Kulkarni explained why the god was asleep on the ocean, and supported and canopied by a giant snake. At the beginning of time, a terrible fire consumed the earth, the Underworld and the sky: this was the first sacrifice. Then clouds gathered and the rain submerged the universe. Vishnu now became the guardian of all the creatures, made of mud and fire, whose lives were yet to come, and then he fell asleep for ever on the cosmic ocean.

'And the ocean is a sea of milk,' the yogi concluded.

'A sea of milk!' said Theo. 'Better tell Nestlé!'

'No,' said Aunt Martha, 'because the milk is churned.'

'In that case it's butter,' Theo decided.

Not butter either, because in India they used clarified butter, *ghee*, produced by boiling ordinary butter five times to remove the impurities. This purified ghee was so sacred that it was poured over dead bodies just before cremation.

'What a dish!' said Theo. 'And what about the giant snake?'

The snake belonged to the vast underground empire of the Nagas, which lay beneath the waters. That was why the ashes of the dead must return to the river, and why a handful of their ashes was thrown into the Ganges, because after the sacrifice to fire, with cremation, came the sacrifice to water. And according to tradition, the victim thus offered was the body itself.

'I see,' said Theo. 'You burn like a little joint of meat, basted in butter. But in the end it's better than rotting underground, I think.'

Mr Kulkarni objected to this, because what happened to the body had nothing to do with the immortal soul, and it was his job to train the soul to be better prepared for death. Finding that the conversation was drifting towards topics she wanted to avoid, Aunt Martha decided that the time had come to leave Hinduism to its colourful mythology and turn towards the Buddha, who had nothing to do with these exotic fantasies.

The fabulous legend of the Buddha

So next day they visited Sarnath, on the outskirts of Benares, just a few kilometres north of the city, because it was there, in the place called the Deer Park, that the Buddha had spoken his first sermon, and first set in motion the wheel of the law, the wheel of dharma.

It was only a vast and beautiful garden, planted with towering trees, where not far from some anonymous ruins stood a tall round monument made of brick and stone. Feeling a touch disappointed, Theo sat down in the shade: how was he to imagine the Buddha in this peaceful landscape?

Aunt Martha explained, in considerable detail, that the wheel was the chief symbol of Buddhism, the emblem of the everlasting cycle of birth and reincarnation: it was release from the wheel that brought serenity. The same wheel appeared in the middle of the national flag of modern India, in memory of the first Buddhist ruler, and unifier of the country, the Emperor Asoka. Then she embarked on the great monument standing among ancient trees: the first 'stupa' of Buddhism, which contained some of the Buddha's relics. Buddhist stupas – mound-shaped shrines – often held relics of the first Buddha or his successors. Theo yawned.

After that, she went on to list all the successive names of the son of King Suddhodana and Queen Maya, of the Sakya clan – how his given name was Siddhartha, meaning 'He who hits the mark', the expert bowman, his family name Gautama, and how his name became Sakya-muni, wise one of the Sakya clan, and afterwards Buddha, the Awakened. Theo nearly dozed off.

'If I'm boring you, just say so!' his piqued enlightener grumbled.

'Er, well . . .' mumbled her nephew, glazed with apathy. 'I liked Mr Kulkarni's stories better.'

'Over to you, guru-ji,' Aunt Martha sighed, and the very learned yogi obeyed.

Prince Siddhartha was born in Kapilavastu, in a small kingdom in what is now Nepal, in April or possibly May of a year sometimes given as 566, sometimes as 563 or 558 BCE, and was eighty years old when he died. He married at the age of sixteen, abandoned his wife and his palace when he was twenty-nine, and achieved illumination in 523, or it might have been 517 . . .

'I've had enough of all this classroom stuff,' Theo burst out. 'What does it matter whether it was 517 or 523? Who cares? Only bookworms! And what good are *they*, unless you can stretch them into a belt for Ganesa?'

Luckily, the legends went much further. For instance, the man who was about to become the Buddha had chosen his own parents. He had entered his mother's side in the shape of a snow-white elephant . . .

'No, no,' Aunt Martha protested. 'If she really existed, which we don't know for certain, it was a dream Queen Maya had about her son, that's all!'

'Shh!' said Theo.

. . . And he did not grow inside his mother's womb, but in a shrine of precious stone. He was not born in the usual way, but emerged from his mother the same way he had entered. The moment he was born the infant roared like a lion, announcing loud and clear that he was the best in the world, and oldest in the world, and that this would be his final rebirth.

'Ridiculous,' snapped Aunt Martha. 'Roared like a lion? It doesn't match his teaching at all.'

'Do be quiet!' cried Theo. 'It's a lot better than the different names of the Buddha.'

When the future Buddha visited the temple for the first time, the statues of the gods bowed down to him. A wise old man flew from the

Himalayas and asked to see the miraculous child. He took him in his
arms and wept at the thought that he would not live long enough to
follow his future teachings. When the king asked whether his son would
grow up to become a great sovereign like himself, the wise man
answered that the child would be lord of the world. Seven days later,
Maya died. His father now decided to bring up his son to become a
great king, and kept him shut inside the palace with all its pleasures.
The young prince married two princesses and had a son. It was then,
when he was twenty-nine years old, that thanks to the watchful gods,
he slipped out of his gilded prison and saw on different visits to the
streets of the town a sick man, an old man, and a dead man . . .

'Listen to that, Aunt Martha,' said Theo. 'You forgot about the dead
man.'

Then by the roadside he came across a monk with a peaceful face.
The prince realized that in the shelter of the palace he had been kept
away from the essence of life, which was *dukkha*: suffering. But he
also realized that through meditation it was possible to overcome suffering and achieve serenity, and so he made his escape by night, abandoning his wives and child. There ended the legend of the Buddha's
birth.

'And not before time,' said Aunt Martha.

'You'd think it was Jesus,' said Theo. 'No father, then he enters his
mother's body by a miracle, a wise man comes a long way to see him
– they're similar stories.'

But from then on, nothing was the same. The prince who had
renounced the world began his quest with the exercises practised in
his own time: it took him only a year to become a yogi. Then he
withdrew for six years and entered a period of fasting. He managed to
stop eating altogether, and reduced himself to a living skeleton, so
consumed by his own ascetic fire that he wasted almost into dust. Now
came the decisive event: he understood the uselessness of mortification,
and broke his never-ending fast by accepting the gift of boiled rice
offered by a peasant woman. It was such a change of tune that his
baffled first disciples took offence and left him. Give up the ascetic life?
Unthinkable!

Since the prince of renunciation had spanned the whole of the scale
from pleasure, women and fatherhood to yoga and asceticism, now he
could move on to meditation. Sitting beneath a spreading pipal, he
waited to achieve what he already called the Awakening. Death came
to tempt him in the form of demons and monsters, but he resisted.

Then came Love, in the shape of seductive women. In fact, the same deity, Mara, incarnated both love and death: at dawn he admitted defeat. During the first vigil, the Buddha travelled all the worlds in spirit. On the second night he pondered on all his previous lives, and the lives of all men and women. In the third vigil he understood how to stop the cycle of birth and rebirth. By daybreak he had become the Awakened, the Buddha. He found his estranged disciples, brought them to Sarnath, into this garden, and expounded his teaching, based on compassion.

At this point, Mr Kulkarni was content to stop.

Aunt Martha teaches Buddhism

'That's a bit short on the teaching!' said Aunt Martha.

'Why?' said Ila. 'It's the truth, after all.'

Aunt Martha surveyed her companions from the height of her ample self, and criticized their narrow conception. The Buddha had given the world a genuine philosophy, which had nothing to do with a religion of gods and demons. No, the Buddha had discovered so much: the four noble truths alone mattered far more than all these fairy tales.

'Listen, Theo,' she said. 'It's very simple. The first truth is that all existence is suffering.'

'I don't agree with that,' said Theo.

'But it's true,' she insisted. 'Because everything fades. Even happiness, even the joy that comes from meditation. Everything is transitory, the Buddha says, which means . . .'

'It doesn't last, I get it. What else?'

'The second truth is that the cause of suffering is selfish craving, what the Buddha calls "the thirst to be oneself". Even the wish for ecstasy is part of that.'

'OK, so how do you lose it?' Theo asked.

'Through the third truth, you see. To take away the suffering of transience you must achieve nirvana. Nirvana is eliminating thirst, breaking free of attachments. The last of the four truths describes the ways to get there.'

'Tell me about it!' said Theo sceptically.

'Well, it's the Middle Way. Avoid pursuing happiness by seeking pleasures, and also avoid the quest for bliss through asceticism. The right view in everything – right in the middle. So wisdom comes, and it is only then that compassion enters in, not only for all people but for all living beings. Because if the whole sum of everything that exists in the world is transitory, and if even knowledge is perishable, then self no longer exists, there's no room left for selfishness. But most of all, it's not in another life or in some different place that the state of nirvana is achieved, but here and now, in present time.'

'Nirvana's the name of a rock group,' said Theo. 'Apart from that, I don't understand what you're saying.'

'I'll try to explain,' said Aunt Martha. 'As they emerge from contemplation, those who follow the paths of the Buddha can say: "Oh, nirvana! Destruction, calm, an excellent way out!" Because the Buddha speaks literally about "pulling the house down". Of course, that means, not knocking it flat with a bulldozer, but becoming detached from it, destroying it in its protective essence. Just like the body, the house is transitory, and this view is not the Buddha's invention: in fact, in Hinduism the cosmos, the human body and the home obey the same universal order, strictly defined for everyone at birth. Isn't that so, guru-ji?'

'Indeed,' the yogi replied.

'So no more conditionings, says the Buddha. And if you succeed in eradicating the idea of home, body and cosmos, then Hinduism's ancient taboos disappear, and that means no more social rules, and no more castes. Isn't that right, guru-ji?'

Mr Kulkarni, who was a Brahman, nodded and did not protest.

'So it follows that everybody can achieve calm, and perfected thought and action; everybody can escape suffering, and not only the privileged. Do you see?'

'I think I do,' said Theo. 'You're saying that the Buddha did to Hinduism what Jesus did to the religion of the Jews. He made it available to everybody.'

'Bravo!' cried Aunt Martha. 'You skip right past the philosophy of transience, but you're on the right track.'

'You haven't mentioned the Buddha's famous smile,' said Ila.

'Let's go and see it,' said Aunt Martha. 'Seeing is best.'

At the exit to the gardens, in the little museum, was a statue of the Buddha meditating. His peaceful, broad, mysterious smile was more eloquent than all Aunt Martha's lectures. Theo stroked his feet of polished stone and wondered how you could quell that deplorable thirst that he personally identified with life.

'Is it OK to eat, at least?' he asked timidly. 'I feel quite hungry.'

'Who said anything about fasting?' Aunt Martha replied. 'Self-denial can be taken too far. Where would you like to go?'

The tyrant emperor's mosque

On the morning of their last day in Benares, Aunt Martha announced that they mustn't ignore the great mosque. They had almost forgotten that because of its location on a strategic ford over a great river, Benares had been continuously inhabited for over two and a half thousand years, and a key trading centre. The Mughal emperors had held the city for centuries, there was still a big Muslim community, and the mosque had a history of its own.

From its site on Benares's highest ground, the immense mosque, coloured a majestic pink, towered arrogantly over the temples and the Ganges. But access was impossible: the mosque was ringed by barriers.

'This must have something to do with the Hindu fundamentalists,' said Ila unhappily. 'They want to pull it down to purify the city.'

'The way they did with the Babri Masjid mosque in Ayodhya in 1992,' Aunt Martha said. 'What a way to behave!'

'What do they hold against the place?' asked Theo.

The root of the trouble was not the mosque, but its builder, who was Emperor Aurangzeb, one of the children of Shah Jahan. During his own reign, Shah Jahan the tolerant had spent a fortune on building the Taj Mahal, a gigantic tomb for his dead wife. In reaction to his father's laxity, Aurangzeb became a puritanically strict Muslim: he destroyed Hindu temples, reorganized the empire, and built the famous mosque in Benares using stones from the temples he had destroyed. In India, he had bequeathed the memory of a cruel sovereign who would stop at nothing to persecute his Hindu subjects, so the extremist political parties who wanted to restore the Hindutva, the Hindu nation, longed to retaliate by razing his mosque in Benares, even though it was a famous part of their country's heritage.

Aunt Martha pointed out that although the mosque was enormous, the tomb of Aurangzeb was very simple: an enclosure, a white sheet, with a hole in the middle and a basil seedling growing through it, and that was all.

Theo went closer. Inside the sculpted niches, swarms of aggressive wasps had built large nests. The mosque was well defended.

Ganesa on a postcard

When he and Theo parted, Mr Kulkarni sighed and gave his pupil a hug, which was unusual for him. Then he went to catch the train that would bring him to Bombay in three days' time. The return to Delhi was not a happy event, even though Captain Lumba came to collect his wife and her friends at the controls of an Indian Airlines plane. Not even a visit to the cockpit could cheer Theo up. First they were leaving Benares, and second there were yet more blood tests to be endured.

The verdict was stable, and Aunt Martha knew that Melina would be upset when she called Paris to pass on the news.

'Listen, Mel, they're saying his condition is stable,' she bellowed through the crackle of the line. 'That means no change – no better and no worse . . . Come home? What on earth for? Yes, of course he's taking his pills. What's that about Benares? The water? We only drank bottled water . . . Ganges water? You can't be serious. All right, if you don't believe me, ask Theo.'

She handed him the phone.

'Mum? No, not a drop, it's much too dirty. What did I see there? Now you're asking. Lots of things. I did some yoga – yes, with a proper teacher. Do you know there's a snake in your spine? . . . No, I'm not teasing . . . Been away long enough? No, I want to keep going! Yes, I know. What do you mean, how do I know? Because Aunt Martha told me, of course. She says I'm stable, so that means I'm no worse than I was before, doesn't it? What about my lentils? All green already? Yes, I miss you. Yes, I do think about you when I go to bed. And in the morning too. I love you too . . .'

He blew a wet kiss into the phone, and hung up.

'She's really strung out,' he said. 'What can I do?'

'Send her a postcard,' Aunt Martha suggested.

No sooner said than done. Theo chose a picture of Ganesa – the pot-bellied baby elephant, rosy with health, smiling on his throne – and wrote a brief message: 'Darling Mum, here's my guardian god. He's the god of Home, with one tusk missing, all for the sake of literature.' This time it was Melina's turn to solve a riddle.

CHAPTER 14

Blessed Lightnings

Tales of two vehicles

'By the way,' said Theo, doing up his belt, 'seeing that we were already on the Middle Way in the garden at Sarnath, why go to Darjeeling? To buy some tea?'

'Aren't you the sharp one!' Aunt Martha laughed. 'In Darjeeling, you'll meet the other form of Buddhism.'

This caught Theo completely by surprise. 'You mean there are two different kinds?'

'The first is called Hinayana, which is Sanskrit for "the Lesser Vehicle". That is the Buddhism we told you about beneath the trees in Sarnath. The second is called Mahayana, "the Great Vehicle", and that is the form that gradually took hold in the Himalayan countries.'

'Meaning Tibet,' said Theo.

'Yes, but don't forget there's also Nepal, Bhutan and Sikkim, where we are going.'

'I thought Sikkim was in India.'

'So it is, but it hasn't been for long. It's a small ancient kingdom annexed by India, and what used to be its religious capital, Darjeeling, is now in the north of an Indian state called West Bengal. If you'll just let me finish, Theo . . . From the Himalayas, Buddhism spread over into China, and then to Japan. Along the way, it became the Great Vehicle.'

'"Vehicle".' Theo sounded puzzled. 'That's a pretty weird name for a religion!'

'It's a "vehicle" made for driving on the Middle Way,' Aunt Martha told him. 'And it has wheels. You remember that the Buddha's first sermon in Sarnath is called "the setting in motion of the wheel of the law"?'

'Yes,' said Theo, 'and I didn't see why.'

'Because while he was meditating the Buddha had come to understand the cycle of birth and death, a true vicious circle. And the Law is what enables people to escape from this circle of suffering by taking the Middle Way. Shaking the Wheel of the Law means breaking out of the infernal circle with the help of a different wheel, which is certainly another cycle, but this time a cycle of teachings. The first cycle you've already met: it involves the four noble truths. The second is devoted to pure emptiness – come to think of it, Theo, it's the exact opposite of Judaism. For Jews, God is Being, and he is full, he contains everything. Well, for the Buddha it's the reverse. The real has no being, it is pure.'

'Then the Jews' Eternal isn't pure?'

'Oh yes, he is pure,' she replied. 'But as the Buddha sees it, being is impermanence, remember. When the thirst for self has been mastered, emptiness enters and spreads, the heart is open to compassion, the shadows fade away, and that is when the final cycle of teachings leads towards the light, which brings the Awakening. In Darjeeling you'll find out about the Great Vehicle.'

'What went wrong between the lesser and the great?'

'Oh, the usual thing in the history of religions,' Aunt Martha shrugged. 'Once the Buddha was gone, the unity of the movement fell apart. The Buddha had left a question with no answer: had he been awakened from the start, or had he slowly made his way towards awakening?'

'That depends,' said Theo. 'In the legend he's like a god, but in life he isn't.'

'That's exactly where one of the fault lines lies. And some people claimed a solution: the Buddha perceived in his lifetime had been nothing but a figment created by the true Buddha.'

'That's not fair!' Theo protested. 'The one who didn't want to be a god . . .'

'Couldn't prevent it from happening,' she agreed. 'The Buddha showed the way to make a personal link with the divine, but the longing for a guide is very deep-seated in people, so Buddhist theologians produced the idea of saintly individuals willing to keep on deferring the bliss of their final Awakening for the sake of the rest of humanity. They call them "bodhisattvas", learner Buddhas who are already well on the way to awakening, and so filled with holiness and compassion that in

238

their greatness they inspire absolute devotion. Their power is almost godlike ... The sublimated Buddha merges into the inaccessible. Do you see now why your guru annoyed me with his legends?'

'Are you a Buddhist, then?'

'In a way,' Aunt Martha admitted. 'And precisely because it is a philosophy that can do without God. We all have to do the best we can to find our personal peace of mind, and that appeals to me. Believe me, Theo, I'm not the only one to find herself tending towards the Middle Way: these days, you'll find Buddhists all over the world ... In the United States, Canada, Switzerland, Germany ...'

'But not in France, at least!' Theo laughed.

'Of course! What do you think – that French people are immune to compassion? There are plenty of Buddhists in your country. They even have a slot in the religious broadcasts on Sunday mornings. As I see it, that's a good sign. Buddhists have no quarrel with anyone, and they're perfectly tolerant people ... Obviously they'll look quite weird to you at first. Their clothes, their prayer wheels, the way they bow down ... it does look strange. But it makes sense. Oh, I'd better remind you that in Tibet, Buddhism came across a very old religion and had to make some compromises with it.'

'A very old Tibetan religion,' Theo mused. 'Do you mean the religion of the *Bardo Todrol*, the Book of the Dead?'

'Ah,' she exclaimed, 'I was forgetting that you've read it. Well, that book doesn't have a lot to say about the religion I'm talking about, which was called "Bon".'

'B-o-n?'

'That's right. In old Tibetan that means the religion of men, the "Bon-pos". I warn you, the story of the fusion between Bon and Buddhism is strange.'

A rope and six small monkeys

So strange that it took two hours' flying time to tell it.

At the beginning of time, according to the myths of the old Tibetan religion, the gods above dwelled in the mountains, the gods below in the Underworld and the waters, and the people lived in the middle. The first king of Tibet had married a mountain goddess, and from their union came the very first people. In the daytime, the king remained on earth, and at night he returned to the sky by means of a magic rope, the colour of light, that he wore on top of his head.

'You've mentioned these locks of hair before,' Theo recalled. 'Talking about the Sikhs, Brahmans, and Samson the . . . um . . . Naz . . .'

'Nazirite,' Aunt Martha supplied.

The image of the rope that led all the way up to the sky was a universal theme; it appeared even among the Indians of Brazil, and always there was some bungling figure who cut the rope to heaven. That is what happened to the sixth king of Tibet, whose fatal flaw was his vanity. He challenged his stableman to a duel, but refused to pass on his divine powers to him. This was unfair, but the stableman confined himself to asking the king to sever his sky rope, and the king's pride led him to agree. His opponent drove a hundred oxen on to the battle-field, with spears lashed to their horns, and pulling cartloads of burning embers. In the havoc that followed, the stableman killed the reckless monarch, who became the first king to die. For ever after, no king could return to heaven by the sky rope. Only magicians and saints could do the trick. That was the myth of the ancient religion of Tibet.

'What's left of the religion?' Theo asked.

There were still some Bon-pos left, who in marriage ceremonies pre-served the custom of tying a cord to the husband's head, and not so long ago, in the Potala palace, the Dalai Lama's vast fortress in Lhasa, three men used to climb all the way down from the top of the roof, by a rope left dangling in mid-air. Then, with the arrival of Buddhism, the story of the king with the sky rope changed completely, and the origin of people changed too.

At the beginning of time, according to Buddhist teachings, a full-grown monkey wanted to become a convert, under the influence of lessons received from a holy Bodhisattva called Avalokitesvara. The saint dis-patched him into the snows of Tibet, because the closer you are to heaven, the better you concentrate. While the monkey was meditating on com-passion, a rock ogress passed by, fell madly in love with him and took on female form. Bound by his vow of chastity, the monkey rejected her advances, but the ogress coaxed him into letting her sleep by his side. Then when persuasion failed, she threatened to give birth to monsters that would consume the human race. Not knowing what to do for the best, the monkey sneaked off to consult the saint, who ordered him to marry the ogress, out of compassion. The saint had seen it coming.

When her six little monkeys were born, the ogress – true to her nature – wanted to gobble them up, but their monkey father saved them, fled into the forest, and there abandoned them. Three years later, the six had multiplied, as monkeys will. Now there were five hundred, and they were starving to death. Once again, the poor monkey was forced to consult his teacher, who climbed on to a sacred mountain, took from inside it five different kinds of grain, and then sowed them. The monkey brought his five hundred young to the spot, and as they ate the grain they shed their fur and tails. They were the first Tibetans.

'So that means that today's Tibetans are all descended from the big monkey,' Theo concluded.

'Yes,' said Aunt Martha, 'and you've met him before. His name is Hanuman.'

'He gets around!' said Theo. 'And what about the other, Avalo-something?'

'Avalokitesvara? In order to convert Tibet to Buddhism, he had spirited himself to the top of the Potala hill, and there let a beam of light shine out of his palm and turn into a monkey.'

'What a muddle,' said Theo. 'So here we have friend Hanuman hatched from the hand of a Buddhist saint, and an ogress I don't like the sound of.'

'I know what you mean,' said Aunt Martha. 'Because the ogress comes from the Bon religion, and all that's left of the sky rope is the beam of light. You see what a tangle it's become . . .'

'A proper dog's dinner,' Theo decided. 'I wonder what I'm going to see in Darjeeling.'

City in the mist

To start with, Theo saw the tiny airport outside Siliguri, where a chunky little car, an Ambassador, was waiting, its cooling fan too feeble to make a difference. By now it was March, and already very hot, but Aunt Martha assured Theo that the air would be cool, and probably chilly, at the altitude of Darjeeling.

The road wound upwards through vast estates where women dressed in broad straw hats picked leaves from compact, bright green shrubs laid out in orderly rows. They had reached the tea plantations.

'These are the bushes that make your favourite drink,' Aunt Martha said.

'Please can we stop?' asked Theo. 'I'd love to see a fresh leaf.'

Working with practised deftness, the women used their fingernails to pinch off sprigs of tender, acid-green leaves from the tops of the bushes. Theo nibbled at a leaf: the taste was fresh and bitter. There was some way to go from this fragile newness to the desiccated, dark brown shreds and curls of leaf, and scraps of twig, that Theo spooned into his teapot – though not so far as the journey from the illusion of the real to the Buddha's pure light . . . Aunt Martha promised that they would buy a packet in Darjeeling. Meanwhile they drove on towards the town, slowing down when they had to crawl their way through banks of low-lying cloud.

Theo nodded off to sleep, and did not wake again till they came to the outskirts of Darjeeling. When he opened his eyes they encountered a towering wall of snow, flushed with the pink of sunset.

'The Himalayas!' he cried. 'I can't believe I'm here.'

'Better get your parka and boots on right now. Look at the steam when we breathe . . . Quick as you can!'

Straggling in tiers across a good kilometre of rising ground, the town was lost in mist, thickened by the smoke from open-air cooking fires. The air was grey, with shadows of darker grey striding though the haze or clustered around a kettle put to boil on a small fire. Darjeeling at dusk was like a ghost town. The Himalayas faded into the gathering night, and Theo felt frozen. Luckily the hotel selected by Aunt Martha was in the colonial style, with a big open fireplace and deep armchairs. The hotel's owner was a friendly, garrulous woman who insisted on telling them all about the important people who had stayed beneath its roof, among them the famous traveller and writer Alexandra David-Neel, who had become a true initiate and expert on the lore and wisdom of Tibet.

'So expert that she was able to keep her body warm in the freezing cold,' Aunt Martha added.

'Surely that's not so hard, with fire,' said Theo.

'Yes,' said Aunt Martha, 'but not if you don't use wood and matches. It's a classic technique used by Tibetan yogis. They sit in the snow stark naked, wrap themselves in a sheet dipped in freezing cold water, and the sheet has to dry on their skin. The fire comes from inside them, through their control of breathing.'

'Oh, sure,' said Theo. 'And I'm supposed to believe that?'

'It's up to you,' Aunt Martha told him. 'Alexandra David-Neel claims that she did it. Now off you go and warm up the sheets in your bed.'

The Tibetan temple

Next day they paid a visit to a temple at the top of the town. By the roadside there were wisps of fabric fluttering on bamboo poles or strung along a line like streamers. They came in all sorts of colours, including pink, pale blue and sea green. Some were in tatters, and grey with dust.

'Do they hang their hankies out to dry in front of their temples?' asked Theo in surprise.

'Have a close look,' said Aunt Martha. 'There's writing on them. Those are not hankies, they're prayer flags. You write a sacred message on the fabric, and then it hangs in the wind till it frays away completely.'

'So that's why they're all in a mess,' said Theo. 'Oh, look at that pretty new red one!'

'Somebody begging the god for a favour,' Aunt Martha remarked.

'What god?'

'Who knows? There are so many!'

That is how Theo learned that the world of Tibetan Buddhism was inhabited by monstrous gods and demons. The gods were terrible but basically peaceful, and the demons as common as the world's illusions. As a token of their triumph, the victors always assumed the form of the vanquished, and it was hard to distinguish the kindly goddess from the demon she had crushed.

'You'll see them in the frescos on the walls,' his aunt informed him. 'Now we must find my friend Lama Gampo.'

'This is too much,' sighed Theo. 'My aunt has a lama friend . . .'

'Lama means "teacher",' she replied. 'Lamas teach the doctrine they learned in the monasteries.'

There was something ominous about the silent mass of the temple that loomed over them, with its golden roof and whitewashed walls daubed with pink clouds outlined in red. Inside the temple, drum beats punctuated the insistent ringing of a bell: di-didi-boom-di-didi-didi-boom . . . A young monk robed in red rushed out of the temple carrying a censer, and swung it in an arc to whack a sleepy dog in the rear. Another boy objected, and they scuffled and laughed. Suddenly the intimidating temple looked more like a playground. Aunt Martha used her hand as an eyeshade and scanned for her lama friend, who finally emerged, all smiles, and rubbing his hands in delight.

Lama Gampo wore a plum-coloured robe. His skull was shaved, and perched on the end of his nose was a small pair of steel-rimmed spectacles that slid off when he bowed to Aunt Martha.

'Hello, young man,' he said as he bent to retrieve them. 'How are you?' He spoke in impeccable French.

Theo was taken by surprise. 'You speak French!' he blurted.

'Naturally,' the Lama replied. 'I left Tibet with our Dalai Lama when he had to flee into exile in 1959. He took refuge in India, in Dharamsala, and since then we have spread all over the world. My destiny took me to France – to Asnières, to be exact.'

'In 1959!' Theo exclaimed. 'How old you must be!'

'Who knows?' said the Lama mischievously.

'But if you live in Asnières, what are you doing here?'

The Lama gestured towards the Himalayas. He had to breathe snowy mountain air from time to time, and feel the presence of his native land beyond the high peaks.

'Let's go inside,' he said, pushing his glasses up the ridge of his nose.

But when Theo reached the peristyle, the Lama stopped him. First of all you turned the prayer wheels. Inside the entrance to the temple there were two huge yellow ones, so heavy that even when he heaved with all his strength, Theo could not shift one.

'First, that's not the right direction,' the Lama told him. 'That's not good, and some say it is harmful. Always turn a prayer wheel clockwise.'

Theo pushed the other way, and as if by magic, the massive wheel revolved.

'Done it!' he shouted. 'By the way, how does it work?'

The Lama explained that inside the wheel there were scrolls inscribed with holy texts and prayers. If you turned the wheel devoutly, you were saying a prayer.

'Convenient,' said Theo.

'Yes, but you have to turn them a lot,' said the Lama. 'And if you do it insincerely, it doesn't count. Is your heart pure and sincere?'

Theo shuffled his feet, and stared down in bafflement at the toes of his trainers. If only he could tell!

'I honestly don't know,' he admitted.

'Perfect,' said the Lama. 'Awareness of ignorance is the beginning of doubt, and that leads on to wisdom. Now you can look at the frescos on the walls.'

At first, Theo saw nothing but a seething pack of monstrous black and red figures with contorted, pop-eyed faces and dripping swords, fighting among themselves against a background of swirling storm clouds. They were so hideous that it took him a while to get used to them. In one corner, dead bodies were being sliced to pieces by demons wielding an enormous saw, while others were being turned on a grill, and others had spikes thrust through their tongues.

'It looks like hell!' cried Theo.

'Because those are hells,' the Lama murmured. 'Or rather, it is the riot of the demons that strikes our imaginations. Look at the centre, young man. You'll find that there are more views of paradise than hell.'

When Theo looked closer, he made out a geometrical shape so complex that he had to make an effort to identify the Buddhas in the lotus position and eight-armed deities positioned inside concentric circles. Eventually, as his eyes became adjusted, he realized that one of the images was simple: a woman, possibly a goddess, seen from the back, sat astride the thighs of a man who faced towards her in the lotus position, with her arms twined amorously round his neck.

'Now this takes some explaining,' he said casually. 'The fighting devils, the beautiful round and square designs, and the porno pose.'

The Lama smiled more widely, and explained. The hellish scenes illustrated the gods' eternal struggle against the demons of the vicious circle, the wheel of existence. Gods in the lotus position sat in the middle of circles in this traditional shape called a mandala: made up of a square enclosed in a circle, itself surrounded by circles enclosed in a larger square, the mandala contained four gateways, and its central, smallest ring stood for the cosmic universe where supreme wisdom floated in an ocean of joy. The mandala was a vision of the ideal palace of godhood, which Buddhists called 'divinity': in the middle sat the embracing couple.

In order to understand the mandala and the ocean of joy, said the Lama, you must look more closely at the fresco that Theo saw as pornographic. Obviously it displayed the sexual union between man and woman, joined together in one of the best-known positions in the world. But that was not the central reference, because what this sacred image symbolized above all was the fusion of the god with female energy: *shakti*. By showing the sexual act at its purest, the image actually illustrated the infinite fulfilment of meditation: the divine union of the male with the female principle was the perfect object through which to achieve that concentration of the spirit from which the ocean of joy would suddenly gush out, and drown awareness.

'Is this where the snake in the backbone comes in?' Theo asked. 'My guru told me something like that. I suppose they're joined for ever, like Shiva and Parvati?'

The delighted Lama informed his visitor that he supposed correctly, except that the focus was no longer on Shiva and Parvati, but on the meditator uniting with his own female side. And this was a lot more complicated, because although the branch of Hinduism called Tantrism involved ritual sexual union, with the semen retained, in Tibetan Buddhism, on the contrary, the monk had no partner. If the Buddha took the form of a married couple making love, then the purpose was to show the complementary link between the groom, who was compassion, and the bride, who was emptiness. The monk entered meditation by concentrating on feminine energy, the source of enlightenment. Just in case, Theo took a photo so that he could show the divine union to Fatou, because after all, the way he saw it, his own *shakti* was a girl from Senegal.

'Now we can go inside,' said the Lama politely.

On the polished wooden floor a row of young novices dressed in their plum-coloured robes were chanting prayers in a low drone, sometimes stumbling over the words, each of them holding a big tambourine and beating time with a curved drumstick. From time to time a thickset monk, armed with a whip, would brandish it over the boys if they made a mistake, and sometimes he struck them lightly. Right in the middle of the temple, a lama was performing a strange routine: he stood up straight, raised his joined hands above his head, lowered them to the level of his neck, and then his heart, and finally lay flat on a wide wooden board, before standing up again with the help of pulley blocks placed on the ground, and starting all over again.

'What are the children chanting?' was Theo's first question.

'The teachings of the bodhisattvas,' the Lama replied. 'But one particular saying of ours is the one you'll hear our pilgrims reciting on the road: "*Om mani padme hum*". The Buddha gave the world a whole lot of words and phrases that we call "mantras": that is the one that everybody knows, but the mantras our future monks have to learn are so difficult that they sometimes make mistakes.'

'That's no reason to hit them with a whip!' Theo protested.

'It's a question of discipline,' the Lama replied. 'First, it removes the cramps in the novices' backs, and second, a teacher must always be a little bit harsh with his pupils – there's no avoiding it.'

'I had some of that in Jerusalem,' said Theo ruefully. 'And what about the gymnast?'

'Those prostrations are tiring but necessary,' Lama Gampo explained. 'It's the cure for pride. Let's look around.'

Then, in the half-light, Theo spied the giant statue of what looked like a smiling, golden Buddha, with outstretched hands. Round his neck he wore some coloured scarves, and draped over his shoulders an enormous cloak of yellow satin. On the altar in front of him stood some sprays of coloured daisies that might have been sculpted in wax.

'The Buddha,' Theo whispered, moved by the sight.

'No, that is a bodhisattva,' the Lama corrected him. 'But you can think of him as the Buddha if you like, because each bodhisattva is travelling the path to Awakening.'

'Those flowers are pretty,' Theo remarked.

'They're made of yak's butter,' said Aunt Martha.

Butter? Theo couldn't believe his ears. He went over to the altar, stroked a single petal with his fingertip, and tasted: a rancid tang came through. The flowers really were carved out of butter.

'But they'll melt!' he said out loud.

'Hush . . .' his aunt whispered. 'In the Himalayas, there is no shortage of water, but people get cold. Here, fat is a staple of life, so butter here is as precious as water is in India. Anyway, in a climate like this one, butter doesn't melt.'

Theo moved closer. The Buddha stared back at him with heavy eyes half closed. His full lips hinted at a smile, sealing a silent eternity. The novices chanted louder, the whip cracked, a gong clanged sonorously, making the wooden floor vibrate. Incense, sculpted butter, the fatty smell, syllables chanted in a monotone, the boy monks' look of concentration - a solemn gravity pervaded it all. Theo did not feel well. The thudding tambourines throbbed so heavily that he saw the huge statue with its shuttered eyelids lean towards him . . . His head spun, and he fell beneath the golden smile.

Lama Gampo caught Theo just in time. Aunt Martha was horrified to see that her nephew had a nosebleed. Moving with swift efficiency, the lama carried Theo outside, tipped his head back, scooped a handful of snow from the edge of the roof and rubbed it over his nose.

'There,' he said calmly. 'That will stop the bleeding. It's probably the altitude, don't worry.'

'You know very well that he's sick!' cried Aunt Martha. 'And where am I going to find a hospital?'

'We can do better than the hospital,' the Lama murmured. 'Let him come round and I'll take you there.'

Darjeeling's unusual doctor

'Tell me what happened, my boy,' the Lama asked when they were sitting in the car.

'I don't know,' Theo told him. '*Shakti*, the demons, the smile, I suddenly felt giddy.'

'Hmm,' breathed Lama Gampo. 'It's not just the altitude.'

'It certainly isn't!' snapped Aunt Martha. 'I've told you before, there's enough horror in those frescos to give nightmares to a regiment.'

'The world of self-illusion is like that – terrifying,' said the Lama. 'That's why we represent it, to tame the fear. Now, exactly what fear is involved here? Theo must look for himself. For the moment, we'll take care of him.'

The Ambassador drew up in front of a little booth with a line of people outside it. The Lama went straight to the front, pleading Theo's condition – the nosebleed worked wonders.

'An emergency, Doctor Lobsang,' he said, propelling Theo into the dark interior.

An ageless woman in a long woollen dress, gathered beneath her breasts, sat on a stool and gazed at Theo without a word. Then she beckoned him to sit facing her, and her beautiful face grew taut. After that she put a series of questions to the Lama, who translated both ways. Did he sleep well? Did he rest in the afternoon? Did he often yawn? Did he have pains in his hips, or fits of giddiness or nausea? One by one she folded his fingers, making the joints crack. Then she examined his tongue and made a remark that the Lama repeated word for word.

'She says that Theo's temperament is *rLung* – air – and the seat of the trouble is the liver. She'll check your pulse to verify the diagnosis.'

Doctor Lobsang closed her eyes, visibly relaxed her body, breathed deeply, then held her breath and placed the three middle fingers of her right hand over the veins of Theo's left wrist, pressing incredibly hard. Seconds elapsed, and turned to minutes, then she went through the same procedure with her left-hand fingers probing Theo's right wrist. The silence was total. Finally the doctor opened her eyes with a sigh, and then spoke at length to the Lama.

'It's as she thought,' he confirmed. 'The illness is serious. It doesn't come from diet, or climate, or sexual excess, obviously, or any accidental event. Doctor Lobsang believes that this is a case of very bad karma, and that a hidden spirit is eating at Theo's health – someone he killed in his latest previous life, without a doubt.'

'Naturally,' said Theo wryly, groping for courage. 'You can tell from my face I'm a natural-born killer.'

'The pulse is shallow, with abnormal pauses,' Lama Gampo continued. 'That indicates extreme internal tension. With her left-hand middle finger, Doctor Lobsang detected the path of the disturbed channels . . . You must act as fast as possible. First, avoid tart and bitter foods, and drink less tea.'

'I'll never succeed with the tea,' Theo muttered.

'Second,' said the Lama, 'take more sweet, sharp, acid drinks: lemonade is ideal for the purpose. By way of medicines, the doctor can supply what you need: silver, saltpetre, iron, shellfish powder, crocus flowers and pig's liver fat.'

Theo felt frightened to death. 'Pig's liver and silver-plated crocus, with metal and shellfish on the side?' he joked. 'I'll have to buy the recipe!'

Already the doctor was busy opening tins and packets and taking pinches and scraps of unknown substances that she weighed carefully before tipping them into little paper sachets and telling the Lama the name to write on each, with a pen she provided. Aunt Martha took them and paid. The doctor gave the ghost of a smile, patted Theo's cheek, and spoke to the Lama again.

'She says that you must also have massage with avocado oil, but that if you follow the treatment properly you will certainly get better, because only Tibetan medicine has the power to cure your illness.'

Theo felt terrified, but he did his best to thank the Tibetan lady by extending a shaking hand. The doctor took it carefully and brushed it with her lips, where he wore his mother's ring. It wasn't much, the smallest kiss, enough to reassure Theo, and mainly on the ring. The grip of terror loosened, and again the doctor smiled.

'Who is she?' asked Aunt Martha, when they were back outside.

'Doctor Lobsang Dorje is one of our greatest medical experts,' Lama Gampo replied. 'People come a long way to consult her, you know.'

'How could she find out so quickly?'

'That's how the Tibetan diagnosis technique works,' he answered straight away. 'If the course of the channels is measured by pressing the points on both wrists, with enough concentration it is possible to localize the trouble and then to treat the humours.'

'Ah!' cried Aunt Martha. 'Concentration. That's why she held her breath.'

'Yes, so as to be able to sense the different pulse beats,' the Lama told her. 'These are very ancient practices, originally from China.'

'Magic!' said Theo.

'That's right,' said the Lama with a smile. 'As long as you realize that there's nothing illogical about magic. The mind has great power over the body. But in order to be cured, it's necessary to follow both the diet and the course of medicine prescribed. Oh, I nearly forgot. In my opinion it would be better to give up the other treatments. I feel that Theo's illness is beyond your Western medicines. But it's just my advice, nothing more.'

A difficult choice

Give up the other treatments! What were Theo's parents going to say?

'Before doing that, I must have permission from Paris,' said Aunt Martha.

'Paris?' the Lama protested. 'When you've told me over and over that there was nothing the doctors there could do?'

'But his parents, you're forgetting about them . . .'

'It's what I truly believe is for the best,' the Lama declared. 'So I will pray for their consent.'

On the telephone, Melina burst into tears. They were killing her Theo. She'd always known that this journey was madness, and Theo would never survive it.

Aunt Martha's reply was a cruel question: 'Do you really believe that in Paris he will live?'

Melina's sobbing jarred on Aunt Martha, who did what she could to console her before asking for her brother, because with Jerome the scientist all hope was not lost.

'Listen, Jerome, what have we got to lose? The tests are getting nowhere. All right, they're no worse, but there's no improvement either. Let me try . . .'

'Do you realize what a serious decision this is?' Jerome asked her.

'Why do you think I'm calling from Darjeeling?' she replied. 'Of course it's serious.'

There was silence at the end of the line, then the sound of her brother clearing his throat.

'OK,' he decided. 'I think you're right. Anyway, I know that some French doctors are starting to investigate Tibetan medicine. Well, all right, I agree. We drop it.'

'Aah,' said Aunt Martha, and heaved a long sigh of relief. 'We agree.'

'Wait . . . But instead of phoning once a week, you're to call us every day.'

It was settled. Theo put away his capsules and started the Tibetan treatment. The fact is that next day he felt better. During the night he had dreamed that he was merging into the form of a strange shape in which black arms and white legs were so tightly intertwined that he woke with a start.

An abbot, tea, butter and prayer

The Lama thanked the peaceful deities for having defeated the demons of darkness, and he set the prayer wheels turning.

'Do you know what?' Theo whispered in Aunt Martha's ear. 'He looks like Blessed Lightning.'

'Blessed Lightning?' She gasped. 'What are you talking about?'

'The monk in *Tintin in Tibet*, the one who levitates and has visions. Without his glasses, Lama Gampo looks just like him, I swear! Do you think he can float in the air too?'

'Oh no,' sighed Aunt Martha. 'You're not going to ask him? You are? Theo!'

Too late. Theo had gone running to the Lama to ask his question, and the monk gave a chuckle.

'Do excuse him,' she fussed. 'It's because of Tintin.'

'No need,' the Lama smiled. 'In France, it's the usual question. Anyway, Theo, I'm sure you don't know the meaning of the word "Darjeeling": it stands for "thunder town". Now, let's pay a visit to our abbot.'

The Abbot was a bed-ridden old man with a threadbare robe, a sparse goatee beard, a bald head and dreaming eyes, who lived in a tiny hut with a tin roof. In fact he was so old that they had to be content with his blessing and some tea. He did not notice their arrival but went on reading, bringing long sheets of paper covered with handwriting close to his tired eyes, then restoring these sacred texts to their yellow satin wrappings when he was done. When the Lama bowed low at his bedside, the Abbot looked up, crinkled his eyes, gave a brief childlike chuckle, and gestured just once. The Lama ran to fetch him what he wanted, which was a Thermos flask printed with a floral design, made in the People's Republic of China and full of the famous butter tea.

'Ugh,' said Theo, pulling a sour face. 'It tastes like salted coffee.'

'Because we put salt in it,' the Lama explained. 'We also add lime. Can you see the orange reflection?'

'Yes, and some blobs of fat on the surface,' Theo noticed.

'That's the butter.'

'So really it's a soup then.'

'Quite right,' said the Lama. 'It's a fine way to keep out the cold. Two days from now, you won't be able to do without it.'

'You might say thank you,' Aunt Martha whispered.

Not knowing how, Theo pressed his palms together. The old man's

251

face lit up, and he blessed the boy with a shaky hand. Then they left, the Lama and Theo hand in hand, while Aunt Martha trailed behind, as usual.

'I've never seen anyone so old,' said Theo, as soon they were out.

'Probably not,' the Lama replied. 'He's over a hundred.'

'How do you manage that?' asked Theo, with a quaver of dread in his voice. 'I can't be sure of reaching fifteen!'

'Don't drink alcohol, or smoke, or overdo things. Do pray, and do drink butter tea,' the Lama replied in a flash. 'You've only to try, and you'll see.'

'The soup, all right, but praying, I don't know,' said Theo.

'Yes you do,' said the Lama. 'It happened in front of the bodhisattva.'

'A nosebleed is praying?'

'No,' said the Lama enigmatically. 'Just before.'

Just before? What happened just before? The statue had swayed, and . . .

'And the smile knocked you over,' said the Lama. 'Didn't it?'

'Yes,' Theo agreed. 'If that is praying, then I know how.'

The Lama squeezed Theo's hand and fell silent. Surrounded by peace, Theo took deep, easy breaths. Suddenly the silence was shattered by Aunt Martha's sharp voice, as she caught up with them.

'What are you two talking about?' she cried. 'Don't say you're turning my shrimp into a mystic!'

'No need for that,' said the Lama. 'He was born that way. A previous life, for certain.'

The thunder-dagger

Next day the Lama guided them to the busy confusion of the Tibetan refugee centre. At the entrance they sold all sorts of objects of prayer that Theo wanted to buy. Cymbals made of an alloy of eight different metals that made a marvellous sound; musical bowls, that when you rubbed the rim with a wooden rod gave off strange harmonies that tingled in the air. A small copper prayer wheel that revolved round a carved handle . . .

'Why don't you open it,' the Lama suggested. 'You'll see what prayers it holds.'

Theo obeyed. Wrapped round the spindle inside he found a tiny scroll of paper.

'Open it,' the Lama instructed him. 'You've got to read it.'

'But I don't know Tibetan . . .'

'Just try.'

Theo was baffled, but he obeyed, and found words that he could read. *Hidden at the heart of the largest city on one of the largest among many islands, I inspire wisdom in expatriates. For I am neither god nor saint: I am the horribly ugly Sage.*

'That's tricky,' said Theo.

'Now you must think,' said the Lama. 'And thought is like prayer: you know how.'

'I thought I did,' said Theo. 'But after everything that's happened, I'm not so sure. You and your magic tricks, demons, goddesses, smiles – I don't know what to make of it.'

'Very good,' said the Lama. 'That's an essential feeling. Anyway, thinking is also a part of the exercise. Oh, I want to give you this.' He reached to a shelf and took down an odd-looking dagger made of gilded bronze. The blade was three-sided, the pommel ended in an ugly face crowned by death's heads, and the hilt was carved in the shape of a dragon. It was also very heavy.

'Thank you,' Theo mumbled, staring at the mysterious object.

'It looks quite frightening, doesn't it?' said the Lama. 'Let me explain.'

Like the yogis of India, the monks of Tibet spent much of their time in meditation on death. Since nearly everybody could be practically certain of not being perfect, they were not going to dissolve into infinity, and that meant that they were bound to be reincarnated, and therefore bound to die. There was no cause to be afraid. Hence death's heads were a common theme in objects of prayer. Sometimes the top of a skull, lined with metal, was used as a drinking cup.

'A real skull?' Theo shuddered.

Yes, a real one. A way to know the nature of impermanence, one of whose heaviest shackles was the body. Some day, Lama Gampo's own skull might be reduced to this: a cup for another lama. This was no cause to be frightened; instead, it gave substance to life, as bodhisattvas did their best to guide the Buddhists of Tibet along the path to wisdom. The greater your knowledge of death, the better you felt. It was a sure-fire recipe for cheerfulness.

'Centuries ago,' Aunt Martha added, 'there were devout Catholics in France who kept human skulls as aids to meditation. The idea was the same, and connected with the old biblical saying: "Vanity of vanities, all is vanity . . ."'

'That is not exactly our doctrine,' the Lama corrected. 'We do not

253

meditate in despair – not at all! The Middle Way is not the contemplation of nothingness. Certainly we too can say: "Illusion, all is illusion." But our great teachers, the very precious ones, have the power to communicate with us when they are reincarnated, and there is nothing illusory in that. When they die, we embalm them and wait for a year before we bury their remains. Then we set out in search of a child whose body houses the soul of our precious departed.'

'I know!' cried Theo. 'You have a system for recognizing the right . . .'

'We show the children a few everyday objects, till one of them reaches of his own accord for the one object that belonged to the teacher. This little boy who's sometimes still a toddler will be recognized as the new incarnation, because the presence of our very precious one has been with us continually for centuries. So death is nothing. A skull is just a temporary lodging.'

'It's not my thing,' said Theo, putting the dagger back on the shelf.

'Wait,' said the Lama. So far he had only explained about the death's heads, but Theo mustn't get a false impression: the dagger was not made for shedding blood – certainly not: the rule of compassion for all living beings forbade it. But thrust it into the ground, and it could skewer the demons of the underworld. It was called *phurbu*, 'the thunder-dagger'.

To make it clearer, Lama Gampo drew a sketch. 'There are five human skulls,' he explained, 'because the elements, the passions, go in fives – the number of wisdom. The empty skull stands for the person whose brain doesn't teem with the pretences of the Self, that busy kind of brain that won't stop thinking . . .'

'Hey,' said Theo, 'that's just what Sheikh Suleiman told me in Jerusalem!'

'Yes, you see, not easy to switch off one's own ideas. They are illusion, Theo . . . What matters most is far above: we call it the jewel. The skull is appearance. Reality, the jewel, bright light.'

'You're giving it to me so that I'll stop fussing and fighting,' Theo whispered.

'As you compared me to Blessed Lightning, I thought . . .' the Lama murmured shyly.

'That's kind of you,' Theo replied.

'The thunder-dagger will help you find peace, I'm sure of it.'

'All right,' said Theo, picking up his trophy. 'But for the skull, the answer's No.'

The Lama smiled. No skulls were on sale in the tourist shop at the entrance to the camp. The goods they offered were harmless, sold to aid refugees from Tibet.

'Exile,' sighed the Lama.

'You know,' said Theo, 'there's something about that in my new message.'

The ugliest of sages

Back at the hotel, Theo started thinking. *An island among islands* . . . an archipelago. He opened his atlas: lots of archipelagos here. Japan matched the definition perfectly. Was it Tokyo?

'There aren't any expatriate communities in Japan,' said Aunt Martha.

'By the way, what are expatriates?'

'They're people who've chosen to work away from their own country.'

'It must be Indonesia,' he decided. 'What are they over there?'

'Mostly Muslims,' she replied, 'but also Christians, and quite a few Hindus. Originally they were all animists, as in some parts of Africa, but people came to trade from other countries, and they stayed on.'

'Then you could say that these traders are expatriates?'

Apparently you could. So where did they come from?

'You'd do better to look for the horribly ugly Sage,' said Aunt Martha. 'Try your dictionary of religions.'

There were ugly gods all over the place. In Greece, Hephaestus the blacksmith, hideous. In India, Kali, repulsive. In Tibet, the demons, grotesque. Then look at Mexico, Brazil, Africa . . . A chamber of horrors.

'But the message doesn't mention a god,' said Aunt Martha. 'What if it refers to a man?'

Theo pored over the book. Socrates: not an exile. Jesus: but he was handsome. Then he came across the broad face of a man with a shock of bristling hair, bulging eyes, and two buckteeth protruding over his lower lip.

'He's no beauty,' said Theo. 'What is his name? Confuses us? Confucius! And what is he? Ah, Chinese. Did your traders come from China?'

China it was. The one thing left to do was to locate the largest city on one of the largest islands in the Indonesian archipelago, and that was Jakarta, on the island of Java.

'Well done!' said Aunt Martha. 'And very fast, this time.'

'See!' said Theo proudly. 'It's the Blessed Lightning effect.'

'And your new medicines?'

'Don't even ask!' Theo pulled a nauseated face. 'Will we see doctors in Jakarta too?'

'Where there are Chinese people, there are always first-rate doctors,' Aunt Martha assured him. 'Rather like your doctor in Darjeeling.'

'Why not go straight to China?' asked Theo in surprise. 'It's simpler.'

Not as simple as he thought. First, China's most ancient religion spread across space and time, and was not easy to see. Obviously a visitor could climb the seven thousand steps of the great sanctuary of Taishan, in eastern China, where at the top, 1,545 metres high, there was nothing except the tablets where Chinese sovereigns had left a record of their visit, and the view of far horizons. The steep little climb up the 'stairway of Heaven' was the most important pilgrimage in China, because it was there that souls flew to be born into earthly life. But Theo's health was not equal to such an exhausting exercise, which took hours to complete and required a whole lot of effort from everybody. Because in this case, the prayer *was* the effort.

'Let's say you're right, then,' said Theo. 'And there's truly nowhere else?'

Aunt Martha wriggled in her armchair. Yes, there were a few other holy places, but you see, the snag was that to enter the People's Republic of China you needed a visa, and she would never be granted one. A few years before, in Beijing, she'd got rather too closely involved with some illegal demonstrations: she'd fought by their side, and now she was on file . . .

'Brilliant,' said Theo. 'So now we're in a jam . . .'

No, because the religions of China had survived in exile, and it was in Jakarta that they could best be seen.

'If you say so,' Theo sighed. 'All the same, I would have loved to see Beijing. Oh well, I can go when I'm grown up. By the way, isn't it time to call Paris? Dad will give us hell if we don't.'

It occurred to Aunt Martha that this was the first time that Theo had mentioned a possible future in her presence.

Two white scarves

Before they left, Theo worked his way one by one through the shops on the main square where sturdy blonde-maned ponies roamed. He was questing for tea. He must have his tea! On one of the stalls Aunt Martha reached for a cone-shaped block of some brownish stuff and put it into Theo's hand.

'Funny-looking thing,' said Theo, sniffing suspiciously at the solid mass. 'It looks messy and it doesn't smell so good. What is it? Tobacco?'

'It's your tea,' Aunt Martha replied.

Theo gaped in disbelief at the object. The Tibetans squeezed the leaves together using a press to make compact cones of tea, and it was this brown substance that produced the soup they served with butter. It was an odd sort of tea.

'But it's good Darjeeling tea that I'm looking for,' he pleaded.

There was none to be had. The best tea in India was reserved for export. Theo was furious, and swore to find something really different for a souvenir. In Hadjeet Mehta's Kuryo shop – curiosities for tourists – he bought a painting on fabric showing the couple locked in their embrace in defiance of the demons prowling round them. Then a gilded bronze statuette of a smiling goddess sitting in the lotus position and crowned with an elaborate golden diadem; her name was Tara, and at least she had a kindly look. Wearing a smile as friendly as the goddess's, Mr Hadjeet Mehta, who was not a Buddhist but a Hindu, made a point of explaining that Tara, herself a bodhisattva, was a kind of female partner of Avalokitesvara, born from his tears, and loved for her good works and compassion.

'Sounds a bit like a nurse, but I'll take her all the same,' said Theo. 'And the big one, is that the Buddha?'

The statue was as tall as Theo, and Aunt Martha rebelled.

'Think what it would cost in excess luggage,' she cried. 'He's far too heavy.'

Theo was forced to give up, but Lama Gampo had another present waiting for him. Just when he was about to get into the Ambassador, the monk held out a thin white scarf, draped across his upturned hands.

'This is how we say hello,' the Lama said. 'I didn't give it to you when you arrived because I get absent-minded sometimes, and I dropped my glasses when we met. So I'm making up for it now that you're leaving.'

'Here, Theo,' said Aunt Martha, extracting an absolutely identical scarf from her handbag. 'Give this to Blessed Lightning. Exchanging scarves is the custom in Tibet.'

Theo took the scarf, arranged it ceremoniously on his spread hands, and presented it to the monk, who bowed as he received it.

'I'll miss you,' he sighed. 'What will I do without you?'

'Well, Blessed Lightning will just have to visit you in your dreams,' said the Lama, with a broad smile. 'That's a promise.'

CHAPTER 15

Between Heaven and Earth

Stop-off in Calcutta

The journey to Jakarta was no day-trip. They had to drive back to Siliguri, fly from there to Calcutta, then catch a plane to Bangkok, and another to Jakarta. Aunt Martha had taken the precaution of booking a room in Calcutta's best hotel for the night.

On the way down from the hills, Theo kept his eyes wide open. A little toy train ran alongside the road, hauled by a sky-blue locomotive and crammed with exuberant children. The snowy peaks retreated into the mist, the temples and stupas petered out; in the distance, threads of silver winding across the plain signalled the arms of a river, the Brahmaputra. The air grew dry and the soil yellow. On the plane to Calcutta, Theo quickly dozed off, and he stayed fast asleep until he was shaken awake.

'We're landing,' said Aunt Martha.

'Where?' mumbled Theo, still drowsy.

'In Calcutta.'

'Not much of a place,' he answered. 'I've heard it's the most deprived city.'

'Then you've heard wrong, young man,' she snapped in reply. 'Look around you at the airport instead of talking nonsense.'

The lobby of the passenger terminal in Calcutta airport was luxurious and modern, decorated with lanterns of red and blue fabric, and sparkling clean. At the exit, Aunt Martha looked for her taxi and majestically

259

dismissed the swarm of beggars. Some were dreadfully mutilated, armless, or with legs reduced to stumps.

'You see,' said Theo.

'There were just as many in Benares,' she blared.

'But Mahantji said it was a religious tradition.'

'That's right. And in India they beg. For those who have renounced the world, it's actually a duty. I don't say that these people are that sort, but you must revise your image of Calcutta. Where there are tourists you'll always find beggars. To them, we're made of money . . . But after all, you're used to being rich.'

'Me?' Theo protested. 'But I'm sick!'

'So are they,' she answered bluntly. 'But they haven't got an aunt to make them better, you see. Half of the world is like that, while the other half stuff themselves so full that dieting's an industry!'

'So give them some money!' Theo argued.

'To the old man over there who isn't begging, yes I will,' she said, and took out a note from her purse. 'The rest of them . . . Do you know that in India there are gangsters who will cut off a newborn baby's arms to make a potential beggar? My Indian friends insist that the only way to stop that happening is never to give alms to people disabled that way . . .'

'Don't the scum who do it ever get caught?'

'Yes,' she said bleakly. 'But for each one they lock up, there are thousands they miss . . . Come on, let's keep moving!'

The road from the airport was lined with ponds where children dived and swam. Everywhere there were huge hoardings proclaiming CALCUTTA, CITY OF JOY, and all things considered, it seemed to be true. As everywhere in India, streams of pedestrians flowed endlessly to and fro, but more of them wore smiles.

This was all they would see of Calcutta. In any case, the whole town lived in the shadow either of Durga, the slayer of the buffalo-demon, or Kali, her ghastly twin: as he loathed both of these murderous goddesses, it was no loss to Theo. Aunt Martha wanted to eat Chinese for a change, but Theo refused. China could wait: on their last night in India . . .

For the sake of peace and quiet, she gave in. They dined on dhal, hot nan, fresh lassi and boiled rice

Majorities versus minorities

'We're nearly halfway through,' Aunt Martha remarked. 'Tell me what you make of the trip so far.'

Theo stopped to think, before beginning: 'Well, there are things to say for and against. As I see it, where there's God there are also massacres.'

'As bad as that?'

'I'll try to list the killings. One, the Jews; two, the Bahais; three, the Sikhs; four, today's Indian Muslims; five, the Christian martyrs; six, the Cathars; seven, Hypatia . . . And I know I've left some out.'

'Do you think there's a pattern to them all?'

'Whenever a new religion comes into the world?'

'That's almost it. Except for the Muslims in India today.'

'Then it's where there are too few believers in the country they live in,' Theo suggested. 'The secret of avoiding persecution is strength of numbers and sticking together.'

'Exactly. Minority religions are nearly always ill-treated. But you know, the same applies to individuals: if you're too different you'll have trouble!'

'Do you think so? In class, the teachers tell me I'm unusual, but there's no one who hassles me.'

'Well, in the olden days you might have been burned as a witch . . . Till the seventeenth century, having one brown eye and the other blue was enough to condemn you to the stake. Or in our country, for a woman to wear a green dress, the devil's colour, could have had her hauled up in front of an Inquisition court.'

Theo was startled. 'In France, you say?'

'Haven't they taught you anything about the Wars of Religion? Saint Bartholomew's Day? The massacre of the Huguenots?'

'Yes,' said Theo. 'But that's all in the past.'

'We've come some way since then,' Aunt Martha admitted. 'But our country was no exception.'

'Because the bigger group always has it in for the smaller one.'

'Use the right language, shrimp: when we talk about the larger group we say "majority", and the rest are "minorities".'

'The majority always resents the minority,' he repeated obediently. 'And then when the minority turns into the majority it starts all over again! They get their own back by murdering the losers. Did you notice the Christians? Don Ottavio gave a good description: first you make

261

martyrs, then you make war. You deal with the Cathars, then you charge off on the Crusades.'

'Yet till recently Hindus didn't persecute other beliefs,' Aunt Martha said. 'Nor do the Tibetan Buddhists. What do you make of that?'

'It's true.' The thought caught Theo by surprise. 'Basically, who are the ones who've gone to war? Christians and Muslims.'

'Jews too, from time to time,' his aunt reminded him.

'Because they'd had martyrs, it follows.'

'Because they are monotheists, Theo . . . They recognize only one God. And monotheists tend not to make compromises, you see. Remember Jerusalem: each faith defending its own god, and not other people's, whether his name is God the Father, or Allah, or Adonai Elohim. Do you know, at this very moment, to work on the masses more effectively, Hindu extremists are trying to reduce the number of Hindu gods. Of all those millions, they've chosen the Rama of the *Ramayana*. They want to turn him into the one and only god of the Hindu fatherland.'

'You're telling me that people who believe in a whole lot of gods are more tolerant,' Theo observed. 'But I don't see why that is.'

What is syncretism?

Aunt Martha set about explaining, giving plenty of examples. When, in the sixteenth century, the first Christian missionaries began to preach to the Hindus, they drew comparisons between the many gods of Hinduism and the holy figures of Christendom. Jesus was Krishna . . .

'Minus his eleven thousand girlfriends, I imagine,' said Theo.

Naturally. As for Mary, she was a mother goddess who trampled the serpent underfoot, just as Durga destroyed the buffalo-demon. The Holy Trinity was a piece of cake, because after some centuries the Hindus had grouped Brahma, Vishnu and Shiva into a trinity called the Trimurti. And as the Holy Trinity consisted of a bearded god, the Father, a handsome young man, the Son, and a dove, the Holy Ghost, Hindus concluded that all they had to do was to include a group of three gods with a goddess at their side and they would become Christians.

'So they fell for it!' said Theo.

In much the same way, rather than openly fight them, the Great Vehicle had made itself a patchwork coat out of the religions it converted. Here it sewed a pocket for devils, there it let goddesses shed tears, patiently redesigning the divine and adding new bits and pieces as it moved from country to country. This artful procedure was known as syncretism, from a Greek word meaning something like 'joining together'. One of the champions of syncretism had been Mahatma Gandhi, who never went anywhere without his three sacred books: the Koran for Islam, the Gospels for Christianity and the *Bhagavad Gita* for Hinduism.

'The what?' said Theo. 'Never heard of it.'

But he had. It was the key episode when the god Krishna, in order to force people to fight among themselves, revealed himself to them in his full glory.

'Now I remember,' Theo glowered. 'All for the sake of war. And the Mahatma used it? The Gospels and the Koran, all right, but the *Bag of Agitators* . . .'

'*Bhagavad Gita*,' Aunt Martha corrected him irritably. 'You can call it the *Gita* for short.'

The *Gita* was not the only sacred text that prompted people to kill: the Koran approved jihad, and in the gospels Jesus had spoken words that sent chills up your spine: 'Think not that I am come to send peace on earth: I came not to send peace, but a sword.' People interpreted that as referring to war. Faith in God, whatever the name he was called by, often required a military kind of commitment from the faithful . . . But that was not the heart of the matter, because for Jesus what counted most was love, for Mohammad justice, and for the *Gita* the radiance of divinity. The holy war of the Koran was first of all a war against oneself, a struggle against injustices of one's own making. What appeared to be threats from Jesus Christ were appeals for Christians to be brave. The *Gita* threw light for Hindus on the luminous truth of the Order of the world.

'What about the Mahatma?' Theo persisted.

In his own way, Gandhi was a true warrior! Non-violent, of course, and a pacifist, but a man who rallied his strength every morning for a long battle against himself and the occupying power. From war, he had taken the best it had to offer: discipline and courage. And out of the sacred texts he had made a syncretism of his own invention: justice, love and courage united in worship of God.

'And on top of that, to reunify the different peoples of India was a great achievement,' said Aunt Martha. 'Do you see what I'm getting at this time?'

'It amounts to saying that through syncretism, if people wanted they could unite the whole world instead of picking fights all the time.'

At daybreak, awakened by the shouts of rickshaw wallahs arguing under the windows, Theo looked out over the city where traffic was building up already. In the distance rose a sort of Greek temple and an incongruous Gothic cathedral.

'More syncretism!' he exclaimed. 'Look, Aunt M, they've built a church to Durga!'

But the church was the Anglican cathedral of Calcutta, a city built by the British and once the capital of their whole Indian empire. As for the Greek temple, it turned out to be the Victoria Memorial, a monument to the British queen-empress. There was nothing syncretic about this hymn to the triumphant colonialism that Calcutta's citizens managed to take pleasure in, now that it was gone.

Sacrifices: from man to animal, from animal to bread

In the plane to Bangkok, Aunt Martha snored like a chainsaw. Theo took out his notebook and decided to add some more drawings, in honour of India. Shiva and his trident, Krishna and his favourite shepherdess, Durga with her weapons and her tiger, the four heads of the god Brahma. Impossible to combine them. Fired by the spirit of syncretism, he tried to amalgamate Horus, the jackal-god, with Ganesa the elephant and Hanuman the monkey, but it didn't work.

Then, in retracing his journey, he came to the sacrifice of Abraham. It was the starting-point for a complicated game of religions. From here came the ram sacrificed in Isaac's place, Christ expiring on the cross, and the corpses cremated on the bank of the Ganges, where the body was committed to the flames as a sacrificial victim following physical death. A shudder ran through him: so crucifixion and cremation were forms of human sacrifice! Whereas with Islam, Judaism and the Sikh religion it was only animals that were sacrificed to God. He drew a tree with two branches: on one side, the sacrificed bodies; on the other, a book out of which letters flew skywards, surrounded by the smoke from burnt animals.

'Aunt Martha!' said Theo, shaking her arm.

'Mmm . . . hmm?' she mumbled. 'Are we there?'

'No,' he said sheepishly. 'Tell me whether there are still human sacrifices.'

'What?' she exploded. 'You wake me up for that, you little horror?'

'Sorree,' he said.

She shook herself, took out a handkerchief, mopped her face and ordered tea for two.

'All right,' she sniffed, 'what's this about human sacrifices?'

Theo explained his tree, and his questions.

'You can go further than that,' she advised. 'Forget the beginnings and think about what is actually sacrificed afterwards. For instance, in Christianity, instead of the flesh and blood of Christ they sacrifice bread and wine. It's all in there! No matter what the religion, it replaces human sacrifice with a sacrifice of a different kind.'

Theo wrote a list of examples. CHRISTIANITY = BREAD & WINE. BUDDHISM = BUTTER & INCENSE. HINDUISM = MILK, FLOWERS, FRUIT. JUDAISM, ISLAM, SIKHISM = NOTHING, BUT A BOOK.

'Not bad,' she admitted. 'But remember that, even though the practice has now been abandoned, the Eternal's commandments once required Jewish priests to sacrifice bulls and chickens. Not long ago a strange thing happened in the State of Israel. A completely red heifer was born. Now keep in mind that in the Bible the liquid used for ritual purification, in accordance with the law of the Eternal, was spring water mixed with the ashes of a red heifer. Red ones without a single hair of another colour are so rare that since the foundation of the Temple only nine had been recorded! The rabbis in exile concluded from this that the tenth would be a sign that the Messiah was coming.'

'Another one!' said Theo. 'And did the Israeli rabbis burn the modern heifer?'

'There was a serious debate, and now I forget what they decided. The land and State of Israel aren't what they were in ancient times. The Jews in the Bible were not hunters but stock breeders. Now a calf is important for a herder. What else can he offer to his God but his dearest possession, I ask you. And as that is no longer his son, then let it be his bull, the sire of the herd. That is why animal sacrifices still go on all over the world. In Nepal, the Hindus slit the throats of buffaloes. In Calcutta they still offer headless goats to Kali. Actually, animal sacrifices have been banned in India since the 1950s.'

'As late as that?' Theo exclaimed.

'Oh, but human sacrifice is never far below the surface . . . You were wondering whether it still existed? The answer is yes. Every now and then some really gruesome story crops up in the Indian press: a couple have their daughter's throat cut by a priest, to make sure that their next child is a son . . .'

'This goes on today?' said Theo. 'But still, they're sent to jail, I suppose?'

'Of course. But it's not just in India that such things happen: in the

Sixties there were Satanic cults in the United States who practised ritual murder. If you think about it, the idea of sacrificing a human being hasn't completely died out.'

'Still, at least there aren't any cannibals left,' Theo sighed.

'You think not? In some tribes in Brazil, they eat the body of their enemy so as to absorb his powers. As long as the loser is going to die and be buried in any case, the victor's stomach is no worse than a hole in the ground, don't you think?'

'*Malaish,*' said Theo. 'So on the "Against" list, I only see Judaism and Islam rejecting human sacrifice altogether. With Jesus, it isn't quite clear. God the Father didn't mind letting him die to redeem the sins of the world.'

'That's an interesting way to look at it,' she remarked. 'You haven't read Freud, have you?'

'The guy who thinks Moses is Egyptian?'

Sigmund Freud had given a lot of thought to human sacrifice, and had come up with a fable of his own. He theorized that at the dawn of human time there was a primitive clan dominated by a leader so powerful that he kept all the women to himself. The other men grew jealous. They murdered and ate him, and then felt so riddled with guilt that they founded a cult of their victim, and called him 'Father'. According to Freud, the origin of all gods lay in this original sacrifice.

'It's not a cheerful theory,' Theo commented.

Patience . . . Later, the human race had changed. The Jews were the first to ban all human sacrifice and bow to the authority of an invisible, invincible, and therefore inedible Father. But the Hebrew people often evaded the paternal commandments. Here, Freud had his own explanation: observing the law of the invisible Father was so difficult, he said, so contrary to the original parricide, that the Hebrews fell back on the statue of the Golden Calf, a relic of their slavery in Egypt.

'The goddess Hathor,' cried Theo, pleased to show off his talents as a budding Egyptologist.

So it was easier for them to worship an edible animal than an invisible god. But this was reckoning without God's representative. When he came down from Sinai, where God had dictated the ten commandments to him, Moses screwed down the lid of a cauldron that bubbled with guilt, blood-lust and a horde of gods. The Eternal's punishment was terrible. Moses put three thousand heathen Jews to the sword, three thousand died of the plague, and another three thousand caught leprosy. The Hebrew people did not succumb again. But when Christianity was born, said Grandpa Freud, human sacrifice returned, only this time in the shape, not of the Father of the primitive horde, but of a Son. It was God in person who sacrificed his child. People found this idea more bearable, hence the massive success of the new religion.

'Why more bearable?' asked Theo.

'Because according to Freud, it is better not to completely repress the original murder of the Father,' Aunt Martha replied.

'Repress, the way some police forces do?' The term was new to Theo.

'Something like that,' said his aunt. 'Repressing means distancing, containing, and most of all forgetting. But in the long run the forgotten event always does harm. You never think about it, you don't know what it is, and one day the buried secret breaks out into the open. Some people may fall ill, and some may even die as a result – these things do happen. When the police repress demonstrators, the situation turns explosive, doesn't it?'

'OK,' said Theo. 'So the Jews repressed the murder of God. Then what about the Christians?'

'It's not so hard a case. With the sacrifice of the only Son, the original repression loosened its grip.'

'Might as well sacrifice babies alive while they're at it!' Theo exploded. 'He talks rubbish, your Grandpa Freud.'

Aunt Martha disagreed. The genius of Christianity was that it also substituted bread for flesh and wine for blood. In India, after a dark age of human sacrifices followed by whole centuries when they sacrificed stallions, something similar had happened: a small figurine of a human was enclosed in the altar, and that was enough. The rest of the sacrifice became flowers, fruit, honey or milk. The point was to find the right substitute.

'I'd rather have none at all,' said Theo. 'Like Judaism and Islam.'

'Which aren't very kind,' Aunt Martha added. 'What if there's some connection there?'

But as the plane was coming in to land, the question was deferred.

The roads to Heaven

All the way from Bangkok to Jakarta, Theo was immersed in his notebook. This time his theme was images of ropes and braided hair. He sketched a Sikh with his hair coiled inside his turban, a Tibetan king with a rope on the crown of his head, a Brahman with his single lock of hair, and lastly a shaggy Samson and a pair of open scissors.

'Put in Heaven,' said Aunt Martha, 'and Hell.'

Obediently he added fleecy clouds in the sky and some figures dancing on flames.

'Your tree idea's not bad,' Aunt Martha told him. 'All religions try to link Heaven and Earth – with a hair, a rope, a ladder, it doesn't matter. In myths there's always a man who climbs the stairs to Heaven from a tree, and always a fool who cuts off the way.'

'Come to think of it, the cross of Christ is a tree,' Theo realized.

'Absolutely. And the minarets on a mosque point their spires upwards. But in both cases, it's to get back in touch with God.'

'Uh-huh, but what about Hell?'

'People have to learn fear, otherwise anything goes. When the Buddha simply suggests the Middle Way and inner joy, the frescos in Tibetan temples depict the battle between the gods and the demons of illusion . . . And if it isn't ghastly tortures, then for Jews it's Sheol, an empty darkness, or for Hindus the pain of reincarnation. People want to be punished.'

'Well, they get what they ask for. Luckily there's something else.'

'You think so?' she said. 'What is it?'

'I don't know yet. Good moments. Something like a feeling of contact. Strange, but reassuring.'

'Do you mean contact with God?'

'More with the people who believe in him,' he replied. 'And who do me good.'

Aunt Martha said no more. This was not the moment to badger her nephew about these strange contacts that might have the power to cure him.

China, or the Order of the world

Theo turned the page pensively, and drew a tree in the form of a cross, with a curly-haired child perched on top of it, his arms raised to the sun.

'And the Chinese, what do they do?' he inquired at last, closing his precious notebook.

'It's totally different there,' she replied. 'Their principle is absolute Order. Keep in step, and everything is fine. One foot wrong, and you're lost.'

'OK, it's like the Hindus.'

'Yes and no. You'll find very few religions that don't invent their own cosmology, in other words their own explanation of the birth of the world. You know the Jewish and Christian version . . .'

'Wait . . . God created Paradise, is that it?'

'You really don't know much,' Aunt Martha sighed. 'In the beginning there was darkness, and the spirit of the Eternal moved on the face of the waters. He said: "Let there be light," and there was light. He called it "Day", and the darkness he called "Night". Then he divided the sky from the water, created the dry land, and called it "Earth", and then named the plants, the stars and planets, and the animals. Lastly he created Man, then took a rib from the new body and used it to create Woman. That took him six days, and on the seventh day God rested . . .'

'I know!' said Theo. 'He did nothing!'

'We'll even be meeting some people who believe that he fell asleep for ever,' she said. 'But for the Hindus, it's a different story. Their cosmology comes from a primordial egg, and out of it the Creator brought likenesses: the world, the house and the body all have the same construction. The Chinese start from a similar principle. The world is a vast whole where mountains and body, colours and directions, food and the cycle of the seasons were all conceived as a kind of giant Meccano set that no one is detached from.'

'What does that mean, though?'

'For example, a mountain's ridge is linked to a hunchback's hump by an invisible connection.'

'Because mountains have hunched backs?'

'Exactly. The Chinese worked out an entire system of likenesses. The north was winter, water, the fourth note of the musical scale, and the number 6. The south was summer, fire, the second note on the scale, and the number 7. The east was spring, wood, the fifth note and the number 8. The west was autumn, metal, the third note, the number 9, and in the middle was the Centre, earth, the first note, and the number 10, which could be reduced to $1 + 0 = 0$.'

'Oh,' said Theo, 'I've come across this before. Mum reads articles about it in *Elle* magazine: it's numerology.'

So it was, but numerology out of context was just a simplified astrology. You had to go further than that to understand the cosmic Meccano set, because in China space and time formed an intricate whole: cyclical as the alternation of the seasons, time was reflected in the circle, whereas space was related to the square. As a result, the whole earth was divided into squares. House walls, city ramparts, fields and religious congregations came square-shaped, so that the sacred square stood for the whole of the Chinese empire, in other words the entire world. As for time, it was harnessed to the rhythm of agricultural work: the period of intense activity to till and fertilize the earth was succeeded by the period of people gathering together for festivals, harvest, and celebration of the sacred. Every year, the assembled community recreated the time to come by chanting: 'Ten thousand years! Ten thousand years!' Because just as in Egypt the sun did not rise without the people's prayers, so in China without these communal gatherings time stopped dead in its tracks.

But most of all, two principles, Yin and Yang, shared the two cycles of time between them: the first had charge of the wet, the dark, the Moon and the feminine, the second ruled the dry, the light, the Sun and the masculine.

'Haven't we talked about this before?' Theo murmured. 'Just a minute . . . Ganesa was involved, and - got it! Skanda, his father's fire, and Ganesa, his mother's waters.'

'Exactly,' said Aunt Martha. 'The two are complementary, as you'll see.'

The alternation of the wet season and the dry depended on these two principles. The sunny Yang, seduced by the dark of the Yin, went underneath the earth, and emerged again by stamping its heel on the ground to break the ice and waken the springs once again. So Yang and Yin would breed the whole of life in a perfect community. Their interaction formed a lovely design, which Aunt Martha drew in his notebook.

'That's pretty,' said Theo. 'And what are those two spots?'

Each one embedded in the opposite principle, they represented the measure of feminine Yin in the masculine Yang, and of male Yang in the female Yin.

'It's India all over again,' said Theo. 'Is it true that I have some female in me?'

Aunt Martha remarked that geneticists had recently discovered the existence of chromosomes of the opposite sex in all human beings, which confirmed the intuition of the Asiatic religions.

'Hmm,' said Theo, feeling overwhelmed with information. 'Rabbi Eliezer talked about a veiled lady, the feminine presence of God, didn't he?'

But the Rabbi hadn't found this in the Bible. The Shekhinah, the lady in the veil, had been added in exile, by way of consolation.

'I don't see where Confucius comes in,' Theo said.

But Confucius was simply the Sage: it wasn't he who had originated the chief religion of China, because the Chinese religion was Taoism, whose central concept was the Tao, which meant Order, the Path, or the Way.

Tao

It was the Tao which had yielded the principles of Yin and Yang: 'A Yin aspect, a Yang aspect, that is the Tao,' said the sacred text. The Tao was the principle of their alternation and perfect regulation. The Tao was by no means a god: it did not create, but it ruled, it guaranteed. To pay their tribute to the Tao, that is to the Order of the world, and in the world, Taoists simply savoured time and space. For instance, those seven thousand steps that had to be climbed, one by one, so as to come, in good time, to infinite space. But there were some hard-core Taoists who preferred the solitude of caves and mountain tops to crowded pilgrimages.

'They meditate,' said Theo. 'That's no big deal.'

'They don't just meditate,' Aunt Martha replied. 'They also interpret.'

Because in order to look deeper into the signs of Yin and Yang, Taoist philosophers created sophisticated systems of mathematical calculation and divination, the scientific foundations of great advances made in physics, chemistry and medicine. But they had an odd obsession: just as in Europe the alchemists sought the philosopher's stone, as a source of everlasting life, so the Taoists were determined to find the philosophical pathway towards rejuvenation. These recipes for long life made unusual demands. The first was to preserve the vital powers that a trio of demons, the Three Worms, kept consuming by forcing them out through the orifices of the body. The next was to feed on dew and cosmic breath: so one breathed the air of the moon, the sun and the stars. Lastly, it was also possible to carry out various so-called bedroom practices that involved retention of sperm during sexual intercourse, and channelling it to repair the brain.

'Hey,' said Theo, 'I've heard this somewhere else.'

In addition, Taoist science looked for the basic minerals needed to secure true immortality. Gold and jade, because they were Yang, gave protection against decay. And cinnabar brought regeneration, because of its blood-red colour.

'Cinnabar?' said Theo. 'What's that?'

'A mineral, sulphide of mercury,' Aunt Martha replied. 'Have you ever seen mercury, Theo?'

'Yes. I once broke an old thermometer, and the stuff poured out in a flash. Mum told me it was quicksilver.'

'And I'll bet you were fascinated by the way it behaved . . . That's why cinnabar, which came from mercury, was so interesting to the Taoists. A great Chinese alchemist prescribed taking ten pills of cinnabar and honey for a year. After that, he said, your hair would turn black, and lost teeth grow again.'

'The Chinese were mad, then,' said Theo. 'Lots and lots of Japanese people have died of mercury poisoning caused by toxic wastes dumped in the sea.'

'In tiny doses, mercury can be useful as a trace element. It's found in fish, poultry, and even raspberries . . .'

'Which are red,' Theo noted.

'But cinnabar is not only a blood-red mineral. Matching the order of the world, in a secret region of the brain, itself connected with a legendary mountain in the Western sea, lies the "cinnabar field". Taoists had the power to rouse its effects by distilling semen in their brain. Then, so they said, it was possible to enter a state of chaos comparable to the peaceful, blissful state of the world before its creation.'

'Brilliant,' said Theo, 'but absolutely crazy.'

'So much so that through its obsession with magic recipes the Taoist religion lapsed into orgies, you see.'

'Orgies . . . ? Shame on them,' said Theo dutifully.

The ugly sage and the hidden sage

'It was bound to end in chaos,' Aunt Martha continued.

Then, some time in the sixth century BC, came Confucius, who should really be called by his true name: Kung Fu-tse, Master Kung. He did not go questing for immortality, he rejected magic and obscurantism,

272

and he said: 'Peering into mystery, working wonders and going down to posterity as a man with recipes is what I do not want.'

What did he want? Respect for Order. Obedience to the rules of society, defined in keeping with the laws of the Cosmos and governed by the sovereign. One had only to observe to understand the signals sent by the world, and Master Kung was an observer of genius. He discovered fossils, and the names of the most unfamiliar animals, but instead of 'I know', he would only say: 'I am informed that . . .' Because he invented nothing. He interpreted the tradition that descended from the distant past. Of men, he asked only one thing: an order worthy of them. That meant self-respect, good faith, kindness and efficiency. 'The man of honour cultivates his person,' he said, 'and by doing so he can respect other people.'

'Is that all?' asked Theo, sounding surprised.

That is exactly what his pupils asked him, so he added: 'The man of honour cultivates his person and gives peace of mind to others.' When this was still too little, he added: 'The man of honour cultivates his person and gives peace of mind to the people as a whole.' Because when the order of things is respected, society thrives. That was not at all the view taken by the greatest Taoist teacher, Lao-tzu, who, as a good Taoist, set his mind on immortality and solitary meditation.

'Never heard of him,' said Theo.

Lao-tzu – meaning 'old philosopher' – was credited with writing the most sacred of Chinese texts, the *Tao-te ching*. He was also known as Lao-tan, and also Lao-chun, and was deified under that name. Like Master Kung, he may have been an archivist at the court of the very ancient dynasty that came to power after the victory of Duke Chou.

'More of a sneeze than a name,' said Theo. 'Who was he?'

Chou was a duke who later became a very great king. He ended the rule of a monstrous tyranny and was the founder of China. Lao-tzu belonged to his court, then he left to travel westward and dictated his famous book. Later, because he knew the secrets of long life, he was reputed to have lived for two whole centuries before quitting the world by discarding his mortal remains in the same way a cicada sheds its coat, which is why cicadas were also held sacred.

'That's why I've never managed to catch one in Provence,' said Theo.

'Maybe worshipping invisible cicadas makes Provençals a little bit Chinese,' Aunt Martha conceded. 'All right, may I go on?'

Because in order to reconcile the two great teachers – the sage of meditation, Lao-tzu, and the sage of action, Master Kung – the Chinese had invented a legend. In the days when Lao-tzu had not yet assumed his celestial form, Master Kung had twice paid him visits. On the first occasion, Lao-tzu was very rude. 'Get rid of your arrogance,' he told him. 'Eliminate all those desires, that bumptious air and overdone zeal: it will not help you. That is all I have to say.' Master Kung went back to his pupils with his tail between his legs and told them that it was no good his knowing all the animals, there was one he didn't know, and that was the dragon Lao-tzu, who soared on wind and clouds into the sky.

The second time, Master Kung found Lao-tzu utterly lifeless, like a corpse. He waited, then Lao-tzu opened his eyes. 'Am I mistaken?' said Master Kung. 'You were like a block of dried wood, you had left this world, locked in unreachable solitude . . .'

'Yes,' said Lao-tzu, 'I was thinking about the Origin of all things.'

'What a nerve!' said Theo. 'Dabbling in the origin of everything. How phoney can you get? . . . How about you? Which one do you prefer?'

Aunt Martha hesitated. Master Kung might be too disciplined for her liking. There was a kind of greatness in the meditative Lao-tzu, but his trances weren't much help with running ordinary human affairs. 'He does nothing, and yet there is nothing that's not done,' Taoists said about Lao-tzu. Actually, this didn't matter very much, because although historians were sure that there had been a Master Kung, the figure called Lao-tzu, and known as 'the hidden Sage', was fictitious. If she absolutely had to choose, Aunt Martha would go for Master Kung.

'He was a humanist,' she said, 'and a great sage.'

'But very ugly,' said Theo. 'Apart from that, you'd take him for the Buddha.'

Aunt Martha thought definitely not, because the Buddha opened the Middle Way to all without distinction of caste, whereas Master Kung was a scholar of genius who accepted the world as it is, with its injustices, inequalities and punishments.

'All the same, he talked about making your way through a lifetime, not looking for the hereafter?' Theo asked, in a deceptively casual voice.

'Of course,' said Aunt Martha, off her guard.

'Then it's the same,' he asserted. 'It's a way of keeping to the middle.'

'But without illumination,' she bridled.

'Don't worry,' said Theo. 'Your Buddha's safe with me.'

The mysterious Mr Sudharto

Jakarta had the best-looking airport in the world – a cluster of pretty pavilions roofed with pink tiles and surrounded by gardens. It looked like a series of temples signposted for international visitors: EXIT – BAGGAGE – CUSTOMS – PASSPORT CONTROL. Theo wondered what new genie called up from his aunt's address book would greet them at the exit.

'A man or a woman?' he asked.

'A man, and Chinese,' she replied. 'So he's sure to be on time.'

Their new guide didn't let her down. Mr Sudharto was a man in his forties, short, thickset, and smartly dressed. He gave her an energetic handshake.

'Meet my young nephew, Theo,' she said, pushing him forward.

'What is your first name?' Theo asked.

'In Indonesia, there's no such thing,' said the man in the well-cut suit. 'Call me Sudharto. Now, after such a long flight you must be feeling tired. My car is here, and I've booked a suite at the Borobudur Intercontinental, my dear Martha. I hope you'll like it.'

It took two hours to reach the hotel, making painful progress through hectic traffic jams and air that reeked with pollution. Through windows necessarily closed, Theo surveyed the city's neat tree-lined avenues, skyscrapers, tower blocks, busy public squares, and in the distance a giant dome.

'A temple!' he cried. 'Is it Chinese?'

'In Indonesia,' Mr Sudharto informed him, 'the chief religion is Islam. What you are looking at is the great Istiqlal mosque. All by itself it has room for twelve thousand worshippers, both male and female – though segregated, of course.'

'Twelve thousand! It must be the biggest mosque in the world.'

'One of them, anyway. Islam is booming at present, and doing a whole lot of building.'

'But you are not a Muslim?'

'Isn't this a country that respects religious freedom?' Mr Sudharto replied.

'You're bothering our friend with all these questions,' Aunt Martha interrupted.

'Why?' asked Theo, taken by surprise.

'Not again!' She caught his eye and glared. 'That's enough.'

Theo realized that he was treading on dangerous ground, though unintentionally. In any case they had reached the hotel, an impressive building surrounded by coconut palms, banana trees and scented frangipanis. The Kirtamani gardens were famous for their lush varieties of jasmine and for the exceptional size of their traveller's palms, the graceful arcs of their alternating leaves reaching three metres in length.

'Tell me what I did wrong,' said Theo, as soon as Mr Sudharto had seen them to their room.

'You weren't to know, of course. Like all Chinese people in Indonesia, my friend Sudharto has changed his name. His true name is Koon Tai-kwan. The Chinese are very cautious in Indonesia.'

'OK, no need to tell me,' Theo sighed. 'They're scapegoats, right?'

'It happens. In 1965 the Indonesian Communist Party grew a bit too powerful, and rumours spread that it was planning a coup, with the backing of Mao Zedong, the leader of Communist China in those days. The Indonesian military stepped in, and a large-scale massacre followed, with up to a million people slaughtered, including many Indonesian Chinese.'

'They were all Communists?'

The answer was no. Nor did it matter that they had been born in Indonesia, and involved in business for generations. They were suspected of treason and paid the ultimate price for it simply because they were still Chinese. And the mud had stuck. On the thinnest of excuses, the Chinese could see their shops burned to the ground, because they were hard-working people, and often did better than their neighbours, which also meant that some of them lent money at interest . . .

'Which is never a good thing to do,' said Aunt Martha. 'My friend Sudharto is a big industrialist, and owns a multinational company specializing in textiles and timber, but he keeps a private plane in a flying club, in case . . .'

'In case of what?'

'If he had to get out in a hurry, he's ready.'

'Is it because of their religion?'

'To some extent,' Aunt Martha reckoned. 'It's better to be a Muslim around here.'

CHAPTER 16

Ancestors and Immortals

A snake's-blood cocktail

There was no getting round it: now that they had reached Jakarta, Theo must go to hospital.

'But the lady in Darjeeling treated me,' Theo protested. 'That's enough.'

Aunt Martha took no notice. It was nearly a month since Theo's last blood test, and she had given her word: yes, they would continue Doctor Lobsang Dorje's treatment, but only on condition that Theo must receive regular tests to monitor its progress. So he steeled himself for the routine procedure of disinfectant swabs, needles, syringes, and dark blood stored in small labelled tubes. Mr Sudharto saw to it that the samples were couriered to a specialist hospital in Singapore, the best-equipped in the region. They would have the results back in a few days.

'Hell,' said Theo. 'Mum will start flapping again.'

'Don't worry, Theo,' Aunt Martha tried to reassure him.

'Not me,' said Theo. 'I'm fine, and I'm feeling much better.'

'Maybe the boy would like to try something else,' Mr Sudharto suggested. 'I know a pagoda in my neighbourhood . . .'

'Good idea,' said Aunt Martha.

It wasn't far away, but because of the infuriating traffic jams it took nearly an hour to reach the Chinese quarter, with its narrow alleyways, red motorized trishaws, vendors selling mauve orchids or little pies, and open-air cauldrons with unknown dishes simmering inside. All at once

Theo gave a start. They had come to a stall where a man stood peeling the skin off a snake, while the living animal writhed in all directions.

'Do you see that, Aunt Martha?' Theo could hardly speak.

'What? Oh, the snake! The server will slit its throat, then squeeze the blood into a glass. Then he adds brandy, and you drink it all down. It really bucks you up. Would you like some?'

'No chance!' he gulped.

'Would you rather have tiger's penis in sauce, or grilled bear's paw?' Aunt Martha teased.

'Spaghetti!' Theo croaked. 'In tomato sauce!'

'Would you like some noodles, young man?' asked Mr Sudharto. 'I can get you some easily.' And he bought a bowlful of delicious pasta that Theo wolfed down, not feeling the least bit put off. After that they walked to a spacious square where the entrance to the temple stood, a tall gateway painted white and yellow, with a curved, unmistakably Chinese roof.

Divination in the pagoda

Inside the pagoda, everything was red – the walls, the giant altar candles, the candle-holders, all ox-blood red. Light shone at the far end on a group of bizarre golden statues. In front of a bowl of sand planted with lighted sticks of incense a woman held a long tube filled with slivers of bamboo. She rotated it over the smoking incense, tilted it forward, not too sharply, and shook it gently till one of the slivers fell to the ground. In a flash she bent to pick it up and read what was written on its blackened surface.

'Is it a game, Sudharto?' Theo asked. 'Tell me how it's played.'

'I wouldn't say the lady is playing a game,' Mr Sudharto told him. 'No doubt she is here for advice. Perhaps one of her sons is applying for a job, or is seriously ill. In any case, she is here to learn the truth.'

'What's this about?' said Theo. 'The truth in scraps of wood?'

'The Chinese have produced quite a number of manuals on fortune-telling,' Sudharto told him. 'The best-known is called *I Ching*, the Book of Changes. You just have to pick up the sacred container, like this . . . point it in the right direction, hold it over the incense and spin it round, to drive out the evil spirits. Then, if I give it a shake – like this – one of the messages will fall out of its own accord. I do not choose it. After that, I read it, and I have the answer to the question on my mind.'

Mr Sudharto stepped back to read the prophetic message picked up from the temple floor, and his face lit up.

'Excellent,' he murmured. 'The gods have spoken very kindly.'

'You mean you believe in it?' Theo exclaimed.

'Why would I not follow my ancestors' tradition? They have honoured it for thousands of years.'

'Suppose you try it, Theo?' Aunt Martha prompted.

'What have I got to lose?' said Theo. 'And I know what question to ask.'

He took his turn with the tube, and shook it so hard that a sliver flew out, but when he stooped to retrieve it he found that it was inscribed in Chinese. Sudharto volunteered to translate.

' "A time for refinement, a time for quiet",' he read.

'I don't understand,' said Theo.

'Maybe you forgot about the incense,' Mr Sudharto suggested.

'You're right,' said Theo. 'I'll have another go.'

And in spite of Aunt Martha's objections, he started again, this time following the procedure, rotating the tube over the incense, and shaking it gently. A second sliver emerged and fell. Mr Sudharto took it out of Theo's hand.

'Although it's not the custom to try again, I respect our young friend's wish,' he said in mitigation. 'This is the translation: "The Yang calls, the Yin answers." '

Theo thought hard. The Yang was sun, and the Yin was moon; the Yang was dry, the Yin wet; the Yang was boy . . . and the Yin was girl.

'I've got it! The Yang is me. I call Fatou on the phone . . . She is Yin, and she answers. So I'm going to marry Fatou.' Theo was overjoyed.

'You're jumping to conclusions,' Aunt Martha warned.

'Not at all! And do you realize it also means I'm going to get better?'

'What about the first message, Theo?' Mr Sudharto asked.

'No problem!' Theo replied. 'The time for refinement is this journey. The time for quiet is when I return to Paris, isn't it?'

Aunt Martha admitted defeat.

'That's just fantastic!' Theo proclaimed. 'If this is the Tao, I'll go for it!'

At the sound of his raised voice, some women turned and frowned. A bonze raised his eyebrows. Offended worshippers gathered around Theo and stared. Mr Sudharto took him by the arm.

'It's a pity you can't celebrate, young man, but we are in a place of worship, and . . .'

Theo clapped his hand over his mouth in embarrassment, then clasped both hands behind his back and set about exploring the smoke-filled pagoda.

'Those enormous candles, over there . . . ?' he whispered for a start.

'They're made to last all year,' Mr Sudharto replied. 'Then they're renewed.'

'To recreate time?' said Theo. 'And what about the statues?'

Evil and friendly spirits

Sometimes they looked like deities, sometimes like demons, but in reality the same energy impelled them both, the power of the ancestors. The demons were ghosts, or *kuei*: Mr Sudharto listed a few of them.

'Usually,' he said, 'they are spirits taking revenge on the living, or reincarnations of wicked animals. You see a pretty girl when it is actually a wandering soul that preys on corpses, the spirit of a fox ten thousand years old; you can recognize it by the purple hair in the left eyebrow.'

'If she wears make-up you could be mistaken,' said Theo.

'I can also tell you about the spirit in the form of a hideous old woman that creeps inside children's stomachs by night and steals their souls. Spirits are very fond of the souls of the living . . .'

'Charming,' said Theo. 'Are there many still around?'

Hordes of them. Some were not unpleasant: an old carp became a girl in mourning weeping by the water's edge and doing harm to no one . . . Sometimes they were even beneficial: the spirit of worn-out gold pieces roamed about as an adolescent girl with red feet, holding a torch in her hand; a boy, the spirit of pieces of silver, played with a fish by the roadside.

'No sweat with those, at least,' said Theo in relief. 'But what do you do about the evil spirits?'

'With the help of the divine powers, people can outwit the evil spirits,' Mr Sudharto explained. 'In very ancient times, Taoist scholars summoned powerful celestial armies from inside their own bodies by drawing a talisman in scarlet on a piece of yellow fabric, then burning it and swallowing the ashes. And the famous "dance of Yu" is still performed.'

'Famous? I've never heard of it.'

'Oh, it's very well known. To fight the flood, the Great Yu travelled the world, but the strain of building so many dams paralysed one side of him, so the "dance of Yu" is performed with a limp.'

'Like this?' said Theo, hobbling along on one leg.

'But you are not a Taoist priest!' Aunt Martha protested.

'What does that matter?' said Theo. 'I'm allowed to drive ghosts away if I want to . . . Hey, I could launch it on TV, old Yu's ghost dance, like the lambada. It'll be a smash!'

'You have no respect for the sacred,' she sighed.

'And who's that over there? She's so beautiful.'

He walked over to a statue whose sweet face was shrouded by the wing of a gigantic bird; around the goddess her golden attendants danced in the candlelight.

'That's no ghost, you can see,' he whispered. 'Tell me who she is, Sudharto.'

'The lady dressed in feathers,' Mr Sudharto murmured. 'She is the Queen Mother of the West, Hsi Wang Mu, the greatest goddess in China. One day, Emperor Mu of Chou met the Queen Mother of the West, and took such pleasure in her company that he forgot to return to his land.'

'That's nice,' said Theo admiringly. 'It sounds like a poem.'

'The Chinese love the Queen Mother of the West,' said Mr Sudharto earnestly. 'She reigns in a palace of jade surrounded by walls of gold: the immortals live there – males in the right wing, females in the left. Today she is alone, but once upon a time she had a twin, the Venerable King of the East: the same bird shaded the King of the East with its left wing, and with its right wing the Queen Mother of the West. In the course of time, the pilgrims have forgotten the King of the East. Only the Queen remains.'

'But look, they've deprived her of her twin,' said Theo. 'It's not right to do things like that.'

'Someone else could tell you the powers of the Venerable King of the East, but the Queen Mother of the West certainly held the secret of long life – the miraculous peaches. That is why, for us, peaches are the symbol of immortality.'

'I love peaches,' Theo rejoiced. 'So I must be immortal . . .'

'I'm sorry, my boy. Only the Queen Mother's miraculous peaches have that power, and her orchard bears fruit only once in three thousand years.'

In his disappointment, Theo ran towards the light, and found himself outside again, far from the ox-blood interior.

Lunch with Mr Sudharto

In the harbour, huge blue sailing ships nudged their graceful prows against the wharfs. Since the early days of boats, it was here that their cargoes of aromatic precious woods had been unloaded.

'It's an interesting story,' Mr Sudharto explained. 'Here, the first invaders came from Vietnam and China, blown by the monsoon winds to the island of Java. All of them brought their religion – Taoism, Confucianism and Buddhism. Later on, they discovered that clove trees grew in the Moluccas Islands.'

'You know about cloves?' Aunt Martha asked Theo. 'We put them in stews, and with cooked apples.'

'Mum sticks them into oranges,' said Theo. 'When they're dry, they have a gorgeous smell.'

Cloves were spices, flavours and scents of life. In the Middle Ages, when they were very highly prized in the West, these precious cargoes sailed from the Moluccas to Java, from Java to India, and from India to Venice, by way of long caravans strung across the sands of Arabia. But in the fifteenth century the Venetian Republic gained a stranglehold on the clove trade, thanks to the strength of its links with trade routes dominated by Muslim maritime powers, some of them now settled in the islands of Indonesia. To break this intolerable monopoly, destroy the wealth of Venice and bypass the Muslim sphere of influence, a century later the Portuguese conquerors took a different course, sailing southward round Africa and the Cape of Good Hope, then eastward into the Pacific. They brought Christianity to Indonesia, and cloves, nutmeg and mace to Europe. Because the paths of the monsoon winds crossed over the island of Borneo, and immobilized their ships for a whole season, all these visitors had plenty of time to preach the virtues of their gods, and that is why so many religions converged and survived among these scattered islands.

'I can smell cloves, I think,' said Theo, breathing deeply.

'Unless it's tar,' Aunt Martha answered. 'I doubt if they're still warring over the spice trade nowadays.'

'Tar or cloves, I'm starving,' Theo decreed. 'Where can we eat?'

'It's all taken care of, young man,' said Mr Sudharto. 'I'm honoured to invite you to my house.'

They set off through the narrow lanes again. The air was full of enticing smells that made Theo's mouth water: steamed ravioli, clear soups with chopped lemon balm floating around, shiny little fried cakes, and everything smelled and looked delicious. Theo was feeling more and more ravenously hungry when all at once Mr Sudharto turned the corner of a street and stopped in front of a high wall with a tiny door set into it. Inside the door they faced a second, smaller wall that had to be passed in a zigzag, a few paces one way, a few more in the other.

'Please excuse this little detour,' Mr Sudharto apologized. 'It prevents evil spirits coming in, because they only move in straight lines. This is my humble home.'

Humble, compared with palaces of jade and walls of gold. They emerged into a square courtyard with three buildings laid out around it. In the middle of the courtyard, golden carp swam in a circular ornamental pond. The main house stood beyond it like a stately, discreetly dressed old lady. The shady interior was filled with massive pieces of furniture made of a dark wood inlaid with mother-of-pearl. The effect was imposing, but hardly inviting. Theo crept furtively in as if entering a church, and perched on the front edge of a rigid armchair where he didn't feel much like relaxing.

'It's a really nice place you have,' he said for the sake of politeness.

Mr Sudharto smiled. For a man as rich as he was, it was sensible not to attract attention. The house had remained the way it had been since his ancestors had settled there, built in accordance with the rules of Chinese cosmology: three dwellings on the sides of a square, with a round pool in the middle, occupied by sacred fish to bring good luck – a house as wrinkled as the old people who scurried through its warren of darkened rooms, muttering inaudible prayers.

'Nothing has changed since my last visit,' Aunt Martha remarked as she took off her scarf.

'I don't think you've seen our new TV set,' said Mr Sudharto. 'We've had a brand-new satellite dish installed.'

Not far from this piece of state-of-the-art equipment, Theo noticed an odd contraption. On a mother-of-pearl table-top spread with yellow brocade stood a miniature pagoda whose twin doors opened on to a turquoise figurine of a presiding female spirit with a plump belly. Above her a few framed photographs were displayed: an old man with a bald head and a stern expression, a lady with her hair scraped back into a very tight chignon, another lady smiling, and holding a flower in her hand, and an elegant young man with a sad face, his tie neatly pinned. Lastly, in front of the miniature pagoda lay a little bowl of sand with sticks of smoking incense planted in it, next to a silver holder heaped with the familiar chips of wood for consulting the future.

'You keep a pagoda at home?' Theo asked in surprise.

'No, no,' said Aunt Martha. 'That is an altar to your ancestors, isn't it, my friend?'

Mr Sudharto looked embarrassed. 'I fear that our young friend is right,' he replied. 'Our little shrine is a replica of a real pagoda, except that in it we worship the men and women who came before us in this world. That is the custom among those of us who come from China.'

'Custom?' she echoed. 'Why not tell Theo that it's Confucianism you practise?'

'That's not exactly . . .' And Mr Sudharto embarked on a rambling account from which it emerged that the ancestral heritage did indeed derive from the Confucian precepts of respect for one's ancestors and for the social order, but also that the turquoise guardian spirit was the Moon goddess, sitting on her toad companion. The Moon, the toad and divination came from the Taoist tradition.

'So you syncretize Taoism with Confucius,' Theo concluded.

'Oh,' Mr Sudharto protested, 'that would be putting it too strongly: may the immortals spare me from that. I am a humble follower of custom, nothing more.'

'Immortals?' said Theo. 'Then you too have gods?'

You couldn't quite say that. Nevertheless, any reading of the sacred texts was bound to confirm that the original Taoism had made room for a whole family tree of divine beings.

'My son will say much more than I can,' he murmured. 'Man-li! Will you join us in the living room?'

A young man blew in out of nowhere, flopped down in a chair, pulled up his jeans to make himself comfortable, and rested his feet on the low table, trainers and all.

'Hi, guys,' he said, offering his hand to Aunt Martha. 'How you doing?'

'Behave yourself, please,' said Mr Sudharto.

The young man sat up straight and kept quiet. There was a pause, and Mr Sudharto continued.

'Man-li is reading comparative theology at Chicago University. My son, you know our friends Mrs Macquarie, and this is her nephew Theo. Our friends would like to know a little more about our country's gods. Can you enlighten them?'

Chaos, the egg, man and the Sovereigns

The young man stopped to think, and stuck out his legs.

'Please don't keep us waiting,' said Mr Sudharto. 'And sit properly.'

'Yes, father,' said Man-li, folding his beanpole legs again. 'I was wondering how to clarify our many versions of the origin of the world.'

'Well, clarify away, my son!'

Man-li scratched his head and got started. At the beginnings of time reigned a hazy, formless darkness. Then the Tao gave birth to the One, which divided into Two. Two gave birth to Three, which yielded ten thousand beings that wear the Yin on their backs and embrace the Yang. But according to other versions, two deities emerged from the gloom: one took charge of Heaven, the other of Earth, and they became the Father and Mother of all creatures.

'Just a minute,' said Theo. 'So "Two" is the parents' number, and "Three" is the family's.'

Man-li agreed. There was another way of narrating the birth of the world: the Lord of the Southern Ocean met the Lord of the Northern Ocean in the house of the Lord of the Centre, Chaos, who welcomed them both with the greatest courtesy. Wishing to return their host's hospitality, the two lords decided to pierce him the openings that he lacked, to enable him to see, hear, eat and breathe.

'Wait, though,' said Theo. 'What was he then, this king? A ball?'

By definition, Chaos was formless: he was neither round nor square, with no outline and no contours. Cutting holes in Chaos was a brave thing to do. Unfortunately, on the seventh day, Lord Chaos died of their attentions, and . . .

'Simplify, Man-li,' Mr Sudharto interrupted. 'You're not a professor yet.'

To cut it short, Chaos resembled a cosmic egg, and out of it came the very first human, P'an-ku. When he died, after eighteen thousand years, his eyes became the sun and moon, his head a mountain, his fat the seas, his hair the trees and plants. His tears set the Blue and Yellow rivers flowing, his breath was the wind and his voice the thunder. From his black pupil grew the lightning, from his contentment the clear sky, and out of his anger the clouds.

'So it is man who creates the world,' Theo concluded. 'Without God.'

No, because that came later. No one knew exactly when in history the first man, P'an-ku, and the sage of the Tao, Lao-tzu, had merged into a single deity. The left eye of the hidden Sage became the sun, the right eye the moon, his hair the stars, his skeleton the dragons, his flesh the four-footed animals, his entrails the snakes, his belly the seas, his body hair the plants, and his heart a sacred mountain. Finally, a mysterious being named the August Lord broke the connection between Heaven and Earth.

'Here we go again,' Theo whispered in Aunt Martha's ear. 'The statutory idiot spoils it for us.'

'It's rude to whisper,' she answered in the same tone.

These were the myths of Taoism, but you must also know the genealogy of the great kings, as laid down by Master Kung, who loved neither gods nor the supernatural. The first, said Man-li, were the Three Augusts, two men and a woman. By observing the feathers of birds, the variety of the universe and the parts of his own body, the oldest, the August King with a serpent's body, invented the book of divination. The August Woman, his wife, shared with him the same serpent's tail at the base of her spine.

'Hey, Siamese twins,' said Theo.

'Chinese!' Man-li corrected him.

As for the third of the Augusts, the Divine Ploughman, he created agriculture. Then came the Five Emperors. The first, the Yellow Emperor, wrote the treatises on medicine, sexuality, astrology and the art of war. The second was the one who divided Heaven and Earth. The third, the Crow Emperor, had for his wives the mother of ten suns and the mother of twelve moons. The fourth ruled the cycle of the seasons, but passed on their management to a man of the people, Chouen, the most virtuous of all.

'Not to a god, or to a rich man,' said Theo. 'I like that.'

Chouen was no ordinary human. Before choosing him, the Emperor had put him through some cruel ordeals. Chouen had to pass through flames, escape from a flood, dig himself out of the ground when it closed over his head, and face a hurricane, which didn't bother him. The worst ordeal led to his being beaten senseless by his own parents. Chouen managed not to show them disrespect, and founded the tradition of ancestor worship. Later, he drove out four demons through the four gates of the world, before relinquishing power to the fifth and last Emperor, Yu, born from a stone, Emperor of the Soil.

'The Great Yu?' cried Theo. 'The one who dances on one foot?'

The very same. With the Great Yu the holy ancestry of the Three Augusts and the Five Emperors came to an end. After them came the kings of perdition, dreadful tyrants who invented tortures and orgies. One of them flew into such a temper when he was scolded by a sage that he cut him in two to examine his heart. Duke Chou then raised an army, cut off the tyrant's head and hung it from his white standard. From then on, the story joined the history of China.

'Wow!' said Theo. 'It's just as complicated as Grandma Theano's gods.'

Aunt Martha ventured to explain that Theo was half Greek, and that his grandmother had told him bed-time stories from the mythology of her home country. Mr Sudharto asked politely if Theo would agree to tell a few episodes.

'It takes some time,' Theo yawned. 'And I'm starving.'

Aunt Martha's furious elbow dug into his arm.

'You're hurting me,' he yelped. 'What have I done?'

Mr Sudharto was chuckling as he rose to his feet and invited his guests to eat. Lunch was served at a round table with a revolving tray in the middle, Chinese style.

A Chinese meal, and food for thought

'Aunt Martha!' Theo hung back and whispered in her ear. 'I hope we won't be eating tiger's willy.'

'Don't worry,' she told him. 'I know what's on the menu.'

Caramelized jellyfish, translucent and crackling; frogs with garlic and parsley; egg soup; steamed sweet chickens' feet. When the crab and asparagus omelette arrived, Theo begged for mercy.

'Where are your manners?' Aunt Martha chided. 'Eat.'

As he picked halfheartedly at the omelette, Theo's chopsticks encountered something solid: a tiny wooden cylinder was hidden inside.

'Do I eat this?' he asked.

'Not before you open it,' Mr Sudharto smiled.

Theo wiped his fingers, popped open the container, and from it fell a tiny roll of paper.

'Don't tell me this is the next message!' he cried.

'Sure it is,' his aunt replied. 'Now you see how I knew about the menu.'

I am the sun, and I dislike raw horse meat. Come if you want to see me in my shrine.

Raw horse meat? For the sun? What country could this funny sort of deity come from?

'Hard, isn't it?' Aunt Martha crowed.

'Nought out of ten,' he admitted. 'I'll never get it.'

'What if Man-li can help?' asked Mr Sudharto

'I'd like to,' said Man-li, 'but I don't get it either.'

'Then perhaps you should consult the ancestors,' his father suggested mischievously.

The young men both stood up. Theo picked up the silver holder and waved it ceremoniously over the smoking sticks of incense. One shake dislodged a small wooden oblong that must have been balanced on the edge.

' "Then I withdraw, and the world sees night," ' he read out. 'This isn't an oracle.'

'I've got it now,' said Man-li with relief. 'It refers to the oldest goddess in . . .'

'Not another word!' Aunt Martha glared.

'It's a swizz,' said Theo. 'First you fix the oracles, then you won't let Man-li interpret them. If that's how it is, I'm going to call Fatou. Where's my mobile? Oh hell, I've left it at the hotel.'

'Why not use mine?' said Mr Sudharto, reaching into his pocket.

In the land of the festive carp

'Fatou? Yes, I'm fine. But I'm struggling with the message. You're not surprised? I see . . . Can you please give me the clue? Fishes celebrate children, and cherry trees the spring. What use is that? Couldn't you tell me a bit more about the raw horse meat? Skinned? A fat lot of good that does me! Nothing else to tell me? Never mind. Yes, love you too . . . Pretty hot . . . No, I'm not sweating. Yes . . . You too . . . A lot.'

Theo was looking baffled when he switched off the mobile.

'She says the horse is raw because it's flayed,' he muttered. 'Do you get that, Man-li?'

'Of course,' he grinned. 'The goddess's brother threw a flayed horse into her house.'

'That doesn't give me the country's name.'

'You can find it, my lad,' said Aunt Martha. 'Where do they celebrate children with paper carp?'

'Don't know. In Mexico?'

'No,' said Man-li. 'Where do the most beautiful cherry trees in the world grow? What country is it where everything comes to a halt while they view the blossom?'

'Japan!' cried Theo.

'Took you long enough,' Aunt Martha sighed.

'And who's this girl who doesn't like raw horse meat?' asked Theo, annoyed with his own ignorance.

Her name was Amaterasu, an austere, chaste goddess. She lived in a rock cave attended by serving women who wove her a kimono every day, the colour of time. Every morning, Amaterasu emerged to light up the world, until the day when, as a prank, her obnoxious brother Susanoo, god of Thunder, Storm and Rain, threw a flayed horse on to the weaver women's looms. They surged around in terror, and one of them was pierced between the legs by her own shuttle, and died of the wound. The goddess Amaterasu was not amused by practical jokes, and did not like the flayed horse. She was so upset that she hid in her cave, and the light disappeared.

'What an idiot, the brother,' said Theo. 'Did it last long?'

Long enough to cause panic even in heaven, where the gods and goddesses could see no better than the mortals below. They met in consternation, and plotted a scheme of their own. They asked Uzume, the goddess with the best sense of humour, to entertain them outside the cave where Amaterasu had blocked the entrance with a boulder and was brooding. No half-measures for Uzume: she hitched up her dress and broke into a bawdy dance, pulling hilarious faces, and showing off her rump and female treasures. She was so comical that the gods roared with laughter . . . Unable to restrain her curiosity, Amaterasu pushed the boulder aside, but the gods had made a mirror. They held it up, and she saw a shining woman. In her surprise, she stepped forward, so then the gods caught her by the hem of her kimono, and Amaterasu left the cave for ever. The world was saved.

'That's a good tale,' said Theo. 'Still, she had a right to be angry.'

'There are so many marvellous stories in Japan,' Man-li told him. 'You're lucky to be going there.'

But before they could leave for the islands of Japan, they had to wait for the results of the blood tests, and right now it was time for their siesta. Theo was sorry to leave his new friends. As soon as the door closed behind them, Mr Sudharto went to the altar, shook up the urn, consulted his ancestors about the fate in store for Theo, and smiled at the answer.

Surprising results

All the same, when the results arrived from Singapore, they showed no real improvement. Condition stable.

'Stable,' said Aunt Martha. 'That's very worrying . . . What treatment? Well, actually . . .'

The thrill that ran through her was so violent that she dropped the phone and almost passed out.

'Theo!' she cried. 'Do you know what? The blood tests are stable.'

'What's the big deal then?' he answered. 'Same old story.'

'No it isn't. Because you stopped taking the medicine from home, and the new treatment has taken over! The doctor in Darjeeling has succeeded!'

Wild with delight, she grabbed him and whirled him round the room in a headlong dance.

'Aunt Martha,' he panted, shuffling his feet in self-protection, 'why is the phone making that funny noise?'

'My God, I forgot to hang up,' Aunt Martha giggled.

This was the cue for Theo to speak to his parents.

CHAPTER 17

Mothers and Daughters of Japan

Aunt Martha is stuck

Jerome let out a sigh of relief when he heard what his sister had to say. Of course, the preliminary results were still only average, but Tibetan medicine had come to the same conclusions as its Western cousin, and that itself was encouraging. Theo's father insisted they stay another week in Jakarta, to have some more tests done. Martha protested that they would do just as good a job in Tokyo, but Jerome wouldn't hear of it, and she had to give in. Once her brother made up his mind, he would not budge.

'He's a pain, your father,' she grumbled, hanging up. 'A week! We'll end up missing the Japanese cherry blossom!'

'But it's nice here,' said Theo. 'Now we'll be able to see my friend Man-li again. Anyway, who are you going to conjure up in Japan, eh?'

'You'll like her,' replied Aunt Martha.

'Cool!' cried Theo. 'A lady, for a change. What shall we do now? Shall we go to the Mosque?'

Non-Muslims were forbidden to enter the Mosque, especially Aunt Martha, even though it was ladies' day; but they were allowed to peep inside, as long as they remained at the entrance. The women were all dressed in white, and wore white veils; they prostrated themselves rhythmically with impressive discipline, twelve thousand at a time, their faces framed in embroidered lace. Indonesian Islam was not fanatical, but the dictates of the Koran were strictly observed.

291

'You did say there were also animist tribes, didn't you?' asked Theo as they walked along the street.

'Of course,' she replied. 'One of the strangest, three hours from Jakarta, is the Badwi, who reject Islam, dress in white, and allow some of their people to join modern civilization, but only if they're dressed in blue. The Badwi do things like sending an envoy to give a protective talisman to the President and then withdrawing without saying a word. Nobody enters their territory.'

'There are some really strange folk in the world. I hope I live long enough to get to know them all!'

'Then you'll be an ethnologist,' stated Aunt Martha.

'I've heard the word, but I don't know what it means. What's an ethnologist?'

'You'll have to pick on a particular tribe and live among them and share their way of life. That way you'll understand their way of thinking and their gods.'

'But that's what we're doing, travelling from country to country!' exclaimed Theo.

'We have seen peoples, but we haven't seen tribes, and I'm afraid we won't see any. Their life is too harsh for your condition. They live in such poverty . . .'

'No Taoist sanctuary, no tribes, no steps to climb, what else do you want to keep me away from?' burst out Theo.

'Then just get better, you cheeky monkey!'

Maoism and Taoism

The week went by. Aunt Martha took Theo to see the *Ramayana* in a shadow theatre where, once the initial charm had worn off, he was bored to death. After that, they went to see some golden dancers, who flitted around as gracefully as dragonflies, but Theo found them affected. He preferred conversations with Man-li to Indonesian entertainment.

One day, as he was eating raw beef marinated in a red sauce, a rare dish from the island of Sumatra, Theo suddenly felt an overwhelming urge to visit China, the real China. The land of the cruel empresses and of Chairman Mao; millions of Chinese walking the streets of the cities, or working in the fields; fabulous operas and modern buildings; the young people of Shanghai, the trendies of Beijing. The China he dreamed of and that he would see one day, when he grew up.

'Have you been to China?' he asked Man-li.

'Sort of,' he replied, cautiously.

'What did you see of your religion there?'

'Everything and nothing,' answered Man-li. 'At first, there were a lot of different movements in our country. With the first revolution in 1911, the empire collapsed, and with the idea of empire gone, the world order changed. Mao arrived . . .'

'Like Zorro,' cut in Theo. 'The Long March, I know . . .'

'And Chairman Mao's Great Proletarian Cultural Revolution, have you heard of that?' interrupted Aunt Martha grumpily. 'That's what killed religion in China!'

'Cultural Revolution?' asked Theo in amazement. 'What did Mao do? Send everyone to art school?'

'To think you don't know about the horror of it,' she sighed. 'Was it all so long ago? Listen.

Mao did not send everyone to art school. In the years before the Cultural Revolution, he had embarked on a radical economic reform programme, the Great Leap Forward, which led to disastrous famines. It was clearly a failure. One day, in 1966, Mao reappeared to launch a powerful appeal to the young people of China: "They are right to rebel," he thundered, "let them rebel! Let them criticize the leaders of the Communist Party!" Thousands of students whom Mao called the "Red Guards" responded enthusiastically. They brandished the Little Red Book, a collection of Mao's sayings, and were mobilized on his orders. The schools and universities closed, the students began combing China to weed out the Party traitors.'

'But who were they, exactly?' asked Theo confused.

Mao had advised his Red Guards to fight against the four symbols of the 'old': old ideas, old customs, old habits and old traditions. The Red Guards decided to wipe out superstition from the minds of the Chinese. Marshal Lin Piao, even though he was very close to Mao, was violently criticized for having cited Confucius, who the Red Guards had decided was the epitome of feudal injustice. High on the feeling of wielding revolutionary power, in their frantic dedication, the young people tore down the temples, museums and statues. They pillaged people's homes and destroyed everything that came from the past, because Chairman Mao, their guide, encouraged them to do so. They paraded scientists, former landowners, researchers and writers wearing dunces' caps through the streets, all supposedly guilty of conveying the ancient knowledge of China. Many were beaten to death. For the first time in China, children broke the sacred bonds that linked them to their elders.

Civil war broke out between rival factions of fanatical youths. After two years, Mao sent his Red Guards into the fields, with the peasants. How many were killed during this bout of madness? Reportedly millions. At last, after a period of terrible repression, Mao died in 1976.

'Perhaps you're misrepresenting the Cultural Revolution,' objected Man-li shyly. 'The aim of the head of the Chinese Communist Party was to galvanize his country to help it regain its revolutionary momentum. By calling on the young people, he thought he would find uncorrupted forces. There is no doubt that things went out of control, but the initial idea was not so bad.'

'What!' blurted out Aunt Martha indignantly. 'Entrust the re-education of an entire people to teenagers, give them the power to judge and purge – it's insane!'

'What have you got against young people?' asked Theo.

'Nothing, except when they're holding a gun. On the orders of a tyrannical old grandfather, they turned against their own, for goodness sake!'

'Quite natural,' commented Theo.

'Oh, that's enough from you, all right! They themselves regret it now! They can't believe they enjoyed torturing old people, especially women. And you claim to hate religious massacres? Maoism became a murderous religion, Theo!'

'Not to respect our ancestors was revolutionary, it's true,' said Man-li. 'But on the other hand, Confucianism is sometimes such a heavy load for young people to carry.'

'Does that justify such violence, young man?'

'No, of course not,' muttered Man-li. 'Chairman Mao was sometimes wrong. Around thirty per cent of the time.'

'And now he's absolved!' concluded Aunt Martha furiously. 'Embalmed, deified, he lies in state in Tiananmen Square, and is still revered! He's worshipped just like a god. Twice a day, whatever their job, the Chinese had to dance the Dance of Loyalty in his honour! They called him the Red Sun of everybody's heart.'

'You mean the Red Sun was a new god of China,' said Theo.

'Yes!' cried Aunt Martha bitterly. 'Powerful, generous, nurturing, but as violent as a god, and cruel as a god too! An emperor of perdition.'

'You're going too far,' said Theo. 'It's hardly surprising they chucked you out of the People's Republic of China!'

'You don't know the young people of China today,' insisted Man-li, thumping the table. 'China is a great country, capable of coming to terms with its history. What standard are you judging us by?'

'Any faith that kills is bad. And Mao's is no exception. I don't mind the Chinese bowing down to a capitalist god now.'

'Excuse me,' he butted in, 'I don't know what god you're referring to.'

'It's quite simple,' replied Aunt Martha. 'Money!'

'Mrs Macquarie,' said Man-li who had turned a little pale, 'may I remind you that the Chinese have never thought badly of wealth. My father is rich and doesn't see any shame in that.'

'I'm sorry,' murmured Aunt Martha, blushing. 'That's not what I meant, Man-li.'

'But you said it all the same,' he retorted. 'You are wealthy enough to afford to say such things!'

Aunt Martha clammed up and looked sheepish.

'In any case, this red stuff is very good,' said Theo to change the subject.

The uselessness of cherry blossom

Man-li did not show up again and Theo sulked. The week went by. The results of the latest tests showed almost no change. However, the specialists at the Singapore Hospital wrote on the notes that they were 'encouraging'. Martha rushed to the telephone and obtained permission to leave.

'Let me speak to Mum', said Theo. 'Why is it always you who announces the good news?'

'You're right, darling. Here . . .'

'Dad? Yes, it's not bad. Can you put Mum on? Thanks . . . Mum! Are you pleased at least? Listen, "encouraging" – it's better than nothing! Relax, I'm much better . . . How's school? Really? You're off at the moment? You're not ill, are you? Oh. Tired. Giddiness. Have you seen the doctor? Overwork? I think he's absolutely right! So you're going away for the weekend? Bruges? That's great! Will you bring me back a present? Because I'm bringing back tons for you! Yes . . . Of course, Mum. I love you.'

When he hung up, Theo was worried.

'She's off sick,' he said. 'She also feels giddy. The doctor says it's nothing, but Dad is taking her away for the weekend for a rest. Guess where? To Bruges. That's where they went for their honeymoon.'

'Perfect,' commented Aunt Martha. 'It'll do them good.'

'You're worried sick, I can see! What on earth did Mum do to you?'

'Nothing, but you know how nervy she gets. A nice break with Dad will make her feel better, that's all.'

'To think they're going to Bruges.'

'And we're off to Japan! About time too!'

'I say, it sounds as though you really love the place,' muttered Theo.

'You can't imagine how beautiful the cherry blossom is. You have to see it once in your life!'

'I get it,' replied Theo. 'See the cherry blossom in Japan and die.'

'Don't be stupid. You know very well that you're going to get better now.'

'If only I could be sure! Since we've been in Jakarta, we've fallen out with Man-li, I'm bored and my twin hasn't spoken. It's not a good sign. I don't feel very good.'

'Can you explain something to me, Theo?' she asked gently. 'What does this twin mean to you?'

'Dunno,' he whispered. 'It's as though he guides me in the dark. When I'm feeling better, he talks to me. If he doesn't, the results don't improve. And I haven't heard a peep out of him for weeks.'

'Perhaps he needs a period of silence?' ventured Aunt Martha.

'Suppose so,' answered Theo laconically.

'He'll find it in Japan. If there's a country that worships silence, it's Japan. The cherry trees don't talk, and at the sight of the white blossom, people are silent.'

'But I've seen cherry blossom before,' snapped Theo.

'Yes, but in Japan, there's a whole ceremony. You'll see, in Japan, people are in touch with nature.'

'Nature,' said Theo glumly. 'Bound to be polluted!'

Theo's soul in distress

The Garuda Airlines plane bore the eagle emblem of the god Vishnu, proudly displayed on the nose. In fact, the eagle was rather old and slightly wheezy, and the Jakarta–Tokyo flight was several hours late. Theo's gloom had not lifted: he flicked through magazines, half-heartedly listened to rock music, yawned through the film and dozed off. Martha wondered why her nephew seemed so depressed when the Tibetan medicine was starting to work.

What was wrong? Since leaving Paris, Theo had enthusiastically taken in the three monotheistic religions in Jerusalem, the meaning of the papacy in the Vatican, the whole of India, Hinayana and Mahayana Buddhism, Taoism and Confucius. Her beloved Theo who was so keen to understand everything! Was he tiring of the enterprise? She pictured him jumping for joy in the pagoda . . . He seemed so happy, so alive, and suddenly, no more. The flame seemed snuffed out. What would he make of the profundity of the Japanese ceremonies and the strictness of the rites?

'It's too late to turn back now,' she murmured. 'How can I cheer up my little shrimp?'

Theo became restless in his sleep. Jumbled words came out of his mouth. 'Don't leave me! Mum . . . I'm so lonely . . .' Aunt Martha understood. What with the absence of his mother and the disappearance of his twin, Theo felt empty, and this illness was not curable with Tibetan medicine. Should she ask Theo's mother to come out? 'No. First, we're on the other side of the world. And second, Melina would panic, and besides, she's not ready. No, it's definitely too soon. We've got to hold on,' Martha said to herself.

Trust Japan. Let Theo discover the cult of forests and flowers. Let him taste green tea. Ah! Make him resume his morning yoga. Straighten his back. Feed him raw fish, it's full of phosphorus. Martha rummaged in the bag of European medicines to see if she could find anything: it was there, ready just in case. Suddenly, she realized that she herself was in a state.

'He's bringing me down too,' she muttered, 'even when he's asleep.'

Miss Ashiko

In the midst of a crowd of Japanese festooned with cameras, Aunt Martha was looking for the young lady who did not appear to have turned up. In her annoyance, she decided to go to the reception desk and ask them to put out an announcement.

Theo thought she would turn out to be another sensible old woman, with wrinkles and kindly eyes. He heaved a great sigh. Aunt Martha's friends were all delightful, but if only they were a bit younger! Whenever he came across a friend along the way, like Man-li, Aunt Martha got into an argument with them. Scowling, Theo scrutinized the elderly faces. Which one could it be?

'Hi!' said a cheery voice behind him. 'Could I trouble you?'

Theo turned around. A young Japanese girl was smiling at him.

Laughing eyes, round mouth, hair down to her hips, a shiny black mass of it . . . Mini-skirt, red bomber jacket. Thirteen years old? Fifteen?

'Hi,' he said, breaking out into a smile. 'You're not troubling me but I've only just arrived. I'm with my aunt and we're meeting someone. Do you live in Tokyo?'

'No, Kyoto,' she replied. 'I'm also meeting someone. A lady who's French, like you. She should be with a little boy, but I can't see him. Perhaps you've noticed him?'

'What's this lady like?' asked Theo eagerly, taking her hand. 'I'll help you.'

'She always wears weird clothes. She usually wears a Nepalese hat.'

'That's funny!' cried Theo. 'So does my aunt. That makes two weird old ladies at the airport. Ah, here's my aunt. You see, I wasn't kidding. Look at her hat!'

At the sight of the girl, Martha's face lit up.

'There you are, at last!' she exclaimed. 'Where've you been?'

'I'm terribly sorry, Mrs Macquarie,' muttered the teenager sheepishly. 'My taxi got stuck in a traffic jam.'

'I see you found Theo,' grumbled Aunt Martha, staring at their entwined hands.

Open-mouthed, Theo looked from Aunt Martha to the girl whose eyes grew wide in amazement. So this was her Japanese friend!

'So you're Theo?' she murmured. 'Pleased to meet you.'

'Me too,' he rejoined, letting go of her hand.

'I thought you were younger,' she said, blushing. 'Mrs Macquarie was always talking about her "little Theo".'

'And what's your name?'

'Ah ha! You found each other without knowing who you were!' guffawed Aunt Martha. 'But that's wonderful . . . Theo, this is Miss Ashiko Okara, a French student.'

'Student?' asked Theo in surprise.

'Ashiko is very talented,' added Aunt Martha. 'She's only sixteen.'

Sixteen! Slightly disappointed, Theo took a step back.

'We must be about the same age, I think,' murmured Miss Ashiko shyly.

'I'm only fourteen,' he whispered, mortified.

'I thought you were sixteen,' replied the girl. 'You're so tall.'

'Tall? Theo?' protested Aunt Martha. 'He's exactly the same height as me! Come here, Theo.'

And, taking him by the shoulders, she made him stand next to her.

Theo was a head taller. Flabbergasted, she began again. Theo had definitely grown.

'Just look at that,' she gasped. 'It's crazy! How did that happen?'

'Travel helps young people grow, old girl,' replied Theo, delighted.

'I shan't call you "little shrimp" any more, but "beanpole",' she retorted. 'Come on, children, let's go!'

Naturally, the hotel suited Aunt Martha's usual style: old-fashioned, opulent and comfortable. Except for the bathrobes and slippers, there was nothing Japanese about it. The beds weren't futons, the screens weren't made of paper and the hotel was not built of wood.

'I thought the Japanese spent their whole time kneeling on mats,' exclaimed Theo in surprise.

'That's the old way,' replied Aunt Martha. 'Would you have preferred tatamis? Ridiculous! Do you know that the Japanese make fun of Westerners who ape their traditions?'

'But what's Japanese in all this?'

'The single flower in the vase,' she said.

'Mum can do that. She took ikana lessons.'

'Ikebana!' corrected Aunt Martha. 'You're in such a rush to remember everything that you leave bits out, beanpole.'

'By the way, your friend's really nice.'

'I've known her since she was a baby. She was such a podgy little thing, and look at her now, pretty as a picture, don't you think?'

'Oh yes,' agreed Theo. 'She looks like Sophie Marceau. So what else does she do, apart from being a student?'

'Wait and see . . .' she replied. 'In the meantime, take your Tibetan whatsits and have a rest!'

But Theo could not get to sleep. Seeing the cherry trees with Miss Ashiko promised to be much more fun than visiting the Vatican with the Cardinal. He dreamed of cherry blossom petals on her incredibly long black hair, and of a cold little hand that he was trying to warm up.

The cruelty of raw fish

In the late afternoon, Aunt Martha woke him up. Stretching, Theo realized that it was nearly dinner time.

'At six o'clock in the evening?' she teased. 'You've forgotten the time lag again.'

'Drat,' said Theo, adjusting his watch. 'I'd do better to use the alarm clock that Irene gave me. Six o'clock. That's a hell of a long time till dinner. What shall we do?'

'Stroll around the streets till we find a fish restaurant. How does that suit you?'

'If you mean sushi, I've had it before,' grumbled Theo.

'Your grumpiness is beginning to get on my nerves. And supposing I told you we were having dinner with Ashiko?'

'That's different,' admitted Theo. 'But I warn you, I hate raw fish.'

The minute he was outside, Theo was fascinated by the gadget stores. Aunt Martha gave him a small allowance to indulge his fancy. He lingered in front of the latest miniature television model and eventually tore himself away. By now he was starving, and he stood for ages outside a restaurant window displaying giant lacquered pink prawns, sumptuous carrot rosettes and bowls filled with squid cut in star shapes.

'Does that make your mouth water?' asked Aunt Martha. 'Well, it's fake. Those appetizing dishes are made of plastic.'

As he was unable to eat for real, Theo shopped for imitation food to play tricks on his sisters: vegetables, shellfish, and a glass of Coca-Cola with ice cubes. Meanwhile, Aunt Martha bought a pale blue kimono decorated with huge purple birds and a heavy, black cast-iron kettle from a street stall.

'Hey, think of the excess baggage!' scoffed Theo.

'It's for your mother,' she snapped.

'That blue kimono's hideous,' muttered Theo. 'Can I choose one for her?'

Aunt Martha didn't have a chance to reply. In no time at all, Theo had grabbed a kimono embroidered with delicate flowers in old gold against a creamy white background. With a great sigh, Aunt Martha scrunched up her ugly kimono like a bin bag and hailed a taxi.

'Aren't we walking any more?' asked Theo in surprise.

'I sometimes get a bit tired too,' she muttered with tears in her eyes.

Poor Aunt Martha . . . Theo felt a surge of affection and gently kissed her hand. She blew her nose noisily.

'At least, you didn't criticize the kettle,' she said.

Theo didn't answer. Melina already had one like it and he couldn't stand raw fish. Luckily Miss Ashiko would be there!

She was waiting for them, looking very schoolgirlish in a navy blue dress brightened up by a demure white collar.

'Don't you ever wear a kimono?' asked Theo wistfully.

'Yes, she does,' replied Aunt Martha before Ashiko could say anything.

'Kimonos of a particular kind, you'll see. Don't be too impatient. And decide what you want to eat.'

'Grilled fish,' decided Theo.

There wasn't any. The seafood was eaten raw, the minute the fish had been cut up on the chopping board where some parts were still wriggling. His stomach churning, Theo watched Miss Ashiko devour octopus slices that quivered horrifically. Soon, he had to go outside to avoid being sick. The garish neon lights dazzled him, customers hurried in and out of brightly lit bars, drunks yelled into the night and Theo was starving.

'Is something the matter, Theo?' murmured Ashiko's voice. 'Come back inside with me.'

'No. I'll never eat raw fish!'

'Is eating it cooked any better?' retorted Aunt Martha's gruff voice.

'Don't care!' cried Theo. 'I can't watch it, it makes me feel sick and I'm starving!'

Ashiko took things in hand, found another restaurant and asked for the menu. A few moments later, having washed his face with a hot flannel, Theo delightedly watched the thin slices of beef simmering in a huge cast-iron skillet over blue flames. You picked a piece up with chopsticks and dipped it in raw, beaten egg.

'You Japanese are so cruel,' he said after swallowing the first mouthful. 'At least cooked meat is humane!'

'Raw or cooked, it's still living creatures you're eating!' said Aunt Martha. 'Correct me if I'm wrong.'

'I understand how he feels,' cut in Ashiko, embarrassed.

'Oh you do!' protested Aunt Martha. 'As someone who defends the most traditional rites, you venture to make such a criticism? That's not very Japanese!'

'For many long centuries, our civilization was dominated by warrior principles,' she replied. 'You know that their code of honour had its cruel side.'

'Ah! You're thinking of *seppuku*. You know this death rite, Theo. In Europe, it's known as *hara-kiri*.'

'Daddy's got some back issues of a magazine called *Hara-kiri*,' said Theo. 'But I've never heard of the death rite in Japan.'

The story of a girl, a boy and a divine sword

It was the last act of the Japanese warrior. If he had behaved dis-
honourably, or been defeated, if he had betrayed, or if his master simply
took it into his head to command him to do so, he would commit
suicide according to an iron ritual. Dressed in white, he would slit open
his abdomen from top to bottom with a short-handled dagger, before
his assembled friends. In olden times, the worthiest person present,
chosen by him, would cut off his head to curtail his suffering.

'Is that what *hara-kiri* is?' cried Theo in amazement.

'*Seppuku*,' corrected Miss Ashiko. 'It's almost extinct now.'

'But each year you commemorate the forty-seven brave samurai who
decided to avenge their master and, once their duty was accomplished,
slit open their stomachs one by one,' said Aunt Martha.

'The forty-seven *rōnin*?' smiled Ashiko. 'The masterless samurai? They
symbolize the duty of loyalty. The fate of those *rōnin* was harsh. Either
their master was dead, or he no longer had the means to pay them, so
that in either case, they wandered pathetically from place to place with
their useless swords. The forty-seven set themselves a specific task. We
revere them for their tenacity and their sense of honour, not for the
seppuku.'

'Don't be so sure,' said Aunt Martha. 'The great writer Mishima committed suicide in this way not very long ago, and what a death! Listen
to this, Theo. First he entered the office of the chief-of-staff of the
Japanese army and tied him up neatly. Then, in front of the TV cameras,
he deplored the loss of the ancient Japanese values that he was going
to demonstrate in all their splendour. And once his speech was over,
he slit open his stomach. His friend cut off his head and then did
likewise. That happened in the Seventies.'

'Mishima lived in a bygone era,' replied Ashiko. 'We young people
live in the modern world.'

'Since when?' asked Theo.

'Come, you haven't forgotten the atomic bomb on Hiroshima,' cut in
Aunt Martha.

'No, but what date was that?' protested Theo.

'In 1945, to end World War Two, the Americans tested this new
weapon on Japan. Since the beginning of the conflict, Japan had been
an ally of Nazi Germany and Fascist Italy. The other two countries had
already surrendered, but every day Japan sent *kamikaze* bombers to
attack enemy ships.'

'I've heard of *kamikaze*,' declared Theo. 'It means "suicide".'

'Not exactly,' Miss Ashiko explained. '*Kamikaze* means "divine wind", but it is true that the pilots committed suicide by crashing their planes on to their target.'

'Incredible courage,' commented Theo.

That, and the sense of their divine mission, was precisely the meaning of the Samurai code of honour. Ever since the nineteenth century, the Emperor had been a god, a direct descendant of the goddess Amaterasu. As he was of divine origin, all Japanese had a duty to sacrifice their lives to him. When, after the Hiroshima bomb, the Emperor decided to surrender, some soldiers refused the inconceivable and fought alone on some Pacific islands, for years. For in their eyes, the Emperor-god could not fall and his people could not abandon him.

'More human sacrifice in the air,' thought Theo. 'What's that nice Amaterasu got to do with this war? I thought that after leaving her cave, she illuminated the world!'

True, but Amaterasu was the daughter of a pair of founder gods whose tragic story left a profound impression on the Japanese mind. Japan's father god was called Izanagi, and the mother goddess Izanami. Before the earth came into being, the community of gods pushed them onto a rainbow bridge to create Japan. The young Izanagi was so handsome that the goddess Izanami stopped in the middle of the bridge of transparent colours and said to him: 'Will you marry me' They were wed, but, to their great horror, their first children were monstrous creatures – jellyfish, octopuses and other gelatinous beings. It was a disaster.

In despair, the two deities went back to the celestial kingdom, but the gods sent them back onto the rainbow, insisting that they obey the will of nature. So, in the middle of the bridge, the god Izanagi stopped and said to the goddess: 'Will you marry me?' and, as this time the male had behaved as he should in proposing to the female, Izanami gave birth to the most splendid children, the islands of Japan.

'So far, it's not too tragic,' commented Theo.

But, on giving birth to her last-born, Izanami died. Crazed with grief, Izanagi decided to go and seek her in Hell. Miraculously, he obtained permission to bring her back to the world of the living, but under no circumstances was he to turn around. Alas, Izanagi disobeyed. So his beloved was turned into a rotting corpse, who pursued him to eat him alive. The god managed to escape by throwing her a comb, pulled out of his hair, and he never saw Izanami again.

'That reminds me of Grandma Theano's story,' murmured Theo. 'In

Greece, the woman was called Eurydice, but I can't remember what the man's name was.'

It was Orpheus, the magician, poet and musician. But although Orpheus became one of the sources of inspiration behind a powerful mystical tendency, he didn't have any offspring. Bitten by a deadly poisonous snake, Eurydice never had time to have any children. Izanami on the other hand represented an adorable mother capable of changing into an ogress in the depths of Hell. The supreme and awesome mother, Izanami gave birth to the whole of nature in its divine form: Japan. According to the Shinto religion, Izanami's daughter, the goddess Amaterasu, entrusted her brother Susanoo's sword, the insignia of divinity, to the first Emperor of Japan. Susanoo was a violent god, representing the dark side of the universe, while Amaterasu symbolized the bright side. On receiving Susanoo's sword from the hands of the goddess, the Emperor-god inherited the two principles of masculine and feminine.

'Right,' said Theo. 'It's a way of holding on to power.'

Ashiko protested. According to religious historians, the cave to which the goddess Amaterasu withdrew probably had echoes of a distant period when the Japanese buried their dead in caves. The return of Izanami's daughter therefore did not only signal the rebirth of light, it was also the sign of life after death. Like the sun, the dead disappeared and reappeared, often in the form of mournful ghosts who had to be appeased. As the holder of the divine sword, the Emperor thus also guaranteed the immortality of the Japanese.

'I have one question,' ventured Theo. 'What does Shinto mean?'

The way of the gods. Early Shinto, Japan's most ancient religion, worshipped the deities in their simplest forms: the sun, the wind, rocks, mountains, the flower in bloom, the woods and the clouds. And the influence of the natural deities, which Shinto called the *kami*, extended over the whole earth, and the gods were accessible. It did not take much to placate them: a cord tied around an item of clothing, a pennon or a prayer. For a long time, Shinto was the simplest of all the religions: an ecstatic relationship with Japan's natural environment, which was volcanic, threatening, lush and peaceful, misty, snowy, tropical in the south and glacial in the north.

'If that's what Shinto was,' asked Theo warily, 'does that mean it's changed then?'

Yes, because it had been buried under layers of religions from elsewhere: Chinese Confucianism and Mahayana Buddhism. Shinto had not disappeared, on the contrary, it had survived very well, but it had accommodated the new religions. Out of this magma, Shinto-Buddhism had emerged.

'Here we go again, syncretism, don't tell me!' exclaimed Theo.

As everywhere, Buddhism had no difficulty grafting itself onto a religion which was content to worship the gods of nature without any real philosophy. The first Buddhist monks began by praying in the Shinto shrines to the deities known as the 'gods of golden light': nobody raised any objections. Then they made up all sorts of legends in which the Shinto gods explained how they were in fact bodhisattvas. Some contradictions were not easy to resolve: for example, how to reconcile compassion for living things with the dead fish that were sacrificed to the gods of golden light.

'Good question,' observed Theo.

So, the gods explained to a holy monk unable to devise a reply that they had taken upon themselves the fault of humans who acted without thinking. Incidentally, the gods took care to collect up all the old fish that had come to the end of their lives as fish, so that if men caught them, it was through divine will. Thus they entered the way of the Buddha.

'Those Buddhists were crafty,' said Theo.

Not crafty enough to avoid fighting among themselves, though. For a very long time, the Buddhists were divided into warring sects, which gave rise to the famous warriors' code of honour, *bushido*. After centuries of bloody conflicts, the Emperor regained power and made Shinto the official religion. Ever since, the official religion of the Japanese nation has been the same as that of the Emperor, who, thanks to Susanoo's sword, was revered as the direct descendant of the Sun, indisputable and, therefore, undisputed until 1945.

'So the Emperor of Japan is no longer a god,' concluded Theo. 'Although I saw on TV that people bow down to him and all that.'

The terms of Japan's surrender imposed by the American General MacArthur specifically required the Emperor to give up his divine status, but the Japanese soul preserved its zeal. The Emperor was respected, even though he was now no more than a sovereign like any other, at the head of a parliamentary democracy. The transition to a democracy had been complicated, because the word 'freedom' meant nothing in the old Japan, neither did the word 'individual'. Previously, the entire society lived for the god-emperor, who was himself the incarnation of Japan. The idea of a free decision was foreign to a system where only the country and its god counted. General MacArthur had also demanded the vote for women, which was an even greater scandal. What, Izanami's daughters were to be allowed to vote? So Japan would once again pay the penalty for the disastrous action of the ill-mannered goddess on the rainbow bridge! That would spell the end of absolute rule by men . . . the old Japan would collapse!

'But it didn't collapse,' said Ashiko quietly. 'That's why I understand the cruelty you spoke of, Theo. The old misogynist traditions are still alive.'

'And a jolly good thing too!' blurted out Aunt Martha. 'Besides, why does it matter so much to you to preserve Shinto, my dear child?'

'Because it is in tune with nature. The *kami* mean respect for living beings in a country so narrow that we have to crowd together on the coasts. What would become of us without the trees and the plants? Where would oxygen and life come from? Look at our cities of concrete and glass, they can no longer breathe . . . is nature really full of gods? I don't know, but I worship nature with all my heart.'

'So you're not a Buddhist,' concluded Theo.

'For some things I am,' she replied. 'When it comes to the flower cult or the tea ceremony. When it's not being applied to the art of war, Zen suits me.'

Theo opened his eyes wide. Zen? War? Tea? What was the connection?

First lesson in Zen

'Wait, a minute,' he murmured. 'For me, "Zen" means "cool". At school in France, we say that you have to be "Zen" when you've just had a bad mark. In other words, when you've got problems. War isn't Zen!'

'Japan of old had perfected the rules of combat to the highest degree,' replied Aunt Martha, 'and that's where Zen comes in. I don't think you know what it is. It is not thinking, thought unthought, purging the mind of all notions and concepts.'

'I'm lost,' said Theo. 'Thought unthought?'

'If you think that you are thinking, you're still thinking, right?' she told him. 'You'll learn about it later on at school, when you study Descartes's philosophy: when I think that I am thinking, I exist. For Zen, it's the opposite: to accomplish the perfect act, you have to be without thought.'

'I think that I'm picking up this bowl, and I pick it up,' retorted Theo, matching action and words. 'It is a perfect act, and that's that.'

'No, because you spilt a few drops of tea,' said Aunt Martha wryly. 'For the perfect act, you should no longer be thinking about the bowl, and your hand should pick it up all by itself, without you.'

Theo closed his eyes, concentrated, reached out a hesitant hand and upset the whole bowl. Ashiko started to laugh.

'You try then if you're so clever!' he cried, furious.

'This is not the place,' replied Ashiko. 'You have to be in a calm, quiet room.'

'Anyway, I don't see what the bowl of tea's got to do with war,' he grumbled, wiping his sleeve.

'Tell him about archery,' instructed Aunt Martha. 'He'll love it.'

The art of war inherited from the Zen tradition consisted of forgetting the self the better to match the movements of the enemy. And archery was never more effective than when the arrow flew alone as a result of a perfect gesture, in other words, performed in a state of emptiness. If you aimed carefully, you were too tense to hit the target; if, on the contrary, you were one with the arrow, if the mind let go, then the bow and the arrow would hit the mark. To achieve this, you had to abandon yourself completely.

'I get it,' said Theo. 'That's what they teach athletes to help them relax. I heard that during the Olympic Games.'

'Zen has crossed frontiers,' said Ashiko a little wistfully. 'Now it's used for everything in your world: to help businessmen relax, to loosen up athletes, to make everyday life easier . . . Even here, it's becoming commercial.'

'Come, child,' said Aunt Martha. 'You're a pacifist, you're not going to mourn the art of war, are you?!'

'For me, Zen is at its best in the tea ceremony,' she replied.

'That's great,' said Theo. 'You make a ceremony out of drinking tea?'

'That's an understatement,' snorted Aunt Martha. 'Wait until you've seen one before you get excited. We'll talk about it then.'

'Why, Mrs Macquarie?' asked Ashiko in surprise. 'Didn't you enjoy it last time we shared the experience?'

'Oh yes, of course I did. Let's just say it went on for rather a long time.'

'Mrs Macquarie, you haven't yet attained the Zen state. You feel anxious a lot of the time. I can see it only too clearly.'

'Cool, aunty!' exclaimed Theo. 'Be Zen!'

'You set my nerves on edge,' she replied. 'With someone like you around, I don't see how I'll ever empty my mind!'

'I'm sure Theo will get there,' Ashiko went on. 'You need a sharp mind and a simple trust in others. He has those qualities.'

'May as well call me a suspicious old fool,' grumbled Aunt Martha. 'I know the principles of Zen, but I want to think in peace, that's all.'

'But, Aunt Martha, Ashiko isn't the first person to talk to me about abandoning the self,' objected Theo. 'The Sheikh in Jerusalem said the same thing. And my strange, dear old guru in Benares said it to me every day . . . and your friend Lama Gampo, didn't he talk to me about prayer when I passed out in front of the Buddha?'

'You fainted before the Buddha?' asked Ashiko in surprise. 'You see, Mrs Macquarie!'

'Theo's responding well to Asia, for sure,' muttered Aunt Martha. 'But we've still got a long way to go before our journey's over!'

'You don't like abandoning the self?' asked Ashiko.

'No!' cried Aunt Martha. 'I want to be free, I do!'

'What greater freedom than abandoning yourself?' questioned Ashiko.

'Controlling yourself, child. In our culture, we prize self-control. We try to think clearly. By the way, why are you studying French, if you don't mind my asking?'

'To get a job,' replied Ashiko. 'And also because I know a little about France, where you choose your own husband. Whereas here, that's not the case.'

'She wants to choose her husband freely!' sniggered Aunt Martha. 'What a contradiction! When it comes to finding a husband, you're not prepared to submit to your parents' choice! Now where's your famous abandonment of the self?'

Ashiko blushed and looked sheepish.

'Don't worry,' said Theo, taking her hand. 'Her bark is worse than her bite. She always wants to be right. But I understand what you're saying.'

'Really?' murmured Ashiko, her eyes closed.

'You want to choose your happiness and abandon yourself afterwards,' whispered Theo. 'Come on, look at me.'

Slowly she looked up and reluctantly met his gaze.

'You can do better than that,' urged Theo. 'Don't think about it!'

Ashiko gave him a radiant look.

'You see, Aunt Martha, that's Zen,' said Theo, thrilled.

'Cheeky little Romeo,' she muttered. 'Come on, you two lovebirds, I'm tired. Time to go home.'

Embarrassed, Ashiko jerked her hand away. It was Theo's turn to blush. Him, a Romeo? He was only trying to come to the rescue of a damsel in distress.

CHAPTER 18

Flower, Women, Tea

Ashiko's secret

On the way back, Aunt Martha did not open her mouth once; and as soon as they were in their room, she made for the bathroom, slamming the door. Theo undressed quickly, slid between the sheets and pretended to be asleep. Her face impassive, Aunt Martha reappeared in a pair of black silk pyjamas with a pink lace nightcap on her head. Theo couldn't help sniggering.

'You are impossible!' she cried, thumping the pillow. 'If you carry on like this, I warn you, we'll go home!'

'What on earth . . . why?' stuttered Theo, taken unawares.

'Why? Because you've changed! You used to be affectionate, and now you bite my head off. You fight with me and flirt with a girl!'

'What's that supposed to mean? All this because we're both young!'

'Here we go again! Ever since Indonesia, you've been harping on about my age.'

'You're amazing for your years, you know . . .' he said sincerely. 'But Ashiko is my age, isn't she?'

'She's two years older than you, Theo. She's almost an adult. You're not.'

'We think alike,' murmured Theo. 'We're just friends.'

'Be careful with her,' said Aunt Martha in a different tone of voice.

'What? Is she ill too?'

311

'No, but . . .' Aunt Martha cleared her throat discreetly. 'I'm not supposed to talk to you about it. But, if you swear you'll keep it a secret . . .'

Ashiko's story was bound up with the history of Japan. Ashiko's grandparents, shielded by a hill, had survived the atomic explosion over the town of Nagasaki, the second one, which killed 39,000 people. Aunt Martha had met them at an annual pacifist memorial rally in Hiroshima. Their shared horror of war had brought them together, and Aunt Martha became friends with the Okaras, who adored their only son, Hiro. At twenty, like many young Japanese of his generation, he left to study in an American university where he fell in love with a French girl, and married her. The young Mrs Okara became pregnant and Ashiko was born.

'So she's half French?' Theo was astounded. 'I'd never have guessed.'

'There's more to come,' replied Aunt Martha.

Despite the birth of their child, the marriage was a disaster. The French woman wanted to work, the Japanese man wouldn't let her. After a painful divorce, Hiro returned to Japan with baby Ashiko, and his parents found him a new wife in the traditional manner, without consulting him. The second Mrs Okara brought Ashiko up as her own child. Ashiko became a true daughter of Japan. Miss Ashiko was not one of those brazen young Japanese girls who dyed their hair red and earned pocket money through legal prostitution by offering telephone sex . . . Quite the opposite, Ashiko was doubly faithful to traditional values. Her story was all the more unusual in that she knew nothing whatsoever about her real mother and was unaware of the inner reason for wanting to study French.

'But it's strange, I find her changed,' said Aunt Martha. 'I've never heard her criticize Japanese discipline. She used to be so submissive, so traditional . . .'

'I'll be careful, I promise,' murmured Theo, disconcerted.

'With me too?' she asked gruffly.

'Sure! Truce?'

She ruffled his air in response.

A strange theatre

The next day, Theo bent over backwards to make amends. He brought Aunt Martha breakfast in bed, took his Tibetan medicine without needing to be reminded, brought her her boots, her tonic and her moisturizer.

'Don't overdo it, I might get into the habit,' she said. 'You'd do better to get yourself ready for the day ahead of us.'

'Why, are we going to see a temple?'

'Sort of. We're going to the theatre.'

'If it's all in Japanese, I won't have the foggiest idea what they're on about,' he moaned.

Well, he was right there. For the play they were going to see was chanted and sung in Japanese. It was Japan's most ancient form of drama, Nō theatre.

'But you do buy tickets and sit down?' asked Theo.

'You can even follow the dialogue in a booklet if you want, like at church,' she replied, laughing.

'And what's Nō all about?' asked Theo, perking up.

'Ghosts, demons, warriors, gods, madness.'

'With sheets and rattling chains! Great!'

Whether he would find this type of ghost as exciting was another matter. The first time she had seen Nō, Aunt Martha had been bored to death. Then, towards the end, half asleep, she had let herself be carried away by the poetic atmosphere of the eerie performance. She had returned the following morning for a whole day during which several Nō plays alternated with crude popular farces, *kyōgen*, which made the Japanese audience laugh until tears ran down their faces. Aunt Martha did not find the *kyōgen* funny, but she fell in love with the magic of Nō. But to fire Theo's interest from the start . . .

Aunt Martha had invited Ashiko to come and explain what they would see. They met in the hotel lounge, and sat sipping a delicious green tea that Theo drank delicately, his little finger crooked.

'Why the little finger?' asked Aunt Martha in surprise.

'I thought you had to drink tea with ceremony,' he said. 'Isn't that how you do it?'

'Not at all! Never mind about your finger, and listen to Ashiko.'

'First,' began Ashiko, 'the setting is very simple, it's always the same: in the background is a tall pine tree, a bridge and a few reeds, and at the rear are a few musicians dressed in black and grey. The stage is made entirely of wood, as a reminder of the Shinto shrines which are also made of wood.'

'Is that important?' asked Theo.

'Yes, because they are demolished and rebuilt every twenty years. The thing about our shrines is that they aren't meant to last forever. We honour our divinities by renewing their shrines. As in nature, nothing must be left of the old; everything changes with every age and season.

'Aren't there any ancient monuments in Japan?' he cried in amazement.

'Yes, Buddhist temples, palaces, residences . . . But no Shinto shrines. The scenery in Nō theatre is similar: unchanging, but continually being renewed. The Nō stories are supposed to be set outdoors. The action takes place by a river or beside a road, or on a ferryboat, because it often involves crossing water. The characters are divided into three groups: the narrator, the commentator and the victim of suffering. The narrator tells the story, accompanied by the chorus, like in the Greek tragedies. But the true hero, the person who suffers, wears a wooden mask, with no hole for the mouth.'

'So if there's nowhere for his lips, how does he speak his part?' exclaimed Theo.

'He always embodies misfortune,' she replied. 'Naturally, because of the mask, he talks in a muffled voice, which gives the impression of suffering. Nō actors have a special timbre to their voices: the breath comes from the stomach, like a wild cry. The main character does not speak in human language.'

'Is he a god?' asked Theo.

'The main character is a man or a woman, but their suffering is so great that their howl seems to come from another world. The Nō hero is almost holy, he rants, he groans, he cries . . . Ah! I must tell you one thing that's very important. To cry, the actor raises the end of his long sleeve to his eyes, that's all. Sometimes, he starts to dance, as the Japanese once did in front of the Shinto gods.'

'And then?' asked Theo, intrigued.

'Then nothing,' she smiled. 'The narrator is filled with compassion for the weeping hero, the chorus too, the hero dances and disappears forlornly into the darkness.'

'That's not much fun. So what are we going to see today?'

'It's the story of a poor madwoman who is treated as an outcast. The narrator, a ferryman who was about to take her over the river, had heard about this wandering woman who haunted the banks, waving her arms as she roamed. Once on board, the madwoman tells him that she is looking for her son who was kidnapped by slave merchants, and suddenly the narrator remembers an abandoned child found on that shore. Before dying of exhaustion, the poor little thing had begged the people looking after him to build a burial mound in his memory and to plant a willow tree on it. The madwoman begins to cry: it was her lost son. The narrator takes her to the grave, the mother calls her son, and he appears. They reach out to each other, but the child returns inside the mound, and the mother is left alone, on her knees.'

'It's not exactly a bundle of laughs,' said Theo.

'Well if you get bored, Theo my love, we'll leave,' Aunt Martha interjected hastily.

'Is the actress who plays the mother good?' he asked.

'Only men are allowed to practise the art of Nō,' Ashiko informed him. 'But this actor is perfect in the role of the mother.'

'A transvestite!' exclaimed Theo.

'You won't even be aware of it,' declared Ashiko.

'Tell me, Ashiko, haven't you forgotten one important thing about Nō?' asked Aunt Martha.

'Yes, I have,' she confessed. 'Theo, when you hear the words "*Namu Amida-butsu*", you should know that it is the Buddhist prayer that the Japanese recite all the time.'

'So is it Shinto or Buddhist, this thing?' he queried.

'Both – as always in Japan,' she concluded.

The ghost child

The theatre was sold out and the audience all had copies of the famous booklet. There was no curtain. An elegant shape on a backcloth, the pine tree spread its branches over the wooden bridge. A bamboo frame covered with green gauze with a thin branch on top of it was brought out and placed at the front of the stage.

'The burial mound and the willow,' said Ashiko.

'I say, they don't take too much trouble with the setting,' commented Theo.

The musicians made their entrance, bowed and took their seats at the rear of the stage. A drum banged, followed by a reedy flute, accompanied by a hoarse, solemn chant.

'Sounds like mewing,' Theo whispered in Ashiko's ear.

But Ashiko did not laugh. She was concentrating on the prelude to the Nō drama. The lengthy incantation at the foot of the huge, dark pine went on for ages. Then the ferryman entered and, at last, the mother, wearing a wide hat and carrying a bamboo branch.

'The bamboo branch stands for madness,' murmured Ashiko. 'Now, watch.'

The character's mask was an oval face, dazzlingly white, etched with thin eyebrows and a thin red mouth. The actor was huge and he had strong hands: how could you think of him as a woman? Theo felt uncomfortable and wedged himself in his seat. It was a puppet show for grownups, he was going to be bored out of his mind.

But the hieratic figure turned slowly on his heels to face the audience, and began to speak. On hearing the sound that emerged from the depths of the soul, Theo shuddered. The poor mad woman was suffering to the very core. No sobbing, no tear in the world could have attained the depth of that inhuman howl, so tragic and heart-rending that it brought tears to Theo's eyes. Without understanding a word, he followed the slow movements, listened to the agonized groans and let himself go. Soon, he felt deliciously light-headed. The mewings were closer together, the drums beat with an urgency, the mother grabbed a bell whose sound echoed to infinity, and suddenly, the dead child with curly locks appeared chanting '*Namu Amida-butsu, Namu Amida-butsu, Namu Amida-butsu . . .*'

Theo felt dizzy. The dead child was talking to him. 'My brother!' sang the ghost child in his other-worldly voice, 'I was born with you and I live in your life . . . Tell Mummy! *Namu-Amida-butsu . . .*'

Panic-stricken, Theo buried his face in his hands and watched the scene between his fingers. As if by magic, the white silhouette of the child disappeared inside the mound, and the mother left the stage weeping, the end of her sleeve brushing her eyes.

'Wake up, Theo . . .' murmured Aunt Martha. 'It's over!'

'I don't think he's asleep,' said Ashiko. 'He's very pale.'

'Theo? Answer me!' panicked Aunt Martha. 'Are you all right?'

'No,' groaned Theo. 'I feel giddy . . .'

'Quick, go and get the theatre doctor,' she told Ashiko. 'Lie down, darling. Did you faint again?'

'Mmm,' moaned Theo. 'I feel giddy . . . Where's Ashiko?'

'A giddy spell. That's bad,' said Aunt Martha. 'Ah! Here's the doctor.'

The doctor made Theo stretch out on a seat, took his pulse, listened to his heart, switched on the electrocardiograph, examined his skin, felt his stomach and looked up satisfied. Then he took a sugar lump out of his pocket and popped it into Theo's mouth.

'Nothing to worry about,' Ashiko told Aunt Martha. 'Just a touch of hypoglycaemia.'

'Is that all?' asked Aunt Martha in amazement.

'Nothing at all, Mrs Macquarie,' she confirmed. 'I promise you.'

'But did you explain?'

'I told him everything,' replied Ashiko. 'But it's not Theo's illness, it's just low blood sugar.'

'Did you hear that, darling?' exclaimed Aunt Martha.

'Uurgh,' he grunted, sucking his sugar lump. 'I . . . aw . . . y . . . in.'

'Don't talk with your mouth full!' she said. 'Go on, bite it. Now, what was that?'

'I saw my twin,' he replied, able to speak again. 'The child in the play, it was him! He talked to me!'

Ashiko stared dumbfounded at Aunt Martha. Mrs Macquarie didn't seem upset. Quite the opposite . . .

'You'd never seen him before, had you?' she murmured, holding her nephew close.

'No,' he whispered. 'He's got hair just like mine! I'm glad . . .'

'You're right,' she said. 'Keep lying down for a bit, he'll watch over you.'

She softly tiptoed away. Ashiko took her to one side.

'Mrs Macquarie, there was no child on the stage,' she said in a hushed voice. 'In this Nō, the mother is supposed to be the only person who can see him, but the spectator only hears him.'

'I know,' cut in Aunt Martha.

'Did you see him?'

'Of course not! I'm not mad.'

'So how could Theo have seen a child appear?'

'He didn't see a child, he saw his twin from the Underworld,' sighed Aunt Martha. 'Theo has a ghost in his life, you see.'

'A hallucination?' she asked, anxiously.

'Could be,' replied Aunt Martha, sounding evasive. 'But I'm not sure.'

'Do you believe in ghosts, by any chance, Mrs Macquarie?'

'Why, don't you?' retorted Aunt Martha looking her straight in the eye.

The art of the flower

Once he had eaten the sugar, Theo sat up, full of beans again. After his giddy spells, he always felt as right as rain. Aunt Martha had noticed that the deeper he went into the loss of self, the hungrier he was. They went off to a little restaurant and lunched on delicious soups with daisies carved from turnips floating on top.

317

'Anyway, I wasn't bored by Nō,' he said, licking his chops. 'How do you learn that weird wail?'

'From the stomach,' replied Aunt Martha. 'Like the "om" in yoga.'

'Yes, I see!' he exclaimed.

And he tried at once, pulling his chin into his neck. 'A-o-ou-u-m-mi-a-o-u-hi . . .'

'Sounds like a cross between a yowling cat and a squeaking door,' commented Aunt Martha.

'Nō is a difficult art,' explained Ashiko. 'It takes years of practice to make the sounds come from deep down inside. On stage, you have to forget your natural voice . . .'

'Just like the opera,' said Aunt Martha. 'Not everybody can sing like that.'

'Talent alone is not enough. It also requires meditation. The actors sometimes take thirty years before they attain the art of the flower . . .'

'Flowers again!' said Theo.

It wasn't easy to understand the connection between the flower and Nō. When this unusual form of theatre was born in the fourteenth century, Buddhism and Shinto had been interwoven for a long time. Shinto could be found in the gestures of the *kyōgen* plays, similar to the *kagura*, grotesque dances of the deities, like the dance performed by the goddess Uzume to lure Amaterasu out of her cave. But the Nō master, the great Zeami, probably drew his inspiration from Zen when he wrote about the nature of his art . . .

'That's all very well, but what about the flower?' Theo reminded her.

She was coming to that. According to Zeami, the art of Nō had to achieve the ephemeral lightness of the flower. The gestures, the play of light on the wooden mask, the neck movement and the slow steps all helped evoke the emotion aroused by a fully opened flower about to wither. Therefore, the actor's prime came when he reached maturity, when he no longer had the energy of youth but was not yet bowed by age. This perfect moment was the point of nothingness, the time of non-interpretation: the fortunate actor who went up on stage after long years of practice must simply appear and refrain from expression. The less he sought to feel emotion, the deeper the emotion of the audience: for a flower does not speak, it blooms and fades. That was the essence of Nō.

'It'd be perfect for my aunt,' yawned Theo. 'Just before she turns decrepit . . .'

'Theo!' she cried. 'You promised!'

Ashiko chipped in to add that the main character often carried a fan that he unfurled to balance the dance: then the image of the flower took on a poetic meaning. By emptying his mind, the actor rediscovered the movement of the stem and the naturalness of the leaves and the fan evoked the petals. These huge Nō fans were some of the most beautiful in Japan. The masks were also highly prized, and if Theo wanted, they could buy one like the mask he had been so taken with . . .

'Dunno,' purred Theo, half asleep. 'It was . . . the voice . . .'

And he flopped onto the table.

'This time, he really is asleep,' murmured Aunt Martha. 'All that emotion was too much for him.'

'Because of the ghost?' asked Ashiko. 'Is that the cause of his illness?'

'Probably,' she replied. 'Theo is suffering from an unknown secret, and that type of secret is harmful.'

'I know,' replied Ashiko with a blush.

'Good,' burbled Aunt Martha heedlessly. 'Call us a taxi, dear.'

In the car, Theo snored like a pig. Aunt Martha stared out wistfully at the first cherry trees in blossom. Lost in the city, they seemed as artificial as the glass of Coca-Cola Theo had bought.

Exchange between Aunt Martha and Melina

Theo slept until dusk. Martha tried to do likewise, but her head was buzzing. This twin, for goodness sake! If Theo was starting to see him, the whole thing was coming to a head. Martha concluded that she ought to tell Melina. She pulled the phone cord to its full extent and locked herself in the bathroom. This time, she was going to talk to Melina about the true problem.

'It's Martha,' she began. 'No . . . Don't worry, he's asleep. What? Just the usual nap, that's all. Yes, but I have to talk to you about something important. Listen to me very carefully, Melina, I swear it's not about Theo's illness. On what?'

She relaxed her grip on the receiver and thought.

'Melina? I swear on my mother's grave, is that enough? Good, now listen. Theo is still going on about his twin. Please, darling, don't screech at me . . . Don't imagine for a second that I've told him! How does he know? That's the point, he doesn't!'

Melina sobbed so loudly that Martha held the receiver away from her ear.

'Please, darling,' she entreated. 'In certain situations, Theo hears his twin talking to him . . . Yes, he's the one who calls him his twin. His twin from the Underworld. Yes, I'm astonished too . . . What circumstances? Well, there has to be quiet, sometimes the chime of a bell, or music . . . No, I can't explain it. But today he saw him. Yes, you heard right, saw, s-a-w! No, not actually. On the stage in a theatre. Oh, a play about a mother looking for her dead son. Why? But it's a beautiful Nō play! Stop him? Theo isn't ten any more! Melina, please . . .'

Martha sighed with irritation and held the phone at arm's length.

'Are you going to calm down or not?' she bellowed. 'I haven't finished . . . Visibly, his twin makes him happy. He sleeps better. In his dreams? No. Like an inner voice. Of course, it's essential. Wait . . . I'm sure he's going to tell you about it. I wanted to warn you. Try not to cry, it would upset him. There, you understand. Tell him the truth? Ah, that I don't know, darling. Talk to Jerome about it. Me? No way. What if he guesses all by himself? That's a different matter. Yes, you do that, call me back. Love you too.'

Relieved, Aunt Martha sank down onto the edge of the bath. For the first time, Melina had been willing to listen.

'With a bit of luck, she'll finally tell him her secret . . .'

'Who?' asked Theo, standing in the doorway. 'What secret?'

'Oh, it's you!' she replied, sheepishly. 'You're awake! I . . . Er, I was talking to Ashiko's mother.'

'What? You know her?'

'Vaguely,' she lied.

'Would you like Ashiko to meet her real mother?'

'It would be better. Family secrets are always harmful. People bear the shame of them for years, and when they come out, it's like a shell-burst . . .'

'Luckily we don't have any!' said Theo.

'Are you quite sure, my love?' she replied carelessly.

'I thought . . .' mumbled Theo, disconcerted. 'Unless . . . No, I must be wrong.'

'What were you thinking of?'

'My twin,' he blurted out. 'I wonder where I get him from. Have to talk to Mum.'

'We'll see about that later!' she said firmly. 'Get ready for dinner. We'll need an early night. Tomorrow we're catching the train for Kyoto.'

'With Ashiko?

'Of course,' she replied. 'It's her home town.'

Priestesses and shamans

The bullet train, the famous Shinkansen, travelled so fast that through the windows the houses seemed to tremble. And, as there was a fine drizzle running down the window panes, the trees were blurred. Ashiko told Theo how important rain was in Japan, but he wasn't listening. His forehead pressed to the glass, he stared out at the unending towns and the grey mountains.

'So when are we going to see these cherry trees?' he asked.

'Not straight away,' replied Ashiko. 'Of course, in Kyoto, we have magnificent cherry trees. But you'll see them at their most spectacular on the shores of the lake, near Hakone.'

'And what are we going to do in Kyoto?'

'Learn about the way of tea,' she said.

'And what's so special about tea?'

'What's so special about this, and what's so special about that! You're beginning to get on my nerves!' broke in Aunt Martha. 'What's the matter with you?'

'I don't like rain,' he grumbled.

'In Japan, it rains, and there's nothing anyone can do about it,' stated Aunt Martha.

'It won't last long,' added Ashiko. 'In Kyoto, the sun always shines. And, there's a surprise awaiting you! Because in Hakone, Mrs Macquarie has booked into a Japanese house, one of those inns known as a *ryōkan* . . .'

'With paper walls and tatamis?'

'And big tubs where you bath naked with other guests,' added Aunt Martha.

'Oh,' said Theo with a note of alarm in his voice. 'With Ashiko too?'

'Wishful thinking,' replied Aunt Martha. 'Stark-naked with men in a steam bath.'

'That's no fun,' said Theo. 'Why do they always want to keep men and women apart?'

'It's the men who decide,' said Aunt Martha. 'Apparently, they see women as a threat. Take Kali for instance . . . That's some image the Bengalis have of women: dripping with blood and armed from head to toe, and yet they worship her!'

'It's no better here,' Ashiko chimed in. 'A woman turns into a ghost and haunts the footpaths to murder travellers, or she's a vixen who disguises herself as a beauty to rip out her husbands' throats . . . To think that at first we used to have priestesses!'

'Really?' asked Theo, intrigued. 'Female priests?'

'In the Shinto religion, only women were allowed to be inhabited by the spirit of the gods,' she went on. 'They were magicians, they went into trances and were possessed, they spoke on behalf of the *kami* . . .'

'Trances? Possessed?' repeated Theo. 'So they were witches?'

'You're thinking of witches because of the word "possession", like in *The Exorcist*, aren't you?' Aunt Martha chimed in.

'Yes, with green stuff coming out of their mouths and spooky voices, it's fun!'

'Well, forget the green slime and keep your spooky voices. All ancient religions have women in a prophetic role. Anyway, haven't you been to Delphi? Have you forgotten who performed the rites there?'

'The Pythia!' exclaimed Theo. 'A madwoman standing over a cauldron!'

'I'll give you madwoman!' retorted Aunt Martha. 'For a long time, people thought that the Pythia was high on the smoke from laurel leaves . . . In fact, it's not known for certain. But what is certain is that the Pythia was a mouthpiece for the god. She was a prophet, the most important prophet in Ancient Greece!'

'You mean there were others?, asked Theo in amazement.

'In Africa, they still exist,' she said. 'In India, they're known as "mothers", and here, in Japan, Shinto rites were performed by female shamans . . .'

'Shamans?' asked Ashiko. 'I don't know that word.'

'I do,' Theo boasted. 'They're sorcerers in America.'

'No!' exclaimed Aunt Martha. 'The theory of Shamanism derives from observation of the Yakuts . . .'

'The what?' chorused Ashiko and Theo.

The Yakuts were a people in eastern Siberia, where the sorcerers, who were known as 'shamans', enjoyed a strange status. According to the Yakut people, you were destined to be a shaman if you had a slight oddity: a squint, a limp, or simply a tendency to daydream. The Romans believed that epileptics were inspired, for their fits came from the gods: the great Julius Caesar possibly used his own fits to build up his power . . .

'Right!' exclaimed Theo. 'In the film, Elizabeth Taylor shoves a stick in his trap to stop him biting his tongue . . .'

322

Yes, but in *Cleopatra* there was no explanation of this divine illness which for centuries was known as the *grand mal* in Europe, and people were greatly in awe of it. Epileptics could become shamans. All they needed to do was lose consciousness or have a dream . . . Then, to fulfil his destiny, the future shaman would drink herbal brews that sent him on a journey: he descended into Hell, where the occult powers would dismember him and change each of his bones, one by one. The shaman returned from his long voyage with a skeleton of iron and supernatural powers: then, with the help of terrifying ritual dances representing spirits from the Underworld, he could predict the future and cure the sick by spitting out the pernicious disease in the form of a substance that, once it was out, no longer affected the sufferer's body.

'No?' said Theo in disbelief. 'Does it work?'

Perfectly. The sick were cured, so strong was their belief. The Shamanism of the Yakuts was not an isolated case, and ethnologists got into the habit of calling anyone who made the long journey down into Hell under the influence of mysterious substances a shaman. The Pythia was a shaman, and so were the Shinto priestesses.

'But you were saying that in Japan only women are shamans,' remarked Ashiko.

Man or woman, it made no difference, because in those far-off places there was neither good nor evil, neither man nor woman. The shaman came back transformed: whatever his or her sex, he or she was no longer man or woman. That was why male shamans could speak in high-pitched voices and female shamans could speak in the deep tones of a god like Apollo. Shamanism involved the transmutation of the sexes, because shamans no longer quite belonged to the human race. As a result of the journey, they had become supernatural beings, mediators between humans and god. Hence their ability to raise up spirits, or to urge the sick into wild dances for a brief journey into the Underworld.

'By the way,' Theo interrupted. 'Is it possible that the Sheikha in Luxor is a shaman, by any chance?'

'What do you think?' asked Aunt Martha.

'Let's see,' he mused. 'Yes, I think she is. There were fumes, dancing, an underground world, my twin . . . But she called me "the bride"! So does that mean I'm a shaman too?'

'Why not?' she replied. 'After all, you are making a hell of a journey . . .'

'What about me?' Ashiko broke in. 'By performing the rite . . .'

'Ssh!' Aunt Martha stopped her. 'Don't spoil the surprise!'

Theo stared at the girl, who lowered her eyes, blushing. There was nothing so pretty as the pink of Miss Ashiko's cheeks when she tried to conceal her thoughts.

Misunderstanding under a cherry tree

The hotel in Kyoto wasn't quite the traditional house with tatamis: it was called the Mikayo, surrounded by lawns planted with weeping willows and tall pine trees. But to the side, a tree thrust its snowy blooms skywards.

'I've never seen anything so beautiful!' exclaimed Theo.

'A cherry tree . . .' said Aunt Martha.

'That giant tree's a cherry tree?' asked Theo in amazement. 'At home, they're much smaller!'

'I told you, but you wouldn't believe me,' sighed Aunt Martha. 'The splendour of the blossom in Japan . . .'

'It's true,' admitted Theo. 'I'm going to take a photo for Mum.'

He pointed his camera: click! The magnificent tree was captured for posterity.

'Please . . .' whispered Miss Ashiko. 'It's better not . . .'

'There,' he announced, satisfied, brandishing the camera. 'This time I framed it beautifully. I'll send you a print, Ashiko.'

'Thank you, Theo,' she said quietly. 'Photography's all very well, but . . .'

'Aren't you pleased?' he asked in surprise.

'Oh yes!' she exclaimed with a tense smile. 'I'm very touched. But . . .'

'Have I offended you, Ashiko?' he asked, putting his hand on her neck. 'Tell me how, please.'

'In Japan, we respect the fall of the cherry blossom flowers,' she murmured hastily.

'Really?' replied Theo, not understanding. 'So what's the problem?'

'There isn't one,' said Ashiko, lowering her head. 'Perhaps you could simply watch the flowers falling . . .'

Theo quietly obeyed. A gentle breeze was dispersing the open blossoms whose white petals whirled slowly in the sky.

'There,' he said without conviction. 'Well?'

'Like the days of our life the cherry blossom flies away,' murmured Ashiko. 'It is a fleeting, magical moment. Can't you feel the divine presence? The flower opens, its whiteness shines, and a second later, it is no more. Petal after petal, it dies, the wind blows it away like ourselves . . .'

Stunned, Theo gazed at his friend, whose huge eyes seemed to be staring into infinity. Softly, he placed a kiss on her cheek.

'The blossom is you, Ashiko,' he said in a hushed voice. 'Why do you speak of dying? It's sad!'

'We must love the present,' she breathed. 'A photograph betrays it a little. Focus on the beauty of the flower, Theo . . .'

'But seeing that I've told you the flower is you . . .' Theo began to get cross.

'Stop that, Theo!' broke in Aunt Martha. 'Ashiko is trying to tell you something important . . . Here, beauty is in the things that go away. Nothing lasts . . .'

'OK,' moaned Theo, letting go of Ashiko. 'So basically I'm supposed to understand that we're going to grow old. Ashiko, you'll have wrinkles like Aunt Martha, and I'll walk with a stick . . .'

'You're hateful,' replied Aunt Martha, seeing tears in Ashiko's eyes. 'You're making her cry.'

'Me?' asked Theo stunned. 'Are you really crying, Ashiko? Wait . . . I'm contemplating the petals. I see nothing but the petals. They're like white butterflies. Is that better?'

'Very good,' said Ashiko, drying her eyes. 'The cherry trees are so important to us.'

'Next time, I'll shut my big mouth,' mumbled Theo.

'You're not capable of it,' cut in Aunt Martha.

'Oh yes he is!' Ashiko hotly defended him.

'Ah! You see?' crowed Theo. 'At least Ashiko knows what I'm really like!'

'Not at all,' replied Aunt Martha. 'As a worthy daughter of Japan, she is honouring her guest. By the way, what time do we have to be at the ceremony?'

'Mrs Aseki is expecting us in two hours,' replied Ashiko.

'Only two hours!' exclaimed Aunt Martha. 'We've got to unpack, have a bath, get changed . . . Let's get going, children!'

The four virtues of tea

As soon as the door had shut behind them, Aunt Martha had her shower, put on her hideous blue kimono and made Theo wear his best trousers, the black jeans, with a navy blue blazer that she fished out of her bag.

'That?' exclaimed Theo. 'No way!'

'Don't argue with me, please,' she said in a no-nonsense voice. 'For the tea ceremony, you have to be properly dressed.'

'I'll look like a wise monkey,' he groaned.

'A right little Hanuman,' she concluded, kissing him. 'Let's go downstairs, Ashiko's waiting for us.'

She too was wearing a kimono. But unlike Aunt Martha's with its ridiculous birds that only stressed her plumpness, Miss Ashiko's burgundy kimono made her look even more slender. Her long dark hair was tied back with red silk and her face with its white make-up gave her the mysterious air of a goddess of youth. Theo bowed to her.

'I shall no longer dare kiss your neck, Miss Ashiko,' he murmured.

'You should not hesitate, sir,' she replied graciously. 'However, I believe you must now attend your tea lesson.'

First of all, he would have to remain absolutely silent. Then, copy whatever Ashiko did, down to the last detail. And last came the hardest part: he must stay on his knees till the end, even if it made his joints ache.

'For how long?' asked Theo.

'Only a couple of hours,' replied Ashiko.

'Two hours to drink a cup of tea!' cried Theo. 'How do you manage that?'

That was the great mystery of *chanoyu*, the tea ceremony. The tea master welcomed the guests, then, while the water was boiling in the kettle, he cleaned the bowl, added the powdered green tea and then poured the water and let the tea infuse.

'I can do that in ten minutes,' said Theo.

'And how long do you spend cleaning the bowl?' asked Aunt Martha.

'I don't know,' he replied, disconcerted. 'Ten seconds maybe.'

'It takes the tea master at least twenty minutes,' she whispered.

'Does he do everything in slow motion?' asked Theo aghast.

That was more or less the case. Tea drinking had been introduced from China in the ninth century, practised mainly by Zen monks. One of the main contributors to the culture of the tea ceremony as it is practised today was the great tea master Sen no Rikyu, who lived in the sixteenth century. '*Chanoyu*,' he said simply, 'is nothing but this: boil water, make tea and drink, that is all you need to know.'

'Exactly,' grumbled Theo. 'Nothing to make such a song and dance about.'

And yet, master Rikyu forfeited his life for tea ... He was in the service of the governor of the land, the Taiko Hideyoshi, who accorded him his protection and the respect due to the great tea masters. What happened exactly? Nobody knows. The fact remains that master Rikyu offended his lord and in his fury the Taiko unsheathed his samurai sword before regaining control of himself and banishing the fallen servant. The tea master went into exile. Then, he received orders to commit suicide. Now at the very moment when the Taiko declared he was prepared to grant him a pardon, master Rikyu calmly slit his belly open, stating that death was the greatest gift his master could bestow on him.

'Committing suicide over a cup of tea!' exclaimed Theo. 'How stupid!'

The tea masters were almost wholly dependent on the lords who employed them. Sometimes they were revered, sometimes dismissed. They were expensive. Master Rikyu was without question one of the greatest tea artists, and that alone made him vulnerable. There were two ways of interpreting his decision: either he was obeying the warriors' code of honour or, more likely, he saw *seppuku* as the end of a long life of meditation whose sole objective was the divine meaning of tea to which he was sacrificing his life, his soul at peace. For, emphasized Ashiko, the tea ceremony was part of a unique religion, which some contemporary Japanese philosophers call 'teaism'.

'Honestly, they turn everything into a religion,' said Theo.

Shocked, Ashiko stated that it was a pity that enlightened minds should misunderstand the art of tea: true, it was enough to boil the water and to drink. But only a long apprenticeship made it possible to attain perfection. The tea ceremony required four virtues: harmony, respect, purity and serenity. Each of these virtues had both a material and an immaterial sense. Harmony dwelled in the art of the tea room setting, but also in the relationship between the participants in the ceremony. Respect was due not only to the guests, but to each of the utensils: the bowl, the ladle and the wooden spatula. Purity applied to the utensils, which had to be thoroughly cleaned, but above all to purity of heart and simplicity of mind. And lastly, serenity was the outcome of the three previous virtues: when one achieved serenity, one forgot the self and attained nothingness.

'If there's nothingness, then it's a Zen thing,' said Theo. 'But why two hours?'

Two hours for a guest, ten years to come anywhere near the spirit of tea, an entire lifetime to reach perfection . . . Through assiduous practice, you discovered your own limitations: a heavy body, inept fingers, fumbling hands, dropping the utensils, spilling the bowl . . .

'Like me, the other day,' murmured Theo. 'Why the bowl, anyway? Is there only one?'

Of course, because the ceremony was based on harmony of heart. The bowl was passed from hand to hand, to share the tea.

'You see, Theo,' added Aunt Martha, 'that is one of the great secrets of all religions: sharing. Bread and wine are shared at mass, at Passover Jews share the lamb and bitter herbs, and during Ramadan Muslims share the evening meal after the day's fasting. Drinking and eating are something sacred.'

'For me,' said Theo, 'tea is what Mum brings me in bed.'

CHAPTER 19

The Sadness of the Cherry Trees

Mrs Aseki's lesson

At last it was time to go to Mrs Aseki's house. By now it was dark and the cold had descended on Kyoto. Theo snuggled into his parka and wondered when they were going to have dinner. Ashiko stopped the taxi by a dark driveway dimly lit by lanterns. The flagstone path led through a carefully swept garden, where only a few petals on the lawn signalled the presence of a cherry tree. Nestling at the bottom of the garden, the wooden tea house looked like a doll's house. In the entrance, Ashiko unbuttoned her coat, and the other two did likewise. They dipped the light bamboo ladle into the water and rinsed their hands and mouths. Then they were allowed to warm themselves for a few moments. Aunt Martha sank down on a wooden bench and stuck out her legs with a sigh of contentment, Theo stared at his feet and Ashiko closed her eyes.

'Well,' said Theo after a minute, 'shall we go in?'

'Patience,' murmured Aunt Martha. 'Ashiko will tell us when it's time.'

Slightly numbed, Theo was beginning to drift off when Ashiko stood up and walked over to a low entrance, so low that you had to bend over to go in.

'Careful, Theo, bend over,' she whispered.

'Ow!' he cried, banging his head. 'That's clever!'

'It's the door of Humility. I warned you!'

The tea room contained four tatamis and a little alcove, at the back of which hung a scroll depicting a crane with a long beak. On a black table lay a lily only just in flower. Ashiko took Theo's hand to show him the lower shelf on which stood a china pot of water, and the upper one, with a red lacquer box containing the precious green tea powder.

'Can I look?' asked Theo.

'You're not supposed to, but . . . all right then,' replied Ashiko, cautiously lifting the lid.

The thick powder was bright green; it looked like the sort of paint used on green shutters. Theo dipped his finger in the pot and tasted it. The powder was bitter.

'Do you know how rude that is, Theo?' commented Ashiko. 'Only the master is allowed to touch the tea.'

'I like trying new things,' exclaimed Theo defiantly.

'Ssh . . . Come and listen to the cast-iron kettle. Mrs Aseki has put polished pebbles in it to make the water sing, can you hear it?'

'But where is Mrs Aseki?' he asked, mystified.

'There,' said Ashiko pointing to a sliding door. 'You can be sure that she sees everything you do.'

As if by magic, the door slid open, and the tea master appeared, bowing deeply, her hands on her knees. Mrs Aseki smiled, and hundreds of tiny creases appeared around her kindly eyes. Then, with calculated slowness, her body erect, she knelt down. Her guests did the same. In perfect silence, the ceremony began.

Unfold a napkin, immerse it in cold water, wipe the bowl and fold the wet napkin again, picking it up by the centre. Dry the bowl with another napkin of black silk, fold it again, turn the large bronze-glazed ceramic bowl around to display the reflections. Gently open the red lacquer box, take the feather-light wooden spatula and place the green powder in the bottom of the bowl. Remove the kettle lid and place it silently on a china stand. Dip the ladle into the boiling water in the cast-iron kettle and pour delicately over the powder. Take the finely crafted bamboo whisk and whisk the moistened powder . . . A froth appeared on the surface. The tea was ready.

Mrs Aseki's gestures were deft and light as the wings of a bird in flight and seemed so natural that it was impossible to imagine that tea could be prepared any other way. Aunt Martha glanced furtively at her watch: thirty minutes had passed as in a dream, thirty minutes during which Theo hadn't uttered a single word. Transfixed, his hands on his knees, he seemed fascinated. Aunt Martha shifted and her knees cracked painfully. Then Mrs Aseki placed the bowl on a white napkin. Aunt Martha took a delicate sip and passed the bowl to Theo.

He took a huge gulp and pulled a face because of the bitterness. He had drunk so fast that his chin turned green with froth. Ashiko burst out laughing. Theo glared and passed her the bowl. Ashiko turned the bowl around, admired the beauty of the froth and drank in silence. The first part was over.

The second time the tea was served in individual bowls, and by now the froth had dispersed in the water. The taste was completely different, and a strange sweet flavour assailed the palate. Theo loved it and stretched out his hand for more tea. Mrs Aseki was happy to oblige. Then she served each guest a miniature meal on a black lacquered tray: nine carrots carved in flower shapes, three hard-boiled eggs decorated with flowers of raw turnip, and a rolled-up shrimp. Then came a red bowl full of steaming soup, followed by a gilt dish on which fish roe canapés were arranged on a white fan, and lastly, three white cakes, all accompanied by a strange bottle shaped like a samurai and filled with sake. Now was the moment for conversation, and Mrs Aseki turned to Theo.

Had he enjoyed the experience?

'Thoroughly, Mrs Aseki,' murmured Theo. 'Your movements were so graceful, especially when you reached out to pick up the wooden ladle.'

Did he like the taste of the tea?

'Oh yes!' he said. 'I've never tasted green tea before, but it's really alive. It's like drinking the forest . . .'

Had he understood the meaning of the ceremony?

'If it's what I think, it's a way of finding peace,' he replied at once. 'Well, that's what I felt. Have I got it right?'

Mrs Aseki gratified him with a warm smile: the boy had understood the way of tea. Mrs Aseki thanked Ashiko for bringing her such a gifted guest; Ashiko modestly lowered her gaze. Aunt Martha had listened to Theo in amazement: the brat had submitted to the ritual . . . The words had come to him as if he had always been meant to be the disciple of a tea master! While her knees were killing her! It wasn't fair . . .

'This child has the spirit of tea,' Mrs Aseki went on. 'For a young Westerner, that is very rare. Would you leave him with me for a while, Mrs Macquarie? He could perfect the art . . .'

'I . . . er . . .' mumbled Aunt Martha awkwardly.

'My aunt is trying to tell you that I'm ill,' said Theo calmly. 'But when I'm better, I'll gladly come back and study with you.'

'He took the words out of my mouth,' said Aunt Martha. 'Perhaps it's time to . . .'

'. . . Allow me to give him this fan as a reminder of this moment of shared happiness.' And Mrs Aseki pulled from her sleeve a folded fan, which she held out to Theo, bowing from the waist. He nodded, took it and unfolded it . . .

'Oh no . . .' he muttered. 'A message!'

'So it is,' said Mrs Aseki. 'But the spirit of tea will remain with you to help you find the solution. Do not be disappointed, for if you had not followed our rituals, I would not have been able to give you the fan, or the message. You may read it if you like.'

Under the hammer, reaped by the little implement of time, still I survive. The end of the anvil bears my three initials.

'I don't want to think about it now,' said Theo, shutting the fan again. 'I don't think I could.'

'That's good,' replied Mrs Aseki. 'The life of tea is stronger than the illusion of thought. Isn't it, Ashiko?'

'Yes, Mrs Aseki,' said Ashiko. 'The first time you allowed me to prepare the tea, I had not understood. The thought of controlling my movements made my hands shake so badly that I spilled the powder on the tatami.'

'You must learn to forget yourself,' said Mrs Aseki gravely. 'The best tea is prepared with the heart.'

'Which you're certainly not lacking,' said Aunt Martha. 'I'm very grateful to you for agreeing to give Theo his first lesson.'

'That is my job,' sighed Mrs Aseki. 'Nowadays tea masters have to charge for the ceremony. But I have chosen to follow the way of tea, and I'm happy to have brought you a little peace this evening.'

The two hours had gone by: it was time to take their leave. Mrs Aseki bowed down to the ground before withdrawing behind the sliding partition. The guests went away in deep silence.

'Frankly, Theo, you amaze me,' began Aunt Martha clip-clopping on the wooden floor. 'How did you manage to enter a world so far away?'

'By keeping quiet,' sighed Theo. 'And I'd like to keep on for a while, if you don't mind.'

Aunt Martha's surprise

According to Aunt Martha, tomorrow would be a very big day· they were to attend a Shinto rite in a garden. They could not expect it to be as pure as the original rite, for the spectacular re-enactment was a huge tourist attraction. All the same, the rite would be amazing.

'You'll be amazed,' she stressed next morning.

'Hurry up, will you!'

'Always rushing . . . When will you learn to take things slowly?'

'Well, well, well, you've changed your tune!'

'It's Ashiko,' he murmured. 'Or the tea, it's the same. Will she be there?'

'That I promise you,' replied Aunt Martha, laughing to herself.

But the punctual Ashiko did not turn up. In front of a majestic red portico, a row of priests had already taken up their positions. Their robes, the same colour as the portico, spread out behind them. They wore conical black silk hats and stood perfectly still, like statues.

'What are they waiting for?' asked Theo.

'The priestesses,' whispered Aunt Martha.

They arrived clad in red skirts and white surplices, their black hair tied back. To the sound of strange flutes and booming drums, they formed a line and danced slowly. Then, from the back, came the first priestess. Her clothes were so heavy that she walked with tiny steps. She wore a kimono the colour of old-rose over another embroidered with gold, hiding yet another kimono of which they could only see the hem, brocades, silks, ribbons . . . And lastly, a white veil floated around her feet.

'How many kimonos is she wearing?' asked Theo.

'Twelve,' replied Aunt Martha. 'All antiques, I'll have you know. Look at her hair. Do you see those strange ribbons that come down to her knees?'

'The problem is, that with those things you can't see her face,' muttered Theo.

The statuesque priestess with the twelve kimonos had come to a halt. With a modest air, she arched her graceful neck . . . and Theo, flabbergasted, recognized Ashiko.

'I must be dreaming!' he cried.

'Didn't I tell you that you were in for a surprise?' replied Aunt Martha mischievously.

'So Ashiko is a priestess!'

333

'You could say that. Actually, like lots of other students, she earns a bit of pocket money by taking part in these ceremonies, that's all. But you know what she's like, she doesn't do anything without committing herself one hundred percent. I'll bet she believes in it whole-heartedly.'

'I won't dare speak to her any more,' murmured Theo. 'I found her intimidating enough in one kimono, let alone twelve!'

When the rite was over, Ashiko made her exit, walking backwards, stooping under the weight of her kimonos. A short while later, she reappeared in a miniskirt and tee-shirt, her hair in plaits.

'Phew!' she said, shaking her head. 'They're so heavy! I thought I was going to fall this time . . .'

'Do you often do that?'

'Once or twice a year,' she replied. 'It makes my father happy, and I enjoy it too.'

'Even if you're more of an actress than a priestess?' objected Aunt Martha. 'It's a show . . .'

'Oh! I'm quite aware of that!' she cried. 'I also know that Shinto became the official religion in 1868 simply because the Emperor wanted to make his power divine. And at the same time he issued a decree outlawing Buddhism from the temples, forbidding the comparison of the *kami* with the Buddhas, and banishing Catholic priests.'

'You're very well informed,' remarked Aunt Martha. 'Doesn't it bother you belonging to a religion that is so xenophobic and supports such a dangerous kind of nationalism?'

'My personal brand of Shinto isn't like that, as you know very well. These clothes remind me of the splendour of this city when it was the capital of Japan. It wasn't called Kyoto then, but Heian-Kyo, which means "the capital of peace and tranquillity".'

'The kimonos you were wearing date from that period, don't they?' prompted Aunt Martha.

'They're real museum pieces!' the girl exclaimed. 'It's an honour to wear them.'

'You really were the goddess of Japan,' Theo told her.

She burst out laughing, shaking her plaits. Then her expression clouded over and she bowed her head.

'For a long time, I have preferred to live in this city, in memory of that bygone world,' she murmured. 'But I don't think I can stay much longer.'

'What do you mean?' Aunt Martha bristled.

'I'll always worship nature, and I love the serenity of yesterday evening's ceremony,' she said. 'But women aren't free in my country.'

'Does your father want you to get married, by any chance?'

'He's already talking about it,' she sighed.

'What are you going to do?' said Theo, taking her hand.

'Leave. That's why I'm learning French.'

'And you won't act the priestess any more.' The thought saddened Theo. 'You won't wear a kimono any more, you won't prepare tea . . .'

'Of course I will, why not?' she asked in surprise. 'You can find green tea in Paris, can't you? That's where I want to live.'

'Traitor,' sighed Aunt Martha. 'At least you won't chop off your hair though?'

'No,' she replied. 'Japan will never leave me altogether.'

'Will you come with us to the temples of Ise?' asked Aunt Martha.

'Of course,' said Ashiko. 'I'm not going to abandon Theo!'

The road to Ise

The temples of Ise were the biggest Shinto shrines in Japan. They were not very far from Kyoto, a few hours' drive at most. On the way, Aunt Martha urged Theo to think about his message, which he seemed to have put right out of his mind.

'I don't feel like it,' he moaned. 'Look at the scenery, it's so beautiful . . .'

'Listen, Theo, I know you've gone Japanese overnight, but we're not going to be here for long,' she nagged.

'Tonight, when I'm in bed, I promise.'

'We know all about your promises. I said now!'

'Mrs Macquarie is right,' broke in Ashiko. 'I can help you if you like . . .'

'*Under the hammer, reaped by the little implement of time, still I survive. The end of the anvil bears my three initials*,' Theo repeated, peering at the crumpled message. 'What city do you find a hammer in?'

'And a scythe,' added Ashiko. 'The implement of time.'

'A clock?' wondered Theo. 'I've seen that on old mediaeval belfries. A skeleton with a scythe, and he's striking . . .'

'But not with a hammer,' commented Aunt Martha. 'And then this character says that he is reaped himself.'

'Then he must be dead,' Ashiko deduced. 'In that case, how could he survive?'

335

'Ah! That's the question!' said Aunt Martha. 'Don't think you'll find the answer that easily.'

'Initials on an anvil,' said Theo. 'Some sort of blacksmith? Vulcan? No, we've already been to Rome.'

'Under the hammer,' pondered Ashiko. 'In which religion do you find a hammer? We certainly don't have one in Japan.'

'Why don't you call Fatou, Theo,' said Aunt Martha.

'Who's that?' asked Ashiko.

'A schoolfriend,' blurted Theo, going crimson. 'When I'm stuck, I'm allowed to phone her and she gives me a clue.'

'Call her from your mobile,' urged Aunt Martha. 'We'll stop the car and hey presto!'

'No,' said Theo awkwardly. 'Anyway, at this hour she'll be asleep.'

'Come on,' cried Aunt Martha. 'When we were in India you weren't worried about waking your beloved Fatou!'

'Beloved?' murmured Ashiko.

'It's nothing,' groaned Theo. 'She's nuts. I only have to talk to a girl and she thinks I'm up to something.'

Feigning a sulk, Martha sank back into the upholstery and kept her beady eyes on the young people. Perhaps she was nuts, but those two were falling in love. She pretended to doze off, and saw them holding hands. Poor Fatou!

Amaterasu's veil

They had started surreptitiously caressing when the car reached Yamada, home to the temples of Ise. Aunt Martha gruffly asked Ashiko to give them the necessary background.

'Since the year 690,' began Ashiko, 'as I've already told you, these shrines have been destroyed and rebuilt nearby every twenty years. This tradition is called *sengu*: at first, it was supposed to purify the place to help regenerate the world, especially when the ruler died. The last time they were rebuilt was in 1993, the sixty-first *sengu*. But apparently the cost is so fantastic that they won't be doing it again.'

'I know your mind's on other things, but I'd rather you didn't just parrot the guidebook,' complained Aunt Martha.

'I'm sorry, Mrs Macquarie,' said Ashiko, blushing. 'I don't know what to say.'

'That raising the veil of the shrine is forbidden,' she said. 'That in 1889, Viscount Mori dared to lift it with the tip of his walking stick, and six months later he was murdered by a fanatical schoolteacher. The murderer died, but Japan honours his memory. And above all, you could say that the shrine of Ise belongs to the goddess Amaterasu . . .'

'Only the Emperor is allowed inside,' added Ashiko emphatically. 'You'd better be careful, Theo. Don't try and take any photos! The guards will arrest you!'

'But what's inside?' asked Theo.

'Two symbols,' replied Aunt Martha. 'The Sacred Mirror, given to Amaterasu by Uzume on leaving the cave, and her brother Susanoo's sacred sword. The emblems of Japan's eternal life.'

'Have you seen them?'

'No, but I've read books,' replied Aunt Martha. 'You won't see anything but huge wooden structures, brand-new but very beautiful, very simple. But you can throw coins under the veil, and even a message if you like.'

'I could slip my message under, couldn't I?' suggested Theo. 'The goddess might help me . . . Does she answer?'

'We'll see,' said Aunt Martha.

Across the bridge rose the entrance to the Inner Shrine, flanked by a giant camphor tree, six metres high. Not far from it was the main shrine, built of timber with a thatched roof, barely higher than the big camphor tree. Above the fence they could see the sloping roofs and the ridge-poles pointing skywards from the gable. A pool awaited the pilgrims.

'First we have to purify ourselves,' said Ashiko. 'We wash our hands and our mouths. Take the bamboo ladle, but don't open your mouth, the water is muddy.'

Faintly disgusted, Theo performed his ablutions and wiped his hands on his cuff.

'Now, take off your jacket,' she murmured, removing her own. 'It's the custom. We're going to greet the goddess without raising the veil that separates her from humanity.'

On the temple steps, pilgrims knelt down to touch the stone with their foreheads. Ashiko went up and prostrated herself. Aunt Martha and Theo stood still and saw the mysterious veil flutter. Then the girl rose and went back to her companions.

'There, that's it. Shinto is a religion without books or statues, without images and without words.'

'It looks like a big hut,' said Theo. 'Actually, it's better.'

'Better than what?' asked Aunt Martha.

'Better than a big operation with all that paraphernalia and stuff,' he replied. 'In Jerusalem too, there was a veil to hide the emptiness.'

'Let's go to the other Shrine,' suggested Aunt Martha.

Amaterasu's shrine was six kilometres away from the Outer Shrine, at the end of an avenue where the two young people broke into a run, leaving Aunt Martha to puff and pant behind. They stopped for breath under a giant cedar. With not a pilgrim in sight, the area was miraculously deserted.

'It's good to be on our own for a bit,' said Theo, and took her hands.

'What about Mrs Macquarie?' asked Ashiko, looking back.

'Bah! She'll catch up with us in the end,' he answered carelessly. 'Shall we go on?'

Far behind them, Aunt Martha was wailing pitifully.

'Poor Aunty! She's no good at walking . . .'

'This isn't right, Theo,' sighed Ashiko. 'We ought to . . .'

On the other side of the fence, the roofs of the Outer Shrine looked just like the first one. But Theo didn't even glance at the Temple of the Passing Seasons. He ran behind a tree and took Ashiko in his arms.

'We shouldn't . . .' repeated Ashiko, putting up a feeble struggle.

'What's that?' he murmured, stopping her mouth.

Ashiko let herself go. Theo closed his eyes. He had lifted the goddess's veil, he had kissed Ashiko. But why was she squirming?

'Mrs Macquarie,' she whispered, breaking free. 'Just behind us.'

Aunt Martha's eyes were bulging and she had no breath left to shout. Shaking a menacing fist in their direction, she flopped down onto the ground.

'Aunt Martha!' cried Theo. 'You haven't broken anything?'

'Little scoundrel,' she murmured breathlessly.

'It's my fault, Mrs Macquarie,' said Ashiko, kneeling beside her. 'I shouldn't have let him . . .'

'No, it was me!' said Theo, trying to outdo her.

'I don't give a damn about your shenanigans. Just help me up.'

They heaved Aunt Martha onto her feet and anxiously brushed her down.

'My shoes. Brush off the dust. There. Now listen to me, you two. Ashiko, I could tell your father everything . . . Oh, don't pull that sorry face . . . Oh yes I could! I won't though, if you promise to be good. As for you, Theo, any more misbehaviour and we'll go back home. I mean it!'

'Huh,' muttered Theo defiantly.

Thwack! The slap rang out. Scarlet, Theo touched his cheek incredulously.

'Honestly,' she scolded, crossing her arms. 'I don't know what stops me giving you one too, Ashiko. Never mind about canoodling behind my back, but leaving me behind while you run on ahead too fast for my poor old legs, that's outrageous!'

The young people swore that they'd never do it again.

'A pretty performance, but you don't mean it. I know you!'

'We're both very inconsiderate, Mrs Macquarie,' sighed Ashiko.

'A fault confessed is half redressed,' she said, magnanimously. 'I saw some amulets on the way and I bought you one, Theo. But listen, you can't have it till you've solved your message.'

'Very well, Aunt,' replied Theo, with his tail between his legs.

Cross purposes

That evening, Theo consulted his dictionaries without finding the town whose emblem was a hammer. The character who survived death remained a mystery. As for the signature on the anvil, it was utterly baffling.

'So phone Fatou then,' hinted Aunt Martha.

'Do you think I can?' said a shamefaced Theo.

'I bet you don't dare . . .'

Rising to the bait, Theo dialled the number.

'Fatou? It's me . . . I know. I haven't had time . . . I promise you, we're forever rushing from one place to the next. Of course I'm thinking of you. Hey, I need the next clue . . . You can say that again! OK, will you give it to me? What about my voice? It's the same as it always is! Hurry up, will you! Me, being nasty? Not at all! I'm a bit uptight, it's true, but it's nothing . . . That's enough! I'm ordering you to give me my clue . . . Fatou!'

Theo stared at the receiver. He looked stunned.

'She hung up on me,' he muttered.

'Girls sense these things, you know . . . Call her back at once!'

'She sounded angry!'

'Exactly. Do it right away!'

'Fatou? I'm sorry . . . Yes, I'm tired. Very. No, nothing serious. It's cold and it's raining. Japan? Not bad. Please will you give me my clue? *You'll find me in the pole and in the flower. . .* You're going too fast and there's a crackle on the line. Wait . . . *The town has two letters for the city*. Have you decided to give me a hard time or what? What on earth are you thinking of! Stay in Japan, me? You sometimes get the weirdest ideas in your head . . . I don't know, in two or three months . . . Yes, it's a long time. Yes. Me too. Even more. Very much.'

He replaced the receiver gently, feeling uneasy.

'Which one do you prefer, Theo?' said Aunt Martha harshly.

'Shut up!' he cried. 'Fatou's upset . . .'

'So is Ashiko,' added Aunt Martha. 'In a week's time, she won't be seeing you any more.'

'A week . . .' murmured Theo. 'Just my luck!'

'Here's a Theo who's learning to suffer,' she said. 'You'd better concentrate on your message.'

Pulling a face, Theo sat down at his table again. *Find me in the pole and the flower.* . . Maybe capital P for pole? Somewhere in Poland?

'You're going round in circles,' commented Aunt Martha. 'You should think more about the *little* tool.'

'A little scythe? A sickle?'

'Well done! The hammer and sickle . . .'

'A communist country!' cried Theo. 'No, there aren't any more.'

'Think about what's inside, *the pollen in the flower*,' hinted Aunt Martha.

'Did you say "the pollen in the flower"? But Fatou said . . .'

Aunt Martha burst out laughing. 'Now I see. You were both so busy quarrelling that you got it all mixed up – she rattled it off, and you wouldn't ask her to repeat it. You heard "pole and" when she said "pollen". All right, I'll have to set you straight. Now, let's go back to the original clue. Think about the letters: the last three letters in . . .'

'The last three letters in "anvil" are V-I-L,' Theo burst out. 'It isn't a code, it's a crossword clue. And if the initials are V-I-L, the surname begins with L.'

He leafed through the dictionary again. 'Laclos, La Fayette, La Fontaine, Lampedusa, Lawrence . . . hey, Lenin. Vladimir Ilyich Lenin. V.I.L. And it's Lenin who appears in "pollen in". Who thought this up? I bet it was Dad. You don't do crosswords and Mum would have made it easier.'

'You've still got to find the city,' Aunt Martha reminded him.

'Of course, it must be Moscow. Anyway, the town has two letters for the city. The O and W in "town" are the last two letters in Moscow.'

'A promise is a promise,' she concluded, taking a little scroll from her pocket. 'Here's your amulet. It's written in Japanese: "Man's greatest virtue is fidelity."'

'Thanks very much!' muttered Theo. 'You had it written specially, I bet.'

'Maybe I did, maybe I didn't. Supposing it's a message from the gods, eh?'

Pangs of conscience

The drive back to Tokyo was depressing. Ashiko avoided Theo and Theo bit his nails. Swathed in her dignity, Aunt Martha kept her jaws clamped shut. The journey seemed endless. The next day, a hospital day, was not exactly fun. Three days until they got the results, three days during which Ashiko gave no sign of life. Theo traipsed despondently around the museums. He didn't like anything. He picked at his food, slept badly and woke up looking drawn. Taking pity on him, Aunt Martha allowed him a telephone call.

'I mustn't,' he mumbled. 'I don't want to hurt Fatou. Besides, you're right, what's the point?'

'Come on, pull yourself together for goodness sake! Don't let yourself go! Think of your twin . . . Do you think he's proud of you?'

'He's gone quiet,' said Theo. 'I don't think he likes Ashiko.'

'Your conscience is pricking you,' she relented. 'Well, you two deserve a nice outing on a lake. You can say your farewells – just you wait, "Parting is such sweet sorrow . . ."'

There was nothing to be done. Theo stayed in his room and flopped on the couch watching television. Martha watched the clock. At last, after two days of gloom, the results arrived. For the very first time, they showed a slight improvement.

'Wonderful, Theo! You're going to get better!' cried Aunt Martha.

'Yeah, yeah,' he said without enthusiasm, 'and then what?'

'Get a grip on yourself. Or else you'll fall ill again!'

'It might be better if I did,' he sighed.

'Enough,' she said firmly. 'We're leaving with Ashiko tomorrow, for Hakone. And you will be so good as not to spoil our last few days. In the meantime, grab the phone and call your mother. Now!'

'I don't feel like it,' he mumbled.

'What's happened to the spirit of tea? Be Zen!'

Theo picked up the receiver with a huge sigh. The news was excellent, but her son sounded so sad that Melina was worried.

'Honestly, Mum, I swear there's nothing wrong,' he repeated earnestly. 'With Aunt Martha? Sometimes. No, not real arguments. Like the other day I ran on ahead, she was miles behind and she was hopping mad! Why are you laughing? You think that's funny? Well, she didn't! She even clouted me! Afterwards? Afterwards, she gave me a hug. You see, it's not serious . . . By the way, Mum, I saw my twin. You're not surprised? What do you mean? There's a family history? That's interesting. Do you think I'm hankering for a younger brother? No, tell me now . . . Mum?'

Theo replaced the receiver. Now Mum had hung up on him too.

'Well?' murmured Aunt Martha.

'Mum's not too good,' he said. 'When she hangs up like that it's because she's going to start crying. But the results were good!'

'She's probably too excited, Theo,' replied Aunt Martha. 'I can't think of any other reason.'

'I expect so,' he said, feeling puzzled. 'All the same, I can't help wondering.'

'Stop! Aren't you happy to be going to Moscow? The basilicas with their golden domes, the priests in their wonderful attire, the polyphonic singing . . .'

'And Lenin's mummy,' added Theo.

'OK,' she sighed. 'After all, it's good to get acquainted with the last gods created by humanity.'

Farewells on Lake Ashi

Two days later, they left for the region of Hakone with Ashiko. Composed and smiling, she kissed Theo on both cheeks as if nothing had happened. Theo looked more cheerful and took her hand. Aunt Martha had booked rooms in a *ryokan* on the shores of Lake Ashi, from where, on a clear day, you could see the eternal snows of the legendary Mount Fuji.

Theo loved the sliding paper screens and the futons on the floor, and ran in stockinged feet to sit on his beloved tatamis. The kimono-clad waitresses glided about silently tending the huge cooking pots – he would be spared raw fish – and you could wander around in a Japanese bathrobe. In short, he was thrilled. But when bedtime came, that was another story.

'Hey, this bed's a bit hard,' he moaned, after five minutes.

'Do you want a Japanese pillow?' asked Aunt Martha with a smile. 'I'll have one brought to you.'

A girl brought Theo a kind of porcelain brick with a blue floral pattern. 'What the hell's this?' he asked his aunt.

'Your pillow,' she replied in deadly earnest. 'You might find it strange, but true Japanese can't do without it. Try it!'

Theo placed the cube under his neck and kept quiet. But when he wanted to curl up, he winced with pain.

'It hurts!' he moaned.

'That'll teach you. That's what happens when you want to go Japanese. You can't get away from your background, my lad. Your pillow at home is a nice soft cushion that you can shape as you like. Here, it's a discipline for the neck.'

'So people don't sleep the same way everywhere?'

'You can see they don't. And you'll have a job to find universal habits . . .'

'All the same, boys pee the same way all over the world,' he answered confidently.

'Oh no they don't! Some stand, some crouch . . .'

'What about giving birth then?'

'No . . . There are regions where women give birth clinging to the branch of a tree, others where they lie down, and others where they stand up . . .'

'Well you can't stop people breathing with their chests!' he cried.

'What did Mr Kulkarni teach you? To breathe from the stomach, I believe!'

'That's true,' muttered Theo, defeated. 'The only thing left is death.'

'Not even that,' she said. 'Yogis can decide to stop living by taking leave of their bodies in a state of ecstasy.'

'What about thinking?'

'You're right,' she agreed. 'Even though thinking isn't the same all over the world – Europe and Asia have different approaches to mastering thought, whether to control it or free it – it is universal. Now go to sleep, with or without your Japanese pillow!'

The next day was their last in Japan. The sky was blue and a few fluffy clouds cast fleeting shadows over the cherry trees on the hills. A strange boat was waiting for the passengers. A three-master with scarlet-painted sides and an ornate gold stern, like something out of a storybook.

'It looks like Peter Pan's ship!' cried Theo. 'Does it come from the Heian period as well?'

'By way of Disneyland,' replied Aunt Martha. 'I'm paying for the trip, but you're going alone. I'd rather wait for you here. Off you go!'

'I see,' murmured Theo. 'Are you coming, Ashiko?'

So this was the place Aunt Martha had chosen for their last meeting. Peter Pan's ship set sail across the waters. The two young people went up on deck on the pretext of gazing at the outline of Mount Fuji.

'The cherry trees are more beautiful than ever,' said Theo.

'Very beautiful.'

'The light's beautiful too,' he added.

'Very. Theo, I have to tell you . . .'

'Me too,' he broke in. 'You know . . .'

'Yes, but there's something you don't know . . .'

'And there's something I have to tell you,' he said. 'About Fatou, you remember? I told you a bit of a fib. She's not a schoolfriend, she's my girlfriend.'

'I realized that,' she murmured. 'I've got a sweetheart too.'

'No way!' he exclaimed. 'A Japanese guy?'

'French,' she said, blushing. 'He's a secretary at the Embassy. My father doesn't know about it, but Olivier gave me a letter from my mother. My real mother.'

'So you know the truth! Are you going to see her?'

'I don't know yet,' she replied. 'When I found out, I cried for ages. I love my Japanese mother so much, you understand . . . Olivier wanted to comfort me and . . .'

'And he succeeded,' concluded Theo. 'What are you going to do?'

'Leave,' she whispered. 'Olivier says he wants to marry me.'

'Wow!' groaned Theo. 'Are you serious?'

'Very!' she replied vehemently.

'So where do I fit in?'

'You were so sweet, so French, and besides, you're sick, and I thought . . .' she stumbled. 'Nothing happened. You've got your Fatou, and I've got my Olivier.'

'Yeah,' he sighed. 'There was a kiss, though.'

'Oh that, we can do that again if you like!'

And she stretched up on tiptoe to proffer her lips. Theo took her in his arms and kissed her.

'There,' she murmured, breaking free. 'Like the cherry blossom. It blows away . . . But its memory lasts forever.'

Aunt Martha watched them walking back, hand in hand, half sad and half happy. That evening, when he went to bed, Theo cried.

'Well, how did the farewell go?' asked Aunt Martha, casually.

'Leave me alone!'

'I'm going to tell you a Zen story,' she began. 'One day, a monk went to visit a master and he said: "I have come empty-handed." Do you know what the master replied? "Well, put it down."'

'But he didn't have anything!'

'Oh yes he did. Coming empty-handed means having the notion that you might have something. The monk didn't get it at all. He lost his temper. Then the master said to him calmly: "Please pick it up again and go home." Put down today's nothing, Theo. For you have lost nothing.'

'Yes, the cherry trees,' he muttered. 'This time, I have understood the meaning of the blossom falling.'

CHAPTER 20

The Religion of Suffering

Theo cracks up

At two o'clock in the morning, Aunt Martha was woken up by Theo's sobs.

'You're not going to cry all night, Theo dear . . .' she said, switching on the light. 'I'll give you a sedative!'

'It'll pass,' he groaned.

'That's what you think . . . That kind of pain doesn't go away so easily.'

'But I'm not in pain!' he cried. 'I'm just cracking up a bit . . .'

'Because you've got a crush on Ashiko? Don't worry, there are plenty more fish in the sea!'

'Spare me the lecture.'

'You see, I think it's good to suffer sometimes. Have you ever suffered, Theo?'

'Not like this,' he groaned.

'Didn't you sob your heart out when you said goodbye to your mother, in Rome? Parting is always painful. It leaves an ache inside you, and you only see the benefits with time.'

'The benefits of suffering. Give me a break.'

'Naturally, it's hard to believe. You feel sad and then, one fine day, you suddenly feel better. To start with, you lose your appetite, you can't see the trees or the flowers, until the day when, without knowing why, you wake up feeling yourself again. You look around you and you notice that life carries on and that, having got through the ordeal, you're stronger than before.'

'You're not going to give me all that Buddha stuff again, are you?'

'No, I'm not,' she sighed. 'I'm talking about ordinary things that nobody can avoid.'

'So what about you then?' he asked aggressively. 'What do you know about suffering?'

'What do you think? I lost the husband I loved.'

'That's the first time you've mentioned him,' he said, sympathetically. 'Were you very unhappy?'

'Oh, Theo . . . What a question! And to think I'm sitting here like an idiot trying to comfort you . . .'

Suddenly, Theo began to sob so uncontrollably that she had to put her arms around him. After a very long time, he fell asleep, hiccuping like a baby from having cried so much. Aunt Martha eased him out of her arms and laid his head on the pillow.

'At last that busy head has to listen to his heart,' she murmured.

When Theo woke up, his eyes were puffy and he looked somewhat frayed at the edges. Aunt Martha left him alone. She packed the suitcases without a word and turned on the TV at random. Theo stood at the window watching the crowds go by, searching for Ashiko. Then, for lack of anything else to do, he flopped in front of the TV set.

'What is it?' she asked as though nothing had happened.

'Some crap. A French film with Japanese subtitles.'

'Who's in it?'

'An old actress, Bardot. She looks so naff with that beehive!'

'I used to have one too,' she murmured nostalgically.

Theo didn't respond, but stared at the floor with a huge sigh. Aunt Martha called Reception and the porter started carrying the baggage down, which ended up taking some time. Theo didn't budge.

'Come on, beanpole, we're leaving,' she said, putting her arm around his shoulders.

'Couldn't we stay a bit longer, please?'

'What about our appointment in Moscow? If only you knew the hassles that can happen over there!'

'We'll freeze,' he grumbled. 'It's going to be grim!'

'Just what you need,' she retorted. 'You look to me as though you're just in the right frame of mind to understand "Holy Russia".'

A Russian-Soviet hash

In the plane, Theo's appetite came back. He was certainly not very talkative, but he ate. Moving with care, Aunt Martha began to fish around.

'What do you actually know about Russia?' she asked.

'I don't feel like talking about it.'

'Don't be so pig-headed! Go on, for me . . . What do you know about the country we're about to land in?'

'That it used to be called the Soviet Union,' he replied reluctantly. 'That it was totalitarian because of a beast called Stalin. That there's a red star on a sort of fortress in Moscow, because the TV correspondents are always shown in front of it. The Kremlin.'

'Good. What about the fall of the Berlin wall?'

'Dunno. I was too little. My parents were glued to the telly, and people picked up lumps of concrete and looked glad.'

'And before Stalin?'

'Before, there were the tsars, like Lenin,' he said confidently.

'Oh dear!' she wailed. 'Do you know that Lenin is the man who organized the Russian Revolution in 1917?'

'Just before the end of the war,' he replied. 'Things were very bad in Russia . . . He had the Tsar shot and seized power with the backing of the workers he'd called on to rebel. And he called that Communism, but in the end the Russians were as unhappy as ever. Our teacher said that Lenin was the first communist tsar. I don't know, but Lenin sounds to me like a classic tyrant!'

'So, you can talk when you feel like it,' she said. 'Do you have any idea what Russian Communism was?'

'It was awful, a Gulag!' he cried. 'There were loads of concentration camps, the people weren't free, when they said what they thought they were locked up in lunatic asylums. But Dad says it's full of poor people nowadays.'

'He's not wrong there. What about religion?'

'No idea. On telly, there are priests with these sort of mitres . . . hang on . . . patriarchs. They're some sort of Christians, aren't they?'

'But you know what they're called, Theo. The Orthodox Church.'

'No they're not!' he cried. 'That's the Greeks.'

'Or Russian,' she insisted. 'Remember Jerusalem. The visit to the Holy Sepulchre . . .'

'Of everything we've seen, that was the most complicated!' he exclaimed. 'There were four or five Churches all squabbling in there . . .'

'Father Dubourg told you about a schism in the Christian Church, remember. It was one of the first, the one that divided the Catholic Churches of Europe from those of the Orient. The Church of Europe obeys the Pope, and the Oriental Churches their patriarchs.'

'Because there are several Churches in the Orient?'

'The Greek Orthodox, the Copts, the Syrian Catholic Church . . .'

'Syrian Catholic Church? Never heard of it.'

'That's not surprising. Syrian Catholics are found mainly in Lebanon and India. The Syrian Catholics speak their own language and have their own form of worship. Some parts of their mass are in Aramaic, an ancient language of Palestine, perhaps the language that Jesus spoke.'

'This stuff gets right up my nose,' sighed Theo. 'What's so special about the Russian Orthodox then?'

'The whole of Russia. That's not to be sneezed at.'

'I don't get it. Are we going to see Russia or the Russian religion?'

'The two go together,' replied Aunt Martha. 'For seventy years, the communist governments fought to keep them separate . . . They persecuted priests and tried to suppress the Russian religion. But as soon as their régime collapsed, the great Russian myth was suddenly revived.'

'All the same, if they're Christians, they believe in Jesus, like the others . . .'

'Yes, but for them, the Russian land is a mother who suffers as Christ did during the Passion. The main thing is to suffer.'

'Like your beloved Buddha? "All is suffering . . ."'

'Don't be silly! It's only the first of four truths. With the other three, Buddha showed how to find release from suffering. Whereas in Russia, suffering is worshipped . . .'

'Great,' said Theo sarcastically. 'What do you have to do to suffer?'

'It's not difficult. Just let life go on. But the Russian Orthodox sometimes go further. Throw themselves in the fire, for example.'

'Don't tell me we're going to see that!' he cried.

The red death

No, in Moscow Theo would not see any such suicide. But it had happened in Russia. In the late seventeenth century, thousands of believers locked themselves in wooden *izbas* and set fire to them. Men, women and children all preferred to die rather than abandon their faith.

'Persecuted martyrs,' said Theo.

In a way, but in this instance, the strange thing was the nature of the persecutor. Pressed by his nobles or by simple priests, the very pious Tsar Alexis wanted to reform the Russian Orthodox Church, where all sorts of strange behaviour was going on. He appealed to the Archbishop of Novgorod, the patriarch Nikon, who demanded total obedience from the Tsar.

Nikon had been chosen because, as a good Russian patriarch, he was against the Greek patriarchs. For the Russian hierarchy was fiercely hostile to two other Churches – to the Catholic Church because of the Pope, and to the Greek Orthodox Church as its great rival and heir to Byzantium, which had broken away from Russia more than a century earlier.

And now Nikon set about betraying his own side! He brought some of the Russian rituals into line with those of the Greek Orthodox Church. The followers rebelled. Their Church belonged to the ordinary people and the poor, the independent Russian people, inspired by their own zeal. And the real tyrant was their Orthodox patriarch, who had tried to reform their religion.

'Right,' said Theo. 'What did he change that was so important?'

The reform required them to say three 'alleluias' instead of two, delete a word from the creed – cosmetic stuff. But worst of all, the patriarch Nikon changed the way of crossing oneself.

'What? Are there several ways of making the sign of the cross?' asked Theo in amazement. 'You do it with your hand, it's quite simple!'

Yes, but with which fingers? Until then the Russians had crossed themselves with two fingers. The reforming patriarch decreed that from now on the Russians would cross themselves with three fingers, the index, the middle and the third finger together, like the Greeks. So they had to include the third finger. And the rebellion against the power of those known as the 'Old Believers' began, led by Avvakum, an inspired holy man, one of the humble priests who had actually been in favour of reform. With the support of the merchants and the nobles, known as *boyars*, it lasted a long time and ended with collective suicides by fire, 'the red death'. The believers entered the blaze dressed in white and holding lighted candles.

'Dying for a finger is going a bit far!' said Theo.

But the extra finger in the patriarch's reform symbolized the entire identity of the Russian Church. The popular religion had been forged in the villages, and came from the heart. This decree whipped up a storm because it was brutally imposed from above. In rebelling, the Old

Believers were not protecting just their sign of the cross: they wanted to keep intact a faith that was deeply involved with the life of their land. Suddenly, an authoritarian central power was deciding in their place. They fought and they burned. Twenty thousand died in twenty years.

'Yet another massacre!' commented Theo. 'Japan was so much better . . . At least it was only themselves the warriors killed! But here, for a finger, people died . . .'

Not all of them died. The Old Believers did manage to preserve their sign of the cross, the symbol of their freedom in opposition to the government. There were still three million of them in Russia and they did not always subscribe to the official dogma. For, after the violent reform of the Russian Church, Nikon was driven out. Too late . . . A new tsar came to the throne. Peter the Great was a military-minded man, in the Prussian mould, who wanted to modernize his country and bring it closer to the West. He made no concessions to the Church – he did not appoint any more patriarchs, and the Russian Orthodox Church was brought entirely under State control.

'So what did that matter?' asked Theo.

'What do you mean, what did it matter,' replied Aunt Martha indignantly. 'Do you know that in France, the separation of Church and State nearly led to civil war?'

'The massacre of the Protestants?'

'No, you blockhead! At the beginning of the twentieth century, in 1905 . . . Until then, the Catholic Church wielded enormous power, in particular over the nation's education. The Republicans, as self-respecting descendants of the French Revolution, decided once and for all to cut the umbilical cord between the clergy and the State, which till then had always paid the priests.'

'OK,' said Theo. 'So what difference does it make if the State pays them?'

'But that makes Catholicism the official religion, so what happens to the minorities, eh? Before 1905, you would have had compulsory catechism at school, and so would your Fatou!'

'So what?' said Theo with a grin. 'We'd both have had a good laugh.'

'Do you want to turn Fatou into a Christian? And who did you like best in Israel, the secular people or the religious ones?'

'The secular ones,' he admitted. 'But that doesn't mean you shouldn't teach religion at school!'

'If you make that religions plural, I quite agree with you,' she said. 'They should teach the history of religion at school, but that means all religions.'

'Mind you, if that were the case, you wouldn't have needed to take me on this trip,' said Theo.

'If people knew more about religion, we wouldn't be witnessing the eruption of fundamentalism everywhere. And sects wouldn't be killing so many innocent people.'

'Like those nutters who went and burned themselves in their *izbas*,' yawned Theo. 'I've had enough of your stories about loonies. Every time we go somewhere, you come out with a new one . . .'

'It's true, I do feel a bit like a recording. But what can I do, it's always the same story! Just think, religious massacres are the worst problem . . .'

'I want to go to sleep,' moaned Theo.

'Fine. You've earned it.'

Houses on hen's legs

But just as Aunt Martha closed her eyes, Theo shook her arm.

'I can't get to sleep!' he whispered.

'Don't be a nuisance. Try harder.'

'I can't,' he said sheepishly. 'I'm frightened . . .'

'Frightened?' she asked, sitting up. 'Of what?'

'Aren't there witches in Russia? When I was little, Mum used to read me Russian fairy tales with forest huts perched on hen's legs and ugly old ogresses inside who cooked and ate children . . .'

'That's a good one. You weren't afraid of Tibetan demons or Indian gods, but folk tales give you the shivers. Are you afraid of fairies?'

'No, but it's different with the Russian ones.'

'Not at all. Our fairies and elves come down to us from the Roman gods, whereas for the Russians, the ogress *Baba Yaga* and her forest hut on chickens' legs hark back to the old beliefs crushed by the Orthodox Church. Thank goodness they've survived! They're charming . . .'

'You're kidding!' shuddered Theo. 'They used to give me nightmares . . .'

'That's because your mother didn't read you the legends of the *rusalki*, the spirits of the forest. Like many other plains of the world, Russia has often been invaded, and for a long time the Russians were occupied by the Mongols. As often happens when conquerors settle in a country, the vanquished region adopts their beliefs, and the Mongols left behind some wonderful legends where good always triumphs over evil. Now what do you think we are supposed to do about evil?'

'Fight it. For once the answer's straightforward.'

'And people start by giving it a face, in the hope of uprooting it. The devil, sorcerers, heretics, Jews, Muslims, the list of "baddies" goes on for ever. But, to represent Evil, people also draw on the repertoire of the past, dredging up ghosts and reviving deities, good and bad. There is no country in the world without its good fairies and its evil witches, its good and bad spirits, its saints and werewolves. Because long before it went Christian, Russia was a land of animists, and that never dies out completely.'

'So we're all a little bit African?'

'All,' she declared. 'Or rather polytheist, if you don't mind. A polytheist is someone who has several gods.'

'Yet another complicated word!' he sighed. 'Couldn't you find a nice simple religion for me – I don't know, just three or four nice gods and no demons?'

'Sorry, we don't stock that item, but you don't need to be a genius to understand the Russian religion of suffering.'

'Here we go again . . .'

'I promise you won't touch any chickens' legs in Russia,' she said with mock seriousness. 'But I also promise that you will see chickens' legs elsewhere.'

'Hey! That sounds like another message!'

'It's a bit soon,' she smiled. 'We're not even there yet!'

'I'm not going to like this country,' he grumbled.

'Oh aren't you? Why not just say you'd rather have stayed in Japan?'

'Not at all. Ashiko's got a boyfriend . . .'

'So that's why you're so unhappy! I bet you'll love Russia. It's the beginning of spring, the willows will be covered in catkins . . .'

'When you've seen the cherry blossom, willows don't count!'

'That's pretty much what you said about the cherry blossom in Japan before Ashiko,' she remarked.

Alexei Ephraimovich

Moscow's huge, crowded airport far exceeded Theo's worst fears. Amid utter chaos, travellers retrieved their baggage under the indifferent gaze of the customs officials, while Aunt Martha checked her suitcases one by one.

'God knows how much I hated the Soviet Union,' she grumbled, 'but at least, in those days, baggage wasn't stolen!'

'Who by?' asked Theo, taken aback.

'When order breaks down, anything is possible,' she decreed sententiously. 'You used to have to wait for ages at passport control, allow the customs officials to rummage around. They were very pernickety but there was no thieving . . . Mind you, I've locked all the cases.'

'You've got friends in Moscow, haven't you?' asked Theo anxiously.

'Yes, over there,' she said, pointing to the area behind the glass partition. 'Keep an eye on the luggage, I'll go and get them.'

She was soon back accompanied by a dark-haired woman with feline features.

'I wasn't able to get Alyosha through,' sighed Aunt Martha, out of breath, 'but this is Irina, his wife.'

'*Grüss Gott!*' cried the pretty woman, crinkling her eyes affectionately. '*Theo, mein Kind . . . Ich bin so glücklich!*'

'Is that Russian?' asked Theo in surprise.

'Irina learned German in Austria,' Aunt Martha explained. 'She says she's delighted to see you.'

'*Ich auch,*' replied Theo, bowing his head. 'How are we going to manage?'

'Alyosha, her husband, speaks perfect French,' she said. 'Alyosha . . .'

'*Alyosha, mein Mann,*' broke in the woman, pointing to herself. '*Und ich, seine Frau.*'

'That's right,' said Aunt Martha nudging them both forward. 'Let's get a move on and find the husband.'

A lanky fellow with floppy curls, Alyosha flung his arms around Aunt Martha in a great bear hug.

'*Martha Grigorievna, dorogaia* . . . I am so happy!' he murmured, with tears in his eyes.

'Dear Alyosha . . .' said Aunt Martha, hugging him.

'It's such a joy,' he sniffed, taking out his handkerchief to wipe his eyes.

'Why's he crying like that? Has he got conjunctivitis?' whispered Theo.

'Ssh . . .' hissed Martha. 'I'll explain.'

'And how's our Theo?' asked Alyosha, turning his blond locks towards him. 'Is he well? We've prepared supper for him, back at the house. And a nice warm bed.'

'What about a car?' asked Aunt Martha.

'I've got Vladimir Ivanovich's,' replied Alyosha, brandishing the keys. 'Of course we might need a taxi for all the luggage . . .'

They piled the suitcases and Irina into the taxi, and Aunt Martha climbed into Vladimir's old banger with Alyosha and Theo.

'Where are we going?' asked Theo, glowering at the buildings rolling past in the fog.

'To our flat,' replied Alyosha. 'Aunt Martha will have the back bedroom and you will sleep on the bed in my office.'

'So we're not going to a hotel?'

'Allow my friends to stay in a hotel!' he said indignantly. 'When she comes to Moscow, Martha Grigorievna stays with us!'

'But why does he call you that all the time?' asked Theo.

'In Russia, people are called by their first names followed by their father's first name,' replied Aunt Martha. 'Your grandfather was called George, which is Grigor in Russian, which makes me *Grigorievna*, Grigor's daughter.'

'And I'm Theo Jeromovich, aren't I?'

'Fyodor Yeremeievich,' Alyosha corrected him.

'That's nice,' he said. 'And what about you?'

'Alexei Ephraimovich. But we prefer nicknames. I'd rather you called me Alyosha. As for my wife, whatever you do, don't call her Irina Borissevna, she'd be furious!'

'Really?' asked Theo, dumbfounded. 'Isn't Boris a nice name?'

'Ssh . . .' repeated Aunt Martha. 'I'll explain later . . .'

Tired of these mysteries, Theo contemplated the fortresses silhouetted in the distance under the red sky. The road was still bordered with white, but in the streets, people were squelching through the slush. Barely illuminated by the sun's dying rays, the sky was slowly dimming.

'We're lucky, the weather's good,' volunteered Alyosha. 'It looks as though we're in for a magnificent spring . . .'

'With all that mud!' retorted Theo thoughtlessly.

'The snow has to thaw some time,' apologized Alyosha. 'We have a word for the mud: *rasputitza*. It's the first sign of the thaw, hearts open up after the winter, life is reborn . . .'

'How cold did it get this year?' chimed in Aunt Martha.

'Minus fifteen. It wasn't very cold.'

'And now, what's the temperature,' asked Theo nervously.

'Minus two,' he replied, 'and the sunshine is mag-ni-fi-cent!'

'Huh, great if you're a winter sports fan.' Theo shivered as he did up his parka.

But Alyosha's flat was beautifully warm and Theo's bed comfortable, with a brown velvet bedspread. The walls were lined with books; a guitar and a violin were lying in the hall. The higgledy-piggledy corridors led to secret nooks and crannies where countless bags were piled on top of each other, and on every available surface was a freshly cut flower. Theo felt at ease. It was a real home, with real people and real musical instruments. The lace chairbacks on the armchairs made the dining room look like something out of a storybook. When Irina brought in a floral tray bearing the teapot, Theo jumped for joy.

'*Tchaï; oder Kirschenkonfitüre mit Wasser?*' she asked.

'I prefer tea,' replied Theo warily. '*Kirschen* means cherries, doesn't it?'

'You should try, it's very good,' advised Aunt Martha. 'It's morello jam mixed with water.'

'Actually, I'm quite peckish,' murmured Theo.

Alyosha disappeared and returned with two plates of smoked fish garnished with giant gherkins. After three trips to the kitchen, the table was covered with bread, cold meats and stuffed hard-boiled eggs. A peaceful silence fell on the room, and then Irina launched into a great speech in a mixture of Russian and German which she embellished with graceful birdlike gestures. Martha responded in a similar vein, and Alyosha smiled as he stroked Theo's head.

'Let them talk,' he whispered. 'They can understand each other. Eat!'

Theo didn't need asking twice. The room was not very well lit, but the glow from the lamps produced a strange feeling of well-being. Through the double-glazed windows, they glimpsed the tiny pinpoints of light in the sky. Alyosha's house seemed to be shielded from danger. Irina's delightful babble had a musical ring, and Alyosha took Theo's hand as his head began to nod.

'The boy is sleepy,' he murmured. 'I'm going to put him to bed.'

He gently pulled back the covers and helped Theo undress. When Theo had slipped between the sheets with a contented sigh, Irina poked her feline face around the door and placed a kiss on his hair before tiptoeing away. Theo sank into a cocooned state of bliss. The vast, menacing city faded away.

Don't touch the *doucha*

In the morning, Theo was woken by a terrifying rumbling sound just as Aunt Martha came and perched on the edge of his bed.

'What's going on? An earthquake?'

'It's only the plumbing . . . With these old buildings from the Stalinist era, something's always going wrong.'

'By the way,' he said out of the blue, 'why did you shut me up yesterday at the airport? Twice! When I asked you whether Alyosha was ill . . .'

'Well it's like this, you can't keep feelings out of a Russian reunion. Here, when you meet up with your friends again, you cry, it's perfectly normal.'

'Really,' murmured Theo. 'So they don't know what happiness is?'

'But that is happiness, Theo! Russian tears express joy, nostalgia, suffering or bliss. It is the sign of the soul, a state between pleasure and pain. In Russia, it's called *doucha*, "soul". It is warm, enveloping, pleasant. Back home, affection comes dry; here it comes wet. Alyosha is absolutely fine: his tears are proof of that . . .'

'I'd find it hard to do the same,' he said, puzzled. 'What's his job?'

'He teaches history and music at the university. And Irina's a translator.'

'Yesterday, there was something about her, and a name . . . Boris! You told me not to mention that word.'

'That was political,' smiled Aunt Martha. 'When it comes to the Russian government, Irina has wild enthusiasms followed by violent disappointments. She was an ardent supporter of her beloved Boris before turning against him with equal passion.'

'She sounds like Mum,' said Theo sympathetically. 'Do you remember when she smashed the plates during the elections?'

'And you remember above all that, for nearly a century, the Russians weren't able to speak freely. The police bugged everyone, and if you protested, you were sent to a psychiatrist who diagnosed anti-social behaviour and prescribed some mind-numbing drugs.'

'What about the psychoanalysts, what use were they?' asked Theo.

'Strictly forbidden. Freud wasn't translated. Science for the petit bourgeois, throw it in the fire! Banned books circulated underground, from one person to another . . . People had to keep quiet.'

'I've never experienced that. I'd never be able to keep my mouth shut.'

'Please God you'll never know what it's like to live under a dictatorship. People suffer great hardship So when they are finally able to talk without fear, they get carried away. It's wonderful!'

'I disagree,' said Theo with a frown. 'I don't like fights. In every country we go to you dig up some massacre, and now it's politics as well!'

'But democracy requires debate, Theo. You should understand that, you're forever arguing!'

'Yes, but I don't break anything,' he said proudly 'At school, I wear myself out patching things up between my friends, and I even get thumped in the process!'

'That doesn't surprise me,' she murmured pensively. 'Now, take your tablets, eat your breakfast and get dressed. Then, phone your mother and don't forget to tell her the flat is nice and warm, that you put on your parka and boots. In other words, reassure her. Then we'll go to the Kremlin.'

'Cool!' exclaimed Theo. 'I'm going to see a modern mummy!'

'I'm sick of you and your mummies. I warn you, we'll have to queue.'

'Like for the mummy room at the Cairo museum, only this time I'll go in!' he declared, jumping off the bed.

The passion-sufferers

Alyosha did not share Theo's enthusiasm for Lenin's mummy. The embalmed body was a symbol of the tyranny that had oppressed his country since 1917.

'But I'm telling you that Theo simply wants to see a mummy!' Aunt Martha argued herself hoarse.

'Out of the question,' repeated Alyosha, shocked. 'You know how much my family suffered. I can't allow it.'

'It won't take long,' Theo broke in. 'I promise you I won't like him, so there you are!'

'It's an insult to my father's soul,' said Alyosha gravely. 'Because of the Communists, he spent twenty years in the Gulag, and when he came home, he was an old man.'

'I know, Alyosha darling,' said Aunt Martha, embracing him. 'But the boy wants to know about all the different religions, you understand?'

'Communism, a religion?' he snorted. 'Perish the thought!'

'Forget it, Aunt M,' murmured Theo. 'I didn't know about your father, Alyosha, I'm sorry.'

So they would begin with the churches of the Kremlin, whose golden domes glittered under the blue sky. It was here, in this huge square, amid great pomp and ceremony, that the patriarch used to crown the tsars with the heavy burden of Russia, condemning the appointed sovereign to the curse of power – so grievous an affliction that sometimes the new tsar was reluctant to accept this dubious honour. The prospective tsar would be approached by the boyars and then withdraw to a monastery, refuse the crown, and only give in when begged by the crowds to accept it. Of course, he might have been shamming, but behind this gesture of withdrawal lay a holy kind of truth.

Under the embroidered coat, the *chapka*, and the furs, the tsar became the Father of the people, sometimes fearsome and sometimes generous, bogeyman or loving father, depending on the situation. This role was so painful that the tsar sometimes renounced the world and became a monk. In the sixteenth century, the aptly named Ivan the Terrible decided to give up his throne on a whim when he was criticized for his harshness. He went off to a monastery, exchanged his gold and brocades for a black monk's habit, and devoted himself to mortification. The people, having previously accused him of all sorts of evils, went down on their knees and implored him to come back. Ivan prolonged their entreaties before returning to Moscow having consolidated his power, which he wielded with legendary cruelty while protecting his vulnerable country.

It was the sheer enormity of Russia that made the tsar suffer. When he chastised, he suffered. When he failed, he suffered. A victim of Russia, he suffered for having the right to punish. The tsar spent his time heaping insults on his own head: he called himself a slave, unworthy, a sinner, incapable, but from this dejection he drew his power, and the obligation to kill if necessary. The long history of the tsars was studded with bloody crimes and assassinations, and the fate reserved by Lenin for the last of the Romanov dynasty, Tsar Nicholas II, was simply the logical conclusion of this. Killed together with his entire family, the last crowned tsar paid a very high price for being the established ruler. The Father was finally dead. Soon after Lenin's death, Stalin was to agree to be called 'Little Father of the Peoples': people had become peoples because of the diversity of the regions in Soviet Russia. The Father was back with a vengeance.

'Hold on, I'm lost,' said Theo. 'Did they kill the tsar, or was it the tsar who killed?'

That was the nub of the question. Several Russian tsars had killed their own sons. Ivan the Terrible and Peter the Great had been through agony, but had not flinched from the demands of power: they had had their heir executed for being weak-minded or rebellious. Then the tsar suffered like God the Father, who allowed his son to die on the cross. The tsar represented God, and took upon his own shoulders all the sins of his people. His heir, the tsarevich, was by definition destined for the Passion.

'What families!' cried Theo.

'The Kings of Western Europe weren't so different,' Aunt Martha reminded him.

But other sovereigns weren't required to suffer. Whereas in Russia, the double suffering of the father and the son was profoundly rooted in Russian mysticism. For the first Russian saints were two young princes who were murdered, Boris and Gleb. Even though the murderer was their brother and not their father, the tsars' criminal history started with the sainthood of the two martyred princes, who allowed their throats to be slit without putting up a fight, like lambs of God. At once, the Russian people were fired with a tremendous zeal: the assassinated princes revived the Passion. A word was coined for them that does not exist anywhere else: the passion-sufferers. And when the tsars executed their own son, the tsarevich, they made him into a saint, whom the people worshipped as they did the Son of God, which wasn't entirely in line with the Orthodox religion.

'They didn't give a damn about children's rights,' growled Theo. 'Your tsars are a bunch of child-murderers!'

Herods, the people called them, like the king who had all the first-born children in Palestine killed to prevent the victory of Jesus the Messiah. In the sixteenth century, one hapless tsar even had to take the blame for the murder of a young prince which he did not commit. Tsar Boris Godunov suffered because it was his job, then died of remorse. And this cult of suffering had an additional dimension: murdered tsareviches often mysteriously came back to life again.

'Really?' cried Theo. 'That's not possible!'

No, that's just it. But the people believed in their resurrection: since they had suffered the Passion, why shouldn't they come back to life? So there were tales of strange princes who appeared at the frontiers, miraculously spared by Heaven, and who were marching on Moscow to punish the guilty tsar. One of them actually succeeded. Nobody knew who he was, where he came from, or what his real story was, and yet, the Empress recognized him as her resurrected son, who had died before her eyes. He was crowned in the Kremlin under the name of Tsar Dimitri, succeeding poor Boris Godunov, who died for a crime he had not committed. Dimitri was also the first of a long line of imposters all passing themselves off as princes come back to life and whom the people followed blindly.

The martyred child's strength was his innocence. Christ had said: 'Suffer the little children to come unto me and forbid them not: for such is the kingdom of God.' In their innocence, children were able to reveal the hidden truth. The revived tsarevich therefore told the truth. The saintliness of the murdered princes later spread to the entire nation: the weak, the elderly, women and children were destined to become passion-sufferers, but, by way of compensation for their agonies, only they could express themselves freely.

'That's what I think too,' said Theo. 'No need to suffer though!'

Oh yes there was, said Alyosha. From this suffering of the weak was born one of the strangest figures in the Russian religion: the holy fool, the *yurodstvo*. These people were not necessarily mad. They pretended to act crazy by rigging themselves out in a spectacular outfit. Half-naked, they wore rags, even in winter, with heavy chains around their neck or sometimes a crown of thorns on their head like Christ in disgrace. The wretched fools would hobble around the public squares, where the people would listen to them predicting prosperity or disaster. Passers-by would laugh and throw stones at them, but nobody dared kill the holy fools.

For they were the only ones who dared shout the truth in the face of the tsar and condemn abuses of power. One *yurodstvo* had the temerity to present Ivan the Terrible with raw meat in a pool of fresh blood in criticism of the Tsar's murderous reign. Another accused Boris Godunov of infanticide. Even though he was innocent, Tsar Boris couldn't answer back. He simply asked the fool to pray for him, for nobody could question the word of a holy fool. As long as he wore rags and could endure the bitter cold of the Russian winter, this sacred clown could behave with impunity.

'I suppose they disappeared with the arrival of the Soviet regime,' said Aunt Martha.

'Can you imagine a stark-naked guy with chains here?' guffawed Theo. 'The police would take him straight to the loony bin!'

'Just look to your right,' smiled Alyosha.

Theo did not believe his eyes. Huddled against the steps of the basilica, an old woman in rags wore a battered shoe dangling from heavy chains around her neck and was brandishing a flag embroidered with a sickle, a hammer and a cross. She said nothing, she wasn't raving, she was content just to be there and wait for the powers that be.

'Incredible!' cried Aunt Martha. 'The fools are back!'

'There's no end to popular zeal,' said Alyosha. 'They're rebuilding churches all over Moscow. Just behind the Kremlin, the Cathedral of Christ our Saviour was blown up by the Communists and turned into a swimming pool. Now it's been rebuilt exactly as it was.'

'What's the meaning of the flag she's waving?' she asked. 'The emblem of the Communist Party and the cross? I thought I was dreaming!'

'In her deranged mind, Christ came down to Earth to save the world, and the Communist Party to save the people. The Party lost, but Christ came back. Which is the old world, which is the new? The woman doesn't know any more . . .'

'Has she lost her memory?' asked Theo.

'No,' replied Alyosha. 'It's just that these old women have lost their bearings. During the War, my country sacrificed millions of soldiers in the fight against the Nazi invaders. Stalin won the war, Stalin became the Father of the People. He enslaved them, but he fed them. No freedom, but guaranteed work, a pension, free health care . . .'

'True,' said Aunt Martha. 'But what a price to pay!'

'Appalling. By the time the Soviet regime collapsed like a house of cards, these women were elderly. Within a few months, their world had vanished . . . With the Party in tatters, pensions weren't paid and speculation rocketed. Elderly people are poor. They get confused. So the cross, the hammer and the sickle are all mixed up together. It's a protest.'

'Deep down, they are believers,' murmured Aunt Martha. 'The distant past is coming back in its most Russian form.'

'Believers or not, they loathe democracy,' added Alyosha softly. 'I don't like them.'

'Poor old things,' said Theo.

'Well, you wanted to understand suffering in Russia?' exclaimed Aunt Martha. 'Now you know!'

'The Russian religion isn't only about suffering,' said Alyosha. 'There's the adoration of beauty. The chants and the icons, the worship of Christ, the angels, just you wait . . .'

'I didn't know you'd gone back to the Church,' said Aunt Martha in amazement.

'Our operas are full of it, our music is so mystical,' Alyosha said by way of excuse.

'Shall we go in?' asked Theo.

'Wait till we get to the Trinity Monastery of Saint Sergius,' he said. 'It's much better than the Kremlin for learning about the faith. Too many tourists.'

The museum of atheism

'Excellent,' said Aunt Martha. 'Let Theo see his Lenin, since we're right here.'

'Count me out!' cried Alyosha. 'I'll wait for you at the entrance to the new church, on the other side of Red Square.'

'What new church?' asked Aunt Martha. 'I don't know it!'

'That's because you haven't been here for a long time. Look over there, to your right . . .'

Leaning against a greenish building, the tiny church displayed its pink arches, its various bells and new domes. An endless procession of people filed in and out.

'Where did this church spring from?' she cried in utter amazement.

'From out of the ground,' replied Alyosha with a smile. 'From freedom. It appeared when Russia was revived. It is continually full . . .'

'How extraordinary!' remarked Aunt Martha.

'You must understand, Martha Grigorievna,' he said. 'From 1930, the persecuted Russian Church went underground, the way the early Christians did, so it was known, quite naturally as the Church of the Catacombs. The League of Militant Atheists massacred the clergy and their congregations. Between 1918 and 1938, forty thousand priests and six hundred bishops were murdered!'

'I didn't know it was so many,' she murmured.

'All so as to turn the Russian people into atheists! Do you know that under Communism, in Leningrad, the Soviets closed down the most beautiful church and converted it into a museum of Religion and Atheism?'

'I remember only too well,' she retorted. 'I saw it in the Sixties. With paintings depicting the priests as sinful and violent, with long wild beards. It was utterly ludicrous . . .'

'Well, as a result, we have Russian zeal! With the defeat of Communist propaganda, the Cathedral of the Virgin of Kazan was handed back to the Orthodox Church and the city got its old name back: St Petersburg. People were in such a hurry that they would install plywood icons in our churches before the buildings had been converted back to religious use – a lot of them had been turned into warehouses.'

'But in Red Square, they did even better,' pointed out Aunt Martha.

'It looks like a strawberry charlotte,' commented Theo acerbically.

Alyosha ruffled his hair and walked off in silence.

'You've upset him,' remarked Aunt Martha.

'He's so touchy,' grumbled Theo. 'Are all Russians like that?'

'They are sensitive,' replied Aunt Martha. 'We're pretty thick-skinned by comparison. Alyosha isn't religious, but he loves his country, that's all.'

'OK, shall we go and see the old man?' suggested Theo.

Lenin's mummy

The soldiers standing guard in front of the dark marble mausoleum looked bored. A few odd visitors scurried in and out. People weren't falling over each other to see Lenin's mummy.

'When I think what it used to be like before!' exclaimed Aunt Martha. 'An endless queue, newly-married couples with the groom in a dark suit and the bride in a white dress who had come on a pilgrimage . . . What a change!'

'Sounds like they don't like him any more,' said Theo dismissively. 'Why do they keep him here?'

'They removed Stalin's mummy and discreetly buried it. Lenin's different. He made the Revolution, he embodied hope . . . Why do we keep Napoleon's tomb in Paris, eh?'

'Because he still stood for something,' mused Theo. 'Napoleon wasn't bad at first either. OK, shall we go?'

But Theo was disappointed. Lenin's face was yellow and dull, it told him nothing, not even about death. Theo stood for a long time in front of the small body lying there, seeking some mystery of which there remained not the slightest trace.

'And to think that the whole of Russia quaked in front of him,' he sighed. 'Why do they want to keep that old carcass?'

'For the same reason that the Christians divide up the bodies of their saints after their death, I think. Not everybody agrees with keeping him here, but no one will take the initiative to remove him. This human fondness for preserving remains is truly bizarre! People want to believe that the body isn't really perishable.'

'Supposing that were true?'

'Christianity has a lot more to offer than mummies: we will be resurrected at the Last Judgement, with the body intact in all its glory. The flesh too. That takes care of everything!'

'But he wasn't a Christian, was he?' protested Theo, pointing at Lenin.

'Not at all. Nor was Mao. The mummies of the founders of Communism prove that it is a proper religion, home-grown in Russia. Naturally!'

'Why naturally?' asked Theo.

'Well, in 1918, a year after Lenin came to power, a great Russian poet wrote a powerful poem celebrating the Revolution, *The Twelve*. It is a description of the march of a shady band of twelve Red Army men, looting and killing their way through a fierce blizzard during the St Petersburg uprising in 1917–18. These revolutionaries wanted no more "Holy Russia", "fat-arsed Russia", as they called the Russia of the *izbas*. They shot at people in the streets, sobbed with remorse and dragged the old world with them. Do you know who was leading the men?'

'Lenin!' cried Theo.

'Jesus Christ, wearing a crown of roses and waving a bloodstained flag. For in Russia, the saviour is Jesus. Salvation through bloodshed and fire, maybe, but in their own way the Russians understood Jesus' protest against the injustice of this world, which the holy Father allows to persist.'

'I knew Lenin was onto something,' said Theo.

'More or less the same thing as Jesus. Equality for everyone, no more rich and poor, perfect happiness, earthly paradise . . . but paradise grows out of the end of a gun.'

'What was your poet's name?'

'Alexandr Blok. His poem didn't do him much good. He just had time to see the first mistakes of his beloved revolution, then he died writing: "She gobbled me up, this filthy, snorting, honking native mother Russia, like a sow with her farrow."'

'You know it by heart!' exclaimed Theo.

'Oh yes!' she replied. 'I'm very wary of native mothers. Listen, I know of a great Hindu mystic who sang the praises of the Terror in France, because the duty of Mother Revolution was to devour her children.'

'Brill!' cried Theo. 'Mum can fry me with onions.'

'Human sacrifice!' she said, wagging her finger at him. 'You see it's never far beneath the surface.'

'But poor old Lenin wasn't an ogre,' he moaned. 'He just got it wrong . . .'

'Oh, is that all! What about the millions who died in the Gulag? I grant you that Lenin was an austere man. He didn't drive around in a carriage, he didn't live like a king. But what crimes! Wonderful ideas, police-state methods. Massacres, intolerance, seventy years of dictatorship.'

'Well, the Russians really do go in for suffering in a big way,' concluded Theo.

'Suffering in Christ,' she retorted. 'It's not the same thing.'

'I have to say that keeping that old guy with the closed eyes . . .' murmured Theo with a final backward glance at Lenin.

'A bit of respect for the dead,' she scolded. 'It's not his fault if they refuse to give him a grave.'

CHAPTER 21

Mother Earth and the Gift of Tears

Aunt Martha is tired

After the lunch that Alyosha had so lovingly prepared, Theo demanded a rest.

'Don't you feel well?' asked Aunt Martha, anxiously.

'No,' murmured Theo. 'I feel like reading quietly. When do I have to go to hospital?'

'We're not going,' she said. 'There have been pay cuts, which doesn't improve the service. We'll do the tests in . . . just wait and see.'

'You nearly said it!' he cried. 'What about the next message?'

'Tomorrow,' she replied. 'Your father doesn't want us to stay here too long. You won't have much time to find the key to the mystery!'

'So, a good book and bed!' yawned Theo.

But by the time they had found Theo a novel, he had already fallen asleep. Irina and Alyosha were drinking tea in the dining room. Martha joined them and sank into a chair with a groan.

'*Dorogaia Martha Grigorievna, welch'eine traurige Sache* . . .' said Irina, stroking her hand.

'What?' said Aunt Martha with a start. 'Oh! I get it. No, Irina, it's not sad. I'm convinced that Theo is on the road to recovery. But from time to time, I do get a little tired . . .'

'How do you know he's getting better?' asked Alyosha.

'The way he stands up to the rigours of travelling makes me optimistic,' she replied. 'I'm knackered, but he's in great shape! For the last

369

two months, the Tibetan medicine seems to have halted the progress of the disease.'

'We're familiar with these methods in Russia,' said Alyosha. 'Our scientists have done a lot of work on hypnosis, which is often more successful than surgery. Could it be that Theo is sick in his soul and not in his body?'

'I don't know,' she sighed. 'His consultations with Eastern healers have done him good, but I wouldn't go so far as to say that they have cured him . . .'

'We were supposed to be going to the museum to see the icons,' said Alyosha, glancing at his watch. 'Let's leave him to sleep.'

'If you'll excuse me, I'm going to do the same. It's strange, when Theo sleeps, I come over all sleepy too . . .'

'It's sympathy in the Greek sense of the word,' concluded Alyosha. 'You're like his mother!'

'Oh no you don't! I'm not falling into that trap. Melina is young enough to have more children, and a jolly good thing too. No, I'm not his mother. Let's say I am what the Greeks call a "psychopomp": a conductor of souls . . .'

'You want to lead him to God,' I believe,' said Alyosha.

'Absolutely not! That's up to him! Anyway, Theo is more drawn to mysticism than to religion.'

'*Du bist also ein bisschen mystisch*,' Irena said softly, with a smile.

'A mystic, me?' protested Aunt Martha. 'I admit I'm interested in the subject, but that's all. I do find it incredible that people always take refuge in God, and as I don't understand, I investigate.'

'That's exactly what the mystics do,' declared Alyosha.

'I mean . . .' she floundered. 'Oh! You're getting on my nerves with your insinuations. I'm going to have a nap, so there!'

Irina and her husband exchanged a smile. When their friend Martha was cornered, she went into a sulk.

The thaw of the wet mother

At around 10 o'clock that night, Irina roused Theo from his slumbers with some hot broth which he sipped before falling back into a deep sleep. As for Aunt Martha, she had surfaced at dinner time, but had barely been any more forthcoming. The next day, they all drove to the Trinity Monastery of Saint Sergius.

'Saint Sergius,' grumbled Aunt Martha, wedging herself into the back seat. 'Why did they change its name? Zagorsk was much nicer!'

'But that wasn't its original name, my dear,' said Alyosha starchily. 'The town where the monastery was built was renamed by the Soviets. Zagorsk was a revolutionary. Instead of Saint Sergius! It was right to go back to its original name.'

'Old name, new name, what madness!' she exclaimed. 'Each generation sees the names of the streets change, it puts you in a spin!'

'I suppose you'd rather have kept the German street signs in Paris after the war?' said Theo, with an edge of sarcasm.

'Theo catches on fast,' said Alyosha. 'It's as if we were coming out of a military occupation.'

Aunt Martha looked away without answering. As they drew further away from the city and the grey buildings ended, dazzling white snow appeared on the plain and on the roofs of the houses. Aunt Martha was spellbound by the dappled whiteness of the silver birches. And, surprise, surprise, Irina began to sing a melancholy dirge, capturing the mood of the tardy spring.

'Isn't the thaw beautiful?' sighed Alyosha. 'Here in Russia, nothing is more important. After being numbed for so long by the cold, the soul awakens.'

'That song sounds familiar,' murmured Aunt Martha. 'What is it?'

'It's from *The Invisible City of Kitezh*, an opera by Rimsky-Korsakov,' replied Alyosha. 'Fevronia, in the last act, when she sinks into the ice. Sublime liberation . . .'

'Freezing to death?' protested Theo, outraged. 'Strange way to liberate herself!'

'You have to know the legend,' said Alyosha. 'Fevronia is a peasant woman who lives in the forest. She is so pure and so good that the Prince of Kitezh marries her, with lavish celebrations. But, on their wedding day, the city is threatened by the Tartars. Protected by a divine charm, Kitezh becomes invisible and the people are saved. Except Fevronia, captured by a ruffian. The young girl is beaten and tortured, but remains as virtuous as ever. When she finally sinks into a frozen pond, she is reunited with the invisible Kitezh where she will reign as queen.'

'OK, but she's dead,' said Theo.

'No! Fevronia is the symbol of the thaw. It is in the spring that the prince discovers her, surrounded by animals and flowers. And when she disappears, it is the end of winter, because the ice gave way. Fevronia is the Russian land, frozen in winter, green in spring, searching for the ideal of the celestial City.'

371

'Like the Jerusalem of the Jews in exile,' said Aunt Martha. 'In another time, another world, next year . . .'

'Theo doesn't know that after the fall of Byzantium, Moscow was designated the third Rome,' Alyosha went on. 'The first was the city of Saint Peter, the second Constantinople, and the third Moscow.'

'Are there even more?' asked Theo.

'There could be,' said Aunt Martha. 'For the Rome of the Christians suffered the same fate as Jerusalem: founding a city often means stealing a little bit of Jerusalem. Like the thrice holy city, Rome has moved three times.'

'Building a city takes some doing!' said Theo, 'You haven't got time to think about God . . .'

'There you're wrong! Their founding rituals always invoke the divine. Remember the Chinese cities, a square in a circle, in accordance with the Tao . . . Before deciding on a site, they plot a sacred furrow and seek a miraculous spring – a supernatural sign – inventing one if need be. How many ramparts have been built over the body of a sacrificed virgin!'

'The Russian land alone is sacrifice,' murmured Alyosha. 'She is the mother who cries at the sight of the battlefield as she contemplates her massacred children. Before Christianity, there was a pagan god, Moist Mother Earth, who would not allow herself to be dug until the day God spoke to her: "Don't cry," he said to her. "You will feed the people, but you will eat them all too." We have kept this Mother Earth goddess. Our land! We bow down to touch it, we kiss it respectfully. We beg it to forgive . . .'

'You're not the only ones,' pointed out Aunt Martha. 'Do you know how the black slaves deported to Brazil used to commit suicide? By eating earth, in despair at having lost their own.'

'We don't eat it,' he said huffily. 'We Russians mix up the earth with the Mother of God. Flooding it with tears is a holy deed . . .'

'Strange irrigation system!'

'Let him finish,' Theo cut in.

'You can talk,' she retorted. 'Are you interested in Mother Earth?'

'Very,' said Theo. 'Mum cries a lot too, even when she's happy. Granny Theano says it's Greece coming out in her.'

'Granny Theano is Theo's Greek grandmother,' explained Aunt Martha. 'That's what makes him sensitive to Russia.'

'Perhaps we're more pagan than the Greeks,' said Alyosha. 'Here, Mother Earth devours the invader, Napoleon, Hitler . . . She defends us.'

Worshipping beauty

When he caught sight of the gold-spangled blue domes, Theo was unable to suppress a cry of admiration. Their huge sparkling crosses were dazzling against the blue sky. The Trinity Monastery of Saint Sergius on its hill seemed to welcome the whole of humanity. Theo walked slowly into the complex. The paths lined with snow-clad bushes led to the churches into which trooped elderly ladies with scarves on their heads, laughing young girls and very solemn-looking youths. Well-dressed priests, fiddling neurotically with the cross around their necks, milled with the crowd of worshippers who kissed their hands and gave them pictures to bless.

'Incredible,' murmured Aunt Martha. 'The last time I came here, I only saw one or two *babushkas*.'

'What's a *babushka*?' asked Theo.

'Elderly mothers,' replied Alyosha. 'They're very respectable. Let's go closer.'

It was difficult, the church was so full. As he elbowed his way through, Theo could hear a host of mysterious voices which created a deep, mournful dirge. Then he saw the thousands of candles burning in the gloom and his heart leapt.

'Where's the music coming from?'

'It's the congregation, singing in parts,' murmured Alyosha.

'They sound like angels,' said Theo in wonderment.

In front of the crowds who beat their breasts as they prayed, Theo saw a huge panel depicting giant haloed figures. They all had the same doleful look, the same sad faces with eyes full of tears . . . The angels and saints seemed to be crying over the believers.

'The icons,' whispered Alyosha. 'Do you see Christ? He's the biggest.'

'He's making eyes at me,' murmured Theo, fascinated.

'Christ is the master of everything, "Pantocrator" in Greek. The true face of man as seen by God. The face of love that suffers while waiting for people to recognize themselves in him. To look Christ in the eyes is to melt in his suffering and his divinity.'

'It makes me feel really weird,' said Theo with a shudder. 'Like when I've got a temperature . . .'

'That's perfectly natural,' whispered Alyosha. 'Looking at the icons, listening to the singing, seeing the candles and smelling the incense, means looking at beauty, and all the senses are affected by the mystery of the Trinity: the Father isn't here, but the Son gazes at us with love, and the Mother who is crying, is you. We call that the "painful joy".'

'That's pretty heavy,' sniffed Theo. 'It makes you want to cry . . .'

'Then cry,' said Alyosha. 'Let your tears flow, it's good for you.'

'But why? I can't help it, it's stronger than me . . .'

'Just let go,' he repeated. 'Now you know what joy is.'

When the liturgy was over, huge tears ran down Theo's radiant cheeks.

'Here,' mumbled Aunt Martha, proffering her handkerchief. 'You've got a runny nose.'

The wellspring of tears and the second baptism

In front of the cathedral people were swarming everywhere like ants. The atmosphere was festive and believers jostled each other around stalls to buy tiny icons and crosses. Sitting to one side, a young man with a bloody nose was holding his head and moaning.

'What's the matter with him?' asked Theo anxiously. 'Has he been in a fight?'

'You see a lot of young people in a right state on Sundays,' replied Alyosha. 'On Saturdays they go out drinking, then at night, they get into a fight. The next day, during the liturgy, they come and pray and then go out the following Saturday and start all over again.'

Filled with pity, Theo began to snivel again.

'That's enough, Theo,' snapped Aunt Martha. 'Getting yourself all wound up – you must have lost your head!'

'Martha Grigorievna, this state that you are complaining about does not come from the head, but from the heart,' said Alyosha irritably. 'Russian faith requires us to do without the head . . .'

'I forgot,' she grumbled. 'What do you call it again? The head in the heart?'

'During prayer, the spirit must come down from the brain into the heart,' he corrected her. 'The head is in charge of intelligence, but the heart is the source of emotion. Now intelligence isn't able to pray. Prayer does not consist of concentrating the mind on words: it's enough to say by rote, like a child, stuttering and stammering, and the spring wells up from the heart.'

'That's childish! Do you know the extremes that the Orthodox monks go to, Theo? They bend double until they can't breathe, stare hard at their navels, and repeat the Lord's Prayer tirelessly until they lose consciousness!'

'It's just another technique for achieving a trance!' protested Alyosha. 'First of all, the monks who invented this practice were Greek, and secondly, their aim, in stopping their breathing, was to allow the brain to descend into the heart.'

'What's the use of the navel, then?' asked Theo.

'It's in the middle of the stomach, at the point where we were separated from our mother. Once the cord is cut, how do you re-establish contact? The navel is the centre of the stomach as it is the centre of the world. To reach a state of trance, all you have to do is breathe and pray in harmony.'

'Like in yoga!' cried Theo. 'It's true, Aunt Martha, it's no different from Professor Wacko's "Om"!'

'Except that yogis don't cry,' she retorted. 'They smile. I don't like all this whingeing.'

'You don't understand the first thing about it, Martha Grigorievna,' said Alyosha angrily. 'I'm going to explain the gift of tears to you.'

As the prophets of Israel had always claimed, he said, the world belonged to suffering, supremely epitomized by Christ crucified. That's why Russians were continually afflicted by a sadness of divine inspiration.

'Heard that one before,' said Theo. 'All is suffering!'

But human sadness could be transformed through the gift of tears. If each of us were to be content merely with individual physical suffering, we would remain sterile. On the other hand, if we went beyond solitary melancholy, then we could indulge in the delicious taste of tears. Crying is not granted to just anyone: the gift of tears is a privilege reserved for pure hearts. In Russia, holy men had the power to provoke tears, which enabled them to cure the faithful. They were known as the *startsy*, the charismatic spiritual guides who could aid others in attaining spiritual progress and success; *starets* in the singular.

There had been a number of very famous *startsy* in the past. In the fifteenth century, when the country was rocked by political disturbances; in the nineteenth century while the Russian Church was under state domination, and lastly under the Soviet yoke at the time of the persecutions. When the Russian people had no one else to turn to, then the *startsy* appeared to calm their fears and stir up their zeal. They weren't married, like the priests. They went off into the desert like Christ and Moses . . .

'Into the desert in the snow?' asked Theo in amazement.

375

Snow or sand, the principle of the wilderness was solitude and empti-ness. The *starets* would retreat to a hermitage where, soon, the kindness of his luminous gaze would attract crowds. He was worshipped by the people: better than a dignitary, more than a priest, even more than a tsar, his simple heart would bring together the Russians in a collective communion. And he knew how to get those tears of joy flowing. These tears alone were capable of irrigating the aridity of the spirit that had at last descended to the heart.

'I call that oversensitivity,' groaned Aunt Martha. 'Crying non-stop, how weak!'

Weak? Yes, human nature was weak and sinful. But people couldn't cry all the time because continual tears meant a callous indifference. True tears were spontaneous, like a second baptism, flooding the heart of the person praying. They cleansed the heart of its impurities, relieved it and gladdened it.

'It's true, isn't it, Theo, that your tears make you feel better?' con-cluded Alyosha.

'I'll say,' replied Theo. 'But it's exhausting. I'm knackered.'

'Now look what you've done!' cried Aunt Martha. 'You've got him into a right state, Alexei Ephraimovich . . . In his condition! Nice work!'

Surprised at his aunt's anger, Theo blew his nose hard.

The city with three names

'Calm down, let's not dramatize things! It's just that all that emotion has made me hungry. I could do with a bite to eat.'

'Would you like some *piroshkis*?' asked Alyosha, looking concerned. 'We can get some near the souvenir shops at the entrance to the Mon-astery.'

'They're little meat pasties,' explained Aunt Martha. 'Will that do?'

Theo stuffed himself with *piroshkis* washed down with Coca-Cola, and inspected the souvenirs – dolls wearing coronets of bluebells and ears of corn, giant Russian dolls representing the tsars, and floral shawls with black fringes.

'Why don't you buy a Russian doll?' suggested Aunt Martha. 'This one, for instance, with plump cheeks and blue eyes.'

'Nah,' he said. 'You've brought me three already. Shawls – one for Mum, one for Attie, and one for Irena.'

'OK, but I'm buying you the *matrioshka*,' she insisted. 'You are requested to open it straight away.'

'I bet there's a message hidden inside,' groaned Theo, picking up the nesting dolls.

Because I am the bridge between two continents, I have often been conquered and I have changed my name three times. If you find me, you can bid farewell to reason . . .

Without a change of expression, Theo slipped the message into his pocket and set about choosing the shawls for his family.

'Have you guessed it already?' asked Aunt Martha in amazement.

'Don't be in such a hurry!' he said, feeling the fabrics. 'We haven't got a plane to catch . . .'

'Oh yes we have,' she replied. 'We're leaving tomorrow. I warned you, you've only got twenty-four hours to find the answer!'

'In the car then,' he conceded. 'Will you pay for the shawls?'

Just then, shattering the stillness, the first bells tolled out their deep, vibrant notes, soon joined by the small bells, ringing for all they were worth. The whole sky clanged. Theo was spellbound, and stood stock-still, clutching his shawls.

'Russian bells are living beings,' said Alyosha. 'When the Russian Church was born, casting a bell was a sacred task, for the sound of the bell echoes the voice of God.'

'I've never heard anything so beautiful,' said Theo.

He literally had to be dragged away from the wonders of Saint Sergius and bundled into the car. Complaining, he took the slip of paper out of his pocket.

'Now,' he sighed. '"A bridge between two continents." I need the map. "I've often been conquered" . . . So have lots of places. What's next? "I've changed my name three times." How am I supposed to know? But the last bit's the killer! "Bid farewell to reason"?'

'I admit it's not easy,' conceded Aunt Martha.

'Between two continents, there's Mexico,' said Alyosha. 'Or Tangier. Or the Bering Strait, between Russia and America . . .'

'No prompting!' she warned.

'Between Greece and Turkey . . . wait a minute . . . Istanbul!'

'You could have spun it out a bit,' said Aunt Martha, feeling miffed. 'What about the city's three names?'

'You're never satisfied,' he replied. 'I'm either too fast or a slowcoach. You want me to tell you the three names? Constantinople, Byzantium and Istanbul, so there! Now I've done my homework, can I get some kip?'

And, resting his head on Alyosha's shoulder, Theo fell asleep.

'Since we left Japan, he's cried a lot,' murmured Aunt Martha. 'He's lovesick . . .'

'He's so delightful,' said Alyosha. 'You'll see, those last tears will have soothed his soul.'

Little pigeon

For their last evening, Irina had really gone to town. Smoked swordfish, vodka, borscht, and orange sorbet. On the table, she had placed candles; the dining room was more welcoming than ever.

'To your health, *galubchik*!' said Alyosha, raising his glass of vodka. Theo did likewise, and drained the glass in a single gulp.

'Wow . . .' he yelped. 'It's incredibly strong! I'll have another glass or two. It makes you feel all warm inside . . .'

'*Otchin etwas Borscht?*' murmured Irina. '*Das ist sehr gut!*'

'*Stratvoutié, Irina, ich habe genug,*' replied Aunt Martha.

'When you've finished talking double Dutch!' snapped Theo, 'I'm going to phone Mum.'

The telephone was in the corridor. From a distance, Martha overheard the usual conversation. Everything was fine, he hadn't caught cold, they'd do the next tests in Istanbul, he sounded funny because of the vodka, he'd only drunk two glasses, very strong, oh yes, Russia was very, very beautiful and how was Fatou? Was she well too? No? Ah . . .

'Tomorrow I've got to call Fatou,' he said, coming back into the room. 'I'm going to pretend to ask her for a clue.'

'Do you need an excuse?' asked Aunt Martha. 'Just phone her now!'

'I have to get ready myself,' he whispered. 'Anyway, I've had too much to drink.' Feeling melancholy, he staggered in the direction of his room. Irina came and planted a kiss on his cheek, followed by Alyosha who sat on the edge of his bed and took his hand.

'Hey, Alyosha, what did you call me earlier? *Galu* something . . .'

'*Galubchik*,' said Alyosha. 'In Russian it means "little pigeon".'

'That's pretty,' yawned Theo tipsily. 'Pigeon fly!'

CHAPTER 22

Islam: Surrender to God

Theo tells a lie

In the morning, Theo groped his way to the telephone. He dialled the number blindly.

'Fatou? It's me-ee . . . Yes, I'm yawning. I've only just woken up, and you see, I'm calling you. Oh, it's night-time? Sorry. What, that long? Are you sure? I haven't called you for three weeks? That is a long time. Is that why you sound so upset? Well you needn't be, silly! Forget you? With your two pendants around my neck? I've got you with me all the time. OK, give me my clue. *Farewell to reason, seeing those who whirl*. I'm stumped. I'll call you later for the other clue. When? After breakfast. Japan? Nice. Who with? A lady. Another old dear, yes. Of course I love you.'

'Liar,' said Aunt Martha behind him.

'I had to,' sighed Theo. 'Anyway, she's already perked up.'

Revived by a glass of black tea, Theo gorged himself on croissants and jam and pondered how to extricate himself from the situation. Decipher the clue, call Fatou back, thank her, tell her that without her, he would never have found it, that without his beloved Pythia he wouldn't get anywhere . . . That what gave the trip its meaning was the return to Paris. That he loved her very much.

Find 'those who whirl'.

'Are we going to see dancers in Istanbul?' he asked.

'Sort of,' replied Aunt Martha. 'I'll help you: they wear white robes.'

'And they whirl,' said Theo pensively. 'I don't get it. All dancers whirl!'

'Not on the spot, and not all the time,' she said. 'You'll never guess. It's the whirling dervishes. Go on, call your girlfriend . . .'

From love to fanaticism

Saying goodbye at the airport was a tearful affair, as Theo had predicted. Standing close together, Irina and Alyosha waved for as long as they could. Aunt Martha kept a jaded eye on the luggage and Theo thought wistfully of Fatou. In the plane, he absently flicked through the Turkish Airways in-flight magazine and stopped at a photograph.

'Istanbul really is full of mosques,' he commented.

'More than anywhere else in the world, and they're the most beautiful,' confirmed Aunt Martha. 'The best place to teach you about Islam.'

'But I thought Mecca was the best place?'

'It is, but unfortunately, non-Muslims aren't allowed there under any circumstances. So how could you and I go there? We haven't got a hope!'

'Couldn't we pretend?'

'No way. The minute you get close to Mecca, there are big signboards saying: STOP. RESTRICTED AREA. MUSLIMS ONLY PERMITTED. I've seen them with my own eyes! Besides, it's dangerous. Every year, during the great pilgrimage, believers are trampled to death by the crowd, it's terrifying!'

'It's not true,' said Theo. 'What a horrible religion!'

'No, it's not . . . In India, during the pilgrimages to the Ganges, several hundred of the twelve million pilgrims die each time. But that's caused by crowd hysteria and has nothing to do with the religious side. It's not the fault of Islam.'

'I want to see for myself,' he replied warily. 'I'm sure not all Muslims are like my Sheikh in Jerusalem.'

'And not all Hindus are Mahantji! There's no religion without fanatics. But no fanaticism without tolerance: that's the rule.'

'But the thing is, you only know the tolerant ones. I see the best, never the worst.'

'The worst wouldn't speak to you. They would never accept that someone wanted to understand all religions at the same time. Theirs is the only true religion and that's that.'

'Why aren't the fundamentalists tolerant? They're starting to make me cross!'

'But it makes sense, don't you see . . . Poverty is the root of fanaticism. Take the poor from the slums anywhere in the world, Bombay, or Cairo, for example. They migrate from their village because they have nothing left. The last drought killed their livestock, and the crops failed. They had neither work nor food, so they left the countryside to look for a job. But not a hope. So now they're trapped. They've lost everything, their village, their herds, their trees and their fields, everything except their religion.'

'What use is that to them, I wonder.'

'It helps them recreate a world for themselves that's more or less intact. At the temple, or the mosque, they regain a sense of community. At home, they can surround themselves with religious paraphernalia, a prayer mat, a portrait, a piece of calligraphy, gods. And then the religious leaders come along and take care of the needy; fundamentalist movements do ever such a lot to help the needy.'

'Really? So they also do good?'

'You have to face facts, the answer is yes, they do,' she said. 'Only, it's rarely without any strings attached. The poor things are financially dependent on the religious community and that's all too often how fanaticism is born.'

'So the religious leaders manipulate them.'

'It's not so simple. What the religious leaders see clearly is that poverty is spreading around the cities. By the year 2020, there'll be six billion people on the Earth, with half of them crammed into the world's major cities. Three billion!'

'As many as that?' said Theo appalled. 'What can we do?'

'Nobody has a clue. For the poor in the slums, religion is there, ready to comfort the dispossessed. It warms the heart and gives hope . . . Do you understand?'

'I understand that some clever bastards take advantage of them,' grumbled Theo.

'Don't be so sure,' she said. 'They want to restore justice, that's understandable.'

'With bombs?' said Theo indignantly.

'I never said I approved. I'm trying to find the causes. Otherwise, it's war!'

'War for the love of God is terrible,' said Theo. 'When you love, you don't want to kill the other person, as far as I'm aware!'

'Hmm . . . Do you know the legend of Tristan and Isolde? They loved each other so much that it killed them both . . .'

'They should have got married.'

'They couldn't! Isolde was married to Tristan's uncle . . .'

'Well, that was hard luck. Aunt and nephew, it's not on. Imagine, you and me? They shouldn't have fallen in love.'

'Believe me, they tried! Love is sometimes fatal, Theo. Sometimes mothers suffocate their child with love and then the child dies. Love is so often war . . .'

'I don't agree,' he said. 'Love is peace, otherwise it's a sham.'

'Let's see. Supposing when you got back, Fatou didn't love you any more. Wouldn't you try and pressure her?'

'That's not possible,' he replied, blushing. 'Fatou and me . . . it's for real. We argue, but we don't fight.'

'Arguments,' she murmured. 'Watch out. That's how wars begin. Byzantium was torn apart by arguments. Arguments cause rifts within religions. People talk seriously, they argue . . . Then, one day, they quarrel, they part, they take up arms and they fight. In the name of God and love.'

'What a nightmare! I simply don't believe you.'

'That's up to you,' she sighed. 'The history of Istanbul might help you understand.'

Nasra the Muslim

Luggage, porters . . . Arrivals were all the same. As in Cairo, the women of Istanbul were sometimes veiled, sometimes not. In the crush, Aunt Martha was looking for their next guide.

'Help me, Theo. She's got dark skin and the blackest eyes you ever saw . . .'

'Not too young?' asked Theo anxiously.

'Neither young nor old. You can't miss her, she's magnificent.'

'That one?' asked Theo, pointing to a plump woman with a laughing face.

'Nasra is as thin as a rake!' she said huffily. 'A gazelle! Look, there she is, I didn't lie to you, did I?'

It was true. Nasra was breathtakingly beautiful. With her doe's eyes, mysterious smile, muslin veil and dangling emerald earrings, she looked as though she had stepped straight out of a miniature. Theo stood gawping, rooted to the spot.

'Hello!' she said in a husky voice. 'Your aunt told me all about you. Aren't you going to give me a kiss?'

He didn't need asking twice. What's more, she smelt nice, and she wore a tiny diamond in her nostril.

'You're Indian,' he murmured as he embraced her. 'I can see it from your little diamond.'

'I'm Pakistani,' she corrected him, smiling.

'What religion is it in your country?' mumbled Theo shyly.

'I'll tell you later,' she replied. 'We won't hang about in this crush.'

Despite her slender build, Nasra did not lack authority. She barked orders to the porters like a real captain. The taxi driver jumped to it and drove off without a murmur. Porters, cars, donkeys, traffic jams, hooters. But, on the hilltops, the minarets floated in a golden haze of dust. They drove past markets, mosques, wooden houses with ornate balconies, concrete apartment blocks, shops and stalls, but everywhere you felt the presence of the sea. Aunt Martha and Theo would be staying in Nasra's seventh-floor flat with a balcony and a view over the Golden Horn.

Nasra liked sofas and tuberoses. She removed her veil, kicked off her court shoes, jangled her diamond bracelets and sat gracefully on the carpet. A silent woman dressed in black brought them sweet coffee. Nasra thanked her in Arabic and invited her to join them.

'A diamond in your nose and tuberoses, and you're not Indian!' exclaimed Theo.

'In 1947, when British rule in India came to an end, India was divided into two separate countries,' said Aunt Martha. 'Most of the population in Pakistan, to the north-west of India, are Muslims, like Nasra.'

'So you were just speaking the Muslim language of your country,' observed Theo.

'At home, we speak Urdu,' said Nasra. 'In Istanbul, we speak Turkish, and I was speaking Arabic to my friend Mariam, who is Palestinian. There is no Muslim language.'

'All the same, Nasra, the Koran is written in literary Arabic,' interrupted Aunt Martha.

'God speaks to the heart of the faithful in their own language,' said Nasra, piously. 'He speaks to Moses in Hebrew, to Jesus in Aramaic and to Muhammad in Arabic. As far as I'm concerned, language is less important than the love of God. Would you like to try these cakes, Theo? Watch out, they're dripping with honey.'

'Baklava!' said Theo, thrilled. 'The honey tastes delicious.'

'Let's not waste too much time, Nasra,' broke in Aunt Martha.

The Koran

Nasra folded her legs under her.

'Let's begin,' she said. 'So, I'm supposed to tell you about the Koran?'

'I've got news for you,' he said in surprise, 'the Sheikh told me about it in Jerusalem. Allah, Muhammad, Abraham . . . I already know all about it!'

'We'll see about that,' she smiled. 'Do you remember what Koran means?'

Theo opened his mouth in surprise and the honey dribbled down his chin.

'Our friend Suleiman told me you'd probably forget,' she observed. 'Yes, he and I know each other, would you believe, and fairly well too. He told you, didn't he, that Koran means "Reading aloud", or "Recitation". Do you know at least who Iblis is in our book?'

No answer.

'I'll tell you. When the Creator made Adam out of clay, he commanded all his angels to worship his creature, his creation. Only one refused, Iblis, because he felt superior: "Me thou hast created of smokeless fire, and shall I reverence a creature made of dust?" The Creator immediately threw him out. "My curse shall be on you till Judgement Day!"'

'But the angel was right, wasn't he?' said Theo.

'No, because he was questioning the Almighty. However, Iblis asked the Creator for time, to entice man. Allah's answer is very mysterious: "You are reprieved till the Appointed Day," he said to him, accepting his entreaty. So the Creator gave the fallen angel the power to entice man into Hell. Iblis, the first infidel, is also known as Satan.'

'So he's the devil!'

'But, unlike the Christian devil, Iblis made a deal with God. It's up to the believer to choose between Iblis and the Prophet, for the Koran warns: if you do not respect Muhammad's word, when the time comes, you will be doomed to hellfire and boiling pitch.'

'As usual.'

'No, worse. The Koran goes on at great length about the horrors of Hell. But it also dwells on the infinite joys of Heaven, magnificent gardens running with rivers of milk and honey, where every desire is satisfied. Young boys in green satin serving delicious nectars, houris dance to delight the senses . . .'

'Houris?'

'Celestial creatures, young girls with kohl-rimmed eyes,' explained

Aunt Martha. 'They are the believers' companions, forever virgins . . .'

'Allah's heaven sounds like a load of fun,' commented Theo. 'Better than the Christian one where you just hang around.'

'They're images, Theo,' went on Nasra, 'to give people something to dream about. Actually, to avoid going to Hell and get to Heaven is very simple. You just have to respect the five pillars of Islam to the letter. One, swear that "there is no God but God and Muhammad is the prophet of God". This profession of faith is called the *shahada*. It means the testimony. Two, observe the five daily public and collective prayers. Three, pay each year the mandatory *zakat* or tithe, a tax for the support of the poor.'

'Tithe?' queried Theo. 'I learned about tithes in history. Farmers used to have to give a tenth of their produce to the priests . . .'

'In Islam, there are no priests. The believer gives to the Lord, his God,' Aunt Martha broke in. 'A contribution to be shared among the poor. I think you can also give to charity voluntarily, can't you, Nasra?'

'It's advisable. The fourth pillar consists of fasting during the month of Ramadan. You must fast completely from dawn until sunset. Not a crumb of bread, not a drop of water. You're not even allowed to swallow your saliva . . .'

'Wow!' exclaimed Theo. 'That's tough!'

'The effort is part of Ramadan,' added Nasra. 'But we celebrate in the evening, with a big family meal. As for the fifth pillar, you have to make the *hajj* – the pilgrimage to Mecca – if you can afford it. As you see, the principles are straightforward. There are other, more detailed regulations, as many as the ones Moses decreed for the Jews.'

'They're often the same,' remarked Aunt Martha. 'You're not allowed to eat pork, or animals that have not been slaughtered in the ritual way, circumcision . . .'

'Which is often thought to mean female excision too, quite wrongly!' spluttered Nasra indignantly. 'When I think that's an African custom and that our traditionalists have turned it into a Muslim precept, even though the Prophet condemns excision!'

'Don't choke, darling,' smiled Aunt Martha. 'But as for wine, it's the Prophet who forbids it, and he alone, there's no doubt about that.'

'He came to do so gradually,' she explained. 'At first, he celebrated the sweetness of wine as a gift from God. But when the early believers kept getting drunk and disorderly, he behaved like a politician, just like Gorbachev when he came to power in the Soviet Union in the Eighties

– his first decision was to ban alcohol. But the Prophet takes a tougher line on gambling, and vain and dangerous idols . . .'

'All the same, you've got to admit, that apart from wine, when it comes to food taboos, the Koran is very similar to the Bible,' Aunt Martha insisted.

'Undeniably! The Prophet is forever saying that before him, Allah sent his messengers to speak to the people. That's why the Creator sent a last message paying tribute to those who came before him. The Prophet sent envoys to the Jews and to the Christians, but, despite the earlier revelations, they wouldn't listen. That's what the Koran says.'

'So is it true what Suleiman said, that no more messengers will come?' asked Theo.

'Careful,' warned Nasra. 'If you go by the Koran, none. But there are countless commentaries, the *hadith*, which make up the *sunna*, the tradition of the Prophet. According to one of the *hadith*, someone will come – the *Mahdi*, which means "the guided one" – who will have the same function as the Hebrews' Messiah. On the whole, believers are not waiting for him in the way the Jews are, they don't believe in his incarnation, like the Christians, they are only waiting for Judgement Day. Then the believers will be rewarded and the infidels will go to hell.'

'Yes, and while we're on the subject of infidels,' Aunt Martha broke in, 'according to the Koran, fighting the infidels is actually an obligation!'

'Are you talking about *Jihad*, holy war?' replied Nasra. 'Do you know that the word primarily means holy militancy, effort in Allah's service?'

'Effort on oneself,' said Theo. 'You see, I haven't forgotten everything.'

'Congratulations, Theo! You understand better than your aunt. What's more, the infidels aren't all non-Muslims!'

'Oh! I know,' said Aunt Martha. 'You're going to tell me that the faithful of the other religions of the Book, Jews and Christians, are tolerated by Islam as long as they pay special taxes. You're going to give me the example of the sultan of the Ottoman Empire who welcomed the Jews with open arms when they were hounded out of Spain by the Inquisition in 1492. I know all that. All the same, if you're animist, Buddhist or Hindu, you'll have to convert to Islam on pain of death!'

'Unfortunately! It's often been called the sixth pillar of Islam. *Jihad* is supposed to be the gateway to Heaven. I prefer the great philosopher Al-Ghazali's version: "It is possible to be a *Jihad* warrior without leaving home." '

'That's a bit simplistic, Nasra. Tell Theo what the Koran says about women. They make such a fuss!'

'Yes, I shouldn't have unveiled myself in front of you, Theo,' laughed Nasra. 'For you are neither my father nor my brother nor a member of my family, and you aren't a little boy any more. Now think. You have to go back to the time before the revelation: the "time of ignorance". It was to men, who were all violent and brutal, that Muhammad spoke first of all. He forbade them to abandon their wives on the slightest excuse. He entreated them, if they divorced, to give their wives material compensation, asked them to be kind to them and, if they beat them, not to be too harsh . . . That gives you an idea of the situation of women in Arabia when the Prophet announced the Word! The Bedouins buried their daughters alive at birth if they felt so inclined . . .'

'All right,' said Aunt Martha. 'And afterwards the Prophet spoke to women.'

'That's true,' she admitted. 'But if you look closely, the Koran is fairly reasonable. Women must be virtuous, good wives, good mothers, lead a decent life, bring their veil down over their breasts and unveil themselves in front of their families. I don't see anything so shocking in that. Do you prefer the naked women on the catwalks of Paris?'

'A naked woman's beautiful,' ventured Theo.

'Does your mother walk around the streets of Paris baring her breasts?' retorted the young woman angrily. 'I'm sure she doesn't. The fact is, there's exaggeration on both sides.'

'Why don't you tell Theo where Muslim exaggeration comes from,' asked Aunt Martha.

'The Muslims have neither pope nor patriarchs to decide on the interpretation of the Koran. The community of believers, the *Umma* in Arabic, has no infallible leader . . . So, for centuries, the learned Muslim doctors have added their commentaries: women must not only cover their breasts, but also their heads and faces. You'll find that as a note in some translations of the Koran. But, in the Book itself, there's nothing of the sort.'

'Why did you take your veil off in front of me?' asked Theo in surprise.

'I adapt to the situation. When I go and visit my friends in India, I don't wear a veil. Nor do I wear one in Europe. But if I stay in a country where people would be shocked, I cover my head with a veil. I'm not a fundamentalist, Theo.'

'So I gathered,' he said. 'And does your husband have several wives?'

'No,' she said. 'Having several wives is called polygamy, which is different from monogamy, the system whereby you can only have one wife. In the Prophet's day, polygamy was usual among the Bedouins. The Prophet himself had twelve wives, but only after the death of his first wife. So the Prophet was monogamous for a long time. Why did he change? Probably because having several wives was the privilege of important chiefs. But, at that time, the Prophet laid down strict laws on polygamy: the number of wives was strictly limited to four, and still is, as long as the believer can afford to keep them. The Koran commands men to honour their wives regularly, in the fairest way: one night each.'

'I can just picture Mum's face if Dad decided to inflict that on her!' cried Theo.

'She wouldn't agree,' said Nasra. 'And quite right too! Oh! I know that there are still learned Muslim commentators around today who will justify polygamy by saying that it's the equivalent of the European social welfare system, that it constitutes a reliable guarantee for women who would otherwise live in solitude and destitution. That means they don't have the right to be financially independent, and so they can't work! It doesn't suit me. I work. I earn my own living. Anyway, my husband's not Muslim, he's Christian.'

'Heretic!' thundered Aunt Martha. 'Infidel! According to the Koran, a Muslim man can marry a Jewish or Christian woman, but not the other way round!'

'Because the commentators on the Koran are stuck in the dark ages,' sighed Nasra. 'The recommendations concerning women haven't changed since Muhammad's day. What's more, they've been adapted to suit different countries. In one, it's forbidden to educate girls, whereas it is possible elsewhere. Some governments impose monogamy, some don't. Allah is one, but the believers are divided.'

'Them as well?' exclaimed Theo in surprise.

The many branches of Islam

Just like all the others. After the death of the Prophet . . .

'Don't tell me!' cried Theo. 'I'll tell you what happened. His successors fought each other to seize power.'

Of course. Who was going to govern the Muslim community? Who would be the caliph, ruler of the Islamic world? On 8 June, in the year 632, the very night of the death of the Prophet, while his wife Aisha 'the beloved' was still weeping, three factions confronted each other. The people of Medina, the Prophet's companions and his closest heir, and Ali, his son-in-law and cousin. This third group immediately found a name, simply *shi'at 'Ali*, 'party of 'Ali'. Some years later, another party broke away because they felt Ali was too weak to lead the community of the faithful, or *Kharijites*. A little later, one of them stabbed Ali, and his son Hussein was brutally murdered during a battle between rival factions.

Muslims had killed the grandson of the Prophet himself! Then Muslims divided into two irreconcilable branches: one followed the Sunna, the words and the acts of the Prophet, appointing their leader by unanimous consensus of the community; and the other was that of the murdered legitimate heir, the Party, *shi'at 'Ali*. After that, those who followed the Sunna became 'Sunnis', and those loyal to the Party, 'Shiites'.

The Sunni caliphs asked scholars to lay down rules of Islam, making peace and solidarity within the community a priority. Sunnism came to dominate the Muslim world. But the bloody battle had divided Islam: the Sunnis, for whom Hussein was only a warrior who had died in battle, and the Shiites, for whom the legitimate heir of the Prophet had become a holy martyr. The Shiites commemorated Hussein's cruel martyrdom each year by holding huge processions during which they re-enacted his wounds and injuries, flagellating themselves and some-times cutting their flesh to make themselves bleed.

'That's something else,' muttered Theo. 'I hope they don't still do that!'

Yes they do. Especially in countries where poverty triggers extreme passions that enable people to express their suffering and thus find temporary relief . . . but the history of the Shiites did not stop with Hussein's martyrdom. At first, they had their imams, their leaders. Then, secondary branches broke off from the original Shiite branch, always at that difficult moment when an imam died, which always raised the dreaded question of who was the Prophet's true descendant. After the death of the seventh imam, some chose to support an imam called Ismail, against the wishes of the others. Ismail died before his father. So who was to succeed him? Faced with this insoluble problem, the 'Ismailis' decided that Ismail wasn't dead and that he would return one day.

'A sort of Messiah,' observed Theo.

So the Ismailis eagerly awaited the Great Resurrection. One day, in 1090, it was solemnly proclaimed by the imam Hasan, in the midst of the Ramadan fast, at a place situated in what is now Iran. The scene was amazing. In the main square of the mountain fortress of Alamut, the imam Hasan had a dais built facing away from Mecca, and addressed the people of the worlds, jinns, men and angels, to announce the existence of the 'Resurrector' personified in himself. Then he made them break the fast and celebrate, doubly transgressing the pillars of Islam: first by making the throne face away from Mecca, and then by breaking Ramadan. The imam Hasan had become the master of truth, the only person with the power to transmit the doctrine.

'Honestly, no religion can resist temptation,' commented Theo. 'It's so good to be the one and only!'

The Ismailis broke clean away from the main branch. The West knew them above all under the name of 'Assassins', for during a turbulent period of their long history a sect born from the Resurrection of Alamut had raised terrorism to the rank of holy action. It was thought that the 'Assassins' acted under the influence of hashish, and that their name came from the effects of the heavenly substance, but according to others the word assassin may derive from the Arabic word *hashishi*, which means 'sectarian'.

'Could they possibly be the inspiration behind the terrorists?' suggested Theo.

The collective violence of the Ismailis could be explained by the imminence of the Resurrection: these new-style Muslims were in a hurry to act, spurred on by the urgency of a world to be conquered. Their doctrine included a public part, based on a cyclical history divided into seven periods, each one announced by a Messenger, the *natiq*, and personified by a 'fundamental man', then by an imam who was master of the hidden truth. For the other part of the doctrine was secret: it was the hidden meaning of the Koran, which would be revealed on the last day, but which the initiated could decipher during their lifetime. After centuries of ups and downs, in the nineteenth century, the Ismailis took refuge in Bombay, in India, under the authority of their leader, the Aga Khan.

'Hey, Aunt M., you forgot the Ismailis when we were in India!' cried Theo.

Aunt Martha protested that, different though they were, the Ismailis were still Muslims, and that besides, they weren't the only ones to have invented their own prophets. The same thing happened to the Shiites when they were once again confronted with an insoluble problem of genealogy: for the eleventh imam died without any heirs. Who would be the twelfth?

'A Holy Book, like the Sikhs?' suggested Theo.

'No,' replied Nasra. 'The Shiites began to wait for their twelfth imam. He was simply hidden from the eyes of men. Sometimes, he moved anonymously among them, but nobody knew his face. One day, he would return to earth . . .'

'Here we go again,' commented Theo.

And again! For the Druze sect was also waiting for the return of the Imam al-Hakim, a strange character who disappeared from his palace one day in 1021. The Druze had their own book, the Epistles of Wisdom; their customs remained extremely secret. But the Shiites had neither the activist impatience of the Ismailis nor the Druze taste for obscurity.

'You have to understand, Theo, the history of Islam is full of surprises,' sighed Nasra. 'The Shiite theology developed around the long absence of the twelfth imam, based on the concept of a single God, the revelation of Muhammad and the legitimacy of the descendants of Ali, the Prophet's son-in-law and cousin, who will one day be reincarnated in the twelfth imam, which is why they are sometimes called "Twelvers". Their faith is more radical than that of the Sunnis, and their hopes wilder . . . For the Shiites believe in the existence of those holy imams with a pure heart, supreme religious leaders, and distant descendants of Hussein the martyr, whose role is to guide humanity on the path to salvation. Obedience to the imams is a holy obligation . . .'

'I don't like the sound of that,' said Theo. 'Blind obedience always spells trouble!'

'Don't be so hasty in your judgement, please,' replied Nasra. 'In Iran, the wait for the twelfth imam sparked off a revolutionary desire for equality, which culminated in 1979 with the Islamic Revolution, when Ayatollah Khomeini flew back and, ignoring Shiite dogma, the crowds in Tehran began to cry "The Imam has come!"'

'Fine,' said Theo, 'but that sounds like messianism and all that stuff. I thought Muhammad was the last Prophet . . .'

'That's exactly the view of the Sunnis who on the one hand respect the Koran in its entirety, and on the other the tradition of the *hadith*. The Koran contains the *Sharia*, the Koranic law. But the whole interpretation of the Koran is a major question, given the lack of an infallible pope to pronounce on its practical applications . . .'

'Seen in that light, the Pope's not such a bad thing,' said Theo thoughtfully. 'Except that women aren't necessarily treated any better by the Catholic Church.'

Nasra pointed out that in twentieth-century Islam there were two trends which had nothing in common with the previous splits. One tendency wanted to stick to the letter of the Koran and follow the *Sharia* in every detail. Those who followed this religious policy had moved from respecting the fundamentals of the Koran to fundamentalism: all or nothing! The second tendency, on the other hand, known as reformist, claimed that the Prophet had managed to tailor his message to the society of his time: therefore there was no reason why the Koran could not be modernized to suit modern times.

'You don't hear very much of them, do you!' exclaimed Theo.

'Because they don't plant bombs and are content just to publish their books! In my view, it's a great mistake to ignore them, for they are trying to put an end to the divisions among Muslims. They often have tremendous clashes with the fundamentalists, who believe there is nothing more dangerous than the modernization of the Koran. And lastly, Theo, I have to tell you there's one more branch of Islam, as old as the Koran, and which has been in existence as long as the Muslim religion itself, without causing any kind of split.'

'Listen carefully, Theo . . .' whispered Aunt Martha. 'For Nasra has kept the best till last.'

These Muslims lived for the love of Allah, of him alone. In their eyes, all religions loved God: that's why the last branch was that of tolerance. Believers in this branch of Islam did not convert the infidels by might, or by sermons and commentaries either. They weren't waiting for any imam, they didn't talk of resurrection, they simply taught how to find divine love directly.

'Directly?' cried Theo. 'They sound like mystics, like Nizamuddin's Sufi!'

The last branch of Islam was indeed Sufism. But as Sufism was based on the concept of allowing each person to express the love of God in their own way, it took on all sorts of different forms. In India, Theo had heard *qawwali* – devotional singing – but in Turkey, for example, the Sufis had discovered two other ways of communicating with God: dance, and sometimes holy howling. The only thing the Sufi in different parts of the world had in common was the love of God, tolerance, and the *dhikr*, the recital of the name of Allah.

'What about you, where do you fit into all that?' asked Theo.

'Into the last branch,' she replied. 'I'm a Sufi.'

'Not only a Sufi, but a dervish,' added Aunt Martha.

'Do you whirl?' Theo marvelled. 'Show us!'

'It's not a circus act,' snapped the young woman. 'Whirling is loving God. You've still got so much to learn about Islam, Theo. It's such a wonderful religion! Pure love, equality and justice . . .'

'Except that men are more equal than women,' said Theo, standing his ground.

'Women haven't always had the right to become dervishes, and yet I've become one,' said Nasra. 'Islam can change when it has to.'

The pilgrimage to Mecca

'What about the great pilgrimage to Mecca, have you done that?' asked Theo.

'Not yet,' admitted Nasra awkwardly.

For her, it was complicated. *Hajj*, the pilgrimage was required of you only once in a lifetime, for the Prophet himself had only made it twice. On this point, he had shown restraint, as usual. Someone had asked him: 'Do we have to make the pilgrimage each year?' The Prophet didn't reply. The man repeated the question three times. At last, the Prophet spoke: 'If I say yes, it will become compulsory, and you won't be able to do it.' That's why only those believers who could afford it were obliged to make the pilgrimage to Mecca. Nasra wasn't short of money, but she couldn't go there with her Christian husband, and scholars were still arguing over whether a woman can make the pilgrimage without being accompanied by a relative. Nasra wasn't certain that she would be allowed to set foot on the soil of Mecca, where the rulers guarded the holy places jealously . . . Her father, however, was a *hajji*, as those who completed the *hajj* were entitled to be called. He had made the greater pilgrimage, followed the whole route and had done everything by the book. He had even talked to his daughter about it, and she was waiting for the right moment.

'It must be incredibly difficult,' commented Theo.

'Not really, but there are very strict guidelines. You just have to follow the four pillars of the pilgrimage to Mecca.'

'Not more pillars!'

'Islam builds,' she said. 'I'm going to tell you what my father told me. The pillar of the first day is the ritual purification, or *ihram*. It is the first act, the true starting-point. The would-be pilgrim has already arrived in Saudi Arabia, and it is there, in places rigidly stipulated by the Prophet according to the pilgrims' place of origin, that they make a solemn declaration of their intention to go on the pilgrimage. Then, as a sign of equality between pilgrims, they exchange their clothes for two simple lengths of white cloth, one covering the lower part of the body and the other draped over the shoulders, the same for everybody. They pray, then they cut their nails and perfume themselves, for all these activities are forbidden once they are in a state of *ihram*.

'What about your father, did he go via Egypt or Iraq?'

'Patience,' said Nasra. 'In the past, long caravans used to wind their way across the deserts from all four corners of the earth, and the Muslims of Kansu, in China, would take up to three years to reach Mecca. Nowadays, the number of pilgrims is at least two million during the holy month that is reserved for the annual pilgrimage. My father went by plane and changed in a cubicle at Jedda airport. He was amazed: tower blocks have mushroomed all over Mecca and minarets rise up between the mountains of the desert. There's nothing left of the ancient city. But he told me that the plain is dotted with thousands of white tents, not to mention the hotels and inns. There are so many people that the Saudi government, whose sacred duty it is, finds the crowding increasingly hazardous. Sometimes there's trouble! Anyway, it all went well for my father.'

'He was lucky,' said Aunt Martha. 'When you go on your own, be careful!'

'If I do decide to go,' said Nasra. 'I'm not sure I want to obey the instructions of the imams! My father was very keen, but he's a man, so of course . . . Anyway, he particularly enjoyed his ninth day as a pilgrim. They go to Arafat, which means "knowledge" in Arabic. It's the place where Adam and Eve ended up after being thrown out of the Garden of Eden: for Adam had landed in India, and Eve in Yemen. In memory of their reunion, the descendants of Adam and Eve must turn to face their Creator to ask him forgiveness, help and guidance in the future. That is the meaning of the second pillar of the pilgrimage to Mecca. The wonderful thing is, that *hajjis* from all over the world meet at the site of the reunion of the first man and woman. My father described Arafat as a sort of Babel where every language under the sun is spoken! From there, on the morning of the tenth day, he went to Muzdalifa to collect seventy stones.'

'Why all those stones?' queried Theo. 'You can't eat them!'

'No, you throw them. The next day, just outside Mecca, at Mina, the pilgrims stone the *shaitans*, three round pillars symbolizing Iblis, the devil, seven times. On that spot, Adam stoned Iblis and chased him away, or was it Ibrahim and his son Ismail? Anyway, my father stoned

Satan too . . . On the same day, he sacrificed a lamb, shaved his head and was no longer in a state of purity. Only then did he go to Mecca to walk seven times around the Kaaba shrine, where the "Black Stone" representing God's right hand on earth is embedded. This ritual is known as *tawaf*.'

'You must have seen photos of the Kaaba, Theo,' said Aunt Martha.

'I've never heard of it,' he mused. 'A black stone? What does it look like?'

'I'll tell you,' said Nasra. 'The Kaaba is a tall building covered with a black cloth embroidered in gold. But the Black Stone is only 30 centimetres in diameter: three simple pieces of reddish-black rock. Thrown by the Angel Gabriel, the Stone was picked up by the Prophet Ibrahim and his son Ismail when they were building the Kaaba. We don't worship the Black Stone, we don't bow down to it, that would be idolatrous. We walk around it anti-clockwise, reciting prayers. My father kissed the stone and placed his hands on God's right hand as a token of his absolute devotion . . . And so he completed the *tawaf*, the essence of the pilgrimage, his third pillar.'

'Whew!' said Theo. 'I hope that's nearly it!'

'Almost, Theo! There's still the last pillar, going backwards and forwards between Mount Safa and Mount Marwa, on foot, seven times, jumping up and down midway each time.'

'What on earth's that about? Sounds weird!'

'Weirder than you think,' replied Nasra affectionately. 'The story behind this ritual is strange, but so moving! It happened when Ibrahim took his wife Hagar into the desert. At this very place, after Ibrahim left Hagar and his son Ismail in the care of the Almighty, the poor mother rushed to and fro between these two hills looking for water for her thirsty baby, to save his life. Miraculously, water gushed out!'

'Of course,' said Theo. 'Otherwise Ismail's descendants wouldn't be here to make the pilgrimage.'

'The water that saved the child was kept in the holy well of Zamzam, and it is in memory of Hagar's frantic dash back and forth that the pilgrim has to tread the same path. As you can imagine, the holy trail is no longer in the middle of the desert. Mount Safa is covered by a dome. And lastly, after walking the path seven times, my father returned to Mina for three nights, stoning the *shaitans* seven times each day with the famous saved-up pebbles.'

'So you do need a good supply,' remarked Theo. 'Best take a big bag.'

'Then my father went to Medina, Islam's second holy city. The

395

pilgrims wash and perfume themselves there, and go and pray in the holy mosque of the Prophet, a magnificent building, with a floor covered in red and grey patterned carpets, which made a huge impression on my father. He prayed on the Prophet's tomb, then in the cemetery of his ten thousand companions, his children and his wives.'

'Is that the end, this time?'

'Yes! My father claims that these rules seem rigid, but the main thing in his view is the four pillars: the moment of purification, walking seven times around the Black Stone, the seven trips between the two hills, and the prayer at Arafat. Through this solemn ritual you honour Adam and Eve, Hagar and her son Ismail, and the symbol of God's right hand on earth, all in one go. I'm telling you what he told me.'

'The pilgrimage to Mecca is incredibly complicated,' sighed Theo.

'No more than others are,' Aunt Martha chimed in. 'Christians often have to climb massive staircases on their knees, there's no one like the Hindus for making believers walk for days on end. And in China . . .'

'They have to climb the seven thousand steps of the shrine,' interrupted Theo. 'It's always about exhausting the body. I wonder why.'

'To make the spirit humble before God,' replied Nasra with a smile. 'You who didn't know the meaning of the word "Koran", do you know what the word "Islam" means?'

'Actually, I don't, now you mention it,' said Theo.

'The meaning of the word "Islam" in Arabic is crystal-clear: Islam means "SURRENDER". The Creator demands obedience, which is why Islam also means "submission". Islam is not the only religion like that . . . All the rites in the world are tough on the body. Do you know that exhaustion is one of the best ways to achieve ecstasy? No need to be Christian, Buddhist or Muslim to get there. Athletes, mountaineers, and long-distance walkers have all gone through it. After the exhaustion comes illumination: the body is free from pain, the spirit expands, dissolves, and suddenly the light dawns. I'll show you how you can exhaust yourself by whirling.'

'At home, when we're exhausted, we rest. What are these crazy recipes?'

'The West has lost the path of the spirit,' said Nasra gravely. 'All comfort, no effort, a narrow existence. No wonder so many young people get swallowed by sects!'

'By the way, I want to ask you something,' Theo went on, puzzled. 'If I faint and then dance without realizing it, is that what you call the path of the spirit?'

'Without a doubt,' she replied. 'I suppose you're thinking of the Sheikha's dance at Luxor.'

'That's not fair, she already knows everything!' protested Theo. 'I'm being tailed!'

'That's right, you complain,' moaned Aunt Martha. 'Who else has as many guardian angels as you, all over the world?'

Istanbul

Theo kept quiet. The bright sunshine was fading and the sky beyond the windows glowed pink. Islam had come nearer, like a frightening shape in a stormy sky, which, seen from close up, was only a big rain cloud. The teachings of the Koran seemed so simple that it was impossible to imagine so much explosive violence, so much blood shed in its name. Weary of thinking, he leaned on the balcony. Amid the din of the city rose the sound of the tankers' sirens, the roar of the steamships, the hooters, sometimes the faint cry of a gull, like a flute drowned by a vast orchestra. A horde of boats swarmed in the Bosphorus – cargo ships, sailing boats, fishing boats, caïques and ocean liners with fluttering flags. On the other side of the strait, regal Istanbul received the noisy greetings with a majestic indifference. Its hills steeped in legend, its mosques reminders of its epic history, the city with three names sank into an untroubled sleep. Here, nobody prayed for the return of the sun. Secure in its past, the city awaited the dawn.

'Elsewhere, Islam is more austere,' murmured Aunt Martha's voice. 'Like Judaism, it's a religion that was born in the desert. Water changes everything; it softens things. But make no mistake, these domes that shine so brightly in the dark have seen unimaginable brutality carried out in the name of God. Don't forget that before these beautiful mosques, Istanbul was called Byzantium, and that Byzantium was wiped out.'

'It's beautiful, isn't it?' breathed Nasra, placing her arm around Theo's shoulder. 'Yes,' he said in a hushed voice. 'Aunt Martha hates silence. With her, there's always a lesson to be taught . . .'

CHAPTER 23

Love in a Whirl

A visit from Lama Gampo

The next day, Theo woke up in a state of great excitement. Lama Gampo had appeared to him in a dream! At first, the Lama had been laughing, brandishing a piece of paper inscribed with unintelligible numbers. Then he grew to an enormous size and turned into a statue of the Buddha. And finally – but things became a bit vague at this point – he and Dad had taken Theo's mother by the hand, for she was having trouble standing. And yet, it was a happy dream, without a shadow of anxiety.

'Well, there you are!' concluded Aunt Martha. 'Didn't he promise he'd come and visit you in your dreams?'

Theo was baffled, and decided to call his mother to find out if she was all right.

'Mum? How are you? Not so tired? How was the second honeymoon? I mean Bruges, of course! Wonderful? Good . . . Mum . . . do your legs sometimes hurt? A bit? Why? Swollen? Be careful! How did I guess? You won't believe me . . . My lama friend showed me in a dream. He did! Well he was right, wasn't he? . . . Did he show me anything else? I think he was bringing me a bit of good news, well, that's my interpretation. He's right, you say? Good. By the way, Mum, about my twin, can you tell me more about this heredity business? No, wait . . . Tell me now, please! Yes, I am inquisitive, that's the way I am! Yeah, yeah, I'm fine. Me too. Big kiss. I love you . . .'

'She doesn't sound too bad,' Aunt Martha concluded in relief.

399

'She did say her legs were giving her trouble,' murmured Theo. 'How did the Lama know?'

'I haven't met Lama Gampo yet,' sighed Nasra, who was listening very closely. 'He seems to be endowed with extraordinary supernatural powers. We Sufis experience that too: our saints are able to appear in two different parts of the world at the same time.'

'Oh, pull the other one,' replied Theo. 'I don't believe in magic.'

'Fine,' she said, unfazed. 'Some other time. Now it's time to go and see Islam in its own surroundings.'

'But let's begin with Hagia Sophia, if you don't mind,' said Aunt Martha. 'The mosque may be abandoned, but I want Theo to soak up a bit of Byzantine atmosphere.'

The icon – caught between cross and crescent

From the outside, it wasn't the most beautiful of Istanbul's mosques. Hagia Sophia looked like a big squashed animal. But it was inside that the beauty of the mosaics struck you. The huge dome decorated with angels was supported by forty ribs, with windows between them, while fragments of mosaics depicted long figures in dalmatics against a background of old gold.

'Gorgeous mosque,' enthused Theo.

But Nasra saw it differently. Hagia Sophia was not a mere mosque. Built originally by Emperor Constantine, the one who enforced Christianity throughout the Roman Empire and gave his name to the city of Constantinople, Hagia Sophia was not built in commemoration of the holy martyr whose name it appeared to bear. Hagia Sophia, in Greek, was something completely different: supreme wisdom, the feminine representation of the divine soul, half-woman, half-angel. Hagia Sophia was once the biggest basilica of the Oriental Church. Destroyed, rebuilt, burnt down, it had been rebuilt once and for all on the orders of the Emperor Justinian, by ten thousand workers, in 537. On entering the finished basilica, the Emperor, who did not suffer from excessive modesty, cried: 'Praise the Lord who judged me worthy to accomplish such a task. I have conquered you, O Solomon . . .'

'Wow, that was tempting providence, wasn't it?' said Theo.

Especially as, twenty years later, the dome was shattered by an earthquake. Every twenty years, the basilica was destroyed by tremors. Each time it was rebuilt, and each time it was more beautiful. The jewel of the Christian Empire of the Orient, Hagia Sophia mirrored the glorious

image of the imperial order of God at the centre of the world, Constantinople. The principle of Byzantium was simple. At the top of the hierarchy reigned the Emperor, the reflection of God on earth. Amid
unrivalled pomp and circumstance, he was worshipped in his legendary
splendour. 'Christ has given the earthly emperors power over everything,' wrote the chroniclers of the day. 'He is omnipotent, and the
lord on this earth is a reflection of the All-powerful.' Nobody had the
right to criticize the Emperor of Byzantium; in his presence, people
held their tongues and prostrated themselves.

'The opposite of democracy, in other words,' said Theo.

Indeed, nothing was more autocratic than the Byzantine pyramid of
power. But few regimes based on religion were so passionately devoted
to art. Painting icons, building churches and creating mosaics were all
ways of paying tribute both to the Emperor and God.

But Islam spread throughout the Byzantine Empire, and the Muslim
taboo on depicting God crossed the borders, gradually influencing the
religion of Byzantium. Eventually, one emperor, Leo III, decided that
the popular zeal for icon worship had gone too far. Didn't the Bible
forbid idolatry? Should Christ be represented by a lamb or by a simple
cross? This scrupulous emperor removed the huge icon depicting Christ
from the main entrance hall of his palace and in its place he erected a
cross. This sparked off a mass movement to destroy icons throughout
the Byzantine Empire, dividing the believers into 'image breakers', the
iconoclasts, and 'image worshippers', the traditionalists.

'The iconoclasts were quite simply thugs,' burst out Aunt Martha.
'They destroyed so many works of art!'

Nasra disagreed. In replacing portraits with crosses, the iconoclast
emperors were bringing Byzantine orthodoxy in line with the pressure
from Islam. The cross was a symbol of unity between all Christians, and
a more powerful means of opposing the crescent of Islam than the
splendid icons of Byzantium. Already, the cross had replaced Christ's
face on the coins circulating outside its frontiers. But in vain . . . After
years of pitched battles between image-breakers and worshippers, the
icon triumphed over the cross. A giant portrait of Christ was set up
once more at the palace entrance, and coins were minted with his
haloed figure. The iconoclasts' cultural revolution was doomed.

Resplendent in its unique glory, Hagia Sophia protected the Western
world from the relentless Muslim attacks. In the shadow of the basilica,
the divine Emperor was in no danger. Until the apocalyptic day in 1453,
when the Turkish conqueror rode into Hagia Sophia on horseback.

'He wasn't too fond of the Orthodox Church,' concluded Theo.

Mehmed the Conqueror was a devout Muslim. The sultan had sworn to capture the capital of Oriental Christianity at all costs. Protected by sturdy ramparts, and by reinforcements from the Christian countries, the city resisted. The siege went on for ages. The fearsome cannon 'Shahi', the Redoutable, cast at Andrianople and pulled by four hundred buffalo, burst under the impact of its own cannon balls, but the Sultan did not give up. A sign spurred him on: an old Sufi sheikh dreamed that a famous companion of the Prophet, Eyüp El Ensari, who had protected him during his stay in Medina, was buried under the wall of Constantinople. In this premonition, the Sheikh and the Sultan appeared side by side in the presence of Muhammad, who raised the red shawl covering his face and said: 'I entrust to you, O Mehmed, the flag of Eyüp El Ensari.' Then the red shawl turned into a green standard. Meanwhile in Byzantium the icons of the Virgin were being smashed amid terrible turmoil.

The Sultan had his men dig up the ground, and the saint's tomb was unearthed. Then, in order to attack Byzantium from its exposed north-eastern side, the Sultan had seventy ships hauled over the hills on enormous wooden runners. Dragged by a workforce of thousands, the Conqueror's fleet was moved from the Bosphorus to the Golden Horn, from which the city was vulnerable. Constantinople fell. The last emperor of Byzantium was killed in the battle, identifiable only by his imperial garb, embroidered with gold. Mehmed had promised his troops free rein to pillage. Once Constantinople had been sacked, the Sultan entered Hagia Sophia where bodies where strewn everywhere.

The next day, the crescent supplanted the cross, the basilica became a mosque, and Constantinople was called Istanbul. The angels and saints were covered over with white roughcast, the name of Allah was inscribed, religion changed both God and symbols. Hagia Sophia remained a mosque until 1935, when Ataturk, the father of modern Turkey and passionately secular, decided to close down the mosque and remove the roughcast from the mosaics of Byzantium. Hagia Sophia became a museum.

'Sometimes,' said Nasra, 'there's talk of restoring the famous basilica to Islam; but there's a lot of uncertainty, for in the city of Istanbul there is no finer example of the symbol of the conversion of the Christian Orient to Islam.'

'And what do you think?' asked Theo.

'There is no God but God,' replied Nasra. 'I'm not interested in the rest. I see God's love in it, as it is, even closed down. I love seeing the name of Allah and the Byzantine angels together, the crescent and the cross side by side.'

Five times a day

Theo remained pensive. What difference was there between Christ's face and the symbol of the cross? What mystery was hidden there?

'Let me ask you something, Nasra,' he said. 'Why does Islam forbid images?'

'For the same reason as Judaism,' she replied. 'Because it is forbidden to make images of the Creator. The God of the Jews never showed himself, he made himself heard, which is not the same. The Bible strictly forbids the representation of God. The same goes for us. God is above humanity. But if you give him Christ's face, then he becomes a man.'

'Exactly!' cried Theo. 'It's much easier to identify with Christ's sorrowful gaze!'

'If you believe that he is the Son of God on earth, yes. But if you don't recognize him, it is an affront to God. Worse, it is the return to the age of ignorance, to worshipping idols and sacred stones.'

'By the way, you haven't explained the meaning of the crescent,' Theo broke in. 'I accept that Islam doesn't worship any image of God, but where does this bit of moon come from?'

'Well, I'll tell you. The Prophet got so furious with the sun worship that was common among the polytheists that he chose the moon as the symbol of Islam. Probably the crescent makes sure that the moon won't be mistaken for the sun.'

'I'll tell you what I think,' mumbled Theo, 'I think it's difficult to pray in a void.'

'Oh no it's not,' retorted Nasra. 'Come and see how easy it is, on the other side of the esplanade, in the Blue Mosque. Here, the Muslim art of the arabesque opens the way to divine joy . . .'

The gigantic Blue Mosque, surrounded by six elegant minarets and crowned with dome upon dome rising up to its golden pinnacle, owed its nickname to the bright blue ceramic tiles depicting plant and flower motifs in the interior. In the same way that the gloom of Hagia Sophia evoked its bloody past, the Blue Mosque was bathed in joy. It had not fallen into disuse; at prayer time, mullahs stopped tourists from entering. Nasra conferred with them, and they waited amid the pigeons for the cry of the muezzin, the call to midday prayer.

Soon a crackling loudspeaker blared its message all over the square. '*Allah o akbar . . .*'

'What's he saying?' asked Theo.

'God is most great,' said Nasra, 'there is no god but God and Muhammad is the messenger of God . . . The profession of faith.'

'Words that you heard chanted by the singers at Nizamuddin,' added Aunt Martha.

'But they sang beautifully,' he said.

Nasra let out a huge sigh: how pure the muezzin's voice had once been, in the days before electronic PA systems . . . In front of the fountains, the faithful were beginning their preparations. Each person washed their face and arms, up to the elbows, and then passed their moist hands over their heads before washing their feet up to the ankles.

'They look as though they're scrubbing themselves,' said Theo. 'Do they do that every time?'

'Ablutions are compulsory before each prayer,' replied Nasra. 'They must wash away all impurities before praying to God. But if you're travelling and there's no water, you can use sand, as long as it's clean.'

'Not very hygienic,' commented Theo.

'Impurity isn't only physical, it's also moral. Obviously, as a result of washing five times a day, the Muslims were clean before the Christians . . .'

'Five times a day!' cried Theo in amazement.

'One, morning prayer, when the sky turns pink,' said Nasra, counting on her fingers. 'Two, midday prayer, which is what you see now. Three, afternoon prayer, between three and five o'clock. Four, evening prayer, at sunset. And lastly, night prayer, before dawn, that makes five.'

'So what do people do when they're working?' he protested.

'They go into a separate room, roll out a little prayer mat facing Mecca, ensure that no animal walks across the prayer area and there you are. It doesn't take very long. Let's go in quietly and keep out of the way, at the back.'

As in Jakarta, the faithful performed the same gestures in unison, with impressive discipline, under the guidance of the imam standing in front of a niche. Touch the shoulders with the open palms, cross the left hand over the right and say the prayer. Bend over until the hands are touching the knees, and pray. Straighten up, and recite the prayer. Prostrate yourself completely, touching the ground with your forehead, rise to a kneeling position, pray.

'But why all together?' whispered Theo.

'Wait till we're outside,' murmured Aunt Martha, 'otherwise we'll cause offence.'

Theo quietly watched the rows of backs bowed under the blue light in honour of the invisible and only God. At last, after a final murmur, they stood up and life went on once more with its chaotic rhythm. Prayer was over.

'Can I ask about it now?' whispered Theo.

'Go on,' said Nasra.

'Which direction is Mecca when you're inside the mosque?'

'That's easy,' she replied. 'That's why the niche where the imam stands is there.'

'Why do they all pray in the same way? In churches, some people kneel, others remain seated, some take communion, others don't . . .'

'But everyone has to bow their head when the priest, after the consecration, raises the host representing Christ's body. In Islam, we pray together to express the voice of the community of believers, it's exactly the same thing.'

'Yeah,' he said, unconvinced. 'Five times a day, you haven't got time to forget.'

'Exactly! The prayers do not allow the believer to forget that he belongs to the community. It's done on purpose.'

'So you can't pray on your own?'

'Of course you can. At night, or when you're travelling, you have to. And any time you so wish, you can. But, according to the Koran, the best prayer is the one said in the mosque, among the believers.'

'Do you do it? I haven't seen you prostrating yourself!'

'I have other ways of praying,' she replied, evasively.

'Because you're a Sufi,' he decided. 'You've got your own stuff!'

'You'll see my stuff this evening,' she retorted. 'In the meantime, your aunt asked me to drive you to the hospital to do your tests.'

Ether

The rotund doctor who greeted Theo could not have been kinder, but, as he never stopped talking, he put the needle in the wrong place and had to try again. The white-tiled room stank of ether; Theo gritted his teeth. Between the third and fourth attempts, the doctor noticed that he'd left the top off a bottle and apologized profusely. Finally, he shut up, concentrated and jabbed the needle into the vein.

'The bastard,' groaned Theo when it was over. 'I've got such a bruise!'

'He's a bit of a chatterbox, but a very good doctor,' Nasra assured him. 'With him, you can rely on the results. Here, take your prescription.'

'A prescription?' exclaimed Theo. 'I've got my own medicines!'

'Just read it,' she suggested. 'Perhaps you'll discover medicines you haven't heard of before . . .'

'But we said we wouldn't change treatments,' he replied stubbornly.

'You really have no curiosity,' insisted Aunt Martha.

Theo read the prescription. Beneath the name and address of the hospital, the message was short and sweet: *Go where we came from when your people deported us in our millions.*

'It's not that blabbermouth doctor who wrote this,' he said, turning pale. 'Is it a message?'

'Of course,' replied Aunt Martha. 'Does it shock you?'

'It's not very nice,' murmured Theo. 'My people deported people? The French did?'

'That's what you have to find out,' said Nasra. 'I assure you the message is not lying.'

'Not the immigrants, because they come of their own accord,' Theo reckoned. 'The penal colonies, but they weren't millions . . . Millions, really?'

'Yes, absolutely,' Aunt Martha confirmed. 'You know this story.'

Theo read and re-read the disturbing riddle. Where and when did the French deport people in such large numbers? Suddenly, the truth hit him. The African slaves! The ships dispatched by the French ship-owners. Fatou's Africa. He hung his head.

'I see you've got it,' observed Aunt Martha. 'Now you have to find out which part of Africa we're going to.'

'Senegal,' he murmured. 'Fatou told me of an island where they put the slaves on board in chains.'

'That's it,' she said. 'That's where we'll be in a few days' time.'

To soften the violent impact of the message, Nasra decided that they would go and have lunch in a restaurant overlooking Istanbul's Egyptian Bazaar. The seats were tiled blue and yellow, the atmosphere lively, and the view over the busy port enjoyable, but Theo didn't say a word. Nasra ordered grilled swordfish served on a skillet, and Theo just picked at it. The waiter was concerned, and brought all sorts of dishes, in vain.

'I'm not hungry, and my arm's sore,' he complained.

'Are you sure it's not the message?' asked Aunt Martha. 'I admit it's a tough one. No? Well say something, for goodness sake! You're not tired, are you?'

No reply. The colour was draining from Theo's cheeks. Suddenly, he ran to the toilet and vomited. Nasra calmly held his forehead and wiped his chin. Meanwhile, Aunt Martha was in a flap. Theo unwell again!

'There,' said Nasra, making him sit down. 'You had a nasty shock earlier on. You must drink water, lots of water. Have you got any sugar in your pocket? Suck it. There.'

'I'd like some tea,' murmured Theo. 'Proper tea, like at home.'

That was no simple matter. Nasra explained to the owner, but nothing doing. There was no Earl Grey to be had in the Istanbul bazaar. Finally, Theo gulped down a liquid that vaguely resembled tea. They made the snap decision to go back to Nasra's house for the rest of the afternoon. There, Theo fell asleep with no more ado.

'And to think he hasn't once been taken poorly since Japan,' sighed Aunt Martha. 'What can be the matter with him?'

'No problem there,' said Nasra straight away. 'The smell of ether! That damned doctor had left a bottle uncorked. I nearly fainted on the spot . . .'

'Do you think so? It's given me such a fright!'

'I know so, darling,' said Nasra soothingly. 'But vomiting isn't one of the symptoms, to my knowledge.'

'That's true,' she admitted. 'But supposing he's going down with hepatitis?'

'He'd be running a temperature,' replied Nasra. 'His forehead felt icy, like any child's when he's sick. Vomiting's necessary, you know! You eliminate the bad, you purge the system . . . I think Theo's body knows what it's doing. The ether and the message were too much for him.'

'I hope he's better this evening,' sighed Aunt Martha. 'The Dervish dance might make him ill!'

'Let him be,' replied Nasra. 'Don't treat him as if he's dying. He's entitled to feel a bit off-colour now and then.'

The woollen coat

Nasra was right: towards the end of the afternoon, Theo woke up starving. The young woman served him 'proper' tea and made him eat a bowlful of boiled rice.

'We're going out this evening, I believe?' he asked.

They were going out. They were going to a *tekke*, as the hall where the Dervishes whirled was called. Guests took their seats on a stand overlooking a floor on which the master would direct the ritual movements. For the Dervish dance was a religious ceremony.

'What's the object of the whirling?' he queried. 'To make your head spin?'

No. The Dervishes' dance was nothing like a dizzy waltz, quite the opposite. When it stopped, the Dervish didn't stagger. It took years to learn to whirl, and the practice itself had existed for centuries.

'Will you show me, please,' begged Theo. 'Go on, just a little.'

Nasra stood up and placed one of her bare feet over the other. Then she raised one arm, her palm upturned, and extended the other, palm downwards. Then she spun on both crossed feet and began to whirl slowly on the spot.

'I can't go any further,' she sighed as she stopped. 'Because before we whirl, we need music. My master isn't here and I'm not in a state of prayer. What I can tell you is why we place one foot on top of the other.'

The story went back to the thirteenth century, when the founder of the Dervish sect Jalal al-Din al-Rumi, who was called the Mawlana, our Master, had collected a group of keen disciples united by the love of God. Among them was a cook. One day, while the Dervishes were whirling, the cook was so overwhelmed with love for his master that he forgot his ovens and burned his foot badly when he dropped a piping-hot dish. So as not to interrupt the prayer, he simply placed his other foot on top of the burned one. Moved by such a sacrifice, the Master decided to honour him: and it was in memory of this humble cook that the Dervishes began their dance by placing one foot on top of the other.

'Hang on a minute,' said Theo. 'Do you love God, or the Master?'

That was a key question, for Sufis sought divine love through the person of a living master. No prayers without the master to teach the Sufi spirit, no Sufi without the master. The master was merely an instrument of God. They owed him obedience, especially when he spoke words that went against common sense and reason. For through the master's strange words came God's messages.

'Weird stuff,' said Theo. 'There's something of the absurd, like in Zen, love, like in Russia, surrender, since it's Islam . . .'

'And complete abandonment, like in yoga,' Nasra went on. 'We say that the disciple in the hands of the master is like a corpse in the hands of the gravedigger. You've had yoga lessons, haven't you? Remember the last posture, isn't it called the "corpse" position?'

Like the Ismailis and the Shiites, the Sufis found a spiritual guide for the practice of Islam among their fellow men, but they were not awaiting any resurrection, or imam. The master was always the descendant of a long line of masters who had handed down the power to guide the Sufis, forming since the dawn of Islam a shining chain of holy luminaries. For only these inspired guides had the power to combine inside each person the outer aspect of God, mere earthly reflections, and his inner aspect, beyond appearances. Sufis withdrew from the world, and lived in poverty . . .

'You'd never think so to look at you,' said Theo, pointing to Nasra's expensive bracelets.

Yes, well, there was no need to take things too far. In any case, in the ceremonies, the dress was very restrained, and the Sufi had to wear a plain coat. In Sufism, nothing was more important than the coat. Sewn together from odds and ends, it was made of wool, *suf* in Arabic, hence the name 'Sufi', the wearer of a woollen coat, like Moses long ago on Mount Sinai.

'Ah! That coat . . .' said Nasra. 'In one of the most famous commentaries on the Koran, it is written that the Prophet in ecstasy entered Heaven. The Angel Gabriel opened the gates and the Prophet caught sight of a casket. Muhammad asked God's permission to open the casket and find out what was inside: and he found it contained spiritual poverty and a coat. "These are the two things I have chosen for you and your people," said the voice of the Creator. "I only give them to those I love, and I have not created anything that is dearer to me." The Prophet returned to earth and gave the coat to his son-in-law and cousin, Ali, who passed it on to his descendants.'

'And do you wear it?' asked Theo.

'Before the ceremony, yes! It's compulsory. A simple woollen coat that's brown like the earth. You'll see all the Dervishes wearing it. On their heads, they wear a very tall domed hat that symbolizes the tomb, which they never forget. But their clothes are white, the colour of the pilgrimage to Mecca. For, contrary to what people say about us, despite the peculiarities that have led to so much persecution, we Sufis are true Muslims. We love God and we give ourselves to him . . . But, on principle, we think that only the external aspect of God is different from one country to another and from one people to another: as for the inner aspect, it's the same for everyone, universal in its light! It is enough to surrender your personal identity to the master who will guide the soul to its true centre, far from the grasp of appearance . . .'

With a hint of irritation, Aunt Martha pointed out that the relationship between master and disciple was found all over the world. Theo flushed with anger.

'Make up your mind!' he exclaimed. 'Are we or aren't we studying all the different religions? If you mix them all up, how am I supposed to understand anything?'

'By not falling for all the religious twaddle,' she muttered.

'You're a bit too much of an atheist,' said Nasra gently. 'The Sufi doctrine annoys you, I can see, but that's no reason to put other people off.'

'Hear, hear,' concluded Theo. 'Can I ask some questions?'

Beyond 'I' and 'You'

Nasra flashed him a brilliant smile.

'What is the centre of the soul?'

'I'm going to reply in verse,' she said. 'Listen to this poem by the Sufi Shabestari:

> ' "I" and "you" are the veil
> that Hell between them wove.
> When this veil in front of you is raised, nothing remains
> of the sects and the credos that fettered us.
> All the authority of laws can bear only
> upon your "I" linked to your body and your soul.
> When the "I" and the "you" are no longer between us
> What are the mosque, temple of Fire or synagogue?'

'Not bad,' he conceded. 'But when is the moment when the "I" and the "you" no longer come between two people?'

'The moment of love,' she replied. 'When two people love each other so deeply that they form one being. That's what happened to the master who founded the order of the Dervishes, the Mawlana. In his youth, he had been just a very traditional Muslim theologian until he met a wandering mystic called Shams al-Din of Tabriz. This Sufi drunk on God came from nowhere; he would reach ecstasy dancing to the sound of the reed pipe. The future Mawlana fell passionately in love with Shams al-Din of Tabriz. Then, one day, Shams vanished, probably murdered by rivals. The Mawlana sought him as one seeks God, but he never returned. The Mawlana could not find words to describe the love he had for this man: a divine union, that led to God.'

'So he was gay, then?' observed Theo.

'It's not important. That kind of love goes far beyond gender. The greatest Sufi in Islam was an Iranian woman.'

'In Iran?' exclaimed Aunt Martha sarkily. 'Well, well!'

'More ignorance! In the eighth century, Rabia was the greatest saint in the Muslim world. All her life, she lived in poverty, consumed with divine love. Sultans came to visit her from afar, scientists admired her, but she barely looked at them. One day, she did not even notice that a splinter had pierced her eye. No pain . . .'

'We've got saints like that in Christianity,' mumbled Aunt Martha. 'It's not only Islam.'

'The love of the Sufis doesn't exclude any religion, I tell you!' cried Nasra, who was getting irritated.

'Divine love, OK, but what about love between a man and a woman?' asked Theo.

'Why should that be forbidden? Do you know the most beautiful love story in all Islam?'

'Cool, is there one?' exclaimed Theo. 'Tell me!'

'Two children loved each other tenderly,' began Nasra. 'But, following custom, the little girl, whose name was Leyla, was married off very young by her father to another man. The boy was supposed to step aside.'

'Why?'

'Because, in Arab society, the father had complete power over his daughters. You didn't argue with his decisions, and love outside marriage is forbidden. Do you know that, under Islamic law, adultery can be punishable by death?'

'Not "can be", it *is* punishable by death,' Theo blurted out. 'I've seen photos! They stone lovers to death!'

'Not in all Muslim countries! Anyway, you understand why our young man would have done better to resign himself. But he didn't! Condemned by society, he stood his ground. He hung around Leyla's house singing of his love with such despair that soon everybody thought he must have lost his mind. The young man thus became "Majnun", the demented one.'

'That's what the children in Jerusalem called after the madmen who thought they were the Messiah,' said Theo.

'There you are! Majnun longed for Leyla as his Messiah . . . He roamed the desert wailing his love for Leyla to the stars, and he died of it. So did she. The inflexible Arab society bowed to the power of a love that had nothing to do with sex and everything to do with the divine flame

411

of holy madness. The story of Majnun and Leyla is still told throughout the Arab Muslim world. That's what love is.'

'As a matter of fact, I prefer Romeo,' said Theo. 'At least he gets to sleep with Juliet.'

'But Romeo wasn't interested in God, whereas Sufis are passionately concerned with the love of God, whichever God he may be. Hatif Isfahani, a Sufi from Persia, fell in love with a Christian woman and accompanied her to church. "Oh you who hold my soul ensnared in her net," he said to her during mass, "each hair of mine stays fastened to your belt! How much longer will you impose on Him who is one the shame of the Trinity? How can the one true God be called both Father and Son and Holy Ghost?"'

'You tell me,' said Theo. 'I bet the Christian woman didn't answer.'

'Oh yes she did, "with a loving smile, as sweet as syrup," said the poet. Listen . . . "If you know the secret of Divine Unity, do not brand us infidels. The eternal beauty in three mirrors sends one pure, dazzling ray of His light." Then the church bell started ringing, and the poet concluded: "Its chimes said to us: "He is One, and he nothing but Himself. There is no other God."'

'So he had the last word,' said Theo.

'But she had replied, and he had understood,' said Nasra with a smile. 'That's an example of our tolerance.'

'Well! Now Theo knows enough to go and watch the Dervishes dance,' said Aunt Martha, rising to her feet.

'Not yet,' said Nasra. 'Two more points. The ceremony you will see is called the *Sama*. The word is impossible to translate literally. Let's call it "hearing" or "listening" if you like. You enter the *Sama*, and it can take you over . . . Some Dervishes in a state of *Sama* tear their clothes and sob. In Iraq, others roll in the embers, or eat them while they're still red hot, or pierce their arms and cheeks without shedding one drop of blood.'

'We won't be seeing that, will we, Aunt Martha?' murmured Theo.

'No you won't,' said Nasra. 'Our *Sama* has nothing in common with these wild trances. We listen to the divine flute, and that is what guides us, strung into a circle at the centre of ourselves. We form a circle around the central star, the invisible face of God. That is why Dervishes whirl like planets in space. The reason they have one hand turned upwards and the other downwards is because their body is the axis that links the two worlds.'

'Like a power circuit,' said Theo.

'Like a metal that conducts electricity,' she concluded. 'The other thing I wanted to explain is the meaning of the songs that precede the dance: "Bid farewell to reason, farewell, farewell, farewell . . ."'

'Ah! My message is complete,' said Theo. 'Bidding farewell to reason, I honestly didn't get it. Another thing where you have to lose your mind!'

'Quite the opposite! You have to find it . . .'

The spinning planets

It was time to go and meet the Dervishes. Muffled up in her Sufi coat, Nasra was silent. Aunt Martha and Theo did not dare disturb her. People filed quietly into the *tekke* and took their seats in the stand, behind the carved wooden balcony. Nasra had warned them: it wasn't 'her' *tekke*, because her master wasn't there. She would not be whirling, she would participate by watching, and in spirit.

The Dervishes entered one by one, barefoot, their arms crossed, dressed in their brown mantles. The master stood in a woollen coat the colour of earth. A sweet, eerie sound cut the air . . . and Nasra's face lit up.

'The music from that reed pipe is a vital part of Dervish ritual. It laments the separation . . .'

Soft strings, deafening kettledrum, the delicate clash of cymbals, and the *Sama* began. The master moved to the centre of the floor. One by one, the Dervishes removed their coats, then filed past the master to place themselves within his orbit. Their shoulders spread . . . In unison, the dancers crossed their feet, turned one palm skywards and the other towards the ground, and began to whirl, slowly. The full white skirts flared into corrollas, the farewell to reason accelerated . . . The men were no longer human beings, but planets shining around an absent sun, cherry blossom doomed to die, candles on the waters of the river, the Buddha's smile, fugitive light. Aunt Martha's head spun and she closed her eyes, but Theo didn't miss a thing. His eyes glued to the slow, insistent whirl, he was listening to the twin voice, soothing and at peace, that spoke to him from within.

The music faded away and the petals closed up again. Nasra did not move. Aunt Martha opened her eyes and saw Theo's faraway expression.

'Hey!' She shook Nasra's arm. 'Look what a state Theo's in . . .'

'Don't touch him,' she replied, sounding perfectly calm. 'It takes a while for reason to return.'

The Dervishes left one by one. On the empty floor, there was nothing left of the planetary dance. Theo ran his fingers through his hair and emerged with casual ease from his dream.

'Where did you get to?' asked Aunt Martha.

'I was here,' he said. 'At the centre. It isn't hard to do.'

'And your twin came too?' she guessed.

'That's right,' he beamed. 'And about time too . . .'

'We are all two,' said Nasra. 'We all have an outer face and a hidden one.'

CHAPTER 24

The Book or the Word?

The work of the mystics

Theo went to bed without saying a word. Aunt Martha slid between the sheets, switched off the light and prepared to go to sleep . . .

'Can I talk to you for a bit?'

'Of course. Do you want me to put the light on?'

'No! I prefer it dark. Is Nasra a mystic?'

'Probably, since she's a Dervish. Why do you ask?'

'Because she said she worked. What's her job?'

'She works at the headquarters of the United Nations High Commission for Refugees, based in Geneva. They take care of refugees all over the world.'

'I bet they're kept busy,' reflected Theo. 'But what does she do in Istanbul?'

'When she's on leave, Nasra comes to join her sheikh. But she's always got her mobile phone with her . . . The rest of the time, she's always off on missions.'

'So you can be a mystic and work,' said Theo pensively. 'I thought you had to be cut off from the world.'

'Not in Islam. The idea of the Community of believers rarely permits isolation. The best prayer is collective, as you saw. Other religions share out prayer between those who are "in the world" and those who withdraw from it. Some Christian monks shut themselves up in their monasteries and are forbidden to speak to each other. The same goes

415

for some orders of nuns . . . In the Christian tradition, the religious orders lead what is known as the contemplative life, because they have only one occupation: praying.'

'Not much use,' Theo commented. 'Leaving the work to everyone else . . .'

'That's not what they think! The prayer of the contemplants rises as much on their behalf as for the sake of the "active" orders. It's a different concept of community: each person carries out their own duty towards God. Look at the Hindus: when they've finished raising their children, they're allowed to leave their family and become "renouncers" roaming the highways . . . Buddhists have their monasteries, and Taoists a preference for solitary retreat. It's not the same with Nasra. She has two types of work. Here in Istanbul she whirls for God, while elsewhere she's a Muslim wife who works.'

'What does her husband do?'

'He's a Swiss industrialist, a decent man who lets her have her freedom. When she gets away to join her master, he never comes with her.'

'Wow, he's not the jealous kind, is he?'

'He knows his wife. Can you imagine Nasra being unfaithful? Impossible!'

'Well I think she's having an affair with God,' he declared. 'Did you see her eyes when we came out of the *tekke*?'

'In that case, there are millions of very pious wives who are unfaithful to their husbands with God . . . From what you say, you prefer real nuns!'

'Yes,' he agreed. 'At least they're legally married to God. What about me? Am I a mystic?'

'You . . . you're an odd customer. You're forever drifting off into a daze, as if you're in a dream! Is your head back to normal now?'

'I can't say. I like it when I go into a daze. By the way, I didn't tell you the best thing! My twin is a girl!'

'How do you know?' she exclaimed, sitting up in bed.

'I know because earlier she whispered it inside me,' he said calmly. 'She said I should ask Mum what her name is. I think Mum's hiding something from me, don't you? A baby cousin who died, maybe?'

'Rub . . . bish,' she replied, overcome by a coughing fit. 'It's . . . your illness.'

'Bet you I'm cured,' said Theo. 'Still, I'll ask Mum all the same.'

Aunt Martha settled down again, and, lying through her teeth, announced that she was sleepy. Theo tried to continue the conversation, but she pretended to snore.

The revelation

The next day, Nasra received a call from the garrulous doctor. The results were astounding: the illness had suddenly regressed. Nasra kissed Theo, regardless of Muslim law, and headed into the kitchen to prepare something to celebrate the good news with.

'You see, I was right,' observed Theo. 'That's why Blessed Lightning looked so pleased! The sheet of paper in my dream was the results of my tests . . .'

'Hold it,' said Aunt Martha. 'Phone your mother now!'

On the phone, Theo struggled to sound calm, but felt far from it, for naturally Melina sobbed her heart out. Suddenly, Martha's ears pricked up.

'. . . Well, are you going to tell me?' demanded Theo. 'Oh, so you know her? Who is she? My twin? I know that, thank you . . . A real one? What do you mean? Wait, say that again . . . Ah . . . All right. No, it's no problem. Why didn't you tell me before? Poor Mum. No, of course I'm not angry. No, you weren't wrong. Stop it! It's not your fault! Just give me another one! Another what? A little sister, hey . . . that's an idea . . .'

When he hung up, Theo was a little pale. He went to sit beside Aunt Martha and nestled against her.

'My twin sister died at birth, just after I was born,' he murmured. 'Did you know about it?'

'I didn't know it was a girl,' confessed Aunt Martha. 'So she told you in the end? That's good. Now you know why you've got a twin inside you.'

'But if she talks to me, she can't be dead. I mean, not completely.'

'You don't sound surprised . . .'

'I'm not stupid. I just want to understand how this thing works. Dead people come and live inside your body?'

'In Africa, you see it everywhere,' she replied. 'And the Africans could be right.'

'Do you think she'll stay with me all my life?' asked Theo anxiously. 'It's not that she bothers me, but all the same!'

'She'll leave when you're better,' Aunt Martha reassured him. 'I bet you she's come to help you.'

'Maybe. Last night, it was as though she knew the results. She was so calm!'

'Enough,' she broke in. 'Don't hang around too long in the realm of the dead. You've come so far already.'

'Huh! I've seen some places, and everywhere people take notice of the dead, except at home. Granny Theano is always going to the cemetery. We never do. What if that's not a good idea?'

'Wait till you get to Africa. They'd think it's no good at all,' she replied with a smile.

While Theo's results hadn't turned Istanbul upside-down, it was a different story in Paris. Jerome called from the lab ten minutes later, demanded to hear the whole report read out, took the phone number of the garrulous doctor, expressed doubts as to the reliability of the tests and suggested a repeat, much to the fury of Theo, who gave such a graphic description of the bruises made by the doctor's needle that his father gave in. At lunchtime, the girls phoned because they were feeling so glad. He just had time to pay a visit to the famous Palace of the Sultans, and then it was Fatou's turn. She said nothing, but laughed for joy.

'What's got into them all,' asked Theo in amazement. 'They've all gone mad!'

'Give them time to get used to it,' advised Aunt Martha. 'They're unbelievers!'

'Except Fatou!' protested Theo. 'I've still got her grigris . . .'

'Grigris?' said Nasra. 'I see you're wearing one grigri round your neck, as well as a Koran. It's not the same thing. Islam is protecting you, Theo!'

'Hang on a sec, Miss Islam . . . You can't sweet-talk me. OK, you're the most beautiful houri in Allah's Paradise, but that doesn't mean you'll have me eating out of your hand!'

'Talks tough too!' laughed Nasra.

The rest of the week was spent in delightful walks. Nasra took her friends to the Mosque of Eyüp, where the believers pressed up against the walls of the saint's tomb, like those at Nizamuddin's shrine. The pigeons pecked at the grains of sugar that leaked from the offerings, and Theo bought an exquisite calligraphy of the name of Allah, with gold letters on a black background. They hired a caïque that took them cruising along the shores lined with ancient villas whose balconies overlooked the water. The cemeteries were poetic, the mosques welcoming, and the swordfish delicious. After protracted conversations with the garrulous doctor, Jerome had cooled off. He was all set to decide that the trip might as well end there and then, seeing that Theo was cured, but Aunt Martha sorted him out. If he came home now, Theo would fall ill again, she was certain of that.

An argument about Black Islam

A few days later, Aunt Martha announced they were leaving for Black Africa.

'You mean African Islam,' Nasra corrected her. 'Senegal is a Muslim country.'

'The oldest democracy in Africa,' Aunt Martha pursued. 'Completely secular.'

'And all the inhabitants are Muslims,' said Nasra.

'No,' replied Aunt Martha. 'You're forgetting the Christians and the animists.'

'No I'm not,' she said. 'All the same, most Senegalese are not only Muslims, but Sufis.'

'Again!' cried Theo. 'African Sufis?'

'Yes,' said Nasra.

'No!' cried Aunt Martha.

Battle raged between the two friends. Nasra claimed that the Muslims of Senegal were genuine Sufis, while Aunt Martha maintained that they were Sufis only in name. Nasra insisted that the sheikhs of Senegal had inherited the tradition of the love of God, Aunt Martha replied that they had substituted the obedience of disciples for love, and the argument hotted up.

'Hey, girls, that's enough!' exclaimed Theo. 'I'm big enough to make up my own mind. Shut up or else . . .'

At this admonition, the two women exchanged sheepish stares.

'Well honestly,' muttered Theo. 'You're not going to turn into fundamentalists on our last evening, are you!'

The heat cooled down. Filled with remorse, Nasra rushed over on her tiny bare feet and kissed Aunt Martha to ask forgiveness.

'I'm going to miss you,' she cooed, holding out her hand to Theo. 'We've been so happy, the three of us.'

'Have you noticed, Aunt Martha?' asked Theo, delighted. 'They all say the same thing!'

'Big-head,' she scolded. 'Go and pack your bags, now you're better.'

'You're my houri with kohl-rimmed eyes,' he whispered in Nasra's ear as she laughingly fended him off.

Their departure from Istanbul was just like all the others. A slim figure waved a scarf at the airport before disappearing under the wings of the plane. For once, Aunt Martha brushed away a tear. Theo gazed out over the Sea of Marmara for the last time.

Peanuts and prayers

As he stepped out onto the gangway at Dakar, Theo felt a gust of hot air.

'Put your hat on,' commanded Aunt Martha. 'The sun's as strong as in Egypt. Keep moving, we're being met and we don't want to be late.'

'Man or woman?' asked Theo.

'Man. Someone you know well.'

Talk about a big surprise. The person meeting them turned out to be none other than Mr Abdoulaye Diop, Fatou's dad wearing a suit and tie, despite the heat.

'How're you doing?' he said, lifting Theo up as if he were a feather. 'Your parents told me to take good care of you. How are you, Martha?'

'Very well, thank you,' replied Aunt Martha. 'And how's your family?'

'Fine,' replied Mr Diop, smiling. 'Let's get your luggage and go to my house. Everyone's waiting for you.'

The streets of Dakar were thronged with men in kaftans and turbaned women in *boubous*, revealing their plump shoulders. Sitting on the pavement, women roasted peanuts by tossing them in scorching hot sand at the bottom of a big iron pot. Hawkers sold plastic watering cans, fluorescent sandals, bags of apples, mosquito nets and cigarette lighters. At each street corner stood a beggar child with huge, appealing eyes. Mr Diop looked away; Aunt Martha began to grumble.

'You see, Theo,' she began, 'these little beggars are called *talibs* . . .'

'Which means "student",' interjected Abdoulaye Diop.

'Yes, like the word "Taliban" in Afghanistan . . . You're not going to tell me that these children are studying while begging in the streets! That's disgraceful!'

'No, they don't study,' sighed Abdoulaye Diop. 'But let me tell you that the tradition of our Sufi brotherhoods can't be summed up by a few stray children.'

'Funny,' said Theo. 'In Istanbul, my aunt and her friend Nasra have already had that argument. Can you explain it to me, Abdoulaye?'

'Of course,' he replied. 'Senegal is divided between four Sufi brotherhoods . . .'

'A brotherhood,' said Theo, 'I saw one of those on telly. They're people dressed up in medieval costume who get together and drink wine. I don't see the connection!'

There wasn't one. As the name indicated, a brotherhood brought together a group of brothers who shared a common belief. Although you might say that French wine was a shared religion, the faith of Islam united numerous believers all over the world in different brotherhoods for a much more serious purpose. In the Muslim regions of Africa, there were Sufi brotherhoods that each united countless believers around a master. This was the case in Senegal, a country where Sufi Islam had unified the many peoples, including the Fulani, the Tukulor, the Lebu, the Mandingue, and lastly the Wolof who made up the majority of believers.

The most ancient brotherhood, the Qadiriyyah, came directly from Baghdad, and from a Sufi school dating back to the twelfth century. The second, that of the illustrious and highly respected Tijaniyyah, had spread throughout the Sahel from the Maghreb under the leadership of a sheikh born in Algeria, who died in Fez in 1815. In the twentieth century, the greatest spiritual master of the Tijaniyyah brotherhood was Tierno Bokar from Mali, the 'Sage of Bandiagara', an enlightened thinker. The third brotherhood in Senegal, that of the 'Layens', followed a new African Prophet, Seydina Laye, sent to the Black race by God, in the nineteenth century. But the last one was something else! It owed its existence to an exceptional African, Amadou Bamba, founder of the Murid sect whose name meant 'religious aspirant'.

Aunt Martha protested. Certainly, the four venerable caliphs from the four brotherhoods exercised a considerable influence, and were respected by the democratic authorities, but while their personal spirituality was undeniable, the heavy supervision of the faithful by the lesser officials was not always so admirable . . . As for the Murids, remember that the founder of the brotherhood had been one of the first to rebel against colonial France, and had been deported to Gabon for political reasons: that was the crucial factor.

Not at all! replied Abdoulaye. Sheikh Amadou Bamba was not interested in overthrowing the colonial power. This grand master had only one goal, and that was to improve the faith of the believers. On his deathbed, his father, a very pious man, had entrusted the fate of his Muslim brothers into his hands, and so the young man had become a theologian within the very ancient Qadiriyyah brotherhood. But he was only interested in meditation. He used to disappear into the forests: he had a quest – somewhere in the country a sacred place awaited him. One day, guided by a strange light, he set out and halted under a baobab tree, at the place where the ray of light had stopped. In the shade of the tree, he understood that he had reached the centre of his soul. He had 'his own' revelation, and laughed for joy, laughter that roared so loud that farmers heard him thirty kilometres away . . . That day, a son was born to him whose name was Muhammad.

That was all very well and good, Aunt Martha replied, but nobody could deny the existence of fake marabouts, those charlatans who were two a penny in the streets of Dakar. One day, one of her Senegalese friends had shown her an instructive sight. A fake marabout in full ceremonial *boubou* arrived at one end of the street, while at the other end his three associates threw themselves flat as soon as they caught sight of him: 'There's the *grand marabout*!' they murmured. People stopped. Then the marabout launched into a long speech: he didn't need money, he wasn't asking for anything, besides, he was wealthy enough to have three wives already. All he wanted was to come to the assistance of the needy.

'Nice guy,' said Theo. 'So what have you got against him?'

Ah! Well! The marabout declared that he would only take eight people, not one more. People rushed towards him. The marabout chose eight and beckoned them close: he then asked each of them for money for their blessing, five hundred CFA francs per finger and per toe . . . The chosen paid up. Then, as Aunt Martha's friend was watching their antics with a scornful expression, the marabout singled him out: 'For you, I'm going to offer a special prayer,' he said. He shepherded him into a corner and slipped him ten thousand CFA francs to shut him up.

Abdoulaye shrugged. He'd heard hundreds of stories like that! OK, so there were con men, but nobody could mistake them for the marabouts of the brotherhoods. These true marabouts enjoyed considerable prestige and were highly respected. They recognized only one higher authority: their caliph. They exploited no one, they led their disciples, supervised their education and collected the money from their congregations for the benefit of the community. No Senegalese worthy of that name could mistake the authenticity of a real marabout: and if there were fools prepared to fall for anything, that was their hard luck!

Theo, who was listening with half an ear, suddenly heard the deafening beat of tomtoms. Parading down the centre of the main avenue, a group of freaks were dancing and laughing their heads off. These strange creatures in multi-coloured coats and leather necklaces, with shaggy hair and cudgels under their arms, were beating their drums with one hand and waving a gourd with the other, prancing like devils, with demonic grins.

'They're great,' cried Theo. 'A band?'

'Oh no!' replied Abdoulaye Diop. They are Baye Fall. They belong to a particular Murid sect, disciples of Sheikh Amadou Bamba.'

'Why don't you tell the truth?' said Aunt Martha irritably. 'Aren't the Baye Fall in fact a religious militia that protects arable farmers at the herders' expense?'

Abdoulaye Diop patiently explained that the history of the Baye Fall was much more complicated than Aunt Martha thought. A prince of royal blood called Ibra Fall heard of a great mystic living somewhere in Senegal and spent nine years looking for him. But in each village he went through, Ibra Fall, a kindly giant, drew water for the women, cut wood, performed a week's work all by himself . . . and left next day on the trail of the Sheikh. At last, after years of toil and wandering, Ibra Fall found him in the place that was to become the Murids' holy city, Touba. Sheikh Amadou Bamba had decided on the name Touba, which came from a Wolof word meaning 'return to God'. Then, after kneeling at the feet of the master he had sought for so long, Ibra Fall took matters in hand. He protected the Sheikh, kept out intruders, introduced discipline and earned a special status from Amadou Bamba: he would be exempt from prayer, and would work instead. Soon, he had his disciples, the Baye Fall, who called him 'the Prophet'.

The religion of work acquired a frenzied following. The Baye Fall were exempt from prayer, provided they could do the hardest labour. In exchange for this dispensation, they had to beg for the pieces of cloth that would be sewn together, one by one, to make their Sufi robe. Their training was rigorous, their devotion blind. There was one thing that was different about them: of all the Murids, they were the only ones to sing and dance to the rhythm of the tom-tom, in keeping with the country's ancient customs. Baye Fall initiates would gather at night in a circle and enter into a trance, repeating the great Sufi invocation . . .

That was waffle, insisted Aunt Martha. The Baye Fall formed a police force! And as for their work ethic, it demonstrated the essence of Murid-ism. The Murids of Senegal had invented an ingenious system: work was prayer. What a godsend! The pact between master and disciples was straightforward: the master fixed salvation for the disciple if the disciple worked for the master for free. The Murids had a flare for business . . . With the labour force formed by disciples who did not need paying, they developed peanut farming in Senegal, the country's main source of revenue. Then they bought shops, acquired markets . . . In other words, the Murids were formidable traders.

One up to Aunt Martha.

'It was the French colonial governors who recognized the economic value of the Murid system!' protested Abdoulaye Diop. 'They used the Murids to harvest the peanuts . . . It was nothing to do with Sheikh Amadou Bamba!'

'France, exploit Muridism?' retorted Aunt Martha. 'The French sent Sheikh Amadou Bamba into exile!'

'But then they brought him back,' he argued. 'You're mixing up colonial policy and the mystical quest of an inspired sheikh. Like a true Sufi, he refused to collaborate with the French authorities. For Sufis do not bow to political powers: sultan, king, emperor, administrator, president, it makes no difference to them. Sheikh Amadou Bamba preached poverty!'

'Who are you trying to kid?' she snapped. 'All that's because you're a Murid yourself!'

Abdoulaye Diop was furious. The historical documents were incontrovertible . . . As for the bartering system between disciple and master, the Sheikh's idea was perfectly straightforward: education came foremost. In passing on his knowledge, the master gave them a precious asset, and in demanding labour, he trained the disciple for life. And by the way, the master housed his pupil, fed him and found him a wife. Furthermore, Sheikh Amadou Bamba emphasized one essential thing: no disciple worked against his will. With his brotherhood, Sheikh Amadou Bamba had brought order and education into a society plagued by violence and war. Thanks to him, at the time when French colonization was causing social upheaval, the Senegalese people were united, they farmed their own land, reached a compromise with the new masters, made the country richer . . .

'That's all economics,' said Theo. 'What's it got to do with Islam?'

Abdoulaye Diop leapt at the opportunity. Had Aunt Martha read Sheikh Amadou Bamba's mystic poetry? Had she read the *Pathways to Paradise*? She hadn't?

> Pursue your meditation, friend
> On Earth and heaven and also on the stars
> ON SUN AND MOON, AND LIKEWISE ON THE TREES,

On fire, water, and even on the stones.
On still more things, such as the night and day,
Then comes enlightenment and peace of heart.

Abdoulaye Diop had equalized.

'Anyone can write poetry,' mumbled Aunt Martha. 'But calling him a mystic is going a bit far!'

'Well go and visit the Murids' holy city of Touba then!' he countered. 'You'll hear authentic Sufi chants in the monumental mosque, and they are the inspired poems of Sheikh Amadou Bamba!'

'I'm going to settle this,' said Theo. 'Tell me: is there a single religion that doesn't make its believers work?'

Silence fell.

'Yes,' said Abdoulaye Diop. 'All religions, without exception. None of them is based on the requirement to work. Each one defines the path to God in its own way.'

'No,' replied Aunt Martha. 'There's no religion that hasn't been transformed into a means of exploitation. There, I agree with Karl Marx: "Religion is the opium of the people." The people are duped into sweating blood and tears.'

'That's a great help,' Theo went on. 'I have another question. What's African about the Murids?'

Another silence.

'Let's say that black Africa never disappears altogether,' ventured Aunt Martha. 'The brotherhoods in Senegal completed the Islamization of the Wolof people. Before the emergence of the brotherhoods, Wolof values were based on the physical effort of working the land. All Sheikh Amadou Bamba did was to Africanize Islam in his own way. Under Muridism, the Wolof values are very much there.'

'I disagree,' replied Abdoulaye Diop. 'The Wolof had castes and slaves. For example, Sheikh Amadou Bamba caused a scandal in trying to emulate the Prophet, who deliberately married his daughter Zanayda to a former slave. When the Murids were offended, the Sheikh reminded them of the principle of equality in Islam The next day, he promoted a group of lower-caste men to the rank of dignitaries. Sheikh Amadou Bamba truly brought equality to the Wolof people, where it was unheard-of.'

'Hang on, just let me go over that again,' said Theo. '"Senegalese Islam = Sufis + castes + slaves + peanuts." You've lost me. Castes and slaves, in Africa?'

That was how Theo discovered that the whites had not invented slavery in Africa. Wolof society was based on a hierarchy with nobles, free men and slaves. The domestic, who belonged to the mother, lived with the master's family and were not badly treated. The father's slaves were treated as nobodies, had nothing and counted for nothing. And finally, the chief's slaves went with him to war, received their share of the plunder, and were allowed to pillage and terrorize the villages, so much so that the 'free men', the poor farmers, often fell victim to arrogant armed slaves.

'Compare that with feudal Europe,' said Mr Diop. 'The peasants were serfs, under the yoke of feudal lords. If you count the lord's house slaves too, you have two categories of wretches who found in Islam the equality that they craved.'

'There's worse,' broke in Aunt Martha. 'The African kings used to make raids on neighbouring villages to sell their populations on the market. Without them, the whites would never have been able to grow rich on the slave trade: they had their suppliers on the spot.'

'Unfortunately!' sighed Mr Diop. 'The fatal flaw of the Islamic conquest in Africa was the black slave trade, which went on till the nineteenth century. How many African empires were built on the subjugated tribes . . . The empire of Gao reached all the way down to Lower Senegal and up to the Sahara. Chief Kongo Moussa of Mali went on a pilgrimage with a huge retinue of black slaves . . . They were traded for horses, they were put to work in the fields! We criticize the whites for having deported our people, but the truth is, part of the blame lies with Africa, I agree.'

The sons of corpses

They had arrived at the Diops' house, a white villa nestling among the bougainvillaea. Abdoulaye propelled Theo into the dining room where, sitting on a velvet-covered sofa, three turbaned women were fanning themselves in silence.

'My mother, my aunt and my sister Anta,' said Mr Diop, introducing them one by one to Aunt Martha. 'Are the children in bed?'

'Yes, but they're not asleep,' whispered the youngest woman. 'Aminata's wide awake, she's teething.'

'That's normal at her age,' said Abdoulaye. 'If she cries, Anta, you may as well bring her in here.'

The conversation about family matters was so relaxed that Theo felt at home. Abdoulaye disappeared and returned wearing a voluminous white *boubou*, and matching oriental slippers on his feet.

'That's better,' he murmured as he sank onto the sofa. 'Is dinner ready?'

Old Mrs Diop rose with silent dignity, and everyone moved to the table. There was a mountain of millet cous-cous, roast chicken, onion sauce, and boiled vegetables. Theo was ravenous. The women spoke little, or conversed in low voices. Amazingly, Aunt Martha followed suit.

'I have a question,' said Theo, looking up from his food. 'You didn't really explain the caste system in Senegal earlier. Is your country like India?'

Old Mrs Diop raised a fastidious eyebrow and the shocked aunt dropped her fork, while Aminata's mother hurriedly stood up, mumbling that her daughter was crying. She came back carrying the baby.

'We'll talk about it after dinner, if you like,' said Abdoulaye with a smile. 'It's rather complicated to explain.'

'All right,' replied Theo. 'So what caste is your family?'

'Do be quiet,' said Aunt Martha under her breath. 'Ooh! What a gorgeous baby . . . How old is she and how much does she weigh?'

All attention was switched to little Aminata. Her eyelids fluttered with sleep and her little mouth puckered as she stared unseeingly at the adults around her. Her mother smiled with a shy modesty, and Theo, fascinated by the child's pretty round head, forgot his questions about castes. At this point, dessert arrived, slices of watermelon, and floating islands. The three women went off to put Aminata to bed, and Abdoulaye resumed his seat on the sofa.

'There,' he sighed. 'We can talk now. The Senegalese aren't too fond of discussing the subject of castes.'

'Especially in front of a little *Toubab*!' exclaimed Aunt Martha.

'Am I the *Toubab*?' asked Theo anxiously. 'Does it mean "idiot"?'

'*Toubabs* are foreigners, and by extension, white Europeans,' said Mr Diop with a smile. 'But in Senegal, we rarely talk about castes with the *Toubabs*. Besides, in theory, there aren't any castes nowadays. But I have to admit that in practice they still count a little.'

'Only a little?' Anta broke in, coming back to sit on the sofa. 'You work in Paris, but I live here, I've got ears! Despite our sociologists, our historians, our learning, we still can't help gossiping about the daughter of a griot family! Let me give you an example: in my classes, I'm determined to tackle the injustice of the caste system. I talk about

427

it, I explain, I criticize . . . I do everything I can to combat it, but is it any use? You tell me.'

'Anta is a sociology lecturer at the university,' said Mr Diop. 'So explain to Theo, you'll do a better job than me.'

'A large part of Africa is riddled with the caste system,' began Anta. 'The "higher" castes didn't even have a name. On the one hand were all the free men, and on the other, right at the bottom, those who were looked down on, whom a girl could not marry without disgracing her family: blacksmiths, potters, shoemakers, jewellers, weavers and griots.'

'Griots are those singing sorcerers,' said Theo. 'Fatou told me about them. Apparently they're very entertaining!'

The griots were one of the most unusual cases. Entrusted with the task of declaiming the chiefs' glorious genealogies, the griots were like strolling players – an essential part of life, but relegated to the outer fringes. Court bards, wandering minstrels, town criers, the griots brought together the people and sang accompanied by their instruments, but were not allowed to enter houses, or to rest underground. Griots were never buried. So, with no room available underground, their bodies were placed upright in the hollows of tall baobabs, and sealed in with clay.

'Gosh,' murmured Theo. 'Do they still do that today?'

No, for the old customs had died out with democracy, and the griots now enjoyed a new status. When an exhibition opened, they were there, and at important official occasions. The only thing they still did was to sing praises, at the tops of their voices, before the crowds, and now they enjoyed the rightful respect that was due to an ancient tradition.

'It's odd,' said Theo, perplexed. 'Why were they outcasts?'

'There are all sorts of legends about the origin of the griots,' she said. 'The strangest is about a particular griot caste, the Nyole. Nobody knows whether to place them right at the bottom of the griot caste or in the caste just above, but what a story. If only you knew!'

'That's all I ask,' said Theo. 'Out with it!'

'One day,' Anta began, 'in the Sahel, a man fell ill with a mysterious disease, and no one could cure him! He grew thinner and thinner and died. But when his neighbours gathered around the body for the funeral ceremony, they noticed to their amazement that the dead man's penis was . . . indecent.'

'Dirty?' asked Theo.

'No,' she said, embarrassed. 'He had an erection. His wife was said to be very beautiful. An old man advised her to lie with her husband for a last goodbye . . . She obeyed, and once the act was over and the body had returned to its normal state, the dead man was buried as usual. But the man's widow, pregnant as a result of her act, gave birth to twins, a girl and a boy.'

'Both live?' asked Theo.

As live as could be. Despite this strange miracle, the birth of the twins was perfectly straightforward. They grew up, married and had many descendants. But, one fine day, the Wolof discovered the curse that afflicted the offspring of the corpse: on their death, their bodies rotted at once! First, the skin cracked in the most horrible manner, then the flesh visibly putrefied . . . The griots weren't quite human. Since that day, the other castes avoided any matrimonial union with those who become known as the 'sons of corpses'. That was why they were hurriedly walled up with clay in the hollow of a baobab.

'Yuck,' Theo pulled a face. 'That's spooky!'

'Doesn't it remind you of anything?' asked Aunt Martha.

'No,' he said. 'Oh yes! It's a bit like the story of when Osiris died, except that poor old Isis never managed to get his willy up again.'

Anta explained that according to certain very influential theories, the first Africans were none other than the Egyptians, the ancestors of Black Africa, and black themselves. Back at the dawn of time, the peoples of Senegal had come from Egypt. Crossing mountains and deserts, they had set out on the long march across the black continent, from the Indian Ocean to the Atlantic, where they had established an Egyptian lineage at the furthest shore of Africa, opposite Brazil. So it was hardly surprising that African myths had distant echoes of Egyptian mythology, like the erect penis of the corpse-father of the griots.

But their story was all the more curious in that the other castes had something in common: blacksmiths, potters, shoemakers and jewellers all worked with their hands. But while they were skilled craftsmen, the griot had only one skill, and that was the power of oratory. Even when they were acclaimed as illustrious artists with a splendid voice and an inspired gift, the griots were still considered cursed creatures. They sometimes died on the battlefield, where they accompanied their chief, but that still didn't entitle them to a normal burial. Into the baobab, like all the rest!

Abdoulaye Diop pointed out that the Muslim faith was opposed to all caste discrimination. All believers had the right to the same burial, including griots.

'There was a time in France when actors weren't allowed to be buried in Catholic cemeteries,' Aunt Martha chipped in. 'The Church ban was only lifted in the nineteenth century, and yet castes had been abolished in France since the French Revolution! I'm not convinced by your story. The way I see it, people are simply afraid of those who carry the word – griots, actors, they're all the same. Those who make a profession out of the word are a threat.'

'Islam respects poets,' said Abdoulaye.

'Really? And this late in the twentieth century, who issued the *fatwa* against the writer Salman Rushdie? No, those who manipulate language arouse curious feelings. Plato, the great Greek philosopher, wanted to keep poets out of cities, and throughout history there's been a constant temptation to ban them. When they don't have complete control, religions don't like wordsmiths. Excluding the griots is no exception to the rule.'

'And yet, there is a story that rescues the griots' reputation,' continued Anta. 'Do you remember, Abdoul? The myth of the Gelwar . . .'

'The princess and the griot,' replied Abdoulaye.

Of all the peoples who made up Senegal, the Serer were the only ones that had established a royal dynasty of foreign origin. The Gelwar, who came from elsewhere, ruled over the Serer kingdom from the fourteenth to the nineteenth century. And yet the sovereigns' stock carried the stigma of scandal.

In the thirteenth century there was a princess, the daughter of a great king of Mali. Who had given her the child she was carrying in her womb? Her betrothed? Her brother-in-law? In any case, her royal father was unaware of his daughter's pregnancy. The child was to be illegitimate. The shamed princess ran away before dawn, at the hour when the village was beginning to stir to the sound of millet being pounded in the huge wooden mortars. She was not alone. A lovesick griot accompanied her. Perhaps he was the father of the unborn child – who knows?

Anyway, the runaways fled four hundred kilometres on foot and found refuge in a stone cave in the heart of the forest. Seven years later, local hunters came across the princess, her griot and their daughters: in the meantime, two more children had been born. Things might have gone badly . . . But they hadn't! The hunters were astonished that the exiles had survived, which they took as an omen. The princess was crowned queen and founded the Gelwar dynasty, which means 'mystery'.

What became of the lovesick griot? Nobody knows. Only the brave princess won the people's admiration. Her long absence, the cave that sheltered her, the miracle of the forest where the hunters had found her, everything contributed to the fervour stirred up by mysterious apparitions. All the same, the children of the first queen of the dynasty were illegitimate, and what's more, descendants of the griots.

'What a wonderful story!' said Aunt Martha. 'Pity the griot disappeared along the way . . .'

'He'd fulfilled his role,' replied Anta. 'He'd sown the gift of the word in the princess's womb. No further trace of the instant decomposition of the body: it's as though the princess purged the griot. The women of the dynasty have always been strong queens.'

The tom-tom and the word

'What's become of the Serers today?' asked Aunt Martha.

'Some are Catholic, but they're mostly Muslims,' replied Anta. 'But whichever they are, the old religions haven't entirely disappeared. Take the Wolof Baye Fall. You should see them gathered around the fire, absorbed in their songs, staring into a vacant space . . . With the tom-tom, they introduced African rhythm into Islam. Thanks to that rhythm, they have preserved the real trance of Africa.'

'What's a trance?' asked Theo.

'A sort of state between sleep and waking,' replied Aunt Martha. 'You lose consciousness, you shiver, you tremble, you spin and you dance, you can suddenly fall down, you're both yourself and someone else both at once.'

'There's an epileptic boy in my class,' murmured Theo. 'Once, he had a fit during break. Was that a trance?'

'Not at all. Epilepsy comes from a lesion in the brain. People are rarely cured of it, but it can be kept under control with medication. When you're in a trance, it's not that you're ill, you move into an altered state of consciousness. Not only is medicine powerless against it, but also the trance can cure you by itself.'

'Why do you say "you"?' asked Theo anxiously. 'Have I ever been in a trance?'

'Of course you have,' she answered. 'In Luxor.'

'Is that all it is!' he cried. 'So I'm an African too?'

'No way!' retorted Aunt Martha indignantly. 'What a cheek!'

'I don't see why you're scolding him,' Abdoulaye stepped in. 'Or why Theo shouldn't be "an African" as he puts it. Wherever I've travelled, in America or in Asia, I've seen people in trances. In my view, it can happen to any of us. The trance caught Theo, and one day it might catch you too, my dear Martha.'

'But I bet you've never seen a trance in Europe. No, Anta's right: the African trance is something special.'

'Excuse me for saying so, but I disagree,' said Abdoulaye. 'Firstly, because a techno concert triggers the same sort of trance you find in Africa.'

'You're right there,' interrupted Theo. 'But my aunt doesn't understand anything about techno.'

'Music for savages,' she grumbled.

'That sounds funny, coming from you!' said Abdoulaye ironically. 'Do you know that here, in the suburbs of Dakar, blonde European girls go into a trance during the most ancient ceremonies of Senegal? You've seen that at home.'

'But your sister was talking about the true African trance!' she insisted. 'I didn't imagine it! What did you mean, Anta?'

'I don't know,' murmured the young woman. 'Our bodies don't dance in the same way . . . The rhythm takes over . . .'

'You see!' triumphed Aunt Martha. 'Don't compare the pale waifs that jiggle around in techno concerts with your wonderful way of dancing!'

'The means of achieving a state of trance are different everywhere,' went on Abdoulaye, 'but the result is the same. The bodies are different, but the eyes of people in a trance always roll upwards in the same way. Of course, there is the true African trance. What does it depend on? On the irresistible sound of the tom-tom. The African trance is rhythm.'

'Nothing else?' asked Theo, disappointed. 'I imagined hen's blood, masks around a fire at night, magic, all sorts of incredible stuff . . . Fatou told me . . .'

'That's Fatou all over,' smiled Abdoulaye. 'Always inventing mysteries . . . yes, there is something else. Only it's not what you think. It's the word. In traditional Africa, the word is decisive. It's not there to convey a message: it continually reconstitutes the world and reconstitutes us. The Book, revealed, offers a prescription. That's different. For, despite their virtues, the Koran, the Bible, those great holy books, do not always manage to reconstitute us. Africans can pray all they like with the Prophet, or Jesus, they will never be cured except through the grace of their original word.'

'You've lost me,' moaned Aunt Martha. 'What are you talking about?'

' "To be naked, is to be speechless",' replied Abdoulaye mysteriously. 'That is what the elders of Mali still say today, in the Bandiagara cliffs.'

'So when I talk, I'm getting dressed?' yawned Theo. 'Oh! Sorry. I think I'm sleepy. I'm talking nonsense.'

'Bed!' decided Anta. 'You're making the child's head spin with your long speeches, Abdoul. Lean on me, Theo. Your room's not far.'

'The best of it is, he's right,' concluded Abdoulaye, following Theo with his gaze.

CHAPTER 25

Matters of Life and Death

Africa's sorrow

The next day, they walked around the city, visiting the Grand Mosque, the cathedral and the smaller mosques. The sky was pale, the sun white, the sea grey. In the distance, Theo could make out a row of pink-roofed houses on an island.

'Gorée,' said Aunt Martha. 'The symbol of the slave trade.'

'We'll be going there later, Theo,' added Abdoulaye. 'I'd like you to discover our Africas first. There'll be plenty of time to see the conditions we started out from.'

'Are we staying in Dakar?' asked Theo. 'Because it looks like a French city, that's why . . .'

'. . . With its town hall, station, and barracks, it's every inch a prefecture. The French built Dakar, and we took it over.'

The pavements teemed with people clad in *boubous* and caftans calmly going about their business. The streets were a hive of activity, hawkers selling parrots, masks and grigris, a whole bustling world filling the straight, tree-lined avenues. This wasn't Fatou's Africa.

Fatou spoke of baobabs, grain stores on stilts, pirogues with eyes painted on the prow, mountains of shells, the flight of the pelicans, and more baobabs. Fatou described the red earth, the green banana trees, the musky taste of mango, the white sands, the silvery trunk of the baobab. Fatou, her eyes half-closed, conjured up sacred trees, the homecoming of the fishermen, skies streaked with lightning before the storm, and yet again, the baobab.

'OK, it's very nice,' he said. 'But what about the baobabs?'

They were going to see them, as they wove in and out of the queues of lorries. They drove through suburbs where the streets were no longer lined with trees, the roads weren't tarmacked and there were no more shop windows. They swerved to avoid children who suddenly ran into the road in pursuit of a dog. They were held up behind a van so crammed with passengers that they were spilling out of the open doors. They drove past misty lakes where egrets fished, and desolate stretches where salt dried in little mounds. They passed roadside stalls fringed with light foliage sheltering pyramids of mangoes, strange bunches of leaves for making infusions, and coloured basketwork. They overtook carts hitched to little horses and donkeys ridden by children. They saw mango orchards, the dark trees bowed under the weight of their golden fruits. They glimpsed strange shapes in the distance, a forest of giant ghosts with spindly arms.

'There are your baobabs, Theo,' said Aunt Martha.

'What?' he exclaimed. 'Those hideous bare trees?'

Abdoulaye braked suddenly, the tyres screeched, and the car came to a halt.

'For us, the baobab is sacred,' he said. 'The bark is used to make rope, the leaves are used to bind sauces, and the fruit is full of a sort of chewing gum, which is soft and sweet. We suck it or soak it, it's delicious. In a week's time, the tops of the baobabs will be covered in thick foliage, and these hideous bare trees will have white flowers bursting with nectar dangling from the ends of their branches. The faithful skin of their trunks holds the trace of past generations, and if for some reason they had to be cut down, we would have to sprinkle them with milk so as not to anger them.'

'Oops, I'm sorry,' said Theo.

'It doesn't matter,' he said. 'But in Africa you have to learn to look. What will you say about our villages if you don't know how to look at a baobab?'

'That big one over there, is that a griot cemetery?' asked Theo timidly.

'Who knows?' replied Abdoulaye Diop with a smile. 'With us savages . . .'

Theo kept quiet. The earth was parched, the ground dusty, the sun scorching and the baobabs disturbing. As in India, people walking by the roadside had scarves wound round their necks, and the women walked with their boubous flapping in the wind, majestically carrying their loads on their heads. Theo felt a lump rising in his throat.

'In August, the rains come and everything's different,' went on Abdoulaye. 'Senegal is covered with fresh green, buds burst into flower, life is reborn, the sky grows dark with clouds and turns blue again after the storm . . .'

'It's true that the Sahel is arid,' murmured Aunt Martha.

'Let's go into the baobab forest,' suggested Abdoulaye. 'I want to show you something.'

Twin souls at the foot of the baobab

It was a forest without foliage, without shelter and without shade, an enchanted forest that had become a wilderness. Goats nibbled at shrubs and zebus lay on their sides waiting for dusk. Abdoulaye spotted a baobab whose huge trunk afforded a little shade where they could sit down. Aunt Martha took out a handkerchief and dabbed at her cleavage.

'In other countries, it's the mountain snows that kill,' said Abdoulaye. 'Here in Senegal it's the sand. For nearly twenty years, we had no rain. The Sahel desert gradually began to encroach on the land. But the rains are back! In two months at the most, we'll be able to sow. Seed is life . . . That's what the elders of the Sahel tell us, the people who live in the Dogon country.'

There, began Mr Diop, the villages were perched on high cliffs of yellow rock, so high that the Dogon had to descend steep steps to fetch water and carry it up to the top, where there wasn't any. The tiniest crevices and crannies in the rock were used for growing onions, which were planted in tiny strips of field. This people had preserved their ancient rituals and religion so carefully that the Dogon had become a tourist attraction just like Westminster Abbey. The Dogon, with their masks, dances and grain stores were now part of the Africa discovery trail. They weren't complaining and benefited from tourism without losing anything of their pride.

'The famous Dogon!' cried Aunt Martha. 'Apparently even their myths have a lot in common with those of Ancient Greece and Rome, don't they?'

'Now listen, my dear Martha, your ethnologists may have drawn parallels between our religions and yours; fair enough, it's better than being called savages. But the Dogon are from Africa, and Africa could well be the mother of all myths.'

437

'Watch out, Theo, you're going to find out about African cosmology,' said Aunt Martha. 'Listen carefully . . .'

Abdoulaye took a deep breath, for the Dogon myth was a long story.

'In the beginning,' he said, 'God created the smallest seed in the world, the cereal seed known as fonio. The "seed of the world" was brought to life by a whirlwind so powerful that it exploded and became the egg of the world. Inside the shell were two pairs of fish who became two sets of twins . . . The egg matured slowly like a child in a woman's womb, and out came a single boy, born prematurely, called Ogo.'

'Interesting,' said Theo. 'All alone . . .'

'Exactly! It wasn't natural! Now this clever premature baby yanked out a bit of his placenta and dropped it, and that was Earth. Ogo entered Earth determined to find his twin, Yasigui, who he believed had been born at the same time as him. He planted the fonio seed in the tainted blood of the placenta earth, but did not find his twin, for God had kept her in the remaining part of the egg.'

'Poor Ogo,' murmured Theo. 'Losing your twin's no joke.'

'Why poor Ogo? He was a bastard! In tainting the "seed of the world" with impure blood, he ruined the earth's food! So God turned the wicked Ogo into a Pale Fox, who is to blame for the evil of the world. Then, to make amends, he sacrificed one of the remaining twins, cut him into sixty-six pieces that he shaped into human forms, and used the placenta to stick his work together. This was the first man, who was called Nommo, which means "give water". Nommo became the master of the word and of water.'

'Sacrificed, dead and resurrected,' commented Theo. 'Sometimes, God repeats himself a bit.'

'Don't make hasty comparisons! Lastly, God sent to the Fox's impure earth four pairs of boy and girl twins, placed at the four corners of an arc made of their joined placentas. The stars were set in motion and the sun lit the purified earth. The nightmare of the failed creation was over. In accordance with the divine calculations, the sacred twins multiplied. But two by two.'

'I like that,' said Theo. 'Everybody had their twin!'

'Not for long! For soon the new creation was once again tainted by the impurity of the fonio reddened by the blood of the cursed placenta. On the fourth day, during the first eclipse of the sun, Yasigui, the lost twin, jumped down onto the earth in the form of a woman.'

'We'd forgotten all about her!'

'Well, we shouldn't have . . . She married one of the twins as though nothing had happened, then tricked him into eating the bloody fonio seed. The husband had to be sacrificed to purify the field.'

'Predictable,' said Theo, picking up a handful of sand. 'The second human sacrifice . . .'

'If you like, but what comes next is unique to the Dogon. The pregnant twin women all had single children . . . Humanity had just lost the precious gift of twins.'

'Shame,' groaned Theo.

'Yes, it was. That is why, in memory of this vanished dream, every person has only one body, but twin souls. One lives in the body: if it is a boy, it's the male soul. If it's a girl, it's the female. But the twin soul is never far from the body: at the bottom of a lake guarded by the Nommo, the resurrected ancestor, the female soul protects the male soul in the boy's body, and the male soul protects the female soul in the girl's body. Each guides their half soul in secret . . . For every human being is descended from the primal Nommo who was killed and resurrected as sets of boy and girl twins.'

'So we all have a twin soul lurking around somewhere,' murmured Theo. 'That's how it is with me, except I've found my twin sister. I'm not like the Pale Fox! Yet I'm French, not Dogon . . . How do you explain that, Abdoulaye?'

'Maybe the Dogon recognize a truth that others have not yet discovered. The whole of Africa is influenced by twins . . . They are either honoured or feared, they are either offered the first harvest or else one of the twins is killed at birth. But they're never ignored.'

'Who dares kill a twin?' asked Aunt Martha, horrified.

'Oh, nobody does it any more! Don't forget that twins are the ancestors of humanity: the birth of twins in today's world has something supernatural about it.'

'If I understand correctly, with my dead twin, I wasn't born normal,' concluded Theo. 'I'm almost divine . . .'

'Quite the opposite!' cried Abdoulaye. 'There's only one of you, so you're normal. The unusual thing about you is that your dead sister is able to talk to you . . .'

'Ah, you know about that?' said Theo, flushing. 'Aunt Martha's been blabbing again!'

'That's exactly why I decided to tell you the story of Nommo,' he replied. 'The sacrificed twin through whom we drink and talk, symbolizes the two essential elements of life: water and the word. When you said yesterday that when you talk you're getting dressed, you were right. For if being naked means being without words, then words do clothe us . . . In the name of the ancestor, words are the fabric! Salvation always comes from the dead ancestor. That is why we Africans are never satisfied with a simple identity card . . . A man is not himself if he is not the son, brother, grandson, nephew, great-nephew or cousin to the members of his family. A boy, or a girl, is never alone in the world. Dead or alive, the relatives dress their body.'

'And where does love come in? Where's its place?'

'Love,' hesitated Abdoulaye. 'Perhaps, in the same way that Yasigui sought Ogo the impure, each half soul goes looking for its twin half . . .'

'I know,' said Theo. 'Love is depositing your baggage of ancestors with the person you love. You put down your suitcase, you're at peace.'

'Here, we make sacrifices to the ancestors,' said Abdoulaye. 'We give the baggage to them, to make amends. That's not bad either.'

He stood up, brushing the dust from his boubou, then, reached to bend down a young branch and showed them a tiny fresh yellow leaf.

'That's what I wanted to show you,' he said. 'Without water, all on its own, the baobab is growing its leaves. Like us, it gets by.'

The birth of the dead

The next stage was water.

As they approached the Serer country, the look of the villages changed. Among the acacia groves, Theo glimpsed his first square huts with thatched roofs, just as Fatou had described them. They arrived at Joal, parked the car and walked across the wooden bridges that spanned the mud of a mangrove swamp.

Fadiouth was truly an extraordinary village. Grain stores on stilts overlooked the murky water lapping around the mangroves covered in oysters. But the most unusual thing lay on the far shore: a cemetery of immaculate shells, dotted with white crosses and centuries-old baobabs. The predominantly Catholic population of Fadiouth had inherited this strange cemetery from the old Serer religion.

The ground crunched underfoot. The tombs were in orderly limestone mounds set in rows on the slopes of the tumulus. Aunt Martha stumbled, swore and tried to regain her balance. Meanwhile, Theo climbed up with the agility of an egret swooping over the Serer country. How high they were, these funeral mounds! Had they not been made of shells, they could have been pyramids built to last for posterity, he observed.

'You never spoke a truer word, Theo,' observed Abdoulaye, sitting down at the foot of the huge cross on the largest mound.

'Are they pyramids?' asked Theo in amazement.

'When a chief died in Serer country,' explained Abdoulaye, 'he was put in a funeral hut made from the roof of his own hut. After a while, the people from the surrounding villages would come and help build the tumulus, where they planted a pole made of palmyra palmwood – a tree with rot-resistant timber and palms shaped like hands. Then, when they were converted, the Catholic Serer built their tombs on the mounds of shells that concealed the food buried with the dead for the long journey to the City of the Ancestors.'

'Strange,' remarked Theo. 'Here too, they prepare food for the journey of the dead, like in Egypt?'

'That's not the only similarity between the Serer country and Egypt! Here too, the bull was man's double, and the high chiefs were sewn up in a bull's hide before being buried. Here, as in Egypt, the spirit of the deceased is restless if it is not fed. From the fourth day, the dead should be given couscous, water or milk, depending on preferences. I've even heard tell of a wealthy Serer patriarch who increased his flocks in the hope that his descendants would give him enough milk . . .'

'Enough milk for what?' asked Theo.

'To get to the City of Ancestors, of course! The journey is similar to the one the Egyptians make: for a proper death, you need provisions, otherwise you don't really die. The man I told you about had eleven sacred ancestors. He was certain to become the twelfth ancestor, provided he had enough milk to get there.'

'Because you might not make it?' said Theo.

Not all the dead succeeded. To attain the status of ancestor, you had to have made a success of your life, had children, planned a splendid funeral in advance, provided the sacrificial ox, in other words, have prepared the lineage to become its protector. For, once an ancestor, the deceased lived on in the thoughts of his descendants. Their mutual survival depended on it. The ancestor had the power to heal his descendants, but without the descendants the deceased would not be an ancestor. The ancestor acted as an intermediary between his sons and God, as long as his family accompanied him throughout the journey. There was a reciprocal need and mutual help between the living and the dead.

The one thing that differed from the Egyptians was the burial ceremony of the Gelwar, the descendants of the princess and the griot. They were buried twice. The first funeral took place at the site of death:

the chief was sewn up in the bull's hide, and the body lowered upright in its coffin into a pit three metres deep. The chief was to become a bull-God, and this burial was secret. The second funeral was an official public ceremony with a coffin filled with earth and amulets. No one was fooled! Everybody knew that the official coffin was empty. But nobody knew the secret whereabouts of the pit where deep inside the dead chief was embarking on his transformation into an immortal being.

'So it wasn't instant?' said Theo.

In Africa, went on Abdoulaye patiently, nothing in a man's life happened instantly. The child in its mother's womb was not created in just nine months, it also stored the heritage of the names of its lineage, some of which would be given to the child at birth. When the child was born, he continued to create himself in stages: circumcision, his initiation. When he died, that creation did not stop half-way. That was the meaning of the double funeral: they celebrated the social death of the Serer chief in front of the empty coffin, but building a life in the next world continued in the pit.

'I don't get it,' protested Theo. 'What happens to the deceased? In ancient Egypt, he was judged, and that was that. But in Africa?'

'Let's take another example, the Yoruba of South Benin,' said Abdoulaye. 'The family begins by burying their dead relative. Before the funeral, the deceased is dressed in new clothes and given some everyday objects so that he has with him something old and something new. Everything else is burned, to free him from the burden of the past. Then there are festivities to celebrate the beginning of a new life. And finally, the long wait begins . . .'

'What on earth are they waiting for?' asked Theo.

'For the mortal frame to disintegrate! Death follows the opposite path to birth. The body gradually discards its flesh, and one fine day, five or six years later, it is ready. Then it can begin its initiation into death.'

'Hang on a sec,' interrupted Theo. 'How do they know it's ready? Does it go "coo-ee, it's me" from under the ground?'

'Almost! Someone falls ill, husbands and wives argue, there's something wrong. That's how they know that the deceased is giving a signal, and it's time. Then, they remove the skull from the grave, wash it with a purifying plant, sacrifice a chicken, pour the blood over the skull and divide the chicken in two, one half for the family, and the other for the deceased. That's the initiation into death.'

'Wait a minute, you're not telling me they initiate a skull!' cried Theo. 'What's that about?'

'It really is an initiation,' insisted Abdoulaye. 'Initiation means "introduction to secrets". The deceased is taught the secrets of death. As if for a young man, the skull is dressed in a white garment. They greet his return, for he has indeed returned! Lastly, the dressed skull is tied up in a bag with the chicken's skull, and the whole thing is hung in the deceased's hut. That's not the end of it. The second funeral hasn't begun yet. The deceased has returned, but he is still alone. With the last rites, he will be reunited with the village community.'

'Aunt Martha, we've never seen such a complicated burial, have we?' exclaimed Theo. 'Death is obviously something you have to live with.'

'Listen to the next bit,' she said. 'You can philosophize afterwards.'

'The next stage involves several families: each one brings the skull of their deceased relative in a basket and places it in front of the collective ancestors' hut. Now the key moment has come. The person in charge of the rite washes the skulls and carefully collects the water. People make their last offerings to the dead before shutting them away in earthenware jars which they dress and parade around, and feed, and show off in the villages, just like new-born babies.'

'New-dead babies!' said Theo.

'Exactly. Then, the deceased is buried once and for all in a big hole in a place that is kept secret. They say that the dead set sail in a pirogue towards the sea.'

'Whew!' said Theo. 'The end!'

'Not yet. The deceased must have his place in the village. Then a sunshade is erected in his name in the ancestors' hut, and that's it, he's established. At last he is an ancestor.'

'That's finally it? It takes a hell of a long time!'

'In your country, there is one burial and it's over in a day. What remains of the deceased in your families afterwards? Every year you go and put flowers on their graves on All Souls' Day. In other words, nothing! You've lost the sense of lineage. In my view, that makes you very unhappy. In Africa, we can't live without our ancestors. They support us, they sustain us. But you don't have the support of your ancestors any more. You are alone!'

'Not at all!' said Theo huffily. 'We've got our families!'

'OK, but then what? Where's the continuity with the past? And what about this family of yours? In your country, the family has died out. You're in tiny groups, crammed into a tiny boat in the middle of the ocean.'

'You don't expect me to go and dig up grandpa and wash his skull, do you?' said Theo.

'That's not your custom. The sad thing is, in Europe you hardly have any customs left. You're happy with just one God who forgives, and that's the end of it! With our ancestors, we create our own divinities. They're more reliable.'

God doesn't take much trouble

Aunt Martha had plonked herself down on the shells among the tombs some time ago. 'We could eat oysters at the restaurant we saw in Joal, couldn't we?' she said. 'These shells are murder to sit on!'

Abdoulaye looked embarrassed and admitted that the place wasn't exactly comfortable. The wind was still blowing over the lagoon where black herons strutted and furtive curlews trailed. They made their way down gingerly, crossing back over the two bridges, and drove to the restaurant to sample the oysters from the mangrove swamps. After the meal, Abdoulaye sipped his fruit juice, Theo his Coca-Cola, and Aunt Martha a glass of white wine.

'Tell me, Abdoulaye, why haven't the Christians changed tombs?' asked Theo.

'Don't you ever get tired!'

'I warned you that this fellow's unstoppable,' Aunt Martha reminded him. 'We'd have to knock him out!'

Theo held his tongue, stared at the coconut palms, examined the oysters and wriggled on his chair.

'I'm bored,' he sighed. 'May I leave the table?'

'Put your hat on!' cried Aunt Martha.

He shot out of the door. Aunt Martha and Abdoulaye both ordered another drink and savoured the peace and quiet. Aunt Martha was very thirsty, and asked for another jug of white wine.

'Theo's a different person,' said Abdoulaye after a silence. 'I barely recognize him! He's grown, he's looking well, you'd never think he was so sick . . .'

'He isn't any more,' grunted Aunt Martha.

'Is that really so? That would be so wonderful!'

'Sure,' she muttered.

'You're not very talkative, Martha. What's wrong?'

'It's the wine,' she groaned, 'it's making me sleepy!'

Abdoulaye felt awkward and concentrated on his drink. One sip and that was it! Propped up on her elbows, Martha was snoring blissfully. From time to time, a hiccup dislodged her, she slid down on her chair and Abdoulaye sat her up again. He looked at his watch. What on earth was Theo up to?

'Ah! There you are at last,' he said when Theo reappeared. 'Wherever did you get to?'

'The market . . . Aunt Martha . . . She's snoring!'

'I think she's had too much to drink,' he said. 'Sit down. You asked me a question earlier. Why did the Christians keep the tumuli?'

'Oh yes!' said Theo. 'I'd forgotten.'

'Well I hadn't. In Africa, it's not forbidden to mix the old and the new. The God of the Christians doesn't bother the ancestors. Quite the opposite! Jesus's resurrection is pretty much in tune with the journey of the dead.'

'Watch out!' cried Theo. 'Aunt Martha's going to fall!'

'Don't worry,' said Abdoulaye, heaving her up again. 'Did you understand what I said?'

'No. I wonder where God is in all this.'

'The God of the Africans doesn't spend too much time with men. The Dogon call him Amma. Here, in Serer country, he's known as Roog-Sen. But whether God is called Roog-Sen or Amma, he's only the creator of the world.'

'That's already quite something!' said Theo.

'But it's not perfect . . . God's intentions aren't evil, he's reasonable, he does what he can. When his creatures get out of hand, he expels the Pale Fox and repairs the damage. It's not he who manages human lives: it's the spirits, the ancestors. God doesn't intervene except in the event of a disaster.'

'A flood?' asked Theo.

'In Serer country, there's worse,' he replied. 'In the beginning, the forest sheltered people, animals and trees. Then, they fought among themselves. One day, while the men and the beasts were killing each other in the forest, the trees became murderers too . . . I must tell you that in those days, trees could talk, hear and move. There was out-and-out war between the three species, trees, animals and humans, and it was up to God to do something. He punished the trees: dumb, blind and paralysed, they were immobilized for ever. But Roog-Sen did not remove their ears. That is why trees are sacred, for they hear everything . . .'

'But they can't repeat it,' said Theo.

445

'I wouldn't be so certain. You have to be careful with trees. As for the animals, Roog-Sen made them mad. They lack control, but Roog-Sen did not take away their instinct. And when it came to humans, Roog-Sen was content to shorten their height, and their life, but not their spirit. He has never intervened since.'

'So people don't worship him,' concluded Theo.

'Oh yes! You'll often see a wooden column to Roog-Sen in the court-yard, and at the foot of it, people put gourds containing horns, roots and stones. If the harvest is good, the head of the family pours milk over the column. But it's the *pangols* whose help they are summoning, not his.'

'Say that again!' cried Theo. 'She's snoring even louder!'

'THE *PANGOLS*!'

Aunt Martha woke up with a start.

'You weren't half snoring, Aunt M.' said Theo.

'What?' she muttered, in a daze. 'What . . . Did I fall asleep? What time is it?'

'Time to go and see the *pangols*,' said Abdoulaye, getting to his feet.

A mermaid's skin and a millet pestle

The road from Joal took them through the eucalyptus forest to a vast stretch of blue water that flowed into the sea, the surface barely ruffled by a glossy ibis fishing.

'Is this lake a *pangol*?' asked Theo.

'No,' he replied. 'A *pangol* is a spirit. But a great Serer poet tells how, in this lake, the mermaids used to come and drink. The fishermen from around here know all about mermaids. To go and catch them in the sea, they must appease their *pangol*. . . You pacify the mermaid with songs and sacrifices. Only then will she allow herself to be caught, for the fishermen have treated her properly.'

'Real mermaids who sing, with real breasts and a fish tail?'

'Well, not exactly. They are manatees, a type of sea cow. As these huge animals have breasts, they have often been taken for the mermaids of the legends. Here, the spirit of the manatees is dressed as a woman, with a white *pagne* . . .'

'I want to see,' said Theo, leaning over the lake. 'If you're there, mermaid manatee, show yourself!'

Startled, the ibis flew away, and the lake rippled. Then nothing. Theo plunged his hand into the water and pulled out a piece of skin, slimy with black mud.

'The mermaid's skin!' he cried. 'A spirit's skin!'

'Or a snake's slough,' said Abdoulaye. 'In any case, you're lucky, Theo. For the spirit of the snake is also a *pangol*.'

'It stinks,' complained Aunt Martha. 'Wash it please . . . In the meantime, put it in this plastic bag.'

'Here, people would put it on a sacred tree like this,' said Abdoulaye, pointing to a group of old trunks covered in bits of cloth. 'That way, you make the *pangol* your ally. Don't you want to give your snake-skin to this tree?'

'No way!' said Theo.

Thus, brandishing his slimy trophy, Theo followed Abdoulaye to the first hut in the village. In the hollow of three huge trees, guarded by two assistants, was the healer in his shack.

Abdoulaye exchanged interminable greetings Senegalese fashion with the guard at the door: 'How are you?' 'I'm well.' 'How's the family?' 'Fine.' 'Your mother?' 'She's fine.' 'The children?' 'They're fine.' 'Work?' 'Fine.' 'Your health?' 'I'm fine', and the guard inquired the same of him. At last, the ritual over, the guard showed Abdoulaye and Theo inside. Aunt Martha preferred to sit beside the lake and sleep off the wine.

Leaning against three huge trunks, the dark shack was tiny. A roof of palm leaves, a fence, a sheet stretched across . . . In the centre stood a giant gourd filled with green water. Chicken feet and slit gizzards were piled to one side. The healer was waiting in the shadows.

He was an old man with only one leg, wearing a woolly hat, his neck muffled up in red scarves, a carved walking stick in his hand and his wooden leg resting sedately on the ground. His wrinkled face wore an expression of circumspect amusement. What could this young *Toubab* understand? The greetings began all over again. The old man looked suspicious. Abdoulaye joked, begged, bent over backwards . . . Finally, after long negotiations, the one-legged man began to laugh. All right, he'd speak!

When he received a patient, the healer started off by sacrificing a chicken: he slit the gizzard in half to discover the cause of the illness. Then he treated the patient by giving him a ritual bath in the huge gourd. With a wooden ladle, the healer poured the therapeutic water over the patient, who crouched naked in the miniature tub. How strange this cloudy, magic water looked . . .

'What's in the bottom?' asked Theo.

'Just put your hand in!' replied Abdoulaye. 'You may.'

Without hesitation, Theo fished out some odd-shaped grey pebbles.

On the surface floated little sticks of wood that the patient would take home after his ritual bath, as protection. But what about the pebbles? With the help of supernatural inspiration, they had been found in the wood at the spot where lightning had struck the ground, a long, long time before their discovery by the healer. But how do you identify stones that have been struck by lightning? Only the healer was able to recognize their divine power.

'Isn't there anything else?' asked Theo with a note of disappointment.

'Yes,' replied the old man, pointing to his toothless mouth. 'There are the words I throw in. If you like, I can also show you the *pangol* that lives here.'

He grabbed his walking stick and rose. Just behind the shack, in the middle of a raked circle, stood a tiny post coated in dried milk. The *pangol*! A pestle for pounding millet driven into the ground, its secret passed on from uncle to nephew for generations. Around the milky spirit, they fell silent. It was only the end of an old pestle in the shade of three trees, but the power of a spirit was locked inside it . . . Theo tried hard to find out more, but the old healer refused vehemently. It was forbidden to talk about the *pangol*.

The Serer star

The sun set fast quickly in Africa; it was time to leave. They drove back the way they had come; the palm trees and acacia groves petered out. Aunt Martha had dozed off. As they drew nearer the town, the tall baobabs reappeared.

'There!' cried Theo. 'That's our baobab!'

Abdoulaye stopped the car.

'Go and see if the griots are there,' he commanded. 'I mean it, Theo. Go!'

Theo tiptoed over to the tree, clutching his slough. He cautiously poked his head into a gaping hole and saw a crumpled piece of paper on the ground.

'Huh, some griots!' he cried. 'It's a message!'

'Yes, but in a sacred tree. You are requested to treat it with respect.'

'What makes this one sacred? You didn't tell me earlier!'

'Perhaps your baobab is enchanted . . . Do you see the ray of the setting sun through the branches? Yes? Well, that's how the spirits appear. One day, two Serers glimpsed the same light at the top of a baobab. But when they drew near, the baobab had vanished! So they went and consulted a soothsayer. She waited in the place they indicated and, towards sunset, she was amazed to see a baobab rise slowly from the ground.'

'Go on. Was it playing hide-and-seek?'

'It was a shy baobab. At night, it came out of the ground to join its baobab brothers, but during the day, it withdrew underground. The soothsayer tied a cloth to the end of a branch, and the baobab stayed above ground.'

'Ooh!' cried Theo. 'I can see a cloth up there, all torn! Is this the enchanted baobab?'

'Who knows,' murmured Abdoulaye with a smile. 'In Serer country, all it takes is a stump of wood erected to represent the male, an overturned pot for the female. But listen to me carefully, Theo: neither the *pangols* nor Roog-Sen mean anything if you don't know the Serer star. Watch.'

Abdoulaye crouched down, brushed the twigs out of the way, and with a simple gesture drew a five-pointed star in the sand.

'There, at the top of the star, is Roog-Sen's place. Here at the bottom, in the space between the two points, is man's place. He is linked to God by the axis of the world, you see, the little fork. Safe at the centre of the star. Still at the centre of the universe. Now, stand under the baobab and read your message please.'

I am white and brown, the goddess of the waters. I await you in my country, in the land of mermaids, read Theo.

'But I'm in the land of mermaids,' he muttered, getting back into the car. 'What on earth does it mean?'

'Consult the soothsayers . . .' whispered Abdoulaye. 'We have some excellent ones.'

'Don't cheat,' scolded Aunt Martha groggily.

'Shut up,' retorted Theo, irritated. 'You're sloshed!'

'How dare you be rude to your aunt!' said Abdoulaye indignantly. 'Aren't you ashamed? Now apologize.'

'Mind your own business!' snapped Theo. 'She's *my* aunt!'

'You don't talk to your elders like that in Africa, my lad. Do as you're told, you cheeky thing!'

Theo gave her a reluctant kiss. Aunt Martha gave a contented sigh and went straight back to sleep again.

'Now for your message. Well?'

'Dunno,' sulked Theo, fiddling with the amulet bag. 'I need a dictionary.'

'OK, I'll give you a clue. There's another land of mermaids. A very long way from here. But also very near.'

'Still in Africa?'

'Yes and no. Another Africa. I'm giving away far too much!'

'Huh!' sniffed Theo. 'Is that why I need my spirit, my mermaid skin?'

Theo gets a fright

When they returned to the house, Aunt Martha went straight to bed. Abdoulaye launched into a long speech to explain to his venerable mother that Madame Martha had felt slightly unwell during their outing, but that it wasn't necessary to make her any herb tea, it really wasn't. Theo showed off his mermaid skin, which he was asked to go and wash immediately. After dinner, he rolled it up and put it under his pillow just in case.

In the dining room, Anta and her brother were commenting on the day's events. Theo eavesdropped.

'So, what do you think of the kid? You know him better than I do.'

'I think . . .' mused Abdoulaye. 'To be honest, I don't quite know. He's a very bright boy and he scoffs too much, so as not to believe in the sacred. But he listens. On the other hand, our poor friend Martha seems exhausted . . .'

'She probably is,' said Anta.

'I think she's depressed. Now that Theo is on the road to recovery, she's losing her grip. I'm worried about her.'

'And yet the hardest part still lies ahead . . .'

'I know! We're leaving tomorrow morning.'

'But it's the day after tomorrow that the going will get tough. I hope that the boy will be able to handle it!'

'If he's afraid, we get out,' said Abdoulaye. 'It would be too dangerous.'

Then they went on in an unfamiliar language sprinkled with words he recognized – 'main hospital', 'trauma', 'faint', 'electric shock treatment' . . . Electric shock? Theo froze. What was going to happen the next morning? Where were they going to take him? Was it some form of treatment, the worst of all? Aunt Martha hadn't prepared him . . . He looked for a means of escape, but the windows had bars. He half-opened the door, but Anta and her brother stood in the way. Aunt Martha snored on. Theo stared in panic at the lights flickering on the garden wall, the silent flight of a big fawn-coloured fruit bat, three stars in a patch of pitch black sky . . . he had nothing but his mermaid for protection.

CHAPTER 26

The Ox, the Goat, the Cockerels and the Initiate

N'Doeup

At breakfast, Abdoulaye launched into an explanation. Aunt Martha had dark rings under her eyes and looked under the weather, though not much more than Theo, who had barely slept.

'Well, Theo,' Abdoulaye began. 'We're going to see a rather special ceremony known as the "N'Doeup".'

'How do you pronounce it?' asked Theo.

'Don't even try. You'd have to say EN-DURP and the Senegalese would make fun of you. *Toubabs* can't pronounce it properly. It's a Lebu healing rite. The Lebu are a fishing community who still live in the Dakar area. This ritual is very important for them. The N'Doeup is also a performance, for that is part of the cure.'

'Performance,' echoed Theo. 'Will there be masks?'

'No, but the N'Doeup is even more impressive than the masked dances. In Africa, we have our own ways of healing. You Europeans use medicine and surgery; that's fine, but not for everything . . .'

'I've paid a high price for the lesson,' said Aunt Martha. 'This trip has cost a fortune! You have no idea . . .'

'But my dear Martha, you know very well . . . As soon as we're dealing with diseases that affect the soul, your medicines are useless. For these illnesses, the community comes together and acts as a group. Only we have our own theatre.'

'A real theatre with a stage and an auditorium?' asked Theo.

No. The theatre was the home, then the beach, and finally, the street, where the drama would come to an end. For drama there was, majestic, pathetic, and violent. A collective catharsis, a mass emotion. A . . .

'That's all psychology,' protested Theo. 'Would you please begin at the beginning!'

'Very well,' said Abdoulaye, concentrating. 'It starts with a woman having dizzy spells. She cries, she stops speaking, she stays in bed all day and has nightmares. She goes to see one of the female healers – for generally they're women. The woman gets her to talk about her dreams, or her hallucinations.'

'Your female specialist sounds like a psychoanalyst,' broke in Aunt Martha.

'I don't think a psychoanalyst would use a gourd with roots floating around in it,' replied Abdoulaye. 'The specialist stirs the water, and depending on the size of the roots that float to the surface, she first of all decides on the type of sacrifice: an ox, or a goat, or a chicken that the patient must pay for.'

'The psychoanalyst is paid in cash, and yours in kind,' continued Aunt Martha. 'There's not much difference!'

'But the ox isn't for the woman!' said Abdoulaye indignantly. 'It's for the *rab*! He demands a sacrifice!'

'Instead of getting annoyed, you'd do better to explain that a *rab* is a spirit,' chided his sister. 'Depending on the content of the dream, the healer knows which *rab* has possessed the patient, whether it's a spirit from the father's side, or from the mother's.'

'In fact, the *rab* often strikes the patient after a trauma,' Abdoulaye resumed. 'A bereavement, an accident, an unusual event. Once the consultation is over, the patient prepares for the ceremony, which can last a week.'

'We're not going to stay a week to watch that!' exclaimed Aunt Martha. 'I'll never last out . . .'

There was no question of following the entire N'Doeup ceremony! In any case, the first part of the ritual was private, involving only the family and the school of the *N'Doeup-kat*, the specialist healing women. They did the patient's hair, poured herbal water over her head, and mothered her. The patient allowed herself to be treated like a baby. Then the chief healer took some curd in her mouth, and sprayed it over the patient and massaged her with it for a long time. Then the rhythms began. Little bells, which the healer rang tirelessly behind the patient's ear. Banging gourds. Griot drums. The healers began to dance, calling on the seven great *rab* leaders for help . . . Goaded by the obsessive ringing of the bells, the patient rose and joined in the dancing.

'I bet she goes into a trance,' said Theo.

'You're right. But the trance alone isn't enough. During her ecstasy, the patient has to utter the name of her *rab*. To achieve this, tambourine players and healers choose different beats corresponding to the many *rabs*. They try each one in turn until they find the right one, and only then, to the beat of her *rab*, does the patient keep screaming out the name of the spirit that possesses her and falls to the ground. And a good job has been done!'

'It sounds like a birth,' said Theo.

Yes, but it was also a death. Then came the second part of the N'Doeup, the public performance, and that was what they were going to see.

'At least I hope it's not too tiring?' asked Aunt Martha sheepishly.

The spirits in a basket

They entered a quiet courtyard surrounded by low houses, out of which trooped sleepy children and women gracefully stretching. They ate millet porridge with curd from gourds, they cooked unhurriedly in huge pots over braziers. In the shade of the tree in the centre of the courtyard, the elderly healer waited for the men to wake up.

'I warn you that we're going to see something unusual,' whispered Abdoulaye. 'For once, it's a man who is possessed, not a woman.'

The patient who sat inert and blank-faced at the old woman's feet looked alarmingly docile. A youngish adult, he wore a leather headband decorated with cowrie shells around his forehead and a simple white percale tunic. He seemed little older than Theo, but he was thirty. The healer explained that he shouted and ran about wildly, that he no longer slept, ate little, in short, that he had lost his mind until the day when he had whispered her name, which was a clear sign!

The healer had diagnosed the disease. The young man was possessed by two spirits on his mother's side, those of the forest and the sea. It was a grievous case. The *rabs* had already killed his mother and his young sister. So she was going to give him the full works and sacrifice a huge bull, a goat and three cockerels. But first they had to perform the secret measuring ritual.

'Measuring?' murmured Theo. 'Are they going to measure his height?'

'They'll measure all sorts of things,' said Abdoulaye. 'But you must be quiet.'

Thanks to Mr Diop, Aunt Martha and Theo were shown barefoot into the room where the healers were going to prepare the patient. The female relatives, lying on mats, were cleaning their teeth with sticks. Sitting in the middle, legs outstretched, the patient submitted to their care. The healers removed his tunic, placed a piece of fabric torn from a sheet and symbolizing the shroud on top of his head, folded it down over his forehead and fastened it with the leather headband. The preparations began in total silence.

From a distaff, the healers pulled seven white threads and stretched them from the forehead to the feet, and then to the knees. Then the chief healer removed a piece of red fabric embroidered with cowries and containing roots and horns from a plastic bag and placed it in a half-full basket of millet. With easy majesty, she blew some millet through a wooden pipe onto the patient's head. The measuring rite began. The basket passed under the patient's legs, brushed his head, and ran along his belt before coming to rest on his knees. The healer whispered a curt order: the man put his hands on the basket, millet was poured into it, and two roots stood up on end. A contented murmur rippled around the room.

'The roots represent the two *rabs*,' whispered Abdoulaye. 'Now, he has to balance the basket on his head, and the *rabs* with it.'

The operation was not a success. The basket obstinately slid off each time. The concentration intensified. The healer struck the millet and the roots authoritatively to force the *rabs* to strike a balance. At last, the basket remained in place: the *rabs* had yielded. The healer leaned towards the patient and spoke to him in a muffled voice, wagging her finger.

'She's making him say the name of his *rabs*,' whispered Abdoulaye.

The patient finally managed to blurt out two names. Then the shroud was removed, his tunic was slipped back on and the dark leather headband replaced.

'The initiation's over,' said Abdoulaye. Now they're going to dress him for the next part.'

When he left the house, the initiate cut a fine figure, with his face framed by a pointed hat, the headband around his forehead, and three blue and black striped cummerbunds around his torso. In his outstretched arms he held up a white rope with seven knots. The russet bull was led in on a rope, the tom-toms started, the initiate began to dance, and a procession of children led him through the narrow streets.

'He must dance outside every house in the village,' said Abdoulaye. 'Let's go to the beach, this is going to take a while.'

The rider has mounted!

They sat inside a straw hut; Aunt Martha leaned her head against a pillar and dozed off. The sun beat down and a strong wind blew. Toddlers ran about, little girls came and stared shyly at them and donkeys wandered around. Soon, the echo of the tom-toms could be heard: the procession reappeared on the edge of the shore. Theo ran over to see. The vast beach teeming with people heaved like an angry ocean.

But the real sea was so calm! The foam on the waves licked the pale sand, the sky had softened, and the bull seemed to be approaching his swim as if it were an innocent bit of fun. The strange thing was the man with the headband, who brandished a taut rope at arm's length, signalling victory. Agile as a young god, he leapt from rock to rock with astonishing grace.

'The bull is herded into the sea,' explained Abdoulaye, 'to be presented to the powerful *rab* of Dakar, who lives in the foam of the waves. Look, the Ox is very reluctant!'

'I thought it was a bull!' said Theo.

'We always say "the Ox",' he explained.

The healer brought the patient to the bull at the water's edge, and he was hoisted onto its back. The initiate raised his arms triumphantly and the crowd gave shouts of joy to the sound of the big drums.

'Do you know what they're saying?' said Abdoulaye. '"The rider has mounted!" Now the initiate is in physical contact with his Ox. All he has to do is sacrifice it, as his spirits require.'

'Don't tell me they're going to kill it!' cried Theo.

'The *rabs* demand it,' replied Abdoulaye. 'Otherwise they'll continue to possess the patient. It's the Ox or him!'

'What can the bull have to do with it?' insisted Theo. 'He's not the patient!'

'Not yet,' said Abdoulaye. 'But he soon will be.'

The bull was dragged into the courtyard of the house and its hoofs hobbled to make it lie down. The patient was laid along its massive back, one arm touching its hide. A goat was brought out to suffer the same fate, quavering with fear. To transform the Ox into a sacred victim, the healer planted three large horn amulets around the animal and

457

placed a black root on its stomach. Then the female relatives threw brightly coloured cloths, known as *pagnes* over the man and the animals.

Apart from the panting of the bull, which made the heavy mound of fabric rise and fall, nothing moved. The healer seized the white cockerels by their bound feet and swung them over the heap of *pagnes* and bodies.

'The rite of the caresses,' whispered Abdoulaye in Theo's ear. 'The feathers of the live cockerels will be soft for the *rabs* when they enter the Ox hide.'

Time passed. The pounding of the tom-toms, the roll of drumfire, then suddenly, silence. The healers led the women of the family in a slow dance around the mound of *pagnes*, chanting to the quiet throb of the drums they held.

'What's he doing under the covers with the poor Ox?' asked Theo anxiously, 'and what are they singing? It sounds like hymns . . .'

'They're beseeching all the spirits,' whispered Abdoulaye. 'They're going to beg the *rabs* to leave the sick man's body and enter the animal. The initiate is going to die and be reborn.'

'What do you mean, die? He looks alive and well to me!'

'Yes, but they pretend he's dead so as to simulate his rebirth. Earlier on, when they passed the basket of millet under his legs, it was to make the *rab* come down from his head to his feet, ready to exit the body. Do you see? He was being prepared for a sort of birth in which he plays the part of the baby.'

'Like for the ancestors?' murmured Theo. 'Dead and resuscitated?'

'You could say that. Now, if they want the *rabs* to go over to the Ox, they have to make them feel sorry for him . . .'

'Is that why the women are crying now?'

'It's essential! The tears must move the spirits to pity at all costs. If they want the patient to be reborn, they must weep. There . . . You see, he's emerging from the *pagnes*. That means the *rabs* have entered the Ox.'

'Why enter a man's body?' asked Theo. 'What a weird idea!'

'The *rabs* are very touchy! If they get angry, they enter your body and take over your mind . . . The only way to get rid of them is to pass them on to an ox, a goat or a white cockerel, whichever they prefer. This time, they're very demanding, probably because there are two of them. Look . . . The healer is going to revive the initiate.'

The women had stopped crying. In the silence, the healer sat the patient on the back of the Ox and baptized him by spraying water over his head through the wooden pipe. Three times she made him straddle the victim before performing the final rite: four new-laid eggs were thrown at the animal, mixing with a well-aimed gob of spittle to form a sticky yellow goo.

'The egg contains the germ of life,' explained Abdoulaye. 'Now, the Ox has been deified and everyone will be able to speak to him. Watch carefully!'

The head of the shackled animal was raised, and his muzzle forced open. The patient leaned over and spoke a few words into the bull's throat. Then he spat. The female relatives came one after the other and dropped a few words and spat into the sacred mouth. What a bizarre sight! Women spitting a breath of humanity into the depths of a contorted muzzle, divine spirit and hobbled bull . . .

'Now, they're going to sacrifice the animals,' murmured Abdoulaye. 'You won't see anything, there's no need to cover your eyes . . . They're already slitting their throats in the backyard . . .'

'Why, if the fellow's cured?' groaned Theo, his hands over his ears.

'Don't worry, they're killed with a single blow to avoid any suffering. Then the blood of the victims is collected and the initiate's body is washed with it.'

'Washed with blood? That's disgusting!'

'But for us, blood cleanses and protects. He'll sleep all night under this protection. The healer will make him a necklace with the Ox's entrails, and two anklets, which also give protection. At dawn, the patient will be allowed to remove the entrails and the dried blood. He will be a new man. Now they've been satisfied, the *rabs* will have left him.'

'Where will they have gone?' asked Theo.

While they skinned the Ox on the sand before quartering it, Mr Diop, with his usual patience, explained that, to contain the *rabs*, the healer was going to build them an altar in the family home. During this operation, she would place the meat from the sacrifice in several gourds, together with the horns, the roots and the millet, then would bury them under the ground and plant the pestle-turned-*pangol* on top. From that moment, the cured patient would become his protective spirits' priest.

The drumming had ceased. Surrounded by the healers, the initiate made his way home. The crowd dispersed. The courtyard was quiet again and the murmur of the sea could once again be heard. Theo felt wobbly and Abdoulaye made him sit down. That was when he realized that Aunt Martha had disappeared.

Snakes and spiders

Aunt Martha was crouching behind a fishing boat, a handkerchief over her mouth, stifling a convulsive hiccup. Abdoulaye helped her to her feet and gave her a hearty slap on the back. The hiccups stopped.

'Oh!' she groaned. 'I couldn't take any more. The blood, the drums, the heat . . .'

'You're very pale,' said Abdoulaye. 'And Theo looks as shaken up as you. Come and sit with him.'

Lying on the sand, the aunt and nephew gradually recovered their spirits. Mr Diop tactfully went off for a walk along the beach, looking for shells, to give Aunt Martha and Theo the opportunity to exchange notes.

'Wow, that was heavy,' murmured Theo. 'Is that what animism's about?'

'Yes,' she said. 'If animism consists of worshipping invisible spirits that can take over people's lives, it certainly is.'

'But I thought the Senegalese were Muslims! None of these spirits is in the Koran!'

'In the Koran, there are the djinns, you know . . . Here, they're called spirits, *pangols* or *rabs*. They sacrifice a bull, but at the same time they chant the name of Allah . . .'

'Ah! It's the same as everywhere else. Syncretism!'

'If only those tom-toms weren't so deafening,' she groaned. 'It makes me ill!'

'It was the sight of blood that did for me,' said Theo.

'Be quiet for a moment,' she murmured, closing her eyes. 'I'm tired.'

A little girl was paddling barefoot in the waves, stroking a marmalade kitten. Theo joined her: she was so cute with her red dress and tiny plaits all over her head. She leaned towards him and held out her cat, a beautiful ginger animal with blue eyes. Theo gently took it from her. The little girl ran off shouting 'It's yours!'

'Aunt Martha won't be too pleased,' muttered Theo, stroking the cat. 'Tough! I'm adopting you, old thing.'

Wrong! Aunt Martha was so shattered that she didn't say a word. Abdoulaye suggested that a little nap before lunch might be a good idea. Aunt Martha and Theo didn't need telling twice: as soon as they reached the house, they collapsed. The kitten curled up in a ball at its new master's feet. Time to rest.

Abdoulaye found Anta in the sitting room.

'Well?' asked his sister.

'Our friend found it all a bit too much. It's understandable that the boy found it hard to take, first time around, but Martha knows Africa!'

'We must treat them like my baby,' said Anta sententiously. 'Let them eat when they wake up.'

Towards evening, Aminata's baby gave the signal for feeding time and all three babies woke up at the same time, Aunt Martha, Theo and his cat. Anta served a bottle, cold chicken and a tart. Perched on Theo's knee, the marmalade cat devoured the chicken leftovers.

'So this is Africa,' mused Theo.

'What is?' said Anta. 'The sacrifice of the Ox? In Asia too, they sacrifice animals. Being possessed by spirits? You find that all over the world, even in France, if you go into the remoter areas.'

'But nowhere else do you find men lying down on the ground and pretending to be animals!' cried Theo.

'Oh yes you do! Don't forget, I'm a sociologist, I've read some books. In southern Italy, women wriggle on the ground like spiders. From what they say, they've been bitten by the creatures called tarantulas while working in the fields. And then, on the anniversary of the bites, they fall ill again. Now, first of all, there are no venomous spiders in that region, and secondly, it's a medical fact that no insect bite ever recurs the following year. So . . .'

'So they're bonkers,' concluded Theo.

'No,' said Anta. 'They're possessed. The proof is that only an orchestra can cure them. The musicians are called in, and the "tarantulized" patient begins to imitate the movements of the spider, crawling on the ground to the sound of the violin. It goes on for days. The woman is cured. The following year, on the same date, the same thing happens. How is that different from our N'Doeup?'

'Spiders aren't *rabs*,' said Theo.

'Oh yes they are! What's so peculiarly African about the N'Doeup?'

'Not the sacrifice, not the possession by spirits . . .' pondered Theo. 'Death and rebirth?'

'That's one difference,' Anta replied. 'Do you think there are any others?'

'The tom-toms,' murmured Aunt Martha, who hadn't uttered a word.

'Oh you and your tom-toms!' Anta laughed. 'You'll be hearing some more tomorrow!'

461

'I know,' said Aunt Martha glumly.

'Cool!' cried Theo. 'The tom-toms on their own?'

Not really.

The possessed

The last part of the N'Doeup took place in a little square. The crowd was attentive, all eyes were turned to the circle drawn in the sand by the healers. For they were all there, the healers, wearing voluminous boubous with leather belts; and with them, the new initiate wearing his headband, the ox blood washed off and rid of his necklace made of entrails. At the edge of the circle, Aunt Martha clutched Theo's hand under Abdoulaye's watchful eye.

The healer rang the little bells in the initiate's ears . . . A shudder ran through the crowd. The initiate began to shake convulsively, and the griots launched into action. They roused the *rabs*, invoking them with their booming drums, summoning them to be incarnated in the healers' bodies . . . They chased the women into the sacred circle, and pursued them. The first ones succumbed, their eyes bulging, choking as they exhaled, whirling round until they lost their balance and threw their heads back with a frenzied jerking of their bodies.

'Why are they doing that?' whispered Theo.

'Because each one of them must honour her *rab* so as to let the initiate into the circle of healers. They must all fall into a trance, and until they do, the rite isn't over.'

'Each one has her own *rab*?' asked Theo, puzzled. 'So they're all possessed?'

'Every single one of them! That's how you become a healer. By having first of all been healed yourself. But the initiate isn't there yet . . . Look.'

The griots surrounded the initiate and would not leave him alone. Taunted by the drums, he stuck out his tongue and eventually fell howling to the ground. But that was not enough. The tom-toms still hungered for felled women, they wanted the one who had not given in. The possessed women were resisting! They held their ground . . . War raged between the women and the tom-toms. The drumbeat became thunderous and cries tore the air.

'Aunt Martha!' cried Theo. 'Watch out!'

Her head nodding gently, a faraway look in her eyes, Aunt Martha was dancing to the rhythm of the tom-toms. Abdoulaye tried to hold her still.

'Stop her!' yelled Theo. 'She'll fall!'

Swaying with a regular motion, she staggered, her eyes closed . . . Panic-stricken, Theo watched Abdoulaye restrain his glassy-eyed aunt. Suddenly, everything stopped. All the healers lay on the ground and the triumphant tom-toms had stopped playing. The victors had stopped drumming. Abdoulaye grabbed Aunt Martha and bundled her hastily into the car.

'Don't talk to her,' he ordered.

'It's not serious, is it?' pleaded Theo.

'Just a little trance. It's nothing. These things happen.'

'Shouldn't we take her to hospital?' urged Theo. 'They'd look after her!'

'They'd knock her out with tranquillizers . . . All she needs is a good sleep and tomorrow she'll be fine.'

'Are you sure?' insisted Theo. 'My aunt's not from Africa! Will she get over it?'

'Just like you in Luxor. Look, she's opening her eyes. Don't say anything!'

Aunt Martha was surfacing. She mumbled incoherently, and Theo gathered that she had seen pretty lights, that she felt light and that she had been very hot. Theo took her hand. No, Aunt Martha didn't look too ill. Simply exhausted, a vague smile playing on her lips. Anta helped her undress, gave her some hot herb tea, and Aunt Martha slept the sleep of the just, with Theo at her bedside. The cat tried to distract him, meowing pathetically, but in vain. At dinner time, Anta found all three of them fast asleep.

Martha entranced

'They're asleep,' she said, coming back into the dining room. 'You were right, Abdou! Something was getting our friend Martha down . . .'

'I can't get over it . . . She really must have needed to get it off her chest!'

'Too many responsibilities! Too much anxiety! Gallivanting around the world with a kid who's half-dying . . . I wouldn't have been able to do that. Her courage has taken its toll!'

'OK, I can understand that at the point when Theo began to get better, she let go. But our Martha, who's so rational, so controlled, in a trance! She's never betrayed the slightest sign of weakness . . .'

'Nor has she ever embarked on an adventure like this,' said Anta. 'Goodness knows what Theo's stirred up inside her!'

Abdoulaye pensively agreed that after all, he didn't know much about Martha's past. On that subject, she was not forthcoming. Her husband's death, perhaps? Martha had not been able to save him. With Theo, she'd strained every nerve . . . Yes, this tough battle against death had probably exhausted her considerable energy.

'Well, I think it's good that she went into a trance,' said Anta. 'It's always better than a real illness.'

'But she doesn't understand a single word of the N'Doeup ceremony, so how come?'

'So, opportunity makes the thief,' said Anta. 'You're forgetting the tom-toms. She can't stand them!'

The tom-toms! The pounding rhythm and the music had been too much for Martha. She'd fought so hard, made such an effort to resist them that in the end, the tom-toms had got the better of her.

'At least she got it out of her system,' said Anta. 'What amazes me is that the boy wasn't affected.'

Abdoulaye had an explanation. Theo had fallen into a trance, without realizing it, at the start of the journey, in Egypt. He had had his share. Especially as he had gradually discovered the story of his still-born twin sister . . . everything was clear now. Theo no longer needed to go into a trance because he was cured.

'Granted,' said Anta. 'But there's still something missing. His twin sister's name. In other words, his twin sister is his *rab*.'

The other Africa

The next day was a hospital day, but this time it was for Aunt Martha. Abdoulaye had insisted on a thorough examination, to ensure that Martha's trance was not masking something more serious. Theo had a blood test. But Aunt Martha was kept for four hours – they took X-rays, checked her blood pressure and her heart, and ran a whole series of blood tests . . .

'It's your turn,' said Theo. 'I'm used to it.'

'OK wise guy,' she grumbled. 'Well, I'm not!'

Basically, Aunt Martha was suffering from exhaustion and low blood pressure, but they would have to wait for the results, which didn't please her. She was angry for allowing herself to be caught flagging, angry with the hospital. Deeply humiliated, she kept cursing the tom-toms of Africa, which were as barbaric as techno music. To take her mind off things, Abdoulaye suggested a brief trip to Casamance, where the sea was beautiful, nature magnificent, and there were masses of pelicans. What's more, it was one of the most mysterious regions. They were to leave the following day.

In the morning Theo woke up with a start: someone was tapping at the window. Half asleep, he went over to the window and found himself face to face with an enormous creature with an incredibly long orange beak. The bird was twisting its neck, banging on the pane with its beak and staring at Theo with its round eyes.

'It's food you want,' said Theo. 'I haven't got anything here, old thing.'

Furious, the bird flew off. The cat meowed. Theo burst out laughing and Aunt Martha opened her eyes.

'Who was knocking at the window?' she asked.

'A kind of toucan with a swan's neck . . .'

'A hornbill. When it flies away, it's said to head straight for Mecca.'

'Mecca,' said Theo. 'Lucky thing!'

'So are you,' she retorted. 'We're going to fly straight to the forests of darkest Africa. Get a move on, the plane leaves in two hours.'

'Not another planc!' protested Theo. 'I'm sick of planes . . .'

But this plane was different. It was a little five-seater crate, a miniature plane. Peering anxiously out of the window, through the clouds Theo glimpsed a sea of trees, long ribbons of blue, and neat little squares of emerald.

'Can you see the paddy-fields?' said Abdoulaye. 'And the arms of the river? They're called the *bolong*.'

'Where are we?' asked Theo anxiously. 'Have we left Senegal?'

'We're flying over the Casamance,' replied Abdoulaye.

'Is the Casamance a country?'

'It's the other Senegal,' cut in Aunt Martha. 'The Africa of the forest.'

'The land of the Diola,' added Abdoulaye. 'They're cousins of the Serer.'

Aguaine and Diambogne, twin sisters from the north of Senegal, the knowledgeable Abdoulaye told them, travelled down the coast to the headland of the Saloum river mouth, not far from the village of the old Serer healer. Across the sound they saw two beautiful trees and a pirogue, into which they both clambered. A tornado broke the pirogue in two . . . the twins would have died in the storm if the water spirits hadn't carried the two sisters onto opposite banks of the River Gambia.

Aguaine, who had remained on the south bank, became the mother of the Diola, while Diambogne, in the north, became the mother of the Serer. Thus the two peoples descended from twins parted by the storm and a river.

'In Africa, there are twins everywhere,' remarked Theo gravely.

The twins had each given birth to a very different region. Serer country was scattered forest, palmyra palms in the savannah and giant baobabs. Diola country lay in the shade of giant silk-cotton trees wrapped in dense curtains of tangled creepers. In Serer country, they grew millet; in Casamance, a round-grained variety of red rice. The Serer country was the home of the star and the *pangols*, while the Diola country hid mysterious initiations in the sacred woods that no stranger was allowed to enter.

'Were the sisters real twins?' asked Theo suspiciously.

'Maybe they weren't homozygotes! For the Diola differed in other ways. Their society was organized to reflect the cosmos: each person was in close contact with the village community, which was ruled by the order of divine energy expressed through phenomena, gestures and ritual. The actions of one person affected the entire community, and yet the Diola seemed fiercely jealous of their individual freedom. They were said to be rebellious, quarrelsome and closed. The Diola religion was kept a closely guarded secret; initiates were not allowed to reveal these secrets without endangering the entire village, in other words, the cosmos. This was probably the reason for the many rumours about the ceremonies in the sacred woods ... Human sacrifices, bloody decapitations, layers of women's corpses arranged on a rack and smoked, to be eaten collectively.'

'What utter rubbish!' Aunt Martha exploded. 'You talk about the Diola the way the Spanish conquistadors did about the "savages", as they called them! Cannibals, backward heathens! Aren't you ashamed, Abdoulaye?'

'It's only hearsay, I tell you!' he protested. 'I imagine that, in the sacred woods, people sacrifice animals like everywhere else in Africa! I really have no idea. I'm not a Diola. We'll be landing in a minute. You see, it's not far.'

The king of the woods

The tiny seaside airport was shrouded in mist. The air was humid and the wind had dropped: the African rains had begun. Despite his efforts, Abdoulaye was unable to smooth over the disastrous effects of his clumsy rumour-mongering. There was nothing to be done before they settled into the hotel bungalows set in beautiful gardens. Vista over the ocean, beach fringed with coconut palms, loungers, straw huts . . . The hotel certainly came up to expectations as a peaceful haven. Theo put on his swimming trunks and Aunt Martha reclined under a parasol. Abdoulaye sighed with relief.

'Isn't it relaxing here, Martha?' he ventured.

'It feels as though we're in California, in an American soap!' cried Theo.

'But there aren't any cannibals in California,' mumbled Aunt Martha. 'You shouldn't repeat such nonsense about the Diola, Abdoulaye. It's not like you!'

'If they weren't so secretive, people wouldn't say such things! Besides, I'm not going to be your guide in Diola country, it'll be one of my friends, Armand Diatta, an expert on ecosystems. I'll wait here for you, I've got a report to write. Anyway, Armand wouldn't show me anything. Not a thing!'

'A new guide?' said Theo. 'Where is he?'

'Here,' replied a soft voice.

Mr Diatta was around fifty, with a brilliant smile, fine eyes and a twinkle of mischief. He made his suggestions in a shy, reserved voice. If Madame Martha agreed, they would go and visit some high-ranking religious dignitaries. Would they like that?

'Yes!' decided Theo. 'California can wait.'

As soon as the words were out of Theo's mouth, then Mr Diatta disappeared to telephone.

'He's going to let them know you're coming,' murmured Abdoulaye. 'Nothing's straightforward in Casamance. For instance, my friend is a member of the royal family, though he might not tell you himself.'

'So there are kings in Casamance?' asked Aunt Martha in surprise.

'It's no secret,' replied Abdoulaye. 'That, I can tell you about.'

In the Diola religion, the king acted as a high priest, with close links to the village gods, who themselves were mediators between God and humans. It was difficult for outsiders to understand how a Diola king was chosen in Casamance. What they did know was that royalty wasn't hereditary, that the dignitaries had to identify the future king from among the royal families by certain signs, and that, once crowned, the king exercised his religious powers under rigorous conditions. He took on a strain of divinity, for he had passed into the other world, that of the spirit.

Once crowned, the king lived alone in the royal forest. He was not allowed to live in public, or to marry, or to eat and drink in the presence of others, except for initiates. One day, the exacting royal duties caused a terrible tragedy in Casamance. In 1903, a Diola king called Sihabele was arrested by the French, and interned with some ordinary prisoners. Because he couldn't eat in front of other men, he allowed himself to starve to death . . .

'My God,' murmured Aunt Martha. 'A real crime of ignorance!'

'So the king really is very, very holy!' concluded Theo. 'Because, to live apart from others, he must be pretty awesome!'

But his role was crucial . . . The king was responsible for peace in his village. The king performed the rain ceremonies so vital for the paddy fields and therefore for life. But if war broke out or there was a drought, then the king's failure could cost him dear!

'That reminds me of a Roman myth, long before the Republic and the Empire,' said Aunt Martha. 'Rome was just a village at the time, and its chief lived in the heart of a dense forest, the Nemi wood. The village ruler was called "the king of the woods". Chosen by the gods, the king of Nemi was seen as a threat to the community. He too lived alone: nobody touched him, for he was taboo. People couldn't do without him, but they feared him because of his powers. After a year, a new king was chosen and the old one was killed.'

'Odd sort of power,' Theo broke in. 'Where's the fun in that?'

'There isn't any,' she replied. 'True royalty is always linked to the divine. The king doesn't choose to be king: power is his destiny, a fate he cannot avoid. True kings rule "by divine right". Do you know that the kings of France were also healers? They had the power to cure swollen glands in the neck!'

'That's a joke,' said Theo. 'Is there any proof?'

'No more than the ritual bath of the Serer healer,' she replied. 'But if that should fail, those with the magic powers are in trouble! I feel sorry for them.'

Abdoulaye nodded. It was easier to submit to Allah's omnipotence than to deal with the awesome sacred force of the cosmos. Armand Diatta reappeared, and Abdoulaye sulked. He knew he wasn't about to learn the secrets of his friend from Casamance.

The sacred colour red

The trip planned by Mr Diatta didn't seem particularly mysterious. In a village, they saw the fetish tree and the huge drum in the middle of the square, a giant hollowed-out trunk booming out messages that could be heard ten miles away, transmitted in the code learned during the initiation in the sacred wood. The village chief offered his guests palm wine which Aunt Martha wisely refused, while Theo tasted it. They glimpsed pelicans and white storks roosting in flocks on the tops of the palmyra palms. In the distance, they could see dense forest, maybe sacred woods, maybe not. They passed tourists in shorts, some on bicycles, others in cars. In a market, they met a healer from Ghana whose stall displayed a painted canvas illustrating the diseases his potions cured: impotence, haemorrhoids, stomach aches, worms and bed-wetting.

'Well, are we going to see your friends soon?' asked Theo, with a hint of disappointment in his voice.

'They're waiting for us at the entrance to the village,' replied Mr Diatta tersely.

'Then what?'

No answer. The car pulled up in front of an old man in a cap. He seemed to be saying there were complications, as Armand Diatta looked very annoyed. In the end, he raised his voice and the man ambled off again without a word.

'He tried to make trouble, but he agreed to act as our guide,' said Mr Diatta authoritatively. 'I'd like to see that man stand up to me! It's a mile away on foot. Mrs Macquarie, would you mind removing your red scarf please . . .'

'My scarf? Is it a problem?'

'It's the colour,' he said. 'Where we're going, you mustn't wear red. Luckily, you're both dressed in blue.'

Bemused, Aunt Martha and Theo followed him along the footpaths, across fields and scrub. They passed huts where women were pounding millet, they met cheeky children, they walked round the leafy trees once, twice, twenty times, and soon they reached the entrance to a dense forest.

'Ah, at last,' sighed Aunt Martha, mopping her brow. 'Is this a sacred wood?'

'Yes. I even have the sacred duty of telling you so. We are at the entrance to the royal area. Let us enter. The king is waiting for us.'

'The king in person?' cried Theo. 'I'm going to meet the king? In the sacred wood? And I've got Mum's ring! Brill! The Pythia from *Wrath of the Gods* was right!'

'Don't shout like that,' said Aunt Martha. 'Control yourself.'

They emerged from the foliage into a shady clearing. Armand Diatta bade his friends be seated on tree trunks. At the back of the clearing, a wall of beautifully plaited palms barred the way. There was a sort of door planted on strange wooden legs but nobody went through it. Perched on the branches of a silk-cotton tree, young vultures lazily stretched their wings. There was absolute calm, and the wait seemed endless.

'What's that wall?' asked Theo to break the silence.

'Let's say it's a bit like a palace,' murmured Armand. 'Actually, it's something else, but if I tell you too much, I'll be betraying our community, you understand? Our religion is too often seen as an old-fashioned tradition, and we have to protect ourselves . . . Our king is very important to us. Don't worry, he'll see you because it's been arranged. Ah! Here he is.'

Aunt Martha and Theo stood up without prompting. A very old man with a white goatee beard emerged noiselessly from the palms. The village king was in red. His felt fez was red, his boubou was red, the king wore red. In one hand he held a besom of dry stalks, and in the other a round stool, on which he sat. Armand Diatta made the introductions and, as this was an audience, Aunt Martha began to thank the king profusely. The king replied with a few words of welcome, but he did not speak French.

'The king is honoured by your presence,' Armand Diatta translated. 'He's sorry not to be able to receive you in greater style, but the village is preparing for a ceremony.'

'Which he will be leading, I understand,' said Aunt Martha.

'Well . . .' hesitated Mr Diatta. 'The king doesn't do. Our king is. He embodies the spirit of the cosmos and is our link to our God, Ata-Emit, the god of Heaven. We only have one absolute God, who is invisible, whom we must not fail. We say: "*Atemit Sembe* – God is power and strength."'

'Don't you have any *pangols*?' asked Theo.

'We have altars and spirits, but we'll talk about those later,' replied Armand Diatta cautiously. 'For here we are in the presence of the king, who safeguards the balance of the divine energy forces.'

'Can I ask the king if he leads his people in war?' said Aunt Martha.

When he heard the translation, the king was transformed. His whole being came to life, his eyes flashed, his body trembled, giving a glimpse of his power . . . Raising his arms to the heavens, he launched into a lengthy speech. Accompanying his words with expansive, graceful gestures, he brandished his besom and spread his hands as if to bless the space around him. Then he was silent.

'Was my question inappropriate?' said Aunt Martha. 'The king looks shocked . . .'

'He said that he is not even allowed to witness bloodshed,' replied Armand. 'That his only weapon is his sceptre, this besom. That his role is not to manage the affairs of men, but those of the sacred, for which he is accountable. But he is not a military leader, quite the opposite! He is no longer of this world. Nothing would be more sacrilegious than for a king of Casamance to spill another man's blood!'

'Can he at least make peace?' asked Theo.

The king said that he rejoiced in peace and blessed it, but that in so saying, he was only speaking for himself. For the Diola communities held respect for the consensus above all else, and that was outside the king's sphere of influence. The village king confined himself to the sacred, of which he was the living guarantor.

'He truly is the King of the Woods,' murmured Aunt Martha. 'The guarantor of the hidden and inaccessible. What majesty . . .'

The audience was over. The king took his leave and vanished among the foliage. All at once the space seemed empty.

'I suppose it's because of his red clothing that I had to remove my scarf,' mused Aunt Martha.

'When he's in ceremonial dress, he alone is allowed to wear the colour of blood,' replied Armand. 'Red is also the colour of fire . . . If he were to be extinguished, it would be terrible! When the villages no longer have a king, they can't function! The king is the central energy force.'

'What's this king's name?' she asked.

'He doesn't have a name. The king isn't called by his name, he's called "*Man*" – not the English word: it has no other meaning than the king's sacred title. Our kings have no power, they represent God . . . and they don't die!'

'Oh yes they do!' cried Theo. 'The one who was arrested by the French allowed himself to die of starvation . . .'

'King Sihalebe didn't die,' replied Armand Diatta gravely. 'He disappeared. On his arrest, people said that the earth was shattered.

When the French burned his royal fez to destroy his power, the smoke rose to Heaven . . .'

'And you buried him in accordance with the rites,' added Aunt Martha.

'Unfortunately,' he sighed, 'King Sihalebe's remains are no longer in Casamance. I shouldn't say where they are, but you are French, so I'm going to tell you. The royal remains are at the Musée de l'Homme, in Paris.'

'How frightful,' murmured Aunt Martha.

'But since he's not dead, let's not speak of it,' Armand said hastily. 'Forget it.'

'Why do we have to be dressed in blue?' asked Theo.

No answer.

'What about the altars, then?' said Theo.

They saw the altars on the way back. They had walked past them without even noticing, for the altars looked like two huts, one large and open, the other tiny and closed, with thatched roofs and a clay pot on top. From a distance, they could make out large drums hanging from pillars, all pointing in the same direction.

'This is where we pray,' said Armand. 'People will tell you that we have fetishes, the *boekin*, but that's not entirely true . . . They are only symbols of the one energy force. You see, we Diola are a bit like the Jews. The high priest of the Hebrews also represented royalty, and if you want to find out more about our sacrifices, I advise you to read Leviticus in the Bible. And the book of Numbers.'

'Leviticus . . .' murmured Theo. 'Eliezer talked to me about it in Jerusalem. If I remember, it's the rules that forbid the hare . . . Something about impurity?'

'Not only,' replied Armand. 'The choice of the sacrificial animal, the method of slaughter, how it is then divided up . . .'

'And what goes on in the little hut?' inquired Theo.

'Don't be so nosy!' scolded Aunt Martha.

'Well, I can tell you quite simply,' replied Armand with a smile. 'In the little hut, the living spirit breathes.'

Aunt Martha and Theo clambered back into the car in silence. Armand Diatta tried to tell them a little more, but was skirting the taboo, and stopped in confusion. The world of the sacred must not be jeopardized by betraying the secret.

The ladies of Bignona

'Anyway, in the place we're going to now, things will be public,' concluded Armand. 'We're going to visit the nuns in Bignona. No more secrets!'

The ladies and musicians were waiting under a huge medlar tree in a vast quadrangle, in the shadow of the Catholic church. The nuns welcomed their guests and sat beside them on chairs set in neat rows. Assembled on one side, a shawl over their *boubous*, rows of cowrie necklaces adorning their chests, the ladies of Bignona chatted as they kept an eye on the tom-toms that the musicians turned by warming the skins over a fire. Suddenly the drumming began . . .

Barefoot, the ladies of Bignona took out from their *boubous* two sticks that they banged together to the beat of the tom-toms, jigging on the spot. Behind the dense shadow stood a dancer wearing a goat-hair head-dress. Suddenly he leapt into the centre of the circle in one bound, his eyes glassy and a smile on his lips. He wore a necklace of blue beads, hair bracelets and trailing scarves on his arms, and in his hand he held a flute . . . Dressed like that, he looked like a young god surrounded by priestesses.

'If he were Hindu, you'd swear he was Krishna,' muttered Aunt Martha.

'Or Dionysus and the Bacchantes,' added Theo. 'You know, the Greek god of wine?'

'Thank you, I know,' she said. 'But . . . Look!'

The dancer was leaping towards her and looked about to jump at her . . . At the last minute, he stopped a foot away from Aunt Martha, one arm extended as if to invite her to dance. Aunt Martha recoiled and blushed. The dancer stepped back with exquisite elegance and Aunt Martha felt sheepish. The ladies of Bignona laughed heartily at the foreign lady's panic, banging their wooden sticks.

One of them stepped forward and launched into frenzied action. Bent double, her arms outstretched, her rear pointing upwards, she stamped on the ground at a furious tempo, then, like the dancer, she stopped dead and resumed her place in the crowd. A second woman stepped into the centre, and then another. From time to time, the dancer began his prodigious leaps again, stopping dead with a smile . . . Two hours went by under the medlar tree, to the sound of the banging sticks and furious tom-toms, two hours of the leaping dancer. Sometimes, he accompanied a girl on the flute, whirling around her to encourage her, but each time the ladies of Bignona would suddenly break off in mid-dance and return to their seats at the most unexpected point. Occasionally, one of the ladies would toss her flimsy shawl into the lap of a young nun.

Laughing in embarrassment, the nun, dressed in white, would rise and join the dance, knotting the shawl around her hips. With the exception of the elderly nuns, they were invited one by one to stamp on the ground without removing their shoes. All complied with a madly joyous though controlled frenzy. Then the ladies of Bignona gathered together, and as the tom-toms reached their climax, they started to move off, smiling, calm, with small steps, filling the entire area like a human tide. The dancer vanished and the drumming died away.

Aunt Martha dabbed at her neck with a handkerchief.

'Whew!' she cried. 'I really thought they were going to make me dance!'

'They didn't dare,' replied Armand. 'But they were dying to . . .'

'Even the nuns joined in!' she said. 'Were they in a trance?'

'Not at all,' he said. 'That wasn't a sacred ceremony, since we're in the quadrangle of a Catholic presbytery. It was simply a dance. Until people have seen our religions at work in a village, they can't understand a thing. Our bodies are made of dance. Did the tom-toms bother you?'

'Not at all!' she replied. 'I felt completely at ease. I'd never have thought it!'

'Well, at least you've seen the Diola drums now!'

'Where's Theo got to?' she said, suddenly anxious. 'I can't see him anywhere . . .'

Theo was in conversation with the youngest nun.

'Her name's Augustine,' he said. 'She's great! She's taught me to dance, look . . .'

He bent double, pointed his rear upwards, spread his arms, jumped up and down on the spot, grabbed his feet and rolled in the dirt. Sister Augustine burst out laughing and dusted him down.

'You'll need some more work on your balance,' commented Aunt Martha. 'When you dance, you look like a lost chick looking for its mother.'

'There's nothing else for me to show you this time,' said Armand. 'Maybe another day . . .'

Back at the hotel, Abdoulaye was pretending to work. He barely looked up from his report . . . Theo rushed over to hug him, but Mr Diop fended him off.

'Well?' he said.

'We saw the King of the Woods!' cried Theo. 'All in red!'

'I told you about him,' he replied. 'And what else?'

'Are you kidding?' said Theo. 'I bet you haven't seen the King?'

'No, but I still know,' he said, irritably. 'I read books about the Diola, I do, I have no alternative . . . One of these days, Armand, you'll have to stop treating me like a barbarian.'

'It's difficult, you know, for the initiated . . . You Muslims consider us as satans, so how can we explain our world to you?' said Armand awkwardly.

'What about them, then? They're not Diola, as far as I know!'

'No,' muttered Armand. 'But they're studying all the world's religions, and ours is one of them. They know that.'

That evening, Aunt Martha rummaged in the suitcases and unearthed Leviticus. The Lord called Moses and gave him the laws concerning sacrifices: for cattle, a young male without blemish, whose blood would be given as an offering on the altar before the animal was flayed and cut up. Anyone who transgressed, even inadvertently, had to sacrifice a bull to the Lord and confess his sin publicly. Only then would the priest, anointed by the Lord, be able to protect the people through God's strength.

'A priest-king, an unblemished bull, a united community, a public confession, an absolute God and altars,' she said. 'Well! It's a true religion, there's no doubt about that.'

'Hang on,' said Theo. 'I'm going to copy all that into my notebook. Right, a King of the Woods, a bull, a confession, an altar, God, of course, . . . You forgot the pure and the impure, Aunt M. Judaism, Hinduism and now the Diola . . . the priests are so pure that they can't be touched. And the others have to be purified through sacrifice. Isn't that right?'

'That sounds plausible. But you're forgetting the community as a whole. Armand also told us to read Numbers, didn't he? Let's see . . .'

In the Book of Numbers, the Lord commanded Moses to number the whole community of Israel by families in the father's line. Then he commanded him to expel the unclean, everyone, man or woman, who suffered from a malignant skin disease or a discharge. Then, once the tribes were expurgated, the Lord gave each one a specific task, laying down also the rations of wine, flour and oil that should accompany the sacrifice of the bull. Only members of the tribe of Levi, called the Levites, would be entitled to carry the Tabernacle of the Tokens.

'What on earth is *that*?' asked Theo, bemused.

'The purpose of *that* was to regulate the tribes within the community,' she said. 'The Levites are the priests, rather like the Brahmans. Our Diatta is like a sort of Diola Levite. Not only is he an initiate, but he is of royal blood . . . The only thing not in Numbers or Leviticus is the sacred wood. I wonder how God's energy flows there.'

The slave island

After Casamance, it was time to leave the Africa of the forests and return to the capital. Abdoulaye tried to coax his friends to tell him the secrets they had witnessed, but apart from telling him about the Bignona dances, they clammed up. Neither Aunt Martha nor Theo felt inclined to elaborate on the King of the Woods, and Abdoulaye was wasting his time.

On their return, concrete reality took over from the invisible. Aunt Martha was anxious about the results of her hospital tests. As for Theo, he had a sore throat and was continually thirsty. But Theo's results showed further improvement. When consulted about his sore throat, the doctor said that it was simply a reaction to all the dust. And Aunt Martha had probably suffered an attack of spasmophilia but it wasn't certain.

'Spasm, trance, it's the same thing,' she complained as they left. 'I tell you, doctors are all stupid. And to think he gave me magnesium! I know what the disease is and I know the cure. In both cases it's the tom-tom.'

And seeing that the patients were cured, Abdoulaye decided that the time had come to visit Gorée island. Aunt Martha insisted on telephoning Paris, and made it a point of honour to tell Theo's parents about her African trance herself.

'No,' she told her brother, 'it's not painful. It was very light, very gentle . . . What did I do? I don't remember. I blacked out . . . Yes, me, fancy that! Well, actually, I am rather proud of myself. That was my little initiation . . . Yes, the hospital, what do you expect? . . . They thought it might be spasmophilia, but they don't know anything about these things. Theo? He was absolutely fine. Abdoulaye said that he'd had his share already. Of what? Of trances, silly! You want to talk to Theo? I'll hand you over. By the way, the results of his blood tests are excellent.'

Theo confirmed Aunt Martha's account and suddenly froze. Fatou, Dad was saying, Fatou! She was so miserable it was heartbreaking . . .

He'd forgotten to phone her again! And what about his message? It had completely slipped his mind . . . What had Aunt Martha been thinking of?

'Goodness me!' cried Aunt Martha. 'That's the first time I've forgotten a message for Theo!'

It was time to knuckle down to it. *I am white and brown, the goddess of the waters. I await you in my country, in the land of mermaids.* Another Africa, Abdoulaye had said. With a white and brown water goddess. White? It didn't make sense! Theo took the opportunity to give Fatou an affectionate call. And supposing she gave him the clue?

'*The goddess came from Africa with your ships,*' stated the Parisian Pythia in a mystical voice.

Theo was as baffled as ever. OK, the black slaves had been deported. But in which former slave country did the water goddess live? There were so many in Central and South America . . . Urging them to hurry, Abdoulaye looked at his watch and warned them that they were going to miss the next boat for Gorée island. Tickets, embarkation, benches, rough sea typical of the rainy season, cormorants flying overhead . . .

'The Wolof, the Serer, the Lebu, the Diola, that makes four,' counted Theo. 'Four peoples for one country!'

'There are more than you think,' said Abdoulaye. 'There are also the Tukulor, the Mandingue, the Soninke, the Bassari and the Fulani. That's nine.'

'More than in India!' exclaimed Theo. 'Senegal's quite something. So what are you?'

'My father is Wolof and my mother's Fulani, but my great, great grandmother was Lebu,' said Abdoulaye. 'And if we looked hard, we'd find a bit of Mandingue blood in the family. Senegal is a melting pot. Whoops! I nearly forgot the Saint-Louisians . . .

'Are they a people?' asked Aunt Martha. 'I thought Saint-Louis was a town!'

'A town that had French deputies who intermarried with blacks, Martha! The people from Saint-Louis are different from everyone else . . . They're very distinguished, highly civilized, very . . .'

'And you're not distinguished, I suppose?' said Theo.

'My grandmother was from Saint-Louis, you see. I know what I'm talking about! A whole way of life . . .'

'I see,' said Theo. 'You're a snob!'

'So what?' retorted Abdoulaye. 'Is snobbery bad?'

Defeated, Theo shut up. After twenty minutes, they landed on Gorée island and walked across the burning sand to the Slaves' House, a huge pink building flanked by magnificent curving steps, a real palace.

The curator of the museum had enhanced the symbolic status of the site. The handwritten notices gave exact figures for the millions of deportees from Africa, retracing their ordeal, their cruel deaths in the holds of slave ships, their suicides when the time came to leave, children separated from their mothers, the barbarism of a trade in human beings treated as live merchandise. He had reverently reconstituted their entreaties, their prayers and their songs. He talked about it with heart-rending sincerity. A group of Black Americans who had come on a pilgrimage wept together . . . Overcome with emotion, Aunt Martha and Theo began to cry too.

In the basement housing the cells where the captives were herded, a narrow door opened onto the Atlantic. There, said the curator, from those forbidding rocks, the fettered Africans were whipped on board the ships. This was the next stage of the long journey that began in the Sahel with the slave raids mounted by the African chiefs. There, the white slave masters rounded up the black human cattle whose trade would enable them to build their magnificent mansions in Bordeaux or Nantes. Dark, sinister, the door opened onto the ocean of exiles bound for the United States, the Caribbean or Brazil.

'Brazil!' cried Theo. 'Is there a water goddess there?'

Yes there was. Her name was Iemanja, and she came from Bénin. When they boarded under the lash of their masters' whips, the black slaves took with them the only possession that nobody could take away from them: their gods. The goddess of the African waters had sailed with her followers. But although her priestesses came from Africa, Iemanja had skin as white as the milk poured over the *pangols*.

CHAPTER 27

The Horses of the Gods

The freighter *Belmonte*

Leaving Dakar was not a wrench. Theo would see Fatou's father again in Paris. And for the first time, he was taking a friend, Arthur the cat. They had given the kitten a tiny fragment of a sleeping pill, and it was sound asleep in an open-work bag. The Air Africa flight took off in the middle of the night for Lisbon, where they would leave the plane.

'Lisbon – Rio, that's a long haul,' grumbled Theo.

'Who says we're flying?' replied Aunt Martha. 'We're going by ship!'

Theo was open-mouthed. Sailing to South America! A luxury white liner with loungers, a swimming pool on deck and a cinema . . .

'Don't get carried away,' she broke in. 'The transatlantic liners from Europe to Brazil stopped years ago. We're travelling by freighter.'

Freighter? In the hold, like the black slaves? Chained up among the containers, next to the roaring engines? What had he done to deserve such a punishment?

'This'll teach you!' she laughed. 'This way you'll understand the trials and tribulations of the first Portuguese navigators . . . After all, they were the first whites to reach the West Indies with their caravels. You've got nothing to complain about: we'll have engines, it's an improvement!'

Aunt Martha couldn't be serious . . . What would his parents say? But she waved aside her nephew's protests. She didn't sound as though she was joking, but Theo didn't believe her until he saw the freighter with his own eyes.

For the *Belmonte*, brand-new with her red funnels and Portuguese flag, was in dock. Aunt Martha strode undaunted up the gangway, dragging Theo, who was dismayed by the appalling weather. The sailors had grabbed the suitcases and bags, which had increased fourfold by now. When they were aboard, the Captain kissed Aunt Martha effusively before showing her to her cabin. On opening the door, Theo discovered a twin-bedded room, furnished in light pine, with armchairs, tables and a bathroom.

'Hang on,' he said. 'Is this a luxury ship or a freighter?'

Aunt Martha burst out laughing. Captain Da Silva explained with a grin that on many freighters there was guest accommodation. True, a freighter didn't have a swimming pool or a cinema. Aunt Martha and Theo would have to be content with sharing the Captain's food in his cabin. But . . .

'Brill!' cried Theo. 'You really conned me, the pair of you . . . So where are the engines? Will you show me how you handle the steering wheel? Pleeease. Will you?'

The Captain promised, except that you only found steering wheels in picture books nowadays. He left them to settle in, and went and shut himself away in his cabin before the *Belmonte* left port. Aunt Martha had barely begun to unpack the first suitcase when the massive structure began to creak. Theo went up on deck, but found neither wheel nor captain: a freighter was steered by a series of electronic dials in the bow of the ship, in an area where nobody was allowed to enter. There was nothing but the heaving Atlantic, which Theo eyed with apprehension.

Prophets and mixtures

'Well, what do you think of my surprise?' asked Aunt Martha when he came back down. 'You were sick and tired of planes. Are you happy?'

'Very,' he assured her. 'I'm just scared of getting seasick.'

'It's not serious. You get used to it.'

He felt happier lying down, just in case. But there was no problem. Arthur was still asleep. After a minute, Theo began to fidget.

'Aunt Martha, I have a question,' he began.

'That makes a change,' she said with a resigned sigh.

'I can't take my mind off that business with the bull the other day . . .'

'There's nothing unusual about the sacrifice of the bull, it happens all over the world. But for us, it certainly is a horrifying sight.'

'Exactly. Why?'

'Think. How often do you watch TV and see children dying of star-vation in various parts of the world? Isn't that a thousand times worse than a bull's throat being slit?'

'Yes, except that on TV you're not seeing it live.'

'Exactly. There's your explanation.'

Couldn't they have given the mad guy some sort of medicine to make him better?'

'He could have been treated in a psychiatric hospital,' she replied with a shrug. 'They'd have drugged him with neuroleptics, and it wouldn't have cured him. But by going back to his African roots, he's got a chance of getting better, do you see?'

'OK,' said Theo. 'So I won't be cured without Granny Theano. Because my roots are in Greece.'

'What about your father?'

He rolled over. Two minutes passed by.

'I've got another question,' he announced.

'Questionitis. Help!'

'What's the most durable religion in Africa? Islam, Christianity or the ancient religions? Because smearing yourself with bull's blood in the name of Allah, I mean . . .'

'Africa is like India,' replied Aunt Martha. 'Both continents have cow's stomachs. They swallow the foreign grass, soak it with their juices, chew it and calmly digest the lot. But however foreign the fodder, Africa remains intact.'

'They're not bothered by the notion of one God?' asked Theo in surprise.

Not at all. Just as the Hindus had integrated Mary into their vast pantheon of gods, the Africans had effortlessly assimilated the supreme God, Jesus and the Prophet. That didn't stop the drums beating, or trances from laying out the body and cleansing the heart of its fears. Open-air Catholic Masses dedicated to the Virgin were punctuated with the piercing cries of the women falling down, which shocked nobody, for this was under the African sun. On the other hand, the story of Christianity was full of mystics who proclaimed themselves prophets and founders of new religions.

Africa had seen some famous examples, such as pastor Harris, who preached in the name of the Angel Gabriel and cleanliness, and Albert Atcho, who healed the sick with the help of telegrams, taking their dossier out of God's huge filing system, or Simon Kimbangu, who served God and the cause of his people's liberation. The colonizers had repressed them, for the African prophets were in direct competition with Christianity. Then, the black mystics got a foothold in their country, succeeded in turn by new prophets who emerged from the forests, armed with Jesus and equipped with the power of fetishes.

'After all, the Africans are entitled to have their own messiahs,' concluded Theo. 'Why inflict white-skinned prophets on them?'

'Exactly,' she said. 'Religions may well travel with the invaders, but they run aground on the people's collective memory. Wait till we get to Brazil!'

'What are they in Brazil? Christian, Muslim, animist or what?'

In Brazil there were Christian Africans, Muslim Africans, animist whites, Christian Indians, Catholic or Protestant whites, Indian mulattos and even plain Indians, who had gone to enormous lengths to protect their own religions against the gold-diggers, roadbuilders and investors. Brazil was the biggest religious melting pot in the world, the place where they had become irretrievably intermingled, the epitome of syncretism, the country of divine madness.

'What about Carnival?' he asked.

Carnival too was part of the religious scenario. Captain Da Silva knew a lot about these matters, as his cousin Brutus came from Brazilian stock.

Indians, Blacks and whites

In Captain Da Silva's comfortable cabin, lunch was set out. There were scallops for starters. Theo set to.

'I hear your cousin's of Brazilian extraction?' he said.

'Brutus?' The Captain looked surprised. 'Who told you so?'

'Aunt Martha, of course. Why?'

The Captain began to laugh. His cousin Brutus was Brazilian, not 'of Brazilian extraction', for the phrase was meaningless in Brazil. True, he had a Portuguese name, Da Silva, to which 'Carneiro' had been added at some stage for greater effect. The Portuguese family archives did indeed confirm that a Da Silva had emigrated to Brazil at the time of the caravels, but after that no more was heard from the American branch. The product of a marriage between the Portuguese line and a gorgeous Greta from a German family that had emigrated at the start of the twentieth century, cousin Brutus claimed that he had Indian blood as the result of intermarriage between his ancestor and a tribal princess, like Pocahontas. For having Indian blood was trendy in Brazil: descent from a native Indian counted as a high-class alliance between the white

482

conqueror and the Indian, distinguished as the country's original inhabitants. But cousin Brutus avoided explaining where his frizzy hair and full lips had come from, for in Brazil, people of good family didn't admit to having Negro blood.

'I'm sure that the Portuguese ancestor fell in love with one of his African slaves,' concluded the Captain. 'Cousin Brutus is so insistent that there is no African blood in his veins that it makes you wonder!'

'What a mix-up,' said Theo. 'Why are Indian ancestors better?'

Ah! Because the Indians weren't slaves, quite the opposite! Of course, there'd been bloodshed at first. Then, a compassionate missionary called Las Casas noticed in time that his fellow citizens, supposedly such good Catholics, were enslaving the pure-hearted vulnerable savages who were too delicate for forced labour and were dying in their hundreds. Determined to halt the genocide committed by his compatriots, and aware that as Catholics they were wanting in Christian charity, the excellent Las Casas had a brainwave: he persuaded his sovereign to replace the Indians with Negro slaves, who were more robust, and better suited to the hard labour of the colonies. The road to Hell is paved with good intentions, and Las Casas had not foreseen the replacement of one genocide by another, which he subsequently denounced in vain . . . That was how, based on a generous thought gone wrong, the black slave trade between Europe and America began.

'But the Portuguese slept with their African slaves,' said Theo.

Not only them! Portuguese colonization was based on a simple principle: as soon as you landed, you took a wife. So in Brazil there were mixed-race black and white, black and Indian, and Indian and white inhabitants. And religions had mingled through the women. From the Indians, the Brazilians had borrowed the animal gods of the forests, the *Curupira*, the spirit of the woods with green teeth, the exquisite pipe-smoking *Caipora*, naked astride a peccary, and the red *Boto* of the Amazon river, a seductive dolphin who made women pregnant. From Africa, the Brazilians had inherited the gods hidden away in the holds of the slave ships, a pantheon from the former kingdom of Dahomey, nowadays called Benin. Forced to become Christians, the African slaves had embraced the worship of the Catholic saints, whom they happily included among their own gods. The result was that the religions of Brazil formed a frenzied Carnival dominated by dancing and drums, in other words, by the power of Africa.

'The tom-toms again, Aunt Martha!' cried Theo. 'Cool!'

Yes, the tom-toms. Thus began the slow reconquest of Africa by the

African slaves. The masters were harsh, but good economists. If the slaves were killing themselves by swallowing earth, that wasn't profitable. To avoid commercial losses, the masters allowed their slaves to play their drums. That was the origin of the *batuques*: all the drums of Africa combined. The gods were dredged up from memory, in secret, along with the African languages. Then followed the appearance of clandestine altars and ceremonies, which were now official. One day in the 1870s, the Africans came down from the hills of Rio and invaded the masters' city with their drums. That was the first Carnival.

There had been magnificent carnivals and religious processions in Portugal. As well as the clergy in their robes, saints, devils, emperors and kings and queens paraded alongside blacksmiths, monkeys, Venus, Bacchus, Saint Sebastian pierced with arrows, Saint Peter, Saint James and Abraham. The wild processions emigrated with the Portuguese. The Africans adopted the kings and queens, embroidered their totems on their banners, and later their guild emblems, and created a feverish atmosphere at Carnival with their dancing and their drums. Samba schools sprang up, and Brazilian Carnival became world-famous. Gradually, Africa made such a healthy recovery that it converted the whites, many of whom joined in Brazil's African religions. And if they weren't mad about Africa, then they turned to the Indians, borrowing their feathers and symbols.

'The Indians bequeathed to the Brazilians the hammock, maize, tobacco, rubber balls and the custom of bathing in the river,' added Aunt Martha.

'And the Africans, palm oil, caresses, pimento, turbans, charms and glass beads!' said Captain Da Silva. 'Not forgetting the influence of the Muslim Africans. That's why I like Brazil. It's at the crossroads of all cultures . . .'

'Why don't you talk to Theo about the motto on the Brazilian flag?' she suggested.

'You're right. In this country where the Indians, the blacks and the whites are all jumbled up together, the Brazilian motto nobly declares: "Order and Progress".'

'Do you know where that comes from, Theo?' asked Aunt Martha. 'From a sort of religion invented by a nineteenth-century French philosopher, Auguste Comte. He decided to replace the religions of God with the religion of Humanity which he called "positivism". The social sciences were positive, he insisted, governed by cause and effect. Then he wrote a positivist Catechism . . .'

'Catechism?' exclaimed Theo. 'Why not a religion while he was about it?'

'But that's exactly what he did! With a calendar celebrating Moses, Charlemagne, Descartes, the proletariat and women ... the founders of the Republic of Brazil were fervent disciples of Auguste Comte: hence the motto. You can still find positivist temples in Brazil.'

'Another religion,' concluded Theo.

'And we, mustn't forget *saudade*,' the Captain went on. 'A strange Brazilian sentiment, half sad, half happy, a mixture of optimism and despair. If it's not a religion, it's a cult.'

'So is samba,' said Aunt Martha.

'I'm going to like it there,' said Theo. 'But what exactly are we going to see?'

'Ah, you'll just have to be patient!' he replied. 'I promise you there'll be drums.'

Professor Carneiro Da Silva

In the middle of the Atlantic Ocean, the *Belmonte* began to pitch and toss. Arthur cowered in a corner. Aunt Martha gingerly paced the deck, clutching Theo's arm. He felt fit as a fiddle. Swaggering around in the spray, he found the waves exhilarating and thought Aunt Martha was being a bit pathetic. Suddenly Theo turned pale and rushed over to the rail. He hadn't got his sea-legs!

He stayed shut up in the guest cabin for three days, ignoring the Captain's advice to go up on deck and get some air. Finally on the fourth day, he gave in. By the time the crossing was over, Theo wasn't seasick any more. Aunt Martha pointed out that that was no great achievement as the ocean was calm now. Theo retorted that Aunt Martha wasn't exactly able to gallop across the deck ... She rose furiously to the challenge and was lurching dangerously when the ship's siren sounded. The *Belmonte* was about to dock and cousin Brutus was waiting for them.

Cousin Brutus cut a dashing figure. His eyes were greener than his splendid three-piece suit, and his hair was undeniably frizzy, with a white mop tumbling over his forehead. He embraced Captain Da Silva warmly, bending down from his great height, and elegantly kissed Aunt Martha's hand.

'This is my friend Professor Brutus Carneiro Da Silva,' she declared. 'Say hello, Theo, please.'

'How are you?' inquired Theo, extending his hand. 'And how's your family?'

'Couldn't be better,' replied cousin Brutus, puzzled. 'How about yourself?'

'I'm fine,' replied Theo. 'And how's your health?'

'Fine,' he muttered with a smile. 'Aren't you a little overtired, my young friend?'

'Not at all,' said Theo. 'And how's your work, everything going fine?'

'STOP!' cried Aunt Martha. 'You're not in Dakar now!'

'What?' said Theo sulkily. 'You told me to be polite, didn't you?'

Cousin Brutus had the luggage loaded into the two cars he had had the foresight to order, picked up the bag that held the meowing Arthur with a look of disgust, and launched into long historical explanations about the founding of Rio by the navigator Gaspar de Lemos, the misfortunes of the expedition of French Protestants led by Admiral Villegaignon, the sack of Rio by Duguay-Trouin, the arrival of Albuquerque . . .

'Where's the Sugar Loaf mountain?' Theo interrupted.

'What do you think that is!' snapped Aunt Martha. 'Shut up!'

Theo absorbed more viceroys and emperors, but gave up at the Republic of 1889.

'What's that white thing up there that looks like a plane?' he asked.

'The statue of Christ the Redeemer on the Corcovado!' cried Aunt Martha.

Cousin Brutus hastened to mention the name of the sculptor, Landowski, a Frenchman, who had given the world the masterpiece dominating the bay of January, 'de Janeiro', in memory of the first of January, the day of the Portuguese discovery . . .

'When are we eating?' said Theo.

'Theo's not very interested in history,' remarked Aunt Martha. 'Please forgive him . . .'

With a flick of a handkerchief, Cousin Brutus dusted his white shoes and fell silent. He settled Theo and his aunt into the hotel without another word, and arranged to meet them at five for coffee. Then, straightening his bow tie, he disappeared.

'Hey, what are we supposed to do with ourselves until then?' grumbled Theo. 'It's lucky we've got Arthur!'

They weren't at a loss for a moment. First they went and had lunch on top of the Sugar Loaf mountain, then they set out along the winding roads for the spectacular statue of Christ the Redeemer, whose gigantic arms seemed to be embracing the world. Theo found him truly enormous. They had to rush back down or they would be late for Cousin Brutus. And Aunt Martha was dawdling.

At six-thirty, Cousin Brutus marched in and ordered a *cafezinho*, a few drops of coffee in a tiny cup. Then he began to explain effusively that they'd be taking the plane to Bahia the following morning – unfortunately, Theo wouldn't have time to climb the Sugar Loaf mountain, or to see the famous statue of Christ close up. Aunt Martha nudged Theo, who didn't say anything. Finally, after giving Aunt Martha's hand an impeccable kiss, Cousin Brutus took his leave.

'This friend of yours is a bit stuffy,' sighed Theo.

'Don't you be so sure,' she replied. 'In Rio, he's always polite, but in Bahia . . .'

Cousin Brutus transformed

In the plane, the professor relaxed a little. He fussed around Aunt Martha, glanced at Arthur in his bag, fastened Theo's safety belt and spoke to him in a more jocular tone, as he glorified the charms of Salvador de Bahia, the most delightful city in Brazil.

'Of course, it's a pity about the dilapidated houses,' he said, 'but we're going to restore them, we have to. But the streets are bursting with life, the smells are wonderful and the fruit! And the cakes . . .'

When Cousin Brutus listed all the types of delicacies to be found in Bahia which included 'coconut kiss' and the gross-sounding 'maiden's saliva', Theo pricked up his ears. Professor Carneiro Da Silva became animated when he talked about food; suddenly he became agreeable. On leaving the airport, he removed his bow tie; in the hotel lobby, he shed his jacket, and by the time they went out for lunch, Cousin Brutus had swapped his suit for a brightly-coloured embroidered shirt. Despite his stoop, he looked younger.

Theo allowed himself to be piloted past the stalls of the dark-skinned market women in white lace, with charms dangling from their necks and scarves on their heads. Cousin Brutus had him taste prawns in banana leaves, doughnuts cooked in palm oil, cassava cakes and coconut custard tarts.

'I won't have any appetite left for lunch,' sighed Theo, now full up.

'But that *was* lunch!' exclaimed Cousin Brutus. 'Don't you like it? Let's go and buy some fruit.'

Theo didn't recognize any of the fruits other than mangoes and custard apples. Unable to choose between a medlar-like fruit and huge round pineapples, he plumped for a strange blue fruit in clusters.

'Bad luck!' hooted Cousin Brutus. 'They're little crabs – they're delicious stuffed. Here, let's console ourselves with a drink of sugar cane juice. Then we'll try the *vatapa*.'

After two hours, Theo begged for mercy. Aunt Martha had vanished into the shops, and Professor Brutus was still gorging himself. Theo sat down on the pavement. Aunt Martha emerged cheerily brandishing some charms.

'I've bought some *figas*!' she cried. 'There's a big one for you, Theo, it's the Brazilian lucky charm . . . Look, it's a hand with two raised fingers.'

'I bet you it opens. No more surprises when it comes to messages, these things always open!'

But the *figa* didn't open. Its tapering fingers pointed mysteriously in an unknown direction. The other tiny *figas* were made of aquamarine, moonstone and pink quartz. In short, Aunt Martha had purchased enough charms to bring luck to an entire regiment. Her shares must be rising on the stock exchange, mused Theo.

The *orishas*

After a long nap, they met up in the hotel restaurant. Aunt Martha asked Professor Brutus to move on to more serious issues.

'Very well,' he began, stooping even more. 'This evening we're going to attend a ceremony . . . Or rather a religious ritual that originated in Africa, which is secret but open to the public. Although it's not easy to gain entrance to the place where it is held, which is called the *terreiro* . . .'

'A *candomblé*, to be precise,' said Aunt Martha.

'You're absolutely right, dearest. In Rio, it's called *macumba*, in Haiti, *voodoo*, a word that is closely related to the word *vodun*, which is practised in Benin. The name doesn't matter, because the rites are almost identical, and here in Bahia, these ceremonies, or Afro-Brazilian rituals, are called . . .'

'*Candomblés*,' she finished. 'Go on!'

'When the black slaves were deported from Africa, they carried with them in the holds, well – not literally, but in their minds and their memories . . .'

'Their gods, we know all that. Your cousin told us on the boat.'

'Oh?' he mumbled, disappointed. 'So there's no point me telling you about the *orishas*.'

'Oh yes there is!' cried Theo. 'Because I haven't a clue what they are!'

Professor Brutus did not need to be asked twice. *Candomblé* was inspired by the cults of the Yoruba people, a common source adopted by slaves from all over Africa. Among the Yoruba, each god had his fraternity, they didn't mingle. But in Brazil, as the slaves were dispersed, all the *orishas* were worshipped at the same time. So they had to establish a hierarchy, and as the ceremonies had been secret for a long time, the slaves disguised the *orishas* as saints of the Catholic calendar.

At the top was the God of Heaven Obatala–Jesus, followed by the God of Lightning, Shango–Saint Jerome, flanked by his three wives, one of whom was the lovely Oshun–Our Lady of Candlemas, the goddess of rivers, and his brother, Ogun–Saint Anthony, God of the Forge. There were twelve *orishas* altogether, including the essential Eshu-the devil, a necessary mediator between the faithful and the *orishas*. In Africa, he was known as Legba, God of Crossroads, saviour or destroyer, breaker of barriers, wicked or kind, in fact, a shady character.

'What about Iemanja?' asked Theo.

Ah! Iemanja . . . Best known and best loved, the beautiful goddess of Sea Water and of Love, whom the Africans had concealed under the features of the Virgin Mary . . .

'With black hair?' asked Theo incredulously.

Professor Brutus pointed out that in the New Testament there was no evidence that Jesus's mother had blonde hair. In Europe, the Virgin was fair-skinned and had blue eyes and flaxen hair. In Brazil, the Virgin of the Seas wore a white dress with a blue belt, but she had black eyes and hair like the women of this country. During *candomblé*, with a bit of luck, she might deign to appear before her worshippers . . .

'What do you mean, appear?' queried Theo.

There was no question of a miraculous apparition. In *candomblé*, the gods didn't show themselves in the guise of sublime, luminous visions like the Virgin of Lourdes or Fatima. The divinities came down into the bodies of the faithful who had been dedicated to them during a long initiation process. The gods possessed the initiates, transformed their faces, imposed their dances and their emblems, then returned to the realm of the invisible until the next occasion. The initiates were known as 'horses' because the gods rode them during the ceremony.

'Is that how I'll see Iemanja?' asked Theo anxiously. 'In the shape of a lady with long black hair?'

A lady or a man, Cousin Brutus corrected him. The gods weren't fussy about the gender of their horses. It all depended on the initiation, which was no mean affair. Then, when the initiate had been dedicated to a particular divinity . . .

Professor Carneiro Da Silva broke off.

'Why have you stopped?' said Aunt Martha. 'Tell us about the initiation!'

'It has its mysteries,' murmured Cousin Brutus, 'and I don't know, dearest Martha . . .'

'Come on! Be brave . . .' she urged. 'Brutus doesn't dare tell you that he himself is an initiate!'

'You?' breathed Theo. 'You're a god's horse?'

The worthy professor nodded in silent acquiescence. It was no easy matter getting him to talk! Aunt Martha repeated that Brutus wasn't in any way obliged to tell all, and swore to high heaven that neither she nor Theo would ever breathe a word to a single soul. At last, on condition that they locked themselves up in Martha's room, Brutus gave in. Arthur immediately came over and rubbed up against his legs.

Three months in a convent

'Here goes,' he began, stroking Arthur. 'One of my friends often used to invite me to the Bahia *candomblés*, which were of interest to me. I'm a specialist in Brazilian history, you see. One night, when I least expected it, I began to shake and I lost consciousness. I was in a deep trance. Since the god had manifested himself, I had to be initiated. That's what my friend advised me. I was very reluctant, as the initiation lasts for around three months, but I couldn't sleep, my head was so heavy that . . . In a word, I agreed.'

'Three months!' exclaimed Theo.

'In Africa, the initiation sometimes lasts twelve years . . . But, to transform a woman or a man, it takes time. My friend was a very elderly man, at the top of the *candomblé* hierarchy: a Father of Saints, is the term we use. I trusted him. So . . .'

'Go on,' encouraged Aunt Martha.

'A week before the initiation, I joined the group of would-be initiates, equipped with white clothing and objects . . . which I can't tell you about. Every day we went to church to pray to receive heaven's blessing on our initiation, and we took holy baths in water and leaves.'

'More syncretism,' said Theo.

'The Church benefits from the prayers, and we from its blessings. We no longer live in the days when sorcerers were burned at the stake!'

'Maybe not,' said Aunt Martha. 'I hope you're right. Go on.'

'Then came the evening of the lying down ritual: we were made to lie down on the ground, were scolded in public and whipped for our mistakes . . .'

'What mistakes?' asked Theo.

'I didn't even know what I was supposed to have done,' confessed Brutus. 'In any case, I was scolded along with the rest! Then a stone was placed on our heads and we danced in procession. Our initiation mistress began to cry, because we were about to die. It was time for us to enter the convent.'

'Meow,' purred Arthur on cue.

'Dying is just a charade, like in the N'Doeup,' remarked Theo. 'But is the convent like ours?'

'The initiation,' said Brutus solemnly, 'is a mystical union with the god. It's similar to the nuns' marriage to God. The convent is the place where we enter into reclusion. I'm not allowed to talk about it. What I can tell you is that I wasn't in my normal state!'

'A sort of trance,' Aunt Martha broke in. 'You were not your normal self, that's for sure! Is it true that the initiate returns to childhood and plays with rags like a kid? That the supervisors don't take their eyes off you for a minute, as if you were three-year-olds? That you can't talk any more? That afterwards the Father of the Saints pulls out a hen's tongue with his teeth, wrings its neck and plasters feathers over your heads with the blood from the sacrifice?'

'Now you're prying,' said Brutus evasively. 'I can tell you that in the convent we have our heads washed to settle the god there. The washing is not with water, but with a mixture of organic substances that we must not remove for the duration of the period of reclusion. For each initiate, the initiation mistress checks the identity of his or her god, and the dedication takes place.'

'They must have made you say the name of your *orisha* yourself,' said Aunt Martha. 'I've read that initiates in reclusion were drugged . . . Don't say a word! Carry on.'

'After three months, we come out in public, dressed in white with our heads shaved. At last we've been resuscitated. We're made to dance before being tempered by fire: we have to fish pancakes out of boiling oil that doesn't scald us. Then we go back into the convent to resume everyday life. Ouch! This cat's scratching me!'

'You don't recall anything of your reclusion, do you?' asked Aunt Martha.

'That's a secret too. I came out changed. I was an ebullient character, sometimes exuberant, sometimes gloomy, always angry, touchy . . .'

'You still are!' she pointed out.

'Sometimes,' he admitted. 'But before I'd have been capable of smacking Theo! But now my *orisha* guides me and calms me down. In exchange, I give him my body so that he can appear, it's as simple as that . . .'

'But who is your god?' asked Theo, his eyes bright.

'Shango,' murmured Brutus. 'The god of thunder, righter of wrongs, violent and virile. Sometimes a bit of a libertine.'

'Shango is Saint Jerome, isn't he?' said Theo. Dad's name. 'That's nice . . .'

Arthur took advantage of the situation to jump up on Brutus's lap.

Oshun, Iemanja and Shango

Brutus had nothing more to add. Soon the ceremony would be starting. At the *terreiro*, they had been preparing food for the gods all day to entice them down to earth . . . It was high time to drive over there, for it was a little way outside Bahia. Theo fed Arthur, who fell asleep on the bed. Aunt Martha seemed nervous as she got herself ready, which set Theo thinking. Of course, she was afraid of going into a trance again!

There was nothing spectacular about the candle-lit entrance to the *terreiro*. With its palms and hangings, under its flat roof, the room where the ritual took place looked vaguely like a beach dance floor, with a tall pole planted bang in the centre. But when the bell spoke, everything changed. The Father of the Saints presided over the opening, dressed in white, and covered in necklaces. Three drums beat out the summons to the first god invoked by the chants of the faithful: Eshu, the Legba of Africa, the messenger. The Father of the Saints inspected all the faithful one by one: when he met Aunt Martha's gaze, she quickly looked away. Theo took her hand and squeezed it as hard as he could . . . Brutus was already being transformed.

A first cry rang out. A woman in a voluminous lace skirt staggered and closed her eyes . . . The Father of the Saints immediately had her removed to the sanctuary. Supported by two assistants, she emerged wearing a spangled tiara from which hung gold beads that veiled her from head to toe. Brutus cried 'Oshun!', for it was the goddess of Rivers, who rode the possessed woman. Her bracelets jangled softly, she was the mirror in which Oshun looked at her reflection . . . A second woman began to tremble gently. When she returned, decked out in the regalia of her *orisha*, she too wore a tiara and held a round fan.

'Two Oshuns!' exclaimed Theo.

'No,' whispered Aunt Martha. 'Look at the colour of her beaded veil. Glass and silver . . . Listen to what people are shouting. Here's your Iemanja at last.'

'Hi, Iemanja!' cried Theo. 'How are you doing?'

The two women whirled around the pole in the middle of the room, under the beady eye of the Father of the Saints, watchful for the slightest hint of trance among the faithful. The third horse was Brutus. Shuddering violently, he too disappeared. When he emerged, he was holding a double wooden axe, and wore a red and white necklace. Was this really Professor Carneiro Da Silva? His eyes shone, his stoop had gone, his mouth was curled in an arrogant sneer, he danced authoritatively, brandishing his double axe . . . Brutus had become Shango.

'I don't believe it!' murmured Theo.

'Isn't he better like that?' said Aunt Martha. 'I like it when Africa comes out in him.'

Aunt Martha seemed perfectly relaxed, not at all frightened. She closed her eyes so as not to see too much; she was playing it safe. She kept quite still – well, almost, shifting gently from one foot to the other. Theo was relieved, but just as he let go of her hand, the Father of the Saints came over to Aunt Martha and took her by the waist, pressing his index finger into her forehead as though he wanted to screw it right in . . . Aunt Martha moaned and opened her eyes.

'Aunt Martha!' cried Theo. 'Are you all right?'

'Let's go outside,' she murmured. 'I feel dizzy.'

Outside, they could hear the three drums and the chanting. Aunt Martha sank down on a seat and got her breath back.

'Did that guy hurt you?' he asked suspiciously.

'Actually, I think he stopped me going into a trance again,' she sighed. 'I could feel it coming on . . . and he pulled me back. I'm indebted to him.'

'Really? Just a finger on your forehead is enough?' asked Theo incredulously.

'His finger,' she said. 'Pointed by a Father of the Saints. Oh! he's got strength, I tell you. I bet I've got a bruise on my forehead . . .'

'Do you think you became a horse?' murmured Theo in awe.

'Not even a mare! I've always been affected by drums, that's all.'

'Now I understand why you hate rock and techno,' he concluded. 'You'd better stick with Mozart, it's safer . . . Shall we go back in?'

'No way! We'll wait for Brutus here.'

They waited until dawn, huddled together, gazing at the candles that spluttered out one by one. When, having let Shango dance in his stead, Professor Carneiro Da Silva found them, they were even more exhausted than he was. Brutus slipped a note into a sleepy Theo's pocket and carried him to the car.

Aunt Martha finds her master

Brutus did not reappear until the following evening. Aunt Martha and Theo had spent the day sleeping. Despite the dark rings under his eyes, the professor looked lively.

'I hear you nearly succumbed to our gods, dearest,' he said affectionately. 'What a pity you didn't carry on. Do you know which one it was?'

'I don't give a damn!' cried Aunt Martha.

'I'll tell you anyway,' he insisted. 'You would have become the horse of Yansan, the goddess of the Storms, the only *orisha* able to control the souls of the dead. Talk about a perfect match for you!'

'I don't want to be a horse,' she muttered.

'You're wrong. Actually, the *orishas* are nothing more than our hidden selves. As Yansan's horse, your legs wouldn't hurt you any more and it would cheer you up . . . but above all, I haven't told you the most important thing, my dear friend: Yansan is Shango's wife . . .'

'Thanks a million,' she muttered. 'It's a marriage of pure fiction.'

'But you could make it a reality, dearest Martha, it's entirely in your hands,' said Brutus solemnly.

'You're joking, I hope,' she breathed.

'Not at all,' he replied, and took her hand. 'We've known each other for such a long time! The gods have spoken, Martha . . .'

'Hey, I can leave you two alone if you want,' Theo cut in. 'Get married, don't get married, do what you like, but Arthur and I are famished.'

And so were they. Theo tried to get Brutus to talk about his memories of Shango. The professor couldn't remember anything, and it was the Father of the Saints who had told him about Aunt Martha's *orisha*. Once out of his trance, Brutus forgot everything and was perfectly happy that way. Aunt Martha dreamily watched him devour a dish of prawns with gusto . . . Cousin Brutus wasn't bad, after all.

In the middle of dessert, he struck his forehead.

'Have you looked in your pocket, Theo?' he said out of the blue. 'I forgot to tell you . . .'

'I get it,' replied Theo, unfolding the note. 'Who's the message from, Shango or Brutus? I prefer Shango, he's more fun! Let's see . . . *Follow the African trail to the Big Apple.*'

'Easy,' said Aunt Martha.

'Big Apple, that rings a bell,' said Theo. 'It'll come back to me when I've had some sleep.'

Theo and Aunt Martha were just nodding off when the phone rang. It was Melina.

'Mum?' yawned Theo. 'What's going on? No, it's one o'clock in the morning here . . . You've got the time difference wrong! Are you all right? Your legs aren't bothering you any more? What on earth's the matter? Why are you laughing like that? Yes you are, you're giggling like mad . . . Are you sure? Are you sleeping well? We're knackered. Oh nothing, an all-night party, it was brill! The tests? Aunt Martha hasn't said anything to me . . . What do you mean, we can do them in New York? The doctors think it can wait? So I'm better! Mind you, I thought so . . . Hey, you did say New York, didn't you? Ah. You just let the cat out of the bag. We're leaving for New York . . . OK. No, she won't be angry. Don't worry, she's got other things on her mind. No, no, she's absolutely fine. What? Ah! That's a secret . . . Me too, big hugs. For the others too . . .'

She had hung up. Theo went straight back to sleep, despite Arthur's purring.

But he was mistaken. Aunt Martha went berserk. What! After all the trouble she'd taken in thinking up the messages, one of them got ruined in the middle of the night! An easy, fun message to boot!

'Easy?' said Brutus, buttering his croissant. 'I'd never have got it. The Big Apple?'

'What, don't you know that it's the nickname for New York?' she retorted. 'Where have you been?'

'In my Brazil,' he confessed. 'I've never had the chance to taste the apple. Would you have guessed, Theo?'

'I already had,' fibbed Theo. 'It's not Mum's fault . . . I was pleased because she sounded cheerful. Forget it, Aunt Martha. When are we leaving?'

'First, we'll get your tests done,' cried Aunt Martha, still incensed. 'Your mother always overdoes it. Before, she fretted too much, and now her mind is wandering! I don't know what's got into her, but there's no question of relaxing our vigilance. What's more, we won't wait for an appointment, we're going to the hospital now. So there!'

'We'll do whatever you wish,' said Brutus, 'but please don't be angry any more . . . Listen, Theo, I'll take you to the hospital while our dear Martha has a rest.'

'A rest? I don't need one!'

'Well, you're going to have a rest anyway!' cried Brutus, getting to his feet. 'It'll calm you down!'

Aunt Martha was speechless. Theo grabbed Cousin Brutus's hand, and Brutus winked.

'Not bad,' said Theo in the lift. 'Nobody's ever spoken to her like that before.'

'Really?' replied Brutus. 'Well, there you go, it's my hidden nature . . .'

Fatal error

After the hospital, Brutus took Theo to gorge himself on local delicacies. Then they went for a stroll on the beach, among the crowds of bathers. Brutus bought ice creams, played a guitar borrowed from a street musician, sang lyrics in a surprisingly attractive voice and was quite a success, for his age. When they got back from their aunt, they found Aunt Martha with puffy red eyes.

'We should have gone back to Rio for the tests,' she wailed. 'I wasn't thinking . . . Why didn't you say something, Brutus?'

'Theo's much healthier than you are, dearest . . . Look how energetic he is! Ill, Theo? Those tests weren't necessary! You were simply asserting your authority, Martha, that's all.'

'I assure you . . .' she said plaintively. 'Brutus, you must believe me . . .'

'I believe you, I believe you,' he replied hastily. 'Don't cry. Now, this is what we're going to do . . .'

While awaiting the results, they would go to Belém, at the mouth of the Pará River, where the luxuriant vegetation tempered the humid heat. Brutus took them to the magic market where they discovered protective amulets and love potions, snakes embalmed in strange fluids, or dried vaginas of female dolphins, a powerful aphrodisiac. Aunt Martha didn't want to touch these disgusting-looking blue mammal organs, and made do with a transparent phial, which she chose for the label showing two smiling lovers embracing. Theo bought three philtres at random, and a mummified snake's head for Arthur to play with. Brutus examined the products, felt a few skins, sniffed various salves, and decided on an armadillo claw.

'Here, the Indian spirit prevails,' he said. 'I feel inspired by the blood of my African ancestors.'

'Your African ancestors?' exclaimed Theo. 'So you know about them!'

'Of course. In Belém, they practise the cult of the *caboclos*, mixed-race black and Indian people. I'm lucky enough to be descended from three branches at the same time, white, black and Indian. I'm a one-man Brazil!'

'You see, Aunt Martha, he's not denying his African roots,' observed Theo. 'Your cousin said . . .'

'My cousin!' snorted Brutus. 'He's wild at being merely Portuguese . . . Come, you're going to taste an interesting food.'

The duck stew and spinach purée didn't look especially exciting, but Brutus warned Aunt Martha and Theo that the duck with chilli would set their mouths on fire, and the *tucupi* herb purée extinguished the fire. A mouthful of duck, then one of *tucupi*. The minute she tasted the spicy bird, Aunt Martha choked; Brutus forced a spoonful of purée into her mouth . . .

'I can't taste a thing any more,' she exclaimed in surprise. 'My tongue feels completely numb!'

That was the secret of the strange relationship between the chilli pepper and the *tucupi* herb, an anaesthetic worthy of a dental surgery. In fact, with the fire of the chilli and the numbing effect of the plant, it wasn't possible to taste a thing. Theo took revenge on the pastries. Without consulting Aunt Martha, Brutus decided to put her on a diet. No cakes or sweets!

'What right do you have to tell me what to do?' she grumbled. 'Nobody has ever bossed me around before!'

'There's a first time for everything, my dear Martha,' decreed Brutus, removing her plate. 'I'm too thin, and you're too well covered.'

As a consolation, he bought the emblems of Aunt Martha's *orisha*, a big wooden sword, a horse tail, a garnet necklace, the Storm goddess's stone.

'When you get angry, dearest, you can wield your sword,' he said affectionately. 'You'll look terrific . . .'

Jaunts on the grey Amazon, boats laden with used hammocks, the screeching of birds in the forest, the wrinkled faces of the market women, porters bowed under the weight of heavy bags, giant fish with scales as hard as wood, manatees, the end of the earth . . . The Amazon was sad, but Brutus was bubbling. Aunt Martha was won over, and allowed Brutus to persuade her to visit the curious towns of the Brazilian interior. One thing led to another, and Brutus ended up travelling with them for three weeks. At last, Aunt Martha's conscience pricked her, and she decided they should return to Bahia to get the results.

Calamity! Contrary to all expectations, they were disastrous . . . Aunt Martha rushed to the phone and called her contact in New York, to have Theo hospitalized. Perhaps the Americans would work a miracle? But to make matters worse, their New York 'guide' was bedridden with a bad attack of hepatitis. Aunt Martha's network was collapsing.

Brutus vanished. Aunt Martha called him every name under the sun, swore revenge for his unspeakable cowardice, telephoned all over the place, but couldn't find anyone to help. Panic stations. Theo cuddled Arthur and cried quietly. The worst thing would be telling Mum. It was all over! In an hour, the adventure had turned into a nightmare. Aunt Martha collapsed. When Brutus came tiptoeing back, she was sobbing and panting for breath.

'Martha, it's all a mistake,' he murmured.

'A fatal mistake!' she moaned. 'How could I have believed . . . It's all my fault! And yours too!'

'The hospital mixed up the files,' he said, taking out a wad of papers from his pocket. 'It was a genuine mistake. We left it too long . . . These are the right results. There's an improvement.'

She flung her arms around his neck for joy. And as their New York guide was out of action, Aunt Martha invited Brutus to go to the Big Apple with them, since he'd never been there. To their delight, Brutus accepted.

'Do you know what?' said Theo to his cat as he watched Aunt Martha adjust Professor Carneiro Da Silva's bow tie. 'First of all, I knew perfectly well that I was cured. And secondly, those two will end up getting married . . .'

CHAPTER 28

The Gentleman Doth Protest

A bad start in the Big Apple

It was the first time that no one came to meet them at the airport. Stuck in the queue for American immigration control, Aunt Martha fumed.

'It's always the same here, it takes hours!'

'Wooden sword!' replied Brutus.

Aunt Martha stared at him blankly.

'Draw your goddess's sword, dearest,' he said, bowing. 'Your anger will be more effective . . .'

She began to laugh. Excited by the outburst, Arthur, smuggled onto the plane in Brutus's bag, began to meow at the worst possible moment, attracting the attention of the police. There was a heavy fine; things had got off to a bad start in New York. Given the task of finding a taxi, Brutus returned with a black limousine with tinted windows, to the horror of his beloved who knew how much things cost.

'I'll pay,' he nobly offered.

'You're broke!' retorted Aunt Martha.

'I'll sell my books,' he sighed.

'Don't talk nonsense,' she murmured affectionately. 'I'm rich enough for two!'

'When you two have finished, we'll go to the hotel,' said Theo.

The hotel! In the panic, Aunt Martha had forgotten to make the reservations! They were supposed to stay with Naomi, but Naomi was ill. In the end, they drove around in the limo for two hours before they managed to find two shabby rooms in a student hostel near New York University. Aunt Martha swore that the Big Apple had lost its charm, but Theo loved the glass façades, the strange-shaped roofs of the sky-scrapers, the little public gardens, the fenced-in football pitches and, in the streets, weird people, everyone isolated in the midst of this human sea . . . He let Aunt Martha fulminate and Brutus calm her down.

Once Arthur had been fed, the luggage sorted out and clothes changed, they had to contact Theo's parents, give them the hotel phone number, and explain their long silence and the business of the mistaken results. If it hadn't been for Brutus . . . !

'Who's Brutus?' asked Jerome.

'Brutus?' cried Aunt Martha. 'Of course you know him. Professor Carneiro Da Silva. Yes, the Brazilian historian. An odd name, you think? I don't dislike it. He's in New York with us. Why? Jerome, you're a bore with all your questions . . . Because I like having him with us, so there!'

Bang! She had hung up. Dad hadn't improved Aunt Martha's temper. She decided they would drop Arthur off at Naomi's, so he wouldn't be a nuisance. In spite of Theo's pleas Aunt Martha stuffed the cat in her bag, leaped into a taxi and came back an hour later wearing a poker face.

'Why did you do that?' whined Theo. 'What's going to become of my cat?'

'He jumped onto Naomi's bed,' she said. 'He's being unfaithful to you!'

'Why are you so horrible to me?'

'Because I am!' she replied, exasperated.

Brutus tried to mention the wooden sword, but Aunt Martha didn't want to calm down. She only relaxed in the café, over unlimited coffee, pancakes and maple syrup.

'Huh!' she sniffed. 'There's no freedom in this world. As if you always had to justify yourself . . .'

'By the way,' Theo ventured cautiously, 'we've finished the religious tour, haven't we? Jews, Catholics, Muslims, animists, Hindus, Buddhists, Confucians, Shintoists, haven't we seen them all now?'

'Listen to that!' she exploded. 'Of course not! You find the answer, nephew. Why are we in the United States of America?'

'I don't know,' said Theo. 'For the weirdo sects?'

'You find those everywhere,' she answered. 'Think again!'

'I protest!' declared Brutus. 'You're not helping him enough! Theo, there's still one fundamental religion left, one of the world's main religions, which is in the majority here. I protest . . .'

'Protest, protest, you're always protesting,' retorted Aunt Martha with a note of irony.

'In the majority?' muttered Theo. 'Those guys who preach and rant on telly? Oh! I get it. The Protestants.'

'About time too!' she said. 'Lucky Brutus helped you . . . "I protest" was a clever idea. Brutus, you're wonderful.'

'Yeah,' said Theo. 'A bit obvious. Besides, apart from the fact that loads of Protestants were killed in the Saint Bartholomew's Day massacre in Paris, I don't even know what they believe.'

'To be honest, neither do I,' said Brutus. 'Would you enlighten us, dearest?'

When the Pope became the Antichrist

Aunt Martha took a perverse delight in getting on her anticlerical soap-box.

Who were the Protestants protesting against back in the sixteenth century? Against the countless abuses of the Apostolic Roman Church. The priests were openly depraved, cohabited with women, made virgins pregnant and lined their own pockets with the money that the faithful had to fork out for practically everything. Baptisms, funerals, weddings, registering births, marriages and deaths, charity and above all, Indulgences. For, with the general deterioration of standards, the Church had introduced a system of marketing redemption.

The sinner could purchase 'Indulgences' from the Church, at the going rate. For a major sin, the offender bought a stack of Indulgences, in other words, a guaranteed pardon. It was a profitable business! Haunted by the fear of Hell, the Christians invested in Indulgences the way people speculate on the Stock Exchange nowadays, except that, instead of a pension to look forward to, they bought eternal retirement – cheap at the price . . . And the poor just fell by the wayside.

That wasn't the Church's only trade. It sold relics, pieces of the real Cross, hairs from Saint Ursula, Saint Sebastian's metacarpus, Saint Joseph's shroud, hairs from Saint James's beard and the Virgin's tears. If all that junk had been collected under one roof, it would have looked something like the magic market in Belém. In short, the Church was on its way to downright paganism. Now, who was the head of the Church? The Pope. And who behaved like an armour-clad warlord leading his troops into battle in the name of the Church? The Pope. Who controlled the wealth of his states? Who dared have mistresses, and children, in defiance of his holy calling? The Pope.

'Really?' cried Theo. 'All the popes?'

Only one, actually, Alexander Borgia. But the others weren't blameless. Who allowed the Inquisition to do as it pleased, burning anyone who protested at the stake? The Pope. Lawless, unjust, unworthy of the legacy of Saint Peter, the Pope, whoever he was, had become the 'Antichrist'.

Rebellion had been brewing for a long time when a Catholic monk by the name of Martin Luther proposed the reformation of the Church. Certainly, the idea of purging it of its sins was nothing new; any number of learned priests had dreamed of doing so for nearly a century. So Luther wasn't the first reformer, but unlike his distant predecessors, his views didn't cost him his life. Commanded to recant in 1520, Luther solemnly burned the papal bull that gave the order. Worse, he made public a document entitled: *Why the books of the Pope and his disciples were burned by Doctor Martin Luther*. Had he lived at another time, he would have been burned at the stake. That didn't happen. But he was excommunicated in 1521.

The German princes, weary of the Church's excesses, rallied to Luther's cause. They helped him evade arrest, shielded him from threats, hid him under a false name, and Luther survived. A great victory! Entire states converted to what became known as the Reformation, a widespread movement of protest against the authority of the Church and of the Pope. Soon, the reformers had nothing but scorn for those they called 'the papists'.

Like many others before him, Martin Luther wanted to return to the original Christianity, with no popes, no convents and no holy commerce. No hierarchy or clergy either – a religion that did not violate the equality of the children of Christ. In the early days of the Church, it was not forbidden for priests to marry, that was imposed later by the popes – there was no mention of such a ban in the Gospels. Luther threw it out of the window, along with his monk's habit, and in 1525, he married a nun, Katherina von Bora, who had run away from a convent with her rebel sisters. The idea of the Reformation was simple: strip the Church of its hypocrisy, stop the lying, the faking, and the use of spurious writings as holy Scriptures. Go back to the Bible, and be guided by it. Above all, accept the grace of faith, experience it with intensity, with all one's heart. Only the grace of God could save the soul. For Luther was not content merely to criticize the Roman Church: he passionately longed to renew the contact with God.

'A mystic!' cried Theo. 'Did he go into ecstasies and all that?'

Almost. His fate had been a strange one . . . Terrified by a storm, the young Martin Luther had vowed that if he escaped with his life, he would enter a monastery. He bravely strove to be a good monk. He fasted, kept vigil and endured the terrible cold. But it was no good. Despite his sincerity, the monk Martin Luther was unable to overcome his violent mood swings and the lust for the flesh that tormented him. The fact is that he desperately loved life. He accused Satan of having terrified him in order to capture his soul, was filled with self-doubt and questioned the monastery, and Christianity, until the day he discovered the illumination of a faith without affectations. Far from the bondage of the Church, how simple faith was!

'Odd,' said Theo. 'Sounds like the Buddha when he broke his fast . . . You torture your body in every possible way, and the divine returns in beauty.'

Very true. But, unlike Buddha, all through his life, Luther suffered the same torments. Sometimes exalted, sometimes gloomy; sometimes inspired, at others defeated. Racked by headaches, Luther was given to alternate bursts of frenetic activity and bouts of melancholy and inertia. Living life to the full when he was high, drinking and eating well, the ogre of God broke down for months on end. This temperament steeped in holy violence had the strength to launch the Reformation, and the weakness not to be a saint.

'Human, too human . . .' Aunt Martha concluded.

'Unjust, full of contradictions, excessive,' said Brutus. 'Luther attacked his chief enemies: the Pope, the devil, the Turk . . . and the Jews. He had no hesitation in supporting the massacre of the peasants by the German princes. Luther didn't give in, it's true, but wielded cold iron and fire, just like the Pope!'

'But you said you knew nothing about Protestantism!' Aunt Martha marvelled.

'Well, the fact is . . . I have an admission to make. I told a slight fib so as to hear what you had to say, dearest! And a good thing too, for I don't share your views on the Reformation at all . . .'

The Christian world in fragments

Brutus had his own version of events. Martin Luther would never have emerged from obscurity if his strength hadn't shown itself at the right moment. The sixteenth century was the end of a long road. For centuries, cracks had been appearing in the Christian world. Decimated by the Black Death, obsessed with mortality, ravaged by wars and famines, under threat from the Ottoman Empire, it didn't know which way to turn. History no longer made sense, so the Last Judgement was nigh. Preachers began to curse the damned, hunt witches, and threaten disaster to the faithful for the slightest fault ... There were horrendous murders, suicide sects, children sacrificed ... Panic-stricken, the believers thought of nothing but death, the gateway to Hell gaped, and the priests raved on about hellfire and brimstone.

'Sounds like the modern world!' commented Theo.

Indeed it did. From the fear of eternal damnation sprang the mania for relics and the trade in Indulgences. Was the Pope to blame for the collective crisis of a world that was falling apart? No, he was powerless to stop it. But he was the head, the scapegoat of a floundering Church. So, leaderless, the Christians sought paths of their own. Some found a reassuring figure in the Mother of Christ, Our Lady of Charity. They threw in the mother of the Mother, Saint Anne, Jesus's grandmother: it was to her that Luther had made the vow to enter a monastery. Others sought relief from a gruesome world through ecstasy. And lastly, some thought that if the Church could no longer fulfil its role, then you'd better rely on yourself, without further ado. Every single Christian was responsible for spreading the Gospel, so every Christian, no matter how humble, could be right, and the Pope wrong. It was up to one and all to get down to work.

Another important factor: by Luther's time, printing from movable type, invented by Gutenberg some time in the 1430s, had spread all over Europe. The clergy and the monks were no longer the only people with access to the books of the Bible: if you could learn to read you could discover it for yourself. Published and translated into various languages, the Bible became accessible to thousands of people: this was not a lot, but it was enough for the new readers to be able to interpret it for themselves. Suddenly, information circulated as it had never done before. Europe entered a state of upheaval: the world that people had believed closed was beginning to open up.

'So the book was the sixteenth-century Internet!' cried Theo.

The book no, but printing certainly. Just when the Christianity of the clergy was collapsing, the faithful masses seized on the Bible and made their voices heard. Luther translated the Bible into German. He was one of those faithful, one believer among others, a hothead raised by the passion of his rebellion. That is why Brutus didn't really admire the founder of the Reformation, particularly because others came after him and finished off the job he began.

'The classic routine,' said Theo. 'You can't found a religion on your own. You die and hey presto! the others change everything.'

Aunt Martha flared up: the others' hadn't 'changed everything'. Luther had laid the true foundations of the Reformation: the inner quest, giving oneself to God, the only master. The grace of faith depended on Him: thus God had enlightened Martin Luther when the poor tormented monk had sunk into the torpor of doubt. Without God, man was helpless to achieve faith. He was not free to do good or evil, since everything depended on God. Till then, who had protected Christians from the devil, who guaranteed their salvation? The Church and its leader, the Pope. Now, Luther was offering proof that people could dispense with the Church by putting their trust in God, in other words, in faith. Short-circuited, the Church became superfluous.

'Hey,' said Theo. 'Then it was the Pope himself who had broken the bond between Heaven and Earth?'

In Luther's view, yes. The founder of the Reformation re-established the link with God.

'There's nothing new in that,' said Brutus.

'Oh yes there is!' she snapped, miffed. 'Because Luther wasn't content to keep God for himself. The true Church is in people's hearts, he said. He went back to the literal meaning of the word Church, *ecclesia*, the assembly of believers around the Gospels.'

'That wasn't Luther,' replied Brutus. 'That was Calvin!'

'You've forgotten Jan Hus!' she parried.

'Come on, you two lovebirds,' interrupted Theo. 'Instead of shouting names at each other, you'd do better to tell me what the Protestants do. They pray, don't they, they have a religious service! What's it like?'

'I wonder,' said Brutus. 'The ones I know aren't exactly brimming with trust in God. They're as miserable as sin!'

'Well, I'm going to make you change your mind,' she said. 'Wait till tomorrow, you're in for a great big surprise.'

505

African emotions

The next day was Sunday, the Lord's day. Aunt Martha, Brutus and Theo went over to 130th St, where African families dressed in their Sunday best were filing into the Abyssinian church. Their hair smoothed with gel, the little girls wore flounced dresses, the women hats with little veils and sometimes frilly evening dresses, and the men their best suits. The crowd was so dense that they had to wait outside the church before going inside. Next to the harmonium on the left-hand side was the choir, made up of three women wearing royal blue surplices.

'There are hardly any whites,' said Theo, kicking his heels. 'Is it a Church exclusively for Africans?'

'Not specially,' replied Aunt Martha. 'But think a little. The Africa trail was laid by the slaves! There were millions of them in the United States of America . . . and mixed marriage between whites and "Negroes" was strictly forbidden. The Afro-American slaves weren't freed until the Civil War . . .'

'Thanks to Abraham Lincoln,' Theo broke in.

'By that time, intermarriage had already made Brazil a cultural melting pot. But here, where did you still find Africa enslaved? In the wretched shacks and the fields of the plantation owners. Africa was baptized by force. How could people get back in touch with it if not through songs and rhythm in the cotton fields? The African slaves sang. Once freed, it was another matter. Before the Civil War, the slaves' and the masters' children lived together . . . but afterwards!'

'You're not going to tell me that things were worse after they were freed?'

'It was hardly any better,' she sighed. 'The fallen masters rejected them . . . The two societies, black and white, were separated by a ruthless segregation. That's how the black ghettos were born. In a sense, they preserved Africa in the United States. Cut off from the whites, the blacks were able to live in their own way.'

'I don't call them "blacks",' said Theo. 'I prefer Afro-Americans, otherwise it's racist, so there!'

'Oh, if you like, Theo. I'm not going to quibble. So, as in the cotton plantations of the past, the poor districts were home to the Negro spiritual, gospel singing and the blues, consoling laments, beyond the control of the whites. Then, because they were only allowed two or three musical instruments, the Afro-Americans invented jazz, their first victory over the masters' world.'

'Fine, but what's that got to do with religion?'

'You'll see. The service is about to start.'

The congregation sat in pews facing a podium where an elderly man in a golden yellow surplice stood. The minister. His hands resting on the Bible, he slowly began his sermon. He was barely audible; he was working himself up. Then his voice rose, became fired with passion . . . He started to shout, wagging his finger at the crowd.

'The devil is among you!'

'Yeah!' replied the congregation, clapping their hands.

'You don't know his face, but he's prowling, yes, he's there!'

'Yeah!' cried the congregation.

'Is it you?' he accused, pointing at one man, 'or is it you, my brother?'

'No!' replied the crowd.

'You're wrong! He sneaks in everywhere . . . I've seen him, seen him enter my very own church . . . He was all red! Yes, I've seen him sit in the front row and glare right back! He gave me the evil eye!'

'Shame on him!' groaned the crowd.

'I chased him away with the Book!'

'Hallelujah!' the congregation chorused.

'Who'll keep him out, brothers and sisters?' he cried. 'Who will save you?'

'JE-SUS!' replied the crowd, swaying in unison.

At an invisible signal, the preacher and the crowd began to sing and dance, clapping their hands to the beat. It was a huge wave, rolling from pew to pew, a single voice, a single body. The little girls' plaits, the hats and the flowers on their brims, the white-gloved hands, everything billowed on the tide . . . Nobody fell. No one fell into a trance in this turbulent sea. No drum rolls, but the single smack of clapping hands. A multiple God pitching to the rhythm of Jesus's name. Aunt Martha and Theo stood still, not daring to disturb the harmonious movement. Brutus joined in the dance.

'But you chose baptism!' cried the preacher.

'Yeah . . .' murmured the ecstatic congregation.

'You have been purified by immersion in the faith! Do you know what you believe in?'

'Yeah!'

'The Bible!' he yelled. 'The Bible alone is our guide! Thanks to the Bible, you live and breathe your faith!'

'Amen . . .'

'The Bible alone, brothers and sisters, will fight the devil's drugs, the evil that eats up our children, rots their minds and kills their bodies!'

'Lord have mercy . . .'

'He is the one, the red devil, who turns you away from God, who leads you into poverty!'

'Yes he is . . .'

'Equality for all within our Church! No separation, no injustice! Each of us is only one among others! Who gives us brotherhood, who gives us sisterhood? Give me a name!'

'JE-SUS!' replied the congregation with a stamping of feet.

Arms were thrown up in the air, shrill cries rose, women keeled over, their eyes closed in joy, bodies shook, hands began to clap alternating rhythms, syncopations, counterpoints, music. It was the trance again, controlled and guided by song at the height of its power. Brutus froze.

'Love one another!' cried the minister.

'Let's love one another!' replied the congregation.

In the pews, people were kissing each other to the words: 'I love you, brother. I love you, sister.'

'Wow . . .' whispered Theo. 'And they're Christians?'

'Absolutely,' replied Aunt Martha. 'Baptists.'

'I'd like to go,' murmured Brutus. 'This isn't my Africa at all.'

Freedom, and its excesses

They found themselves sitting in front of a plate of cream-filled pastries. Claiming that the service had upset him, Brutus stuffed himself as usual.

'You did tell me those Afro-Americans were Baptists, didn't you?' Theo asked Aunt Martha. 'Explain!'

'I warn you, it'll take a while, won't it, Brutus?'

'Umm!' he replied, his mouth full of chocolate.

'You don't know anything about it, anyway.'

The Reformation begun by Martin Luther had triggered an unstoppable movement. Soon, whole regions of Europe were swept by a craving to rid the Church of corruption. Flanders, Germany . . . everywhere, revolutionary preachers were springing up, calling for equality and denouncing the wealthy: echoing Christ's suffering on the cross, the sorrows of the people were about to smash the laws. Appointed on Luther's recommendation, one of these preachers stood out from the others. An inspired orator, Thomas Müntzer went further than Luther in urging the poor to revolt . . . But the worthy Luther, frightened by the chaos in the cities, declared outright that the princes had a divine right to put down the rebellions inspired by his former pupil.

Thomas Müntzer rose up against his master, founded a democracy of the pure, preached freedom as a condition of God's word, and was executed with Luther's approval. He was one of the first of what became known as the 'Anabaptists', advocating baptism in adulthood.

But, after his death, the preacher of the democracy of the pure inspired a messianic movement that was radical in a different way. In the town of Münster, in Westphalia, a baker and a tailor set up a sort of communist theocracy. The Dutchman Jan Mathijis wanted to eliminate the unclean, and organized a complete system of common ownership. Another Dutchman, John of Leiden, called himself 'King of Justice', authorized polygamy and behaved as if he were a god. Anabaptism was running riot! For the Catholic Church, it was going too far . . . The 'Antichrist's' bishop sent his troops into the celestial city of Münster, and the utopian kingdom was wiped out in a bloodbath. The bodies of the Anabaptist leaders were displayed in iron cages that still hang from the towers of the Lambertikirche, Münster's Gothic church.

'I still don't see where the Baptists come in!' exclaimed Theo. 'It's all madness and massacre . . .'

The birth of the Reformation was long and painful . . . Luther's ideas were taken further by small groups of believers who wanted to organize freely, with their own rules. These rules often included adult baptism, a free choice, with total immersion of the subject in the water of the Jordan, as John the Baptist did with Jesus.

'I get it!' said Theo. 'The Baptists!'

In those days, they were called the Anabaptists. But the dreadful siege of the crazy city of Münster left scars that took a long time to heal. It took at least a century for the true Baptist faith to come to England. English Baptist doctrine rested on a set of solid principles: the Bible is the supreme authority, baptism is reserved for believers only, the Church is made up only of believers, who are all equal, and is completely independent of the state and the ruling authority. And each person must bear witness to their faith with integrity and simplicity, without dogma, rules or sacraments. The Baptist faith was later exported to the United States, the land of freedom, and of refuge for many persecuted Protestants. In the United States, the Baptist Church had worked for liberty and equality: its most famous ambassador was Martin Luther King . . .

'Him?' cried Theo. 'The pacifist who was assassinated, like Gandhi?'

The very man. Yes, the defender of civil liberties for Afro-Americans, the ardent pacifist fighter, was a Baptist minister who was faithful to the ideals of his Church.

'I understand why Afro-Americans became Baptists,' said Theo. 'And they were right!'

But to follow the history of the Baptist Church in detail, they would have to make a long detour by way of England.

In the sixteenth century, when Europe was changing dramatically, the Reformation met a curious fate. The King of England fell in love. But he was already married. Because the Pope wouldn't grant him a divorce, King Henry VIII had Parliament recognize him as the head of the Anglican Church of England. He granted himself the divorce refused by the Pope, and that was that.

At first, Anglicanism was simply Catholicism without a pope. Then, a few years later, reinforced by Queen Elizabeth I, it developed towards a strict Protestantism before giving rise to all-out warfare between the English 'papists' and those who became known as the 'Puritans'. Obsessed with purity as Thomas Müntzer had been before them, the Puritans would not accept any other authority than the Bible, while the papists obeyed the pope, as their name suggests. Then the Anglican kings were succeeded by Charles I, a Catholic sovereign, who authorized the persecution of the Puritans: much to his subsequent regret! Rebellion brewed, an army rose up, and Oliver Cromwell, leader of the Puritan party, had King Charles beheaded in public.

'Puritan means someone who's a bit of a stick-in-the-mud, doesn't it?' said Theo.

The true Puritan sought purity and was wary of the devil's temptations: in Cromwell's day, to combat lust, men and women wore high collars and black clothes, and shunned life's pleasures. Enjoyment was reprehensible, music was suspicious . . .

'Fundamentalists in other words!' cried Theo.

That was the other side of the coin: often, the Protestants were too afraid of the devil . . . Outside the Bible, there was no salvation! Woe to the lost sheep led astray by the fiend! There was no forgiveness in Protestantism: you were saved or damned, and nothing in between. In the seventeenth century, in the little town of Salem, in the United States, Protestant communities obsessed with Satan executed nineteen witches, guilty of everything and nothing, purely on the grounds of their beauty,

THE GENTLEMAN DOTH PROTEST

their language, the look in their eyes ... in other words they killed innocent women. The wounds from this outbreak of collective madness never healed. Scarred by the rigid Protestantism of the early immigrants, the United States of America regularly witnessed waves of Puritanism and witch hunts that kept returning in different guises ... American liberty turned against itself, purity wreaked havoc, the ideal of the Reformation was lost.

'That's what I said, stick-in-the-muds!' Theo concluded.

'Pessimists!' Brutus corrected him. The English Anglicans believed in the knowledge of good through reason alone; but the Puritans believed that man had been completely corrupted by original sin. The Anglicans wanted to reform the world as it was, but the Puritans tried to build the heavenly city by changing society from the top down. The Anglicans had a softer life, but the Puritans displayed more energy. And it was in the midst of this schism that the Baptist Church was established in England. Libertarians without dogma, preferring emotion to the work of reason, and direct faith to theology, they had a foot in both camps. They reformed the world as it was, but were also building the Jerusalem of their dreams.

'You like the Baptists, don't you?' said Theo.

'Yes, I do,' she confessed. 'When Martin Luther King was assassinated, I cried.'

'This time, we've pretty much covered the Protestants,' concluded Theo.

'No!' cried Brutus. 'You've left out Calvin!'

'Oh, you've finished your cakes, have you?' retorted Aunt Martha, wiping his mouth.

Noughts and crosses

Sunday was spent roaming the lively streets of Greenwich Village, visiting exhibitions and diving into bookshops. Theo loved the skate-boarders, the showers under the fountains and the atmosphere of free-dom. They walked for hours and were dead beat by the time they reached Little Italy, where Aunt Martha knew an excellent pasta res-taurant. But the Italian restaurant had become Chinese: Chinatown was eating into Italy. Sweet and sour pork, prawns with ginger, beef and green peppers, Theo was familiar with Chinese food.

The next day, Monday, was a hospital day, Aunt Martha had taken care not to tell Theo about the conversation she'd had with Jerome on the quiet. No, Theo shouldn't be told that he was better, or that the doctors, through looking for the causes of this extraordinary change, had possibly identified his mysterious illness . . . He would complete his journey as planned, by the rules. In any case, Theo didn't mind. One injection more or less . . . but Brutus insisted that Aunt Martha have one final blood pressure test, much to Theo's amusement.

He couldn't get a word in about Calvin, poor old Brutus. Every time he challenged Aunt Martha on this major figure, she ducked the issue. She would suddenly see an absolutely magnificent Tibetan hat on the other side of the road, or she claimed she was tired, and when they stopped in a café, the mere mention of Calvin's name sent her looking for the rest room. Brutus gently pointed this out to her and she flared up.

'No, I've got nothing against Calvin! I just wanted a breather . . .'

Fishy behaviour, but apart from that, she made her peace with the Big Apple that night, on Broadway, after a tear-jerking musical. Brutus turned her feelings to advantage to press home his marital ambitions: for when she felt emotional, Aunt Martha became softer. In those rare moments, she no longer entirely dismissed the idea of marriage . . . The next day, she was back to her old self. Get married? Impossible, where on earth would they live? In Bahia? Los Angeles? Besides, to settle down after a life of independence? Poor old Brutus, it was just a futile dream . . .

And it was back to square one. Theo put crosses on the calendar for the noes and noughts for the yeses. Monday, two crosses, no yeses, a bad day. Tuesday, two noughts, one cross, progress. Wednesday, two noughts, two crosses, a draw. They visited one museum after another, went to concerts; the days went by with no conclusive outcome. But they still hadn't tackled Calvin.

On the Thursday, after three positive noughts and a single negative cross, Brutus, his heart full of hope, spotted a splendid-looking Belgian restaurant.

'A Belgian restaurant!' she exclaimed. 'You do have some weird ideas, Brutus!'

'I love Belgian beer,' he said, licking his lips. 'And I love Belgium too.'

His luck was in: the restaurant served raspberry, cherry and peach beers, and Aunt Martha tried them all, especially the peach. Beer was her drink; she became very merry. When Aunt Martha was nice and tipsy, Brutus gently steered the conversation round to Calvin.

'There's more than just fruit beers in Belgium, dearest,' he said. 'You could tell Theo about the Beguines, for example!'

Ah! the Beguines! Delighted, Aunt Martha was off and running. Well before the Reformation instigated by Luther, the Beguines and Beghards had established lay communities dedicated to solitary meditation and charity. The Beguines lived a secluded life in buildings grouped inside a walled flower garden. Being neither nuns locked up in a convent nor lay women prey to the life of this world, they were true Protestants before their time. Their emblem was the phoenix, the symbol of rebirth and Christ's resurrection . . . Of course, some of them were burned for witchcraft. But there were still some surviving *béguinages* in Belgium, a testimony to a simple, mystical current born in the valley of the Rhine, for Rhineland Germany was fertile ground for mystics . . .

'A lot of major reformers came from German-speaking areas,' added Brutus. 'Wasn't Calvin born in Geneva?'

'Harping on about Calvin again,' grumbled Aunt Martha. 'Actually, he wasn't born in Geneva, but in France. One, Calvin came from Picardy, and two, he fled to Geneva. That'll teach you, Brutus! Of course we have to talk about Calvin, but I've had too much to drink . . .'

'You know where he was born, and you claim you're out of it?' said Theo. 'You're kidding!'

'I'll tell you,' confessed Aunt Martha, her head drooping over her beer, 'on the subject of Calvin's doctrine, I . . . Well, I . . . er, I don't know a thing . . .'

'My poor darling,' said Brutus, sympathetically taking her hand. 'Would you like me to tell Theo all about Calvin?'

'All right, Brutus,' she said.

'You see, you can't live without me,' he concluded.

'Yes,' she sighed, her eyes brimming.

Four noughts in one day! Theo couldn't get over it.

The strength of the Spirit

And Brutus told him all about Calvin.

Luther's life was drawing to a close when the young Jean Calvin became involved in the Reformation by challenging the King of France, François I, who was persecuting the first Protestants. What appalled Calvin was the injustice of the powerful. The suffering of the Protestants aroused the young man's sympathy for their cause. But, unlike Luther, Calvin was not a monk. He was a scholar, an intellectual, someone who dealt with ideas. Luckily he was around to give substance to Luther's often woolly enthusiasms . . .

'Woolly?' cried Aunt Martha. 'Call them "intense"!'

Woolly, insisted Brutus. With Calvin, on the other hand, some coherent principles emerged. The basis of faith was the absolute sovereignty of almighty God, who decided everything – not only the feelings and awareness, but above all the grace he granted the believer . . . The believers were therefore completely dependent on God, whose will determined both the ends and the means of all that affected human salvation: some were destined for eternal life, and others for eternal damnation.

'Hang on,' said Theo. 'If I'm damned in advance, does that mean I can't do anything to save myself?'

'No, because you don't know that you are damned,' he replied. 'You only have to put the question of eternal life to be saved: you are not the author of your question, it is God who enlightens you, it is God who has elected you from the start. You are predestined. Your destiny is part of God's scheme.'

'That's not fair!' protested Theo.

God was neither 'fair' nor 'unfair': who was to judge his heavenly designs? Nobody! That was the basis of this radical principle: God had *sovereign* power to decide the allocation of grace. His chosen were strengthened by a powerful feeling of solidarity, especially when faced with inevitable persecution. For those to whom God had given the gift of grace were by definition his protégés: they would win the struggle. Calvin's disciples, known as Calvinists, soon became invincible fighters, so deeply ingrained was their faith. The principle of God's chosen, which Calvin called predestination, might sound odd today, but in the sixteenth century the wars between 'papists' and Protestants created the need for a doctrine to boost the new followers. Calvin had been right: knowing that you are one of God's chosen makes people invincible.

'But there's already a chosen people, Israel!' Aunt Martha intervened.

Calvin understood that so clearly that his Church drew inspiration from Israel's misfortunes. The long persecution of the Protestants was comparable to the Jews' slavery in Egypt, the defeats and victories to those of the Hebrews, and the exodus from Egypt would come one day, when the Church had rebuilt the world. That was why Jean Calvin decided not to wait, but to found a divine republic in his lifetime, far removed from governments, states and wars. The Jews had not succeeded, the Temple had been destroyed ... The Catholic Church in turn had grievously sinned. It was time to find something new: Calvin wanted to build the city dedicated to divine glory, the Jerusalem that man had twice failed to achieve.

Following in Luther's wake, he transformed the idea of the sacraments, namely baptism and the Eucharist, which were too magical in his view. The sacraments, he said, were only external signs of an inner reality, but they did not bring about this reality. Bread was not the body of Christ, it was the symbol of sharing; yeast was not the physical sign of resurrection, but the idea of raising the dough, in other words, the world. Eating the bread didn't mean that the believer was consuming the real body of Christ: it was only bread, a symbol evoking Jesus's last supper.

'I don't think that's so daft,' said Theo. 'It's true that you can want to see justice on earth and share bread ...'

But not without Scripture, for that was the only sign from God. The Bible did not depend on the Church at all, but on the Holy Ghost, and was supposed to enlighten the believer ... If they were among the elect, the believers had sufficient inner light to govern their lives freely according to the Scripture, guided only by the Holy Spirit. As long as predestination was in your favour, and you weren't condemned in advance to eternal damnation!

'You said it,' commented Aunt Martha. 'This religion with no chance for clemency has always got my back up! I don't know why, I always feel I'm on the side of the damned ...'

Brutus wasn't having that. Aunt Martha was one of the elect, you could tell at first sight! Even her brief trance was a sign from above! For Jean Calvin had also preached tolerance ...

'That's why he had his friend Miguel Serveto burned as a heretic for denying the Trinity and saying that Christ was not the son of God,' Aunt Martha added.

'Nobody's perfect,' sighed Brutus. 'All the same, for Calvin, anyone who expresses faith in Scripture, however they express it, is one of God's elect. Words aren't important, only deeds count. Calvin wrote it down in black and white.'

'How come you know so much about Protestantism, dear Brutus?' she asked warily. 'You, the son of a Saint and a *candomblé* follower!'

Brutus gave two explanations. The first belonged to Brazil's most recent history, on which, he took the chance to remind them, he was one of the leading experts. In the south of the country, there had been a mushrooming of Pentecostal Churches: a third of Brazilians in the huge city of São Paulo were Pentecostalists. The poor, illiterate shanty town dwellers all flocked to join, for Pentecostalism seemed to be specially made for them. Like all Protestants, the Pentecostalists wanted to go back to the roots of the Christian Church: but instead of taking baptism as the key issue, the Pentecostalists, as their name suggests, focused on the event of Pentecost. They believed that the supernatural event when the Holy Ghost descended upon Christ's apostles was crucial, and their services faithfully recreated that miracle.

'What do you mean?' asked Theo in surprise.

The Pentecostalists believed in direct communication with God, in miracles as everyday happenings, and in 'speaking in tongues'. When the congregation reached the point of sufficient communion, suddenly one of them would begin to speak an unknown language. Often, the language was incomprehensible, but sometimes it was an existing language, which the speaker did not know. The miracle of the Holy Ghost! Faith thus made it possible to revive the Pentecostal state . . .

'Aunt Martha's already told me about it,' said Theo. 'Glossolila . . . Glossolalia! Obviously, they make it all up.'

No more than the sons and daughters of the Saints ridden by *orishas*! Why shouldn't people speak languages they didn't know? Wasn't memory able to span the centuries? Perhaps these unknown tongues had existed a long time ago, as the African languages had survived in Brazil . . . That was the second reason why Professor Carneiro was interested in the history of Protestantism, and its strange developments. In his own country, Brazil, *candomblé* in the north and Pentecostalism in the south enabled the poor, who could neither read nor write, to express themselves in their own words, with their own characters, their own tongues. Pentecostalism, like *candomblé*, healed the sick! He, Brutus, for example, had no difficulty in combining the Bible and *candomblé*, Africa and the Scripture, since the Saints riding the initiates was a means of expression just like any other, wasn't it?

'You'd make a marvellous preacher, dearest,' said Aunt Martha half-heartedly. 'Pastor Carneiro Da Silva converts French kids . . .'

'Oh stop it,' said Theo. 'This French kid understands what the preacher said!'

The preacher had more to add. The influence of inspiration through grace caught on so widely that, in the Sixties, after the liberal transformation of the Catholic Church under Pope John XXIII, a powerful tendency developed within the Church which, like the Pentecostal Church, included 'speaking in tongues': far from the established rites, the Charismatic Renewal movement also sought the living source of Christianity, for that was the legacy of Jean Calvin and his active commitment in the earthly city. Calvinism had greatly favoured social development towards more justice and equality. Luther scorned it . . . Luther encouraged the German princes to crush the peasants' revolt. Luther only cared about one thing: destroying the Pope and his power. Calvin, Brutus insisted, was the force of the Spirit, freedom in action . . .

'According to the books I've read,' grumbled Aunt Martha, 'Calvin was at the root of capitalism! What an achievement . . . Grinding down the poor, do you approve of that?'

'Just a sec,' said Theo. 'Brutus said precisely the opposite. What's capitalism got to do with all this?'

Aunt Martha was not entirely wrong, conceded Brutus. For, to build the earthly city without delay, the Protestants worked hard and accumulated private wealth. In short, they had established that form of modern economy called capitalism, without help from the state, and far removed from the political authorities. The Calvinist city demanded this commercial effort, aiming to put social justice into practice in their communities. Yes, capitalism was partly inspired by Protestantism! It was every Protestant's duty to create a better world for the glory of God, and success in business was proof indeed of the divine presence. It made sense. So much so that in twentieth-century Spain, although he was not at all Protestant by birth, a Catholic reformer, Josémaria Escriva de Balaguer, founded in the province of Navarra a solid movement dedicated to sanctifying the Catholic believer through work: *Opus Dei*, 'work of God'.

'They sound like the Murids,' said Theo.

'Modernist theologians all make a connection between work and prayer,' muttered Aunt Martha. 'But social progress isn't always on the agenda!'

Brutus was outraged. It wasn't the Calvinists' fault if capitalism had spiralled out of control and become destructive and mindless! Quite the opposite, they tried to make amends!

'Well, it hasn't worked,' said Aunt Martha. 'I don't share that concept of equality of wealth, you see.'

'But you're a capitalist!' cried Theo. 'Every day you check out your share prices . . .'

'That's what's made it possible for me to bring you on this trip!' she retorted angrily.

'Predestination, dearest, predestination again,' murmured Brutus affectionately. 'Theo and I believe in it: you are one of the chosen.'

Martha was peeved and drank her raspberry beer with a vengeance.

Naomi

The next day, Aunt Martha had a call from her sick friend. Naomi was better, Arthur was delightful, a great companion . . . she would like to have met Theo. No sooner said than done: Aunt Martha decided they would go and visit Naomi. Theo was thrilled. He'd see Arthur!

Naomi was waiting for them at the door to her antiquated apartment full of bric-à-brac and paintings. How old she was! Even older than all Aunt Martha's other friends, but she had parchment skin, frizzy hair and such a luminous gaze that Theo adored her at once.

'Your cat's fine!' she reassured him at once. 'Thank you for leaving him with me . . . Arthur's been a great comfort to me.'

'Good,' murmured Theo. 'I'm really pleased. Where is he?'

On my pillow,' she said. 'He's really missing you. Go see him, quick! Third door on the right . . .'

Aunt Martha introduced Brutus with such ceremony that Naomi smiled mischievously. Very much at ease, Professor Carneiro Da Silva treated her to his high-class hand-kissing routine. Tea was waiting for them on the table, and Theo came back cuddling Arthur.

'Well, Theo, what have you discovered in New York?' asked Naomi.

'Everything!' replied Theo enthusiastically. 'Roller blades, fun people in the streets, food, sidewalk cafés . . .'

'I was talking about your "odyssey",' she added. 'I'm so sorry that I couldn't come with you!'

'Are you a Baptist?' asked Theo.

'Yes,' she replied. 'The faith of the heart agrees with me.'

'But you're not African!' said Theo, confused.

'What does it matter? We are all equal!'

'Naomi has always fought on the side of the Afro-Americans,' Aunt Martha broke in. 'She even knew Martin Luther King.'

'A long time before you were born,' murmured Naomi. 'But let's talk about you, Theo. Do you understand what our Church is about?'

'It's great!' cried Theo. 'People sing and dance, there's a feeling of togetherness . . . If it weren't for the devil, it'd be perfect.'

'The devil's not that important,' she sighed. 'What matters is getting close to God through feeling. Social action depends on it: it really does take faith to move mountains! And nowadays, the mountains are huge. All those wars of religion . . .'

'Like in the sixteenth century between Protestants and Catholics,' said Brutus. 'The supporters of the Reformation were just as fanatical as their persecutors.'

'I know,' replied Naomi. 'Think of the tortures they inflicted on Catholic women! Blowing up their stomachs by cramming gunpowder into their vaginas, it was appalling! But the Catholics weren't any more merciful. One of my ancestors was disembowelled. The papists pulled the child she was carrying out of her womb and smashed its skull against a wall . . .'

'One of your ancestors? Where?' asked Theo, open-mouthed.

'In France, in the Cévennes. I belong to a Protestant family that hid in the mountains to practise the underground faith, in the days of the Wilderness.'

'The days of the Wilderness? That sounds like the Jews in Egypt . . .'

'Precisely,' she said. 'We call the long period when we were deprived of religious freedom "the Wilderness". After King Louis XIV decided to abolish the laws that protected us, in 1685, his dragoons massacred us. We fought back . . . Then we were forced into hiding. We didn't regain our rights till a century later, in 1787. But in the meantime, one of my ancestors had managed to set sail for America, and that's how I came to be born an American. His name in French was the same as your Greek name: Theo. Dieudonné. God-given.'

'Do you ever go back to the Cévennes?' asked Theo.

'Every year, I go to Mialet, in spite of my age. The Protestants meet up there every September to commemorate the assemblies of the Wilderness years, out in the open, under the shady trees. It's the most beautiful church! Now, I wonder whether I'll be able to go this year? With this hepatitis . . .'

'Of course you'll go,' Aunt Martha reassured her. 'You'll get better!'

'By the way, I've got an idea, Theo,' said Naomi. 'Do you know Psalm 139? I can see you don't. The Psalms are poetic prayers that King David is supposed to have transcribed in his own hand. I'm going to read part of it for you and me. Listen.

> *Where can I escape from thy spirit?*
> *Where can I flee from thy presence?*
> *If I climb up to heaven, thou art there;*
> *if I make my bed in Sheol, again I find thee.*

If I take my flight to the frontiers of the morning
or dwell at the limit of the western sea,
even there, thy hand will meet me
and thy right arm will hold me fast.

'It's beautiful,' said Theo.

'You see,' murmured Naomi, closing the Bible, 'the hand of the Lord has led you across the seas and has cured you. It will be the same for me, if that is His will.'

'I'm sure it is!' said Aunt Martha. 'My dear Naomi, perhaps we should . . .'

'Ah! It's true,' she said. 'Theo, it's my job to give you your message. Martha wanted to slip it under your plate, but I don't like mysteries. Here it is.'

I am the city of the castle, the city of the Lion, the city of the alchemists.

'Venice?' murmured Theo. 'There's a lion on its flag . . .'

'But no castle,' interrupted Aunt Martha.

'Versailles?' ventured Theo. 'No, that's not it. I'm stumped, but I'll find it.'

'You should concentrate on the castle,' commented Brutus. 'It's not just any old castle!'

'Nor any old lion,' said Naomi. 'Martha, your riddle is too difficult. I'll help you: in German, this lion is called *Löwe*.'

'A castle in Germany?' said Theo. 'I dunno. I don't even remember what an alchemist is!'

Brutus explained that an alchemist was a scholar who tried to find the philosopher's stone by heating various materials in a retort and fusing them together.

'The what stone?' asked Theo. 'Philosophical?'

'Phi-lo-so-pher's! This substance was supposed to bring them immortality by transforming the base lead of the sinful soul into spiritual gold!'

'I get it,' said Theo. 'The alchemists are like the Taoists in China . . . Magic and all that!'

'Not at all,' said Brutus. The alchemists weren't sorcerers, but the forerunners of the chemists who eventually gave up magic and took the hocus pocus out of alchemy. No alchemist ever found the philosopher's stone, but often, in their search, one of them would discover some of nature's wonderful secrets . . . the chemists simplified the alchemists' system and made it into a science.'

'That doesn't tell me the name of the town where we're going,' remarked Theo, stroking his cat. 'I'll find it, won't I, Arthur?'

'Can I keep him a bit longer?' asked Naomi. 'Arthur is such a gifted healer . . .'

Theo magnanimously held out the cat, who nestled in the crook of Naomi's arm. She needed a rest. Theo was sad to say goodbye to the elderly blue-eyed Baptist lady.

Theo cheats

Determined to find the answer to his riddle, Theo flicked through his books without success. There were alchemists, lions and castles all over the place. What's more, Aunt Martha was laughing at him! Furious, he lost patience and rushed out, saying he was going for a walk around the block as he needed some fresh air . . . Then he sat on a bench and took out his mobile phone.

'Fatou? I'm calling you from the street . . . To get a bit of peace and quiet. Do I love . . . ? Very, very much! Yes, they seem to think I'm cured. Oh, I've thought so for ages! You too? I'm not surprised. Oh no! I can't come back straight away! What would Aunt Martha say? I owe her that at least, don't you think? . . . Exactly. Tell me the next stage. No, not the clue. Just tell me. Cheating . . . OK, it's a game, but what the hell! That's enough nonsense! Yes, I'm sick of riddles. Aunt Martha? Honestly, she doesn't give a damn! You'll never guess what she's up to . . . She's in love! I promise you! A Brazilian professor. What does he look like? Not bad for an old man. He wants to marry her. She almost said yes . . . Ah! So you see it doesn't matter any more . . . Go on, tell me the name of the town with the castle. Speak up! PRAGUE?'

'Drat,' he murmured, staring at his phone. 'She hung up. I can't be expected to spit out the word Prague without prompting! Anyway, where the hell is Prague?'

He went back up . . . Aunt Martha had gone off with Brutus, which suited him fine. Dictionary. Prague, capital of the Czech Republic. No trace of any castle, or a lion. Czechoslovakia: Soviet invasion 1968, Velvet Revolution 1989; became the Czech Republic after separation from Slovakia, 1992. Prague, university; Prague, former capital of Bohemia. Still nothing! Weary from his efforts, he picked up his mobile and locked himself in the bathroom.

'Fatou? If you don't explain the lion, the castle and all that to me, I've had it! I must at least pretend . . . The clue? Go on then . . . Bohemia,

I've got that. But what about the castle? It overlooks the city, good. What about the lion? It's the name of a rabbi? Are you sure? Rabbi Löw, I'm writing it down. The alchemists? They have a street in the castle? Golden Lane? I adore you. Oh yes, big kisses! Speak to you soon . . .'

'With that,' he said, putting away the phone, 'I'm going to fix Aunt M.'

At dinner, he planned his coup. Pretended to rack his brains. Buried his head in his hands, closed his eyes . . .

'Call Fatou,' suggested Aunt Martha obligingly.

'I'll find it all by myself,' he murmured, concentrating. 'Let's see . . . the lion in German . . . Could it be a rabbi? Rabbi Löw's very famous! Now where did he live? In a city dominated by a big castle . . . but of course, it's Prague!'

Aunt Martha's jaw dropped.

'This kid's a genius,' she breathed. 'I always knew it!'

'When did this famous rabbi live in Prague?' asked Brutus suspiciously.

'When?' stammered Theo. 'Er . . . The Middle Ages!'

'The sixteenth century,' Brutus corrected him. 'What's the Golem, Theo?'

'It's the name of the castle!' cried Theo. 'Why all these questions?'

'Because you must have cheated,' Brutus laughed. 'The Golem is a clay figure created by the rabbi you've never heard of. You've been caught out.'

'Theo! You didn't phone Fatou?' cried Aunt Martha.

'I did. I was afraid I wouldn't find it, and anyway, I'm sick and tired of riddles!'

'How you've changed . . .' she murmured.

'I've grown up. And it's partly your fault, old girl!'

'Don't be rude to your aunt, or I'll get angry!' declared Brutus. 'Martha is the picture of youth . . .'

'By the way, has the picture of youth agreed to marry you?' asked Theo.

Embarrassed, Aunt Martha displayed her left hand, where a magnificent translucent red stone sparkled.

'I don't believe it!' exclaimed Theo. 'An engagement ring?'

'A garnet – Oshun's stone,' said Brutus modestly. 'I brought it with me just in case.'

The universal chapel

There was only one more visit scheduled in Aunt Martha's New York programme before they left for Europe. Strangely, she dropped into the UN building on the East River. ID checks, badges, security, friendly guards with caps, queues of visitors . . . Theo wondered what such a place had to do with religion. The UN?

'In this machine for settling conflicts?' muttered Brutus, who was asking himself the same question. 'Don't tell me that it's the temple of peace!'

After consulting one of the security guards, Aunt Martha managed to get them to open a door near the main entrance. It led into the UN chapel.

It had been built onto the side of the building in the Fifties, and was intended for believers in all the world's religions. There was no cross, nor any image, name, altar, post, statue or fetish, no trees and no smile. A narrow beam of light shone onto a huge dressed stone, a block of black haematite dug from the mines of Sweden as a gift. There were rows of pews for those who wanted to pray or meditate. That was all.

'Splendid, isn't it?' enthused Aunt Martha.

'But soulless,' murmured Brutus. 'Religion's a living thing!'

'I like it,' said Theo. 'Religion without frontiers – no dogmas, no quarrels. I like it here.'

CHAPTER 29

Return to the Source

Brutus and Aunt Martha say goodbye

Departures were suddenly different. Before, with every farewell, Theo
had lost a new friend. Since Dakar, the script had changed. They'd said
'Bye, see you in Paris!' to Abdoulaye Diop. They'd left for the States
with Professor Carneiro in tow ... And they were leaving New York
without him, even though he and Martha were engaged. The only novelty was Arthur the cat, meowing in his bag like a stray. Aunt Martha's
and Brutus's goodbyes at the airport were rather forlorn, but this time
it had nothing to do with Theo.

'You know I've got to go back to the university, dearest,' said Brutus.

'Of course,' sighed Aunt Martha. 'It's all to your credit, but when will
I see you again?'

'Soon! Do you think I'm any less impatient than you are? Give me a
while to find our future home!'

'Where will it be?' She looked anxious. 'Not in Brazil, I hope?'

'What,' he murmured, turning pale, 'you don't want to live in my
country? I thought ...'

'We haven't yet decided where to live,' she reminded him. 'I don't
want Rio or Bahia!'

'Neither Rio nor Bahia, agreed. But right now, put down your big
wooden sword, kiss me and look at your garnet often, dearest ...'

'Come to Prague! Life's so dull when you're not around ...'

'Thanks a lot!' cried Theo. 'Am I boring or something?'

They didn't hear him. The elderly lovers couldn't tear themselves away from each other. Theo turned on his heel and went off to mooch around the duty-free shops, where he found a fun lighter for Dad, jazzy and smart but not too expensive or heavy; Aunt Martha wouldn't be able to complain for once. Poor Aunt Martha, it was heartbreaking to hear her sniffing back her tears . . .

She was still blowing her nose on the plane. Feeling rather awkward, Theo buried his head in the newspapers and pretended to be engrossed. She didn't stop. Theo ordered a whisky and proffered it without a word.

'Who do you think I am?' she protested. 'I'm not Liz Taylor!'

'You can say that again,' laughed Theo. 'But we've got to cheer you up. You'll see your man again!'

'That's what you think, and then . . . Do you think he really loves me?'

'Er . . .' stammered Theo. 'Do you doubt it?'

'No,' she said, gulping down her whisky. 'I mean, at my age, you never know.'

And that set her sobbing all the more . . .

'Now the boot's on the other foot,' said Theo, taking her hand. 'Before, you were the one to comfort me, and now it's my turn. Come on, Aunt M., be brave! How about telling me what we're going to do in Prague? After Protestantism, I've no idea what happened . . .'

'Good question,' she replied, fishing out her handkerchief. 'Let me blow my nose again . . .'

'This is the last time!' threatened Theo.

'That's better,' she said, after a good, loud blow. 'All over. I'll tell you why we're going to Prague. Do you remember Rabbi Eliezer?'

'In Jerusalem? Of course I do! He wouldn't let me go!'

'Quite. What did he say to us at the airport? That you hadn't seen anything of Judaism. And do you remember what I replied: "Others will complete what you've begun." Well, that's why we're going to Prague, because you still don't know anything about the practice of Judaism, Theo.'

'I've seen the Wailing Wall, the prayers, the lamentations, the religious district, a school, what else is there?'

'A synagogue,' she replied. 'A Sabbath. The meal, the lights, the blessing, sharing the bread. The Jewish religion in daily life . . . You haven't the foggiest idea.'

'It's no accident you chose Prague. I know you. Are there any Jews left there? I thought they'd all been massacred during the war . . .'

'Not all of them, fortunately,' she replied. 'But that's not the only reason for my choice.

Why Prague?

In Prague there was a ghetto unlike any of the others. First of all, it was intact: four synagogues, an old cemetery, old houses, a whole district, famous throughout the world. Then again, the reason it had been preserved was appalling. After devising the 'Final Solution', in other words, the mass extermination of the Jews of Europe, Adolf Hitler had decreed that the Prague ghetto would serve as a museum for a vanished race. Destined to be a showcase for a lost past, the Prague ghetto had thus been spared on the Führer's orders. The Nazis began to store Jewish art treasures there, precious liturgical objects, tabernacle curtains, exquisite hangings. The war ended and Hitler committed suicide in his Berlin bunker. But the ghetto survived. After the break-up of the Soviet Empire in 1989, ownership of the ghetto was handed back to the Jewish community of Prague. Now it ran the Jewish Museum, housed in a former synagogue, and managed the other synagogues and the cemetery, crammed with ancient, crooked gravestones some only an inch or two apart.

'I've already seen a ghetto,' Theo reminded her. 'At Me'a She'arim.'

But faithful as it was to tradition, the ghetto of Me'a She'arim in Jerusalem was only a successful revival. The Prague ghetto on the other hand was living history. Of course, in the street you didn't meet men with curls wearing long black robes, or boys in velvet knickerbockers. On the other hand, the walls had not changed, the stones spoke, and the magic graves were places of pilgrimage . . .

'Magic graves?' asked Theo in amazement. 'In the Jewish religion?'

Yes, magic, in the Jewish religion. After the fall of the Temple of Jerusalem, the Jews in exile built synagogues wherever they settled, but Solomon's Temple no longer stood, except inside their hearts. Their Jerusalem became a fabulous construction of Holy Books. Tradition had it that on Mount Sinai Moses had received from the God with the unutterable name words that were only for the ears of a handful of exceptional men. The Commandments were for all the Hebrew people, but the words of God were for the purest of the pure. These men were the Prophets of Israel, the 'Nabi': Isaiah, Jeremiah, Ezekiel and Daniel, men with a divine calling from which there was no escape.

'Like John the Baptist and Muhammad, in other words,' said Theo.

The word 'Nabi' had in fact remained in the Arabic of the Koran where, under the name of *al-Nabi*, it meant the prophet Muhammad. The four great prophets were followed by twelve others and, when the children of Israel were in exile, the tradition continued. But there were two Jewish traditions. The first, which was not prophetic, placed the emphasis on study or learning, 'Talmud' in Hebrew. The second, which appeared at the time of the second Temple of Jerusalem, was simply called 'tradition', in Hebrew, 'Kabbala'. Soon, the two tendencies divided: the Talmudists were dedicated to the interpretation of the complex written Law, while the Kabbalists were interested only in esoteric mysticism, and man's direct relationship with God.

'I'm interested in that too,' said Theo.

The fact is that the Kabbalists never lacked inspiration . . . After the expulsion of the Jews from Spain, those who returned to Palestine settled in Safed, a little town built on a steep hillside in the mountains of Galilee. It was there, in this idyllic setting among the hills with their flower-covered slopes, that the most mystical branch of Kabbala developed in the sixteenth century, under the saintly influence of the young rabbi Isaac Luria. Born in Jerusalem into a family that had been driven out of Germany, Rabbi Luria had withdrawn to Egypt on the banks of the Nile, in the manner of the early Christian ascetics. Then he travelled to Safed and developed his doctrine.

Human souls were descended from Adam's, but they were not all located in the same parts of Adam's body. Those that came from the lower organs, the bad ones, had been attributed to the pagans, the others, those from the noble parts, to the Jews. To make amends for the original sin, the 'good' souls had to migrate across the bodies of other human beings, or across animals, rivers, trees and stones. Thus good would spread through the world. That is why Rabbi Luria spoke the language of the insects, called upon the souls interred in the grave-yards, fell into the state of ecstasy there, and promoted the idea of the reincarnation of individual souls all derived from the soul of the first man . . . Rabbi Luria was nicknamed 'Ari', the Lion, and his disciples were known as 'the lion cubs', and to this day people still came to visit his tomb in the ancient hillside graveyard of Safed.

'Unless I'm mistaken,' observed Theo, 'this speaking the language of insects is pretty way-out stuff . . . Rabbi Eliezer wouldn't like it!'

Perhaps not. But Rabbi Eliezer, as a good citizen of Israel, dreamed of the return of all the world's Jews to the Promised Land. Others did not always share his desire. Often, the Jews of the diaspora preferred to stay put, in places steeped in memories, where they had their families and their lives. That had been the case for many Prague Jews. Now in the seventeenth century Prague had been home to the famous Rabbi Löw, the Lion, about whom there were fabulous legends that people still told in the streets of the ghetto: the tourist guides were full of them!

Using Jewish magic, Rabbi Löw made a clay servant that he could bring to life at will, the Golem, the artificial man dear old Brutus had referred to. He could build a palace in a trice, fly from one place to another, invoke the spirits, make wishes come true . . .

'A bit like that other crazy lion, loopy Luria,' said Theo. 'So Rabbi Löw was also a Kabbalist . . .'

No one knew for sure. For the Prague rabbi's magic was probably legendary . . . The historical truth was simpler, but also braver. A learned scholar, skilled politician, and good negotiator, the excellent Rabbi Löw managed to protect the Jews of the ghetto from the antisemitism of the local population. He enjoyed such authority that the Emperor himself was intrigued by him, and summoned him in secret to his castle . . . Never had any Rabbi ever met an emperor in Europe! Rabbi Löw went to the palace. For a whole night, he talked to the Emperor . . .

'Did they talk about magic?' asked Theo.

We don't know what he talked about, but the Emperor of Austria certainly did! And this wasn't just any old Emperor. Rudolf II, of the Habsburg dynasty, had chosen to live in Prague and to make it the capital of his empire. He enlarged his castle there, making it into a city within the city; he filled it with incredible collections of stuffed animals, rhinoceros horns, snakes' tongues, sharks' teeth, ostrich eggs, strange corals, wooden pegs from Noah's Ark, poison antidotes, a bezoar from a goat's gut, and even the lump of clay from which God fashioned Adam. He converted the moat into a . . . Anyway, in a lane in his castle precincts this kindly madman installed a colony of alchemists whose job was to discover the secret of manufacturing gold . . .

'The castle, the alchemists, the Golden Lane!' cried Theo. 'All we need now is the lion.'

The true and only lion of Prague was its venerable rabbi. For in Rabbi Löw's day, the Jews lived in prosperity and peace. That was the only genuine miracle achieved by the man whose followers nicknamed him the *Maharal*, 'our good master'. After his death, legends grew up attributing other miracles to him, none of which has been confirmed. Jews come from all over the world and place little chits of paper on his tomb, on which they have written their dearest wishes, as in the cracks of the Western Wall in Jerusalem.

'So this business of magic tombs seems quite common,' said Theo. 'Can I leave a message with my wish on it too?'

Of course. But Prague was not only the home of the best-preserved ghetto in Europe. Despite the extermination of a large proportion of the Jewish community during World War Two, the remaining Jews in their new-found freedom still worshipped simply, as their people had done for centuries in Europe. And since Theo had begun his journey in Jerusalem, Aunt Martha wanted him to end it in Prague, in the company of the Jews of Europe.

'Do you mean that after Prague it's over, that we're going back to Paris?' asked Theo despondently.

'Not quite yet,' she replied. 'There's one last stop.'

'Another riddle!' he cried.

'You'll get it straight away,' she said. 'This riddle's transparent as the day.'

The chalice of freedom

The guide Aunt Martha had chosen for their visit to Prague was called Miss Riva Oppenheimer, and she taught French at the Institut Français in Stepanska. To Theo she looked neither young nor old, neither ugly nor attractive. She was dressed in black, walked with her eyes lowered, spoke timidly, and kept apologizing for her bad grammar – in other words, Miss Riva wasn't what you'd call a bundle of laughs. What's more, in the taxi back to the hotel, she got the name of the street wrong and apologized even more profusely . . .

'Relax, Rivkele,' sighed Aunt Martha.

'What did you call her?' blurted out Theo. 'You told me her name was Riva . . .'

'Rivkele is Riva's delightful nickname in Yiddish,' explained Aunt Martha. 'And Yiddish is the language of the Jews of Central Europe: it's two-thirds German and a third Hebrew.'

'In fact, Riva means Rebecca,' murmured the shy young lady. 'You can call me Rivkele, Theo.'

'Rivkele's pretty,' granted Theo. 'It sounds like a brook . . .'

At last, they reached their hotel, a magnificent newly renovated 1920s building, with the stucco restored and flowering vines repainted on the walls. The splendid lobby signalled that this was one of the top Prague hotels. But when Aunt Martha opened the door to their room, she froze. It was so tiny that two people could barely stand up in it . . .

'What's this tiny rabbit hutch?' she cried. 'The hotel's just been renovated!'

'I really am most very sorry,' replied Rivkele. 'Unfortunately they have kept the rooms from the Soviet period . . .'

'Totalitarian austerity!' thundered Aunt Martha. 'Herding human beings like animals . . . Never mind, we'll manage. Where are you taking us first?'

'For today, I've planned a visit to the castle and the Cathedral, the Museum, the baroque churches and the Mala Strana hill,' replied Rivkele solemnly.

'Are you trying to kill us?' protested Aunt Martha. 'That's far too much. Let's go and have a drink in the square, in front of the Astronomical Clock. We'll discuss our schedule, if you don't mind.'

'Yes, Madame Macquarie,' murmured Rivkele timorously.

'Call me Martha!' she snapped. 'Pick up Arthur's bag, and for heaven's sake relax, Rivkele . . .'

As they came to the vast square in the Old Town, Theo gasped in admiration. The belfry with its pointed roofs, golden church spires, the green bell tower domes – the city already felt magical. On a platform, people were singing; a clown was entertaining the children; a violinist played Haydn. The air hummed with music and chatter. It was very hard for Rivkele to find them a free table.

'What a lot of people!' sighed Aunt Martha. 'And to think it's September too . . .'

'I'm so sorry, Madame Martha,' said Rivkele, 'but since the Revolution and the big change, we get as many tourists here in Prague as they do in Venice. Apparently it's good for our economy.'

'Right, a hot chocolate, a cup of tea, milk and water for Arthur, and what will you have, dear?'

A lemonade and silence. Rivkele was a real wet blanket. Even when Arthur poked his head out of his bag and meowed pathetically, Rivkele held her tongue.

'Look, Theo . . . Do you see that big statue in the middle of the square?' asked Aunt Martha.

'That weird guy all in green, wearing a robe with folds?' replied Theo. 'Who is he?'

'A very famous man. A century before Luther, he wanted to reform

531

the Catholic Church. But unlike Luther, he was burned at the stake, in Konstanz. Remember his name, Theo. Jan Hus.'

'Why was he burned?' Theo frowned. 'Was his thinking wrong?'

'He thought freely,' she said. 'It often comes to the same thing.'

Jan Hus was born in the fourteenth century, of a peasant family in Husinec, in southern Bohemia, from which he took his name. He was an honest theologian who took an interest in new ideas. All the Catholic thinkers were trying to find ways of reviving their Church. Jan Hus was among them, and he did his job as a theologian: he made known his ideas, which were not at all shocking. The printing press had not yet been invented, but Jan Hus had a way with words. He was such a gifted orator that he quickly captivated the mass of Catholics who flocked to hear him preach in the Bethlehem Chapel in Prague, of which he was in charge. Newly built, the chapel could hold a congregation of three thousand, and Jan Hus preached there in Czech, the language of the people. In the other churches, they preached in German for the rich . . . His fame soon spread, and, although he did not know it, that put his life in jeopardy.

What did he say? That they should return to the source of Christianity, to the authentic celebration of Mass. That a true Catholic should take communion in both kinds (bread and wine) as Jesus had done during his last supper. All Catholics were entitled to share the divine flesh and blood, as Jesus had commanded that evening. A good Catholic should eat the bread and drink the wine from the chalice, like the priest.

'That's nothing to make a song and dance about,' said Theo. 'Is it, Arthur?'

The Catholic hierarchy did not share his view. What was this Czech priest meddling with? Trying to change the ritual of Mass! What had become of the pope's authority? Now if this Jan Hus would just keep a low profile . . . But no! The people of Prague loved him! Soon, things started getting sticky for him. He was summoned by the authorities and given a lecture. He took note and stood by his ideas. Inspired by an ideal of freedom, he even developed them further, and became so popular that a few years later he earned himself a lengthy trial. For the honest Catholic Jan Hus, the choice was straightforward: either he renounced his ideas in public, or he would be sentenced to death. Nobody had actually decided to burn him at the stake, and everyone hoped that, like so many other men of his day, Jan Hus would quietly choose to repent and admit his wrongdoings to save his life. But he did the opposite. Yes, the choice was simple. Jan Hus preferred to die for his beliefs.

'That takes guts,' murmured Theo.

And so Hus burned. The Czech people immediately rose up against the Catholic Church in a widespread, powerful grassroots rebellion. Jan Hus's followers were not prepared to renounce the ideas of their national hero. The chalice from which the worshipper drank Christ's blood became the symbol of the revolt. In the name of their chalice, the 'Hussites' took up arms and fought. The Hussite movement was born, with communion at Mass in both bread and wine. Driven out of the churches by the traditional clergy, the Hussites celebrated Mass in the open air – in the woods and fields . . . And with this forbidden practice were sown the first seeds of the Reformation that was to come to fruition with Martin Luther.

A hero emerged from the nobility, a military commander and former mercenary and master of the King's Hunt, Count Jan Zizka. He took command of the holy war under the name Brother Zizka of the Chalice and founded the Hussites' holy city, Tabor. Bohemia had broken faith with the Roman Church! The Pope sent out a crusade to crush the rebellion, but it failed. And a second crusade, which also failed. The third time, the crusaders massacred the Hussites mercilessly.

Since that bloody era, Jan Hus had been the symbol of Czech freedom. Not for the bread and the wine, but because he had had the courage to die for his ideas. Five centuries later, in the middle of the twentieth century, when Czechoslovakia suffered under the yoke of the Soviet Empire, a young man imitated Jan Hus. He doused himself in petrol and set himself alight. Like Jan Hus, the student Jan Palach was willing to die for his ideas, in the name of the freedom stolen from the Czech people.

'Has he got a statue too?' asked Theo.

'He has his place,' replied Rivkele, looking up. 'But, if you like, we can lay flowers at the spot where he set fire to himself. It's something I often do.'

Rivkele's eyes lit up for the first time.

'Your parents suffered terribly during that period,' said Aunt Martha. 'Fired from their jobs for political reasons, reduced to poverty . . . You were only little at the time.'

'I did as I was told,' said the young woman, sounding more lively now. 'I read the Books and I prayed to the Almighty to free us from slavery. Today we are free.'

'Do you know, you look much prettier when people can see your dark eyes?' said Theo.

'Of course I know it,' replied Rivkele. 'But I'm shy. We had to keep quiet for so long . . .'

Fair-haired John and dark-haired John

Just as she was starting to relax, two young men wearing ties stopped in front of the café. They unfolded a little table, methodically laid out pamphlets on it, and waited.

'I'm going to see what they're selling,' said Theo. 'Are you coming, Rivkele?'

The young men weren't selling anything. They answered in halting Czech and gave their pamphlets to those who were interested in their ideas. Rivkele asked them some questions, which they answered with the utmost seriousness.

'They're Mormon missionaries,' she told Theo.

'Aunt Martha!' exclaimed Theo. 'Mormons, just think! Mormons in Prague!'

'Why shouldn't the Mormons come to Prague?' retorted Aunt Martha without budging. 'Take this opportunity to find out more! I'll keep an eye on Arthur . . .'

So, with Rivkele's help, Theo conversed with the two young men. They were both called John. John 1 was fair and John 2 dark. They weren't related, and they had just arrived from Salt Lake City, the holy city of all the Mormons of the world, 'the city of the Saints,' 'the new Jerusalem', as it had been baptized after many trials and tribulations by Brigham Young, the successor to the visionary Joseph Smith, founder of the Mormon Church.

'What trials and tribulations?' asked Theo.

After the lynching of Joseph Smith, the council of the New Church decided to go and settle far from their persecutors. It took the first Mormons a year and a half to travel more than two thousand kilometres westwards in appalling conditions. When they finally reached the heights of the Rocky Mountains, they saw a lake in the middle of the desert. It was a salt-water lake, and they named their town Salt Lake City. Nowadays, the Mormon city was prosperous, with a booming economy. Building the kingdom of God required a highly developed sense of social governance.

'So what are they doing in Prague? Ask them, Rivkele.'

As in every devout Mormon family, their parents had decided to send their eldest sons on a mission for one year; that was the rule. Of course, they were entitled to refuse, but their parents would have been so hurt that in the end they decided to face up to the big test. The Church of Jesus Christ of Latter-Day Saints chose the country they would be sent to and carefully prepared them for their mission, and after that they were on their own. Their task was to spread the principles of the faith contained in the Book of Mormon and to help people – in other words, the standard duties of missionaries of all religions.

'Tell me what you do in your ceremonies,' asked Theo enthusiastically.

'To find that out, you first have to be one of us,' replied fair-haired John. 'In any case, we don't have crosses in our churches, because the living Christ is among us.'

'We can tell you about our code of behaviour,' added dark-haired John. 'We don't commit any excesses. We don't drink alcohol or coffee, we don't take drugs and we don't smoke. We don't have a clergy, there's absolute equality between us: every boy over the age of twelve can take part in the service . . . Our life is austere and simple, the way the tribes of Israel lived.'

'For, according to our Book, we are the lost tribes of Israel, rediscovered in North America,' added fair-haired John. 'Four centuries after his resurrection, Jesus Christ came to visit our distant ancestors . . . Thanks to him, we know: what God did for his Son, he does for everyone. We are all destined for resurrection.'

'That's why we have a sacred duty to baptize the dead souls of the whole world since the beginning of time,' explained dark-haired John. 'We want to bring them back into God's fold to guarantee their resurrection.'

'Since the beginning of time?' asked Theo, amazed. 'But that's impossible!'

'It's possible,' replied dark-haired John. 'In Salt Lake City, we're computerizing all the genealogies of the world. Of course it will take us several decades, but thanks to the many Mormons in our communities, we're making rapid progress! Family after family, we're piecing together the past and discovering the lost ancestors . . . Then we baptize their souls.'

'That way we'll save the whole world,' added fair-haired John. 'Our ideal is simple!'

'Is it true that you practise polygamy?' asked Rivkele, looking them straight in the eyes.

'No,' replied dark-haired John. 'Polygamy is illegal in the United States and we are law-abiding citizens.'

'But our founders considered it a duty to protect women,' fair-haired John continued. 'That's the honest truth.'

'So, you do or you don't?' demanded Theo impatiently. 'What are they saying, Rivkele?'

John and John exchanged glances without replying.

'No,' admitted fair-haired John, after a pause. 'What does it matter, since we are all potential Gods . . . Our Christ is not the Christ of the Passion, but the Christ of the Resurrection. See how he shines!'

'He looks like a star in an American soap,' muttered Theo, looking at the picture. 'Jesus in *Bay Watch*.'

'Don't be rude,' hissed Rivkele. 'I'm not translating that.'

'So ask them if life as a missionary isn't too depressing, so far from their salt lake,' he said.

Dark-haired John declared he was very happy to preach in Central Europe. Fair-haired John mechanically echoed his sentiments. Sometimes, young Mormon missionaries cracked under the pressure of the task, and returned home mortified, even destroyed. But John 1 and John 2 had been lucky: others had been sent into the slums of Latin America, whereas in Prague in September . . .

'Let me ask you something,' said Theo. 'Why can only the boys take part in the service after the age of twelve?'

John 1 and John 2 stood there in awkward silence. When it came to women, the Church of Jesus Christ of Latter-Day Saints was not very forthcoming.

Citrons, palm branches, horns and crowns

The next day, they visited the Prague ghetto. The adamant Rivkele was determined to start with the Jewish Museum, housed in a former synagogue.

'A museum!' moaned Theo. 'What for?'

'She's right,' said Aunt Martha. 'You'll see all the religious objects that you know nothing whatever about.'

In the display cases, Theo saw magnificent crowns surmounted by golden lions, embroidered velvet hangings, lamps, candelabra, mysterious little cylinders, animal horns decorated with gold and silver work, and a whole collection of long sticks with a silver hand and pointing finger on the end. They looked like Christian chalices and monstrances,

536

but, since they were in the Jewish Museum, what were these strange objects?

Rivkele set out to explain. The hand on the end of the long stick was a pointer, used for following the lines of the sacred Hebrew texts, and the finger showed the letter and its vowel. The little cylinder, the *mezuzah*, was fixed to the door-jamb of a Jewish home: you touched it as you went in and out, for it contained a miniature scroll of the Torah, the holy book. The hangings were placed in front of the tabernacle to conceal the Torah, those enormous scrolls containing the first five books of the Bible, which were taken out during the service. The candelabra . . .

'With seven branches, I know about them,' cut in Theo.

The origin of the famous seven-branched candelabrum went far back into the Jewish past. According to the book of Exodus, its design was one of the instructions delivered to Moses on Mount Sinai. A candelabrum appeared on the Arch of Titus in Rome, on a bas-relief depicting the objects looted during the sack of Jerusalem. Had it belonged to the destroyed Temple? Most likely. Carried shoulder-high before the victorious Emperor, its presence in Rome signified the defeat of the Hebrew people . . . This candelabrum, called a *menorah*, had become, together with the star of David, the living symbol of Judaism. As for the lamps, they were reserved for the beautiful Festival of Lights, *Hanukkah*, which commemorated the Maccabee victory over the Hellenists and the miraculous lasting of the holy oil for eight days rather than one.

'And that sort of pineapple you see all over?' asked Theo. 'There, on the crown, and on the velvet curtain . . .'

It wasn't a pineapple, but a giant citron. Among the silverwork objects, Rivkele showed Theo a myrtle, a palm and a willow branch: the citron, the palm, the willow and the myrtle made up the ritual bouquet of 'the four species' used in the Feast of Tabernacles, *Sukkot* in Hebrew. On leaving Egypt, the Hebrews had roamed for many years in the desert before they finally reached the promised land: in memory of those nomadic times, during the Feast of Tabernacles Jews reconstructed the tents of branches and leaves that provided shelter for the wandering Hebrews.

'But what about the horns, are they for the sacrifices?' insisted Theo.

No! Taken from the forehead of a ram in memory of the animal which, at the last moment, replaced Isaac just as Abraham was about to sacrifice him, the horn, called the *shofar*, also referred to in Exodus, was a holy trumpet with a deep, lowing sound that resounded like the voice of Adonai Elohim. As for the royal crowns of gold and silver, these capped the Torah scrolls, giving them an aura of glory and eternity.

'There aren't half a lot of Jewish festivals,' commented Theo. 'The feast of Tabernacles, Lights, are there any more?'

Oh yes! There was the joyous festival of Purim, the Feast of Lots, which recalled how the beautiful Esther, who was married to the pagan king Ahasuerus, had saved her people by revealing that she was a Jew. On Purim, people dressed up, and sang: it was a real carnival! They celebrated the New Year at the end of summer, wishing each other happy new year as people did all over the world, except that it wasn't the first of January. Eight days later came the celebration of the Day of Atonement, Yom Kippur, but this ceremony was very solemn. Its purpose was to atone for the sins committed the previous year. The Jews implored God's forgiveness and prayed for the dead.

'There is at least one Jewish festival that you know, Theo,' Aunt Martha reminded him. 'We talked about it even before we arrived in Jerusalem.'

'Before Jerusalem?' Theo racked his brains. 'It feels such a long time ago . . . Hang on! Do you mean Passover, by any chance?'

'Yes,' she said, '*Pessach* in Hebrew. Not to be confused with Easter, although it's often held at the same time, do you remember?'

'Sort of,' said Theo. 'For the Jews, Jesus isn't the Messiah resurrected. Their thing is about the night they left Egypt, when they eat those lovely crackers that Dad brings home. But which of all these festivals is the most important?'

'*Pessach*,' replied Rivkele. 'Nothing is more important than the end of slavery in Egypt. You have to know what it is to lose your freedom in order to appreciate what it means to regain it.'

The Maharal's tomb

Rivkele had chosen the best time to visit the tiny old Jewish cemetery: the tourist buses were leaving, and so was the sun. Under the foliage of the tall trees stood thousands of gravestones in a chaotic jumble, some upright, others slanting, others lying flat and some of them were smashed.

'Is this a cemetery?' asked Theo in amazement. 'This mess?'

'It is the most revered of Jewish cemeteries, Theo,' said Rivkele. 'Between the thirteenth and the fourteenth century, eleven thousand

Jews were buried in this tiny area. Under each gravestone were piled layers of bodies, deep under the ground . . .'

'Why didn't they find somewhere bigger?' he asked.

'Ghetto rules,' broke in Aunt Martha. 'The Jews were crammed together, alive or dead.'

Theo wandered along the paths in silence as the last rays of the setting sun lit only the tops of the graves. The sparse grass had been trampled, and the paths were overhung with branches; the thrushes and crows cast dark shadows over the neglected graveyard. Despite the autumn gold of the foliage, peace did not reign in the old cemetery. An immense feeling of sadness welled up in Theo, and he barely glanced at the names engraved in Hebrew on the tombstones.

'Stop, Theo!' cried Rivkele. 'Here's the famous tomb of the Maharal, Rabbi Judah Löw Bezalel, the Lion.'

'It's superb,' admitted Theo, gazing at the two majestic arches, 'and it's been beautifully restored. Ah! The rampant lion on the medallion . . .'

'And the citron at the top,' added Rivkele. 'At the bottom, the bunches of grapes symbolizing fertility. Have you got your wish?'

'Yes,' replied Theo, taking a folded paper out of his pocket. 'Where do I put it?'

'Under the lion, next to the others. Take a stone and wedge the paper underneath it . . . Now kiss the stone and concentrate. Then the Maharal will grant your wish.'

'This rabbi's a one-man Wailing Wall!' cried Theo. 'Is it because of the Golem?'

'Probably,' she said. 'Come and sit on the seat over there. There's still a little time before dusk. I'm going to tell you the story of the Golem.'

As they walked off, Aunt Martha unobtrusively pushed a piece of paper under a black stone, just next to Theo's, before drifting over to join them. Speaking softly, Rivkele began the legendary tale.

The Maharal did not invent the name of the Golem, or the secret of his making. According to the Talmud, Golem was a word used to describe incomplete substances – an unfinished pitcher, a childless woman. Before the divine breath brought him to life, Adam was a Golem. Then, a learned rabbi found out how to emulate God.

When, in 1580, the Maharal realized that he had to protect the Jews of the ghetto against attacks by the people of Prague, he decided to bring to life a Golem. First, he took a ritual purification bath and put on a white hooded robe. Then, accompanied by his son-in-law and one of his disciples, he went down to the river bank by night and collected a huge mass of clay. He had to fashion the statue, then walk round it four hundred and sixty-two times, reciting the sacred letters. Then, the Maharal pushed into the clay mouth the piece of paper on which the sacred letters were written. And now the clay giant began to move. The Maharal called him Yossele. He did not speak, he was content to obey, and as he was huge, Yossele Golem frightened people: that was what the ghetto needed him for. That evening, the Maharal removed the sacred paper from the Golem's mouth, and he remained lifeless until dawn.

'Tell me what was written on the paper,' asked Theo.

'The Hebrew word for "truth",' she replied. 'But if you take away the first letter, you have the word for "death".'

It all went wrong when Perl, the Maharal's wife, took the Golem to market. Oh! he was very well-behaved, and strong! But of course he didn't understand a thing. One day, she asked him to pick up a bag of apples. While she was paying, the Golem picked up the vendor with his stall and hoisted him onto his shoulders, creating panic in the market-place. The clay servant was causing Perl endless trouble. Then, one evening, exasperated by his wife's nagging, the Maharal forgot to remove the famous paper. In the middle of the night, poor Yossele Golem began to wander the streets of the ghetto, his heavy clay feet crashing down, damaging everything in his path . . .

He had to be destroyed in the proper way. For if the same procedures were not performed in reverse with the utmost care, there would be complications, as with the Baal Shem Tov who, so the story went, had stupidly asked his Golem to lean forward so that he could remove the paper from his mouth . . .

'Well, well, an old friend!' cried Theo. 'Nobody told me that the Baal Shem made silly mistakes . . .'

The Baal Shem Tov's Golem leaned so far forward that he crushed the Rabbi underneath his weight . . . The Maharal was more cautious. He erased the first letter, removed the paper, and walked round Yossele in the opposite direction the requisite number of times, reciting the letters backwards. When he had finished, the Golem became a huge mound of clay again. The Maharal took the clay back to the river bank and put it back where he had taken it from. Unless he hid it in the synagogue attic, for after the destruction of Yossele Golem, the Maharal put it out of bounds.

'Pity it's only a story,' sighed Theo. 'I'd like to have seen Yossele.'

'Oh!' whispered Rivkele, pointing in terror at the wall. 'The giant shadow over there, behind the tree . . . It's Yossele Golem! It's him!'

'Calm down, Rivkele!' said Aunt Martha. 'This is the twentieth century and there's no Golem any more . . .'

'They say he reappears when the Jews are in danger,' said Rivkele with a shudder. 'The last time he was seen was in 1939, just before the Holocaust . . .'

'Come on,' sighed Aunt Martha. 'It's dark. How can you make out a giant shadow?'

'But look, Madame Martha,' murmured the young woman, trembling, 'it's moving!'

'Goodness me, you're right,' she grumbled, half convinced.

'I'll go and see,' offered Theo gallantly.

Behind a tree trunk, there really was a giant hiding. A tall man wearing a voluminous mud-coloured hooded cloak . . . Brutus?

'Sssh!' murmured Brutus, putting a finger to his lips. 'She doesn't know I'm in Prague.'

'OK,' said Theo. 'I won't say a word. Get going!'

Brutus sneaked away and Theo reassured the ladies. There was no trace of any Golem . . . Apart from a visitor who'd come back to retrieve his coat, he hadn't seen a thing. Oh! Yes, a huge fallen branch.

To revive their spirits, Aunt Martha and Rivkele ordered two hot chocolates at the nearby café. Meanwhile, Theo rummaged around in the antiques shop, bought a gruesome terracotta Golem, a supposed portrait of the Maharal, and a postcard of his tomb to send to Rabbi Eliezer in Jerusalem.

The Sabbath queen

Then there was an evening and a morning. On the Friday, Rivkele invited her friends to join her for Shabbat, which her elderly parents celebrated with quiet simplicity. The Oppenheimers' apartment was near the ghetto, on one of the wide avenues built at the time of its restoration. A retired teacher, the very elderly Mr Oppenheimer was waiting for them in the doorway with its tarnished copper mezuzah. From within, his wife greeted the visitors warmly:

'*Shabbat shalom.*'

'*Shabbat shalom,*' echoed Mr Oppenheimer.

'*Shabbat shalom*, David,' said Aunt Martha, kissing him on both cheeks. 'We've brought an unexpected guest – Arthur, Theo's cat.'

'*Shabbat shalom*, everyone!' Ruth's voice rang out from the other end of the passage. 'I'll be with you in a minute! Do you want some milk for the cat?'

Ruth Oppenheimer radiated an infectious joy. Up to her elbows in flour, she covered Theo in kisses and white smudges, then steered him into the kitchen where she was preparing the meal. Rivkele spread a white cloth on the table and placed two candles, a wine cup, the plates, the cutlery and the wine on it. In a corner of the dining room, a stove blazed.

'Mummy, you're late with the *hallot*!' she cried.

'I know,' retorted Ruth. 'They're baking! Why don't you try and find someone to put out the fire instead of bothering me!'

'Be quiet!' snapped Rivkele. 'You know we must never ask anyone to do that . . .'

'Your mother's forgetful today,' observed Mr Oppenheimer. 'Don't scold her, Rivkele, she's doing her best . . .'

Poking his head into the dining room, Theo had no idea what the mother and daughter were squabbling about. Seeing that the temperature dropped as night fell, the lighted stove was rather a good idea! Why put it out? Why did they have to ask, or not ask?

Mr Oppenheimer shot a meaningful glance at Aunt Martha.

'Very well, David,' she said. 'I'll do it.'

Confused by all these mysteries, Theo went back into the kitchen to crush hard-boiled eggs with a fork, as Mama Ruth had asked him to do. She was chopping raw onion, cursing as her eyes watered. She quickly mixed it in with the chopped chicken livers, pepper, salt . . . She opened the oven and checked the plaited bread that was turning golden brown. On a large dish, a magnificent cold fish was already prepared: Arthur took an active interest in it. Ruth wiped her forehead with a floury hand and heaved a sigh of relief.

'What have I forgotten?' she muttered. 'Ah! The cake. Of course, I got back late, but at last we're ready. Keep your eye on that cat . . . I'm going to get changed.'

When Ruth had slipped her velvet dress over her plump form, it was just time. With a gentle movement, she struck a match and lit the wicks of the candles, murmuring the blessing for the lighting of the candles. Shabbat had begun. Then, as if at an agreed signal, Aunt Martha got up and extinguished the stove.

'During Shabbat, the Jews are not allowed to tend the fire,' explained Rivkele. 'Only a non-Jew can help them, but the Jews aren't allowed to ask them to perform this service. Madame Martha has often done this for us . . . And now, my father is going to say the prayers.'

'The *hallot* aren't on the table, Ruth,' complained David. 'What have you done with them this time?'

'They're still in the oven!' cried Ruth, rushing into the kitchen. 'Martha, come and turn off the gas, please . . .'

The *hallot*, plaited loaves eaten on Friday night, looked perfect: crisp and golden. Ruth placed them in a basket and covered them with a cloth decorated with embroidered letters.

'It says in Hebrew: "Holy Shabbat",' said Rivkele solemnly. 'Each time we celebrate the arrival of the queen of silence . . . The Holy Shabbat is like a bride who lives with us during this wonderful time. The Shabbat queen brings us the warmth of the heart, and peace. My father is going to say the blessing over the *hallot* and distribute them in a minute.'

'I'm not able to walk much any more and so it's hard to go to Synagogue every Saturday,' sighed the elderly David. 'But I can still praise the virtuous woman, for her price is far above rubies, even if she is running late today . . . Isn't that right, Ruth? Then, Theo, it's time for Kiddush, the most important part of Shabbat. Listen . . .'

Mr Oppenheimer filled the cup with wine, placed it on the palm of his hand and everybody rose.

' "Evening came and morning came, a sixth day. Thus heaven and earth were completed with all their mighty throng. On the sixth day God completed all the work he had been doing, and on the seventh day he ceased from all his work. God blessed the seventh day and made it holy, because on that day he ceased from all the work he had set himself to do." '

Then he drank a sip of wine and passed the cup to his wife. After each person had drunk from the cup, the elderly man washed his hands with a little water and raised them to say the blessing over the washing of the hands. To bless the plaited bread, he raised the cloth and laid his fingers on it, reciting the blessing before breaking it into pieces.

'Ruth, your *hallot* aren't cooked,' he chided gently. 'They're burned on the outside and soggy inside . . .'

'I'm losing my mind,' groaned Ruth. 'I'm old, David . . .'

'But more precious than pearls, my love,' he repeated, smiling. 'We can sit down now and eat.'

Theo sat down awkwardly. Aunt Martha attacked the fish with relish. Arthur took a keen interest in the chopped chicken liver. Rivkele was flushed and lively as she chattered nineteen to the dozen. The elderly

David ate slowly, contemplating the Sabbath table, while Ruth plied Theo with food. The candles shed a warm glow over their faces and cast mysterious shadows onto the white tablecloth. It was as splendid as a wedding feast in honour of the bride's arrival at the conjugal home.

After the meal, David Oppenheimer began the evening prayers, chanting in Hebrew.

'What does it mean?' asked Theo.

'He's reciting the *Shema*,' whispered Aunt Martha. 'The central prayer of the Jewish liturgy, Theo. "Hear O Israel, the Eternal One is our God, the Eternal God is One. You shall love the Lord your God with all your heart, and with all your soul, with all your might. Let these words, which I command you this day, be always in your heart. Teach them diligently to your children; speak of them in your home and on your way, when you lie down and when you rise up. Bind them as a sign upon your hand; let them be like frontlets between your eyes; inscribe them on the doorposts of your house, and on your gates."'

When Aunt Martha and Theo got back to their hotel room, it felt rather gloomy. Even Arthur complained, and went to sleep under one of the beds.

The Old-New Synagogue

On the Saturday, the Sabbath day, Rivkele did not appear. Aunt Martha and Theo spent the day at the castle that dominated the city of Prague. There were hordes of tourists and they had to queue to get into the narrow Golden Lane, the former home of Emperor Rudolf's alchemists ... They escaped to the gardens that occupied the moat and looked out over the rooftops and green domes of Prague, the city bathed in golden mist.

'It's not bad,' commented Theo. 'But much more complicated than the ghetto!'

'Here you'll see Baroque art at its greatest. Pay attention,' warned Aunt Martha. 'To fight the Protestant Reformation, the Catholic Church used various means. War, massacres and the Crusades to begin with. Then, a clean-up of its habits and customs. And lastly, Baroque art, which you can see before you. Glorification through beauty was the Catholic Counter-Reformation's strongest weapon in Europe.'

'They could have thought of it earlier . . .'

'But we would have been deprived of these masterpieces. Don't rewrite history!'

'When will we see Rivkele again?'

'Tomorrow evening. This year, the Day of Atonement begins on Sunday, at dusk. You must also see a Synagogue service . . .'

On Sunday, Theo was back in his beloved ghetto. Aunt Martha had insisted on coming early to show Theo the façade of the Old-New Synagogue. Old because it was the oldest, and New because, a long time ago, it had been restored. The Old-New Synagogue was supposed to be eternal: angels had brought the stones from the Temple in Jerusalem . . . The fact was that it had survived, intact, with the dust of Yossele Golem hidden by the Maharal in the attic.

At the arranged time, the Oppenheimer family arrived, Rivkele and her mother supporting the elderly gentleman whose legs could barely carry him. At the entrance to the Synagogue, Theo was given a *kippah* and a white prayer shawl with black stripes, which was draped over his shoulders. David had his own, which he unfolded carefully. Then the women went to one side, and the men to the other.

Surrounded by the group of worshippers with their white shawls, Theo glimpsed the women sitting in rows, all with smart hats. The curtain around the Ark was of red velvet and gold. And when it was drawn back to open the doors, when they took out the magnificent scrolls of the Torah, a holy shudder rippled through the congregation. Moved, Theo trembled. He understood nothing of the cantor's high-pitched singing, couldn't make out the mumbled prayers, he had no idea what the rabbi was saying, but he felt as though he were being transported three thousand years back in time, to the dawn of the religions of the world, to Jerusalem or elsewhere.

'It's the day of Atonement for Jews,' murmured David beside him. 'But it is also the day of welcome for the stranger, Theo. Welcome among us, my boy . . .'

Suddenly, as he turned round to adjust his shawl, Theo caught sight of Brutus wearing a white and black shawl, a *kippah* on his head and a smile hovering on his lips. Professor Carneiro bang in the middle of the Synagogue looked as much at home as in the Abyssinian church or in his *candomblé terreiro*. . . Brutus winked and intoned the refrain to the song. What's more, he was singing in Hebrew!

Who was it who nearly fell over backwards as they left the service? Aunt Martha, at the sight of Brutus folding up his prayer shawl and handing it back to the official. Who was furious with him when she learned about his stupid prank in the old Jewish cemetery? Aunt Martha. Who flung herself into his arms in the end? Aunt Martha.

'I've applied for retirement, dearest,' he said, hugging her. 'My only job will be living with you.'

'Not in Rio or Bahia, I hope?'

'I've inherited an old house in a quaint little town called Olinda,' he murmured. 'You'll live under my roof, my darling, which is as it should be . . .'

'Promise me I'll keep my independence,' she answered warily. 'And that I'll be able to travel around when I feel like it?'

'Wherever you like, dearest. But not alone.'

'Really, you won't ever leave me?'

'When's the wedding?' asked Theo.

'When we get back to Paris,' replied Aunt Martha. 'You've only got one more message, and one more place. Wait till tomorrow!'

Theo had no trouble guessing where to find the message. Sitting under a stone on the Maharal's tomb, a piece of paper signalled the end of the journey.

And now, be reunited with your Pythia in her sanctuary.

Two days later, they left for Greece with Rivkele, bound for Delphi.

CHAPTER 30

The End of the Road

Granny Theano

Theo knew Athens airport inside out. The window where you bought tokens for the luggage trolleys. The baggage claim area, tactics for avoiding the crowds. He took command and gave orders to his troops, Rivkele, Brutus and Aunt Martha, who obeyed meekly. And this time, he knew exactly what lay in store for them outside. Granny Theano, his grandmother, standing up straight with her white hair.

He hurled himself at her, and she hugged him so hard he nearly suffocated.

'My darling who I nearly lost,' she sobbed. 'My Theo, my darling . . .'

'It's over, Granny Theano, I'm cured,' he murmured, squeezing her. 'Stop crying . . .'

'A true miracle! I prayed so hard . . .'

'A good thing you did. It helped, just look at me.'

'How you've grown!' she cried, holding him at arm's length. 'At least five inches!'

'Travel makes young people grow,' concluded Theo. 'Careful with that blue bag! My cat's in there, a ginger tom called Arthur . . .'

'You've travelled all that way with a cat? Didn't Martha say anything?'

'No, because he was only given to me in Africa, and besides, he's so cute, look at him . . .'

'He's got blue eyes,' she admitted. 'What's his name again?'

'Arthur!' repeated Theo. 'Right, Granny, the others are waiting, be

547

nice to them please. Rivkele comes from Prague where she's a teacher. The tall gentleman is Aunt Martha's future husband. His name's Brutus and he's Brazilian. Don't look so shocked . . . He's great!'

'Martha's remarrying!' exclaimed Granny Theano. 'About time too. With a bit of luck, marriage will knock some sense into that feather-brained skull . . .'

Granny Theano sometimes had a spiteful tongue, as the family well knew, but as she was on her best behaviour she congratulated Aunt Martha effusively and was charmed when Brutus kissed her hand. As for the shy Rivkele, she instantly became part of the family.

That evening, Granny Theano sent the three outsiders off for dinner in a cheap restaurant in Plaka, for she wanted to be alone with her grandson.

Sitting in the dining room where he had spent so much time during his holidays, Theo eyed the icons on the wall, the old photographs of his grandfather, the Demeter's head bought in Alexandria, the violin, the music stand and the scores.

'Do you still play?' he asked.

'Of course,' replied Granny Theano. 'Sometimes I even give concerts! Why are you laughing? Anyone would think you don't take me seriously.'

'I just can't believe you're a violinist,' he sighed. 'For me, you're my grandmother and you make chicken soup with egg and lemon. It's silly, isn't it?'

'No. But you're certainly growing up! You never used to ask me about my music. Even as a child, you were always buried in your books. You weren't interested in my profession.'

'Well, I've changed. I've moved on from books to the real world, which isn't as bad as they say.'

'That's a good start. And what have you gained from this tour of the world's religions?'

'Whoa!' cried Theo. 'Is this a quiz show or what? Double or quits? Win a luxury cruise or a fitted kitchen?'

'You've got all the time in the world, and you can take as long as you like, but I'd like to know. Not that I'm an expert on religion, but when you've got a genius in the family . . .

The genius scratched his head and yawned.

'OK. But over Greek coffee and baklava.'

'It's all ready,' she said, lifting a cloth. 'I know you!'

Theo's tree

'Good,' he muttered, taking out his notebook. 'Here goes. While we were travelling I jotted things down and did drawings, you see? The last one is just a tree. Let me explain. Listen ... I see the different religions as the branches of a tree. One big tree with underground roots that spread under the whole Earth ... All the branches are growing in the same direction, towards the sky. That's natural, that's what branches do. Then the trunk emerges from the ground, nice and straight, nice and clean. The tree is an African baobab, because you can carve anything you want on the bark. Read it for yourself: "God is for the good of humanity", that's what's written on the trunk.'

'So you didn't meet any evil gods,' she concluded.

'Hold on! The common trunk of all the religions doesn't just state that God is good! Next to it, on a sign, I've put his instructions, which don't fit on the trunk. Directions for use, if you prefer. God is for the good of humanity, but there are certain conditions: that we honour him, pray to him and make sacrifices to him. Otherwise God gets angry! He causes floods, exile, war, drought, lightning – you name it.'

'So people have duties towards God,' added Granny Theano.

'That also comes in the common trunk. The directions for the tree are endless. All religions want to unite and protect. To achieve this, they're very demanding – you can't stray an inch. A tree has to be watered with clean water. You mustn't pee on it, or damage it by dumping waste. We don't want any more pollution! So religions are very hot on purity. That too, protection against pollution, is in the common trunk. Fertilizer too, which is called sacrifice. So far, they're all the same.'

'I see. And then what happens?'

'It happens that God's first gardeners die. The next ones fall out – it seems that's only human. All gardeners have their own ideas about fertilizer. One thinks animal blood's best, another one thinks wine and breadcrumbs are better, a third says just water, the fourth wants mineral water, the fifth says filtered water, the sixth only wants fire to burn the dead leaves, and the seventh only air – in other words, they're environmentalists at war. One fine day, they each publish their instructions for looking after the tree. That's it. All the religions begin to squabble. So things go wrong. And when the tree grows each spring, each of the gardeners takes one branch, each with a different God.'

'Interesting,' said Granny Theano. 'What do you think of the branches?'

'It's a tree, so it grows branches, that's what trees do! And you know what happens to the tree? If it's not pruned, it dies . . . Well! When a main branch of the tree no longer produces any leaves, a new gardener appears to cut it off. And each time, it grows anew. When Judaism was drying up, the gardener Jesus cut off the dead branch. So then there were two strong branches instead of one. One old, and one new. When the branch of Christianity started mouldering, the gardener Luther ripped off the branch without treating it. And the same thing happened. When the branch of Brahmanism stopped growing in the spring, the gardener Buddha cut it back. And so it goes on and on . . .'

'From what you say, you like gardeners . . . But where do they all come from?'

'I'm not sure. They say they're God's messengers. Apparently, they were tipped off about the tree, and that's what they call their revelations. They went up the mountain, or withdrew into the desert, the forest, the snow, the sand, a long way away in any case. They're a bit crazy and very wise . . . They're all so alike! Moses, Jesus, Muhammad, Buddha, Joseph Smith . . .'

'Who?' exclaimed Granny Theano.

'The American that God sent the Book of Mormon to. Oh, that reminds me . . . They're wonderful gardeners, right? So why do they do such a bad job? Because they don't bother to train apprentices . . . The minute they're dead, all hell breaks loose! Instead of one pretty branch, you get three, six, as many as there are new gardeners! I like tree-surgeons, but when they've finished pruning, that's it, away they go.'

'It's not exactly their fault if they die,' she went on. 'But you're making me talk nonsense! Christ isn't dead, that's the whole point . . .'

'Well, he's not the only one!' cried Theo. 'Muhammad flew off on his mare from the roof of the mosque in Jerusalem, Buddha attained Nirvana, and I can tell you about loads of imams who've passed away but haven't died . . . Moses, yes, he's well and truly dead. But not the others! Nobody will admit that these extraordinary gardeners are men.'

'But Christ is the Son of God, all the same!' Granny Theano was getting irritated.

'He's the only gardener who says where he comes from,' Theo conceded. 'After that, you've got to believe. Personally, I don't know. You do. But I'm interested in the whole tree. Loads of things happen to a tree. Ivy can grow at its foot, or a creeper. If the gardeners aren't careful, the ivy chokes the tree . . . Then you get fundamentalism, and that kills.'

'All right,' she admitted. 'How does your tree end?'

'It doesn't. My tree's tenacious. The healthy branches resist. When they're pruned, they grow again, or produce more branches. The others arc sawn off, or end up rotting . . . But the tree still grows '

'You're beginning to irritate me. Anyone would think you'd never heard of the tree of knowledge in the Garden of Eden . . .'

'Of course I have! I'm going to tell you how I see it. In the beginning was the tree. People only wanted one thing: to climb as high as they could, right to the top where the leaves touched the clouds. They invented the ladder, which worked perfectly. One day, a troublemaker broke the ladder, to see what would happen. No way to climb up any more. In all the religions, you find someone who breaks the ladder between heaven and earth. Then, the gardeners arrived to try and find some other way. Grow the tree as high as possible, allow people to climb up. They never stopped climbing . . .'

'What about the evil serpent? And the apple, what do you do with the forbidden fruit of knowledge?' she objected.

'Not so fast . . . you talk about the evil serpent, but I know about Indian branches of the tree where serpents are very nice creatures, very holy! And besides, I can't believe that God would forbid knowledge. Otherwise, what am I doing at school, huh? You tell me!'

'So you don't believe in sin,' she said anxiously.

'What sin? Drinking alcohol, smoking, eating beef or pork, or letting people see your hair when you're a woman? There are as many definitions of sin as there are branches! It's written on the trunk: God forbids. What? That depends on the gardeners.'

'My God,' she sighed. 'Martha's certainly done a fine job. You've come back an atheist, like her!'

'Not at all, Granny! I felt the power of God, I promise you! It's just that I found it everywhere, that's all. It's the roots talking through the branches. But if I have to choose one branch, then I'm in trouble!'

'Wait . . . So you want to climb the tree too?'

'It seems as if we have no choice,' he murmured. 'It's as though the root is growing inside people's bodies: it has to grow deeper and deeper. And when they fight against religions, it's yet another religious war, so . . .'

'You haven't answered my question, Theo.'

'Yes, I want to climb. Not too high. I'd like to stop at quite a low branch where I could keep an eye on the ivy. Watch the gardener at

551

work, tell him not to cut too much off, to saw neatly, not to damage the tree by sending bits flying everywhere. I would also tell him to leave it alone in spring: there's a season for pruning, a season for fertilizing. I'd ask him not to fence in the branches. Not to remove the birds' nests, even if there are bird droppings everywhere. They're part of the life of the tree.'

'So you're still an environmentalist!' she sighed. 'I don't see anything religious in what you're saying.'

'I'm sorry, Granny Theano,' he said after a silence. 'You've found your branch. I'm still looking for mine. That's the difference.'

'Stop going on about this tree that doesn't bear any fruit!' she cried.

'Oh yes it does! Citrons, grapes, ears of corn or fonio, peaches of youth, a whole basketful of fruit . . . My tree is amazing: it can grow all the fruits of the world all by itself! And there are all kinds of animals living under it . . . The bull, the goat, the ram, the cockerel, the serpent, the eagle, the lamb, the heron, the rat, not to mention all Saint Francis's birds. That's the tree of the Garden of Eden!'

'Just you wait till sin comes along, my boy,' she threatened. 'You're soon thrown out of Paradise!'

'That's the annoying thing with God. He's incredibly violent! When he's cross, he sends lightning, it's a bit much.'

'And who are you to judge God, you little worm?' she cried.

'I'm just me. OK, that's not much. But if you think about it, you'll admit that God created me as I am.'

'Well, he's made some mistakes in his time!'

'Ah! You see, you're being judgemental too! Why won't you allow me to have my branch?'

'Because . . . I don't know. You're making my head spin. It's not the way I see things. I wasn't expecting . . . Anyway, who cured you, Theo?'

'People. Good gardeners. You find them everywhere.'

'So it wasn't God?' she asked anxiously.

'It's the tree,' he replied stubbornly. 'I'll call it God if it makes you happy.'

'You've changed so, Theo,' she groaned. 'Give me time to get used to it! Come and eat. I've made you . . .'

'Chicken soup with egg and lemon?' exclaimed Theo. 'Brill! Because all that talk of the tree and fruits has made me hungry!'

When the cargo ship arrives

At breakfast the next morning, Granny Theano looked drawn. She swore she hadn't slept a wink because of Theo's tree. She'd spent four hours thinking, then in the end she'd picked up her violin and played Bartok to soothe her mind.

'I didn't hear anything,' yawned Theo, with Arthur snuggled in his lap. 'Did you really play?'

'Softly, so as not to wake you,' she said. 'I'd like to go back to your tree. Without disturbing you, Theo. But tell me something . . . Are all the branches equally valid in your view?'

'Valid!' exclaimed Theo. 'Does a tree judge its branches? Some die and fall off. But sometimes, there are tiny branches with pretty green leaves! Aren't they as good as the big ones?'

'Just what I thought!' she exploded. 'You justify the existence of sects!'

'Ah! So that's what was bothering you! You see, I racked my brains over this business of sects and my tree. Sects are awful . . . But actually, now it's clear in my mind. The minute some joker claims to be a prophet and is forever asking his followers for money, then shuts them up and makes them work only for him, it's a sect. Don't worry, I know all about them.'

'Yes, but are the sects on your tree, Theo? It's important!'

'They're not on the tree. They're at the foot of the tree. You know, when you get suckers? Like on your strawberry plants . . . If the gardener doesn't remove them, no strawberries! Sects are exactly the same. Not only are they not part of the tree, but they damage it. They're bad news!'

'I'm not convinced. Let's take an example. Aunt Martha told you about the Cargo cults, I imagine?'

'Cargo?' queried Theo. 'No. Have you heard of them, Arthur?'

'Odd,' mused Granny Theano. 'And yet it was she who told me about these strange sects in Melanesia . . .'

'We didn't go there,' confessed Theo. 'What are they about?'

'I'll try and remember,' she hesitated. 'In some Melanesian islands, in the middle of the Pacific, the natives . . .'

'The local people,' Theo corrected her, 'We're all natives.'

'Anyway, they saw the first Europeans arrive on ships. The whites unloaded all sorts of crates, weird contraptions, unknown drinks, and one fine day, the Cargo cults were born.'

'Because the miraculous ships were cargo ships,' concluded Theo.

'The nati . . . the local people worship cargo. Before, on these islands, they used to practise ancestor worship; they believed the ancestors used to come back and spend some time among the living, to protect them. One day, some huge ships full of cargo docked in these Melanesian islands, provisions and treasures were shared among everyone with absolute equality . . .'

'Very important, equality,' declared Theo. 'I bet they're waiting for their Messiah!'

'I don't know. Their belief is so strong that often, in anticipation of the arrival of the cargo ships, the people destroy all their possessions in the hope that the divine navigators will take pity on them! Now that's a destructive sect!'

'So you think the Cargo cults are sects,' murmured Theo pensively. 'But who's at the helm of the ships? The whites?'

'Oh no! It's the ancestors returning!'

'You left out the most important thing!' he cried. 'So if the ancestors are involved, it's not a sect. It's the Melanesian branch growing back. Why shouldn't the roots of my tree grow under the Pacific islands? I find the idea of the cargo ships interesting. It's true! Paradise arrives by sea . . . The ancestors unload the ships, distribute the food, give out presents. They're always terrific, ancestors. I learned that in Africa. Hooray for the ancestors!'

'Destroying everything for an illusion,' she fumed.

'Would you say that the pantheon of Greek gods was an illusion, Granny Theano?'

'Now listen, Theo, you can't compare the Greek gods to . . .'

'To those savages?' Theo finished the phrase. 'Isn't that what you were going to say? Aren't you ashamed?'

'All right,' she conceded. 'Let's say I'm afraid you're a bit too tolerant of all those phoney sects.'

'My tree knows the difference. You see why it needs gardeners . . . I don't think I'm too bad a gardener. Don't worry, Granny Theano.'

'All right, I won't,' she concluded, rising to her feet. 'Now, we've got work to do. Tomorrow, big picnic at Delphi! We're going shopping.'

As usual, Granny Theano bought ten times the amount she needed for Brutus, Aunt Martha, Rivkele, herself and him, even a hundred times too much, she was so happy. Theo tried to reason with her, but she wouldn't listen. Ten bottles of raki, twenty boxes of halva, five kilos of olives, three tins of cat food for Arthur, thirty kilos of tomatoes. Thirty!

Granny Theano slept on the question of Theo's tree, and in the morning she seemed to accept it. Instead, she railed against the incompetence of the doctors who hadn't realized, didn't know, hadn't found, hadn't . . .

'They did their best,' Theo broke in. 'Leave them alone! Nobody's able to explain how I got better . . .'

'They say you were misdiagnosed!'

'So what? What does it matter? Seeing that I'm alive . . .'

'I'd like to understand,' she stubbornly insisted.

'I'll tell you something,' he murmured. 'The first time I heard my twin sister's voice, I felt a weight pressing down on me . . . Until Mum told me her secret. After that, I was definitely a lot better.'

'Ah! Your little sister who died,' groaned Granny Theano. 'I've always nagged Melina to tell you the truth. She wouldn't listen. She was afraid for you. She was so anxious . . .'

'So anxious that I really did fall seriously ill,' he said. 'Well, not too seriously, but it was close. That's the tree again! It needed cutting . . .'

'I've always said she was too protective,' added Granny Theano hastily.

'I loved . . . But you mustn't prune too drastically! Breakfast in bed, for example . . .'

'Lazybones,' she retorted. 'You're too old for that now!'

'By the way, Granny Theano, did you know my twin sister's name?'

'Stillborn babies aren't given a name,' she murmured. 'She would have been called Theodora, I think.'

'I should have guessed,' mused Theo. 'Theodora hardly talks to me any more. Hey, how come Mum hasn't called? She's all right, isn't she?'

'Couldn't be better,' replied Granny Theano with a mysterious smile. 'I mean . . . When you see her, you'll understand why she hasn't phoned.'

'When will I see her?' he cried excitedly. 'Tomorrow?'

'Tomorrow. When we get to Delphi. Don't miss the end of your odyssey, Theo.'

'Now you've lost me,' he muttered. 'There are no more gods at Delphi . . .'

'I may belong to the Orthodox Church, but I think that the spirit is still alive in Greece!' Granny Theano protested. 'Don't try to take the Greek gods away from me! Then I would get angry.'

'My grandmother's a pagan!' taunted Theo, jumping up and down. 'The branch is growing back . . . Three cheers for God!'

The Pythia's oracle

Aunt Martha, Brutus and Rivkele set out on their own. Granny Theano
slid behind the wheel of her new car, a convertible that she drove at
breakneck speed. Weaving between the lorries, the outrageous grandmother overtook everything, ignored yellow lines, honked furiously and
generally drove like a maniac . . . Theo gripped his seat and didn't dare
say a word: when she drove, Granny Theano was a different person.
Arthur stuck his head out of his bag and meowed as if he were being
strangled . . . small towns, bends, skids, villages, traffic jams, brakes
slammed on, screeching tyres . . . Mind that kid by the roadside! Look
out for that dog!

Her hair streaming in the wind, Granny Theano proudly reached Delphi
in record time. It was around midday: the sun was high in the sky, the
cicadas chirped in a raucous chorus. At this time of year, there were few
tourists. Theo counted the cars: one, two, three minibuses . . . That was
OK. Strangely, when they began to walk up the steps of the ancient site,
there was no one to be seen. It was as though the tourists from the minibuses had vanished into the shadows of the sanctuary.

'I must go and find the Pythia,' he muttered pensively. 'The problem
is, you've always told me that nobody knows exactly where she was to
be found.'

'Since you're so fond of climbing, then climb!' commanded Granny
Theano. 'Apollo also loved heights.'

'Hey, didn't he have a twin sister too?'

'Absolutely,' she replied. 'The goddess Artemis, born under a palm
tree at the same time as him. Apollo the sun, and Artemis the moon.
They rarely meet, and that's all for the best.'

'Why?' asked Theo, shocked. 'How sad!'

'Each god has a place, and each one has a job to do,' she said sancti-
moniously. 'Nobody asks them their opinion. Artemis presides over
women giving birth, and Apollo over the oracle. She works at night,
and he by day. Supposing they met . . . The world would be turned
upside-down!'

'Now, where would the oracle have hidden herself? Is there one last
message for me to find?'

'What's written on the paper, Theo?' she suggested. 'That you must
be reunited with *your* Pythia. Your own. Look around.'

Theo opened his eyes but could only see stones under the hot sun.
A lizard basking on a marble hand. A stray sparrow. A buzzard in the

sky. Olive and cypress trees. Pebbles everywhere. A fluted column lying on its side and, perched on the column . . .

Perched on the column, a shape shrouded in white! An illusion? But the illusion wriggled its toes inside their floral socks . . .

'I don't believe it,' he cried. 'Aunt Martha's really unearthed a Pythia!'

'First of all, I'm not just any old Pythia,' cried the veiled figure. 'I'm your very own Pythia, you idiot!'

Fatou! How come it hadn't occurred to him? He ran, raised the veil and kissed the plaits from which dangled beads of every colour. Kissed Fatou's cheeks, forehead, chin and lips. And Fatou's dark eyes.

'Give me my oracle, my love,' he murmured.

'Learn to read,' she retorted.

'Are you teasing me?' he protested. 'Are you saying I can't read?'

'Not your last message!' she replied. 'It said "your" Pythia. It was obvious, wasn't it? Unless you've met another Pythia on your travels?'

'No, oh no! I love you, and you know it.'

'We'll see,' she said, jumping down off the column. 'Now look carefully, Theo.'

Emerging from the ruined temples, Theo's guides were all making their way through the cypresses and olives, with smiles on their faces. Stunned, Theo recognized Ila's pink sari, Amal's earrings, the flimsy white veil covering Nasra's hair, Rivkele's beautiful eyes, the *kippah* on Rabbi Eliezer's blond head, Abdoulaye's embroidered boubou, Blessed Lightning's purple robe next to the Cardinal's red one, Father Dubourg's black beard, Sudharto in a pair of ultra-trendy jeans, and behind them Alyosha, hand in hand with Irina, tears of emotion running down his cheeks.

'You're all here . . .' he murmured. 'It's the best cargo in the world!'

None of them spoke. Instead they surrounded Theo and looked at him, their faces full of joy. They didn't dare touch him, they just gazed at him fondly. Theo took Ila's hand in one of his, and Amal's in the other, and gathered his guides around him.

'This is my Jerusalem,' he murmured. 'We're all together in Delphi. Incredible!'

'Nearly all,' commented Nasra after a brief silence.

'It's true, there's one missing! Where's Sheikh Suleiman?' asked Theo. 'Is he late?'

'He couldn't come,' replied Rabbi Eliezer awkwardly. 'I'm afraid I have some sad news for you.'

'Our old friend left us a month ago, Theo,' sighed Father Dubourg. 'We were both at his bedside.'

'Is he dead?' whispered Theo. 'Why did he do that?'

'Because his time had come,' replied the Rabbi. 'He passed away peacefully. He knew you were cured. He was very fond of you, Theo . . .'

Theo sat down on a rock and began to cry. His guides' arms comforted him, a whole tree of loving arms . . .

'One of us was destined not to survive,' said Blessed Lightning. 'It was written in the stars. He was the oldest of your guides, Theo . . . But his soul will stay with you, as you know.'

'It's not the same!' sobbed Theo. 'There's someone missing!'

'Someone else is missing, now what's her name? . . .' said Granny Theano, scanning the list. 'Mrs Ashiko Desrosiers.'

'Ashiko?' cried Theo, looking up. 'Married, already? She hasn't wasted much time!'

'She sent you a telegram about cherry blossom, but I left it at home,' Granny Theano apologized.

'There's no hurry,' muttered Theo. 'Ashiko's not dead. That's the main thing.'

'Our holy friend has gone up to Allah's Paradise,' went on Father Dubourg. 'You couldn't find a kinder heart, could you, Eliezer?'

'He'll live on in our memories,' replied the Rabbi. 'That's how we Jews think of eternity. The dead live on in us. Look into your heart, Theo! You'll find our friend there.'

'I can picture him surrounded by houris,' murmured Theo, tears in his eyes. 'That must be difficult for him! What's he going to do with all those girls at his age?'

'Theo!' scolded the Rabbi. 'You don't joke about things like that! Suleiman was an excellent Muslim . . . I can imagine him having a great time with the houris. You didn't know him when he was young!'

'So now there are only two of you to make peace among the religions?' asked Theo wistfully.

'With you, that makes three of us,' replied the Rabbi. 'We'll wait for you. You remember, "next year in Jerusalem"? I told you that you would come through . . . You must come!'

'I like that idea!' cried Theo. 'I'll come back, I'll be just like Suleiman. When I've finished university, would you like that?'

'Next year, son,' insisted the Rabbi. 'Peace won't wait!'

'I haven't forgotten,' said Theo. 'But give me time to think! So many things have happened to me . . . By the way, where are Aunt Martha and Brutus? And my parents?'

'Patience,' said Fatou solemnly. 'At Delphi, I give the orders. I've planned a procession. My dear guides, please form a circle and take your bow! Daddy, show them . . .'

Under Abdoulaye's direction, the women sat down in a circle and the men stood behind them. Fatou climbed up onto the column and adjusted her veil.

Be kind to yourself

'The fiancés!' she announced. 'Martha Macquarie and Brutus Carneiro Da Silva!'

'*Mazel Tov*!' cried Rabbi Eliezer. 'Everybody clap their hands!'

Aunt Martha stepped out of the coppice wearing a very chic, soft black dress. On her arm, Brutus beamed with happiness. Theo rushed over to kiss them.

'You look fabulous,' he whispered in Aunt Martha's ear. 'For once, you're not dressed up.'

'Brutus chose it,' she replied softly. 'Do you really like it?'

'Very much,' he said. 'Are you happy, Aunt M.?'

'Oh yes! You will come and see us in Olinda, won't you?'

'Of course I will, Mrs Da Silva,' he replied. 'With Fatou.'

'You won't forget your odyssey, will you?'

'You've got to be kidding,' groaned Theo. 'She saved my life and she asks me not to forget! My wonderful daft Aunt Martha . . .'

'Daft Aunt Martha kept one wish for the end of the odyssey,' she murmured, slipping a note into his hand. 'Read it with Fatou when you're alone together.'

'Have you two finished whispering, dearest?' inquired Brutus. 'The Pythia's waiting!'

'Theo's sisters, led by Athena,' announced Fatou from her column, introducing Attie who had cut her hair. 'Followed by Irene Fournay and Jeff Malard!'

Theo frowned. Jeff Malard? Who the hell was he? A tall blond guy holding Irene's hand . . .

'My boyfriend,' said Irene, introducing him. 'Jean-François, but you can call him Jeff.'

'Make way!' commanded the Pythia. 'Now, Theo's father!'

Alone? Theo shivered.

'Where's Mum?' he asked, hugging him. 'Isn't she here?'

'Of course she is,' laughed Dad, 'don't be so impatient!'

'And at last, here's our star!' boomed Fatou. 'Theo's mum!'

Melina looked radiant and blooming as she walked carefully, protecting her slightly protruding stomach with her hands. Theo stared at his mother wide-eyed in amazement. Mum, pregnant? Overjoyed, he rushed towards her and swept her off her feet.

'Theo, careful!' cried Dad. 'I want her in one piece!'

'Don't worry, I've grown as strong as an ox!' cried Theo, putting her back down on the ground. 'So when's it due?'

'At the end of the year,' she breathed. 'Gently, Theo! It's a girl.'

'The little sister I asked for!' exclaimed Theo. 'Great! What are you going to call her?'

'Zoë,' replied Mum. 'In Greek, Zoë means "life". Do you like it?'

'Zoë Fournay,' he said. 'Not bad. I'll call her Zozo.'

'Poor thing,' groaned Mum. 'Now, give me back my ring, at once!'

Theo pulled off the wedding ring and slipped it onto his mother's finger, kissing her hand.

The Pythia from *Wrath of the Gods* hadn't lied: at the end of the odyssey, he would find his whole family. The circle of guides from all around the world closed in, a wreath of smiles pressed around Melina and Theo.

A pair of German tourists who were puffing and panting along the path stopped in their tracks when they caught sight of Fatou standing on her column.

'*Was ist das?*' cried the portly gentleman. '*Ein Film?*'

'You've hit the nail on the head, Fred,' replied Fatou, jumping down from her perch. 'In glorious Technicolor, for the big screen, in stereo, with a happy ending. I play the Pythia.'

'*Ach, eine schwarze Pythia!*' said the lady, moving off. '*Etwas ganz neues, wie interessant!*'

Granny Theano had begun organizing everybody. It was time to pile back into the minibuses and go for a picnic on the beach. But Theo's guides were a rabble ... Irene and Alyosha were dawdling, Sudharto had taken Rivkele in hand, Irina was speaking German with Father Dubourg, Rabbi Eliezer was congratulating Aunt Martha effusively, Nasra was nattering to Brutus, Don Ottavio was chatting to Ila, Abdoulaye to Attie, Dad to Mum, and Blessed Lightning was flirting with Amal.

'Let's go!' yelled Granny Theano. 'Order, my friends, please! Cardinal, would you take care of the cat?'

'Can we go for a swim, Mrs Chakros?' chimed in Don Ottavio, grabbing Arthur by the scruff of his neck.

'Oh,' cried Ila in a flutter. 'I haven't got my swimming costume . . .'

'Walk into the sea in your sari, dear child,' he replied paternally. 'That's what the women do in your country, isn't it?'

'I love the sea,' said Alyosha to Theo's sister. 'Don't you, Irina Yeremeievich?'

'Not really,' whispered Irene.

'I'm not going swimming,' declared Nasra. 'The water's too cold in September.'

'I thought as much,' said Sudharto. 'I've brought my wetsuit!'

'He thinks of everything . . .'

'Do you think there are sharks?'

'In the Mediterranean! Of course not . . .'

'Oh! I've heard that sometimes . . .'

'What about the cat? What are we going to do with the cat?'

'I'll keep him . . .'

'Let me have him, dearest . . .'

'Are you sure cats don't like water?'

'Maybe . . .'

Their words faded as they disappeared among the ruins. Theo remained alone with Fatou.

'My poor old mate from Jerusalem,' he sighed. 'The first person who never despaired of curing me . . .'

'I'm sorry I never met him,' said Fatou. 'He was very old, wasn't he?'

'Very,' said Theo. 'Bursting with kindness. We'll go to Jerusalem and lay a rose on his grave.'

'For Christmas?' she asked, her eyes shining.

'You're forgetting Zoë's birth! We'll go there one day . . . Because you know, one day, you and I are going to travel!'

'So Theo's odyssey is over,' she murmured. 'It's been so long.'

'That long? From Christmas to September . . . Only nine short months!'

'I've been so longing to see you!' she sighed. 'Allah is great! You've come back alive.'

'I've just remembered,' he exclaimed. Aunt Martha gave me a prayer for us to read together. Here, read it to me.'

'*Go placidly amid the noise and the haste,*' began Fatou in a half whisper, '*and remember what peace there may be in silence. As far*

561

as possible without surrender be on good terms with all persons. Speak your truth quietly and clearly, and listen to others, even the dull and ignorant; they too have their story. Avoid loud and aggressive persons, they are vexations to the spirit. If you compare yourself to others you may become vain and bitter, for always there will be greater and lesser persons than yourself . . .'

'That's certainly true,' said Theo. 'Let me read now. *Enjoy your achievements as well as your plans. Keep interested in your career however humble: it is a real possession in the changing fortunes of time. Exercise caution in your business affairs for the world is full of trickery.'*

'I don't like that bit very much,' said Fatou. 'Let's see the rest. *But let this not blind you to what virtue there is: many persons strive for high ideals, and everywhere life is full of heroism. Be yourself, especially do not feign affection! Neither be cynical about love; for in the face of all aridity and disenchantment it is as perennial as the grass . . .'*

'Up with grass!' exclaimed Theo. 'I'll go on. *Take kindly the counsel of the years, gracefully surrendering the things of youth. Nurture the strength of spirit to shield you in sudden misfortune. But do not distress yourself with imaginings! Many fears are born of fatigue and loneliness . . . Beyond a wholesome discipline, be gentle with yourself. You are a child of the universe, no less than the trees and the stars: you have a right to be here . . .'*

'Do you hear?' he said. 'We're entitled to be here . . .'

'Let me read the last bit,' begged Fatou. *'And whether or not it is clear to you, no doubt the universe is unfolding as it should. Therefore be at peace with God, whatever you conceive Him to be, and whatever your labours and aspirations, in the noisy confusion of life, keep peace with your soul. With all its shams, drudgery and broken dreams, it is still a beautiful world! Be careful. Strive to be happy.'*

'Who wrote it?' murmured Theo.

'Here, at the bottom of the page,' she said. 'Look . . . There's just one line: "Found in St Paul's Church, Baltimore, dated 1692. Anonymous."'

'Aunt Martha could have written it,' he mused. 'She's managed to find the most beautiful prayer for the whole world.'

Fatou folded up Aunt Martha's prayer and snuggled against Theo.

'Be careful,' she whispered, 'strive to be happy . . . What are you going to do tomorrow, Theo?'

'Me? Go back to Paris, unpack the presents, catch up with my school work and see my mates . . . I'm dying to play football! Right, shall we go to the beach?'

'Sacrifice the bull?' she asked mischievously.

'Dive into the waves!'

'. . . THEO!' cried Melina's voice. 'Have you seen what time it is? It's lunchtime! THEO . . .'

Fatou and Theo exchanged smiles and bounded down the steps of the sanctuary at Delphi like two young mountain goats. On the fallen column lay the Pythia's forgotten veil. Calm was restored to the realm of the cicadas, the chariot of the sun burned onwards across the azure sky, the lizard basked in peace, and solitude reigned once more over the scene. Somewhere in the distance, under the olive trees, Theo's laughter rang out.

INDEX

giving oneself to God (Lutherism) 505
Godfrey of Bouillon 30
Godunov, Boris 362
Golden Calf 266
Golem, Yossele 522, 529, 539–41, 545
Golgotha 32, 69
Goliath 60
Gospels 51, 95, 158, 161, 172, 263, 502, 504, 505
Granth Sahib 190
Greek Orthodox Church 68, 351
griots 428–31, 436, 441, 448, 455, 462
Grotto of the Milk 94
gurdwara 180, 189

hadith 386, 391
Hadrian, Emperor 63, 166
Hagar 54, 56, 395, 396
Hagia Sophia 400–2
hajji 15, 393, 394
hallot 542, 543
Hanukkah 537
Hanuman 204, 205, 208, 241, 264, 326
hara-kiri 301, 302; see also seppuku
Harijan 200; see also untouchables
Harris, Pastor 481
Hasan, Imam 389–90
Hasidim 86, 87, 90, 92
Hasidism 86, 88, 89
Hathor 101, 266
Hebron 54
Heian-Kyo 334; see also Kyoto
Helena, St 68
Hell 244–5, 268, 303, 304, 323, 384–5, 410, 501, 504; see also Underworld
Henry VIII, King of England 510
Hephaestus 255
Hera 134, 183; see also Juno
Hermes 134; see also Mercury
Herod 60, 63, 66, 78, 94, 361
Herzl, Theodor 64–5
Hinduism 171, 177–89, 202, 208, 209–22, 225, 229, 233–4, 245, 257, 262–5, 268, 416, 475
Hindutva 234
Holy Ghost 15, 48, 67, 143, 262, 516
Holy Latin Church 68–70
Holy Places 30, 67, 75, 94, 393
Holy Sepulchre 52, 53, 68, 69, 71, 74, 75, 81, 92, 101
Holy Trinity 48, 106, 262
horse (Brazil) 489, 493, 494
Horus 101, 121, 132, 264
host 15, 48, 207, 405

houri 384, 419, 558
Hus, Jan 505, 532–3
Hussein 389, 391
Hussites 533
Hypatia 102–3

Iblis 384, 394; see also Satan
Ibrahim 54, 56, 57, 395; see also Abraham
iconoclasm 401, 402
Iemanja 478, 489, 492, 493
ihram 393–4
initiation 442, 443, 466, 469, 489–91
Inquisition 33, 64, 85, 141, 142, 261, 502
Irenaeus 47
Isaac 54–6, 90, 189, 264, 537
Isaiah 527
Ise, temples of 335, 336
Isfahani, Hatif 412
Ishmael 54, 56, 395, 396
Isis 101, 121, 132, 135, 136, 429
Islam 38, 51, 54–7, 66, 86, 95, 103, 146, 172, 177, 181, 185, 189–91, 194, 261, 264–7, 275, 292, 379–97, 401–5, 408, 409, 411, 415–21, 424–6, 430, 431, 481
Ismail 389–90
Ismailis 389–90, 409
Israel 14, 27, 29, 33, 42, 43, 64, 77, 89, 90, 98, 375, 475, 514, 527, 544
Istanbul 70, 90, 377, 380–3, 397, 402, 406, 415, 416, 418, 420; see also Byzantium; Constantinople
Ivan the Terrible 360, 361, 362
Izanagi 303
Izanami 303–4

Jacob 42, 43, 114, 115, 151
Jainism 177, 179–80
Jeremiah 527
Jerusalem 14, 20, 23–98, 141, 143, 338, 372, 511, 515, 527–8, 530, 537, 538, 545, 550
syndrome 34
Temple of 52, 60, 61, 527, 545
see also Aelia Capitolina; Al-Quds; Yerushalayim; Zion
Jesus Christ 15, 26–33, 35, 37, 44–51, 55, 68–70, 75, 80, 90, 105, 135–46, 150, 153, 154, 156, 160, 161, 206, 263–7, 350, 362–3, 373–5, 401–5, 486, 487, 502–8, 513–16, 533–8, 550
Jihad 51, 146, 263, 386
Joan, Pope 150
Job 44, 55
John XXIII, Pope 76, 161, 516
John Paul II, Pope 76, 142, 144

ACKNOWLEDGEMENTS

Professeur Pierre Amado, Louise Avon, Chotte Baranyi, R. P. Joseph Roger de Benoist, docteur J.-P. Bernoux. Jacques Binsztok, Patrick Carré, Claude Cherki, Jean-Christophe Deberre, professeur Suleymane Bachir Diagne, professeur Christian-Sina Diatta, Babacar Diouf, Gérard Fontaine, docteur Erik Gbodossou, Françoise Gründ, Lilyan Kesteloot, Jacqueline Laporte, Nathalie Loiseau-Ducoulombier, Veer Badhra Mishra, Lionel Pasquier, Alexandre Eulalio Pimenta da Cunha, Françoise Pingaud, Jean-Louis Schlegel, Daniel Sibony, Man Mohan Singh, Françoise Verny, et naturellement A. L.

Marilyn Bowering

Visible Worlds

Shortlisted for the Orange Prize for Fiction

'Marilyn Bowering's second novel is a *tour de force*, lavish in its scale, complication and information . . . *Visible Worlds* is written with such panache and is so much fun to read that it seems churlish to resist its more fantastic moments. It is a wonderful piece of storytelling.'

LAVINIA GREENLAW, *Independent on Sunday*

'The pivotal characters are twins brought up in rural Canada during the 1930s. One of them is dispatched to Germany to study music and gets caught up with the Hitler Youth movement. The other, quieter one leads a voyeuristic existence, trying to make sense of the lives of his parents and their friends. There is a lot to make sense of. His father believes in a weird science known as Personal Magnetism and takes a clairvoyant for his mistress. His mother is haunted by the spectre of an earlier love affair and an abandoned child. And what about Fika, the young Russian woman who, in a parallel narrative, is busy trying to ski across the ice-cap to Canada in 1960? *Visible Worlds* blossoms into a real page-turner . . . Those willing to follow where Bowering leads will find themselves enthralled.'   *Sunday Telegraph*

'The characters are thousands of miles apart and there are points when we desperately want the two narratives to rub up close. But Bowering keeps us hanging on like icicles until the dark and wonderful end.'   ALEX O'CONNELL, *The Times*

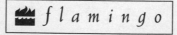 *flamingo*

Peter Hedges

An Ocean in Iowa

'An accomplished follow-up to the much praised *What's Eating Gilbert Grape* . . . The dialogue is fresh and natural, the comedy perfectly pitched: a beautiful book'

JUDY COOKE, *Independent*

'A heart-rending but beautifully economical child's-eye view of break-up in an early Sixties family, when middle America's suburban idyll was about to explode. Creative, unfulfilled mum drinks. Seven-year-old Scotty watches the first astronauts leave Earth during his mother's final row with his insensitive dad. Scotty learns to tell the time, gets kissed by a girl in a lip-crunching mouth brace, and hoards a grenade lost by a boy whose dad used to booby-trap Vietnamese children in order to blow up their parents. An elegantly vivid masterpiece: unpretentious, unsentimental, unforgettable.'

SOPHIE HUNTER, *Mail on Sunday*

'Hedges' prose effortlessly conjures up the numinous clarity with which such episodes are experienced early in life. Scotty himself does the rest: he's quirky and sparky enough to hold our interest, regardless of his tribulations. Hedges is also excellent on exterior detail and successfully captures the magic of a 1960s childhood.' PETER CARTY, *Time Out*

'A fresh, funny and tender picture of family life in Middle America.' OWEN KELLY, *Irish News*

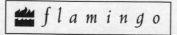

Gretta Mulrooney

Araby

'Tenderly funny and genuinely moving. I loved it.'

FIONA MORROW, *Time Out*

'On hearing of Kitty Keenan's admittance to hospital, her grown-up son Rory returns to Ireland to comfort his father and await the diagnosis . . . Rory's narrative, charting the steady decline of her health, is interspersed with a series of flashbacks through which Kitty emerges larger than life. For Rory, these snapshots of the past are part of a process of unpicking the odd tangle of love and petty grievances that characterise familial relationships. Mulrooney's ability to make sense of the contradictions in clear, precise prose is the most remarkable achievement of the novel. A beautifully observed study of reconciliation, *Araby* makes astute points about conflict and shifting values between generations.'

JAMES EVE, *The Times*

'Kitty is a magnificent diva of discontent: contradictory, ludicrous, sharp-witted, thick-skinned, the sort of character best enjoyed from a distance . . . The narrative of her decline and death is worked with frequent flashbacks to Kitty's heyday, and her enthusiasm for Catholicism, medicament, hobbies and quarrelling . . . What is admirable about Mulrooney's writing is the way she manages to keep the tone buoyant, while alluding to many heartbreaking strands of family history. For both Kitty and Rory, this is a story of gallant survival.'

RUTH PAVEY, *Independent*

flamingo

Suzannah Dunn

Tenterhooks

'I really love *Tenterhooks* . . . Divinely sarcastic and packed full of perky observations, it is very hard to resist.'

In *Slipping the Clutch*, Miranda walks out of Boots one day into beautiful, beloved, fast-living Uncle Robbie who, years beforehand, taught her to drive in his Alpha Romeo and then died in his Lagonda. Well, what's past is past. Or is it?

In *Stood Up and Thinking of England*, Gillian's family are refugees from the 70s recession, bankrupted in Britain, surviving in Spain. But then from back home come the King family, very definitely on holiday. And it is at the local disco with Tracey King that Gillian catches sight of Pedro . . .

Possibility of Electricity, was the dubious claim made for the Spanish farmhouse that becomes the Paulin family's holiday home. Arriving the following summer as company for Renee's frazzled mother is Auntie Fay. Bond-girl blonde, injecting insulin, tanning to the hue of a blood-blister, and telling Irish jokes. Summertime, but the living isn't easy; and, soon, electricity is the least of their problems.

'Dunn has a sharp eye for the quiet moments of conversation that contain emotional truths.'

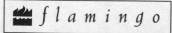